"A Journey to the Gallows brir
overlooked American original,
Stevens. Authors Vic Butsch ar … coax their subject from the shadows into the spotlight of 19th century U.S. history, asking readers to decide for themselves if Stevens was a homegrown terrorist or an unsung American hero. Butsch and Coletti's book is a hybrid of sorts: an impeccably researched biography rendered with fictional flourishes that animate Dwight Stevens and give him voice. Readers will enjoy cameo appearances from some of the legendary figures whose lives intersected with Stevens's, among them Kit Carson, Jefferson Davis, and, most significantly, abolitionist John Brown, with whom Stevens sought to foment a slave insurrection via the infamous Harper's Ferry raid. I read A Journey to the Gallows compulsively and enthusiastically and recommend it to readers who, like me, enjoy connecting the dots between contemporary America and our collective American past."

~ Wally Lamb,
New York Times Best-selling Author of
This Much I know Is True; *We Are Water*;
She's Come Undone, and others.

"This turbulent time in the nation's history produced horrific acts of violence and amazing acts of courage. In this novel, we experience all the drama of this era through the extraordinary journey of one man whom almost no one realizes was at the center of it all. After reading this book, I'll never again question how one person can change the entire course of history."

~ Karen Cook,
Head of Social Studies and History at
Norwich Free Academy

"You are both to be congratulated on a truly impressive body of research!"

~ Dale Plummer,
Norwich, Connecticut City Historian

A JOURNEY *to the* GALLOWS

A JOURNEY
to the
GALLOWS

VIC BUTSCH & TOMMY COLETTI

A Journey to the Gallows

Published by Next Century Publishing
www.NextCenturyPublishing.com
Las Vegas, NV

Aaron Dwight Stevens' picture on cover is courtesy of the West Virginia State Archives

ISBN: 978-1-62903-826-1

Printed in the United States of America

ACKNOWLEDGEMENTS

Our thanks to Kim Baker who performed outstanding research for us in Kansas with the Kansas State Historical Society; to Greg Carroll and Debra Basham at the West Virginia State Archives; to William Gorenfeld who gave great assistance and suggestions about the dragoons in that era of our history; to Tricia Noel, the Research Archivist at the Library of Virginia in Richmond, Virginia; and a special thanks to the people at the Special Collections, Green Library at Stanford University, for all your help.

To Head of Research, Terry Ramsey, at the Bushwhacker Museum in Vernon County, Missouri, your help was greatly appreciated; to Kathleen Wieland at the Otis Library in Norwich, Connecticut, who helped us in gathering information to write this book, thank you. Also, thanks to the wonderful ladies of the Faith Trumbull Chapter of the DAR in Norwich, Connecticut, who invited us to research information, pictures, and artifacts they had of Aaron Dwight Stevens.

To our mutual friend and former co-worker, T. Fred Thompson, who meticulously performed the first editing of this book, our thanks. To Karen Cook, Head of the Social Studies Department, The Norwich Free Academy, Norwich, Connecticut, thank you for your effort, comments, and suggestions. To Wally Lamb, who took time from his busy schedule of writing his own book to read our first draft, sat with us, commented, and suggested on how to make this book a better read, thank you. To Richard White, for his comments and guidance; to Maryanne Mistretta of Pear Tree Enterprises who performed our first professional edit, our sincere thanks.

Special thanks to our wives, Gail and Donna, for their love, encouragement, and patience during the years it took to research and write this book. Many times we temporarily covered our dining room tables, bedroom dressers, and kitchen countertops with research papers, notes, and books, and explained that they couldn't be moved until we had captured all the data from them. We both thank you for allowing us to turn our homes into research centers. And thanks to our many relatives and friends who continuously encouraged us and often asked us how the book was coming along.

Table of Contents

A JOURNEY
to the
GALLOWS

FOREWORD

Being a part of the resurrection of the amazing story of Aaron Dwight Stevens has been a true highlight in my life, which I am happy to say has had more than its fair share of high points. Dwight Stevens, as he was called by his family and friends, had been on my mind since I was first introduced to him by Norwich City Historian, Dale Plummer, more than twelve years ago. My research of Stevens throughout these 12 years has been an "on again-off again" effort, depending on whatever other factors were going on in my life, such as my job at Electric Boat.

Several years ago I found out that Tommy Coletti, a man I had known, respected, and worked with for many years, had written and published a novel. I purchased a copy of *Special Delivery* and found that he had come up with a very good story.

Previously, I had played with the idea of writing the story of Aaron Dwight Stevens, but since I do not consider myself an experienced writer, I never really saw it as an achievable project. I approached Tommy one day in September 2010, told him about Aaron Dwight Stevens, and outlined the highlights of his short but interesting life. Surprisingly, he was immediately excited about doing the book, and said he would like to work with me to tell Dwight's story. He could do the predominance of the fictional writing, while I could provide him with the historical timelines, facts, and background.

However, at the time, he had another book, *Dishonorably Interred*, that was in the final stages of publication, and he wanted to complete the commitment to his publisher before heading out on a new book venture. At the end of 2010, he was available and ready to go, so we started the book in January 2011.

I will never forget reading the first chapter Tommy had written and given me to look over. It was the beginning of the re-creation of a real person, during a real time in our nation's past; Dwight had his own inner thoughts as he talked and related to others, he had friends, he laughed, he loved, and he had tough times. It was wonderful to see Dwight and his story take shape. That feeling never dimmed throughout the long process and now, for me, Dwight has fully come back to life.

Tommy and I have tried very hard to be extremely accurate and informative with all of the historic people, places, and events that touched the life of Dwight Stevens. We have included fictional accounts of how we believed he would have behaved given the circumstances he encountered. **Please note that all actual historical quotes, letters and documents, or portions of documents, are written in bold print.** I must confess that I have grown to respect Dwight even more through the fictional portrayal Tommy created of what Dwight became, what he believed in, and his unfailing commitment to those values and beliefs.

Aaron Dwight Stevens, John Brown, and the small group of raiders that attacked Harper's Ferry in October of 1859 were so far ahead of their time that I wonder if we aren't still trying to emulate what they did. Brown, Stevens, and the others firmly believed in the true equality of all mankind, regardless of race or sex. This sounds kind of passé, and we've all heard similar words like that so many, many times before, but John Brown and his followers meant it in a very literal way.

The abolitionists of the mid-1800s were all in favor of freedom for Negroes, but they didn't necessarily think that Negroes were honestly equal to themselves. They certainly didn't want to share their dinner tables, schools, neighborhoods, jobs, and numerous other qualities of life with them. However, John Brown and Aaron Dwight Stevens were representatives of a small number of people who truly did believe that we were all equal in the eyes of God, regardless of what or who each of us thought our God was. Furthermore, they staked their lives on that belief.

I have grown to admire Aaron Dwight Stevens as a person, even though he was obviously not a hero in the South at the time of his hanging, and still may not be a favorite today in some areas of this country. He was certainly considered a villain when he killed the unfortunate Mr. Cruise while capturing and freeing (or stealing, as many Missourians thought at the time) his slave.

Dwight grew up a soldier and adventurer, and evolved into an individual who, of course, had his faults, but also had an unwavering sense of right and wrong. He had that strong American trait of fighting and sticking up for the underdog, the oppressed, and those who could not fight for themselves. In all the letters he wrote, and all the words written about him, I have never found any of complaint or weakness. In fact, he was called, by one who knew him well, "the noblest man he ever knew." He was also a rugged individual who you would probably not want as an enemy. He was the type of person that most of us would be proud to call a friend. It was Annie Brown, John Brown's daughter, who wrote that of all the men in the group, Dwight "tried hardest to be good."

Vic Butsch

PREFACE

On the rainy night of October 16, 1859, the small town of Harper's Ferry, Virginia lay quietly asleep, nestled between the Potomac and Shenandoah Rivers. The town was home to the United States Armory and Arsenal. The only other facility like it in the country was up north in Springfield, Massachusetts.

Harper's Ferry had become somewhat famous in 1803, when Meriwether Lewis came to the town to obtain rifles and other equipment, including a custom-built boat, in preparation for the historic Lewis and Clark Expedition to the Pacific Ocean. But on that memorable October night in 1859, John Brown, Aaron Dwight Stevens, John Kagi, and nineteen more men, some black and some white, quietly and unobtrusively walked the five miles from the Kennedy farm in Maryland, across the Potomac River to the Federal Armory in Harper's Ferry.

The raiders' ambitious plan was to surprise the guards at the Armory, capture wagonloads of rifles, distribute them to the numerous slaves expected to join their revolt, and then escape into the mountains. From there they would fight a guerilla war against the slaveholders of the South. It was to be a full uprising of slaves against their masters, leading to the end of that most horrible industry.

These men woke up the nation that morning to the start of a new day and the end of slavery. The Civil War would start a little over a year later , and the death of over 620,000 Americans would finally put an end to the institution.

These are the Raiders:

21 raiders accompanied John Brown to Harper's Ferry

The 10 raiders Raiders who died at Harper's Ferry

Pictures courtesy of the National Park Service, U.S. Department of the Interior
Harper's Ferry National Historical Park

1. **Dangerfield Newby**, approximately 35, was born into slavery despite having a white father who was not his master. He tried to buy the freedom of his wife and children, but the owner refused, leading Newby to join John Brown. He was the first raider killed on October 18, 1859.

2. **Watson Brown**, 24, was mortally wounded on October 17, 1859, while carrying a white flag and trying to negotiate with the responding militia. He died two days later.

West Virginia State Archives

3. **William Leeman**, 20, was a veteran of Brown's efforts in Kansas. He was killed while attempting to escape across the Potomac River on October 17, 1859.

4. **Stewart Taylor**, 22, was born a Canadian. He was killed while defending the Engine House on October 17, 1859.

5. **Oliver Brown**, 21, was the youngest of John Brown's three sons to participate in the action. He was mortally wounded on October 17, 1859, and died the next day.

6. **William Thompson**, 26, was captured when he and others emerged carrying a flag of truce. After Harper's Ferry Mayor Fontaine Beckham was killed, the mob shot Thompson in the head and tossed his body into the Shenandoah River to use for target practice on October 18, 1859.

7. **John Kagi**, 24, was Brown's second in command, stationed in the U.S. Rifle Factory during the raid. Realizing he was hopelessly outnumbered, Kagi attempted to escape across the Shenandoah River, but was shot and killed on October 18, 1859.

8. **Lewis Leary**, 24, was another free African American. He was stationed in the U.S. Rifle Factory with Kagi and was shot while trying to escape across the Shenandoah River. He died on October 18, 1859.

9. Jeremiah Anderson, 26, was mortally wounded on October 18, 1859, by a U.S. Marine's bayonet during the final assault on the Engine House.

10. Dauphin Thompson, 21, was one of two brothers in the raid. He died October 18, 1859, of a bayonet wound as the U.S. Marines stormed the Engine House.

The 6 raiders who were executed at Charlestown

Pictures courtesy of the National Park Service, U.S. Department of the Interior
Harper's Ferry National Historical Park

1. John Copeland, 25, was a free African American student at Oberlin College, Ohio, and joined the raiders along with his uncle, Lewis Leary. He was captured and executed at Charlestown on December 16, 1859.

2. Shields Green, approximately 23, was an escaped slave from South Carolina. He was captured in the Engine House and executed at Charlestown on December 16, 1859.

3. John Cook, 30, was the effort's chief quartermaster but not present at Harper's Ferry during the raid itself. He reunited with the survivors as they made their way north, was captured in Pennsylvania and executed at Charlestown on December 16, 1859.

4. Edwin Coppoc, 24, shot and killed Harper's Ferry mayor Fontaine Beckham during the raid. He was executed at Charlestown on December 16, 1859.

5. Albert Hazlett, 22, held the Armory building himself during the raid and escaped across the Potomac River as the situation worsened. He was captured at Carlisle, Pennsylvania, on October 22, 1859, and executed at Charlestown on March 16, 1860.

6. Aaron Dwight Stevens, 29, was a former dragoon and free state militiaman. He trained John Brown's Raiders and was third in command. He was severely wounded at Harper's Ferry, but recovered from his wounds before he was executed at Charlestown on March 16, 1860.

The 5 raiders who survived the raid

Pictures courtesy of the National Park Service, U.S. Department of the Interior
Harper's Ferry National Historical Park

1. Barclay Coppoc, 20, unlike his older brother, Edwin, escaped and went on to become a lieutentaunt in the 3rd Kansas Infintry. He died on Septenber 3, 1861, with injuries sustained when his train fell into the Platt River from a bridge sabotaged by Confederates.

2. Francis Merriam, 21, was blind in one eye, but served as one of three members of Brown's rear guard. Stationed in Maryland, he escaped the raid and went on to serve as a captain in the 3rd South Carolina Colored Infintry. He died in 1865.

3 Charles Tidd, 25, returned to Maryland for more supplies after the raid commenced, and escaped along with the rest of the rear guard. He went on to enlist in the 21st Massachusetts, but died of fever in February 1862.

4. Osborne Anderson, 29, was a free African American who was living in Canada when he was recruited for the raid; he survived and escaped back to Canada. He went on to write a memoir of the raid, and served in the Union Army before dying of tuberculosis in 1872.

5. Owen Brown, 34, was the only one of John Brown's sons to survive the raid. He later moved to California with the remaining members of the family.

John Brown, leader of the raiders, as he appeared at Harper's Ferry – 1859
He was the first to be hanged
Photo courtesy of the National Park Service, U.S. Department of the Interior
Harper's Ferry National Historical Park

Chapter One

The Assault on Harper's Ferry

As the rain continued throughout the morning, the men packed into the indoor areas. Some chose to wait out the rain in makeshift canvas tents. In the farmhouse and the shed across the road, the men sharpened knives and checked and rechecked the rifles and other gear they would need for their assault. No breakfast or noon meal was served that day, and the men fended for themselves until John Brown ordered a dinner meal be prepared. Brown's sons Watson, Oliver, and Owen, along with John Kagi, and Aaron Dwight Stevens rustled up a makeshift dinner consisting of bacon, bread, beans, and garden vegetables. With their stores now depleted, they would all need to search for their next meal.

Everyone was in good spirits despite the anticipation. Brown called the group together for a prayer service before the meal and then left to be alone while the men finished eating. He returned later to read more from the Bible, but he soon relinquished the duty as he looked around at the assembled men. They waited until he picked Shields Green to read. It was a privilege for any of the men to be asked by Brown to read. When Green finished, the men and Brown silently reflected on the holy words for a few moments. Then Brown looked at his pocket watch. It was 8:00 p.m. He rose, looked around at his small army, and with a robust voice, said, ***"Men, get on your arms. We will proceed to the Ferry."*** For an instant, no one moved until Dwight rose. "You heard the captain…move!" Dwight left the farmhouse first; at his command, everyone quickly followed. Within a short time, the men had gathered their weapons and gear. Many wore heavy wool shawls that served as overcoats. The horses were hitched to the wagon that would soon be loaded with men, crowbars, sledgehammers, and a bundle of pikes. According to the plan, John Brown would be the teamster. Dwight checked with Kagi, John Cook, and Charles Tidd, to make sure their men were ready. He called over to his captain, "We are ready, sir."

Brown nodded and climbed onto the wagon. Dwight watched him and quietly said to Kagi, "He seems to be in deep thought."

"I'm sure he is. He's definitely with the Almighty this very moment."

Brown glanced at the Kennedy farmhouse as he grabbed the reins. Dwight and Kagi looked in the same direction. Owen Brown and two other men stood silhouetted by the lantern Owen held at the kitchen door. Dwight felt the wagon move as Brown commanded the pair of horses. Two men, Barclay Coppoc and Francis Jackson Merriam, were assigned to assist Owen in guarding the remaining weapons in the basement. The plan was to keep them safe until after the revolution started.

Earlier, Dwight had suggested that one of Brown's sons be in charge of protecting the weapons. He had reminded Brown that he already had two of his other sons with him. When he recommended that his third son, Owen, remain behind just in case his two other sons were killed during the assault, Dwight didn't have to explain any further. He had also convinced Brown that it would be better if the youngest and most inexperienced men be left with Owen. Dwight emphasized that Barclay Coppoc was barely twenty years old and the least experienced. The other guard was Francis Jackson Merriam. John Kagi had suggested the importance of Merriam's ties to potential money that could not be risked. Kagi reminded Brown that Merriam had brought over six hundred dollars in gold when he'd reported to the farm. The money had come from his wealthy abolitionist grandfather, Francis Jackson, and Brown understood that Jackson would never be approachable again if his grandson were harmed in any way.

The captain looked up again as the wagon passed the farmhouse, and Dwight noticed Owen moving the lantern side to side as a salute. The wagon and men moved slowly away from the farmhouse and disappeared into the night. After a short period on the road, Dwight called out to Tidd and Cook who were walking ahead, "Stay far enough ahead, but not out of hearing range, in case you run into anyone."

Dwight planned this to make sure Tidd and Cook could seize anyone they met on the road to prevent them from possibly sending a warning to the town.

The drizzle continued to dampen everyone's outer garments until, eventually, the smell of damp wool suffused them all. Dwight rode quietly with his eyes fixed on the dirt road. It was dark and the weather was miserable. When they reached Maryland Heights, the lights of Harper's Ferry came into view. The whistle from a railroad engine broke the stillness of the night.

"That's the B&O engineer signaling to cross the bridge."

Dwight nodded at Kagi's remark. Brown never responded except to give a gentle slap to the reins of the horses as they began the descent into the quiet town of three thousand sleeping residents.

As the wagon moved, Dwight softly called out to Tidd and Cook and pointed to the telegraph line. "It's time now. When you're finished, catch up as soon as you can. We'll wait for you by the covered railroad bridge."

As soon as he was able, Tidd climbed the closest telegraph pole and cut the lines. Several minutes passed before the wagon and its occupants reached the bridge.

Dwight checked his pocket watch as Tidd and Cook caught up to them.

Kagi opened his mouth to speak, but Tidd, a little winded, said, "It is done. The wire is useless."

"Good." Kagi jumped off the wagon with Dwight.

Dwight entered the covered bridge that served both rail and commercial traffic. He checked his watch again.

It was 10:15 p.m. So far, all had gone according to plan.

Dwight crouched down when he saw the silhouette of a watchman walking from one side to the other at the opposite end of the bridge. He motioned to Kagi, who had seen him at almost the same time, to get down. They signaled for the rest of the party to stop. Dwight whispered to Cook, "Follow me and John. No firing weapons unless I fire first. Understood?"

Cook nodded.

They slowly walked across the bridge, but stayed to the side and in the shadows. Suddenly, the watchman turned toward them. They stopped, still unseen. The watchman walked to the center of the bridge before he turned and left.

All three men watched as he walked to the end of the bridge again. Dwight strained to see the hands on his pocket watch and whispered to Kagi, "It's ten thirty. It must be part of his job."

The watchman's movement didn't matter to Dwight as he began to walk slowly behind him, with the others following. When the watchman saw Dwight, he was startled.

Kagi called out, "You are under arrest."

The watchman laughed when he saw Cook with Kagi and Stevens. He had seen Cook in town on numerous occasions. The watchman looked at Kagi. "Is this a practical joke, sir?"

"It is not. You are under arrest."

When the watchman got a clear glimpse of the Sharps rifles hanging from the men's shoulders, his smile turned to a look of shock and then fear. He stepped aside as Brown and the others in the wagon emerged from the shadows of the bridge and slowly moved past him.

Brown spoke as he pulled on the reins of the wagon and stopped. "Dwight, move ahead. Watson and Stewart will guard the bridge. Take the watchman with you. We will proceed to the Armory."

Watson Brown and Stewart Taylor jumped off the wagon, and Dwight pointed to where he wanted them positioned. Kagi and Cook followed Dwight as he walked alongside the wagon Brown had started to drive again. Tidd caught up as he pushed the watchman ahead to follow behind the other men, asking the man what his name was.

"It's William Williams, sir."

Tidd spoke softly. "Well, Mr. Williams, as was said, you are under arrest." He then questioned Williams while they walked. "What did you do to that time clock?"

"I put this key into it and turned it. I perform that duty every thirty minutes. It's part of my job. I will need to do it again at eleven o'clock."

"Not tonight you won't." Tidd pushed him ahead and told him to keep quiet.

William Williams obeyed.

The men could see the outline of the Armory despite the dismal wet conditions as they moved straight ahead. Dwight, Kagi, and Cook moved to the right and away from the wagon as Tidd pushed Williams along. They looked through the windows of the large railroad depot that also served, at times, as the local hotel. A few lanterns were lit, but there was no sign of anyone being awake. A small sign over one of the several doors read *Wager Hotel.* The next building was the firehouse. There was no activity visible there either. The three men continued to look around as the wagon of men headed to the Armory building's main gate, with Tidd and Williams right beside them.

A watchman named Daniel Whelan lounged beside the locked gate, oblivious to the approaching danger. Suddenly, he heard the noise of the wagon despite the slow pace.

Dwight saw the watchman get up and move near the gate, and before Whalen could react, Dwight pressed the pistol barrel to his chest and told him to open the gate.

Whelan did not react at first, and Dwight spoke again. "Give us the key." He pushed the pistol harder against Whelan's chest.

"I cannot do that, sir," Whelan replied.

Dwight raised his voice. "Didn't you hear what I said?"

Whelan recognized Williams and was about to say something when Dwight pushed the pistol even harder against his chest and then cocked it.

Brown watched to see how Whelan reacted, but there was no reaction and Brown realized that Whelan was disoriented and becoming a problem. He also didn't want Dwight killing him and waking the sleeping town with the pistol shot.

Brown called out to Tidd, "Apprehend him. When we break the lock, put him with the other one." He turned to several of the men close to him in the wagon. "Use the crowbars. Break the lock."

Dwight caught one of the crowbars as they were tossed from the wagon. Cook helped him as they inserted the crowbar into the lock that secured a chain holding the iron gate closed. Kagi assisted with another. Together they twisted and forced the lock, and within a minute the lock was broken.

Whelan never moved from his position as he watched the events unfolding in front of him. He was taken into custody.

John Kagi took several raiders and entered the Armory. Williams and Whelan stood silently under guard as Brown's men searched the building. Dwight remained outside with Cook and several others in anticipation of other watchmen coming to check on the open gate. Finally, Kagi came outside and reported that he was satisfied that no other watchmen were in the building.

Hearing the Armory was secure, Brown's face lit up. He turned to his two prisoners. ***"I came here from Kansas and this is a Slave State. I want to free all the Negros in this state. I have possession now of the United States Armory and if the citizens interfere with me I must only burn the town and have their blood."*** As he walked into the Armory, Brown ordered Albert Hazlett and Edwin Coppoc to keep watch outside the gate.

Tidd handed Williams and Whelan over to Kagi, who pushed them into the Armory behind Brown. Seeing Hazlett and Coppoc take their positions on watch at the gate and the two prisoners under Kagi's responsibility, Dwight looked to Brown for his own orders.

Brown took Dwight aside. "The plan has run well. Now take your men and seize Colonel Washington.[1]"

"Yes, sir," Dwight responded, and called to his men. "Cook, Tidd." He paused, and then found the other men he wanted. "Anderson, Leary, and Green, come with me."

He knew it was important that some of the men assisting him were black.

The night and the town remained quiet. The drizzle had stopped, but it was still cold and damp. The breath of Dwight and the men following him could be seen as they moved quickly to the residence of Colonel Lewis W. Washington, the great-grandnephew of the first U.S. president, which was approximately five miles from the Armory. They headed south on the Charlestown Road. Dwight checked his pocket watch again. The time was nearing 11:00 p.m. He picked up the pace in

[1] **Colonel Lewis William Washington** was a great-grandnephew of George Washington, and is best remembered as a hostage of John Brown and a prosecution witness in the resulting trial.

hopes that they would arrive at their destination by midnight. The men struggled to keep pace with the veteran soldier as they moved through the night. Dwight remembered the specific instructions Brown had given him: ***"Bring back the pistol Lafayette[1] had given General Washington and the sword of Frederick the Great[2] that had been presented to him. Bring them and the Colonel with you."***

Cook had seen the historical items at the Washington home when he had the occasion to be invited into the house, and had informed Brown. Dwight wanted Cook to verify that these were the historical items that Brown wanted for their great psychological value. Dwight understood the point Brown wanted to make, but he felt guilty taking them, knowing how devastated he would feel if someone stole similar items from his family. He prepared for the worst if Colonel Washington vehemently protested. The word was passed among the men that only Dwight would deal directly with Colonel Washington.

Back in the Armory, tension could be seen on the men's faces despite the fact that everything was going so well. Brown found a clerk's chair and pulled it up to a desk that was situated in a small office to the side of the entranceway. By the look of the papers on the desk and the other articles in the room, he guessed it was an accounting office.

John Kagi saw Brown sit, and he approached only to the office entrance. "Any further orders, sir?"

Brown shook his head, paused, and then spoke. "No, we will wait a while."

Kagi waited while Brown watched the others standing in a group not far from the entrance door.

The captain looked back and smiled. "Tell Oliver and William Thompson to help guard the bridge. We need to keep these men busy."

Kagi relayed the orders. The entrance door creaked as the two men

---

[1] **Marquis de Lafayette** was born in 1757 in Auvergne, France. His full given name was Marie Joseph Paul Yves Roch Gilbert du Motier. When his mother and grandfather died, he inherited a large fortune. In 1777, Lafayette purchased a ship, and with a crew of adventurers set sail for America to fight in the revolution against the British. Lafayette joined as a major general, assigned to the staff of George Washington. He served with distinction, leading American forces to several victories, and becoming an American hero of the war.

[2] **The Sword of Frederick the Great.** This sword is reputed to be the sword sent to Washington in 1780 by Frederick the Great with a verbal message: *"From the oldest General in the World to the Greatest."* This was one of the five swords left to his nephews. The sword was passed down through his son Colonel George Corbin Washington, then to his grandson Colonel Lewis William Washington. Unfortunately, the sword was very badly damaged in the New York capitol building fire in 1911. This fire also destroyed the original records of New York during the American Revolution.

set out. The door made a loud clanking noise when it shut, and it echoed throughout the building.

After some time had passed, Brown looked at his pocket watch and then at Kagi. "John, it is time. Take Copeland and go to the rifleworks down the road. Try to keep to the rock side, and in the shadows. Remember, it is a little less than a mile up the road."

Kagi nodded, turned, and addressed his men. As they were about to leave, Kagi instructed Copeland to close the door softly to reduce the noise the heavy door made.

Kagi and his men quietly approached the rifleworks about fifteen minutes later. They gained access easily and captured several of the ordnance men working the night shift. Within the hour, Kagi sent a messenger to Brown at the Armory. His note indicated that he had captured the rifleworks as well as some prisoners. He also informed Brown that he would wait for his orders after Dwight returned with his captives.

Brown relaxed, feeling things were going well.

About midnight, Dwight and his men approached the Washington home. Two white raiders moved to the slave quarters, woke them, and told them they were all free. They found a large wagon and hitched four horses to it. They then asked the slaves to get into the wagon.

COLONEL WASHINGTON.—[Drawn by Porte Crayon.]

Lewis Washington

Harper's Weekly, November12, 1859

West Virginia State Archives

Dwight and three of the black raiders entered the house and found the colonel sleeping in his bedroom. Dwight shook and awoke Colonel

Washington. Before the colonel had any idea what was happening, Dwight called out, "Sir, you are my prisoner. Get dressed as quickly as possible. You will be escorted back to Harper's Ferry."

"Who are you, sir?" Washington demanded.

"I am Dwight Stevens, at your service. My captain, John Brown, has ordered me to free your slaves and take you back to the Armory, which we have captured."

Washington did not respond as he slowly began to dress. Dwight stopped the man's progress when he ordered, "Colonel, you will surrender your great-great-uncle's pistol presented to him by Lafayette, and the sword of Frederick the Great."

Colonel Washington glared at Dwight before he spoke.

Dwight anticipated the reaction and tensed as he waited to see if Washington would react violently.

The colonel spoke slowly, "What use does your captain have for these precious items? Is he to sell them like a common thief?"

"No, sir. We believe they will serve to instill a psychological effect. We hope to make a point that we came to free the slaves of this town," Dwight answered.

"You are mad to think that this country will allow you to keep these precious items, and to free slaves which are private property."

Dwight watched the colonel carefully to ensure that he did not reach for a weapon or try to escape. Satisfied that he did not, he responded, "Yes, sir. Maybe today we are mad, but tomorrow we will be seen as sane men doing something that has needed to be done since slavery began in this country."

The Colonel did not respond, but only shook his head in disagreement as he finished dressing. Dwight accompanied him to his study to fetch the items that had been demanded. Washington took the sword off the wall, and then obtained the pistol from a case located on a shelf in the same room. Colonel Washington held the two items, one in each hand.

Dwight looked at the African American raider, Osborne Anderson, and told him to come forward. With Anderson standing next to him, Dwight said, "Colonel, please present the sword to this man."

The Colonel responded with a look of bewilderment on his face as he handed the sword to Anderson. The black man bowed as he took the sacred sword.

Dwight took the Lafayette pistol and tucked it into a pocket under his wool shawl. A short time later, Dwight and his men took Colonel Washington with the freed slaves and loaded them onto the commandeered wagon. It was a little after 1:00 a.m., and they still had another mission to complete before they returned to the Armory.

In Harper's Ferry, a second watchman named Patrick Higgins became suspicious when he was unable to make contact with William Williams. As he walked across the bridge looking for the man he was to replace, he came face to face with Watson Brown and Stewart Taylor.

Watson Brown yelled to him to surrender, but with quick reflexes the stubborn Higgins punched Watson, knocking him down. Higgins turned tail and ran back across the bridge, while both Watson and Taylor yelled for him to halt. When he refused, they fired their weapons. One bullet grazed Higgins's scalp, but he was fortunate enough to reach the lobby of the Wager Hotel and sound the alarm.

The occupants of the hotel feared the worst, knowing that the 1:25 a.m. locomotive could possibly be running onto an unstable bridge or tampered tracks. Even worse, the bridge could have been rigged with explosives.

Higgins convinced several others that the bridge and Armory were under threat of demolition, and was then given permission to stop the train.

After the train was hailed down, the conductor, a man named Phelps, said he believed Higgins's story that the bridge had been compromised. He immediately ordered the locomotive engineer, William McKay, and baggage master, Jacob Cromwell, to investigate.

Both men left the train and cautiously approached the covered bridge. They held lanterns as they slowly walked until they heard shots, followed by bullets flying past their heads. McKay retreated back to the train, where he reversed the locomotive and backed it a few hundred feet down the track. His companion, Jacob Cromwell, crouched down until the shooting had stopped, and while the men who fired were reloading, he continued. He was soon joined by another man, a free Negro baggage handler and local resident named Hayward Shepherd, who had come to see what all the commotion was about. They both reached the end of the bridge, where Brown's men immediately confronted them and fired again. Cromwell was fortunate enough to dodge the bullets, and he made it back to safety in the hotel. Shepherd was less fortunate. He was shot in the back while he ran with Cromwell. The bullet exited at his left nipple and he staggered to the end of the bridge, where he crawled to the station platform and collapsed. He lay there for twelve hours, even though local physician Dr. John D. Starry[1] attended him for a short period. Because of

[1] **Dr. John D. Starry** was 35 at the time of the raid, a resident of Harper's Ferry, and a practicing physician. He was an important figure in the actions at Harper's Ferry, and a

Shepherd's condition, the doctor did not want to move him. He eventually succumbed to his wounds and, ironically, John Brown's first casualty at Harper's Ferry was a well-liked local free black man.

The men, women, and children on the train were evacuated into the Wager Hotel as soon as they all realized that there was a small-arms fight in progress. As the train passengers departed, they came upon the sight of Shepherd suffering on the platform, slowly bleeding to death. This induced complete fear and confusion among the passengers. A few women fainted after seeing the bleeding Negro, moaning in agony, while they passed by him to enter the hotel. The train's other baggage man also approached the bridge.

Luther Simpson[1] did not know that his companion, Jacob Cromwell, had earlier retreated to the safety of the Wager Hotel. Simpson slowly walked across the bridge, where he was captured and brought to the Armory to be questioned by John Brown. He was retained there for about an hour and then released to report back to the train. When questioned on what he had seen, he convincingly stated that he had seen five or six hundred armed Negros, and half as many rifle-bearing whites. When asked who the leader was, he said that it was a man who called himself Captain Smith. It was about 4:00 a.m. on the 17th, and still no one knew John Brown had captured the Armory, as well as the rifleworks, and that he controlled much of Harper's Ferry.

Elsewhere, Dwight and his men reached their planned second objective, the fine home and rich farm of prominent townsman John Allstadt[2]. Dwight ordered Osborn Anderson, Lewis Leary, and Shields Green to guard Colonel Washington and keep watch on the slaves in the wagon while he, Cook, and Tidd entered the home, arrested Allstadt and his son, and freed six more slaves. The Allstadts were loaded into the large Washington wagon along with the Colonel and his slaves, and driven to the Armory. Dwight drove the large wagon through the gates of the Armory, where Brown awaited his return.

"I presume your missions went well? Do you have the articles I requested?"

---

valuable witness in understanding what occurred.

[1] **Luther Simpson** was held captive, and talked to John Brown prior to being released. It was Luther who reported that there were "five or six hundred Negros, all having arms; there were two or three hundred white men with them…"

[2] **John Allstadt** was a farmer who lived with his 18-year-old son and his six slaves. One of the slaves got sick during the affair and died. The male slave was 20 years old and the "most valuable" one he had. The rest were returned to him.

Dwight jumped down off the wagon and handed Brown the Lafayette pistol. "Yes, sir, the missions went well."

Brown smiled as he looked over the pistol. Before he could request the sword, Osborne Anderson handed it to him.

Dwight saw the contentment in Brown's facial expression. "Captain, I asked that Colonel Washington surrender the sword to Osborne."

Brown looked it over before answering, "It was the appropriate thing to do." He looked up into the wagon and saw Washington and Allstadt. He instructed several of his men to escort the Colonel and John Allstadt out of the wagon.

Dwight assisted, and when they all were in front of Brown, Dwight introduced them. "Colonel Washington, Mr. Allstadt, may I present Captain John Brown."

Neither man said a word as their slaves brushed by them and were taken to a holding area inside the Armory.

Brown looked at Washington first, and smiled before he spoke. ***"I think, after a while, possibly, I shall be enabled to release you but only on the condition of getting your friends to send in a Negro man as a ransom. I shall be very attentive to you, sir, for I may get the worst of it in my first encounter, and if so, your life is worth as much as mine. I shall be very particular to pay attention to you. My particular reason for taking you first was that, as the aide to the Governor of Virginia, I knew you would endeavor to perform your duty, and perhaps you would have been a troublesome customer to me; and, apart from that, I wanted you particularly for the moral effect it would give our cause having one of your name as 'prisoner.'"*** He turned to Allstadt and said, ***"My statement to you, sir, is that you are a prominent member of this town. The townspeople will be more agreeable to my demands with you and your son under my guard."***

He motioned for them to enter the Armory. They quietly obliged, and were instructed to be seated on several wooden chairs that had been hastily arranged outside the office that Brown was using as his headquarters.

During the quick introduction Brown had with Colonel Washington and Allstadt, the town's doctor, Dr. Starry, was hiding in the shadows just outside the Armory gate. He had seen the four-horsed wagon filled to capacity with Negros and white men entering the Armory gate, and listened to see if he could find out who was the leader of the group. Dr. Starry had been the physician who tried to aid the wounded free Negro Hayward Shepherd but decided not to move him while all the unknown men were around.. Dr. Starry was left alone by the raiders because he was a physician trying to give aid. No one paid any attention to him.

Brown turned to Dwight after the prisoners were out of hearing range, not knowing Dr. Starry was watching them. "It is time to send a wagon back to the farmhouse. Use the larger one from the Washington and Allstadt homes to assist Tidd and Cook. With the help of Owen and the men I left with him, they should be able to load the rifles, pistols, and bundles of pikes quickly."

"Yes, sir. I will instruct them to be quick about it. I suspect more people will wake up soon and become curious about what has developed."

"You worry too much, Dwight. I am convinced the Almighty has granted us good fortune in our plan."

"I'm pleased you feel that way, but yes, I still worry. We have been most fortunate, Captain, but I am convinced that the sleeping citizens will awaken, and they could cause us problems."

Brown motioned for Dwight to carry out his orders.

As the wagon disappeared across the river, Dr. Starry was convinced that whoever they were, they had stolen the safe from the paymaster's office and that was the reason for the assault. He still didn't know who had invaded the town.

Dwight understood that John Brown wanted to hand out weapons as soon as daylight came. He wasn't as sure as Brown was that a multitude of slaves would begin to arrive and join their revolt. Even though the word that they had taken the Armory would spread quickly, Dwight was sure that when daylight came, some form of resistance would be given. He cautioned Brown on that fact again, just as he had done when the plans were initially developed. "Sir, we should watch to see if more opposition arrives. As soon as day comes, we must be prepared to retreat into the mountains with whomever joins us, to avoid capture. We should be prepared to move to the hills as planned and distribute the weapons at a more secure location."

Brown did not respond at first. He looked away and then back to Dwight. "They will come, my son. They will come."

Dwight only nodded. He thought to himself, *The only blacks here are the ones we have freed.* He then went about checking on the rest of the men and realized he needed to separate the prisoners from his men and reduce the numbers needed to guard them. He made plans, after consulting with John Kagi by messenger, to move them to the Engine House.

Dwight looked at his watch. It was almost 4:00 a.m. when he heard Brown strike up another conversation with the train conductor, Phelps, who had returned under guard. Phelps requested assurance that the bridge had not been compromised and that the train could pass over it.

Brown assured him that it could.

Phelps returned to the train, still feeling uneasy that the bridge was somehow unsafe for the train to cross.

Dwight waited for Kagi's messenger to return from moving the prisoners to the Engine House. He read the message that Kagi had sent:

Looking inside the Engine House
Photo by Tommy Coletti

We are losing our advantage of surprise. There must be others organizing. I do not see any indication that a mass of Negros will join us. Look at the ones we have freed. They are scared to death of what may happen to them. They are scared of us, too. I agree that we should take them, and what weapons we have, and leave soon.

Dwight scribbled down a quick reply:

I agree, but we must stick with the plan a little longer. When daylight is full and our weapons arrive, we can decide our exit strategy with the Captain. He looked at his watch, then scribbled a little more: *Let's move all the prisoners to the Engine House. It's half past four o'clock. The weapons should be here soon. At five o'clock I will talk with the Captain again, if nothing changes.*

Dwight sent the messenger.

The train was now ready to move, but its passengers were hiding away in the Wager House, still worried that they would be harmed. Dr. Starry watched the conductor leave and be escorted back across the bridge to the train. With one of the town's most prominent citizens held captive, the wagon that he thought was holding the safe from the paymaster's office missing, and Hayward Shepherd lying half dead on the platform of the station, Dr. Starry decided it was his duty to alert the superintendent of the government arsenal. He snuck away, saddled his horse, and rode to the home of A. M. Kitzmiller[1].

After being informed, Kitzmiller went directly to the Armory only to become one more of John Brown's hostages.

Brown gave orders to move the prisoners into the Engine House after Dwight received another message from Kagi that he would send his prisoners. Dwight waited until the move had been completed before he approached Brown. It was now 5:15 a.m. on October 17th. Kagi was still holding the rifleworks, Dwight was in charge at the Armory, and John Brown sat at the clerk's desk waiting for word from his men that slaves were entering the town to support them.

Unknown to Brown, Stevens, and Kagi, Cook and a freed Negro from the Allstadt home made it only half way back to the Harper's Ferry Armory with the wagon full of weapons before they took a detour. Cook ordered the man to stop at the one-room schoolhouse that had just started classes at 7:00 a.m. It had taken longer than planned to load the wagon and make the trip from the Kennedy farm. Schoolmaster Lind Currie watched as Cook entered the schoolhouse and demanded that he needed the building as a storehouse. Currie resisted, until he was shown the weapons Cook carried to back up his demand. Currie reluctantly agreed, but not before suggesting that he dismiss his students for the day and that he needed to escort one particular student home.

---

[1] **Archibald M. Kitzmiller** was the chief clerk to the superintendent of the armory, Colonel Barbour, who was out of town when the raid occurred. Mr. Kitzmiller was then the acting superintendent.

SCHOOL-HOUSE TAKEN POSSESSION OF BY CAPT. COOK.—FROM A SKETCH BY OUR OWN CORRESPONDENT.

The Schoolhouse, Leslie's, November 26, 1859
West Virginia State Archives

Cook agreed to Currie's request.

The schoolmaster escorted the boy home and then returned despite the opportunity he had to escape. He stayed with Cook for little over an hour but eventually convinced Cook to release him by giving his word that he would return home and not mention what had occurred at the schoolhouse.

Surprisingly, Cook agreed again, and the weapons that Brown waited on to give out to those who came to their cause never arrived that morning. They stayed at the schoolhouse guarded by Cook and the freed Negro assistant.

The day grew brighter as the sun rose higher. The streets in front of the Armory and rifleworks were quiet and desolate, with only the occasional squirrel collecting acorns from several large oak trees. Kagi and Dwight both feared that events taking place were going to result in some form of fierce resistance.

In the meantime, Dr. Starry continued to busy himself in his efforts to inform the locals. He had managed to rouse the pastor of the local Lutheran church and urged him to sound the alarm.

As the church bell began to ring, Dwight looked at his pocket watch and frowned. He approached Brown, who now was reading from his well-worn Bible. "Captain, there is a church bell ringing from the heights above the town. Someone is sounding the alarm."

"I hear it, son. It will also waken the slaves that we expect to come. It is a sign from the Almighty that things are about to happen."

"I believe it could be a double-edged sword, Captain. It may bring some of those we hope to see, but it will also bring the U.S. Army."

"The militia, yes, but the army will take better than a day to get here even if they have been alerted. Remember, most of the militia are just storekeepers and farmers. You know that. They will be no match for your boys."

Brown rose and put his Bible down. He opened the door of the Armory and looked down the street. He smiled when he saw no one. "Have you been in contact with John Kagi recently?"

"No, not since about four o'clock."

Both men heard the whistle from the train and looked at each other. Brown ordered, "Send a messenger to Kagi and find out his status."

Several minutes later the message was on its way.

A short time later, Kagi heard the messenger pounding on the rifleworks door. He opened it after the man identified himself. He hoped and prayed that Dwight had convinced the Captain to send orders for him and his men to abandon the rifleworks, and join up for an organized withdrawal from town. He opened Dwight's message and read it to himself:

The Captain requests your status. Please reply immediately.

Kagi's first response was going to be a damned sarcastic one, until he read further.

Church bells ringing and whistle from train blowing. Not good for us. I will work to convince the Captain to withdraw. Request you support the same.

Kagi wrote hastily:

Status is good. Bells and whistle a bad sign. Agree that resistance is forthcoming. Advise the Captain to leave prisoners and withdraw with men and slaves we have. Where are the weapons?

Dwight received the message about fifteen minutes later. He read it and handed it to John Brown.

The Captain didn't remark on the contents of the message except to say, "We remain where we are. The streets are still quiet."

Dwight went around and made contact with all his men. He double-checked to see how much ammunition and extra weapons they had. If the wagonload of weapons didn't arrive soon, he was concerned that their mission would be in jeopardy.

Dr. Starry remained a driven man. He had managed to send a messenger upriver to stop any other trains coming from the west. Another messenger was sent to Charlestown to inform the county seat of what had occurred in Harper's Ferry. The messenger succeeded in alarming the city into thinking that a slave uprising was underway.

The residents of Charlestown panicked, thinking that another bloody insurrection was happening. Every church bell in Charlestown was ringing within an hour of the messenger's arrival. The telegraph was in constant use as requests, then demands, were made from city officials to send help. Dr. Starry arrived in Charlestown after his messenger had panicked its citizens. At the sight of Dr. Starry's sweat-drenched horse breathing laboriously, many citizens feared the massacring slaves were following directly behind him.

The doctor found the local militia, known as the Jefferson Guards[1], forming to begin their move to Harper's Ferry. He explained what he knew had happened, and within a short period, more joined the guard and swelled its ranks. Dr. Starry observed that most were too old or too young to be of real value, and that they brought only knives and squirrel guns with them. It was obvious that they had nothing that would match the Sharps rifles he had seen the mysterious outlaws carrying. He returned to Harper's Ferry while Charlestown prepared to come and help. When he returned, he found that some of the citizens had armed themselves, but he also knew that they were no formal challenge to the raiders. The streets were still empty.

By 8:00 a.m., John Brown wondered where his weapons were. He knew they should have arrived by now. He also wanted his son Owen, and the others he had ordered to stay at the farm, to be here helping him now. Brown didn't know that Owen, Tidd, Barclay Coppoc, and Merriam had encountered Terrence Byrne on the road. He was the owner of a farm they passed en route to Harper's Ferry. The group had stopped the farmer just out of sight of his farm, knowing he had slaves and demanding that he turn them over to the group.

Byrne objected and explained that his slaves were not at the farm that day. Unconvinced, the group escorted him to his home, thus further delaying their arrival to Harper's Ferry for several more hours.

Throughout the early morning hours, residents of Harper's Ferry,

---

[1] **The Jefferson Guard** was the Charlestown militia organized in 1858 and commanded by Captain John Rowan. They were on duty from Oct 17, 1859, until April 1860, when they were discharged after guarding the prisoners and witnessing all the hangings. During the Civil War, the unit became Company A of the 2nd Virginia Infantry in the "Stonewall Brigade."

one by one, became aware that an unknown number of raiders were intent on taking over their town. Some individual citizens became targets of Brown's men, who were strategically stationed on the streets. A man named Thomas Boerly was shot and killed as he attempted to walk the town's streets carrying a shotgun. Other men preparing to start the workday were surrounded, made prisoners, and escorted at gunpoint to the Armory, the Engine House , or the watch house next to it.

Before breakfast time had ended, Dwight became concerned that he had over sixty prisoners collected. He approached Brown. "Captain, I am expending too much manpower guarding the prisoners. It won't take long for them to realize they could overrun the few men holding them."

"They won't, Dwight. Look at the fear in their eyes. But I suggest you assign several Negros armed with pikes to assist your guards. An armed Negro will make them think twice. Put the minimum you see fit with rifles. Instruct them to keep them cocked and let the prisoners know about it. That should deter any thoughts they might have of overrunning the guards."

Dwight realized that his captain wasn't paying attention to any of his advice. Brown left the Armory to check the streets himself. Dwight issued the orders for guarding the prisoners and then followed Brown.

They came upon a townsman who was resisting arrest. The man identified himself as Joseph Barry and said that he had done nothing wrong and would not be arrested.

Brown ordered that the man be taken. Brown's plan was to take Barry to the temporary jailhouse. Clearly, neither Barry or Brown's men understood Brown's order.

Hearing Brown's orders, Barry ran away as a few of Brown's men prepared to shoot him. Dwight watched as a Negro woman suddenly rushed between Barry and his would-be assassins to keep Brown's men from shooting. Alarmed that even the town's blacks were aiding the town's whites and resisting Brown's men, Dwight returned to the Armory. He summoned another messenger and jotted down a message to alert Kagi of his concerns:

I have failed to convince the Captain that we are running out of time. We have no weapons or numbers to withstand an organized attack. I see no indication that the Negros will respond to our cause. It's only a matter of hours before we are entrapped.

Kagi received the message a little after 10:00 a.m. His stomach turned. Even though he had not seen any resistance brewing from his position at the rifleworks, he had complete trust in his friend. He responded:

I will join you by noon to discuss our situation with the Captain.

When Dwight read the reply, he hoped Kagi would be convincing enough for Brown to issue the retreat. He looked at his watch again. He realized he was looking at it every five to ten minutes. The time was 10:15 a.m.

Dwight looked up when Brown entered the Armory and pointed to one of the prisoners. "You there, come here." He waited as the nervous man approached. "Your name, sir?" he asked.

"Watty Kemp."

"Mr. Kemp, I want you to go to the Wager Hotel and call upon the manager. Tell him that he needs to prepare forty-five breakfast meals as soon as he can. Do you understand?"

Kemp nodded.

"Good, now be gone with you and remember that if I do not receive the meals, the prisoners will be very upset with you. I assume that you know some of these people, and that they will remember you if you do not return. I do not have to say anything further, do I? You understand the consequences if I do not receive the food I have requested?"

Kemp nervously nodded again.

Dwight didn't like Brown's idea. His men didn't need food. His men needed to retreat to the mountains, though so far he had seen no hope of that happening. Dwight also worried that Kemp would give too much information of what was going on when he relayed Brown's message to the manager. So far no one knew their strength, but now Brown had given them a number even though it was not representative of their men. Before Dwight could consider protesting, Kemp was out the door and on his mission.

Watty Kemp informed the owner of the Wager Hotel of the leader's demand for food. Only after Kemp pleaded and desperately communicated Brown's threats did John Foulke, the owner, reluctantly give in and prepare the food. Kemp made many trips back and forth before all the meals Brown had requested were delivered. The men, as well as some of the prisoners, quickly consumed the plates of bacon and eggs. Brown, Washington, and Allstadt did not eat.

Dwight noticed that. "Sir, you ordered the food, but why do you not eat?"

Brown looked at his lieutenant very seriously and said, "I fear poisoning could be a possibility."

Dwight understood his captain's point, but replied, "You still let the men and prisoners eat. You do not worry that they could be harmed?"

Brown never replied. Instead, he turned to Washington and Allstadt and said, "Gentlemen, the air still has a chill in it. Warm yourselves nearer to the stove."

Neither Washington nor Allstadt replied, but did oblige Brown and moved their chairs closer to the pot-bellied stove.

Dwight could feel his temper getting the best of him. He wanted to yell at his leader, who refused to take sound advice from him or Kagi concerning leaving but acted as a gracious host to his prisoners.

"Dwight, there are no indications anything is happening. Let us keep peace with our prisoners," Brown said. "The word will spread that we do not aim to harm them."

Dwight could not have disagreed more. There were already dead men in the street. He decided to lend no more advice. He'd wait for Kagi to return to the Armory.

Brown recognized Dwight's concerns, and turned to Dwight and said, "You have reason to be concerned. Your nature and experience warrant it. But you should remember that I am a student of history. I have traveled the European continent and visited the battlefields where the victories and defeats of Napoleon took place, and I know the advantages of numbers and arms when pitched decisively. We have the element of surprise and have arms nearby. I have sent for them, so do not despair. No form of resistance has been seen. Our plan is working. Have patience. Our support will come soon."

Dwight did not respond. For a man who traveled and had knowledge of military tactics, Brown seemed oblivious to the signs that were becoming clearly evident. Although they both had seen the situation differently at times, Brown was acting as if he never had any experience in dealing with making decisions as problems arose. Dwight realized he was relying heavily on both Kagi's arrival and his attempt to convince Brown to withdraw. He was still worried that active resistance would increase and counter their attack on Harper's Ferry. He watched as Brown sent William Thompson out of the Armory with orders to cross the bridge and go up the road toward Maryland Heights to find Owen Brown with the wagonload of arms.

The Wager Hotel
Harper's Ferry
Public Domain photo

Dwight didn't know how right he was about resistance. Two companies from Charlestown were quickly approaching Harper's Ferry, while others were coming from Martinsburg and Shepherdstown. The President of the United States, James Buchanan[1], was now aware of the seizing of the town, and he ordered Secretary of War John B. Floyd[2] to immediately send federal troops from Richmond, Baltimore, and

---

[1] **James Buchanan** was the 15th U.S. president, 1857–1861. He was a lifelong bachelor and the only president from Pennsylvania. When he left office, popular opinion had turned against him and the Democratic Party had split in two. Buchanan, who aspired to a presidency that would rank in history with that of George Washington, could not impose peace on the sharply divided country which was on the brink of the Civil War. That led to his consistent ranking by historians as one of the worst presidents in history.

[2] **John B. Floyd** was the secretary of war, but had poor administrative skills and was asked to resign by President Buchanan. He was later accused of sending large amounts of arms to arsenals in the south in anticipation of the Civil War. Though he was appointed a brigadier general early in the Civil War, he turned over his command at Ft. Donalson to General Pillow, who then surrendered to Grant as Floyd escaped. He was relieved of command by CSA President Jefferson Davis.

Frederick. Being informed that it would take many hours for the troops from those cities to arrive in Harper's Ferry, the President pressed Floyd to find troops that could respond more quickly. The closest troops that could be mustered were U.S. Marines stationed at the Washington Navy Yard. Luckily for Secretary Floyd, one experienced officer was available from the area to lead the small group of marines. Floyd sent a young cavalry lieutenant named James Ewell Brown Stuart[1], who was already waiting to see Floyd on other business that day, to fetch the chosen officer. Lieutenant Stuart dashed with the secretary's message to the home of the officer in Arlington, Virginia. Upon learning of the content of the letter, Stuart asked the superior officer if he could join him on his mission to free Harper's Ferry.

Unknown to Dwight Stevens, he and his men would have to deal with defending their position, outnumbered forty to one, against a lieutenant colonel named Robert E. Lee[2] and Lieutenant J.E.B. Stuart.

At 1:30 p.m., the President wired Mr. Garrett of the B&O Railroad that ninety-three officers and men were already en route to Harper's Ferry. Garrett returned a wire expressing that ninety-three men were too few, and that it was too late to stem the tide of at least seven hundred armed white and black men who were controlling the town.

Misinformation was abundant and contributed to additional panic within the federal and state governments. The military organization being put into motion to combat the insurrection in Harper's Ferry became further hindered as all realized that mobilizing a sufficient force to combat the numbers of raiders being reported could take days and possibly a week to complete. By noon, the state and local militias began to concentrate their fire at the raiders, but they would delay any assault on them until the U. S. Marines arrived late in the day on October 17th.

---

1 **James Ewell Brown (J.E.B.) Stuart** was a famous Confederate cavalry commander. He had a "cavalier," yet brave and daring image, and was the trusted "eyes and ears of Robert E. Lee's Army." General Stuart became one of the most well-known personalities of the Civil War. He was killed at the Battle of Yellow Tavern on May 12, 1864, at the age of 31.

2 **Robert E. Lee** was a career military officer best known for commanding the Confederate Army of Northern Virginia in the Civil War. The son of U.S. Revolutionary War hero Henry "Light Horse Harry" Lee III and a top graduate of West Point, Robert E. Lee was an exceptional officer and combat engineer in the United States Army for 32 years before resigning to join the Confederate cause. By the end of the American Civil War, he was commanding general of the Confederate army. He became a hero of the South's "lost cause," and is still admired to this day.

J.E.B. Stuart as he appeared at about the time of the Harper's Ferry Raid
Public Domain photo

Robert E. Lee as he looked at the time of the raid at Harper's Ferry
Public Domain photo

With Dwight in the Armory and John Kagi holding his own in the rifleworks, the first shots of gunfire were heard around noon. Despite the men Brown had strategically placed throughout the town, an organized attempt had formed against them and was beginning to take aim.

Dwight looked to Brown and said, "Captain, we must withdraw. The organized resistance has started." But before he could say anything further, Brown struck up a conversation with Colonel Washington and several other prominent citizens.

An argument ensued about whether Brown should give up his position and leave the town. Brown paced back and forth in the Armory, holding the sword of Frederick the Great in one hand and a Sharps rifle in his other. He listened to the comments from Allstadt and the others.

Dwight intervened again as the argument continued. "Captain, we must withdraw."

Brown did not respond.

Suddenly, Dwight heard the Armory door open. He hoped it was Kagi, but instead, Jeremiah Anderson staggered into the Armory. He had been shot and was bleeding from a wound in his side. Dwight ran to assist him and gently moved him to a place in the corner of the room. He looked at Brown, who was oblivious to the importance of seeing the man wounded.

Several minutes later, as Dwight attended to Anderson's wounds, Brown remarked to his prisoners, ***"If you know me and understand my motives as well as I and others understand them, you would not blame me for what I am doing. If you knew my heart and history you would not think evil of me."***

The prominent citizens looked at each other as Brown opened the Armory door and looked out to see and hear the sporadic shooting that had developed.

He yelled out, ***"Hold on a little longer boys. Hold on until I get matters arranged."***

Dwight concentrated on Anderson's injury. He still hoped Kagi would arrive soon.

Watson Brown and Stewart Taylor saw a group of men descend upon the bridge they were guarding but they could not distinguish if they were militia or just armed citizens. As Brown and Taylor watched the group of men approach the bridge, gunfire erupted. They managed to wound one of the attackers, but both men were then forced to withdraw. They realized the citizens they fired on were militia who constantly yelled that they were the Jefferson Guard. The guard quickly approached the Wager Hotel and set up their headquarters there after securing the bridge.

After entering the hotel, Captain Rowan of the Jefferson Guard remarked that the Sharps rifles they had just faced were weapons he had never experienced. He urged his men to be aware of the rapidity of the gunfire that the raiders could employ.

The word spread quickly, and Brown and his men were afforded more time due to the respect the militia had for the quick-reloading Sharps rifle.

As the time approached 1:00 p.m. and the firing increased, Brown finally realized the futility of his situation. Not realizing that the additional arms and the men he sent to get them were still at the schoolhouse, Brown pondered his next move.

Dwight suggested to Brown, "Captain, we should withdraw in a rear-guard action. I feel we could retreat through the Armory courtyard and head for the residential area upriver. The Blue Ridge Mountains could hide us until we reorganize. I'm confident John Kagi would agree. Let me send for him." Dwight paused to let Brown ponder his advice, then spoke again. "Captain, as you must know, no amount of the training we went through will help us if we are boxed up in these buildings. We will simply be fish in a barrel for everyone out there."

Still, Brown did not answer. He seemed incapable of making a decision.

Dwight knew what Brown needed to do, but he was unable to assume command, or even consider taking it, from the Captain. It never occurred to him. Maybe it was because he had too much love and respect for John Brown, or it also could have been due to his years of military life and training. Deep in his soul, there was simply no such option, and Dwight forbid himself from even thinking in that regard. So, he continued to wait for Brown.

Others, however, were capable of making key decisions as the afternoon continued.

Captain John Avis,[1] of the Charlestown irregulars, ordered his men to begin concentrated fire from the houses overlooking the Armory. Just as they starting firing, the main thrust from the Jefferson Guards drove Oliver Brown, William Thompson, and Dangerfield Newby from the safety of their positions. Richard Washington, of Avis's command, took aim at the three fleeing raiders. He concentrated on the lead man, Newby, and fired and killed him instantly with a shot to the throat. Dangerfield

---

[1] **Captain John Avis** served in the war with Mexico, and fought for the South in the Civil War in Company K, 5th Regiment of the Old Continentals. He was also an officer in the local militia. He and his wife became somewhat like outcasts in Harper's Ferry due to the friendship and care given to John Brown and Dwight Stevens during the time he was their jailor. He was called the "Good Jailor" by John Brown and Dwight Stevens.

Newby, one of the last to join the raid, was the first of John Brown's men to die. Word reached the Armory that Newby had been shot and killed.

As the firing increased, Dwight realized that Kagi would not be able to reach the Armory from the rifleworks. He could see everything very clearly now, and it was too late to do anything. He finished assisting with Jeremiah Anderson's wounds and hoped the man would survive despite the amount of blood he had lost. Dwight collected his thoughts and tried to assess the developing situation. He knew Kagi was with Lewis Leary and John Copeland, and he began to develop a plan to rescue them from their position. He needed more men.

Dwight began receiving updates that Owen Brown, Merriam, and Barclay Coppoc were now cut off from the group by the newly arrived guardsmen. Cook and Tidd were now separated as well, with the arrival of the militia. Even if they attempted to deliver the arms they had to the Armory, they would be quickly overcome.

Dwight remembered that Albert Hazlett and Osborne Anderson were in the arsenal across the street, but no guardsmen were shooting at them. He contemplated leaving the Armory, crossing the street, and recruiting Hazlett and Anderson to assist him in freeing Kagi and his men at the rifleworks. He wondered if he could get Kagi and his men back to the Armory.

To his surprise, Brown ordered that his men move Washington and some of the other prominent prisoners inside the Engine House.

The Captain spoke once all the chosen prisoners were together. ***"Gentlemen, perhaps you wonder why I have selected you from the others."*** He looked around at all of them before he continued. ***"It is because I believe you to be more influential; and I have to say now, that you will have to share precisely the same fate that your friends extend to my men."***

Dwight became irritated, hearing the Captain speak in this manner. He felt that Brown had now resolved himself to a standoff, and possible death to his prisoners, if the approaching militia and Jefferson Guard continued their assault. But the old man surprised him.

As the Jefferson Guard approached the iron gate of the Armory, Brown ordered Dwight and several of the men to take aim at the advancing guardsmen from their positions in and around the Armory. When the attacking guardsmen were within approximately sixty yards of the gate, he ordered them to fire their Sharps. Dwight saw several guardsmen fall. The rapid fire panicked those of higher ranks, and they withdrew quickly. From that point on, the guardsmen stayed at a safe distance.

When Brown's men stopped firing, Brown addressed Dwight. "I

am not fooled and I am completely aware of the seriousness of the situation. I will send a truce to their commander for a cease fire. I shall ask for a volunteer."

Dwight did not answer him immediately, instead pondering Brown's decision.

A prisoner overheard Brown talking and responded, "Sir, I will volunteer to go."

Brown was surprised as he looked at the man. "Your name, sir? Why should you volunteer?"

"I am Resin Cross. I am just a resident of Harper's Ferry. I would hope that the shooting would stop and the blood-spilling ends on behalf of this gesture."

Brown smiled and nodded to the man.

William Thompson spoke up. "Captain, I'll go with him."

"Good, then it is done." John Brown looked at Dwight. "Make a flag of truce."

Dwight looked around until he found what he needed. Allstadt's son was wearing a white shirt under his coat, and Dwight commanded the youth to remove it quickly. Within minutes a makeshift white flag of truce was handed to Thompson as Cross opened the Armory door and departed with his hands held high to show that he was unarmed. Thompson followed, still clutching his Sharps rifle in one hand and the flag of truce in the other. The two men walked approximately forty feet past the gates of the Armory before they were descended upon and captured by the guardsmen, the flag of truce completely disregarded.

Shocked at what he saw, Dwight remarked, "They have no honor at all. We are dealing with an uncontrolled mob. We must use more convincing tactics with this enemy."

Brown turned to face the prisoners, who also had witnessed the incident. Some were terrified, believing Brown would take out his frustration on them for the lack of fairness and honor on the part of the guardsmen.

At that moment, A. M. Kitzmiller, the acting superintendent of the Armory, volunteered to take another flag of truce on their behalf.

Brown asked him why he should volunteer.

"Because, sir, I am well known by the citizens of Harper's Ferry. They will listen to me and hear the words you have to relay to them."

"Tell them the bloodshed can end if they adhere to the truce. We shall talk further once they comply." Brown looked at his son Watson. "Go and assure them I am a man of my word." He looked to Dwight. "Please go and protect them. I have the utmost trust in you to see this through."

Dwight did not answer. He grabbed the remainder of the shirt cloth he had taken from the Allstadt youth and arranged it into another flag of truce. He opened the Armory door, motioned for the other two to follow, and led the way out. His eyes swept the scene in front of him as he cautiously walked, carrying the white flag. The only noise Dwight could hear was the sound of their boots grinding the sandy soil beneath them. The shirt cloth waved as he moved it above his head. The smell of gun smoke filled the eerily silent air. The silence was suddenly broken as Dwight heard the shot from a musket and felt the whiz of a bullet pass by his head. The sound of the lead hitting flesh was familiar to the seasoned veteran. He heard the scream of Watson Brown as he fell to the ground.

Watching the scene unfold from the second floor of the Galt House, which was near the Armory, was an armed citizen named George Chambers, a saloonkeeper who either never saw the flag of truce or simply didn't care. He took aim with his double-barreled shotgun. Meanwhile Dwight watched Watson drag himself back toward the Armory. At the sight of Watson being wounded and dragging himself, Kitzmiller fled to safety before Dwight could react. As Dwight turned back and contemplated his choices to either to go forward or retreat, he never heard the sound of the two shots that came from Chambers's shotgun. Both shots hit him, and he fell in the street, unmoving and unconscious.

John Brown watched in horror as his son painfully crawled back toward him and Dwight appeared to be dead in the street. Brown did not notice that a prisoner had run past him and escaped.

Prisoner Joseph Brewer ran out of the Engine House to where Dwight lay still and bleeding from his face and chest wounds. No one knew where Brewer, an average-sized man, got the strength to lift a man of Dwight's size. The firing of weapons ceased. Some thought that it was adrenaline induced by sheer fear that enabled Brewer to carry the injured man to the Wager Hotel. Whatever it was, Dwight Stevens was able to receive immediate emergency care from several women who had volunteered to help treat the wounded. Several rooms in the Wager Hotel had been commandeered for the injured. Dwight was the first critically wounded man to be treated in a clean bed. As soon as Brewer saw Dwight receiving the emergency treatment he needed, he did an unusual thing. He casually left the side of Dwight's bed, went outside, and returned to the Armory again as one of Brown's prisoners.

Dwight was imminently close to death, although he was unconscious and not aware of that fact. He lay completely still, unresponsive to the touch of his caretakers and the outside world. Yet his mind was still working healthily; images of the adventure that was the story of his life gently unfolded behind his eyes.

Looking at the Armory from the Shenandoah River side.
The firehouse is in the center.
http://johnsmilitaryhistory.com/harpersferry.html

Chapter Two

The Secret Trip

He was just a common young man, hiding in a cold, moving train. Several hours had passed since he'd stowed away on that train. He found warmth and comfort among the bales of cloth stacked in the boxcar. Watching the bales being loaded at the Greenville stop earlier that evening had given him the idea to stow away. He had saved almost two dollars to pay for his trip to Boston, but stowing away would afford him a better chance of reaching his destination with at least some money still in his pocket. After sneaking onboard, he had arranged some bales into a makeshift bed; he didn't know where the bales were being shipped, but his thrown-together bed offered the security he needed. Thursday, February 4, 1847, commenced the beginning of a new and important chapter in the life of young Aaron Dwight Stevens, who had left his home in Norwich, Connecticut to fight in the war against Mexico.

The smell of smoke from the steam engine permeated the boxcar, but the cold New England air coming in through the small spaces between the wood sheathing quickly cleared it away. Dwight, as he had been called for most of his life, slept in short intervals as the train slowly pulled its load through the early morning hours. Quite often, he awoke as the noisy engine slowed to a stop at another station. Dwight remembered hearing the conductor yelling each time. He always became apprehensive, thinking that this stop might be where the cloth bales would be unloaded. He had gone over a plan several times in his mind, determining what he would do when that scenario happened. So far, eight or nine stops had occurred and no one had entered the boxcar.

Dwight heard someone yell, "Cranston Station." Based on his geography schooling, he knew the train had made it to Rhode Island. Keeping still, he listened for anyone who might be approaching. He was prepared to bolt. He could hear talking, laughing, and swearing as they loaded more cargo into a boxcar next to his. For the next twenty or so minutes, he remained still and tense in his temporary hideaway.

When he no longer heard any noises, he knew the loading and unloading was finished. Still, the pitch-black night, cold winds, and chance of being caught kept him alert. After a while, he heard muffled voices and knew it had to be the passengers boarding or exiting the one passenger car he had seen back at the Greenville stop. Smoke permeated the boxcar again, and he grabbed some loose cloth to cover his mouth and nose. Dwight knew that his coughing could alert someone who happened to be passing by the boxcar. A chill slowly began to overcome him as he piled more cloth over his face.

The engine began to pull the train from Cranston Station. It was a welcomed feeling, and he began to relax as the train slowly moved into the night. The dim light from the disappearing station flickered through the spaces in the wood sheathing, and then quickly faded as the train increased its speed. Before long the air was clean and cold again, and the interior of the boxcar was dark, but he felt secure. As Dwight lay awake, he couldn't help but think of the home and family he had left not more than eight hours ago.

He pulled more cloth from a bale until he was almost completely buried, trying hard to stay warm. As he lay there, he thought about what his family might think had happened to him. One rule his father had insisted upon was to be home no later than 6:00 p.m. on winter evenings. He wondered whether his father would have asked some of the neighbors around the Norwichtown Green if they had seen his son. His father had always said that one of Dwight's biggest problems was that he constantly roamed about. Dwight felt bad knowing that his sister Lydia would be worried sick when their father returned with no information on him, and for the concern she would have to endure until he could write to tell her his new location and the path he had chosen to pursue. He made a mental note to obtain quill, ink, and paper so he could explain everything to his family as soon as he was able. He was also saddened that he had not confided in Charles.

Charles Whipple and Dwight had been best friends their entire lives. Even though they were cousins, Charles was more like a brother than a cousin. It was only hours ago they had left each other's company after ice skating. He wondered if people would think he had fallen into the pond where they had skated, but he knew that Charles would explain he had seen him after skating, heading home. At least people would know that he had not succumbed to a cold, watery grave.

His stomach growled as he faded in and out of sleep. The clicking of the train's wheels was hypnotic and contributed to his semi-unconsciousness, until the emptiness of his stomach fully awakened him. He reached into his overcoat pocket and retrieved several biscuits he had taken from his stepmother's pantry. When asked why he needed more food after just completing a warm noon meal of venison stew, Dwight had remarked that he and Charles would need something to snack on while returning from skating. His stepmother thought it was a reasonable request from an almost-seventeen-year-old who looked more like a man every day, but when she observed him filling several pockets, she told him to only take a couple to share with his cousin. She would recall that event several days later, which would add to the speculation that Dwight was still alive. She and his father would conclude that Dwight had planned all along to leave Norwich.

The two biscuits were cold and hard. Dwight bit into and slowly ate one, deciding to save the other until later. He had no other plan for his next meal. The several biscuits he had eaten at home had been delicious when they had been served warm with the venison stew, but the one he ate cold barely stopped the growling in his stomach. He became somewhat hypnotized again with the clicking of the wheels on the tracks as he thought about his mother. Her face was becoming difficult to remember. He had only been nine when she died. He couldn't remember why, but his memory kept flashing to her crying and holding a child wrapped in cloth. He saw her lay the child in a tiny coffin. It was then that he saw her anguish. He thought of her often, but he always became sad when he thought of her and his older brother, who had died when Dwight was only two years old.

Dwight vaguely remembered Charles Lester now; he did, however, clearly remember reading the lettering on his headstone. It had been next to his mother's. He recalled the sadness when he visited their gravesites with his family. The visits had occurred less and less as the years passed, especially when his stepmother came into the family. Dwight had known her all his life, since she was his mother's sister. Aunt Adeline became Mother. He couldn't remember when he last visited his mother's grave. He realized that those visits had steadily declined once his half-brother Lemuel and his half-sister, Little Susan, were born. Little Susan was now eight and the center of attention for his parents. Lemuel and Dwight got along well because their five-year age difference minimized the normal sibling rivalries. Dwight didn't resent either of them, and he knew they would obtain all the attention now and was fine with that.

Leaving home was the best thing he had done. He did not hate his family. In fact, he loved them all deeply. But Dwight knew as well as they did that he was vastly different. He did not want to live the life they did. He wanted and needed something else. His family seemed to diligently avoid any excitement, adventure, or anything different, while he craved it. They led a quiet, pious life, but he silently dreamed about a life that was much different. Dwight felt he was not running away from home, but toward something new and exciting. One thing he felt bad about was that others would have to perform the chores he normally did at home. Chopping wood for the fireplaces and cooking stoves was the first chore he thought about. His older brother, Henry ,came to his mind. But Henry was a busy man, and his father would probably hire someone to perform that duty. He thought, *The chore will cost money. They will hate me for this.* But he never thought to turn around and go home. He was committed. Deep down inside, Dwight did not think they would be horribly surprised to find him gone.

Besides roaming, his stubbornness had been a big problem. He always knew he was too stubborn for his stepmother to handle, which resulted in an occasional whipping from his father. That never did change his attitude, however, and his father often commented to relatives and friends that ***"correction could hardly be administered by a properly applied birch stick."*** The pain his father induced was delivered by the strength of a stonemason, which in fact he was.

Dwight smiled, thinking how many times he had been stung by the stick yet had never given his father the satisfaction of knowing how much it hurt him. He laughed to himself, remembering one time when the stick had actually broken and subsequently shortened the punishment. Dwight's biggest problem was his temper. His parents often worried that his short temper would get him in the worst trouble.

He continued to think about the siblings and friends he had left behind. There was warmth amongst the cloth bales now, but his mind was still wandering. He needed something with which to occupy himself. He began to think of the hymns he enjoyed singing in his father's choir. Being the son of the choir director had provided him with the opportunity to become an outstanding singer. Dwight began singing softly, and then realized that his baritone voice was hindered by his effort to keep the volume low. He laughed to himself. Unless someone was in the boxcar with him, no one would ever hear him singing as the train moved noisily along. Before long, he had sung everything he could remember. He wished that he had one of the hymnals his father always carried to church on Sundays and to choir rehearsals. The hymnal had all the words he hadn't spent the time to memorize. While he sang, he laughed as he occasionally made up words to some of the songs. Singing in the choir had been one of the most enjoyable things about his childhood, and the choir had been the reason they had moved from Lisbon to Norwich. His father had been offered the job of choir director of the Congregational Church on the Norwichtown Green, and the family had moved into a home on East Towne Street. It had been an easy decision for his father to make. It offered a larger income and an important position in the church. As Dwight rested his voice, he realized he would miss Sunday service. He couldn't remember when he had ever missed one. Maybe the regiment held services. If they did, he'd be sure to attend.

He cleared his mind and thought about the many times he and Charles played in the streets and on the green. He smiled, thinking of the time the city officials passed a law declaring all ball playing in any public street illegal. Somehow, Charles and Dwight never got caught despite all the times they had played cricket in the streets. Kite flying was another happy memory. The March and April winds would whip up the streets from the Yantic River and over the plain of the green, making the kites fly almost out of sight. The drilling of the militia on the green was also a memorable event. The dark blue jackets and gray trousers the men wore had always impressed him. He thought of the young ladies that watched their beaus, brothers, fathers, and husbands drill until the sergeant major thought they had performed to his perfection. But the close-order drills with fixed bayonets that reflected the sunlight and flashed about when right and left turn orders were commanded were the most impressive.

Parading and drilling on the snow-covered town green had become more frequent during the winter months since the war with Mexico had been declared. When he had heard the news, Dwight decided to join up before the hostilities ended. He was only fifteen when war was declared, but he figured that once he turned sixteen, no one would question his age if he left town and joined up at some other location. He continued to read the postings at the green that described new units that were forming in Connecticut. He planned to join the one farthest from Norwich. When he read a posting that the First Massachusetts Regiment of Volunteers was forming in Boston, his plans changed. Dwight was sure that his height and size would convince those soliciting recruits that he was older than his sixteen years, though his size would only help him enlist if no one recognized him. Boston afforded him the anonymity to ensure no one would.

He decided that if anyone did ask, he would say he was over eighteen. It wouldn't be a lie, because he planned to place a piece of paper in the bottom of his shoe with the number eighteen on it. The paper was his absolution. He relaxed, knowing the act would save his soul from the lie he would need to tell about his age. It was these ideas he had been incessantly thinking about since he had heard about the declaration of war in April of last year. He knew that many people in church and throughout the area did not support the war, but that did not affect his plans.

Dwight wondered what his great-grandfather and grandfather would have thought of this war. He had known since he could remember that his great-grandfather had been a captain in Swift's Regiment during the Revolutionary War. He was sure that the old man, if he had still been alive, would have joined up again. His grandfather had soldiered during the War of 1812. He was sure that he, also, would have joined the fight. The many evenings he had spent in front of the fireplace listening to the heroic stories of Great-grandfather Moses and Grandfather Aaron had been etched in his mind. Dwight had memorized the stories, which only enhanced his desire to fight for his country like they had. His great-grandfather's sword was a constant reminder to him of the family's proud military history. He also remembered, with a smile, how often he was punished for removing the sword from its scabbard and swinging it around the house. He often wondered about how his great-grandfather had used the sword in battle and fantasized many times about who his hapless victims had been.

Military life had skipped his father and his oldest brother, who both were mainly interested in music. They led the family in singing almost every night that they weren't in choir practice or singing at Sunday service. Father and Henry always talked about music and rarely commented on anything concerning the military. When Dwight did mention the war, their general reaction was that he was too young to understand why they thought it was an unnecessary war. His father's stonemasonry work, choir duties, strict Puritan ethics, and musical interests had occupied his life, and his interest in music was what influenced Henry the most. Dwight had heard Henry talk many times with their father about pursuing music as a career and possibly opening up a music store in town. Both men were preoccupied with music, whether it involved instruments or singing. The fact that there had been over twenty-five years of peace in the country, coupled with his father's and brother's association with the Puritan church, only solidified their disinterest in the military and enhanced their pacifist thinking.

Dwight's senses were awakened when he heard and felt the train slow. He tensed, wondering if his boxcar was going to be unloaded at this stop. He strained to hear the conductor's voice identify the station for what seemed like an eternity. Finally the man yelled out, "Attleboro Station."

Dwight wondered, *What distance is it from Boston?* He knew it was in Massachusetts. The thought of his boxcar being opened became his priority. The sounds of horses and wagon wheels on the cobblestone street became louder as he prepared for the door to be opened. As he was thinking of the direction he would flee, the door opened wide, surprising him, and he lost the opportunity to bolt.

Dwight lay still and squinted to adjust his eyes to the morning light. Tension built as he kept motionless in his isolated corner. Expecting the bales to be unloaded any minute, he listened intently to the orders someone was barking at the men who had entered the car. Dwight didn't know what had happened except that, after what seemed to be an eternity, the workers suddenly left. They did not close the door, however, and his wondering of what was happening overcame his desire to remain hidden. He moved out of his hideaway and peeked over the stacked bales of cloth.

A glimpse of a partially loaded wagon revealed that the rail workers had unloaded only a portion of the cloth bales. He relaxed, knowing that he still had not been seen. He froze when he saw a rail worker jump up into the boxcar. Dwight ducked back down and prayed that the man had not seen him. There were more sounds as another worker entered, then the two began talking. Eventually they both were ordered to get to work. Dwight peeked and could see they were stacking wooden crates on top of each other. The sounds went on for almost longer than Dwight's nerves could endure, until the men were told to get out of the boxcar. Within moments the workers were gone, but the door was still open. He checked again and saw that one worker had left a hat and canteen on one of the crates. His thirst was becoming overwhelming. Within seconds he had the canteen in hand and was back in his cloth cave.

The youth poured a small portion on his hand to be sure it was water. Satisfied, he gulped the cool liquid, but realized he'd have to conserve it for the rest of his journey. Dwight hoped that the owner of the canteen would not return, but he did. Dwight heard him yell to his co-workers, asking if they had seen his canteen. The worker mumbled to himself that he had at least found his hat. Hearing laughter, Dwight assumed that the other workers had joked with the man for losing his canteen. Before long the door closed and the darkness returned. The light flickered again into the boxcar as the train jolted to life and continued the journey to Boston.

The light of day was becoming stronger as it filtered through the spaces of the sheathing. His muscles were becoming stiff, so he stood and stretched to limber up. Curiosity overcame his caution and he ventured over to the stacked wooden crates. They were filled with muskets and he realized that maybe these muskets were on their way to the same destination he was hoping to reach. Another plan developed in his head. If the muskets were unloaded near Boston, he could follow the wagon to its final destination, which might be some military unit or storage area where he could obtain information on the First Massachusetts Regiment of Volunteers.

Hunger overtook the famished youth again, and he broke out the last biscuit and ate it. This time he was glad he had some water with which to wash it down. Finished, he secured the cork in the canteen and lay back in his makeshift bed, thinking of the men who would be issued the muskets. He wondered if one of the muskets was going to be issued to him. Dwight drifted off to sleep, exhausted. He slept soundly until awakened again by the sounds and sensations of the train slowing.

"Foxboro Station!" yelled the conductor, and Dwight tensed, preparing for what could happen at this next stop. But nothing did. The conductor yelled for passengers to begin boarding. Dwight relaxed when he distinctly heard him yell, "Sharon, Canton, Hyde, Roxbury, and Boston Stations! All aboard!"

Five more station stops and he would be at his destination. He had lost track of time during his journey and he guessed it had been about twelve hours since he had left the Greenville stop. Not waiting for the train to move, and feeling secure that no one would be entering his boxcar, he ventured out and sat on a musket crate near the door. He looked through a slit for a view of the outside world. Luckily, there was a large station clock that indicated it was a few minutes after 9:00 a.m.

Dwight saw several men in uniform pass by. *They must be soldiers heading to Boston*, he thought. That idea was confirmed when he saw more men trot by to catch up with the ones that had just passed.

The whistle blew and the conductor announced the same list of stations. Within a minute, Dwight felt the familiar jolt as the train began to move. He sat on the musket crate until he was cold from the frigid air entering the car, then he returned to the protection of his makeshift bed. More time passed and he slept, awakened periodically by the blast of the whistle and feeling, again, the train slowing. He vaguely recollected the stops prior to Roxbury, as they had been passenger stops. He relaxed, thinking this stop at Roxbury Station would be like the others—uneventful. Suddenly, he heard horses and wagons approaching his boxcar. Quickly exiting the warmth of his makeshift bed, he ventured out, hoping they would pass by while he peeked through the wood sheathing. To his horror, the first wagon stopped in front of the door. He quickly retreated. Crouching, he waited to see if the wagon had come for the bales or the crates. The door screeched as it slid open. The afternoon light was weaker now that the winter evening was approaching, but Dwight was still able to peek over the bales.

A soldier jumped up. Several moments later, more men were ordered to assist in unloading the crates. Dwight retreated again to keep hidden. He listened and waited, hearing the grunting and swearing from the men and the constant orders from another voice. He slung the canteen over his shoulder and waited to execute his plan. Finally, the unloading was complete and the soldiers and wagon departed. For an instant the boxcar was quiet. He peeked over and saw the empty space where the crates had been stored. Stretching his neck in the direction of another sound, he saw a second wagon begin to pull in front of the open door. He knew this wagon was here to unload the bales and reacted quickly. He bolted out from the cover of the cloth bales and headed directly for the open door.

Exploding through the door, he bumped into a rail worker who was attempting to enter the boxcar. The force from the large youth knocked the worker off-balance, and he fell back onto the cobblestone road. As Dwight jumped from the boxcar to the empty wagon, he could hear the cussing coming from the startled rail worker. A second rail worker, who had been sitting next to the teamster, reached toward Dwight but only managed to grab the sling attached to the canteen. Dwight's speed caused the sling to be yanked from his shoulder. The rail worker could only watch with the canteen and its sling in his hand as Dwight jumped from the wagon to the cobblestone road below. Within moments, the stowaway was running in the same direction he had last seen the wagon of crates being driven off.

Other rail workers heard the commotion coming from the open boxcar and reacted to the youth running past them in his haste to exit the scene. They yelled for him to stop, but to no avail. Dwight increased his speed. He found an alley between the station and a small warehouse. He ran down it and was soon out of sight of the workers. The alley was muddy, and he struggled to keep his balance until he came to its end and stopped before entering the street. The wooden sidewalk offered him some stable footing before he crossed through the busy traffic, moving slowly through the mud mixed with horse manure. He relaxed a little, knowing the rail workers were not interested in pursuit. But then his sense of smell reacted to the stench of the street mud.

The crossing was difficult as he slid through the soft mixture and nearly gagged from the smell. The activity of the traffic kept the mud loose despite the cold. He found himself standing on the wooden sidewalk in front of a mercantile, catching his breath as people, oblivious to his existence, walked about and in and out of the store. A few times, he was brushed past by some men who only grumbled for the youth to get out of the way. His breathing was hindered by the abundance of wood and coal smoke in the air. Finally getting his bearings, he slowly walked in the same direction he thought the wagon of musket crates had gone. Several minutes passed, and he attempted to blow his nose to clear his sinuses with a bit of material he had taken from a clothbale. Despite the foul smell from the street, his nose and then his eyes soon found a bakery. He slipped inside and approached the counter.

"What can I get ya, boy?" the smiling man who was covered partially with white flour asked behind a long counter. He didn't respond at first until the man repeated, "What can I get ya, son? I'm closing soon. It's Friday and I'd a long day." He waited a few seconds. "Cat got ya tongue? Speak up boy, I'm a busy man."

Dwight was looking at several types of breads and biscuits displayed in wicker baskets on the top of the counter. "How much for a biscuit, sir?"

"Oh, yer a polite one, aren't ya? They're two cents apiece. Twenty-five for a baker's dozen. How many ya want?"

"I'll take two. No, three. Yes, I'll take three," he said.

The baker wiped his hands on his apron, pulled three biscuits from the wicker basket, and put them on the wooden counter. "That'll be six cents, son."

The exchange was made and Dwight put his purchase into his coat pocket and turned to leave.

"Ye're not from around here, are ya?"

He paused and turned back. "No, sir, I ain't. I come from Norwich, Connecticut. How'd you know I was from another place?"

"Ya talk a little funny. Could tell right up. Where ya heading to?"

"On my way to join the Massachusetts Volunteers."

"Oh, are ya? You are big enough, but ya look a little young to be killing Santa Anna's boys. Ya know they shoot back at ya." He laughed as Dwight stared straight into his eyes.

"Old enough last March. I had to wait until I got some money to travel here."

"Ya parents let you go off to kill Mexicans, did they?"

Dwight stumbled to answer, but remained silent.

"Oh, so ye're off to defend the country on yer own, are ya? Well, good for ya. I wish ya luck. Not too many boys are running to join up. Mexico is not a popular place to go. I think them Texans should fight 'em. They started this dang thing."

"Could you tell me where the signing up is at?"

"Ya need to keep walking the way you was heading. About four miles down is the commons. Caleb Cushing is forming the unit there. My crazy nephew joined just last week. Can't understand why. His name is Jeremiah. Jeremiah Taggard. Ask for him when ya get signed up."

"Thank you, I will," Dwight said as he turned again to leave.

"By the way, son. What's ya name?"

"Aaron Dwight Stevens, sir."

"Well, Stevens, I wish ya luck. Don't want to see ya in the casualty list someday. Ask for my nephew. Ya two will get along."

Dwight left and turned in the direction he had been directed. He kept to the sidewalk when it was available. The street traffic had lessened as dusk began to settle in. Some streetlights were being lit has he walked and ate the second of the three biscuits he had bought. The temperature was dropping, and he realized that he would have to find some place to sleep until he could reach the commons. By the time he finished the third biscuit, he saw a livery sign up ahead on the opposite side of the street.

Light still steamed through the partially open doors.

Dwight crossed the street and almost turned his ankle in the partially frozen ruts left by the many wagon wheels. The glow of the light from the livery doors brightened as he approached. He could hear the clanking of metal and then saw several men working at a blacksmith's furnace. Watching for several minutes, he got an idea that this type of place would afford him some protection from the dropping temperatures. He slid into the livery stable, unnoticed by the two men.

The men were too busy hammering and the noise was too loud for them to notice him as he found the loft ladder and scurried up it. He slowly moved through the loose hay until he was above where the two men were working below. The heat from the furnace rose and warmed the section of the loft where he lay. He nestled into that area and waited to see how long the blacksmiths would work into the evening. He lay still, hoping that no one would be coming up to remove hay to feed the several horses that were bordered in the stalls he had seen below. The clanking rhythm coming from the blacksmiths and the sweet odor of hay mixed with the smell of the horses relaxed him, and he soon fell asleep. He awakened to sheer quiet after the blacksmiths had stopped working. The door to the livery stable closed and the whale-oil lights were extinguished as the two men left the stable by a rear door, but the glow of the furnace still illuminated the stable. Dwight realized he needed to relieve his bowels for the first time since the start of the trip.

He exited the loft, found a pile of horse manure, and finished his business as quickly as possible. He covered his waste using a pitchfork and went to the blacksmith furnace. The heat was still intense enough to warm him. Staying close to the furnace until his overcoat, trousers, hat, and mittens were almost too hot to keep wearing, he returned to the loft, made a softer bed with more hay he managed to ruffle, and relaxed in the security of the loft. He wondered if the blacksmiths would return to stoke the furnace fire. Too tired to stay awake, he fell off to sleep despite the noises from the horses below and the occasional barking from the dogs that roamed the street outside.

Sometime later, a noise from below awakened him. As quietly as he could, he rolled over onto his stomach, crawled to the edge of the hayloft, and peeked down at the furnace below. He quickly backed out of sight as a whale-oil lamp was lit by one of the blacksmiths. The man went about his task to stoke the furnace as Dwight remained still in the loft above. Minutes went by. Before long, he saw the light extinguish, heard the rear door close, and relaxed as the quiet returned. He fell off to a much-needed sleep for several more hours.

The early morning crow of a rooster finally awakened him. His mouth and throat were parched. Quenching his thirst was his first priority. Descending the ladder, he found a trough and broke the thin layer of ice that had formed over the water during the night. He cupped his hands and drank until his thirst was satisfied. The stable door squeaked as he peeked out to observe the street in the early morning light. He thought that fog was obscuring his sight, but realized it was only the early morning cold with the wood and coal smoke from hundreds of chimneys settling over the city. The stench from the previous day still permeated the air. Heading in the direction he remembered, he set out, hopefully toward the commons. It was Saturday morning. The air was still and the only noises he heard were an occasional dog's bark and his boots on the wood sidewalk. No businesses or shops were open. He came upon an area of the street that seemed narrow and realized the two- and three-story buildings that were built so close together were what contributed to his feeling of near claustrophobia. Moving off the sidewalk and onto the edge of the street lessened his phobia. Luckily, he narrowly missed the contents of a chamber pot that was hastily emptied from a window several stories above him. Several more instances of this nature occurred, and he quickly learned to steer toward the center of the street in order to walk in relative safety.

Soon, horse- or ox-drawn wagons delivering goods could be seen as he passed intersections of the street. He noticed very few horsemen or pedestrians during his walk, but assumed few would be venturing out in the early Saturday morning cold.

He startled when a voice called out to him from behind, "Out early this morning, aren't ya, son?"

He stopped and turned around as a policeman approached him. Recognizing the authority figure in his dark uniform, Dwight responded, "Yes, sir. I'm heading for the commons."

"Not much there these days except soldiers."

"I know. I came to join up."

"Where ya from, lad?"

"Norwich, Connecticut. I've been on travel a while to get here."

"You're heading the right way. Caleb Cushing is the man you ask for."

"Yes, sir. The baker down a ways told me the same."

"Baker Taggard, did he? His nephew done the same thing last week. Be on your way and good luck to ya."

Dwight smiled and relaxed. Thanking the policeman, he continued on his journey as his stomach began to growl. He hoped he'd find another bakery, or a general store or diner, where he could purchase a bit to eat.

The clock on a church steeple he passed rang six times. A small diner with lamps lit, indicating it was open for business, lie ahead. Being the only welcome in sight from the morning cold, he opened the door that touched a small bell and announced his arrival. Several men at various tables looked up as he found an empty table close to the fireplace and sat down. The heat afforded some relief to his cold feet, hands, and face. Uninterested in the stranger, the patrons went back to their conversations and breakfast.

The owner called out, "What will ya be having?"

Dwight looked up to make sure the man was speaking at him as others looked again while they ate. "Breakfast, sir. I'm famished."

"Eggs, bacon, biscuits, and coffee be all right?"

Dwight nodded.

"Be twelve cents, lad, and you can pick up your food and drink at the counter when it's ready."

He rose and paid the fee, then waited back at the table to absorb the warmth. In a short time he was called to pick up his order. He finished the meal in haste, but slowly sipped his coffee to lengthen his stay next to the fireplace. He thought about ordering some apple pie he'd seen behind the counter. He already missed the pot apple pie his stepmother always made. Though it looked good, he decided against it to conserve his money. Finished sipping the last drop of the strong black coffee, he braved the outside again, but this time with the satisfaction of a full stomach and the knowledge that his final destination was only a few miles away. The smoke-filled air cleared a little as a cold wind picked up and bit his face again. The wind also helped to diminish the smell of the city as he headed in the direction of the commons.

Caleb Cushing
Public Domain photo

Caleb Cushing was an American ambassador to China in 1843. He became colonel of the First Massachusetts Volunteer Regiment in Mexico in 1847, rising to the rank of brigadier general. He lost a bid for election to the governorship of Massachusetts in 1848, and was appointed to the Massachusetts Supreme Judicial Court soon afterward. In 1853, he was appointed attorney general of the Unites States.

Chapter Three

The Commons

Dwight occasionally asked for directions to Tremont Avenue, to ensure he was walking in the right direction. The avenue widened as he approached his final destination. The traffic had also increased as the morning progressed. The air had warmed enough to allow him to remove his gloves and loosen his coat. The mud was thawing from the heat of the morning sun and the steady wagon traffic. The clocks on several of the banks and other municipal buildings he passed kept him aware of the time. The widening of the street continued until he saw an open field behind a row of large trees. It was soon after that he saw a row of pitched tents at the far edge of the field. Exhilarated, he quickened his gait. He could see several hundred soldiers marching and drilling on the partially snow-covered plain. Several men on horseback were watching as figures marched along with the groups ordering them about.

He approached one of the men watching and asked, "Sir, would this be the First Massachusetts Volunteers?"

The man looked a little perplexed at the unexpected question.

"Sir, is this the First Massachusetts?" Dwight repeated.

"Oh, yeah, but that's not what we call 'em. Cushing's Regiment is what most people call 'em around here. They're off to Mexico in a day or two. That's what we hear. Thank the Lord. Maybe we get back the commons now with some peace 'n quiet. Look at all the mud they made from marchin' around in the snow all the time."

Dwight ignored the man's comment. "Do you know where to sign up?"

"Not me, boy. Don't want any part of killing Mexicans. No need to. Look yonder up ahead. I think there is a posting somewhere showing where the quartermaster's tent is at. You can most likely sign up there." He pointed, and Dwight nodded and thanked him.

Walking in that direction, Dwight continued to watch the soldiers executing orders that he could barely hear. He reached the edge of a row of wedge tents. The mud he encountered made it difficult to walk. A few soldiers around the two-man tents looked like they were preparing food over open fires. He asked for directions to the quartermaster's tent. Hearing Dwight's question, a large man in full uniform approached him. Based on the number of stripes sewn on his sleeves, Dwight knew he had made contact with someone of authority.

"Ya looking to join, are ya?"

"Yes, sir, I am."

"You'll address me as Sergeant Major Ross.[1] You should know that right away. Follow me. I will take ya to the quartermaster's tent. Quartermaster Sergeant Reed will sign ya up."

"Yes, sir."

Dwight realized his first mistake as the sergeant major glared in response to the answer he had just given. He corrected his response immediately. "Yes, Sergeant Major."

Dwight followed him as they quickly walked in the direction of the quartermaster's tent. He heard the man grumble at the soldiers spreading hay, "Move your asses."

Within a minute, they arrived at a large-wall tent. "Wait here."

Dwight nodded as the sergeant major opened the flap of the tent and entered. He could hear a muffled conversation taking place as he waited and looked around, noticing the National Colors and the banner of the First Massachusetts moving in the wind outside the tent.

The sergeant major reappeared. "The quartermaster sergeant is expecting ya."

Dwight only smiled, bent forward, and entered through the open flap the sergeant major held for him. Straightening up, he found himself staring at another sergeant with almost as many stripes as Ross had.

"I'm Quartermaster Sergeant Joseph Reed. State your name and where you are from, son. Stand erect at attention when you talk in front of the quartermaster."

Dwight immediately stood at attention and noticed a man rise from a chair that was behind a small field desk. It was positioned close to a stove in the back of the tent. He knew the man must be the quartermaster the sergeant had just mentioned.

The quartermaster approached him and spoke. "At ease, recruit. What is your name?"

"Aaron Dwight Stevens. I have come from Norwich, Connecticut, to join up with the First Massachusetts."

"I'm Captain Daniel. Why didn't you join up in a Connecticut regiment, Stevens?"

"Heard about the First and thought it would be a better unit to join."

---

[1] **The last names and the ranks of all the men depicted** in the First Massachusetts Volunteer Regiment were listed on the actual roster. First names of the officers are also on the roster, but not the first names of the enlisted men. First names for the enlisted, as well as relationships and conversations, are fictional.

"A better unit to join, *sir*," the quartermaster sergeant corrected.

"A better unit, sir."

"Well—Stevens, is it? How old are you?"

"I'm over eighteen, sir."

"You are big enough, but your face tells me you are a bit younger."

"No, sir. I am what I said. I don't lie." Dwight relaxed, knowing the paper with *eighteen* written on it was still in his boot and would stand to justify his statement, if needed.

"What do you think, Sergeant Reed? Can we believe this man?"

"Don't think we have a choice, sir. We'll be leaving soon and we need twenty or so more recruits before we go in a few days. Colonel Cushing is counting on it."

The captain only smiled, shook his head, and motioned to the sergeant to begin the procedure.

"You can read and write, Stevens?"

"Yes, Sergeant Reed, I can, and very well."

The sergeant ignored the response as he opened a ledger and began recording the personal information of Aaron Dwight Stevens. The sergeant mumbled, and Dwight heard his name again and something about him being almost nineteen, as the sergeant entered information into the regiment ledger. Dwight did not attempt to correct the man. The sergeant continued to mumble as he wrote, "Saturday, the sixth of February, eighteen hundred and forty-seven."

Several minutes passed as personal information was asked, answered, and repeated to ensure accuracy. Upon completion, Quartermaster Sergeant Reed ordered the recruit to stand at attention. Dwight immediately obeyed as Captain Daniel walked back to him from the tent stove. He stood directly in front of Stevens and administered the oath of allegiance. With the quick ceremony completed, Captain Daniel shook Dwight's hand and welcomed the new recruit to the First Massachusetts Volunteers.

Quartermaster Sergeant Reed instructed, "Salute the captain after he addresses you, recruit."

Stevens attempted his first salute.

The captain responded, "You're dismissed, Stevens."

The quartermaster sergeant, who now carried several pieces of paper, led the new recruit out of the tent and took him to the next tent. It was another wall tent that had a large sign hung on it that read *Dispensary*.

"Wait here, Stevens," the quartermaster sergeant said and disappeared inside. The wind shifted, and the smell of bacon cooking was the first pleasant smell Dwight noticed since he'd left the diner. The quartermaster sergeant reappeared from inside the dispensary tent.

"Come in, Stevens. The surgeon will see you now."

Dwight obeyed, and both men waited as a middle-aged gentleman read a paper through spectacles that he kept adjusting. Dwight looked around as he waited for the man to address him and saw several military cots placed near a tent stove. He realized what *dispensary* meant. This was the doctor's tent.

Finally, the man looked up at him. "Says here you are nineteen years."

Dwight began to respond, but was cut off by the quartermaster sergeant. "Yes, sir. Nineteen and looks strong and fit. He's a rugged lad, I might say."

The surgeon looked over the top of his spectacles. "I can see that, Sergeant. You can wait outside until I'm finished examining this man."

The sergeant's facial expressions changed and his cheeks reddened. "Yes, sir." He exited the tent.

"Take off your coat, son. Stand over by the stove. I only need to examine a few things before you freeze from the damned cold."

Dwight obliged and removed his coat.

"You look fit for"—he paused—"nineteen? You look younger. Haven't been shaving long, have you?"

Dwight remained silent.

"Open your mouth, son." He obeyed. "You might be nineteen. Your molars are in. Teeth look good. Oh, you chipped one. How'd you do that?"

"Can't remember, sir."

"You have any sicknesses as a youth you can remember?"

"None I recall."

"Your parents alive?"

"Both, sir." He corrected himself. "My real mother died when I was nine. I don't remember from what."

The surgeon didn't remark, but only shook his head. "Take off your boots."

Dwight slid them off and stood on the cold dead grass inside the tent.

"Take off your stockings." The surgeon waited. "You look clean enough. When's the last time you bathed?"

"Four days ago, sir. Just before I left to come to Boston."

"Remember to keep your feet and behind clean, Stevens. You'll avoid trouble with your body that way."

Dwight nodded to acknowledge his instructions.

"Get dressed." The surgeon then yelled out, "Sergeant Reed! You may escort this man to his company!"

Reed appeared as Dwight struggled to get his boots back on. "Hurry, Private. Get your coat back on."

Within moments, they departed the surgeon's tent.

Reed brought Dwight over to a group of men who were talking. He immediately recognized the sergeant major laughing in the middle of the group. Reed called out, "Sergeant Major, Stevens is our newest recruit. Duly sworn in and assigned to Company I." He handed him a piece of paper.

"Well, Private Stevens. Welcome to the Regiment." He read the paper and turned to a tall soldier who had been part of the group of men. "Sergeant Murphy, Stevens is yours now. Get a corporal to get him outfitted, and assign him quarters in one of the company tents." The sergeant major handed Sergeant Murphy the paper the quartermaster sergeant had given him earlier.

"Yes, Sergeant Major. Private, follow me."

The two men walked together but did not talk as they passed several small signs that looked more like cemetery crosses than company signs. They passed the first one that indicated the location of Company E. Companies F, G, and H followed until they reached a sign in front of a line of tents indicating they had arrived at Company I. Sergeant Murphy yelled toward a wall tent positioned in front of several rows of wedge tents, "Corporal Mallard, front and center."

A few seconds later, a short and stocky man exited the wall tent, quickly buttoning a coat with two stripes sewn on the sleeves and adjusting his cap. He approached the sergeant and new private. "At your request, Sergeant."

Sergeant Murphy handed him the paper. "Take Stevens to get outfitted. When you're done, feed him the noon meal. I will meet you there."

"Yes, Sergeant Murphy". Mallard motioned for Dwight to follow.

Stevens followed the corporal through some slippery mud that had not yet been covered with hay. The mud deepened until both men found it difficult to walk, and a sucking sound was heard each time they lifted their boots in their attempt to move another step forward.

"Frigging mud, I hate walking in this shit," the corporal muttered. He looked at Stevens, who remained quiet. "Ya don't talk much, do ya? Where ya from, Stevens?"

"I'm from Norwich, Connecticut, most of my life. Born in Lisbon, though, in..." He hesitated, knowing the year would reveal his real age. "Lisbon is a few miles from the center of Norwich."

"I'm from Roxbury. Just down the road a piece."

Stevens nodded as they reached one of the large four-wall tents located away from the main tents. He could see several wagons with soldiers loading crates on them. Several more were waiting, with their horses expelling clouds of vapor into the cold. The corporal opened a flap of the first tent that had *Commissary* stenciled in black on it. He motioned for Stevens to enter. The smell of leather, damp wool, and other strange smells permeated it.

Corporal Mallard yelled to another corporal who was watching the soldiers moving crates.

That corporal turned and motioned to Mallard to wait. "Go easy with that one. Ya break it and we'll be spittin' at the enemy," he said to a soldier, who remarked how heavy the crate was. "What do ya expect, fool, it's lead you're hauling." Satisfied the soldiers got his message, he turned to Mallard. "What ya got here, corporal?"

"Stevens is his name. Assigned to Company I. Need him outfitted." He handed over the paper Sergeant Murphy had given him.

"Step over here, Private." The corporal paused as he passed a tent stove to warm his hands. "What size boot ya take?"

"Eleven."

"Ya lucky, I got only two pairs left in that size." He threw him one pair. "Ya look to be a large for a blouse and coat. Thirty-inch grays should fit ya. You need to hem the trousers if they are too long. The colonel frowns on long trousers." He threw all three articles of clothing at him. "A cap now." He reached for several sizes and threw them at him. "Try 'em. Choose the one that feels right."

Dwight tried on the first. It fit. He handed back the other caps while the corporal issued a set of wool undergarments, stockings, suspenders, a blanket, sewing kit, musket ball pouch, powder container, several blankets, and a haversack to place all his articles in. The last article of clothing issued was a heavy overcoat.

Corporal Mallard laughed when Dwight dropped the articles as he attempted to catch the overcoat. "Stevens, for Christ's sake, stuff 'em in the haversack. Quickly, man, quickly."

The commissary corporal smirked. "Sign here, Stevens, that I issued all this to you. You can write?"

Dwight grabbed the paper and quill and signed his name.

"You'll be charged for the clothes in case no one has told ya. It will come out of your pay. Army rules, not mine. Walk over there." He pointed. "You get your musket and bayonet there."

Dwight and Corporal Mallard followed. The corporal reached into an open crate very much like the ones Dwight had seen on the train and pulled out a musket. "This is the standard-issue musket. It's a sixty-nine caliber smooth-bore flintlock musket. You ever use one?"

"I shot a shotgun—"

"Clean it before you use it," the corporal said as he handed Dwight the bayonet that accompanied it. "We don't want you shooting anyone once you figure how to use it, so the powder and lead will be issued to you later. We don't keep the powder in here next to the tent stoves for good reason."

Both corporals laughed.

"Corporal, is this a new man?"

Corporal Mallard looked over his shoulder and recognized the officer. He yelled, "Attention!"

The three soldiers came to attention. Dwight dropped his bayonet onto the dirt floor of the tent.

"At ease, men."

The officer walked over to Dwight and looked him up and down, and then looked at Mallard. "Corporal, I want this man dressed in his uniform immediately. I want you two to instruct him properly. I don't appreciate the pathetic amusement you have been having with him. Do I make myself clear to both of you?"

"Yes, sir. Perfectly clear, Major."

"Good. Then carry on."

"Yes, sir. Attention!"

The major left and began watching the soldiers loading the wagons. Mallard yelled out, "At ease."

All three men relaxed.

Mallard looked at Stevens. "You heard the major, get dressed now."

Dwight moved closer to the tent stove, stripped to his undergarments, and dressed in his new uniform. Surprisingly, everything fit well. No alterations were required. The boots were stiff and cold compared to the pair he had arrived in, and he was happy to find there was enough room around the calf for him to hide the sheathed knife he had kept there since he was about ten years old. The boots were only the second new pair he had ever received. The first had been six months ago when he had out grown the secondhand boots he had received from his older brother. Neither corporal noticed the knife.

The new wool stockings began to itch as soon as he finished dressing. Dwight gathered his civilian clothes and stuffed them into his haversack. He put on the overcoat as Corporal Mallard handed him his musket ball pouch and powder container. Dwight then strapped the haversack on over the overcoat.

"Christ, ya look like a soldier now, even though ya don't know shit. Here, hold on to this." The corporal attached the bayonet to the musket.

"And don't be sticking anyone."

Dwight grabbed the musket and followed Mallard as he turned to leave. "Corporal Mallard, who was the major?"

Mallard didn't answer until they were outside the commissary tent. "That's our commissary officer. Major Kendall Tyler. Real proper Boston family, as ya could hear. Pain in my ass at times." He pulled at his pocket watch. "Let's get you to your tent and then get you some rations. Follow me."

When they arrived back at Company I, Dwight was assigned to a two-man tent.

"There is another man already assigned here. You'll meet him when all of them are finished drilling. That cot is yours. Stow your gear under it. Lay the musket on the cot."

Dwight did as he was instructed. He looked at how small the tent was. The iron stove in it was almost out of wood.

Mallard looked at him. "You might want to add some wood to stoke up the fire before those coals burn out. Your tent mate will thank you. Look yonder out back. You'll see the wood we've been stacking."

After accomplishing the task, Dwight then followed Mallard to another large wall tent that was filled with wood tables. The corporal explained, "This is one of our rations tents. We eat in these. Don't matter which one you pick. You get ya food outside where the pots and pits are. Follow me, I'll show ya."

Dwight saw men coming in from the outside carrying tin plates of food. Some carried tin cups of coffee nestled on top of their food.

A rations sergeant was busy giving instructions as other troops began to line up for the noon meal. "Move it along, lads, we got plenty of food. If you need more, come back for it. Don't be wasting any, either. You don't want to piss me or my boys off. Move along, move along."

Dwight followed Mallard and grabbed a tin plate and cup, and a fork and spoon. He watched the rations sergeant carry on with one of the attendants.

"Fer Christ sake, Sullivan, make the beans and salt pork last, will ya? Use that other spoon I told ya to get."

Dwight didn't say anything as some of the troops smirked and two laughed out loud. They quickly learned that that was the worst thing to do when the sergeant was talking.

"You think that's funny, boys? You two, get out of my rations line. Fall to the rear. I'll make sure Private Sullivan takes care of ya. You two will be the last two in line. Move it, now!"

No argument was given as the two sheepishly moved back to the rear of the line. The sergeant yelled one more time, "Make sure you two are the last two or you get none! I'll be watchin'!"

"Is that sergeant always like that?"

"This is a good day. I've seen him go toe to toe with the sergeant major. He's a tuff old codger. Don't be pissing him off. You just saw what happens." Mallard walked to a row of tables, and Dwight noticed a group of men watch Mallard as he sat at their table. No one said anything until Mallard spoke. "New man is Stevens. He came in today."

He looked around at them and spoke directly to one. "Avery, Stevens is in your tent. He stoked up the fire for ya. You should thank him when ya get back to your tent."

Only Avery spoke. "Where ya from, Stevens?"

"Norwich. I come from Norwich, Connecticut."

Avery just nodded as he bit into a biscuit, chewed, and then swallowed. "I come from right here. Spent most of my time on the docks. I could walk home if they let me."

A few troops from Company I laughed. No one else said a word as the noon meal was consumed.

Sergeant Murphy appeared behind Corporal Mallard while he ate. "Mallard, Stevens taken care of?"

"Yes, Sergeant, as you ordered. His gear is in his tent."

"Good. Carry on, men."

The sergeant was out of hearing range when a private named Bryant made a comment. "*Carry on*—you hear the man? The way he worked our asses on the parade field, we are lucky we can still carry anything."

A few troops laughed.

Corporal Mallard spoke up. "Bryant, you better watch your mouth. Don't let Sergeant Murphy hear ya. The sum of you will pay for it."

Another private piped up, "Bryant, he's right. We've done enough marching today. We don't need any extra 'cause of your mouth."

Some grumbling could be heard as the men continued finishing their meal.

"Back to the company, gents. Muster in ten minutes," Corporal Mallard stated loudly as he rose from the table. Stevens gulped down the several remaining bits of his meal and shoved a biscuit in his pocket as he moved to keep pace with the corporal.

"Don't get caught with food in your pocket, Stevens," one man whispered. "The rations sergeant will raise hell if he catches you."

"Seen it happen too many times," another private said.

"Here, then you eat it." Dwight quickly handed the biscuit to the private.

The man smiled as he took the food and bit into it.

"That was a shitty way to get another biscuit, Cross," Avery casually commented.

Stevens looked at Avery, but only shook his head.

Cross spoke up. "I just saved the man some bullshit from the rations sergeant if he saw him munching on a biscuit, that's all."

Stevens saw more soldiers carrying pails of boiling water over to the barrels where they had just deposited their tins. The water had come from the metal pots attached to iron tripods over several open fires. The rations sergeant was busy watching the entire clean-up being performed. Occasionally, he barked some needed direction to the soldiers doing the cleaning. "Company I gets its turn tomorrow, Stevens. The regiment rotates the companies for clean-up duty. You get to work for him for the whole day. Breakfast, lunch, and supper. It's a day off to the sergeants and corporals of Company I." Mallard laughed. "Shit, Stevens, tomorrow is Sunday. The whole regiment will be off except you and the others with duty to perform. I forgot about that. It happens like that sometimes." He laughed again.

Both men returned to the company. Mallard instructed Stevens to get his musket and to wait outside his tent until the company was ordered to muster. Several soldiers were already lining up in anticipation of Sergeant Murphy's call. Stevens realized that none of the men preparing for muster had their bayonets attached. After a few seconds, he detached the bayonet and remembered that his powder belt had a bayonet scabbard. It felt good that he had learned something on his own. He stood and waited for the call for muster as Avery, Bryant, and Cross approached.

Avery entered the tent Dwight had been assigned to share with him. When he reappeared, he looked over at Stevens. "The tent's good 'n warm. Good job, new man."

"It's Stevens!" he called out. "Dwight Stevens, and you're welcome."

Several more minutes passed as the men slowly arrived in groups of twos and threes. A few men sat on canvas cots outside their tents in the welcome warmth of the noonday sun. One private kept flipping a bayonet into a chopping block. Dwight marveled how he was able to get the bayonet to stick into the wood block almost every time. Dwight then caught sight of Sergeant Murphy. The private didn't notice him approaching with several officers until it was too late.

"Private, if I ever catch you throwing your bayonet again, I'll be takin' it from you and sticking it up your ass, sideways!" Sergeant Murphy told him. He then yelled out, "Company I, fall in for muster."

Within seconds, about eighty men lined up in two straight lines.

Dwight found himself in the middle of the second line. Sergeant Murphy observed the two lines until he decided they were dressed properly. He yelled out, "Company I, attention!" as another officer approached.

For the first time, Dwight felt and heard the strange sound that was made when nearly a hundred men came to attention. There was complete silence until Dwight heard one of the officers address Sergeant Murphy, "Ease the men, Sergeant."

Sergeant Murphy yelled, "Company I, parade rest!"

Another strange sound came as the company obeyed the command in unison. There was silence except for an occasional cough coming from a few soldiers.

"Men of Company I, as your captain, I was privileged to be informed this morning by our regimental commander, Colonel Cushing, that the regiment will leave Boston within a few days. Our destination will be revealed once we embark. We have been training for this for months, and I know that every one of you will do your duty when called upon to perform. I have instructed my officers and sergeants to make preparations to break camp for embarkation once it is announced. That is all."

Sergeant Murphy jumped to attention, did an about face, and yelled, "Company I, attention!" He did an about face again and saluted the captain.

The officer returned his salute. "Carry on, Sergeant Murphy."

He yelled out, "Yes, sir. Company I dismissed!"

The men broke ranks as Dwight stood still and watched the officers walk away. "Hey, new man. You gonna stand out in the cold watching those officers heading for the warm houses they live in?"

Dwight looked over and realized that Avery was speaking to him. "They don't live in tents?"

"Nope. They stay in the bigger wall tents during the day issuing orders, but at dusk they hightail it to the house they are billeted in. Shit, you think they'd be putting wood in a stove tent every few hours to keep warm?"

Avery led the way back into the tent. As both men entered, he quickly flipped the stove's door open to check the fire. "Damn, that's hot." He shook his hand and quickly flipped it shut again. "It should last for an hour or two. New guy, grab a few pieces from the company wood pile for the next time we need stoking, will ya?"

"Avery, the name is Stevens, Dwight Stevens. Don't call me 'new guy.'"

"Only kidding ya. We'll take turns keepin' the fire hot. Ain't too much room to store wood, as ya can see. With you here now, I can sleep a little longer, not having to get up to stoke it."

Dwight realized that he didn't have much better conditions here than he had on the train.

Avery continued, "Be glad when we leave here. Even a ship should be warmer than sleeping near a stove in the middle of a New England field in February. So far, I hear only a few recruits needed tending to for frostbite. They were sent to the city hospital to recover. So, Stevens, keep your ass warm and your feet dry, and you'll make it out of here."

After returning with more wood, Dwight opened up his haversack and placed his two blankets on his canvas cot.

Avery watched for a few minutes and remarked, "Get some of the clean hay before it gets mixed with the mud. Stuff it under your cot. That keeps the cold from creeping up to your back. Put your musket on the hay; it keeps it from spreading around. Get some more and lay it on your cot. Put one blanket over the hay but keep it loose to wrap in. The second on top of that folded the long way. Ya get the most out of it folding it that way. I put your cot closer to the stove like mine while ya was getting wood. But not too close, 'cause it will cook ya. We don't want ya for breakfast, do we?" He laughed.

Dwight followed Avery's directions until he was satisfied. He sat on his cot, looking at Avery reading a newspaper. "That the local paper?"

Avery didn't answer immediately.

He was about to ask him again when Avery put the paper down. "There's a piece in here talking about a writer named Thoreau.[1] If ya ain't heard of him, he's popular in the city. Written some books. He's been in jail once for not paying his poll taxes. He says paying the tax only advances slavery in the south. It says here that this war will be doing the same thing."

"Never heard of him. What paper is that?"

"The *Boston Evening Transcript.* I read it when one of the paper boys comes through camp selling papers he couldn't sell on the street." Avery continued, "I found out not many people like this war that we are going off to fight."

"How's that, I wonder?"

"Well, if you're asking, it's simple. When we win this war, there will be more open land in the south. The Southern people will want to expand slavery. Most people up here do not take kindly to slavery. We don't want to live with the slaves, but they deserve to be free. That's the way I think

---

[1] **Henry David Thoreau** was an American author, poet, naturalist, avid tax resister, as well as a civil disobedience leader and lifelong abolitionist. He influenced the thoughts and actions of Leo Tolstoy, Mahatma Gandhi, and Reverend Martin Luther King, Jr.

it should be."

Dwight didn't respond at first. He chose his words before he spoke. "All people should live free and be allowed to live where they choose." Dwight stared at Avery for a few uncomfortable moments.

Avery didn't challenge Dwight's statement, but changed the subject. "You have time to clean your musket yet?"

"No."

"I have some gun oil and rags. Ya need to clean out the inside of the barrel. I've seen one recruit shoot a musket without cleaning it first and there was a lot of smoke from the powder burning the inside of the barrel. Ya couldn't see anythin' for minutes. It really pissed off the sergeant major." He handed Dwight the cleaning material. Several minutes later, he inspected Dwight's labor and nodded his approval. "You'll be set now when they issue us powder and lead again. We won't be getting any to practice with, I reckon. We'll be sailing soon. Tomorrow we get rations duty with that miserable sergeant while everyone else has time off." Avery looked at his pocket watch. "Better get some rest now that we have been given the time. We eat supper in a while. I hope ya like bacon, beans, and biscuits again? It's been steady with that for a couple of days now."

Dwight lay back on his cot. The lower blanket with hay under it actually felt soft enough to sleep on. He piled on the second blanket and within minutes, felt warm.

"Make sure ya take off your overcoat and boots when ya snuggle up. Keepin' them on will make ya sweat. When ya sweat, it makes water, and water gets cold real quick."

Dwight did as Avery had suggested. He felt cold taking off his overcoat and boots, but soon felt the warmth being generated by his body now that he had insulated his cot. He napped for an hour until he was awakened by a tug from his tent mate.

"Rise and shine, Stevens. We need to get some rations."

Several minutes later, both men left their tent as light snow began to fall on the commons. Avery looked up at the darkening sky. "Damn snow. God, how I hate this shit."

"I have a question for you, Avery. Who is the officer that talked to us this afternoon?"

"That's our CO, our commanding officer. His name is Davis. Captain Davis. He has three or four letters in front of his name. Nobody knows what they stand for."

"Who were the other officers with him?"

"The first lieutenant was Smith. The two second lieutenants with him were Austin and Reed."

"Is Reed any relation to Quartermaster Sergeant Reed?"

"Don't know, never asked. Don't think so. Would you let a relative freeze his ass off in a tent while ya lived in a warm house? The sergeants sleep outside in tents like the troops do. They got bigger tents, but cold is cold. I can't imagine that they are related."

As they walked to their evening meal snow flurries stuck to their overcoats. Some of the other recruits followed, and they all ended up in a steady stream of men heading for food. Dwight noticed some men stop, come to attention, and salute. Before he could react, Avery had assumed the same position. It took a few moments for him to realize that the National Colors were being lowered for the night. When the bugle stopped, the men went about their business.

After dinner, they returned to the Company I tent and turned in for the night. The word had been passed around that they were to report for rations duty by 0500 hours.

Avery looked at his pocket watch. "That gives us about eleven hours before we have to start the next day, Stevens. I suggest you turn in like I am."

"Avery, you got any paper and a pencil I can use until I get my own?"

"Yep, I can lend ya a few pieces. Need to be writing home, do ya?"

"Yes. To let my sister know where I am."

Before long, Avery furnished the paper and pencil. "Turn down the lamp when you're finished. Don't want it to burn all night."

"Avery?"

"Yeah?"

"What's your first name?"

"Alfred. Call me Al."

"Thanks, Al, for all the help and for lending me paper to write home."

Avery smiled. "Use the flat part of my haversack to write on. Sorry, no room for a table in here." Avery removed his overcoat and boots, then slid into his homemade cocoon to weather the night.

Dwight sat for a few moments and gathered his thoughts. He positioned Avery's haversack as he had suggested, and began to write:

6th of February, 1847

Dearest Lydia,

I write you from the City of Boston. I arrived yesterday by train. It will be easier for all concerned if they do not know of my location. I have joined the First Massachusetts Volunteers and have received uniform and sustenance. The regiment will be embarking soon for the Mexican campaign. I regret that I did not confide in you before my departure, but it was necessary in my opinion to leave quietly and secretly. Please understand and respect my decision to become involved in this conflict. I feel it is my duty to do as others in our family have done in years past. I will be pleased that this correspondence is destroyed once read by you. I will post another letter as soon as possible.

Your loving brother,

Dwight Stevens

After finishing the letter, he felt bad about instructing his sister to keep silent on his whereabouts. Was he asking her to sin? Could he even ask her to do that? Would Lydia figure out how to handle the predicament he was putting her in? Looking over to Avery, he was about to ask for an envelope, but could hear a faint snoring coming from the cocooned figure. He rummaged through Avery's haversack and found one. He addressed the letter, sealed it, and prepared to turn in. Then he realized he needed to relieve himself.

He found the latrine. A few torches were lit along the way. He reached the walled tent and entered. The smell of human waste was strong. Several other men were using the facility. He quickly urinated and departed, deciding that he would return early in the morning to perform his daily constitutional, hopefully before too many of the others. He wanted privacy while he defecated into a barrel on two boards suspended over a dug ditch. One thing he did miss about Norwich was the privy. His father had paid good money to put a rather luxurious family privy in their backyard on Towne Street.

He returned to the Company I woodpile, grabbed several more pieces, and returned to his tent. After he finished stoking the fire again, he prepared for bed. He was surprised that he was warm within minutes. Avery's instructions had been good ones. He fell asleep to the sounds of the popping and crackling of wood burning.

Sometime later, he felt someone rocking him. He thought his brother was waking him for chores and was about to tell Henry to stop shaking him when Avery's words brought him back to reality. "Wake up, Stevens, wake up. Time to rise and shine."

"What time is it?"

"Four fifteen. We got rations duty at five, remember?"

"Right."

Within minutes both men had slipped on their boots. The boots had remained relatively warm placed near the tent stove. Both men shuddered as they put on their overcoats folded their blankets, and spread hay under the cots.

"Remind me to get some more hay when we return tonight," Avery remarked.

They left the tent and headed for the latrine. Luckily, for Dwight's first experience, only Avery was there in the latrine performing on another barrel several feet away from him. It was 4:45 a.m. when the two men reported to the pits. The air was cold, but still. There was a half moon, and numerous stars were out. Both men waited for more men from Company I to show up near the pits. They warmed themselves standing near the hot coals.

"Ah, you figured out the place to be standing and waiting, didn't ya?"

Both men turned to see the old ration sergeant smiling at them.

"You be the first two, are ya?"

"Yes, Ration Sergeant, we are," Avery responded.

"I be kindly to that on this cold morning. You two keep the pits hot today for all the servings. I don't want to be telling ya to keep the fires hot now, do I?"

"No, Ration Sergeant, ya won't have to," Avery said.

Both men stood for a few seconds until the sergeant barked, "Well, get yer asses moving and stoke 'em up!"

They moved quickly, and within minutes, the four pits they were assigned to were illuminated with three-foot flames. Avery remarked to Stevens as they watched the flames rise, "Not a bad place to be this morning, mate."

Dwight didn't respond, but smiled contently in the glimmer of the morning light that was rising in the east.

Dwight thought more about the letter to his sister. He felt guilty that she would have to lie if anyone asked her if she had heard from him. As he opened the pocket of his overcoat and pulled out the letter, he saw that Avery noticed him standing and staring at one of the blazing pit fires. Dwight didn't said a single word as he suddenly tossed the letter into the flames. It disappeared in seconds.

"Change ya mind, Stevens?"

Dwight didn't answer.

"Change ya mind about home, did ya?"

Dwight looked up. "Yeah, no need to write home just yet. Maybe I'll write another time."

Avery didn't respond as he turned to gather more wood to feed the fires.

At six thirty the two fire watchers were relieved of their duties and given permission to eat breakfast. They had 30 minutes to eat and return, so they ate quickly. The breakfast didn't look much different from last night's supper, although Dwight did manage to get a fried egg placed on his bacon. It was a small taste of home. As he finished his breakfast and sipped his coffee, he heard a name that he recognized. He waited until the several soldiers were finished with their conversation before he spoke directly to one in particular, "Might you be Jeremiah Taggard?"

Taggard looked perplexed. Another soldier piped up before Taggard could respond. "He is, and who might you be, soldier?"

Dwight ignored the other soldier. "Your uncle owns a bakery in Roxbury?"

Taggard smiled. "Yeah, he does. Do ya know him?"

"I do, only briefly. I'd just gotten off the train when I purchased some biscuits from his shop. He was friendly. He asked me where I was heading. When I told him, he laughed. Told me you'd done the same. Told me to look you up."

"Well, ya have. What's ya name, soldier?"

"Dwight Stevens."

Taggard put out his hand. "I'm Jeremiah. Glad to be shaking your hand."

"Your uncle was not pleased with either of us for joining the First."

"No, he and I had many an argument over the war. He thinks the Texans should be fighting it."

"Yeah, he made that clear when we were talking."

Avery spoke up and reminded Dwight that they needed to report back to the fire pits.

"It was nice to meet ya, Dwight. Ya can find me in Company C. I'll write and let my uncle know that we met."

Dwight nodded as he left with Avery.

The two men maintained the fires for several more hours. The day was a clear one and the temperature was rising to the mid-forties. Dwight saw some soldiers leaving the commons in small groups. He called over to Avery, "Al, where might they be going? They get time off the commons?"

"Yep, it's Sunday, Stevens. They got eight hours of free time to do what they want. Only on Sundays does that happen."

"When do we get time for services?"

Avery laughed. "Dwight Stevens, you don't figure fast, do ya? We don't get shit off when we got rations duty. Sunday or no Sunday, we are stuck here. Now those boys ain't wasting any time finding some reverend to preach to them about evil. They'll be finding evil on their own before we leave Boston. Too bad for you, 'cause you look to be needing some of what they be looking for."

Thirteen hours later, Avery and Dwight returned to a cold tent. They did find a fresh supply of hay thrown in between their cots, however, and Avery started the stove while Dwight relocated the hay in and around each man's cot. "Some of the men in the company must've been given hay spreading duty," Avery said. "That was one thing good for havin' the mess duty. ya don't have hay duty."

Finished with their immediate chores in their tent, and tired from the constant hauling of firewood to feed the fire pits, they both turned in for the night.

Chapter Four

Embarkation

Dwight was awakened by Avery again. "What time is it? I felt like I just went to sleep."

"Stop complaining. Today we should be finding out when we're leavin'."

Dwight rose and quickly slipped on his boots and overcoat. "I'm heading to the latrine."

"Don't be gone too long. I figure Sergeant Murphy will be calling muster before six. Probably be an inspection too. Usually is on Monday mornings."

Dwight returned within minutes.

"I straightened your gear out so Murphy won't be bothering us."

"You should show me so I can do it myself, but I appreciate it."

"I fluffed ya hay and put your haversack at the base of your cot. Look at the way I folded the blankets. They are all the same. Just need to keep things neat and no one will bother ya. Take your musket with you. I looked it over. It will pass, seeing as you have never fired it yet. Now we go outside and make sure the area outside our tent is neat while we wait for the sergeant and whoever else comes with him to give us news about when we're leaving."

As the two men checked their immediate area, Dwight saw Bryant and Cross standing and waiting for Avery to approach.

Bryant yelled, "Stevens, attach your bayonet to the musket. Bring it here and pitch it with the three of ours."

Dwight was confused at first, but then realized the men were stacking their muskets together. He remembered seeing that done at home. Avery assured that all four were locked securely together and then backed away and fell into position, waiting for muster to be called. Dwight fell in next to him and lined up on Bryant. They waited as more men of Company I stacked their muskets and got into company formation.

"Here they come. Got the captain with 'em and…shit, looks like all the officers and sergeants of the company are right behind Murphy," Private Cross remarked.

"Cross, keep your mouth shut," Corporal Mallard whispered as he walked behind the men.

Dwight saw three other corporals following Mallard as they walked to the front of the two lines. Mallard waited until Sergeant Murphy was within twenty yards of the company.

Sergeant Murphy nodded his head to Mallard. "Company I, fall in, dress right, dress."

Dwight followed the actions of Avery, Bryant, and Cross. Aligned and separated equally, Mallard waited for the sergeant, who yelled, "Company I, attention!"

A rumble of boots coming together in unison ensued. Sergeant Murphy did an about face and saluted the approaching captain and his staff of officers and NCOs.

The captain returned the salute, then spoke to the sergeant. "Ease the men, Sergeant."

"Yes, sir. Company I, parade rest."

The men responded. Dwight had seen parade rest performed many times at the Norwichtown Green. Avery smiled when he saw the newest recruit in unison with the company.

There was silence while the captain took a paper from his overcoat pocket. Dwight could hear several men coughing as they all waited in silence for the man to speak.

He cleared his throat and spoke: "Men of Company I, last night at a meeting with our regimental commander, Colonel Cushing, we were informed that the First Massachusetts Regiment of Volunteers will prepare to break camp by noon today. All tents, tent stoves, and cots with blankets will be broken down, folded, and prepared for removal by wagon to the quartermaster corps within the hour. All personal items will be packed in your haversacks. Your haversack and musket, with bayonet attached, will be carried during the regimental march through the city en route to the ships waiting in the harbor. Embarkation will commence immediately at the city wharf, per orders of the fleet commander. Departure will begin at the readiness of the regiment and tides. Our final destination will be announced while we're at sea. All sergeants, take command of your men and follow the orders you have been given. That is all." He nodded to Sergeant Murphy.

"Company I, attention."

The men responded, and Sergeant Murphy saluted the captain.

The captain returned it, then turned to talk with the rest of his staff.

Murphy called out, "At ease, Company I, fall out."

"Well, this is it, Stevens. You made it just in time. We're off to Mexico," Avery kidded.

"We don't know that for sure. We're going *somewhere*," Dwight responded.

"You better learn how to shoot that musket, Stevens. Maybe ya can shoot at some fish on the way to Mexico," Bryant said and laughed.

Avery defended his tent mate. "Bryant, ya haven't hit shit yet with your musket. Ya better be standing next to him on the ship if he gets a chance to shoot. You sure need the practice."

Several men laughed. Bryant even smiled as they began to break camp.

"Never mind the laughing, fellas. Move your asses and break down the tents like the man ordered!" Corporal Mallard yelled out.

Dwight followed Avery's lead and went to work.

After nearly an hour, they were finished with their tasks.

Avery instructed Stevens, "Spread out the hay. Put your haversack on your back, pick up ya musket, and stand easy."

Corporal Mallard looked at the two men and called out to them, "Move to the NCO and corporal's tents. Take 'em down."

Avery looked at Mallard.

"Ya heard me. You and Stevens take 'em down."

Avery looked at Stevens and motioned with his head for him to follow.

A few soldiers could be heard chuckling as they moved about, breaking down their gear.

Someone yelled out while Mallard had his back turned, "That's what ya get for being too quick, fellas!"

Mallard turned and yelled, "Keep moving! Keep moving!"

Avery and Stevens found the NCO and corporal's tents empty except for the stoves and completed the breakdown within ten minutes.

Corporal Mallard checked their work. "You two, stand easy." He saw several quartermaster wagons pull up to Company I and yelled to the men standing near the piles of tent, stoves, and other gear, "Follow the teamster's lead! He'll tell ya how he wants the wagons loaded!"

Avery nudged Stevens. "I guess being too quick wasn't such a bad thing, now was it?"

Both men stood at ease as the rest of Company I loaded the quartermaster wagons.

Within a half hour, the wagons were loaded and Corporal Mallard called out, "Company I fall in, columns of four! Move it, move it!" Mallard watched, and continued to call out, "Move it, move it, columns of four!"

Sergeant Murphy and three other sergeants lined up to the right of the columns. Stevens noticed Murphy at the lead.

Sergeant Murphy yelled out, "Company I, forward, march!"

The men began to move in unison. Within minutes, four mounted officers joined in to lead the company. Dwight concentrated on keeping in step with the soldiers near him. Occasionally, he could hear Mallard calling cadence to keep the men in step.

Dwight saw several more companies marching in the same direction. Before long the companies merged into a long blue line exiting the commons, followed by lines of wagons and carts. Dwight could see the regimental colors alongside the Stars and Stripes fluttering in the wind as the lead portion of the regiment passed by the State House.

The long line of men came to a halt as the company sergeants gave orders. The men stood at attention with their muskets shouldered until the regimental band struck up a tune and they all began to move out in step. Dwight had never been so proud. The whole scene made him feel very patriotic in his shining military splendor.

Avery commented,"Looks like we are going down Tremont, Stevens. This should be a good show for the city folk. They're glad we're leaving."

"Keep it quiet in the ranks!" Corporal Mallard yelled.

Avery ignored him. "Look sharp, boys, they might throw shit at us. Look alive."

Stevens whispered, "What do you mean, they throw shit?"

"Just that. Horse shit, ox shit, any shit in the road. Some of them don't like what we stand for."

Dwight's enthusiasm for the march, the colors flying, the long line of blue, and the regimental band playing quickly ended as the reality of Avery's statement sank in. He understood that strong animosity existed in many places for the men in blue, and it wouldn't be very long before he witnessed it firsthand.

"When we turn down State Street and head for the wharf, get ready for anything!" Avery spoke loud enough so the men immediately around him could hear.

The regimental band turned off onto the sidewalk as they approached State Street, and formed up to play for the regiment as it passed. Dwight watched up ahead as the column turned right and headed in the direction Avery had stated they would go. All seemed quiet as bystanders watched. Occasionally, one or two of them yelled out something, but much of it was inaudible to most of the men passing.

As they progressed further down State Street, Avery called out, "Watch ya heads and faces, boys, ya don't know what's coming."

A few unidentified articles were thrown into the ranks, but no one in Company I was hit. The calls and yells from the sides of the street increased as the column marched on.

Sergeant Murphy called out, "Keep ya cadence, men! Keep in line!"

A horse reared in front of the company, and Avery called out,

"Looks like one of the lieutenants' horses was hit by something!"

The officer maintained his mount and controlled the horse which had been spooked. "Steady, men, steady. Keep in cadence. Keep in line. Steady," Sergeant Murphy yelled.

The music from the regimental band faded as the company marched further down State Street. The company directly in front of Dwight's stopped. Civilians had been throwing object at the soldiers. Several men broke formation as they began to march parallel with their company, their muskets drawn and bayonets pointed toward the crowd..

Sergeant Murphy saw what had happened. He yelled to Corporal Mallard, "Mallard, assign four on the left and four on the right flank with muskets drawn and bayonets pointed outward!"

Mallard screamed, "Avery, Bryant, Cross, Dillon, fall to the left! Leland, Morris, Ryan, Sears, fall on the right! Keep your eyes alert!"

Sergeant Murphy watched for the company ahead to begin to move as he yelled out, "Forward march!"

The company moved ahead as cadence was called out. Each company followed the direction of the previous company as they passed the rowdy crowd, which mostly yelled obscenities, but occasionally a flying object whizzed by, usually a frozen piece of manure, and hit a soldier.

"Not too much longer, lads. The wharf will be our sanctuary!" Avery yelled out.

The men around him laughed out loud.

"Quiet in the ranks! I don't want to be telling ya again!" Sergeant Murphy yelled out. "Mallard, call in the flank men! Have 'em reform in the column!"

"Ya heard the sergeant! Fall back in!"

Avery and the others fell back into the column as the company approached the wharf.

"Company I, halt. Stand at ease. Move forward as space is made. We'll be boarding shortly. Keep awake. Try not to fall in the water," Sergeant Murphy said as he walked among the men.

"Anyone hurt, Corporal?"

"No, Sergeant Murphy. Shit don't hurt."

Several men laughed.

Sergeant Murphy smiled. "Keep in line and move forward. Mallard, keep an eye on 'em."

"Sergeant Murphy, anyone injured?"

Murphy turned to see Sergeant Major Ross standing in front of him. He quickly spoke up, "No, Sergeant Major, Company I has weathered the shit storm."

Ross smirked at Murphy for his flip answer. "Good, Murphy. Thank God it wasn't like what the Irish Brigade had to put up with yesterday. Carry on."

Stevens watched the exchange between the two senior sergeants and whispered to Avery, "They thought this was a joke. Didn't it bother them? I honestly felt a little embarrassed."

"Don't let it bother ya, Stevens. It don't make no difference. We're glad to leave the commons and the people here are glad we're gone. Keep moving."

"What happened to the Irish Brigade, Avery?"

"They left yesterday. They ran into worse than we did, I guess. They'll be waiting for us on one of the ships at the wharf."

Dwight had never seen ships as large as the four he viewed docked in the harbor.

"Pretty big, ain't they?" Avery remarked.

"Never seen them that big back at home. Most of the kinds I've seen before are shallow-hulled ships that run up and down the Thames River from New London. The larger ones stay in New London," Dwight said while looking back and forth, comparing the four ships. "Which one are we going on?"

"Don't know. Too many soldiers bunching up on the wharf to see what dock we'll be directed to." Avery paused and looked over the ships. "I hope we get the one named *Baring and Brothers*[1] back yonder. I've seen her before docked in the harbor. She's pretty new. I ain't seen the other ones before."

Corporal Mallard heard the conversation as the men moved slowly down the wharf. "The one on the right is the *Remittance*."

No one said any more as the men moved along.

"Company I, move left. Move left. Keep moving to the left," could be heard up ahead of the solid line of soldiers.

"Who is calling that out, Corporal?" Avery asked.

"Can't see. Just look sharp and listen."

Stevens could see better than most due to his height. He stretched his neck a little further. "Actually, it looks like Quartermaster Sergeant Reed is givin' the orders up ahead. I can see him pointing to the dock on the left."

"Glad someone can see over this wall of muskets and haversacks!" Cross yelled out.

---

[1] **The ship names are the real ships** that took the First Massachusetts Volunteer Regiment to Mexico.

As they inched closer the men could clearly hear the quartermaster sergeant yelling for Company I to go left and other companies ahead to go right.

Dwight thought about Private Taggard when he heard Company C. He realized Taggard would be on the *Remittance*. The right side of the wharf broke into two lines, one for the *Remittance* and one for the *Baring and Brothers*. No one could make out the name of the third ship that was moored to the left dock off the wharf until the company finally turned left and the entirety of the ship could be seen.

"She's called the *Smyrna*, Avery!" Dwight called out.

"Yep, I can see that. I'd heard about her but never seen her."

"She looks different from the other two!" Corporal Mallard called out.

"She is, Corporal. She's a lot sleeker. Pretty bark, at that. We lucked out, Company I."

Dwight called over to Avery, "The other ship is the *Hamburgh*! She's got soldiers on her watching us!"

"That's where the Irish Brigade ended up, I guess."

Avery laughed as the men moved down the dock, closer to the personnel brow leading to their ship. Up ahead and in front of the brow waited Sergeants Murphy, Winship, Osgood, O'Connell, and a new man unfamiliar to everyone. At the sight of the four NCOs and the other man, Mallard pushed to the front of the line.

Dwight heard someone yell after him, "I'm gettin hungry, Corporal. Is Ration Sergeant O'Connell going to fix us some grub when we get onboard?"

Corporal Mallard never replied.

Avery had heard it too. He pulled out his pocket watch and mumbled, "It's getting close to two o'clock. I'm hungry myself."

By then the front members of the company had stopped as they reached the brow. Within moments all of Company I stood silent and awaited orders to board. More ships could now be seen anchored in the harbor.

"Looks like they'll be the supply ships. Hope they keep up with us on our way down south!" someone called out from the ranks.

Sergeant Murphy spoke first. "Mallard, this is Chief of the Ship Dermody of the *Smyrna*. He's in charge here. He'll be telling ya where the men are to be quartered. Chief?"

"As Sergeant Murphy told ya, I'm the Chief of the Ship. So that means you're boarding my ship. Ya will do it two at a time. My men will count ya in groups of ten and show ya your quarters. Once you're quartered, you'll be fed. The mess feeds at eight bells. That's sixteen hundred hours, or four o'clock, to the sum of ya. Now step lively, boys, step lively. Follow me shipmates. Step lively."

Mallard began organizing the men in twos as they boarded. It took several minutes before Avery and Stevens stepped onto the brow and were onboard the ship. They followed the crew members who were strategically positioned throughout the halls to steer the men to their assigned quarters.

"Eight bells for four o'clock. That don't make sense," Dwight said, looking at Avery.

"I'll tell ya the bell system later. Shut up and listen, before we have the chief on our asses."

"Smells are different in this ship, Al," Stevens remarked.

"Yeah, smells like a mix of ass and fish," was Avery's immediate response.

"Keep moving, soldiers, keep moving," was the only words the company was given by the crew members as they descended into the lower sections of the ship. They reached their assigned quarters.

As the men inched into the tight quarters, Cross began to swear. "For Christ's sake, there are forty damn hammocks and footlockers. That's not big enough to spit in. This will be a long trip, soldiers."

Nobody commented as they each picked a hammock.

Mallard heard the grumbling. "Take out your gear and stow it in the footlocker. Put your haversack on top, and fold ya overcoats on it. There should be two blankets in the hammocks. Stop bitchin'. It's warmer in here than the wedge tents we just come from."

"Where's the rest of the company, Corporal?" Cross asked.

"The next room, I guess. I'll take a look."

The corporal first stowed his gear in the last footlocker next to the bulkhead door.

"Where do ya piss around here? Anyone know?" a soldier asked .

A sailor who had been assigned to watch the soldiers yelled, "The head on this deck is forward two quarters. The mess is aft three quarters, and up two decks. Don't anyone touch the bulkhead doors." He turned and left.

"What the hell is he talkin' about?" Bryant complained.

"The mess is where we eat," Avery said. "The head is the latrine. Forward is heading to the front. Aft is heading to the back. It ain't too hard to understand. Remember, the sailors do."

Everyone laughed as they eased into their new environment.

Avery looked at Stevens. "I worked as a dock hand a few years back, did some loading and unloading cargo. I understand some of the lingo." He looked at his pocket watch. "We got almost two hours before we eat. I'm resting." He jumped into his hammock. "Suggest ya do the same, Dwight."

"What did he mean about the doors?"

"Oh, yeah. They can be locked in case the ship is sinking. It keeps the water from moving through the ship." He laughed as he looked at Stevens' face. "Don't worry, Dwight, we ain't sinking right now."

After half an hour, Dwight couldn't be still and had to get up to see what was going on.

He felt the ship move and staggered a little but quickly regained his balance. He looked out a porthole and could see the dock moving ever so slowly away from the ship. He became excited and rushed back to inform the others that the ship was moving. As he reached his quarters, he found that most of the men were still in their hammocks resting or sleeping.

"We're moving. We're finally moving." He waited for a response from anyone. There was none.

Then Avery opened one eye. "Get some rest, Dwight. We got another hour or so before we eat."

He ignored Avery's suggestion and immediately stood to look out a small porthole. The dock was even farther away from the ship now, and he could feel the movement of the ship below decks. The hammocks moved in unison and his stomach felt funny. He grabbed his jacket and moved aft to find the stairway to the decks above and topside. The cold air settled his stomach, and he looked over the rail to see that the dock and wharf were now only small lines in the distance.

The *Smyrna* was the second ship in line. He couldn't tell which one of the ships was in front or in the rear since he couldn't distinguish enough between the three ships. He noticed that some of the supply ships were already underway but following considerably behind the larger ships. He started roaming and found thirty or so of his fellow soldiers experiencing and enjoying the same feelings and sights he was. He began to mingle, and attempted to stay out of the way of the many sailors that were busy moving about the ship doing their duty. He nodded to one soldier and then remarked, "Looks like we are second in line."

"Not for long", a sailor said "We'll be first in a short time. This ship can run faster than the *Baring and Brothers* up ahead."

Dwight realized that the *Smyrna* would be the lead ship, followed by the *Baring and Brothers*, *Remittance*, *Hamburgh*, and then the supply ships.

As he watched his ship gain on the *Baring and Brothers*, he felt a hand touch his shoulder.

It was Avery. "Looks like the line of ships will be a couple miles long as we pass Provincetown."

Dwight looked strangely at him.

"Provincetown. Up ahead on the right. That's the tip of Cape Cod. We need to round that before we head south to places I ain't even heard about. We'll learn together, Dwight."

The mist from the sea splashing against the side of the *Smyrna* felt colder as the sun sank behind the ship. Avery motioned to Stevens while he pointed to the pocket watch he held in his hand. A few seconds went by, and then eight bells rang out on the deck for all to hear. The two men and the twenty others headed below deck to the mess.

As they approached the mess, they found a line of men waiting. A few sergeants could be heard yelling at the men to form two lines, to grab a tin and a spoon, and to stay in line. The smell was indistinguishable as to what type of food was being served. Avery and Stevens finally reached the beginning of the mess line, followed the orders, and waited to be served. The tins were deeper than the ones Dwight had used at camp. He realized the food being slopped into their tins was a type of stew. He held his with both hands as the navy cook filled his tin. Beef, potato, carrots, and onions floated in a thick gravy broth. Another sailor handed him a large piece of bread. They found space at one of the four long tables and sat.

"Damn, I picked the wrong service to get into," a soldier sitting next to Avery remarked.

Avery smiled as he tasted the navy beef stew. "Can't argue that, soldier. Can't argue that."

Very little conversation was heard as the hungry soldiers of the First Massachusetts got their first taste of Navy food.

"If ya finished, move on. More men need to eat. No time to be bullshitting. Move on," was heard regularly, coming in short intervals from some of the corporals assigned to watch over the supper mess.

Avery and Stevens finished, and immediately placed their tins and ware in the scullery washtub at the exit of the mess. Several sailors took the items and began washing, rinsing, and stacking the tins and utensils for the next users. A chief inside the scullery room could be heard barking orders at the sailors to keep things moving. The two soldiers overheard the sailors in the scullery talking about how they would be feeding over three hundred soldiers for the supper meal.

"I guess the quartermaster sergeant split the regiment up pretty evenly between the four ships, Stevens. If we are three hundred here, then the *Remittance* 'n the *Baring and Brothers* probably got about three hundred a piece, as well. What about the Irish Brigade?"

"About the same, I reckon."

As the men began walking to their quarters, they felt the ship shift abruptly as it turned southeasterly around Provincetown into the darkening winter Atlantic. Neither man said a word as they navigated the halls on the way to their hammocks. The smell of vomit permeated the entrance to their quarters as they arrived. Several men had already vomited due to the constant motion of the ship. Those that hadn't vomited yet complained incessantly to those who had to clean up their mess. Avery and Stevens knew that the situation would become much worse as more men of Company I ate supper and returned to the swinging hammocks and sickening smell.

Later that night, Dwight had to get out into the fresh air. Quietly, he left for topside and, hopefully, some relief from the stench and seasickness. Some of the sailors smiled at him as he made his way to the fresh air. They didn't need to comment to indicate their pleasure in watching the landlubber's first reaction to a swaying ship.

The cold night air quickly awakened his senses. Looking around, he found other men standing in groups near the ship's railings. It seemed that almost every minute someone bent over and retched.

Dwight heard someone come behind him. It was Avery. "By now, most just got the dry heaves. The supper mess has been puked out of 'em. Be six more hours before sunrise. You up to standin' that long?"

"It's got to be better than down below. I just about puked in my hammock. I needed the air," Stevens remarked as he tried to keep from doing what most had already done.

Avery noticed his attempt to hold back his urge to vomit. "That's good. Try to keep it down. Breathe in, and hold it down. Once ya start, it don't stop." Avery smiled and looked out. White caps could be seen on the water as the ship plowed through the swells. "The night watch was tellin' me that by mornin' we might be able to see Nantucket. That will be the last time we see any land unless the captain follows close to the coast going down south."

"Never heard of Nantucket, Al."

"It don't matter. Just an island I heard about from working the docks." The ship's bell rang as Avery finished talking.

"What time is it?" Stevens asked.

"Six bells. It's three o'clock."

"It's confusing, Al."

"Naw, it's simple. Every half hour the sailors ring the bell. They call it the watch bell. The Royal Navy started it years ago. Watches are four-hour shifts so by the time ya get to the fourth hour ya have eight bells."

"So at three thirty a.m., it will be seven bells?"

"Yep, you got it."

"So four a.m. will be eight bells and four thirty a.m. will be one bell because it starts all over again for four hours."

"Yeah, you're a real sailor now, Dwight."

It would be seven more hours until the young recruit and his new companion would venture back down to their quarters to check their hammocks and personal gear. They found Corporal Mallard yelling at some of the men to clean up the messes they had made.

A few sailors stood by the entrance to the quarters with swabs and buckets. Mallard continued to yell as sluggish soldiers grabbed the swabs and buckets and began to clean.

"Our stuff looks safe, Stevens. How's ya footlocker?"

"Looks free from anyone soiling it."

Mallard heard the two men.

"Store ya gear in them. I want to see just folded blankets in ya hammocks. If ya haven't puked, then get to the mess for breakfast. Ya got one hour from now to be topside with your musket."

Both men obliged the corporal and departed.

"Are you hungry, Al?"

"Nope, but a biscuit and a cup of coffee could settle your stomach."

Stevens didn't remark, but he had learned to trust his new friend.

Muster topside proved to be a very interesting first-day event for the seasick soldiers. Avery and Stevens reported with enough time to see the gray-faced and foul-smelling soldiers struggling to follow the screaming orders of the corporals and sergeants trying to assemble them.

"Stay in the back, Stevens. We don't wanna be catchin' puke down our necks now, do we?"

Dwight quickly figured out how wise his companion was. No sooner had he said that than a private puked straight out and just missed Sergeant Murphy standing in front of him.

"Fer Christ's sakes, Goodwin, puke on yer own boots, ya pathetic soul."

The sergeant waited until the corporals had arranged the men in presentable columns, and until one particular officer's head appeared as he climbed the steep stairs topside to observe muster. "Top of the morning to ya, sir," Sergeant Murphy said with a slight grin on his face. "Did the lieutenant sleep well for his first night onboard ship?"

Second Lieutenant John Reed did not answer as he steadied himself once he had climbed to the main deck.

Murphy called the company to attention, turned around, saluted, and said, "Company I ready for inspection, sir." He waited until Reed returned the salute.

"Company, parade rest."

"There'll be no inspection, Sergeant. The men will be given twenty-four hours rest per the order of Captain Davis, who is busy right now with the other officers of Company I planning our daily events for the duration of the voyage to our destination. That is all."

He saluted Sergeant Murphy, but did not wait for the customary return salute.

Murphy made half an attempt to return the man's salute, then called the company to attention as the second lieutenant slowly departed. He watched him disappear down the stairway to the lower decks and yelled, "Dismissed!"

"Well, Stevens, I guess our leadership wasn't feeling too good this morning," Avery said. He then laughed as he headed below decks.

Dwight remained topside a little longer to clear his head and settle his stomach from the coffee and biscuit he had forced himself to consume at breakfast. He scanned the horizon, but there was no land in sight. The sea had settled a little, he thought, or maybe he was becoming accustomed to the swaying. He hoped for the latter. The *Baring and Brothers* was visible on the port stern, and he marveled at the sight of the large vessel in full sail cutting through the sea, causing white foam to splash up against her bow. He strained to see the *Remittance* and the *Hamburgh* following behind her. He thought it was a beautiful sight.

"Looks like the crew of the *Baring and Brothers* has put some more canvas out to catch the wind. It will help her try to keep up with us," a nearby sailor remarked.

Dwight asked, "Is this ship faster than the other three?"

"Yep. The sleek hull makes the difference. The captain is holding her back so that the other three can keep with us. We are sailing at eight knots. That's half-speed for the *Smyrna*, but almost full for those three."

Dwight headed below decks. He had some interesting information to pass on to those who were interested in hearing it.

The smell of soap with a small hint of vomit was still present in his quarters. Most men sat on their footlockers with their faces in their hands and elbows on their knees, but a few had ventured back to lie in their swinging hammocks. He went to the head and found several sailors watching to ensure that no vomit or feces was deposited in a place other than the proper receptacle. Dwight performed his business quickly under their watchful eyes, and departed. It did please him that the navy had attempted to make sure the ship remained clean.

Avery was asleep when he returned to his quarters. The ship seemed to be swaying less, and he chanced sleeping in his hammock. Several minutes later, he was rocked to sleep by the slight movement and the exhaustion he felt from the previous sleepless night.

By the evening of the second day, most of the soldiers seemed to have grown accustomed to the constant rocking and were developing their sea legs like the veterans of the ship said they would. The company welcomed the day's rest, although Avery commented more than once to Stevens that the officers welcomed it more.

The second day began as the first had. Breakfast was at six, followed by muster topside at seven o'clock. The men waited to be called to attention by Sergeant Murphy. This time, all four Company I officers appeared.

Captain Davis took Sergeant Murphy's salute and waited for the sergeant to rest the men before he addressed them. "Men of Company I, I hope that you have grown accustomed to the ways of the sea. I, for one, have not. I have cleaned up my own puke, just as you have done." He smiled as a few of the men laughed. "We, the company officers and I, have developed a schedule that will be given to your NCOs to be implemented as we sail closer to our destination. One event that will take place this morning is musket training. Sergeant, take command of the training. That is all."

"Yes, sir."

Murphy came to attention and, as he saluted, called the company to attention. The officers left, and Murphy yelled for the soldiers to be at ease. "Form lines along the port and starboard railings! Don't be falling overboard while ya wait for the lead and powder to be handed to ya!"

"You heard the man, start lining up like the good sergeant told ya!" a corporal yelled.

Lead and powder began to be placed on the deck by a group of sailors. The men then began to take their portioned powder cartridges and lead balls.

"Follow my lead, Stevens. You'll be fine. Just follow my lead," Avery assured him.

"Avery, front and center," Sergeant Murphy called out, and Avery followed his command. "Private Avery is going to show ya how a proper soldier loads and fires his musket. Be paying attention, lads. We are going to be doin' it until ya get it right. All of ya."

Dwight watched Avery intently as Sergeant Murphy yelled for all to hear. Avery illustrated the proper stance for preparing to load, drawing the powder cartridge, biting off the end and pouring the premeasured amount into the barrel of the musket, stuffing a cloth wad into it and ramming that in to hold the powder, inserting a lead ball and ramming that down until it made contact with the wadding and powder, securing the musket ram, and bringing the musket to a waist-high position to insert a priming cap under a half-cocked hammer.

Avery yelled, "Ready!" as Murphy commanded him to cock his

musket, aim, and fire.

Dwight jumped as the explosion deafened him for a moment. Acrid smoke filled the air for only a short time before the sea breeze eliminated it. No one ever noticed the round lead ball splash into the sea several hundred feet away.

"All corporals, break your men into groups of four on either side of the ship and drill them until you see that they are shooting proper," Murphy ordered.

Mallard motioned to Avery to gather Bryant, Cross, and Stevens and then started splitting the rest of his men up into the required groups.

Dwight was nervous, but he remembered how he and Charles had practiced loading and firing their make-believe stick muskets after watching every detail the militia had performed on the Norwichtown Green. He had never fired a military weapon himself, since his father owned no guns. The only experience he had was occasionally firing Charles's shotgun when they had hunted quail together.

Avery lined the three men up to his satisfaction so they could watch him perform the loading exercise one step at a time. He then watched all of them perform the motions he had just shown them. The three men followed his lead, but at a slower pace. The first session culminated with Avery ordering them to cock their muskets, aim, and fire. They fired almost in unison for the first report from each musket. Stevens was ecstatic that he had fired a military weapon for the first time.

"Not bad even for you, Stevens. Let's do it again, but a little faster…" His voice was suddenly drowned out as the four soldiers fired their muskets somewhat in unison next to him.

More musket firing made it difficult for the three men to hear Avery as they went through the steps again. This continued until each man had shot his musket four times.

Sergeant Murphy yelled out for the company to cease firing. "Corporals, assemble your men in two lines of fifty on the port side."

Within a short time, the company was assembled as instructed.

"We are going to do one more volley, men. Prepare to load your weapons. No ball this time. Just powder and wad. Load." He watched as the men tried quickly not to be the last soldier loading his musket. Murphy patiently waited until, with the urging of some of the corporals, all the men were loaded and waiting. "Front line, kneel on your right knee." He waited. "Fer Christ's sakes, you know how to pray on one knee, don't ya?"

After a little looking around, the men followed.

"Back line, hold your position. Front line, aim." He paused. "Fire!"

The explosion was deafening.

"Front line, remain kneeling. Second line, aim and fire!"

Some of the soldiers in the kneeling position jerked from the sound and feel of a musket being discharged directly above their heads.

"That's what I expected. No need to be moving. You're still alive 'cause we were just shooting powder. I want you to stand up after the back line has fired. You can load your musket easier. Once you are done, kneel again. The Limeys do this very well. That's how the English conquered half the world. Trust me. I've seen this done many a time, and successfully. Remember what we did today. We do it again in the morning. Corporals, get your men to clean their muskets. Make them shine, gents."

"Ya heard the sergeant. Down below and clean ya muskets," Mallard immediately barked.

The remaining corporals followed suit with their men.

"Well, Stevens, ya didn't kill anybody," Cross remarked. "I was scared shitless when I was kneeling near ya while you were firing."

"Shut ya mouth, Cross," Avery barked.

"The boy's a natural. He'll be shooting the balls off a Mexican at a hundred yards by the time we get to shoot at 'em," Bryant said.

They all laughed as they headed below decks.

Dwight Stevens felt content with what he had accomplished. He wondered what his forefathers would have thought of him.

The next day was very rough at sea. The men felt the ship rolling more violently than they had on the first day that they had ventured off into the dark waters of the Atlantic. Most men were up and dressed well before daybreak due to the heavy swaying of the hammocks. Word had come down that no one was to be topside except qualified crew members. There was a marine posted at the deck stairway to ensure that the soldiers went to the mess, the head, or their quarters, with no exceptions.

Stevens had never seen a marine before. He never noticed their presence when the First Massachusetts had initially come onboard the *Smyrna*. "Some men tell me that the soldier standing near the stairway is a marine?" Dwight questioned Avery.

"Yep, but don't call him a soldier. They are part of the crew on all navy ships, and you better not be bothering 'em either."

"Pretty uniform they wear."

"Don't be telling 'im that it's pretty, either. He's in what they call marine dress. I've seen them on the docks in Boston. They can fight like a son of a bitch when they're drunk. Sailors don't like 'em much either."

Stevens continued to observe the details of the marine until Avery nudged him to get going. They needed to get to breakfast before the storm got too violent and they closed down the mess. That rumor was quickly spreading around the quarters.

As they passed the marine, he repeated the orders he had been given. "Stay below decks. Mess, latrine, and your quarters are your only choices." He repeated the orders every time a new group of soldiers passed him.

Avery and Stevens turned when they heard a commotion behind them. One soldier had apparently made a comment that irritated the marine. He ended up pinned against a bulkhead by his musket. Corporal Mallard apologized for the soldier, and the marine let him go.

"That looked like Bryant getting his ass jacked up, but I can't see. Too many are stopping to look," Avery said as Stevens followed him to the mess.

They were served their breakfast as they struggled to keep their balance. Several minutes later Cross, Bryant, and a few other troops from Company I took their seats near them. Bryant was still complaining about the marine as he sat to eat breakfast.

Corporal Mallard heard him from the other table and warned him, "Bryant, shut up. This is the second time I tell ya to shut up and eat."

"Well, well. You're the fool takin' on that marine. Ya got a death wish, Bryant?" Avery said and then laughed.

Several others, including Stevens, smiled.

"Learn to follow orders, Bryant. Ya live a lot longer that way. I'd keep away from him. He's sure to remember ya."

Bryant tried to eat breakfast, but his embarrassment from the incident as well as the effort required to keep his food down was overwhelming. He left the mess and returned to his quarters. Someone yelled out for him to smile at the marine when he passed him. Some laughter was heard from those who had seen Bryant get ruffed up by the marine.

A few minutes later, it was announced that the mess was closing. The mess crew gave soldiers that did not get any breakfast biscuits as they were turned away.

"I guess we got lucky, Stevens, so long as we can keep down what little breakfast we ate."

"Attention. Officer entering the quarters!" Corporal Mallard yelled.

Captain Davis entered with Sergeant Murphy directly behind him. "Put the men at ease, Corporal."

Mallard yelled out and the men came to parade rest.

Before the captain spoke, he found the closest deck stanchion and tightly grasped it. "I am told we are approximately two hundred miles off the Virginia coast while we weather this storm. The ship's captain has made a statement and has granted us a privilege that I am announcing to you. Men of Company I, you stink. That comment includes the NCOs and the officers under my command. We will be in warmer weather and hopefully calmer seas in several days. I have instructed my officers and NCOs to develop a bathing schedule for the company to perform on deck at the first opportunity. Salt water will be brought up in buckets as needed. Each man will be given soap to cleanse himself. The officers, then NCOs, and finally the company, will bathe, in that order. Each man will change his underclothing and wash the soiled ones. Uniforms will be washed, as well as all garments. Everything will be laid on the ship's railings or deck and dried in the sun. There will be no exceptions. Sergeant, you will work out the details with your men. You will also supply men to assist the officers and NCOs during their time to wash. Is that understood?"

Murphy confirmed that it was.

"That is all."

He turned and left as Murphy called the company to attention.

"Is the man crazy?" Cross spoke out, shaking his head. "We'll catch the death being naked out in the middle of the ocean."

"Maybe he hopes some of you will die. There will be less stink with you dead, Cross," Bryant said and laughed.

"How warm do ya think it will be as the ship gets more south?" Dwight asked Avery.

"I think it will be summer warm, based on what I remember hearing."

"What do you know, Avery? You ever been south before?" Bryant yelled over to him.

"Nope, only what I heard on the docks from southern sailors. No matter what, boys, we'll be getting clean. It will be better than the sour-ass smell we have about us now."

Chapter Five

Cleansing Body and Soul

Several days and many miles passed. Sunday morning was just another day on board the *Smyrna.* Following breakfast, the men mustered topside in full uniform and with their muskets. After several minutes in the warmer sun, they began to feel the full effects of wearing wool during formation.

Captain Davis appeared and addressed the men. "Tomorrow is the first day for bathing. The officers of Company I will go in the morning, and the NCOs in the afternoon. Sergeant Murphy, you will supply six men for pail duty for each bathing session on Monday. Tuesday will be the entire Company I. Each corporal will organize his men accordingly. All men will wash themselves, their uniforms, and their undergarments. Other companies will follow Company I on a daily basis. It is imperative that we complete our turn on Tuesday." Davis paused and looked at the men before he spoke again. "At ten o'clock this morning, the ship's chaplain will hold Sunday services for the ship's crew and the First Massachusetts. The chaplain stated that all Christian men are welcome to attend the services. It is mandatory for all in Company I. There are no exceptions."

He looked up and down the ranks and then at Murphy, who yelled, "Attention!"

They returned salutes and the captain left.

Some grumbling could be heard amongst the ranks.

"I don't need to be hearing some preacher in the middle of the ocean. Don't got no need for it on land or at sea," Avery said as he rested his chin on the barrel of his musket and looked out at the ships on the horizon.

Stevens didn't remark as he stood by his companion.

"It'll do you good, ya heathen," Cross said and laughed. "What, no Christian spirit in you, Al?"

"Never had one, according to the priests I knew growing up. No need to start now." Avery unbuttoned his overcoat. "No need for this coat either. We must be gettin' close to Georgia."

Several hours later, Company I reported topside with the other companies Captain Davis said would be present. The chaplain's sermon dealt with each man's duty to his country and preparation for a cleansed soul in case he met his Creator.

For the first time since joining the military, Stevens enjoyed his chance to sing familiar hymns his father's choir had taught him. Several soldiers remarked that his baritone voice was one of the best they had ever heard.

Cross made too many derogatory comments about Stevens' singing below decks after the service, and Dwight's quick temper got the best of him. Cross found himself on his back and rubbed his chin after Dwight landed a right cross with a clenched fist. The brief fight was broken up quickly before any sergeant or corporal could witness the altercation and bring charges. Cross rubbed his chin for the rest of the day and kept clear of Dwight Stevens.

But the incident wasn't over yet. Several hours later, Stevens went to use the head. Bryant, with Cross following slightly behind, followed Stevens and waited just outside the head for him to depart. Avery watched the whole episode unfold and followed just far enough behind so the two would-be brawlers would not suspect anything.

Stevens saw Bryant standing in his way as he was leaving the head, but before Bryant and Cross could make a move, Avery pushed both of them into the confines of the head.

"Now, lads, if ya both have a problem with young Stevens here, then let it be done now, but one at a time," he said, smiled, and looked at Cross first.

"No problem here, Al," Cross said.

Avery looked to Bryant.

Bryant said, "I have a problem; he hit my friend who was only kidding with 'im."

Avery looked back at Cross and said, "It's fair now. Cross, you back away."

Bryant made his move and swung wildly. Dwight sidestepped and used Bryant's off-balance lunge to push him into the steel wall of the head. The impact caused Bryant's lip and nose to instantly start bleeding. Bryant hadn't had enough. He recovered and tried to grab at Stevens. Dwight avoided his advance, spun him around, and delivered one blow to the midsection. Bryant slumped and moaned.

Another blow was about to be delivered when Avery yelled out, "He's had enough, Dwight! He's had enough! Back away! Remember, he's still in ya company." Avery helped Bryant up. "Ya all done now?"

Bryant just nodded.

"Go clean ya face before coming back to quarters. We don't want Mallard asking any questions, do we?" Avery instructed Stevens and Cross to wait with him until Bryant was presentable. When he was ready, Avery asked, "We all good here?"

There was no response.

"Are we all good now? We need to be depending on one another. We good?"

He waited until all of them nodded. "Good, then it is done."

Others later heard what happened in the head that night and that Dwight had been tested twice that day. Word spread around that it was probably not advantageous to test him further. Overnight, Dwight became somewhat of a well-known and accepted fellow soldier among the men of Company I.

That same night, while both Avery and Stevens swayed gently in their hammocks, Avery whispered to Stevens, "You handled ya fists pretty good. Seems ya got a temper. I'm glad you didn't use the knife ya keep in your right boot. You did right, but if you're caught fighting, they be harsh on ya. They be harsh on all of us. Ya know that, right, young fella?"

Stevens stared up at the overhead for several moments before he whispered, "I'd never use my knife unless someone drew one on me. There was no need for that today. I've always had a problem with my anger, Al. Got some whippings from my father and schoolmaster 'cause of fights I had. The stick never did any good on me."

Avery laughed. "I can see that, but ya need to control yourself. They can flog ya in the military. I know the navy does. I've seen the results. Hear that the army does it too. I'll tell the same to the other two. I'll be talking to them in the morning. I never had use for a knife, but I think I might be getting one when I get a chance, seeing where we'll be going."

"Al, how come you know so much?"

"Been around a bit longer than you, Stevens, but ya learn somethin' every day. Your knife is one. I also spent fifteen years on the docks, seen my share of different people from all over. Heard a lot of stories. Some true. Some not so true, but ya learn. The time passes quickly. I'll be thirty this coming August. That makes me twelve years older than you said you be, I figure."

He smiled as he looked at Stevens, who avoided eye contact.

Dwight ignored the questioning look and changed the subject. "Al, you got any family in Boston?"

"Just my Ma's sister and her husband. She's got two kids."

"What about your mother?"

"Never knew her. She died the day I was born."

"Your father?"

"My father dropped dead working on the docks when I was not yet twenty."

"What made you join up?"

"Don't rightly know, Dwight, don't rightly know. But I did, and here I be with ya. Now, let's get some sleep. Morning be here soon."

Early Monday morning before breakfast, the company was informed that there would be no muster. Mallard told the men in his quarters that six men could volunteer, or be picked, for pail duty in support of the officer's bath. No one volunteered. Mallard said again that he needed six men. Again, there was no response.

"Be it that no one volunteered, Avery, Cross, Bryant, Stevens, Tolman, and Wize are picked. You report topside at eight o'clock, to Sergeant Murphy. Understand?"

A few men commented amongst themselves that they were glad they weren't picked for the duty.

Avery piped up after Mallard asked for quiet, "Corporal, we not be expected to wash their asses now, are we?"

The men all laughed.

"No, just keep hauling up the buckets of seawater. Make sure there's nothing but seawater in 'em, Avery."

More laughter erupted.

"Still need six men for the sergeants."

Within a few moments, six men volunteered. Happy with his duty completed, Mallard instructed the rest of the men to clean their muskets and stay clear of the top deck where the bathing would be done. He dismissed the men as the first six picked for duty headed topside to report to Sergeant Murphy.

Being twenty minutes ahead of schedule, the men had time to actually enjoy the warming weather. The crew had provided buckets and ropes, and bars of soap and washtubs had also been set out for the use of the officers. The temperature was rising more as the sun rose higher in the sky. It was comfortable enough for them to strip off their jackets and wait for the officers to arrive.

The men assisted the officers. Buckets of moderately cool water were poured into tubs for the officers to bathe in. Several full buckets were left nearby so they could rinse. They dried off, donned clean underclothes, and then proceeded to wash and hang out their uniforms to dry. By 10:00 a.m., the temperature had reached almost seventy degrees, with a sustained wind which aided in quickly drying the officer's uniforms.

By noon, they were able to wear their trousers and bring their jackets and overcoats down below decks to their quarters to finish whatever drying still needed to take place. The damp wool smell was a welcome change to the odor that had permeated their jackets only hours earlier.

The six privates were then released from duty after the washtubs and buckets had been rinsed with clean seawater and left for the next group. The supper mess conversation for the men centered on what Dwight and the others could tell about the officers who bathed that morning. Laughter, jokes, and comments were hurled at the six to divulge the answers to the questions that were asked.

Avery finally made one comment. "Gents, the officers don't stink no more or less than we do, but right now they be actually smelling a lot better. There be nothing more to say." Sergeant Murphy had explicitly ordered the privates that no comments or information would ever be divulged about the company's officers who bathed that morning. They all knew better than to disobey orders from him.

The next morning came, breakfast was served, and the men assembled topside carrying one pair of their cleanest underclothes and wearing the uniform they had been ordered to wash. Approximately eighty men of Company I were broken up into groups to draw water and fill tubs while others washed, rinsed, and dried themselves. As soon as they finished, they washed their soiled clothes and spread them where there was room to dry. Upon completion, it was their turn to draw the water and fill the tubs while working the task in their underwear.

"God be good this morning, gents. Must be close to mid-seventies. I surely don't miss the commons!" Avery yelled while he sat and scrubbed his soiled uniform. He looked over at Stevens, who had placed his washed uniform on the wood deck to dry. "Keep checking the jacket and overcoat as it dries. If ya push and flatten, it looks a lot better when it dries."

Stevens followed his instructions.

A few others did the same, but most were content to merely sit and enjoy the warmth of the sun and fresh breeze while they let the clothes dry naturally.

By 4:00 p.m., most of the men of Company I were dressed and preparing to eat supper. Below decks, the quarters' smell had been considerably reduced since the company baths. Orders had been sent down that bathing would be weekly. Washing of the uniform would be at the discretion of the individual, unless so ordered by their superiors. The orders for regular bathing couldn't have come at a better moment. For the remainder of the week, while the ships rounded the Florida peninsula en route to Texas, the temperature exceeded eighty degrees topside. The temperature below decks approached ninety, and on some days was even hotter. Complaints were made that New England wasn't so bad when compared to the dreaded heat of Florida. No one could have imagined that it would be more than a year before they would experience New England weather again.

A strict routine was maintained on board the *Smyrna*. Breakfast, muster, inspection, musket drills, mid-day mess, firing practice, musket cleaning and inspection, bayonet instruction, supper mess by 6:00 p.m., with lamps out by nine. The routine continued for ten more days, until the coast of Texas came into sight and, with it, the rumor that debarkation would be in a few days. No one except the officers of the companies had any idea where that would be.

On the evening of February 27, 1847, Dwight Stevens and the men of Company I learned that a place called Matamoros, Mexico, would be their camp while more training continued. By the time they disembarked from the *Smyrna*, the journey had taken the First Massachusetts exactly three weeks to complete. The men were anxious to leave the ship. The night after the announcement, men sat around, both below decks and topside, discussing what Matamoros, Mexico would be like. No one, including Avery and the NCOs and officers, had ever heard of the place.

The morning of the 28th was hot and humid even before the sun rose. The *Smyrna* had dropped anchor several hundred yards off shore, a half-mile south of the Rio Grande. Many men skipped breakfast mess in order to get topside and out of the heat of their quarters below decks.

"Time to eat, Stevens." Avery finished buttoning his jacket and waited for the young private to finish tidying up his area.

"Too hot to eat, Al. I'd puke if I had to eat something."

"You'll be puking more if ya don't get some food and drink in you. The heat will do ya in quick enough, even more if you don't eat. Follow me."

The walk to the mess was difficult in the heat. Both men entered the mess, grabbed some biscuits and coffee, and sat down.

"Why we staying? It's too hot in here," Dwight said.

"We ain't. Put the biscuits in your jacket and drink all ya coffee. We'll be eatin' in our quarters as long as no one sees us. Then we're goin' topside."

The two men hid their food from the mess crew and returned to their quarters. Within minutes, they had eaten, gathered their belongings, and packed them in their haversacks. Both went topside with muskets in hand and spent the rest of the morning waiting for orders. At 11:00 a.m. the bugle sounded for muster. Three hundred men crowded the decks as they waited for the officers to appear.

Avery glanced at Stevens next to him. Perspiration had started to appear on his brow. He glanced in the opposite direction and saw more men sweating profusely. He realized it wouldn't take too long before someone would collapse in the late-morning heat. Avery unbuttoned the top of his jacket, risking a rebuke from Mallard or Murphy. It was worth it, however, to expel some of the heat that was building in his wool military jacket. He nudged Stevens to follow suit.

Three sergeants called in succession for the three main companies to come to attention. There was silence except for the noisy seagulls flying about. The wind blew softly, which eased the heat on the deck as the men waited. A dozen officers appeared and took their positions in front of their respective companies.

Stevens whispered, "Who are we waiting for now?"

"Watch and see," Avery whispered back.

"Got to be Cushing or Wright. Haven't seen either since before we left Boston."

Two men appeared on deck. One immediately stepped onto several large crates that had been placed in succession to form a small elevated stage from which the officer could address the men. "Put the men at ease," said Lieutenant Colonel Wright, as Cushing looked down at the group of officers assembled directly in front of him. The lieutenant colonel turned to Quartermaster Sergeant Reed. who yelled, "Companies!" and waited for the three sergeants to respond for their respective companies, and then he yelled, "Parade rest!"

A rumble was heard and felt on the deck as the men obeyed the order.

"I'm Colonel Caleb Cushing, your commanding officer. I am very proud of all you men who have endured the many rough miles to come and commence this campaign. I thank the dear Lord that he has bestowed his blessing on us who have undertaken this voyage to reach a successful conclusion. We have completed the first part of our duty, and now we embark on our second. That duty begins by orderly disembarking from this vessel, and assembling on the shore in your respective companies. All muskets will be immediately loaded with powder and ball on shore before formation there. U.S. Marines from the *Smyrna*, *Remittance*, *Baring and Brothers*, and *Hamburgh* have secured the shore and will remain until the entire regiment has been reassembled. We will then secure the shore ourselves until our wagons, horses, mules, and supplies have been successfully delivered. We will then march quickly and proudly into Matamoros." He paused and looked over the men, then continued. "First, let me give you a quick background of why you are here and what will be your duty. Mexico refuses to acknowledge the United States annexation of Texas. They are continuously resentful over disputes about our border. The war is being fought mainly on three fronts. On the first front, Brigadier General Zachary Taylor has been fighting in northeastern Mexico for much of the last year. I'm sure you have heard of his victories at Palo Alto, Resaca de Palma, and Monterrey, and very recently at Buena Vista. We are to be operating for a while in the same areas. The second front is in the west. General Stephen Kearny has captured the city of Santa Fe and much of California, while our navy has secured the California coast. The third front is what concerns us the most. General Winfield Scott and his army are currently marching into Mexico City. If successful, it will most likely end this war. We are here as part of that effort. We will maintain the occupation of Mexico, relieve units that require our help, and respond to emergencies and actions as needed. Each man is expected to perform his duty. We are in a hostile environment, men of the First Massachusetts. Be alert and follow orders immediately. That is all. Lieutenant Colonel Wright, dismiss the men and prepare to disembark."

Within a few moments the orders were fulfilled. The men relaxed and unbuttoned their jackets. "I'm surprised nobody dropped to the deck from the heat. I sure know that I was getting woozy standing in this hellish sun," Avery said and leaned against the ship's railing.

Corporal Mallard approached Avery and the ten or so men gathered around him. "Keep your eyes and ears open, and stay in this area. Company I leaves from here. Listen for the deck chief to tell us when he's ready for us to begin getting in the boats."

Cross spoke up as Mallard continued on to another group. "Shit, Avery, they going to be lowering us down to the water in the boats?"

"What did you think was goin' to happen, Cross? We ain't going to swim."

"It's got to be twenty feet to the water," Cross said as he looked over the ship's railing.

Avery smiled and then laughed. The men in the immediate area laughed as well.

Stevens thought the response was more nervousness than humor. "Avery, I don't think most of us like the idea of being lowered onto the water sitting in a boat."

"Dwight, the navy does it all the time. Just follow the chief's orders."

The men watched as the ship's lifeboats were prepared to be lowered. A short but cantankerous navy chief kept barking orders at his men. The men of Company I watched and waited from their assigned section of the deck to be given the signal to climb into the boats.

The order finally came.

"Okay, soldier boys, time to get in. I want only twenty at a time. There are four sailors in each boat to row ya' inta shore. Don't be tipping me boats over. I can't afford to lose the sailors." He laughed and then looked at the men. "Christ, ya heard me. Get in the boats."

Stevens and Avery took the lead, and climbed into the bow of the thirty-foot lifeboat.

Within a short time, the chief gave the order to hoist the boat and bring her over to the side. The lowering began as the sun beat down even harder on the men sitting and watching the ocean come closer to the bottom of the boat. The process would be repeated many times, until all three officers and the men were removed from the *Smyrna*.

Stevens stood in the white sand, looking at the palm trees and odd plants that grew just off the beach. "It ain't Connecticut. It ain't anywhere I've seen before, Al."

"Never ya mind. Load your musket and put on a firing cap. Rest your hammer gently on it. Keep your eyes open. We're in Mexico now. Look at them marines. Their backs are to us, but they be watching."

An hour passed as Company I slowly swelled to full ranks. Corporal Mallard had found all his men, and Sergeant Murphy could be seen trudging about giving orders and organizing groups of them. The men formed rows of four and were prepared to march behind Company K, which had formed right next to them.

The afternoon heat rose into the mid-eighties. Several men from Company I collapsed, forcing the company to stop and recover their exhausted comrades before continuing on to Matamoros. Other companies passed them, yelling derogatory comments and laughing. Within the hour, those same companies endured reciprocated insults as they were passed by Company I on account of their own men fainting.

Company I was the third company to reach the tenting field that had been left by General Taylor's regiments eight months earlier. His men had advanced from Corpus Christi and fought the Battles of Palo Alto and Resaca de la Palma in May of 1846, a few miles north of the city. Taylor's men had then camped at Matamoros before advancing to fight the Battle of Monterey in September of 1846.

The men had to wait until the teamsters arrived with the tents and supplies. There were distinguishing marks left in the field from when General Taylor and his army stayed, which offered a layout of camp for the First Massachusetts. Captain Davis assigned Sergeant Murphy to organize the officer and enlisted tents of Company I. The orders were then given to Corporal Mallard and the other corporals of the company. They organized the men to stand in the areas where they planned to erect their tents.

Avery and Stevens agreed that Avery would get the tent and other gear from the quartermaster wagons, while Stevens stayed to secure their assigned space. Both men, along with their companions, waited in the sun for the teamsters to drive the wagons to the field.

By 5:00 p.m., Avery returned with the tent, cots, and blankets he was issued. Within an hour, the two men had pitched the tent, aligned the cots, folded blankets, and stored their gear. The heat had not diminished, and their empty canteens stood to illustrate the excessive thirst they had while setting up. Stevens refilled both canteens from the river several hundred yards north of their encampment. The water had a faint amber appearance as it flowed over the smooth stones of the river's edge, but despite the color, the water was still cool and refreshing.

By dusk, pit fires could be seen starting across the encampment close to the river. As the men gathered what firewood they could find down by the river, they waited for word on when supper would be available. Scuttlebutt had it that beans and bacon could be ready as late as eight, and more than a little growling could be heard as the news spread through the company.

"Listen to 'em. You might think that some of 'em never missed a meal," Avery said.

"I'm getting hungry myself, Al," Dwight responded.

Avery finished digging a small pit and surrounded it with stones to begin making a campfire. "Well, young Stevens, look at the setting sun over there. We got more to worry about."

Dwight glanced west. "There ain't no sun to be seen."

"That's right. Looks like a storm be here before we eat. Gonna be a good dowsing this evening after all this heat we had today." Avery looked at the tent for a few moments. "Put my blankets on your cot."

Dwight looked perplexed, but followed his instructions.

Avery put all the firewood and kindling on his cot. "It will keep dry that way. Get out your bayonet. We need to dig a ditch around the tent to keep the water from coming in."

The men immediately bivouacked around them began to dig their own ditches until Sergeant Murphy recognized the approaching storm and ordered that all the tents have them.

Thunder and lightning appeared in the west for almost an hour before the rain finally came. Fortunately, they had already eaten supper by then. When the storm did hit the camp, it lasted for less than an hour, though the intensity of the rain overran the ditches the men had dug and the tents were flooded, if only for a short time. The sandy soil absorbed the rain, and an hour after the storm's departure, all was nearly dry.

"Damnedest thing I ever did see. Raining hard one minute and dry the next. This is a crazy place, Stevens," Avery said.

"Al, I'm going for more water to fill the canteens."

"No. You better wait till morning. I'll be with you then."

"It will only take me a few minutes."

"Look, you can't see now what kinda water you'll be filling the canteens with after this rain, and it's not safe going alone to the river. Who knows who or what could be waiting to harm you? We go in the mornin'. I got a little left in mine. It's yours if you want it."

"Thanks, but I can wait."

The thought of a thousand armed men pitched in tents close together had given Dwight a false sense of security, and Avery's statement unnerved him a little. To worsen the matter, at 9:00 p.m. they were informed by Corporal Mallard that they had been assigned the second three-hour shift of perimeter guard duty. From midnight until 3:00 a.m., they and ten other men from other companies would have sentry duty on the north side of the encampment. Mallard would be waking them fifteen minutes before their assigned sentry duty.

"We better turn in. Maybe we can get a few hours shut-eye till midnight." Avery opened the back flap of the tent, hoping for a breeze.

Dwight pulled off his boots and lay on his cot. He used the wool blankets as a makeshift pillow. They both heard Mallard telling Bryant and Cross they had the 3:00 to 6:00 a.m. duty..

A few cuss words from Bryant could be heard as he reluctantly accepted his orders, and some laughs from other members of Company I quickly followed.

At precisely 11:45 p.m., Corporal Mallard awakened Avery and Stevens. Both men shivered as they got up. The temperature had dropped considerably. They put on their jackets and then the overcoats as Mallard went to the different tents to awaken the other men.

Avery murmured, "Christ be damned, it's got cold."

Sergeant Winship oversaw sentry duty. He passed from one sentry to another, giving short instructions including staying awake, keeping the muskets loaded but not cocked, and repeating the sentry password, "Caroline."

Stevens wondered who Caroline was. His guess was that it was the name of some officer's wife or girlfriend. He found out later, at breakfast, that Colonel Cushing's wife was named Caroline.

The quiet of the night was unnerving for the young recruit as he walked and counted a hundred paces. Upon recognizing the outline of the sentry next to him, he turned in the opposite direction and counted another hundred paces. The sentry on this side was Avery, and he waved. Thus began three hours of uneventful sentry duty. Before long, the cold penetrated his boots and his toes became almost as cold as his hands. The only contentment he had was the relief he felt every time he saw Avery's wave. Finally, they were relieved of sentry duty and returned to their tent. They collected a few embers from others who had awakened during the night to stoke and maintain their own fires, and soon they were warm.

Dawn broke at 6:00 a.m. and the sun began to warm the camp during breakfast. By 7:00 a.m. muster, no overcoats were worn as Company I began their marching drills. Firing practice commenced before noon, and then more marching until the mid-afternoon heat reached over eighty. At 3:00, the men were relieved from duty. Some cooled themselves in the river, while others lay in the shade of the trees alongside it. The routine would not change for several more weeks.

The sutlers appeared once word spread that the First Massachusetts had arrived at Matamoros. They brought the goods that the men craved, namely, chewing tobacco, cigars, and liquor, the third being the most craved and on demand. The sale of whiskey had been prohibited by General Taylor's own orders, but that was overlooked by the majority of NCOs and officers, who indulged themselves on many occasions. Secret signs quickly developed between the soldiers to signal which wagons had the illegal beverage for sale. It wasn't long before the men of the First Massachusetts had a steady stream of whiskey being bought and sold by the sutlers that chanced to sell it.

Most of the men of the First Massachusetts were discrete in their consumption of the whiskey, but occasionally a fight developed. The corporals of the companies did a good job of assigning specific soldiers to keep control of the men on Saturday evenings and Sundays, when the men had the free time to consume what they had bought. Avery was one of the few trusted men assigned by Corporal Mallard for Company I, since the men respected him and he could handle his liquor. As long as the corporals controlled their men, the sergeants looked the other way.

The month of March became hotter, and the consumption of whiskey, and occasionally beer, increased. Fistfights increased, as did instances of insubordination. By April, things were getting out of control, and one specific event forced Colonel Cushing to take action. He both reprimanded and court-martialed some men from companies A, C, D, I, and J who were involved in a drunken brawl on a very hot April 10th, which was a Saturday night.

The following Tuesday morning, the entire regiment mustered. As the men of each company filed in rank, several high-ranking officers stood waiting.

"We'll be getting a talking-to, based on the officers lining up over yonder," Avery said.

"You think they going to talk to us about the fight over by the sutler's wagon on Saturday?" asked Stevens.

"Yep, but more than talk, Stevens. They got George Walsh and some others under guard, and we going to hear about what they are planning to do."

More talking and whispering could be heard throughout the ranks until several corporals and sergeants commanded silence. Corporal Mallard walked up and down his ranks, gritting his teeth while he told the men to keep quiet. He took his place in formation as soon as Sergeant Murphy addressed the company to come to attention. For several minutes, approximately a thousand men waited in silence for one of the officers to address them.

Colonel Cushing watched as his adjutant, Major Alfred Adams, handed a piece of paper to Lieutenant Colonel Wright. The lieutenant colonel paused to read the paper before he addressed the men. Colonel Cushing then nodded to Wright.

"Sergeant Major Ross, bring the men to parade rest."

The heat had already reached eighty degrees, but a light breeze cooled them ever so slightly. Lieutenant Colonel Wright began, "Men of the First Massachusetts. I have an order from our commanding officer to read to you concerning the incident that occurred Saturday, the tenth of April, between men of various companies near the sutler's wagons." He paused and looked over the entire regiment, then read,

Order No. 69
Headquarters
April 13th, 1847

The garrison court martial appointed to sit this day will state charge of,

1.) ***The accusation against Thomas Gallagher of Company 'A'.***
2.) ***Any other accused parties belonging to Companies 'A', 'C', 'D', 'J' and 'I'.***
3.) ***Any accused soldier not of the Massachusetts Infantry***
4.) ***Any accused person of the class of civilian assigned to this camp.***

By order of Col. Cushing
Col. Commanding
Alfred Adams, Major
Adjutant

Lieutenant Colonel Wright paused upon completion of reading the order and stated, "Men of the First Massachusetts, information will be posted this afternoon concerning times and locations of the court-martial proceedings. I cannot stress enough the seriousness of this incident, and the consequences that the individuals involved will be subjected to. That is all."

Several minutes later the men were dismissed.

Dwight Stevens knew the name of the soldier in Company I that had been accused, but he was unsure of the ramifications. "You know

George Walsh. Is he in real trouble, Al?"

"Dwight, he is in more trouble than he knows. They are going to court-martial his ass for sure if he's found guilty. Might get time in one of those military prisons. Don't know. Those other men are in just as much horseshit as he is."

More conversation and questions were hurled at Avery by other men who were listening.

Avery waited until all who walked with them had finished. "I don't know what is happening any more than any of you do. We have to look for the postings the colonel talked about, and just wait and see what happens next."

Cross, who had been lucky enough to avoid the fight, had seen the teamster who had drawn a knife and cut Private Gallagher, causing the fight and subsequently involving George Walsh. "I'm curious as to what they are goin' to do to that teamster."

"Just keep your mouth shut, Cross. You don't know anythin'. You don't want anythin' to do with this. You'll be dragged in like Walsh," Avery said and looked about at the men walking with him.

The next day, the men of Company I were informed that Private George Walsh had been found guilty of fighting, sentenced under court-martial, and removed from the company roster. Some other men met the same fate, and the rest watched as the men were put on quartermaster wagons and sent north to serve their jail time. Fort Leavenworth, Kansas was rumored as their place of incarceration. No one knew how long they would be in prison. Three days later, Avery read the last posted information on the incident. Several men, including Stevens, Bryant, and Cross listened while Avery read the posting,

Headquarters
Matamoros
April 16th, 1847

Lieutenant Andrews of Company 'C', First Regiment Massachusetts Infantry, with a corporal's guard to be detailed by the officer on duty in Garrison, will proceed to Palo Alto, and arrest Henry Aldrich, a teamster, in the quartermaster's service accused of assault with intent to kill, and place him in confinement in the garrison.

By order of Cushing, Col.
First Massachusetts
Commander

No one said a word until Cross finally spoke up. "I heard that he ran from camp as soon as he cut Gallagher. I wondered where he was at. He's going to get worse than jail time for cuttin' him?"

No one answered.

He looked around for a response.

Avery finally gave one. "I'd guess they might flog him, but he's a civilian and I don't know if they can. He'll get jail time most likely, if they capture him, up in Texas in a civilian prison, I reckon. Who knows?"

Teamster Henry Aldrich was captured and arrived at the regiment under guard ten days later. He was incarcerated in the garrison stockade until his court session began on April 26th. The military court found him guilty of assault, but not with intent to kill. The knife wound he inflicted on Gallagher, and his fighting with other drunken First Massachusetts volunteers, proved to be defensive. Eyewitnesses stated, on behalf of the accused teamster, that he only defended himself from Gallagher, who had attempted to stick him with his handheld bayonet. The wound was to Gallagher's forearm, which caused him to drop the bayonet. More fighting broke out. Walsh and others were involved, but no further weapons were drawn during the altercation.

The volunteers involved in the fight were sentenced to time in military prison for both fighting and drunkenness. The intent-to-kill charge was dropped for the teamster, but he was found guilty of peddling illegal whiskey to the volunteers. The court sentenced Aldrich to thirty days confinement in the stockade, loss of pay for the same period, and thirty lashes by bullwhip in front of the assembled men of the First Massachusetts and the company of teamsters that supported the regiment.

After breakfast the men assembled for muster, expecting just another day of mundane activities. They did not realize, however, that their detail for this day was guarding a prisoner. Cross noticed that the prisoner was none other than Aldrich.

"You men see who's over there? They brought Aldrich to muster."

The other oddity for the morning muster was that the teamsters were mustering on the opposite side of the parade field.

"I don't think so," Avery said.

"You see the teamsters assembling, Al?" asked Cross.

"Yep, and I see a whipping pole just yonder. We're going to see a whipping today."

After the men were assembled and presented for muster, Major Adams addressed the regiment. He read the findings of the court. After the public reading, Adams instructed that the punishment for the prisoner begin. The teamster was marched to the whipping pole and had his shirt removed before he was tied to it. Sergeant Stearns of Company A, who was known to be skilled with a bullwhip, was assigned to perform the punishment. Stearns snapped the whip several times to ensure he had everyone's attention. He nodded to the major that he was ready to begin. The major paused for what seemed an eternity for the prisoner and the men of the regiment as well. No one knew if the major was having second thoughts, or if he was trying to heighten everyone's anticipation of the flesh-ripping event about to start. Finally, the order was given.

The men of the regiment jerked in unison as the first lash cut into the shoulder flesh of Aldrich. He grunted and clenched his teeth. The second lash was delivered, and Aldrich grunted louder as the whip hit within a few inches of the first bleeding mark. The whipping continued, and around the twelfth strike Aldrich began yelling each time the whip found its mark. Blood had begun to run down his back and stains of dark red could be seen on his light blue trousers. At lash twenty, he screamed when the whip cut into his back.

Some men in formation dropped to the ground at the sight of the unrelenting whipping. No one went to their aid, after several sergeants yelled at the men attempting to assist them to get back into formation. Aldrich never consciously made it to the thirtieth lash. He passed out between the twenty-fifth and twenty-sixth.

Dwight Stevens watched and prayed that the savagery would stop. It finally did at twenty-six lashes. The major stopped the whipping when he saw Aldrich was unconscious. Dwight was sickened when he saw the bloody and raw back of the man

Aldrich was untied and dragged to the stockade by military guards. The look on the faces of the teamsters as they broke up ranks only indicated the hatred the men had for the barbaric way one of theirs had been treated.

When all of the court-martial proceedings were completed, over sixty men from the First Massachusetts Volunteer Infantry Regiment had been found guilty and charged as "incorrigibly mutinous and insubordinate," and placed in confinement for some time.

For almost a month after the flogging of Aldrich, the sutlers sold only tobacco, dry goods, and other items not readily supplied by the army. Conversations about the need for a drink were constantly heard at meals, during free time, and after extensive training in the spring heat of northern Mexico. The only relief the men enjoyed, however, until whiskey infiltrated the encampment again, was the cool water from the Rio Grande.

Dwight was amazed at how all these men could want more whiskey after what they had witnessed at the flogging.

Chapter Six

Regimental Movement

The month of May offered only hotter weather for the men of the First Massachusetts to endure. Despite the heat that reached ninety degrees by midday, the men were drilled incessantly on musket loading, firing drills, and bayonet practice. They honed these skills until they perfected them. With time, musket accuracy improved as well. Most men in the companies could load, aim, and fire twice in less than a minute, hitting their target three out of five times at a distance of a hundred yards.

Dwight Stevens attained a slightly higher accuracy, and Corporal Mallard noted that fact during one particular firing practice. "Stevens, you shoot well. You are most improved of the men I have in this company." He turned to Avery, who smiled as the corporal had complimented his companion. "I give you the credit for teaching this man."

"It was nothing, Corporal. He learned quick, that's all."

"Maybe so, Avery, maybe so. But you still had something to do with it."

Official word came the next morning that the regiment would be ready to move the following day. All regimental drills were cancelled after the noonday meal. The afternoon was spent assisting the teamsters in packing the wagons of food, supplies, and ammunition, and emptying the temporary buildings that housed the goods. The men were instructed to be prepared to break camp at 5:00 a.m. and be ready to march by 8:00 a.m. The lugging of supplies for the teamsters had tired them. They looked forward to supper, relaxation, and a decent night's sleep before they marched.

Stevens returned to the tent to find Avery writing. He was surprised, since he had previously said that he had no one to write to. "Who are you writing to, Al?"

Avery didn't respond at first as he penciled a few more words on the yellow paper. "Just an aunt of mine. Promised I'd write once I got a chance to tell her my whereabouts. My ma's younger sister."

Stevens smiled and went about his business.

"What about you, young Stevens? Surely there's a girl, ma, or pa that is wanting to know your whereabouts. I seen you throw a letter in the fire pit back in Boston. Maybe about time you wrote another?"

Dwight didn't respond to his question as he began checking his musket and gear.

Avery didn't pursue a response and continued to write.

"Maybe soon I'll write my sister and let her know where I am. Maybe when we get to our next camp."

Avery looked up and smiled. "Next camp could be a long time gettin' to, Dwight."

"I don't feel the need to write yet, that's all."

"Suit yourself."

The First Massachusetts began their march from Matamoros on May 20, 1847. Company I was fifth in formation, with Captain Davis and First Lieutenant Smith leading the company. Sergeants Murphy, Winship, and Osgood marched directly behind the two officers. The men were informed that Sergeant O'Connell followed almost a mile in the rear so that he could supervise the teamsters driving the wagons that contained the regiment's food supplies. He was the most envied NCO because he got to ride.

For two hours the regiment trudged on. The arid ground caused considerable dust to rise, hindering the visibility of the men of Company I. At times they could see less than half of the men marching in front of them. Canteens were constantly being raised as the men rinsed their mouths and dampened handkerchiefs to wipe the sweat from their brows and necks. Sergeants and corporals continually yelled out for the men to conserve their water, emphasizing that it would be many hours before they would stop close enough to the river to replenish their canteens.

There was quiet in the ranks of Company I as they marched on. Occasionally, one of the sergeants would yell out for the men to shift their muskets from the left or right shoulder to ease the weight.

Stevens looked at Avery every so often. He had noticed that his tent companion was constantly looking to his right at the field, brush, ditches, and occasional groups of trees that bordered the rutted dirt road they marched on. Sometimes Avery would stretch his neck and look to the left to observe things that had caught his eye in that direction. "What are you looking for?" Dwight asked.

"Nothing particular."

"You are looking for something. You've been doing it for the better part of the last four or five miles we have marched."

Avery continued to look, but knew Stevens would keep asking until he answered him. He turned while stretching his neck to look left and said, "Looking to make sure some Mexican don't decide to take a shot at us while we're concentrating on marching. We were told to keep our eyes open while we marched. Not too many are doing that. Not even the officers. Look at Lieutenant Reed. He almost fell off his horse once. Falling asleep from the heat, I guess."

The thought of a Mexican shooting at the regiment had not

crossed Dwight's mind much since the first day the regiment arrived at Matamoros months earlier. "You think one would?"

"Not right here, 'cause they couldn't get away without one of us catchin' him."

They continued marching as a few more soldiers heard the conversation.

While looking at some hills ahead, Avery said, "I figure we'll get some trouble where those rolling hills are. There's enough cover for someone to take a shot."

"How long before we get there?" Dwight asked.

"By the end of the day we might be close to them. It's hard to tell how far they are away.

Several days later, the regiment still had not reached the rolling hills that separated Matamoros from Monterey. Word had been passed down on the third day that Monterey was the destination of the regiment. In three days they had marched about thirty miles without incident, but the men were not pleased to hear that Monterey was still some hundred miles west of their present position. The closest city was Camargo, still fifty miles northwest. On the third bivouac, the camp conversations centered on sore feet, tired legs, and the ever-present and hated dust.

"Don't be bitching, boys. The dust will stop choking you as soon as we get into the hills," Avery told them.

"You don't know shit, Avery!" someone yelled from a group of men who overheard him talking.

Quite a few men laughed when another piped up and said, "Yeah, you been talking about the rolling hills for days now. We haven't marched up them yet."

More laughter ensued.

"Laugh all you want, gents. Even with no dust, you'll be cryin' when we hit those hills." Avery knew better than to respond to the continued joking that was developing. He turned to Stevens and said, "You smiling with those fools too?"

"Naw, they're just kidding you, Al. I'm enjoying the laughter."

"Enjoy it, young Stevens. See what the story is in a day or two."

The regiment finally approached the hills and began the slow ascent. Within several miles, the effect of the slow climb began to take its toll. Some men dropped out from exhaustion and had to be coaxed and physically escorted by others to keep up with the regiment's speed. The heat exceeded ninety degrees by midday, forcing the regimental commanders to stop and rest the men. This had to be done two or three times a day, and all marching stopped by 3:00 p.m., when the heat was at its height. The miles covered per day decreased by half as the hills continued to rise toward Monterey.

Even Avery found it difficult to concentrate on his marching and scouting as he grew tired. The regiment trudged along as men took occasional drinks from their canteens, officers slouched in their saddles, and NCOs stopped reminding the men to conserve their water. The NCOs had enough to do with making sure no man was left on the side of the road.

And then the unthinkable happened. A lone shot was heard. Then several more, as the men became alert.

Someone yelled, "The lieutenant's been hit!"

Stevens saw Second Lieutenant Reed fall from his horse. He looked to Avery, who had already broken ranks and was heading toward the fallen officer. More yells were heard as men from Company I crouched with muskets at the ready. Several soldiers were sprawled out on the road.

Captain Davis had seen the men directly ahead of him fall the instant the second set of shots were heard. He screamed, "Company I, fall out to the right! Sergeants, follow my lead! Follow my lead!"

Mallard yelled a few seconds later, "Follow the captain, men, quickly now!"

The entire company broke right and into the trees where Captain Davis rode hell-bent, hoping to come upon the snipers who had just injured several of his men. He would learn later that one of his second lieutenants had been killed instantly by a sniper's bullet.

Stevens ran as fast as he could and found himself at the lead of the men trying to follow Captain Davis. Close on his heels was Avery, who said, "Watch those trees to your left, boy. Don't cock your musket until you're sure you see someone."

They reached the tree line beyond which Captain Davis and several other officers on horseback had disappeared. Several pistol shots were heard. Stevens, Avery, and ten or more men followed in the direction the shots came from. In a clearing up ahead, Stevens saw Captain Davis cut down a man with his saber. The man lay still as the captain quickly moved on, and Stevens and Avery approached.

"No need to watch him. The captain made sure of that. He's cut deep from that saber."

Dwight's stomach turned as he saw the deep gash that ran from the back of the man's neck into his right shoulder. "Looks like his neck is broken," Avery said.

More men continued on as Stevens and Avery stood by the dead Mexican.

"He don't look much older than you, Dwight."

"You think he shot at us?"

"He was holding a musket until Captain Davis cut him down."

Another Mexican was shot and killed, but so were Second Lieutenant Reed and two men from Company H. The regiment did not move from their position for the rest of the day, and that night preparations were made and carried out to bury the one officer and two soldiers. The two Mexicans were buried in shallow graves right where they had died. Many men did not sleep well that night. Sentry duty was tripled, and no campfires were lit in an effort to minimize the chance of night sniper fire.

After a restless night, Stevens awoke early to find Avery and Corporal Mallard talking in the pre-morning darkness. He waited until Mallard left and Avery had returned to their tent.

Avery noticed that Stevens was looking at him. "Good morning, young fella. Sleep good?"

"No."

Avery went about finding his two blankets and rolling them up to attach to his haversack. He saw Stevens watching him perform his morning chores and knew he had something on his mind. "Got a question for me?"

"Yes. I saw you talking with Mallard. I don't want to seem nosy, but there has to be something important going on for you to be talking to him this early in the morning."

Avery finished his chores. "You better get ready, Dwight. We'll be doing some flank scouting with Mallard."

Dwight didn't understand, but waited for his companion to explain as he began getting ready.

"We go out ahead on each flank of the regiment and make sure no more Mexicans can pick off another one of us. It was Captain Davis's idea, and headquarters approved some of us from Company I to scout the right flank. Some of the troops from Company H will be doin' the left. To me, it seems proper that the two companies that lost troops be given the chance, and we are some of the best shots in the company."

"What do you mean, getting the chance?" Dwight asked.

Avery paused, looked at him, and smiled. "To get some Mexicans before they get us. You, me, Cross, Bryant, Mallard, and five or six others will have that opportunity."

Dwight Stevens finished his chores without saying another word to Avery. His only concern now was how he would react if he was called upon to shoot at someone who was trying to kill him or someone in his regiment.

Company I assembled and waited for the rest of the companies.

They watched Company K march quickly past them to the rear. Word spread that Company K was being moved to the rear to protect the regimental supplies. Sergeant Murphy called to Mallard to assemble his men for flank duty.

Mallard yelled out the names of the ten men he had picked. Besides Mallard, only Avery knew the entire list of names. Stevens and the others quickly assembled away from the company.

Mallard waited until all ten had gathered. "We have the right flank duty. You were picked for your marksmanship. We will scout several hundred yards out ahead of the regiment. Company H men have the other flank. Keep your eyes open and try to be quiet. We expect more of what we got yesterday. Check your primers. Keep your muskets halfcocked. Spread out but stay in sight of each other at all times. You understand?"

Everyone nodded.

Mallard looked at Avery. "You pick four and lead. I'll be behind with the rest."

Avery called out the names of the four men he wanted, which included Dwight Stevens, and headed through the brush until some open space was found. He spread his men as instructed, but took the farthest position out from the regiment on the right flank. Stevens was right next to him, and within eyesight as instructed. They moved along cautiously, but at a quicker pace than the regiment, which could be heard noisily marching behind and to the left of their position. This continued throughout the morning, with no signs of any ambush activity.

The First Massachusetts saw small villages and cattle ranches as they proceeded toward Monterey. They marched without incident for hours as the heat increased and baked both the regiment and the flank scouts. There was little relief from the constant uphill march, and this caused them to slip below the marching rate of three miles an hour that Colonel Cushing had hoped to maintain. As the uphill march continued, the time it took to cover those miles significantly increased.

The heat was almost unbearable until the afternoon sun was obscured by clouds from an approaching thunderstorm. A downpour could be seen a few miles away, coming directly toward the moving regiment. The men anticipated the relief from the heat as significant thunder and lightning broke in the sky.

The flank scouts, aware of the coming storm, became more alert as the regiment marched. Corporal Mallard had put out the word that snipers might use the rain, thunder, and lightning as a mask for the noise of gunfire.

Avery and Stevens continued to be in the lead of the right flank scouts. As the two walked, they came upon a closely cropped section of trees with underbrush that made it difficult to get through. The road the regiment would use also cut through the same section of trees. The dense brush obscured the sight of the regiment from the position the flank scouts were advancing.

"Can't see shit in this brush. We need to turn to the road before the regiment gets here." Avery signaled to the men to stop. They waited for Mallard's group to catch up.

"Why you stopping?" Mallard asked Avery in a low but obviously irritated tone.

"Can't see anything, Corporal. We need to get closer to the road in case some Mexicans are using the cover to pick off a few. Be a good place to do it."

Mallard nodded in agreement and motioned the men toward the road.

Avery and Stevens took the lead. They advanced about fifty yards when Avery stopped, crouched, and motioned to Stevens. He pointed ahead.

Stevens stopped and crouched. He nodded his understanding and signaled to the men behind him to get their attention. Stevens waited for Mallard to approach him. As soon as he had, he motioned toward Avery.

Mallard immediately saw what Avery had uncovered. Several snipers could be seen waiting for a quick and clean shot at the approaching regiment. Mallard whispered to Avery, "You and Stevens take out the two we can see. Don't take 'em out, though, until we get close enough to see how many others there are. If they turn to shoot or hightail it toward the road, kill 'em. Don't miss."

Avery nodded and waved for Stevens to approach him and Mallard. When he had, Avery whispered, "You take the one on the right. Be ready to shoot if they see Mallard and his troops coming, or if they turn to run. Got it?"

Stevens' stomach turned as he cocked his musket and took a bead on his target. Avery had already aimed and was ready.

Mallard and the remaining flank scouts cautiously and quietly flanked the Mexican snipers. They'd advanced about twenty yards when the sniper Stevens had a bead on turned and saw Mallard and his approaching troops. As the sniper aimed his musket toward the advancing men, Stevens fired at the middle of the man's body. The sniper dropped as the lead ball went through his chest.

Avery immediately fired on his target, who had not turned yet. The sniper screamed in agony as he thrashed about in the brush with a neck wound. Within a few minutes, he died of blood loss. Mallard and his men charged as they flanked the dead and dying snipers. Two more snipers were flushed out, but they ran in the direction of the road.

The flanking scouts of Company H had heard the initial shots from their left-flanking position on the opposite side of the road, and had headed in the direction of the shots. They approached the road at the same time as the fleeing snipers. Four shots sent the two Mexicans to their deaths.

The men of Company A, marching on the road, were ordered to advance on the double as soon as the shots were fired. Several officers led the advance with sabers drawn and galloped ahead. When they reached the wooded area through which the road cut, they found the two dead Mexicans on the roadside. The officers ordered Company A to separate into columns on each side of the road and continue through the wooded area ahead of the regiment.

Avery and Stevens left their victims where they had shot them. They caught up to the right-flank scouts and took the lead again. The flank scouts finally reached open and level country as the thunderstorm let loose. They all walked in the open field several hundred feet off the road but still in advance of the regiment. The men of the left flank could hardly be seen as the rain intensified. It would not be until they camped later that day that the whole incident could be reported to headquarters by Corporal Mallard and his counterpart of Company H.

Stevens finished pitching the tent as Avery returned with firewood.

No words were exchanged until Avery spoke. "Wood's a little damp. The kindling is dry enough, though. I'll get more to help with starting the fire."

Stevens nodded and finished driving the last stake into the ground to secure the tent.

As Avery was about to leave, he said, "Take a walk with me and get some more firewood."

Stevens followed, and they gathered more wood together. No one said a word until both were carrying an armload.

"You want to talk about it?" Avery asked.

"Talk about what?"

"The shooting today."

"Nothing to talk about, Al."

"You're kinda quiet since we camped."

"I have nothing to say except that I didn't like it."

"Nobody does. It's what war is, though. That Mexican coulda shot me, you, or anybody."

"I know, but I still didn't like it."

"Good. Never like it. Just do it when you need to."

"You think more will happen?"

"Yep. We're in their country and they ain't liking it. General Taylor kicked their asses around here a while back. Their main army is down south. These men are just locals who hate us. They'll do it again for sure."

They returned to the camp and built a larger fire with the kindling they had gathered. Several soldiers sat by the bigger fire they had made. They were more interested in hearing about what had happened during the attempted ambush than getting warm.

Avery gave the details. When he praised Dwight for his marksmanship, Dwight never acknowledged or commented. The conversation was broken up when Corporal Mallard and Sergeant Murphy approached the campfire. The men looked surprised to see the two of them.

Sergeant Murphy spoke. "Avery and Stevens, Captain Davis wants to see you in his tent."

Avery stood up, buttoned his jacket, and put on his cap. Dwight followed. The four men walked several hundred feet to where Captain Davis's tent had been pitched. The front flap was open and all four men could see the captain sitting and writing at his camp desk.

Sergeant Murphy said, "At your command, Captain. Avery and Stevens reporting as ordered."

"Very good, Sergeant. Thank you." Captain Davis finished writing and rose. He slowly walked to the four men standing at attention outside his tent. "At ease, gentlemen."

"Yes, sir," Sergeant Murphy replied.

"I wanted the sergeant to bring you three here so that I may commend you for your quick and decisive action in the field today. That was fine work you did, and I feel it helps to at least partially vindicate the loss of our Lieutenant Reed. I wrote to his parents this evening to inform them of his death, and I tried to include consoling words to ease their pain. It is very difficult to do that in writing, but I mentioned your actions today in the letter to hopefully give them the satisfaction of knowing that the enemy paid a price for their actions. You made me and the company very proud. Thank you." He extended his hand to each of the three men to show his appreciation. Once finished, he looked at Sergeant Murphy. "That is all, Sergeant."

"Yes, sir." Murphy saluted.

The captain returned the salute and went back to his tent.

Sergeant Murphy motioned for the three men to follow him. They walked several yards before Murphy turned and addressed them. "Good work, but good work gets you more work. Corporal, you and your same men will be flanking tomorrow. Good night to you all."

"Yes, sergeant," Mallard replied as the four men separated.

Neither Avery nor Stevens talked until they returned to the campfire. There were men still sitting around the fire talking and laughing.

"What did the good captain want?" Cross asked.

"Just to tell us we had more flank scouting to do tomorrow," Dwight said.

Avery never said anything more. The men turned in early.

The next morning, the flanking scout groups were again sent out ahead of the regiment. The morning was uneventful. The scenic land had opened up and only rolling pastures appeared one after another as the flank scouts preceded the regiment. The landscape did not afford any cover for snipers to take shots at the passing regiment, which relaxed the scouts a little. The heat increased and the cloudless blue sky afforded no relief from the scorching sun. The river flowed parallel with the road the regiment used, and on several occasions came very close which gave the men easy access to fetch water for their canteens. It was at one of these areas that Dwight asked permission to fill the canteens of the small group of men he was with.

Mallard agreed, and within a short time Stevens had collected all the canteens from his fellow scouts. He trotted the distance to the riverbank and proceeded to fill the canteens. He quickly finished his task and took a few moments to splash his face and neck with the cool water. He soaked his handkerchief quickly and intended to place it under his cap to cool his head, but with his head down applying the handkerchief, he temporarily lost his concentration to keep watch for any threats on the river's edge. From out of nowhere, he heard the hooves of a horse approaching in front of him.

Before he could turn to grab his musket, a lariat encircled his neck, thrown from the mounted Mexican who had quickly charged him from the opposite side of the narrow and shallow part of the river. Dwight realized the Mexican intended to drag him across the river. As the mounted adversary turned his horse to do just that, Dwight drew out the knife he kept in his boot and quickly cut at the lariat before it tightened and strangled him. His quick thinking saved him from certain death. The Mexican galloped away without his prey.

Dwight reached his musket as he heard a shot fired. He turned to see that Avery had taken aim at the mounted Mexican, but the distance afforded the Mexican at least another day of life as the ball missed its mark.

"You all right, Stevens?"

"Yeah. That was a little too close. I never saw him coming at me, and then it was too late."

"He came on you from the other side. Smart greaser he was. You got to be careful. These bastards will try to kill us any chance they get. Good thing you had your knife in your boot."

Stevens gathered the canteens, his musket, and his thoughts, and the two men left the river's edge and returned to the scouts. Dwight was still shaken, but now didn't feel quite so bad about the man he had shot during the earlier attempted ambush. That emotional burden had just become much lighter.

Six days later, the regiment was within a day's march of Camargo. After they bivouacked for the night, orders were given that four companies were to proceed to Camargo the next morning, while Company I and the remaining companies and supply wagons continued on to Monterey. The regiment also received news from headquarters that Colonel Cushing had been promoted to brigadier general and Lieutenant Colonel Wright had been promoted to colonel. There were two additional promotions that were about to be given, as well—two that would impressed the men of Company I even more.

Corporal Mallard approached a group of Company I men sitting at the campfire, laughing. The men continued to carry on as Corporal Mallard listened to some of the conversation and waited patiently for a few minutes.

Avery finally broke up the conversations and asked, "Corporal Mallard, what brings you down here? Care for a chew?" He held up some of the chewing tobacco he occasionally indulged in.

"Naw. Don't chew. Thanks anyway. The sergeant major wants to see us."

Avery looked a little confused at the request, but regained some humor and said, "Look, Corporal, I can't be takin' over his job."

A few men laughed.

"He wants to see you, me, and Stevens. Don't know why, just that Sergeant Murphy told me to fetch you two."

"Aw, shit, Avery, you done somethin'. The sergeant major don't call for nothing good," Cross said and then laughed.

"Any idea what he wants with me and Stevens, Corporal?" Avery inquired.

Mallard shook his head as the men headed for the sergeant major's tent. As they approached, Sergeant Murphy and several sergeants and corporals were standing with him in conversation.

"Looks like somethin' come down from headquarters, I reckon," Avery said while looking at Mallard.

"Could be. We'll find out soon enough."

Sergeant Major Ross stopped talking to the group as the three men approached. He turned and smiled at them as they reported.

"At your request, Sergeant Major," Mallard said when he saw Ross's smile.

"Glad you came as soon as you could. I have good news for you, gents."

All three men looked at each other.

"On behalf of Captain Davis, the regimental adjutant has seen fit to promote two of you. Congratulations are in order." The sergeants and corporals watched as Sergeant Major Ross handed Mallard a set of light blue sergeant stripes with a paper signed by the adjutant, recognizing Mallard's promotion to sergeant.

Avery clapped as well, as he approved of what he had just witnessed.

Sergeant Major Ross looked at Mallard, who stood motionless.

"You hearing what I just said, Mallard? You look like you have seen a ghost or somethin'. Take the stripes and sew 'em on before mornin'."

"Thank you, Sergeant Major. I don't know what to say."

"No need, you deserve it." He shook Mallard's hand and turned to Avery. "You, Private Avery, have been promoted to corporal." He handed Avery a set of corporal stripes and the accompanying paper. "Congratulations, you deserve it too. Corporal , I mean Sergeant Mallard has been telling Sergeant Murphy here how much you lead the men. You set a fine example stopping that ambush."

Avery looked completely stunned and was speechless.

Ross saw the confusion and said, "Christ, can't you talk either? You got the stripes because you do a good job leading the men. I like men who can lead. Now sew the stripes on by the mornin'."

"By your order, Sergeant Major."

He shook Avery's hand. "Congratulations to you, Corporal."

"Thank ya, Sergeant Major."

The sergeant major looked at Stevens and said, "There's no promotion for you, Stevens, just my thanks for being a crack shot and killing that Mexican. I've heard good things about you. Keep up the good work."

Dwight only nodded as the sergeant major shook his hand. Sergeant Murphy and the other sergeants and corporals shook hands. Good conversation and a few jokes ensued until the three departed back to Company I.

Mallard turned to Avery as they walked and informed him that he would expect him to start sleeping in the corporal's walled tent with the four other corporals as soon as possible.

Avery stopped walking. "You telling me to get out of my tent?"

"Yeah, you need to start sleeping in the corporal's tent. You're a damned corporal now. I moved up when I was promoted, and now you have to do the same."

Avery didn't answer as he looked at Stevens. He didn't like it, but he knew Mallard was right. It was just that he had never thought about the consequences of a promotion, and now that it had come, the realities caught him off guard.

"Corporal Avery, did you understand?"

"Yes, Sergeant, I do."

"Good. I'll be moving out of the corporal's tent as soon as Sergeant Murphy has made arrangements for me to tent with him and the other sergeants of Company I. As soon as I do, you follow me."

Avery just nodded as the three men approached the tents of Company I.

About twenty men of the company had gathered around the camp. Word had spread that Mallard, Avery, and Stevens had been summoned to the sergeant major's tent. Curiosity and growing rumors had fed the interest of some of the men of the company, causing them to assemble at the large campfire.

Several men saw the three approaching. One yelled out, "You still have your asses on you!"

A couple of men laughed.

"How'd you sweet talk the sergeant major to keep those asses?" somebody else yelled out.

"Hold it down. Hold it down," Avery said, sounding a little annoyed.

The group became quiet after hearing the tone in Avery's voice.

He waited until all the jokes and comments had stopped. "Stevens was congratulated on his marksmanship, and Corporal Mallard has been promoted to sergeant. I saw it myself. He has papers signed by the adjutant. Show 'em your stripes, Sergeant."

Mallard obliged, and most of the men congratulated him while several just stood around and watched.

After several moments Mallard thanked the group and turned to Avery. "You going to tell them about you, or am I going to?" Avery didn't respond immediately so Sergeant Mallard announced, "Private Avery is now Corporal Avery. He will be taking my position tomorrow morning. He will be moving up to the corporal's tent soon. Show 'em your corporal's stripes."

The men lined up to congratulate Avery.

One of the last in the group of twenty or so was Dwight Stevens. "Congratulations, Al. I didn't get a chance to tell you in front of all those

NCOs. You deserve it. I'll be proud to serve under you."

"Nothing is changing except where I sleep. Now I need to be sewing these stripes on before morning." Avery started to leave.

Stevens grabbed the sleeve of his jacket. "There will be a lot of changes. You are our corporal now. We all look up to you already, but we'll look to you even more now that you have those stripes. We'll be counting on you." Stevens let go of his jacket sleeve.

"I understand. I just mean you and me ain't no different", Avery said.

The regiment continued toward Monterey for four more weeks. The heat intensified as they moved south. The arid and sandy Rio Grande basin had fallen away to rolling hills, open fields, and more humid and hotter days as May ended and June began. A few more incidents occurred with sniper fire, but no troops or teamsters were wounded. The several deaths that did occur came from sickness or, according to the regimental surgeon, unknown causes.

The First Massachusetts, as with other regular and volunteer regiments, underwent exposure to yellow fever, dysentery, small pox, measles, and various diseases prevalent in Mexico. These diseases were a constant scourge to the U.S. soldiers, and killed more of them than the Mexican bullets did. The lack of hygiene also made them susceptible to illness. Worst was the lack of leadership by the officers in the volunteer regiments because they were either too inexperienced to understand the hardships their men had to endure, or they didn't care. It would be years later before Major General George B. McClellan[1] of Civil War fame would write about his experience as a second lieutenant:

"I have seen more suffering since I came out here than I could have imagined to exist. It is really awful. I allude to the sufferings of the volunteers. They literally die like dogs. Were it known in the States, there would be no more hue and cry against the Army, all would be willing to have so large a regular Army that we could dispense entirely with the volunteer system. The suffering among the Regulars is comparatively trifling, for their officers know their duty and take good care of the men."

The unrest that had begun in the ranks ended when the regiment arrived at Monterey on the 23rd of June, after marching almost three hundred miles from Matamoros. The encampment at Monterey took on

---

[1] **George Brinton McClellan** (December 3, 1826 – October 29, 1885) was a major general during the American Civil War. He organized the famous Army of the Potomac and served briefly (November 1861 – March 1862) as the general-in-chief of the Union army.

the same function as it had in Matamoros. The First Massachusetts was still assigned as the army of occupation. Boredom became a serious problem, and insubordination and desertions increased.

News of General Scott's victories at Vera Cruz and Cerro Gordo had reached the regiment prior to their march to Monterey. More news of Scott's campaign heading toward Mexico City only increased the men's desires for combat duty. The chance to fight never came, as orders were issued for the regiment to split up for assignments to Brazos and Sabonito. These assignments delayed the regiment, and they didn't arrive at Vera Cruz until early October of 1847. This was two weeks after General Scott and his army had won victories around Mexico City at Contreras, Churubusco, Molino Del Ray, and, finally, at Chapultepec.

Heat exhaustion continued to exist, and the "shakes" or "intermittent fever" took its toll on the men of the First Massachusetts, though no one in the U.S. Army would begin to understand what malaria was until after the Civil War. It was not until the turn of the century during the Spanish-American War that this disease was understood and proper treatment was administered. The First Massachusetts would experience the effects of it in its ranks during their encampment at San Angel, eight miles from Mexico City, for almost six months, from December of 1847 until their departure for home in May of 1848.

Dwight Stevens had become one of the most respected men in Company I. His maturity was not only noticeable in his actions and abilities as a soldier, but also in his sheer size. The now-eighteen-year-old youth, listed on the record as twenty, had grown to six feet with obvious strength. His quick temper was known, and his ability to handle himself only increased the respect he had earned in his company. He had also befriended a new tent companion named Michael Fitzgerald within several days of Avery's promotion to corporal. Fitzgerald had lost his previous tent companion to desertion, and Stevens and Fitzgerald developed a strong friendship that was unfortunately short-lived.

"I'm heading to the sutler's wagon to fetch some goods I need. You need anything?" Dwight asked.

The native of Walpole, Massachusetts didn't reply as he lay half naked on his cot. Mike, as Dwight had called him from their first introduction, had been feeling poorly for several days. Sergeant Mallard had chastised him for failing to keep up during marching drills. He had fallen out several times, and was accused of being hung-over from too much liquor. Despite occasionally participating in a drink or two, Stevens had never seen him get drunk or become ill from the effects of whiskey or beer.

"Mike, you need anything?"

"No, I'm just tired and sick to my stomach. I want to rest for a while."

"Be it as you want. I'll be back in a while."

An hour later, Stevens returned to the company tent to find Fitzgerald shivering and perspiring profusely. Dwight covered his companion with a blanket and asked if he needed anything. The young man only shook his head. He continued to shiver, so Stevens added another blanket onto him. The temperature that evening was still in the eighties, after the day's high of almost a hundred degrees.

"You want me to get some supper for you?" Dwight asked.

The quivering soldier only shook his head again and gave a barely audible response.

Stevens left, concerned that his friend was becoming more ill. He sought out Corporal Avery, whom he found sitting outside the corporal's tent sharing some conversation with some of the other corporals.

"Corporal Avery, Fitzgerald is very sick. It looks like the shakes."

"Damn, this sickness is kicking our asses. How bad is he?" Avery asked.

"Bad. He's not wanting to eat anything, and he won't even take water. He's sweating enough to soak a blanket through, but he looks like he's been thrown out in the cold."

"I'll help you get him to the surgeon," Avery said.

An hour later, Fitzgerald was admitted into the regimental dispensary. Avery and Stevens were told that twenty-four men were already in different stages of the shakes. Fitzgerald made the twenty-fifth. The surgeon could not answer the question of what caused the shakes, but hoped that rest and quiet would help.

Stevens was not allowed to stay with Fitzgerald, due to the fact that it was considered contagious if one was exposed to it for an extended period of time. Stevens was not allowed to visit his friend either, and each time he inquired, he found the man in poorer health. The constant fever breaking and returning and the headache, fatigue, nausea, and vomiting took its toll.

Finally, one evening three weeks later, Dwight returned to the dispensary to be informed that his twenty-two-year-old friend had succumbed to the "intermittent fever," as was annotated on his death certificate and signed by the regimental surgeon. Eight more soldiers and two officers would succumb to the effects of malaria before they would leave for home.

Private Michael Fitzgerald, Company I, First Massachusetts Volunteer Regiment, was buried with full military honors on May 5, 1848. Participating as pallbearers were Stevens, Avery, Bryant, and Cross. The entire Company I stood at attention as the plain wood coffin was lowered into the Mexican soil. Ten burials would take place during the month of May at the encampment at San Angel, due to malaria, other diseases, and deaths from "unknown reasons."

Two days later, Private Aaron Dwight Stevens was informed that the First Massachusetts Regiment of Volunteers was being sent home at the end of the month.

Chapter Seven

Going Home

The excitement was felt throughout the encampment as the word spread. The men spent the evenings at their camp in conversation about the food, women, drink, and higher living they had missed back home while campaigning in Mexico. Thoughts of the heat, sickness, death, and other miseries they had endured seemed to disappear as the men fantasized about how good life would be back in old Boston.

One soldier who did not fantasize about his return home was Dwight Stevens. He had never written home except for the one letter he destroyed in the fire pit on his first day of ration duty. Despite a little nudging from his friends Al Avery and Mike Fitzgerald, he had failed to inform his family and friends where he was. It wasn't his fear of confronting his parents, siblings, or friends, the subsequent abuse he knew he deserved for leaving without permission and lying about his age to join the volunteers; it was his lack of respect for them. He felt guilty for never giving them the satisfaction of knowing whether he was alive or dead. He knew in his heart that Norwich would not be his home for long. He decided that he would return long enough to mend the relationships with his family and friends, but life somewhere else always seemed to draw upon him, even more so now as he thought about going home.

Orders for home came down two days before the regiment was to leave for Vera Cruz. The excitement built as each man prepared to depart. An inspection was held to review the men for cleanliness and their state of being. Most were found in great need of washing and uniform repair. The orders were given that all men were to be bathed and their uniforms made presentable prior to boarding navy ships for New Orleans. Bathing sessions were made mandatory for all the men in the regiment. It took two days to accomplish the task to the satisfaction of the officers and NCOs in charge. Despite the attempts, the First Massachusetts looked and smelled poorly. The condition of their uniforms and body odor did not hinder the contentment and smiles each man exhibited, however, on the day they marched out of San Angel heading for Vera Cruz.

Before the regiment boarded the *U.S.S. Vixen* and *U.S.S. Scourge* off the coast of Vera Cruz on June 22, 1848, all powder, shot, and caps issued to the soldiers were returned to the quartermaster. Their destination was New Orleans, Louisiana. It would take them only eight days to arrive at the southern port. The journey was uneventful, except for the joy and relaxation the men enjoyed on the calm-water trip to New

Orleans. No formations or musket drills were ordered during their travel north.

One exception to the casual atmosphere was Colonel Wright's insistence, in a written order, that his men brush, clean, and repair their uniforms as much as reasonably possible. "As much as reasonably possible" meant at the discretion of their immediate company commanders through inspections that were held several times prior to the regiment's arrival at New Orleans.

Dwight had remained topside on the *U.S.S. Vixen* for the last several hours before the ship docked. The trip up the mouth of the Mississippi River amazed the soldier as strange birds and wildlife could be seen on the riverbanks. The brown and brackish water smell permeated his nostrils with strange and sometimes foul smells. The sight of the port city excited him as steam tugs approached the *U.S.S. Vixen* and *U.S.S. Scourge*, following several hundred yards astern. He watched along with many of the other soldiers from the regiment to see the activity the dockhands and tugs were performing.

Noise from the afternoon crowd that assembled on the docks astounded the men. It was quite a different reception from what they had thought would greet them. The sight and sounds of cheering people waving from the docks seemed so opposite from what the regiment had experienced when it departed Boston in February of 1847. The war with Mexico that had been so unpopular when they left now garnered a new surge of patriotism upon their return.

Within the hour, the *U.S.S. Vixen* was docked and secured. Several brows were hoisted into position, waiting for the officers and soldiers to depart. Cheers from civilians, sailors, and soldiers standing on the dock only added to the noise and excitement.

"Are you listening to all that cheering, Corporal Avery?" Stevens remarked as the men of Company I stood ready to be called to attention at any moment.

"Yeah, I hear it. Far cry from ducking shit back in Boston, hey, Stevens?"

Both men and a few other soldiers hearing the conversation laughed in unison with Avery.

The men immediately snapped to attention when Sergeant Murphy yelled the command. Salutes were exchanged between the captain and Murphy as the men were then put at ease. Other companies could be heard being addressed on different sections of the deck topside, as well as in lower decks within the ship.

Captain Davis addressed his men. "Gentlemen of Company I. It has been my pleasure to command you these past eighteen months since the formation of this regiment. We have traveled almost seven thousand miles, according to the regimental records, since we left Boston in February last year. We still have over a thousand miles yet to travel before we gaze upon the scenery of Massachusetts. If you listen, you can hear the appreciation of our citizens for the sacrifices we have made as soldiers. I expect every man in our company to act within the strictest confines of proper military conduct as Massachusetts Volunteers until we are discharged from our duties in Boston. I know that every man in this company will adhere to what is expected of him. That is all." He turned and looked at Murphy. "Sergeant Murphy, prepare the men for debarkation."

"Yes, sir. As you ordered. Company I, attention!" Murphy yelled.

It took another hour before all the companies of the regiment had moved across the brows and down to the dock. Each company formed in columns of eight, led by their company officers and NCOs. Company I was sixth to depart the ship. Cheering residents of the city witnessed the march through the streets of New Orleans on the 30th of June. Flags were waved by adults and children on the streets and from two- and three-story buildings as the men of the First Massachusetts marched by. Some children ran in between the ranks of the soldiers, cheering. Soldiers, sailors, and uniformed policemen on the street saluted the colors. Occasionally, Colonel Wright and his staff tipped their hats at groups of women and men who applauded when they passed.

Avery whispered to Stevens, "No need to be ducking anythin' this time. They're happy to see us."

Stevens did not answer his corporal. He smiled, though, and enjoyed the feeling of pride as he marched with his company through the streets of New Orleans. His musket did not feel as heavy as it used to be. They marched until they reached one of the empty military warehouses that had previously stored goods for the campaign. It was now reserved for the returning troops to stay in until the army had completed arrangements for their shipment home.

The First Massachusetts had originally been ordered to return home by going around the Florida Peninsula and up the eastern United States coast to Boston. Colonel Wright was given permission to instead depart New Orleans by river steamboat.

On their last day in New Orleans, General Taylor visited the First Massachusetts. As soon as it was learned that "Old Zach" had arrived, the men surrounded him. It was a good time, as described by most of those that witnessed it. Some only said that the general did not really care, and that he was only visiting northern troops because he was a Whig candidate for President. Dwight Stevens could not get close enough to shake the general's hand, but enjoyed being able to observe the event.

The next day, on the 2nd of July, the regiment departed New Orleans on the river steamboat *Kate Swinney* up the Mississippi River. They would steam upriver until they reached the junction with the Ohio River. There, they would follow the Ohio to the city of Cincinnati. The trip by steamboat would take nine days. The vessel slowly navigated the many twists and turns of the rivers as the men spent most of their time out on the multiple deck levels during the day, watching the scenery slowly change as the steamboat moved along.

Dwight Stevens was one of the many soldiers that enjoyed the warmth of the sun and the constant breeze that formed over the river, regulating the heat of the day. Their deck activities included playing cards, conversations, and singing songs, accompanied by those who played the harmonica, banjo, guitar, or fiddle. The revelry could be heard on the decks and in the rooms of the steamboat, where men gathered in groups to participate. Dwight especially enjoyed playing a fiddle or guitar when the owners of the instruments got tired or didn't know the song he asked them to play. The trip up the Mississippi would be one of the most memorable times of his first enlistment in the military.

On the last day on the river, Dwight rose to find that the weather had changed and a light drizzle and fog diminished his view of the passing scenery. As he stood on the upper deck, his mind wandered to thoughts of home. Dwight had been away for a year and a half, and now felt unhappy with himself that he had not communicated with his family. He thought, *How are they, and how will they react when they see me for the first time?* He became angry with himself for never writing the letter that he should have written to at least inform his sister that he was alive and serving in the First Massachusetts. *How will they react to seeing me alive, well, and in uniform after not knowing where I've been? Maybe they aren't well, or worse. Please, Lord. I pray that they are well.* His emotions and imaginations were taking control, and he forced himself to think in a positive way, *I am sure they are all well and in good health.*

He cleared his mind again. He remembered his stepmother's pot apple pie. One thing he really missed about home was those pies. Then his thoughts became serious again. He resolved that he would apologize for his behavior and hopefully mend the relationships he had with his relatives and friends. As he began to plan what he would actually say to all of them, he was interrupted.

"Shitty morning. Nothing like it for the past week," Avery said as he approached Stevens, looking out into the fog.

"It's never a shitty morning when you wake up and see a new day, Corporal."

"That's one way to keep your spirits up, Stevens."

Dwight paused as he continued to look out through the drizzle. "What are you going to do when you muster out, Al?"

"Aw, I don't know. Probably work on the docks again for a while."

"You ever think of just staying in the army?"

"Dwight, this regiment will be no more in a month or so. They'll be disbandin' it."

"I know, but maybe you should think about joining the regulars."

"Nope. No need to join the regulars. No need for them either. There ain't any war anymore."

"I heard that there was a need for regulars to be out West in the new Indian territories."

"I heard that too, but they're looking for dragoons, not foot soldiers. You need to be on horseback to cover large areas when you're out chasing red men. I ain't good riding and shooting on horseback. It don't appeal to me. Why, you thinkin' on joining up out West?"

"I don't know. Just asking what you know about it."

"Well, I don't know shit about the West, or dragoons. You hav'ta find out yourself. But if you ask me, Connecticut is a heap safer place to be than out West."

Stevens smiled as his corporal slapped him on the back, reached into his own jacket pocket, and pulled out a small piece of chew. He put it into his mouth and walked away, occasionally stopping to talk with other men who had also risen early.

Stevens thought a little more about the information he had shared with Avery. He would consider all the options he had pondered since he was informed that the regiment was leaving Mexico. He was still leaning on the deck railing when he noticed that the fog had begun to lift on land. Buildings, small docks, river barges, and then houses began to appear as the *Kate Swinney* steamed upriver.

The sun eventually broke through as the steamboat's whistle blew, and the ship slowed as it approached one of the city's riverbank docks. He saw a large white sign with *The City of Cincinnati Welcomes You* painted on it in red and black letters. Excitement raced through him in anticipation of what this city would be like when they marched through.

The reception in Cincinnati rivaled, if not exceeded, what the regiment had experienced in New Orleans. Debarkation from the *Kate Swinney* was much quicker at the Cincinnati dock. Approximately eight hundred and forty men departed the steamboat in less than two hours. The regiment was quartered overnight in an emptied cotton bale warehouse near the Little Miami and Mad River Railroad.

The cotton dust in the warehouse covered the worn dark blue

uniform jackets and lined the nostrils and bronchial tubes of the soldiers. Most men found relief outside the warehouse, where they found temporary sleeping arrangements along the riverbank or on the railroad loading dock. Doing so allowed them to escape both the summer Ohio heat and the dusty conditions that had built up in the warehouse.

The regiment left the following afternoon on the 12th of July, on the Little Miami and Mad River Railroad. They were headed for the city of Sandusky, Ohio, located on the shores of Lake Erie. The rail trip took another two days as the men slept and consumed beef jerky and hard biscuits. Fruits and vegetables had also been handed to some of the troops from citizens of Cincinnati as they marched to their quarters the previous night. An occasional fight broke out on the trip to Sandusky on account of the gifts, as those that received fruit or vegetables were not always willing to share with those that had not. The sergeants and corporals handled the altercations, although no disciplinary actions were ever reported as the regiment drew closer to mustering out into civilian life.

The regiment arrived and departed from Sandusky on the same day, July 13, 1848, on the steamer *Pacific* bound for Buffalo, New York. The two-day trip afforded the best accommodations and food that the First Massachusetts Volunteers had received since their departure from Boston. Fresh bread, summer corn, and garden-fresh tomatoes were some of the staples that the men had not eaten in over a year. Good coffee and clear water added to their comfort level. The men were fully rested when they departed the steamer at the docks of Buffalo. The regiment spent two days waiting for the remaining companies that had been detained in Sandusky. The unit was whole again when it departed Buffalo on a train for Albany.

Their arrival at Albany couldn't have been more spectacular. The railroad depot and the streets leading to the city hall were lined with flag-waving citizens. For the first time since they left Cincinnati, the regiment was ordered into columns of four, with right shoulder arms to march to the city hall. The men were amazed how the people cheered for them as they marched through the city. A feast, unbeknown to the men, had been planned for the regiment at the city hall. Fresh-baked bread, selections of meats, vegetables, fruits, and desserts were given to the men in great quantities. The highlight of the meal was the tobacco and clay pipes that they were given to smoke afterward. The city dignitaries and the families of wealth and influence in Albany treated the officers to a supper in a different section of city hall. The celebration for the officers lasted into the late evening hours. The enlisted men eventually calmed down, rolled up their jackets, and used them as pillows to sleep on the floor overnight.

Colonel Wright and his staff officers were quartered in the elaborate homes of their hosts.

The following morning, a special train was prepared by the Western Railroad at the Greenbush Train Depot, just opposite Albany, and the regiment departed for Boston and their final encampment at Cambridge Crossings. During the train ride, many citizens of towns en route to Boston stood near the tracks and waved flags, cheering for the First Massachusetts Regiment. There were several occasions when cannons were fired to salute the men while the train slowly passed the towns. At Pittsfield, Massachusetts, the train stopped and a speech was given by the city dignitaries, thanking the commanding officers and the men for their service during the war. The men of the regiment hung out the windows to hear Colonel Wright thank the dignitaries who had organized the patriotic reception. The train continued on to Boston, and as they passed more towns, the greetings continued. In all cases, women waving handkerchiefs especially attracted the attention of the men riding in the cars. In one particular instance, a beautiful young girl dressed in white stood alone on one of the depots and waved a flag. This caused a rousing cheer from the men as they passed by.

The regiment arrived in Boston on the afternoon of July 18th, to a rousing reception of cheers, flag waving, formal speeches, and general enthusiasm as they disembarked from the train. The patriotic fever of the citizens continued as the regiment marched from the train station to Cambridge Crossing, where they pitched their encampment for mustering out. From the time they had left Boston in February of 1847 until they returned in July of 1848, the regiment had sailed, steamed, ridden on trains, and marched for over eight thousand miles. They would be the most traveled regiment of the entire U.S. Army during the Mexican–American War. The regiment ceased to exist on July 27, 1848.

On that morning, Company I mustered out. Present were Captain Davis and First Lieutenant Smith. The other officers of the company had resigned their commissions immediately upon their return to Boston and did not attend. Sergeant Major Ross and Quartermaster Sergeant Reed accompanied the two officers while they addressed the NCOs and troops. It was a short speech that mainly dealt with the procedures the men were expected to follow when turning in their muskets and bayonets, canteens, musket ball pouches, powder containers, and blankets. Only uniforms and haversacks were allowed to be kept by the volunteers. When the men were dismissed, they were told to line up at the quartermaster's tent to be processed out of the regiment.

Dwight Stevens found himself directly behind the group of company corporals who were being processed out ahead of the privates.

Al Avery moved out of line and just in front of Dwight so they could talk as they waited to hand in their gear, receive any pay due to them, and be mustered out. "This is it, Stevens. We are free, white, and can do anything we want in a few minutes."

The statement sparked a concern in Dwight, but he didn't comment.

"You heading back to Connecticut today?"

"Well, I guess. I plan to get to the railroad station and buy a ticket to Norwich."

"Why don't I come along with you when you buy it?"

Dwight was perplexed, wondering why his good friend would want to accompany him to purchase a ticket. "You don't have to come with me. You must have somebody to see now that you are home again."

"Not really. I got my aunt, but she don't know when I'll be coming home. I'll go with you to the station and see how long of a wait you have till you go home. But before we go, I'll get you a home-cooked meal."

Dwight smiled as they approached the quartermaster's tent.

Avery handed over all the gear he was expected to turn in.

Dwight was next, and he somehow failed to present a canteen and a blanket.

Avery overheard the quartermaster clerk telling Dwight that he would be docked the cost of the two items from his discharge pay, and he knew that Stevens might begin to show his quick temper toward the sarcastic clerk. "Hold on, quartermaster. Private Stevens lost his canteen to one of the citizens of Boston who grabbed it from him as he was marching by. They would have gotten mine, but I seen it comin' when he lost his. His blanket went to a sick man who had the chills a few days earlier. I've seen it myself. He don't get charged for either."

The quartermaster clerk never challenged Corporal Avery's account and let Stevens pass with no monetary penalty.

Stevens waited for the two men to clear all the discharge stations until he spoke. "Thanks, Corporal."

"No need to be thanking me, and it's Al, not Corporal anymore. We are free men, and all equal now."

"Well, you lied for me so I wouldn't be charged."

"Stevens, I don't lie. I just gave that damn clerk somethin' to put down in his record book. It don't mean shit. Most of the gear we turned in will be thrown away. Don't let it bother you. Now just follow me. I know a good place to get a cool pint and maybe get it free. Then we are going to get a good meal."

They found the pub Avery wanted to stop at just a few streets from the docks. As soon as Avery entered the pub, several patrons recognized the former dockworker. Within minutes, the two volunteers were surrounded by most of the pub patrons who almost fought each other for the privilege of buying them a pint.

To stop what could be the start of a few fistfights, the pub owner announced that a round was on the establishment in honor of the two First Massachusetts Volunteers who had honored his tavern.

Upon hearing the announcement, Avery turned to Dwight and said, "I told you I'd be getting you a free pint. Maybe more." He laughed and patted Dwight on the shoulder. Avery then turned to the patrons and motioned them to quiet down. "I want to thank you all for the hospitality, and to Dan Maguire who was kind enough to give us a round on him." He raised his pint in salute.

The group followed with more calls and yells.

Avery paused for a few seconds as the patrons drank from their pints. "I want to salute my companion here, who was at my side all the time we were away." He turned to Dwight and held up his pint in a salute. "To Dwight Stevens, a Connecticut Yankee who I am proud to call my friend and a good soldier."

A rousing wave of cheers and yells went up, and they all drank from their pints once again.

"This young man will be famous someday. You wait and see. Remember the name." He raised his pint again, and more roaring and drinking followed.

The festive atmosphere continued until each veteran had drunk several pints apiece, then Avery began to move his very relaxed companion and himself to the pub's door. He shook hands along the way, thanked the patrons, and announced that he'd be seeing them again soon once he got settled.

More cheers and yells came from the very excited crowd.

The veterans left the pub and Avery guided Stevens in the direction he wanted him to go. "I told you I'd get you a pint or two free. They are a good bunch of gents. They are proud of what we did."

Dwight did all he could do to keep pace with Avery as they walked up the street. Before long, each man had aired his senses and they continued on to the home of the only relative Al Avery had.

They reached a home on Washington Street.

Stevens read the name on the door and said, "Robert Morrison. Who do you know in here?"

"It's the home of my Aunt Katie. Her husband is a banker. She's the only relative I got. Remember me telling you about her? My mom's younger sister?"

They knocked, and a pretty teenage girl answered the front door.

She immediately yelled out when she recognized Avery, "He's back, everyone, he's back!" She ran into Avery's arms as he picked her up and spun her around on the front steps of the house.

Stevens backed up and watched in delight.

"Uncle Alfred, I'm so happy you are back and safe, but"—she paused—"you stink."

Avery laughed as Stevens had never seen him laugh before.

"You're right, Bridget, and I'm sorry that I do. I was travelin' a lot. I need one of your mom's scented soaps and a good soaking in the tub. Honey, this is my friend Dwight."

"Glad to make your acquaintance, sir." She curtseyed.

"It's my pleasure," Stevens responded.

As quickly as he had answered, another young woman, a little older, came to the door. She looked at Dwight before she addressed Avery. "Uncle Alfred, I'm so glad you have returned unscathed."

Avery could hardly keep from laughing as he said, "Well, Margaret, I'm pleased as well." He hugged her gently and said, "You turned into a young lady in just a short time. You're seventeen now, but you look twenty."

She seemed very uncomfortable as she was released from her uncle's embrace.

Avery noticed her nose twitching. "I know, honey. I stink. Bridget has already told me."

The two men were led into the parlor, where Robert Morrison greeted them. "Welcome, Al. It's good to see you." He extended his hand and the two men gripped palms.

"Bob, this is my friend—"

He never finished. His Aunt Katie came rushing into the room and hugged her nephew. She cried in his embrace for several moments, until Al finally released her.

"Awe, come on, Aunt Katie, there is no need of you cryin'. I'm home safe and that is it."

"For all that is holy, Alfred, you stink to high heaven. Is there no water in all of Mexico?"

"I know, Bridget was telling me that already, and Margaret's nose's been twitching since I arrived."

"Robert, get each one of them one of your evening robes. You two will give me those clothes, including your undergarments, as soon as you have bathed."

She turned and addressed a young woman who had stayed in the background until now, watching. "Molly, please prepare baths for these two gentlemen."

"Yes, missus, as you say."

Stevens looked to Al. He seemed puzzled as the woman disappeared.

Avery recognized his friend's confusion and he whispered to Stevens, "She's the maid. A good Irish girl that my aunt has taken in to help tend to their chores."

"Thank you for your hospitality, Mrs. Morrison, but I don't want to be a bother to you and your family now that Al has returned. You must have a lot to catch up on, and I'll just be on my way."

"Mr. Stevens, it is our pleasure to meet you. Some of Alfred's letters talked about you in great detail. All pleasantries. I will not hear of your leaving, and I insist that you be given the same hospitality my wandering nephew will have." Her voice softened. "Please, I insist."

Stevens and Avery took turns and spent an hour or more using a bathtub, the likes of which they had not seen in eighteen months. They spent the rest of the evening wearing Robert's clothes as they were treated to a home-cooked meal. Their soiled and worn uniforms were taken from them, washed, and mended. The process of refitting the two soldiers to Aunt Katie's satisfaction took until mid-afternoon of the next day.

Stevens especially enjoyed the time he spent there in the company of Avery's two nieces, who entertained them by singing and playing the piano. The girls were very impressed with Dwight's musical and singing abilities as he played and sang the songs he knew with them. Avery enjoyed seeing his youthful partner singing and playing an instrument. He also enjoyed the brief glances exchanged between his seventeen-year-old niece, Margaret, and his young friend, Dwight Stevens.

The men finally left for the rail station donned in their clean and pressed uniforms. Their walk to the station brought pleasant comments from the Bostonians who passed them. Stevens purchased a ticket for the train leaving for Norwich at 8:00 p.m. The trip would take him twelve hours, but it would be a better ride than his first one eighteen months earlier.

"You never told me you came from a wealthy family, Al," Dwight said.

Avery smiled. "My aunt did good when she married Bob Morrison. They helped me a few times when my father died. I paid 'em back. I don't like charity and I worked at the docks until the war got my interest." He smiled at Stevens when he said it.

Dwight changed the subject. "Well I guess it's time to part our ways, Al. It's been a pleasure serving with you. I can never repay you for the training and guidance you gave me. I will never forget it. Now, there's no need for you to be waiting here with me. You get back to your family.

You stay close to those gals. They'll need you to keep all the men away from them."

"I'll shoot the first son-of-bitch that even comes close to 'em." Avery laughed and extended his hand. "Dwight, you take care of yourself. You were a good friend and soldier throughout. There's one question I always wanted to ask but never got a chance to."

"What would that be?"

"How old are you really? That pretty face is always givin' you away, and my Margaret noticed you."

"I was eighteen this past March."

"Shit, I knew it. You was a baby. You bullshitted your way into the regiment. Glory be, but you pulled it off. Go home, young Stevens, and grow old. You already have grown up."

Dwight Stevens smiled and extended his hand. The two men shook hands until Avery pulled him close, hugged him, and said, "Take care, young Stevens. Come see me if you ever return to Boston. You're always welcome."

Dwight got a little choked up and noticed that Avery's eyes had gotten glossy as he stared back at him.

Avery let go and backed away. He turned and walked out of the train station. He never looked back.

Several hours later, Aaron Dwight Stevens departed Boston for Norwich. He would never return to the city.

The trip home was uneventful, and he spent a considerable amount of time dozing on the hard seat of the train. Very little scenery could be seen as the train moved through the warm July night en route to Norwich. Passengers smiled at the tall, handsome soldier who looked dashing in the worn uniform that revealed his identity as a veteran.

A few passengers engaged in conversation to inquire where the young soldier had been. Dwight was polite to all who asked, but never divulged information on what he had done while in the service in Mexico. Most people accepted his brief and vague answers out of respect for a returning veteran who didn't want to talk of the war. Others who overheard these exchanges simply left the young man to his privacy, allowing him to doze while the train moved ever closer to home.

In the morning, Dwight was fully awake and looking out the passenger car window when the train stopped at Greenville. He had the urge to depart the train and walk the remaining miles to his home in Norwich. The reasoning he gave himself was that he needed more time to think about what he would say to his family and friends when he arrived. He decided against it, though, and remained on the train until it reached Norwich. From the train station, Dwight walked to Franklin Square. The city had not changed in the eighteen months he had been away. A few people nodded or tipped their hats as the young soldier continued his fast pace toward home.

He didn't see anyone he knew as he walked the streets of Norwich, and he hoped no one would recognize him until he arrived home. The day was warm, but the breeze afforded him some relief as he reached Washington Street and continued on past the Chelsea Parade grounds. A few riders could be seen on the grounds while children ran and played. He looked for anyone he knew. He relaxed, as no one looked familiar. He did receive a few looks from people who recognized his infantry uniform.

He reached the Leffingwell Inn and debated whether or not he should rent a room for a few days while he mended the relationships with his family members. He decided against it and quickened his pace toward home. He arrived at noon on the 29th of July, a Saturday, and he knew that everyone should be home.

He knocked on the front door and waited. His stepmother answered the door. Her first reaction was worse than Dwight had anticipated. She froze as she looked at the young soldier standing on her front steps. He caught her as she stumbled and began to fall. He knew she thought she had seen a ghost and felt terrible that he had made her faint. She recovered enough to yell for his father as he steadied her and guided her to a wicker chair inside the door.

"Dwight, is it you? I thought I'd seen your spirit. My Lord, son, where have you been?"

As he attempted to answer his recovering stepmother, his father appeared. "Heaven almighty, the prodigal son has returned. Move aside while I attend to your mother. What have you done to her?"

Dwight watched as his father assisted her to a more comfortable chair in the family's parlor. His father did not say another word until he turned and asked, "Where have you been? We had thought that you drowned, but Charles convinced us that you probably ran away. I would ask you why, but I can see what your intentions were."

"Father, I joined the First Massachusetts Volunteer Regiment. I went to Mexico and have returned just today. I have a certificate on my person that proves my enlistment and discharge. I have come home. That is, if I am welcome?"

"Aaron Dwight Stevens, you are always welcome. I am not pleased with your departure, but we will talk of it later."

His stepmother recovered from her shock and her motherly instincts told her she had to feed him. "You must be famished. I'm preparing lunch in the kitchen. You will sit and eat, and you will tell us of your travels."

His youngest sister, Susan, watched from the table as the three of them entered the kitchen. She was now ten years old, and her look was one of caution. She did not know what to say to her older brother. It wasn't long, with a little coaxing from her mother, before she was laughing and bouncing on his knee as she had sometimes done before he had left.

He expected his brothers and sister to come to the noon meal, but his father spoke before he could inquire as to their whereabouts. "Your sister and brothers are at Henry's music store. He opened up the business after you…" He paused, and then continued, "After you left. Lydia and Lemuel spend time assisting him on Saturdays. They will all be home by five o'clock."

Some awkwardness built as the four of them sat for the noon meal. During that hour, Dwight informed them of all the places his regiment had been.

Lydia, Henry, and Lemuel returned to find a grown man in a military uniform sitting on the front steps waiting for them. It was a joyous reunion between the siblings. Lydia broke into tears and sobs as she held Dwight. He apologized over and over as he held her in his arms.

The more he tried to comfort and console her, the more she cried until she said, "I thank the Almighty that you have returned, for I have prayed every day that you were alive and well. Charles would always tell me that you were all right when we talked of you. I am trying to be a lady and it has taken all my fortitude not to thrash you for upsetting me and the entire family with what you did. Why did you not write?"

Dwight could not answer her. He had practiced what he would say to Lydia over and over again as he walked home from the station, but nothing ever sounded right.

He finally said, "I wrote once, but I never posted the letter. I thought of all of you so many times, but I just couldn't write. I am home now and I will do anything in my power to try to mend the hurt that I have caused you and the rest of the family. I do not know what else to say except that I am sorry and I love you all dearly." He hugged Lydia. She relaxed in his arms and they stayed in that embrace for several minutes.

Henry broke the emotional atmosphere when he separated the two of them and said, "You are home now. Let us talk of this no more. You must tell us all of what you have done and seen. On Monday, I will show you my new music store I have opened with Father's help. Lydia has helped me in sales and organization of the instruments I sell."

Lemuel did not say much. He studied Dwight and only remarked how tall he had grown.

Dwight laughed and hugged him. "You will catch me in a few

years, my impatient brother."

Dwight welcomed the break from all the emotion , and the four entered the house. Word was sent out to Charles Whipple that Dwight had returned. His childhood friend immediately headed for the Stevens home as soon as he learned the news.

The family, Dwight, and Charles talked into the late evening hours on numerous subjects. There seemed to be joy in the Stevens family now that the young soldier was home.

Charles commented on that to Dwight as the two stood outside talking after the rest of the family had retired for the night. "Your family is very pleased to see you. You must know how much you are loved here."

"Yes, I am fortunate that it went better than what I expected. I had a plan to stay at the inn if I had been rejected at home."

"At the Leffingwell Inn? Why would you even think of that?"

"I had to, because I expected rejection. It was a poor decision on my part to leave without telling anyone where I planned to go. But you must understand that I knew I would have not been given the permission by my parents to join the volunteers just based on my age alone, never mind their views of the war and the military. I'm sure my father will talk about that later when we are alone."

"I understand all of that, but you should have confided in me or Lydia. At least we could have told everyone where you had gone after you had left."

"It was too important to me to involve anyone in my plan and risk exposure, or put either of you two in a false predicament. It was my decision, and I take full responsibility for what I did."

"You should have trusted me more, Dwight. I am blood, and your closest friend."

"I know, but it is done and no lies or falsehoods were made between us."

"What are you talking about? You were almost sixteen when you left. How did you convince them you were eighteen if not with a lie?"

Dwight laughed heartily. "I never lied to them, Charles." He smiled and told him how he had placed the piece of paper in his shoe with the number eighteen written on it all the time he was questioned about his age.

Charles listened and occasionally shook his head in disbelief. He never let Dwight finish his explanation. "I would think that your size alone convinced them you were older than your years. You have grown a lot more since the last time I saw you. You must be a half foot taller than I even as we stand here."

"I have grown a bit since we were last together."

Charles turned away from Dwight as he contemplated all that had been said in their conversation. He walked a few paces, then turned to Dwight and said, "Promise me you will never do such a thing again."

Dwight smiled at his cousin and closest friend. He walked over and hugged him. "I promise I will tell you of any future thoughts that involve me venturing on some other journey."

He smiled, but Charles did not believe he was sincere. He asked again, "Do you promise me?"

"I do promise."

Charles studied his face. There was a seriousness that he recognized this time.

"Then I forgive you. Now tell me. Did you shoot and kill any Mexicans?"

Dwight paused as the question reminded him of the snipers he and Avery had killed.

Charles noticed the change in his expression. "I have said something that has troubled you. I did not mean it as a joyous occasion. I only asked for curiosity's sake."

"Yes, I did have to kill a young Mexican who was attempting to shoot and kill members of my regiment in ambush. I do not feel any joy in it, but I do feel satisfied that it was a just act. I saved someone in my regiment."

Charles knew not to pursue more details. "Then let us not dwell on it any further. Now tell me of the women, the drink, and the other unmentionables you dare not divulge to anyone but me." He grinned, laughing, and waited for Dwight to tell him anything and everything he could remember.

Dwight began with the incident at the river where a mounted Mexican had thrown a lariat at him and attempted to drag him off behind his horse.

Dwight and Charles talked until the sun rose on the Norwichtown Green. The Stevens and Whipple families attended Sunday services together later that day. They were very happy and thanked God that their son, brother, and cousin had returned home safely from his service in Mexico. The most enjoyable moment for Dwight, besides mending his relationships with his family and friends, was singing in his father's choir during Sunday service.

One other moment rivaled the enjoyment of his singing—eating a piece of his stepmother's pot apple pie at Sunday supper. Everyone who saw Dwight on that first Sunday remarked he had certainly grown into a strong, handsome young man with a bright future ahead of him.

Chapter Eight

Unrest

The summer of 1848 passed, and life for Aaron Dwight Stevens resumed as if he had never left Norwich. All relationships had been mended with his family and friends. All his experiences in the military had been told and discussed. The places he had seen had been described. The only changes evident were his physique and his thoughts. He was an imposing man who stood at about six feet with broad shoulders, good looks, and a mild disposition until provoked.

Dwight did a lot of catching up on different subjects. Perhaps the one that captured his heart and head more than any other was slavery. It seemed to be the one continuous topic of discussion no matter where he was. He had always known it existed, and he had grown up knowing it was evil. Norwich was the third largest city in Connecticut, with a huge manufacturing and trading center, and a good number of Negroes worked in the factories, on the docks, and on the ships. He had also known there had been a large and active black community in the Jail Hill area of Norwich ever since the Revolutionary War. In fact, Dwight knew many of the men and boys from the area, and some of the families could boast of having fighting men in the war. He was pretty sure that some of the older men he knew had been slaves at one time.

Dwight was surprised and horrified that it took until this very year, 1848, for Connecticut to free the blacks by general emancipation of slavery. What disturbed him the most was the fact that Connecticut blacks still could not vote, even though they were free. He was embarrassed for his state. He was even more disappointed in himself that he knew so little about what was going on.

He had been a very young man when he left home, with little knowledge and a lot to learn. But now was a good time to catch up. He had to understand where he stood on the slavery issue and be able to justify and talk about his views. Until he had gone to Boston two years ago, his knowledge had come from his family and church. Now it was different. He knew more about slavery and had heard the hateful talk coming from some of the whites in the army. He was a different person now, and the thought of owning people and keeping them in slavery made him mad.

As time went on, those close to Dwight noticed that he was becoming a new person. One significant change was that he began to question his own religious beliefs, which irritated his family. They wondered whether he had too much free time to ponder such thoughts and ask such questions.

One morning in the summer of 1849, after gold had been discovered in California, all of Norwich gathered at the Thames River waterfront to send off three Norwich men who were headed to the California gold fields to become rich. Dwight saw the crowd gathering while on his way to his brother's music store, and his curiosity overcame him. When he politely pushed his way through the crowd, he recognized two of the three men the crowd had gathered to send off, namely, William Lathrop and Charles Charlton. Dwight was told they were leaving that morning for New York, where they would board a ship and travel to San Francisco by way of Cape Horn. It was quite a morning for the whole town, and everyone wished them well in their quest.

When the men returned to Norwich the following summer, the crowd was as large as it had been for their send-off. Dwight had heard the news of their return and then witnessed the commotion at the waterfront. William Lathrop showed everyone the small bag of gold he had collected, and Charles Charlton exhibited his brown bear that he had brought back in a cage. Everyone wanted to see the bear, including Dwight, who enjoyed watching the children feed it with bread loaves they had broken up and soaked in molasses. Dwight found out months later that the poor bear was eventually sold to a circus. Gold and bears probably amused him at the time, but this was one of the many incidents in his life that influenced Dwight Stevens to think about leaving Norwich for the excitement of the West.

He continued to spend as much time as he had available with Lydia, Henry, and Lemuel at the music store the first year he was home. Dwight used that time to learn how to play new instruments while assisting wage-free in the day-to-day operations of the store. Charles Whipple had already started working at a machine shop as an apprentice in the winter of 1849. He had mentioned to Dwight that being a machinist would be a good profession for him to pursue. Dwight's father had agreed and approached him numerous times about such a job, but Dwight only laughed to himself, knowing that this attempt to interest him in the machinist trade had obviously been discussed between his father and cousin.

On a beautiful Sunday in December of 1849, just three days prior to Christmas, Lydia, Henry, Lemuel, and Dwight were enjoying a slow walk home from church when Dwight remarked, "The Reverend Arms spoke of a man today with whom I am not very familiar. I do recall the name before I left for the volunteers, though. What else does Mr. David Ruggles[1] do? I probably should say *did*? I understood from what the Reverend said at services today that Mr. Ruggles has now passed on."

It was Henry who spoke up first. "Mr. Ruggles was a free black man, originally from Bean Hill, back up the road. He left home at a young age." Henry smiled, and continued, "Kinda like someone else we all know, only Ruggles went to New York City."

They all laughed, and Dwight's face turned a little red from embarrassment. His face turned more serious as they walked, and he asked, "Please, Henry, tell me more about David Ruggles."

Henry sensed the seriousness of Dwight's request by his tone, and continued. "In New York City, David Ruggles opened up the first bookstore ever owned by a black man. His folks still live on Bean Hill and go to the Methodist Church. They just went up to Massachusetts somewhere to get David after he died and brought him back here for burial. The things he has done, Dwight, you would never believe. I have a hard time believing some of the stories myself."

"What kind of stories have you heard?"

"Well, one of the stories says that he helped more than four or five hundred slaves escape to freedom through the New York City Underground Railroad. You've heard of that, haven't you, Dwight?"

"I am aware of it, but of course I have had no personal experience with it."

Henry continued, "From his bookstore, Ruggles published numerous articles against slavery, and against Southern women who allowed their men to keep slave women as mistresses." He paused, seeing that he was in mixed company. "I am sorry, Lydia. I didn't mean to embarrass you."

"You didn't embarrass me, Henry, but of the stories I have heard, the one I like best was when Mr. Ruggles demanded the arrest of a sea captain who was trading in slaves illegally."

"Yes," Henry excitedly interrupted. "His name was Juan Evangelista de Souza. I'll never forget it because he and a rogue policeman named Boudinot, as well as a slave catcher named D.D. Nash, came to Ruggles's house to do him great harm. But Ruggles escaped from them, just as he had evaded so many others who wished to get their hands on him for his anti-slavery views. They intended to put him on a ship

---

[1] **David Ruggles** (1810–1849) was born Norwich, Connecticut, but moved to New York City as a young man. A free black man and anti-slavery activist, he helped more than 400 slaves escape on the Underground Railroad, including Fredrick Douglass.

headed to Savannah, Georgia, and sell him into slavery, but they never could do it. He was too smart for them."

Dwight was spellbound listening to their stories of the black man.

Lydia added, "He's done some wondrous things, Dwight. I don't know if I've ever heard of a braver soul in my life. Everyone says he was not a healthy man, and he died last Sunday, the sixteenth of December, at only thirty-nine-years-old."

Dwight was quite impressed and, more than anything else, he could not believe that someone like David Ruggles, a simple free black man from Norwich, could have actually been such an important person in the major affairs of the country. "He must have been a very special person to fight so hard, and so well, and against such odds," Dwight said. He then thought to himself as they continued to walk, *I wonder if I could ever accomplish something as important as he did.*

Dwight found reading to be another source of enjoyment, and he strove to read as much as he could in his free time. The frequent trips to his brother's music store afforded him the time to visit the library. On one such trip he picked up a book written by someone who would become a major influence in his life.

The author was Thomas Paine, and his book was called *The Age of Reason.*[1] The more Dwight read of Paine's words, the more the foundation of his religious beliefs changed. He mostly kept his beliefs and questions to himself as he read more of the deistic thought and reasoning. His Puritan upbringing began to be challenged in his mind, but his ability to debate the pamphlet with family or friends would be too controversial. So he kept to himself, and inquired into further writings by Paine.

His reading of *The Age of Reason* was the catalyst for his free thinking. This document, combined with published articles and books on the emerging abolitionist movement in the country, convinced Dwight that corruption in religion, politics, and government truly and abundantly existed. No longer could he look at his Puritan Christian beliefs the same way he used to, when the Christian sect he belonged to were members of either the Whig or Democrat Party that addressed slavery as a political issue and not a wrong that must be made right. Later he would write, ***"And therefore I have had to look elsewhere for religion and found it in the great bible of nature."***

Dwight always wanted to express his views on religion and what he

---

[1] ***The Age of Reason*** **by Thomas Paine** – A revolutionary view of religion at the time that was more about spiritualism and nature as God. He criticized organized religion and the Bible.

was learning from Thomas Paine and others, but he had no one to talk with. The last thing he wanted to do was get into a fight with his family. He knew that would happen if he started talking about spiritualism or the corruption of the organized religions at the dinner table. He couldn't imagine his father lasting much longer than the first couple of words before he choked on his meal and forever banned him from the house. He thought about talking to Charles, but he didn't seem open to change either. Dwight kept most of these thoughts to himself as the days passed.

There were many nights when various combinations of neighbors and friends would be in the Stevens home, and discussions over a myriad of subjects would arise. Often, they were about local politics, the westward movement and Indians, the economy, neighborhood gossip, or even just remembering old times and those who had passed away. All acceptable subjects were open for discussion.

However, the one subject that arose more than any other was slavery. It had become more and more the focal point throughout the whole country, and certainly in the Stevens parlor.

One cold February evening, the family and Charles were gathered after dinner when Dwight's father began speaking in a slow, soft voice. "I greatly fear that I cannot see an end to slavery in our lifetimes. It is so entrenched in the South that it will never be washed away completely. Maybe several generations from now, or if we in the North can remain strong without slavery and the South sees that their fears and ways are wrong in the eyes of God and the World, maybe then…maybe then."

Lydia spoke up. "Maybe you are right, Father, but in any case, a basic education is what is missing in their lives, and that needs to be a priority to help them become contributors to society. I know of some free blacks in Norwich that can read and write. They have found work and are generally given wages accordingly. However, too many of the free blacks, and the slaves coming up from the South on the Underground Railroad, can do no writing or reading and know nothing of numbers."

It was a strict rule in the Stevens house that all should have their say without interruptions. There was a rule that absolutely no shouting matches were allowed, no matter how strong the disagreements were.

Charles, who had been patiently waiting for Lydia to finish, jumped in. "You are all talking as though the poor slaves want to be here and are trapped here in a foreign land as slaves forever. If we asked a hundred slaves if they wanted to stay here in this country or return to Africa, I would bet Dwight's right arm that nary a one would respond with a 'yes' to staying here. If things were reversed and we were kept in Africa, and suddenly we were given the choice of staying there, a place we were brought to against our will to begin with, or return home to America and good old Norwich, home of the best-made pot apple pie in the world, we would surely go."

Mrs. Stevens laughed and told Charles to behave himself and to stop hinting around and get himself some pie if any was left.

"I will surely do that, but I have to say in conclusion that I am in favor of the Liberian plan, as proposed by Thomas Jefferson years ago, and the ACS organization, which I believe stands for the American Colonization Society. They are, and have been for several years, sending blacks back to Liberia in Africa. I say we have done enough harm to these poor folks. Let us help them get on ships and head them home as soon as possible, and then guess what?" He paused and looked around at the others in the parlor. "No slave problems and no race issues. All the problems are solved. Now, please excuse me, as I am going to solve my lack of pie problem."

Dwight laughed and punched Charles's arm as he maneuvered past and toward the kitchen. He didn't know quite how he felt at this time, although he was quite positive that no God or spirit ever intended for men to enslave other men and force suffering upon them for the benefit of their masters. He recognized that there was never a time, in the history of the world that he had ever learned about, when slavery did not exist. He had also realized that only through blood and violence, as when the Egyptians were defeated and destroyed by Moses and the parting of the Sea, were slaves made free. But Dwight did not wish to give voice of his thoughts to his family and friends just yet.

He had never talked to anyone about his thoughts on how to rid the country of slavery. However, he knew that someone would have to stick up for the slaves and take their side if anything was ever going to change. He truly didn't think they could win freedom for themselves, as the whole population of the South was strongly united against them with laws, traditions, and economic stability.

The slaves had no money, weapons, or organization to help them. In the North, there was not the urgent motivation needed to do much of anything. The majority of whites were involved with making a living, business opportunities, and day-to-day life, which was apparently much more important than freeing any slaves that were hundreds, or even thousands, of miles away.

That night, as Dwight lay in his bed going over the conversations, he clearly remembered something his father had talked about the day of his tenth birthday. His father had just finished reading the Bible and had set it down on the small table next to his chair, wishing him a happy birthday. Dwight thought hard to remember the exact words his father had used when he slowly and purposely addressed the family that night.

Something of great significance has happened, and although you may not understand it all, it is well that you should become aware of some of the world around you.

Dwight concentrated and continued to remember more of what his father had said. *The supreme court of this land, with the help of Almighty God, has justifiably ruled to release illegally enslaved Africans of the* Amistad.[1] Dwight couldn't remember any more of the words his father had used to describe his feelings on the subject, but he made a promise to himself to look up the court's ruling on the Amistad matter. He closed his eyes in an attempt to fall asleep.

Several days later, he found what he had been looking for at the library. The slaves that had been taken from their homes and families and forced into slavery by the slave traders had simply revolted. After killing the captain and the cook, the slaves took the ship over and attempted to sail back home. Dwight read that the ship was eventually recaptured and forced to dock in New Haven. He remembered that his sister had questioned their father, asking if the slaves had done wrong by killing the captain and the cook. His father had said to her, "Yes Lydia. They did kill, which in most cases is a grievous sin, but listen carefully to me. It is not God's intention for one man to be a slave to another man. It is also not a sin for a man to fight for his freedom from the chains and bonds of those who would make him a slave. God wishes all of us to be free."

Dwight continued to read the details of the trial and outcome. He remembered the statement his father had made after reading the Amistad matter. *No one should ever forget our own fight for freedom, when God blessed us with victory over our oppressors.* As Dwight finished the article, he noted how lawyer John Quincy Adams[2] had used that same logic to convince the court to release the Africans and let them return home. He laughed to himself as he remembered how angry he had been upon hearing what his father explained about the *Amistad*, and how he had wished he could take his grandfather's sword and single-handedly rescue the Africans from the evil enslavers by destroying them all.

In addition to the discussions in the Stevens's parlor, Dwight read the New York, Boston, and Philadelphia newspapers as often as they were available at the library or at some of the shops at the river wharf. He read

---

[1] ***Amistad*** was the name of a ship on which African captives took control off the coast of Long Island in July 1839. There was a resulting U.S. Supreme Court case in 1841.

[2] **John Quincy Adams** (1767–1848) was an American writer, diplomat, U.S. Senator, Representative and the 6th U.S. president. He negotiated several important International Treaties for the U.S., including the Treaty of Ghent, which ended the War of 1812; the annexation of Florida with Spain; and the Monroe Doctrine. A leading opponent of slavery, he successfully defended the African defendants in the *Amistad* affair.

the published writings of abolitionists and pro-slavery opponents, and he also read articles on the Indian Territories, and the dragoons who had been established to protect settlers and miners from the Indians.

The more he read about incidents that took place in the Indian Territories, the more interested he became.

It wasn't too long before he noticed advertisements in the New York papers seeking volunteers to sign up and be trained as dragoons. All the literature he read indicated that the dragoons were the "elite" of the army and could fight on horseback as well as on foot. The dragoons interested him, and he thought of what it would be like to be one. These thoughts continuously occupied his mind as he read, worked at his brother's music store, sang in the church choir, and lackadaisically pursued a trade. In the autumn of 1849, he finally allowed himself to be convinced to work with Charles as a machinist apprentice in the machine shop of Mr. Cole and Mr. Walker in Norwich.

The apprenticeship satisfied his friends and relatives, and provided the allusion that he was now finally settling down. There were no more concerns about his religious beliefs or thoughts. The main reason was because Dwight Stevens kept his thoughts and ideas to himself.

The first year of his apprenticeship seemed to fully occupy Dwight's daily life. His strength became apparent as he completed chores that needed to be performed in the shop. A twelve-hour shop day kept the war veteran busy as he learned the new trade. He adapted well to the apprenticeship, but he kept to himself and did not mingle much with the other machinists with the exception of Charles.

Occasionally, remarks would be made by one machinist who seemed to be the ringleader of the shop. Dwight usually ignored the jokes or innuendos that continued at the expense of the other apprentices, until one day the bully slated him.

That night as they were closing the shop, while the machinists and apprentices were cleaning up in the washroom, the shop bully approached Dwight. The man made comments about his size and apparent strength, which had been observed by the men in the shop. "So you think you're a tough one, do ya?"

Dwight ignored the bully as he continued to wash his hands.

"I'm talking to you, Stevens. You think you are tough?"

"You say I am, then I guess I am."

"You're a smart ass besides, aren't ya, Stevens?"

Dwight again looked at the bully. "Go away. I have nothing to say to you."

The men who were watching laughed at Dwight's response.

Charles called out and told Dwight, "It's time for us to leave,

Dwight. Dry your hands and we'll head for home."

"You better listen to your little friend, Stevens. He's looking out for ya."

Dwight looked at the bully as he finished washing and said, "He doesn't look after me. I look after him."

"I don't like apprentices who talk back." And with that, he slapped Dwight in the face with his soapy hand.

Dwight went crazy, grabbing him by the neck with his wet hands and pushing him up against a wall. The bully tried frantically to loosen Dwight's grip on his neck by scratching and digging into his wrists, but he could not free himself from the death grip Stevens had on him. He attempted to yell for help but his air was drastically reduced, making it very difficult to speak, let alone yell.

The bully's condition alarmed Charles, who felt that in a short time Dwight would kill him. Charles attempted to free Dwight's grip on the bully's neck, but it was fruitless.

"You never know when to stop, do you?" Dwight asked the bully. "Maybe this will be a lesson to you." He slapped the bully numerous times with his other hand until the man's face reddened..

No one except Charles said a word as the man went limp under Dwight's grip. "Dwight, for heaven's sake, release him. You are going to kill him."

Dwight released his grip and the man fell to the floor. He lay there unmoving. Charles checked him to ensure he could breathe on his own. Dwight dried his hands, grabbed his lunch pail, and walked to the door.

On the walk home, Charles cautioned Dwight about his temper. "You were justified in slapping the hell out of that bully after he slapped you first, but you almost strangled him with the grip you had on his neck."

Dwight did not respond to Charles's comment.

"Your temper is extreme when you are provoked, but I have never seen you that mad before. By the way, I am sorry that I scratched your wrists. Why didn't you stop?"

"The man had it coming to him. No one should have to put up with that. I hope he has learned his lesson and doesn't bother anyone further."

The incident was never again talked about, and the bully never approached Dwight for the remainder of his time at the machine shop. Dwight would leave the shop just before his twentieth birthday in March of 1851.

It was while walking home with Charles on that memorable night that Dwight made the decision to leave Norwich. They were talking of work and local events, when the subject of the American frontier came up. They discussed articles they had read concerning the gold and silver the miners were finding, the unrest with the native Indians who interfered and sometimes killed the miners and settlers, and the dragoons who had been organized and trained to go out to the frontier and subdue the Indians.

Dwight told Charles how he frequently thought about what it would be like to live an adventurous life out West, and to live life free. Dwight finally told him of his secret longing to join the dragoons. He explained that he wanted to see the mountains, the prairies, and the herds of wild horses and buffalo. He wanted to see real Indians and live the new experiences he could never have in Connecticut. He told Charles that he often dreamed of riding across the endless territory on horseback.

His confession amazed Charles. "Then why do you stay here, learning a machinist apprenticeship?"

Dwight looked at his best friend and paused a long time before he answered. "I don't know, Charles. I really don't know. I have been reading about the frontier and longing to be part of the life out there. I have army experience and, until just now, never really saw myself leaving and pursuing a life out in the American frontier."

"You promised me when you returned from the army that you would tell me if you entertained the thought of leaving Norwich again. Is that what you are planning to do?"

"I have planned nothing, Charles. But over the past several months I have been thinking about it every waking hour." Dwight contemplated what had transpired.

The two men walked a ways until Charles spoke up again. "Your life here is good. You are learning a respectable trade and earning a good wage. You have women wooing you for the most part, but to my knowledge, you have never picked one to receive any of your charms. You surely do not suffer from a broken heart yet. You seem preoccupied and in a state of unrest."

"Charles, you are my dearest friend and I love you for it, but there is much inside me you do not know."

"If I have overstepped my bounds, I apologize. But you worry me, my good friend."

"Don't worry about me. I'm going to be a dragoon." Dwight reached back as far as he could, holding his lunch pail. He then threw the pail into the middle of a pond they were passing.

Charles remained quiet, knowing in his heart that his best friend was surely going to leave again.

"I will announce my resignation at the shop at week's end and inform my parents that I shall be leaving the next week."

A few nights later, he informed his parents that he would be leaving for New York.

Lydia approached him several days later when she was informed. "So you have decided to leave without informing me."

"No, Lydia, I have just not found the time to sit and explain my reasoning. But now will be a good time."

They sat in the parlor alone.

"You will be joining the dragoons, as I understand it?"

"Yes. That is, if they will have me."

"And if they do not, will you return?"

"No. I have saved enough money to continue on and find my way to the frontier. I am not happy here. I do not mean with present company or the family, but with the way of life here in Norwich. I have read and seen too much to hold me to the ways and customs here. I long for a different life, free of everything that closes in on me here. It is hard for me to explain, but it is how I feel in my heart."

Lydia did not attempt to convince him to stay. She knew that her brother was different from the rest of the family. There was something a little wild about him. She paused for several moments, seeking the right words to convey her heart to her beloved brother. "Go find yourself, Dwight. Go with God, and find your life. Be careful, and write me as often as is reasonably possible. I will pray that you find contentment out on the frontier. I will surely miss your presence at home and your wonderful voice at service. I love you." Her last words were choked with emotion and Dwight barely heard them. She hugged him, and then left the parlor.

It would be many years before he would see her again, and it was the last time he would ever see the rest of his family.

Aaron Dwight Stevens left Norwich by train and arrived in New York City on April 1, 1851. The city's smells, traffic, noise, and smoke-filled air reminded him of Boston, where he had gone when he first joined the army, except on a grander scale. After obtaining directions, he left the train station and walked for several hours until he reached the address he had cut out of the paper. The four-story building he found had the recruitment office on the ground floor, and posters of dragoons in blue with orange piping were displayed for any possible recruit to see as he entered the office.

He paused outside of the recruitment office for a few minutes and watched citizens go by. A young man passed him and opened the door to the recruitment office. Dwight followed, thinking the man had similar intentions of joining the dragoons. He browsed, reading the posters and several pamphlets of literature that were available for prospective recruits while waiting to be recognized by a dragoon sergeant sitting at a desk. Dwight listened as the sergeant spoke to the prospective recruit.

"And what brings you to the recruitment center, lad?"

"I've come to sign up for training in the dragoons."

"You have, lad, so you have. And what age of sense are you bringing with you this fine day?"

"I'm eighteen this past January."

"And you have a birth certificate from home, or a baptismal paper from a good father to prove your claim?"

"Well, no, I don't have the papers with me, but I can bring them in if you must see them."

"Well, lad, I must. You see, the major I work for will be asking me to show proof of your age before he has the surgeon examine you to see how fit you are to be a dragoon. So be a good lad and go home and get what I need to see before we can sign you up. Now be off and make sure you're sober when you do come to sign up." The sergeant mumbled to himself as he waved the young man off.

The prospective recruit quickly exited the recruitment office and scurried down the street.

The sergeant looked at Stevens, who had waited patiently. "And what can I do for you, my good man?"

"Well, Sergeant, I'm interested in joining up."

"That's good, for you look old enough. You had any experience in the military?"

"Yes, Sergeant, I have."

"And what, pray tell, might that be, Mr. …" He paused. "I didn't catch the name."

"I didn't give it, but it's Aaron Dwight Stevens."

"Mr. Stevens it is. My name is Sergeant Dan Malloy. What's the military experience you have?"

"I was a private in the First Massachusetts Volunteer Regiment during the war. I spent eighteen months in Mexico, until I was discharged in July of forty-eight. I have my discharge paper with me." He handed the yellowed paper to the sergeant.

"I'm impressed, Stevens. I know of the First Massachusetts. You followed in a lot of the same places my regiment had been. I served under Captain Kirby Smith in the Third Infantry."

Dwight listened to the sergeant tell a few war stories.

When he finished, he asked, "Do you have experience fighting on horseback, Stevens?"

"No. Only infantry experience."

"We'll teach you. I learned when I joined up in forty-nine. You wait here. I'll get the major to have a talk with you." Sergeant Malloy rose from his desk and proceeded to the rear office. As he disappeared. Dwight noticed that the man had a slight limp. Within a minute, he returned and sat at his desk. "Major May will be with you in a few minutes."

"Sergeant, what brought you back to New York City? Was it recruitment duty for the dragoons?"

"No, you saw that I limp a bit. I got hit with an Apache arrow. It cut a tendon. All the army doctors told me I'd have to live with it, but I got it fixed here in New York. Major May, who you will soon meet, saw to it. He got me to a surgeon who fixes my kind of wound. I served under Major May in the New Mexico Territories. Damn good officer, he is. He asked me to help him recruit men in New York because I'm from here and know the city."

"You lived here all your life?"

"No, I came over alone from Ireland in forty-five. Joined the army and spent time in Mexico like you. But I stayed in. I ended up in the dragoons. Met Major May when he was a first lieutenant."

Sergeant Malloy immediately stood up when Major May entered the room. Out of respect, Dwight followed. "Sir, this is the gent I told you about."

The major extended his hand to Dwight. "Mr. Stevens, welcome to my office. I'm Major Charles May.[1] Sergeant Malloy has informed me of your experience."

"It's my pleasure to meet you, sir."

"Please, follow me into my office so that we may talk. Excuse us, Sergeant."

"Yes, sir."

Major May lead Dwight into his office. "Please be seated, Mr. Stevens."

"Sir, please call me Dwight."

The major nodded and smiled.

"We are looking for experience such as yours, Dwight. I'm familiar with the First Massachusetts and had met Colonel Wright, your old commander, in Mexico when I was on staff at general headquarters. The colonel had a fine reputation there." The major then changed the conversation and directed his questions to Dwight's military knowledge.

---

[1] **Major Charles May** (1818–1864) served in U.S. Army for 25 years. He fought in the Mexican War and led a cavalry charge at the Battle of Resaca de la Palma. He is mentioned in the Maryland State song "Maryland, My Maryland."

Satisfied that his military resume matched what the dragoons were looking for, he ended the conversation. "Dwight, I am going to forward you to our adjutant assistant surgeon. He will examine you and, if you are fit in his professional opinion, then we will sign you up today. You will be billeted at the expense of the army for several days and then transported to Carlisle Barracks, Pennsylvania, for training.[1] Now, if you will follow me, I will lead you to our surgeon."

The two men ascended a flight of stairs that led to a waiting room. Dwight was asked to wait while Major May talked with the surgeon. A few minutes passed and both Major May and the surgeon exited the office door.

"Mr. Stevens, I am pleased to meet you. I am Dr. John Milhau.[2] I will be examining you. Please follow me."

"Good luck, Stevens. Dr. Milhau will send you back downstairs when he has completed the examination."

Dr. Milhau performed his examination of Dwight while asking the standard questions. The examination took a very short time, and Dwight was found to be in excellent health and not under the influence of alcohol. He was informed that he was eligible to serve in the dragoons. While Dr. Milhau entered his examination findings in a record book, he paused, looked up at Dwight, and said, "We cannot recruit men who are not sober at the time of recruitment, and who are not at least five feet five inches tall. You look taller than five feet five inches."

Dwight did not respond, but did notice that the doctor registered him at five feet eight inches. He never attempted to correct the doctor that he was taller than that. It didn't matter. He had been accepted into the dragoons.

The doctor finished his assessment notes and looked up at the new recruit. "Take this paper with you. I'm sending you back to Major May to be officially sworn into the dragoons."

The whole process had been completed in less than an hour. Aaron Dwight Stevens was officially listed on the rolls of the dragoons on April 1, 1851. After a good meal at a local restaurant and a brief overnight stay

---

[1] **Carlisle Barracks** was located in Carlisle, Pennsylvania. In 1838 the School of Cavalry Practice was located here, and it is the second oldest active military facility. The Army War College is on the base.

[2] **Dr. John Milhau** & Son Pharmaceutists and Druggists was located at 183 Broadway, New York City. They were agents for French artificial eyes, manufacturers of the "Original Elixir of Calisaya Bark" and "Chalybeate Elixir of Calisaya Bark," and importers of fresh castor oil and all varieties of foreign remedies.

in New York City at the expense of the army, Private Aaron Dwight Stevens departed for Carlisle Barracks, Pennsylvania, the following day by civilian stagecoach. He had left his home for the second and last time.

The coach ride from New York City to Harrisburg, Pennsylvania, took almost four days to complete. Harrisburg was within a day's ride of Carlisle Barracks. The stage ride involved a sixteen-hour day, during which horses were changed every four hours at predetermined coach stops. At Harrisburg, Dwight found the military storehouse that would supply transportation for him. He arrived at Carlisle Barracks on April 6, 1851 and reported to headquarters.

He entered the headquarters and walked directly to a corporal who was sitting at the main desk. He stood in front of him until he was acknowledged.

Cavalry at Carlisle Barracks circa 1861
Courtesy of House Divided Project, Dickerson College

The corporal looked up and saw a tall young civilian standing in front of this desk. "And who might you be?"

"The name is Aaron Dwight Stevens. I'm reporting for duty."

Dwight handed his orders to the corporal, who took a few moments to read them.

"Welcome to Carlisle Barracks, Stevens. I am Corporal Joshua Reynolds. I'm the quartermaster clerk." He took a few more moments to look at several rosters he had on his desk and then looked up at Dwight. "You'll be assigned to A Troop." Corporal Reynolds looked over as another soldier came into the room. "Baker, take Stevens over to A Troop and have Corporal Moran outfit him."

Private Baker acknowledged the request and addressed Dwight. "Follow me, trooper."

Dwight grabbed his small suitcase and quickly followed him.

The army post was busy as the two men walked to a brick building that housed A Troop. Upon entering, Dwight and Private Baker were immediately standing in front of Corporal Moran. "And what do you have for me today, Baker?"

"This is a new trooper Corporal Reynolds sent."

He took the paperwork and glanced at it. "Says you're from Connecticut?"

"That is correct. I'm from Norwich, Connecticut, Corporal."

"It also says you were discharged from the First Massachusetts?"

Dwight nodded.

"I was out West in California during the war as a dragoon until last year. I came here to train new recruits. Welcome to A Troop, Stevens."

"Thank you, Corporal. I'll do my best to get out to the frontier."

The corporal laughed. "The dragoons don't call it the frontier. Some call it the badlands. Some call it injun country. Some call it wastelands. But it ain't the frontier, Stevens. We have different names for it, just like you know we always called Mexicans greasers, remember?"

"I do, Corporal, I remember."

"You'll learn the lingo and a lot more, like how to soldier while you're riding at top speed on your horse. Now, let's get you in uniform."

Stevens was outfitted with two complete sets of uniforms, two sets of undergarments, one pair of boots, a service cap with plume, a pair of riding gloves, a white leather saber strap, a belt, and an overcoat. The uniforms were different from what he had been accustomed to in the First Massachusetts. The familiar dark blue jacket and gray blue trousers seemed to contrast the bright orange piping on the jacket collar and on the trousers' outer seam.

Corporal Moran made sure that the uniforms fit the new recruit by adjusting certain items and exchanging those that did not fit properly, especially the boots. "Make sure the boots fit and feel proper. The last thing you want is blisters. Even though we ride where we go, we walk a lot, too."

Dwight stood up completely dressed in his new uniform and stomped his boots. "They feel right, Corporal. I'm sure they will feel much better when they wear in." He reached toward his civilian clothes and attempted to place his sheathed knife in his right boot.

The corporal noticed the move. "You won't have need of a knife, Private. We'll teach you to protect yourself with a saber. Leave that with your civilian clothes."

He reminisced about how that knife had saved him from the lariat. His thoughts changed when the corporal handed him the last three items, a model 1840 dragoon saber, a model 1842 percussion pistol, and a .52 caliber Hall-North carbine. He realized that he would always have the saber with him, and that there would be no need to hide a knife in his boot. The dragoons were much different from the volunteers, and the percussion pistol and the carbine only added more proof of that.

Dwight was shown to his second-story quarters in the A Troop barracks. The open room was lined with twenty single cot beds with blankets and footlockers and one coal-burning stove at each end. "This is where you'll bunk. Make a note, the locker number is twenty-three. That number will also be your number for all your stable gear for your mount."

"Will I be able to pick the mount I will be training on, Corporal?"

"No. One will be assigned to you in the morning."

"Well, I'll store my gear and wait for the non-coms."

"The rest of the troops will be returning from training in an hour. You will report to either Sergeant Weston or Corporal Miner. You'll recognize either one of them. They're the only enlisted dragoons with rank."

Chapter Nine
The Dragoons

The afternoon of his first day at Carlisle Barracks seemed uneventful, until Dwight Stevens met the men of A Troop. Corporal Miner was the first authority figure he met. Miner was a man of medium height, about thirty years of age, laughing but relaying orders to the men as they passed by. Some beat on their jackets and slapped their caps to remove the field mud that had dried on them. A few men who walked past Dwight just nodded and continued on to their bunks.

He waited until the men had passed Corporal Miner, then stood at the foot of the corporal's bunk and waited to be recognized.

"You must be a new recruit. What's your name?"

"Dwight Stevens."

"Well, Dwight Stevens, I'll call you 'recruit' when I can't remember your name, and Private Stevens when I can. What bunk you assigned?"

"Twenty-three, Corporal."

"Good. You remembered what Corporal Moran told you. You got any military experience?"

"Yes. I was in the First Massachusetts for eighteen months in forty-seven and forty-eight."

"Where at?"

"I started in Matamoros and ended up in Mexico City."

"Kill any greasers?"

"When I had to."

"Good. That's good, Stevens. Spend any time on a horse?"

"Only as a civilian. No army time."

"We'll teach you to ride and fire a weapon at the same time. Teach you how to use a saber, too. You got all your issued items?"

"Yes, Corporal Moran saw to that."

"Good. You'll start first thing in the morning. Breakfast is at five o'clock. We start training right after that at the stables. Remember your number, Stevens." As Dwight turned to leave, Miner said, "Stevens, welcome to A Troop." He extended his hand, and Dwight shook it. "By the way, supper is in a half hour. Make sure you eat well. Tomorrow's a long day."

Dwight smiled.

He returned to bunk twenty-three and noticed a dragoon sitting on the brass foot rail of his bunk. Dwight paused to evaluate the situation and to choose the right words to tell the man to get off it. "Can I help you? You're sitting on my bunk."

The man realized his encroachment and stood up immediately. "I heard you talkin' when I passed. I'm Sam Sample.[1] I came in a few days before you from New York. I'm from Lancaster, Pennsylvania."

"Dwight Stevens. I came from New York too. Norwich, Connecticut is my home. You could have saved yourself some time if you came straight here from Lancaster, Sam."

"Yeah, I know, but the army only lets you sign up in New York, or I hear Boston too."

"Well, I'm pleased to meet you." Dwight reached out, and the two men shook hands. "Where do you bunk at?"

"I'm right there." He pointed to the adjacent bunk. "I'm number twenty-one."

"The corporal said that supper was coming soon. I'm real hungry from my trip here. Is the food edible?

"It's certainly not home cooking, but there is always plenty."

"Will you show me where to go?"

"Follow me, Dragoon. I'll be your scout for the rest of the day."

Both men laughed as they headed out of the barracks. As they walked, conversation ensued. "I heard you talkin' to the corporal that you was in the war, too."

"Yeah, I was."

"I missed it. I was too busy working in the ironworks trying to make money like my pa tried to. He never did, but he died tryin'. He died just after I turned twenty-five. So I said, 'Shit with this' and decided to finally join up. My older brothers can take care of my ma."

Dwight listened as the Pennsylvania native told him his twenty-five-year life history.

When they reached the chow hall, Sam looked at Dwight and said, "I never did hear about what you were doing before you joined up."

"I was training as a machinist apprentice. I didn't like it that much. Like you, I wanted to go out West. I guess we'll go out and see it together."

They got in line to receive their supper.

During the meal, Dwight was introduced to more of the men. One particular recruit never said a word while the other men bantered at the tables. Dwight asked Sam who the quiet man was.

"That's Starke. His first name is Adolph, I think. He don't say much. He's German."

---

[1] **The names of the men** in the Dragoons are all real. The relationships and conversations are all fiction.

Dwight didn't comment as he finished his meal and began to sip his coffee. "Men come from all over, based on the accents I heard so far," he finally said.

"Yep, we got all kinds that come from England, Ireland, Germany, and men from some of the southern states too. Hell, we got a dragoon that comes from Turkey. I still don't know if he's really Turkish with a name like Smith. He don't talk Turkey. He sounds more like you."

"I believe the language is called Turkish."

"Whatever they call it, Carlisle Barracks has a lot of different folks in it. I was told at the recruitment office that the government wanted only Americans in the dragoons, but that ain't the truth, as you can see."

"I was never told that when I signed up in New York."

"It don't matter, as long as they can fight like Americans."

"From what I have read, Europeans have been fighting a lot longer than Americans have."

"Well, maybe so, Stevens. We'll see how they do. The recruiters sure don't seem to care."

The two men returned to the barracks and prepared for the evening. A few recruits had brought out instruments and were fiddling out tunes to the amusement of the others sitting on their bunks. One young man that joined in a few minutes later had a banjo. Dwight enjoyed listening to the two fiddlers and the banjo player play tunes that they all knew.

While the men played, Adolph came in and sat on bunk number twenty-five.

Dwight nodded to him. "I'm Dwight Stevens."

"Adolph Starke. Pleased to meet you."

"Glad to meet you as well. Sam tells me you are from Germany."

"Yah, from Deutschland in forty-five to farm land. Not much luck back home. The harvest bad. Potatoes no grow. No money to buy farm here though, so I joined dragoons. I save money. Maybe farm after my time is finished."

"Maybe so. I hear there is a lot of cheap land out there to do just about anything a man would want."

Adolph didn't respond.

Dwight saw a man heading toward his bunk holding a fiddle.

"I'm Nelson Sutphen," the man said. "Come from Kentucky. I was in the Mississippi Rifles same time you was in the First Massachusetts." He shook Dwight's hand.

"Pleased to meet you. Mississippi Rifles. I'm impressed. You fellas wore those bright red jackets and white hats. We always wondered why you wore those."

"We made good targets for the greasers."

Both men laughed.

"I guess Colonel Jeff Davis[1] wanted us to stand out. I hear he's a senator from Mississippi now. I followed him from Monterrey to Buena Vista. Good commander he was. I heard he turned down the opportunity for brigadier from President Polk. Maybe he liked politics more."

"Most all the commanders seem to end up in politics somewhere. Mine was Caleb Cushing. Last I heard, he ran for governor of Massachusetts. He didn't make it, but I'm sure he's doing something in politics."

"Well, Stevens, there ain't no politics here that I can see. We'll see you around." Sutphen left to join in the fiddling.

Dwight was impressed at how well the man played.

That night, he found it difficult to fall asleep. It wasn't that he was bothered about leaving his family. It was just trying to sleep in a strange place and becoming accustomed to the smell of the barracks and to the bothersome snoring from some of the men that kept him awake. Occasionally, someone would curse at the snorer to no avail.

As he lay in his bunk, he laughed to himself as he remembered how it was never quiet at night whenever there was a large group of men coughing, snoring, talking in their sleep, farting, belching, and getting up to go to the latrine. He knew it would take a few days before he would get used to it again.

Before light, Dwight rose, dressed, and made his bunk.

Sam Sample heard him. "Up early, ain't you?"

Dwight put his finger to his lips for Sam to keep quiet. Sam understood and quickly got up, dressed, and also made his bunk. Dwight waited until Sam had finished.

Adolph Starke rose and began to dress as others were stirring and doing the same. "You will wait for me, yah?"

Dwight nodded while the man finished dressing and started to make his bunk.

Sam approached. "You ready to go?"

"No, not yet. I'm waiting for Adolph."

"He can catch up. Let's go."

"Sam, I told the man I would wait for him." Dwight stood still and watched Adolph finish his chores.

---

[1] **Jefferson Davis** was a graduate of West Point and a U.S. Senator and U. S. Secretary of War. He fought in the Mexican War and was President of the Confederate States of America (CSA). He is prominent in this book as the U.S. Secretary of War.

Sam Sample wasn't as patient. "Come on, Starke, move your ass. I need breakfast. I'm starved."

Starke looked at Dwight. "Thank you for waitin'."

The three men walked to breakfast together and talked. Sam Sample, Adolph Starke, and Dwight Stevens were different men from different places, but their commonality was that they were now all dragoons.

Following close behind, as he dressed, was Nelson Sutphen. "Wait up, y'all."

After breakfast and muster, the men assembled at the stables. Dwight found the gear and saddle he would need for his mount on a tack bench marked number twenty-three. A stable sergeant addressed the men and instructed them to get their assigned mount, saddle it, and stand by until Sergeant Weston began the daily drills.

Dwight walked to the corral and watched as recruits found their mounts, bridled them, and returned to the stable to saddle them. Realizing he had not taken his bridle, he quickly returned to fetch it. The stable sergeant shook his head and looked annoyed.

Horse number twenty-three was a handsome, gentle-looking bay. He didn't move away as Dwight approached. He noticed that the bay had bright eyes, a long slim neck, high withers to fit his height, and looked to have strong, sleek legs. The chestnut color coat shone in the early morning sun and caught Dwight's eye.

Dwight had just led the bay back to the stable when the sergeant yelled out to him, "Be careful with this one, lad. He's very young and can throw you real quick. He's done that to three recruits this month."

Dwight talked to the bay as he saddled him. He respected the stable sergeant's advice, but wasn't sure if the bay would try to buck him like he had the others.

Sergeant Weston yelled, "Boots and Saddles," and the men mounted and got in line outside the stable. Dwight mounted the bay, and the horse remained obedient as he positioned himself in line. When the command to move out was given, the bay responded. Dwight relaxed a little, seeing the horse had responded positively to his weight and commands and was moving normally with the rest of the mounts.

The order was given to halt.

Dwight pulled back on the reins, completely calm , and thinking that he was bonding with his horse. He listened intently to the next instructions from Sergeant Weston. Again, move out was ordered and then the commands to walk and then trot. The next command would be the gallop. He waited patiently for the command to be given.

Then Sergeant Weston yelled, "At a gallop!"

Dwight's first instinct was to gently use his spurs. The bay didn't respond at first, so he applied a little more pressure. Suddenly, his horse broke away from the rest of the troops and raced across the parade field back toward the stable. Dwight managed to turn him from the stable, but still could not break his speed. The horse continued to run.

Dwight could hear the laughing and catcalls from the men as they watched for the recruit to be thrown, which was inevitable. He saw a fence quickly approaching. Holding on for dear life and trying to slow the horse, Dwight thought he was a goner. The bay never slowed as it easily jumped the fence and continued running. After the jump, he realized that the horse was not responding to anything he had attempted, so he spurred the bay harder, encouraging him to run faster. About two miles down the road, the bay finally slowed.

The stable sergeant met him on his return to A Troop. "I see he's run out of fight, Private."

"Yes, Sergeant. It seems he has, and I thank the Almighty."

"No need to thank the Almighty, Dragoon. That was good horsemanship the way you managed to stop this fella. He's been a pain in my ass for a couple of months now. You keep working with him. He'll be a good mount for another recruit by the time you leave here."

"We thought that you was done for, Dwight. You rode him like hell, though. Good for you," Adolph said.

"I was scared when he wouldn't respond. I was really scared when we jumped the fence. I didn't think he'd clear it, and I sure as hell didn't think I'd be able to stay on."

Sutphen laughed as he heard the last bit of the conversation and slapped Dwight on the back. "You be one Yankee riding fool. I thought that crazy bay was going to kill you."

"The sergeant told me that crazy bay is mine, and to finish breaking him."

"Well, lucky you. I sure don't want him."

Sam Sample didn't say anything to Dwight as he approached all three of them talking. He kept chuckling as he looked at Dwight.

"It wasn't that funny, Sam. I was holding on for my life."

"Sorry, Dwight, but the scared-as-shit look on your face will forever be in my mind. You don't know how funny you looked holding so tightly onto the reins."

During the next week, the drills were frequently repeated until they became mundane for A Troop. There were a few more incidents with the horse , and it quickly became known as "Crazy Bay." The horse would always take longer than the others to stop after a gallop command was given, but in time, he settled down to Dwight's orders. .

A dragoon's saber had been attached to and sheathed on Dwight's belt since his first day of training, but it wasn't until the second week that the dragoons were given instructions on how to effectively use it. They were taken to an area to practice charging on horseback and swinging their sabers. A series of five-foot poles with one foot of straw attached to the top represented hypothetical men on foot who needed to be cut down.

Sergeant Weston first instructed the men to draw and hold the saber during a mounted trot, gallop, and run. The men repeated the instructions until the sergeant thought they were ready to use them. His specific instructions were that each trooper timed and aimed his thrust correctly so that the saber would contact only the straw and not the hard wood pole.

Dwight watched Corporal Miner begin the demonstration. Miner swung his saber and removed the straw from the top of the pole, stopped, turned his mount for a quick return, and performed the second thrust.

Sergeant Weston yelled out, "That, dragoons, is how I expect all of you to perform!"

Weston ordered the first recruit in line to begin. As fifth in line, Dwight watched his four predecessors successfully accomplish the task.

Everyone waited for Dwight's turn with Crazy Bay. To everyone's disappointment, the two executed the move perfectly.

A Troop commanding officer Lieutenant Beverly Robertson had come out to watch them. Dwight observed with slight amusement as a few troopers swung and hit solid wood. One particular recruit swung so hard he lost balance and fell off his mount. Besides the obvious embarrassment, a chastising from Weston, and the chuckling from the rest of the troops, the man suffered a sore wrist and hand for several days.

By the time the training was completed a few weeks later, each man had learned to skillfully attack a target at full riding speed and to hit his mark with the saber. Years later, when Dwight led the Kansas free state militia, he would have a reputation as an experienced guerilla fighter who was known to wield a sword with swift and deadly precision.

The pistol was also a weapon that Dwight quickly learned to use with accuracy. His skills with it were better than most of the recruits in the troop, but his ability to use the .52 caliber carbine exceeded even that. He never lost his ability to load the new weapon quickly and hit his mark, whether mounted or on foot, with great accuracy. Within a month, A Troop was becoming a highly skilled mounted military unit in use of all three weapons.

As May approached, the evenings became longer and the men had more time to relax in and around the barracks after supper. It was during these daily occasions that the men from A Troop, from various parts of the world, would intermingle and talk about different subjects.

Dwight made time during his leisure hours to read when he was not talking, singing, or playing a borrowed fiddle or banjo. One specific source of his interest continued to be *The Age of Reason* by Thomas Paine. He carried the pamphlet in his back pocket so he could pull it out any chance he had free time.

"You read a lot, don't you?" Sam asked.

Dwight did not answer.

"Stevens, what are you reading?"

He broke his concentration. "Oh, I'm sorry, Sam. I'm reading Thomas Paine."

"Never heard of him. You want to play some cards? I got four so far for poker. We need a fifth to make it a good game."

"No, I don't gamble much, and besides I want to read some more. Thanks anyway."

"What's this author writing about that keeps your eyes staring at the words?"

"Well, Sam, I was reading his beliefs about organized religion."

"Organized religion. I don't fancy church-going much, Dwight. Never had time enough to sit and listen to a preacher. I worked every day in the foundry. Had to. Needed to keep the fires hot. My ma went with some of my folk sometimes, though she didn't go after pa died."

"My folks go every Sunday," Dwight told him. "They read Scripture, sing in the choir, and listen to every word preached from the podium. Reading this book has changed my thoughts on religion."

"I ain't got time to read nothing about religion. I got time to play cards, though. Think about playing."

"No thanks. Like I said, I'm not interested."

Sam turned and continued down the row of bunks looking for some players to fill the seat for the game.

"I hear you talking, Dwight," Adolph said. "My English not good, my reading bad. But I see this book in old country. Lutheran priest say book no good. Sin to read. Maybe you tell me what book says, yah?"

The two men sat and talked quietly while others lay listening to the singing and carrying on at the other end of the barracks. During the conversation, a Southern gentleman named William Stuart from Charlestown, South Carolina, turned over on his bunk opposite theirs and called out, "What kind of bullshit is that? My preacher would have the two of you horsewhipped for reading and spreading such evil words."

Both Adolph and Dwight were taken by surprise at his sudden and uninvited outburst.

"Billy, this no business to you," Adolph spoke out.

"I heard about the book and its author. It's anti-Christian, Starke."

Dwight spoke up. "It's a religious view written a while back that has been read around the world. I'm talking to Adolph and I am giving him my interpretation of it."

Stuart got out of his bunk and stood half-dressed in the middle of the aisle. "It's un-Christian to read the book. My preacher said so."

"That's a point that Paine makes in his book, that organized religion sometimes gives its congregations the wrong teachings," Dwight tried to explain.

"If you are a Christian, then you should act like a Christian. Follow the teachings of the Bible and of your church!" Stuart yelled. By this time, he had reached Dwight and Adolph with his fists clenched.

Dwight struggled to keep his emotions under control. "Back away, Stuart. No need to get worked up. It's a book," Dwight said, now standing and facing the man who was infringing on his personal space.

Adolph positioned himself between the two potential adversaries. "We just talking. Go back to bunk, Billy."

"You stay out of it, German man. Stevens is the one spreading heresy."

Stuart had just stepped closer when Corporal Miner approached, grabbed Stuart, spun him around, and said, "Before you get your ass kicked by a much bigger man and then get all of us in trouble, you better back off. A book is a book, and none of us here are good Christians as far as I can see. And you are no different. So stop your 'holier than thou' shit and back down." Miner glared into Stuart's eyes.

After a few moments, Stuart opened his fists and stepped back. "I don't like what they were talking about."

"It don't matter Billy. It's just talk." Miner looked at Starke and Stevens, and motioned for them to return to their bunks.

Both men obeyed, and it was obvious that no friendship would be made between Dwight Stevens and Billy Stuart.

More training continued for A Troop until Weston and Miner felt that the men were ready to be sent out for assignment to one of the various forts in the Indian Territories. Word came down that the A Troop dragoons would be getting orders in a few days. Anticipation of what could be ahead was the topic of conversation during the evenings.

Sam Sample sat cleaning his carbine and looked up at Dwight, who had just returned from the supper meal. "Where do you think we will be gettin' orders to, Dwight?"

"I don't know, Sam. It could be anywhere. They need dragoons all over the west."

"I guess wherever we get assigned will be open and free space, except for the Indians."

"Yes, so don't forget that the reason we are going out there is to keep peace with the Indians."

Sutphen overheard the conversation and commented, "I'll take New Mexico Territory. It'll probably turn into a slave state territory when it's time. Maybe they'll add the Indians to the slave numbers. We'll need them to farm and ranch out there. We never owned slaves in Kentucky where I was raised, but I saw a lot of slaves when I was training with the Mississippi Rifles. Those darkies did all the work for the plantation owners, shopkeepers, and a lot of other chores. It just makes good sense to ranch out there, using Indians and darkies."

"What makes you think it will be a slave state, Sutphen?" Sample asked.

"Ya don't read much, Sample? The Compromise says so. It's law. When California was accepted into statehood as a free state, the Utah and New Mexico territories were left open until they decided whether they were going to be free or slave. There's some fussing going on in Kansas right now over the same issue."

Dwight listened until he could not be quiet any longer. "New Mexico is free, and I've heard no discussion about that changing. The Indians are not slaves, and the tribes are independent nations. The slaves in the South should all be freed, just like they were in England and the rest of Europe. No man should be a slave."

Stuart spoke up after hearing Dwight's remarks. "Stevens, there you go again preaching evil. Slaves are slaves and are only good for working fields, multiplying, and occasionally fulfilling a white man's needs, if you know what I mean."

Sutphen laughed at Stuart's derogatory remarks, but saw the anger beginning to show in Dwight's face. He moved closer to make sure Stuart and Stevens kept off of a collision course.

"No man should own another man!" Dwight yelled.

"Well, you wouldn't understand, Stevens," Sutphen responded. "You're a Yankee from New England, and what Stuart just said is not true about how most slave owners treat their slaves. Hell, a lot of them are treated like family."

"I've heard that argument too," Dwight said, suddenly lowering his voice as he noticed men starting to gather round. "But slavery is wrong, and allowing it to grow across this country will only lead to more evil."

Stuart shook his head and said, "Learn to live with it, Stevens. You'll live a lot longer. You go preaching that shit in my town and they'd lynch you."

Corporal Miner got off his bunk. "You men need to keep your opinions to yourself. Remember, we are all going out West to protect whoever goes out there to settle the territories. Let them that settles there decide these arguments for themselves."

Miner's comment seemed to at least temporarily defuse the situation, and he began to walk down the center aisle of the barracks. All the dragoons saw him approaching and quickly returned to their bunks.

Orders came at the end of the second week for A Troop. The forty men were issued to Jefferson Barracks,[1] Missouri, where they would have more cavalry training before being assigned to their final outposts. The news about leaving Carlisle Barracks was exciting, but no one knew what to expect in Missouri. Additionally, after ten weeks of training in Pennsylvania, the idea that still more training waited for them in Missouri lessened the excitement.

The dragoons of A Troop mustered for the last time in front of Lieutenant Robertson, Sergeant Weston, and Corporal Miner. The lieutenant made a few remarks that he had been pleased to command A Troop and that he felt very confident that all his dragoons would perform admirably in their assignments. His speech did not last very long. He called A Troop to attention as an officer rode up on a black mount.

Dwight recognized the two corporals that accompanied him. He and the other men noticed his rank, and realized this was the commanding officer of Carlisle Barracks. He had come to address them for the first time.

Lieutenant Colonel Philip St. George Cooke looked over the forty dragoons. He steered his black mount in front of the men, who remained at attention bridling their own mounts, as he spoke. "Dragoons of A Troop. I am Lieutenant Colonel Cooke, your commanding officer. Stand at ease, gentlemen. Lieutenant Robertson has informed me that you all have successfully completed your dragoon training here at Carlisle Barracks. His report to me indicates that Sergeant Weston and his assistant, Corporal Miner, have done an outstanding job preparing you for your next assignment at Jefferson Barracks. I expect you to do your duty when called upon. You will all receive individual orders. Congratulations on your accomplishment. And may God go with you throughout your career as a United States Dragoon."

The lieutenant colonel looked at Lieutenant Robertson, who

---

[1] **Jefferson Barracks** was located on the Mississippi River in Lemay, Missouri. In 1832, the dragoons were formed and stationed here. They were trained to fight both mounted and dismounted at this facility. It was active from 1826 to 1946.

immediately saluted and yelled, "Troop, attention!"

Cooke returned the salute, then kicked his stirrups into his horse and galloped away.

Lieutenant Robertson looked to Sergeant Weston to dismiss the troop. The whole event lasted less than ten minutes.

"That was a short ceremony," Sam remarked.

Dwight laughed and turned to Sample. "Sam, that was no ceremony. I had more of a ceremony than that when they were throwing shit chips at us marching to the docks in Boston in forty-seven."

Sam seemed puzzled by the remark, until Dwight explained the story as they returned to the stables. Most men wondered why they had never seen Cooke until that day.

The next day, Saturday, June 14th, was the last full day at Carlisle Barracks for Dwight Stevens and A Troop. The forty dragoons were given their individual orders and instructed to gather all their clothes, gear, and weapons to take to Jefferson Barracks. That night, the men celebrated with conversation, singing, playing instruments, and sneaking drinks from hidden whiskey bottles some had managed to purchase from the sutlers that frequented the barracks on Saturdays.

Dwight was offered, and accepted, a few swigs of the Kentucky bourbon that Sutphen had bought. It was a better grade than the whiskey that some of the other men swallowed and gagged to keep down. As Dwight took his last sip from Sutphen's bottle, he remarked, "Those boys will surely be wishing that they went a little easier on that rotgut. This bourbon is smooth, Nelson."

"Yeah, it's the only kind I'll put my lips to. I've been drinking it since I can remember. Y'all be sleeping well and waking rested after sipping this batch. They, meanwhile, will be puking once that swill sits in their gizzards."

Both men laughed as Dwight handed the half-full bottle back to his Kentuckian host.

Lieutenant Colonel Philip St. George Cooke
"Father of the U.S. Cavalry," was a career army cavalry officer. He served honorably as a Union general during the Civil War. His son-in-law was Confederate cavalry General J.E.B. Stuart.
Public Domain photo

On Sunday morning, June 15th, the sun rose on Carlisle Barracks. The entire A Troop was up, dressed, and packed despite the effects of the previous evening's celebration. They awaited word to leave and begin loading onto the wagons to bring them to the Harrisburg Railroad. The trip on the Harrisburg Railroad lasted a day and ended with a canal boat ride that brought them, after two days, to the base of the Allegheny Mountains.

They marched over the mountain roads until they were able to board another canal boat and head west until they reached Pittsburgh on June 25th. Ten days had passed and they were still in the State of Pennsylvania.

The troops waited several days to board a steamboat that took them to St. Louis. The days on the riverboat were nostalgic for Dwight as he remembered his journey almost three years earlier when he returned from the Mexican War. The sign he'd noticed back then had not changed—*The City of Cincinnati Welcomes You* was still painted in red and black letters.

This time, however, the dragoons were hardly noticed. They were viewed as mere passengers waiting for the steamboat at the dock. No one inquired as to where they were going, and most of the other passengers kept to themselves and read the newspapers that several paperboys had been selling on the docks.

Dwight had bought a newspaper. One of the main stories was of the World's Fair that had just opened in May. The event was taking place in London, England. Columns containing information about the exhibitors and their new inventions filled the paper. Dwight read how Prince Albert was being hailed for organizing the world event. He was amazed that the United States had almost five hundred exhibits on display for the world to see.

He passed the paper to Sample while he explained what he had read to Starke. The men passed the time waiting to depart by discussing some of the other articles in the paper. It would be five days before the steamboat would finally leave the waters of the Ohio River and enter the muddy Mississippi.

The steamboat turned northwest and headed to St. Louis. Another four days would pass before they reached the city where the Mississippi and Missouri met. It then took eight more hours before they arrived at Jefferson Barracks by wagon on the evening of July 2, 1851. After almost three weeks of traveling by wagon, rail, canal boat, foot, and steamboat, the troops finally reached their destination. They were tired but pleased the trip had ended.

The next morning they were mustered, fed, and assigned new saddles and mounts at the stables. By noon, the men had completed drills in weapons handling, saber assaults, and cavalry tactics. The training continued for another week until Starke, Stevens, and Sample were told by the barracks corporal to report to headquarters after brushing down their mounts and storing their gear.

"What they want us for?" Starke looked to Dwight for an answer.

"Don't know, Adolph. We'll find out when we report."

"Why just us three?" Sam Sample asked.

"Sam, like I said to Adolph, we'll find out when we get there."

"Did the three of you hear me? Move your asses and get to headquarters!" the barracks corporal yelled when he noticed the three still talking.

The three privates found the sergeant major sitting at his desk.

He looked up as he heard the door close behind them. "Starke, Stevens, Sample." He read their names slowly as he held up a piece of paper. "It seems the army needs dragoons quicker than I can get them trained. I picked you three based on what I seen you do in the short time you've been here. You will pack your haversacks, grab your weapons, and leave my barracks first thing in the mornin'. A wagon will take you back to Saint Louie, and from there you will get on the next steamer up the river to Fort Leavenworth."[1] He handed each dumbfounded dragoon copies of their orders, and then waved them away. "Now be off with you, and good luck."

Word got around quickly that the three had been given orders to Fort Leavenworth ahead of the rest.

The one most negatively affected was Nelson Sutphen. He approached as they were packing their gear. "Well, I guess we'll find the three of you when we catch up. I'll miss you until then." He shook their hands and wished them all good luck.

None of them realized that they would never meet again.

Shortly after Adolph Starke, Dwight Stevens, and Sam Sample left for Fort Leavenworth, Nelson Sutphen and Billy Stuart received orders and left for the First Mounted Rifles at Fort Kearny, Nebraska.

---

[1] **Fort Leavenworth, Kansas** was the oldest active U.S. Army facility and the key protective fort and destination during the years of westward expansion.

Chapter Ten

Westward

It rained heavily for the first three days of their journey up the Missouri River on the steamboat *Florence.* The rain swelled and widened the river, which was usually narrow and slow-moving at that time of the year. The steamboat struggled to make headway west in the eastward-moving current.

At times Starke and Sample were sure that the steamboat was not moving. They slept outside on the second-level deck during the night. The heat and mugginess prohibited any efforts to sleep in the cabin, and the second-level deck afforded some protection from the constant downpours and strong winds that forced the rain to attack horizontally at times.

The rain eventually stopped and the July heat quickly returned. After three more days, the *Florence* arrived at Portland, Missouri, and offloaded passengers and cargo. It stayed moored for most of the day as cargo was unloaded and new cargo loaded. The three dragoons watched the activity from the second-level deck. New passengers boarded, and fresh coal and water were taken on. It would be six more days until they reached Jefferson City.

The *Florence* then departed the river dock there for its next leg of the trip to Kansas City. The steamboat would pass Arrow Rock, Miami, and Lexington over the next several days.

The *Florence* arrived in Kansas City on July 20, 1851. It would be another full day before the steamboat would dock at a small pier that extended out into the river. It had taken Dwight Stevens, Adolph Starke, and Sam Sample thirty-four days to reach Fort Leavenworth, Kansas, from Carlisle Barracks, Pennsylvania. The three dragoons stood just off the dock and adjusted their haversacks, gathered their weapons, and oriented themselves before their final walk to the fort.

"Better part of a month to get here, Sam," Dwight said as he wiped perspiration from his neck and face with a handkerchief.

"I guess Nelson Sutphen was right. There ain't very much out here in the way of travel options. I wish the army had given us good horses and saddles."

"I be very happy with horse and saddle now," Adolph said as he adjusted his cartridge and saber belt.

"I hope we can find an army wagon that's heading for the fort so we can ask for a ride," Sam said while beginning to climb the riverbank.

"I don't think we will. If there were any, they would have met the *Florence* at the dock to pick up goods. The boat didn't unload any, so I doubt if there is anyone coming," Dwight remarked as he followed Sample.

"We walk maybe one more time. Then we get mounts."

"Let's hope so, Starke," Sample said as he continued walking up the riverbank. When he reached the top, he stopped.

Stevens and Starke found out why as soon as they reached the top. Less than a mile away on the upper portion of the plain, the Stars and Stripes fluttered on a large flagpole straight ahead. The hot wind blew strong enough from the west to keep the large flag almost fully extended.

"There it is, Fort Leavenworth!" Sam exclaimed.

The three dragoons stood there for a moment in silence as each wondered about what Fort Leavenworth would be like. The sight motivated them. The fort was closer than they'd expected, and the anticipation of getting there rejuvenated their strength enough to overcome the heat.

As they reached the open main gate, two soldiers watched them approach. One of them moved from his post to meet the dragoons. "You three reporting in?"

"Yes, we're reporting from Jefferson Barracks," Dwight said and reached into his jacket to show his orders.

"Keep 'em. Headquarters is over there." He pointed to a two-story red brick building with a wide white porch on the front. Several men could be seen casually looking from the second-story porch at the activities that were going on throughout the fort. "Report through the center door on the first floor. Corporal Mallory will sign you in."

"Much obliged," Dwight said. He folded his orders and put them back into his jacket.

The soldier returned to his gate duties, but continued to watch the three head in the direction of the headquarters.

As they walked, they saw numerous soldiers going about their business.

"There are streets and buildings all over," Sample said as he looked around in amazement.

"Yah, it looks like small city," Adolph commented.

When they reached the main door, a lieutenant exited. Dwight moved from holding his carbine in his right hand and switched it to his left and smartly saluted. Sample and Starke followed. The lieutenant quickly returned the salute and continued on past them.

The large room was busy with activity. Several adjoining offices could be seen with officers and NCOs busy at work. Postings and other information had been attached to an open section of the wall, immediately visible to any soldier or officer that entered.

Dwight spotted a corporal standing behind a desk talking to an officer. He approached and waited to be acknowledged. The officer finished his conversation and went back to his office, while the corporal turned his attention to Dwight and the other two men that now stood on each side of him.

"Reporting in, dragoons?"

"Yes, Corporal. We were told to report to Corporal Mallory to be signed in."

"You're lookin' at 'im in the flesh."

"I'm Private Stevens. These are Privates Sample and Starke."

"Isn't it nice that you talk for 'em, Stevens? You're a good man to do that for your friends. Now, I'm assuming that you all have orders, but maybe you carry 'em for the lads, now do you?"

Dwight realized that he wouldn't get anywhere trying to defend himself against the sarcasm. He didn't answer, but instead pulled his orders out of his jacket and handed them to the corporal. Sample and Starke followed.

Mallory read over the three papers and looked up.

"You three will be billeted in the temporary residence barracks until we get enough of you to send to the New Mexico Territory. You'll find fifteen or so dragoons there that will be going out with you once I get a few more." He opened a ledger and instructed the three men to sign in. He then gathered a few papers and made three separate piles. "Now, when you're finished filling in your information, you need to take these papers to the stable, main stores, and payroll office. Keep the last one for the senior NCO at the temporary residence barracks. You understand?"

All three men answered, almost in unison, that they did.

"Good. Now it wouldn't be fitting if I didn't have you meet the commander. Wait here while I see if he has time to see you."

The men waited at parade rest as the corporal knocked and waited to be recognized by the commander. When beckoned, he entered the office and gently closed the door behind him.

Stevens glanced at each man standing next to him, but no one said a word.

The door opened and the corporal exited. He motioned for the three to approach. "The general will see you now. Go in."

The three entered smartly, came to attention, and held a salute in front of the general's desk. The commander looked up and casually saluted. The men stood at attention while the general finished talking with a man sitting in a chair.

Finally, he said, "At ease, gentlemen. Welcome to Fort Leavenworth. I am General Sterling Price. This fine gentleman is Sutler Hiram Rich." The general paused briefly to look over the three dragoons before he said, "Corporal Mallory informs me that you are fresh from Carlisle Barracks by way of Jefferson Barracks, and that your training at Jefferson was shortened due to your abilities being needed here. That's good, because we need men like you in the New Mexico Territory as quickly as possible. Your stay here will be short, gentlemen. That is all."

All three men came to attention.

The general saluted, and the three quickly returned it, turned, and left his office.

Corporal Mallory waited until Starke shut the general's office door. "Remember to go to the stable, main stores, and payroll office. You'll get issued your saddle and gear. The stable sergeant will assign you a mount. At main stores you can buy anythin' you might need. The paper says you're part of the permanent party. But you really ain't. You won't be here that long."

They turned and began to head to the stables, but the corporal stopped them. "I ain't done with you yet. Nobody told you to move. Stop at payroll before anywhere else and sign in so you will get your pay here. Dragoons get seven dollars a month if you're here that long. Now off with you."

The three didn't say a word until they were outside.

Dwight made one comment as they stood on the porch. "He forgot to mention that payroll keeps a dollar a month until your enlistment is up."

"Where'd you hear that, Dwight?" Sam asked.

"I remember reading it when I signed up."

Starke and Sample looked at him and shook their heads as they walked off the porch.

They found the stable, and a sergeant approached. "I'm Stable Sergeant Jeremiah Delaney. You needin' somethin'?"

"Yes, Sergeant, we just reported in and were told to find a mount," Sam Sample informed him.

"Well then, I'm the one you need to talk to." He issued them each a horse blanket, saddle, and bridle. They stored them in the numbered stalls they were assigned and were then allowed to view the corralled mounts. The sergeant explained they were the mounts designated for New Mexico Territory. Sergeant Delaney slowly walked among the horses, whispering and gently touching them all.

Dwight thought to himself, *This man is in the right job. He loves his horses.*

"They're all broken mounts. They ain't been ridden much in a spell, though. You need to come every day and ride 'em so they get used to you before you get to the territories. Pick the one who gets your fancy. They are all about the same," Delaney said.

Dwight immediately picked out a black Morgan. "I like this one."

"Well, get your bridle and see how he likes you," Delaney said as he stood behind the three dragoons.

Starke and Sample found their mounts, and the men bridled and walked them around in a corral that the stable sergeant had opened for them to use. Satisfied that the horses accepted them, the men tied them to the fence and fetched their saddles. Before long all three were saddled and the dragoons were ready to mount.

"Once they have accepted you, there's a lot of prairie out there for them to run in. Don't be heading that way." He pointed to where he didn't want them to go. "There are prairie dogs out there. They leave big enough holes to break a horse's leg. I'd stay within sight of the fort anyway. Don't want you getting lost out there." Delaney laughed, then stood back to open the gate and watch the three men mount.

Starke's brown Morgan never budged as the stocky dragoon mounted him and then moved him toward the open gate at a walk. Sample's chestnut-colored mount with white stockings shied several times, but Sam eventually managed to calm him, mount, and trot out of the corral.

Dwight's black Morgan bucked several times and spun around twice. He reared once in defiance. Dwight pushed his spurs into the horse, galloped out of the corral past his companions, and let the horse run. The horse was much faster than Crazy Bay.

Dwight spurred him again to see what kind of speed the horse had. He liked this horse, and he let him run free for a while, along for the ride. Then it struck him. The freedom of the open spaces, the endless sky, and a magnificent horse beneath him—he loved it all. In that wonderful moment, Dwight felt closer to God than he had at any other time in his life. He was now positive that God was all around him, in the rivers he had traveled, the prairies, and in the mountains. Aaron Dwight Stevens was happy. He was satisfied with his life, and there was nowhere else on Earth that he would rather be.

After several hundred yards, he pulled up gently on the reins to slow the speed of the horse. The mount obeyed, and Dwight turned and slowed to a gallop, then to a walk. He stopped the horse and then pulled on the reigns to have the horse back up. He reared a few times until Dwight settled him and obliged.

By this time Starke and Sample had caught up to him.

"He runs like a champion, Dwight. We couldn't keep up with you," Sample said as he stopped.

"Yah, we try hard. That horse very fast."

"He's a feisty one, I'll say, and the fastest horse I've ever ridden."

"You goin' to call 'im Crazy Bay Two, Dwight?"

"No. He has too much of a free spirit. I think I'm going to call him Spirit. I think it fits him well. He's too smart to be called crazy."

"Ain't found a name yet for this one," Sam said.

"I'll call this one Reup."

"Reup, that's a strange name, Starke," Sample remarked.

"Name of city I come from in Deutschland."

The three men rode their horses for several more miles and then returned back to the fort stable. They unsaddled, stored their gear, and brushed the mounts. They headed for the main stores and the temporary barracks to which they had been instructed to report.

After purchasing some small items, they went to a brick building with a sign on it that said *In-Transit Barracks* and an arrow pointing to a wooden stairway. The three dragoons entered the room at the top of the stairs.

"Reporting in, are you?" a tall sergeant said, approaching them.

"Yes, Sergeant. Just come in this afternoon," Sam said.

"Welcome to in-transit, men. I'm Sergeant Hank Watson. You can bunk over there." He pointed to three bunks with just a thin mattress on each. "I'll have Corporal Rolling get you some blankets when he returns." He gathered their papers and looked at each one for several moments before he talked again. "Adolph Starke, Samuel Sample, and Aaron Stevens. Welcome. Enjoy your free time. There won't be a lot of it soon. Make sure your new mounts are ready to travel. You don't get much time to prepare 'em once it's time to leave. Spend a lot of time with 'em tomorrow. The supper meal is at five-thirty. Make sure you get enough to eat over the next few days. Once we head out, you'll be livin' on hard tack, salted beef, and maybe some buffalo meat if we get lucky. I don't want you spending your time off finding some place to buy whiskey. Don't let me catch you drinkin' while we travel. You stay with your horse tomorrow, and away from any whiskey buyin', and you three will get along with me just fine." He paused long enough to catch a glimpse of each man's reaction to his instructions. "I don't think I missed anythin'." Then he yelled over to a corporal who had just entered the barracks. "Rolling, get these new men some blankets for their bunks!"

All three set up their bunks and followed some of the in-transit troops to the supper meal. They stayed to themselves being the new men, watching the others laughing and talking as they ate. The new men agreed that the meal was actually good. They ate beef, cornbread, and mixed vegetables, and drank coffee. After finishing, the sun hadn't set yet, which gave them time to see the rest of the fort.

Their eventual return to the barracks allowed them to meet most of the men that had been absent during their talk with the sergeant. There were too many names to remember as they introduced themselves. It would be several days before names and faces began to be associated. Soon the three new men began to mix in with the other in-transit dragoons. Several pints of whiskey were brought out and passed among the men, despite the lecture that Sergeant Watson had given.

Corporal Rolling partook with some of the dragoons, taking an occasional swig. "Don't you drink, Stevens?" Corporal Rolling asked as he watched Dwight looking at the men passing a bottle.

"Yes, Corporal, occasionally. I'm just remembering the speech the sergeant gave us."

"That's the sergeant's biggest tale. If I know him, he's down at the sutler's wagon gettin' a pint for himself right now. Buy it by the pint and hide it. Don't be puttin' any in your canteen. The army checks canteens, and sometimes you got to be sharin' it when a detail gets low on water on the trail. Nobody wants whiskey when you're dying of thirst."

He produced his own bottle, and offered Dwight a drink.

"Much obliged, Corporal." Dwight took a healthy drink and returned the bottle. The corporal motioned for him to take a second. "No, thanks. That was enough to quench my thirst for a while."

Dwight prepared for bed. He sat on his bunk and watched the men laugh and talk for a while until the whiskey was put away.

Sam had apparently enjoyed himself a little too much. He slurred when he talked and stumbled while he walked. Adolph helped him to his bunk.

The next morning after breakfast, the three reported to the barracks stable and saddled their horses. They spent the better part of the morning working with them until they were satisfied that they would perform. After the noon meal, they were told to report to the in-transit barracks. Upon arrival, they and the rest of the fifteen dragoons were instructed that their special training would begin the next day.

Sergeant Watson stated that the men should report to the stable and be ready to ride by 0700. No other instructions were given.

The next morning, the dragoons assembled at the stable. Stable Sergeant Delaney looked over the men and horses as they waited for Sergeant Watson. When Corporal Rolling saw the sergeant approaching, he instructed the dragoons to mount up. Rolling waited for Watson and handed him the bridle to his mount, which had been prepared earlier by the stablemen under Delaney's charge.

Watson never said a word to the dragoons as he took the bridle and mounted. He nodded to Rolling, who ordered, "Column of twos, at a walk, forward ho."

The column formed up and slowly moved out of the fort parade grounds, past the main gate.

Rolling ordered, "Dragoons, column at a trot."

The entire column followed in unison and they began heading out onto the prairie.

After a short time, Rolling yelled out, "Dragoons, at a gallop."

Dwight only had to nudge Spirit, and the black Morgan responded immediately. The gallop smoothed out the ride, and Dwight was glad to have a strong mount under his command. He felt a sense of purpose riding with the United States Dragoons and was completely content with his decision to pursue this way of life.

The column maintained the gallop for several miles until Rolling gave the command, "Dragoons, at a trot. Maintain the column of twos."

Within several minutes, the command to halt was issued. Sergeant Watson pulled out of formation and circled back around the column he had taken out into the prairie. After he looked over all the men and their mounts he spoke, "Dragoons, dismount."

He waited a few minutes as he looked out over the prairie, then he pulled out a cigar and bit off the tip. He lit it and nodded at Rolling, who called out, "Dragoons, bridle your mounts, at a walk, single column, forward ho!"

Sam Sample was directly behind Dwight as the men began walking their mounts. They followed behind Watson and Rolling, who carried on a conversation. Occasionally, Dwight and Sam could smell the foul odor coming from the cigar.

"What the hell is he smokin'? I smelled shit better than that," Sam whispered.

"Yes, it does have a unique smell, I'll grant you that."

"Unique? Shit is shit, Dwight. And why the hell are we walking? These horses ain't winded."

"Sam, keep it down. You're talking too loud."

It was too late. The dragoons responded to Corporal Rolling's sharp command to halt. The men stood still and waited as Sergeant Watson smoked his cigar. Watson handed his bridle to Rolling. He walked back slowly toward the column, but stood several feet out so he could see all the dragoons. He spit out some tobacco he had chewed off the cigar and cleared his voice. "I am hearin' talkin'. Dragoons, you don't talk unless talked to by me or Corporal Rolling. You understand that?" He waited for a response. "Did you hear what I said?"

The dragoons answered loudly and in unison that they did.

"Good. The reason is that when we walk, we don't talk. See, the red man has a keen sense of hearing. Your voice carries out here. He don't listen for horse noises, he listens for assholes like you talkin' so he can find and kill you easy. Rolling and me can talk 'cause we know better. When it is real, no one talks. This is training for you and not us, so shut up." He looked up and down the column and spit out some more tobacco pieces. "Now this is your training for today. We are going to walk about three or four miles more in the direction we are going, and then we are going to turn around and walk back the six miles to the fort. A lot of you think we ride everywhere, but we can't. You need to know how to walk, stay alert, and be goddamn quiet." He looked back at Rolling and nodded. "Dragoons, bridle your mounts, at a walk, single column, forward ho!"

Several hours later, and in sight of Fort Leavenworth, they were finally halted.

"Dragoons, mount up," Corporal Rolling commanded.

Sergeant Watson walked his horse past the column of men waiting to be given the command to move out. He mounted it midway among the dragoons. "Gentlemen, we do training differently out here. I know you all can ride, shoot pistols and carbines, and even dazzle me with your saber skills, but you don't know shit about being out here with the red man, who can kill you quicker than you can spit. Keep that in mind when we are out here." He motioned to Rolling, who quickly ordered them forward at a gallop. They would repeat this training many times in the coming days.

Several days passed before the men were introduced to another specialty of Sergeant Watson's training tactics. About ten miles out from the fort, the men were instructed to halt and dismount. The sergeant told the eighteen men to split into groups of three. As the six groups formed in the middle of the prairie, he motioned for Corporal Rolling to approach the groups. "Now the corporal here is gonna take two out of the three horses in each of your groups. You pick which two he's gonna take. If you don't, he'll pick 'em for you. Oh, and take your canteen off your mount."

The men followed the instructions and began getting their canteens while discussing which mount would stay with each group.

Dwight, Sam, and Adolph immediately knew to keep Dwight's Spirit. Sam and Adolph handed the bridles to the corporal as he passed their group.

"Are you three sure of that? It's a long way back to the fort for three of you with only one horse."

The dragoons in the other groups looked at each other. There were debates as to which horse could carry three men until the sergeant finally stopped them. "You all are fools. For Christ's sake. Listen to you. There ain't any way a mount is gonna carry three of you. Figure out a way to get the three of you and the mount back without endin' up dead. That way, I don't got to tell the colonel how dumb you was." He watched while the groups decided which horse would stay. He instructed Rolling to gather up the remaining horses.

Watson then mounted his horse and yelled, "Two out of three men empty your canteen now in front of me so I can see the last drops hitting the ground!"

Adolph and Sam emptied theirs and watched as the rest of the groups followed.

"Now, the dragoon holding the full canteen, make sure that your mount has the water he needs. He will be the one gettin' you back." He turned his mount in the direction of the fort and took off at a gallop without uttering another word.

Corporal Rolling quickly followed him, and the two men rode off with six horses following each of them. The dragoons stood still in disbelief as Watson and Rolling disappeared over the horizon with their extra horses.

The men quickly organized themselves and devised timetables as to how long two men would ride while the third walked, and at what time the horse would be left to walk alone without any riders. The majority of the water in each group's one canteen was primarily saved for the horse. The men made it back to the fort before sunset. More training in "Watson's methods," as the men began to call them, continued for another month until the last week in August.

On August 23rd, Sergeant Watson instructed Corporal Rolling to have the men report to main stores to help load their travel rations into two wagons that would accompany them out West. They spent several hours loading food stores and other supplies for their journey to the New Mexico Territory.

The three newest dragoons learned that Galisteo, New Mexico Territory, was their destination. None of them except Sergeant Watson and Corporal Rolling knew that it would take them approximately two months to arrive there.

They had just finished loading the second covered wagon when the sergeant jumped up on the seat and addressed them. "I'm in need of two teamsters for the wagons. Anybody got teamster experience drivin' oxen? If no one volunteers, I pick 'im." He waited a few moments as the dragoons looked at each other, wondering who would be the volunteers.

"I drive. Not a teamster, but drive many wagons on farm with oxen."

"Good. Starke, ain't it?"

"Yah, Adolph Starke."

"You tie up your saddled mount to the back of the wagon."

Adolph nodded as the sergeant finished his instructions. "I still need a second teamster. Any volunteer?" He waited for several uncomfortable moments for the remaining dragoons to volunteer. Finally, a man named Powel raised his hand. "Good." He pointed to Powel and gave him the same instructions. "We leave at sunrise. Eat on the trail. No time for breakfast. Get used to it. We eat one meal a day. We cover more miles that way. We will stop every four hours to water the horses and oxen. Starke, you keep an eye on the water. There are four barrels in your wagon. When two get empty, you tell me. Pick two men to help you fill 'em when we stop for water. You understand?"

"Yah, Sergeant. I pick Sample and Stevens."

"Powel, your job is to make camp. Pick two dragoons to get firewood while you hand out rations." He looked out at all the men listening to his instructions to Powel. He looked around at the eighteen new men. He waited for any questions. There were none. "Be mounted by sunrise. Starke and Powel, the stable sergeant will get the wagons hitched to the oxen. That's all."

The dragoons broke up and returned to the barracks. Very little conversation took place as each man thought about what they would encounter on their trip to Galisteo. Adolph, Sam, and Dwight talked a little about the trip as they sat down for their last supper at Fort Leavenworth.

"Starke, your ass is going to be sore sitting and bouncing around on that pine wagon seat for a few days. What made you volunteer for the duty?" Sam asked.

"Get sore ass in saddle too. I safe in wagon. Have water. Nobody leave me, yah?"

"Yeah, I guess they'll be watching the water supply."

"You okay with helping me?" He looked at both men.

They both smiled and nodded.

The next morning, the men were up, dressed, had saddled their mounts, and were waiting at the stable for Sergeant Watson and Corporal Rolling. The two wagons had been hitched up to four oxen each, and Starke and Powel had taken their teamster positions. Stable Sergeant Delaney walked among the dragoons, occasionally checking horseshoes and glancing over the men as they stood next to their mounts. He walked over to the oxen and double-checked the yolks around each animal. "Watch these and make sure you don't tighten any of them. They're set for each animal. Make sure you keep 'em that way."

Starke and Powel answered that they understood.

Delaney turned as he heard Watson and Rolling talking behind him. He extended his hand as the two men approached, and both men shook hands with Delaney.

"We'll see you in the late fall, Jeremiah. Rolling and me will be back for more recruits."

"Hank, keep safe. I'll be looking for you come Christmastime. Remember, you gotta bring back my oxen."

Sergeant Watson looked to Corporal Rolling and nodded.

The corporal yelled out, "Mount up, dragoons! Teamsters at the ready!"

Watson trotted over to the two wagons, looked them over, and nodded to the two teamsters. He then turned his mount around and trotted around the sixteen mounted men for one last look. He turned to Corporal Rolling and nodded again as he pulled up alongside the corporal.

Rolling yelled out, "Forward ho! At a walk! Column of twos!"

Sergeant Watson and Corporal Rolling led the column and the two wagons slowly out of Fort Leavenworth as the sun's rays began to spread over the prairie. Starke and Powel quickly realized that they would be eating dust for the next few days as it began to rise from the column. Each man had donned a handkerchief over his nose and mouth before the first mile had been covered.

The men headed west from Fort Leavenworth. A day's ride from the fort, they reached a wooded area.

Sergeant Watson yelled back so the few in front could hear, "We keep on the Leavenworth branch of the Santa Fe Trail[1] till we reach the main trail, hopefully by tomorrow. This will be our first camp. It will be more than eight hundred miles before we get to Galisteo. Pass the word."

Before the sun set, the men had cooked bacon and made corn flour biscuits flavored with bacon drippings. The coffee was boiled and served as the men relaxed and talked about the first day on the trail. The conversation was brief, as the long day had tired them all.

Guard watch was set to change every two hours. Dwight drew that

---

[1] **Santa Fe Trail** was an old passage or trail used extensively by traders from Missouri who took manufactured goods to Santa Fe to exchange for furs and valuables. Mexican traders likewise had caravans going to Missouri. There were several U.S. Army forts established along the way for protection from Indians.

duty from 10:00 p.m. until midnight. He didn't mind despite being tired. It was a chance for him to enjoy two hours of peace and quiet. He looked at the open sky with thousands of stars glittering from the slim light of the first quarter moon that had risen from the horizon. Occasional howls from a coyote or a snort from one of the mounts were the only noises the sentry could hear. He felt good about coming out to the frontier.

Several days later, the southwestward-bound dragoons sighted a wagon train ahead. Sergeant Watson passed the word that the column would follow the wagon train and camp next to it. He wanted the dragoons to understand that the wagon train members needed to know that the United States Dragoons were there for their protection. He emphasized that each man must be on his best behavior around the mixed company in the train's camp. He was sure that the wagon master would invite them to an evening of conversation and possibly some musical entertainment.

As the day went on, the column eventually gained on the thirty-three covered wagons. Sergeant Watson sent Corporal Rolling to find the wagon master and inform him that the dragoons were at his service if he needed it, and that they would be camping next to him for the night. As expected, the wagon master extended an invitation to the dragoons to visit the camp in the evening. As word spread that they would have a chance to mingle with the pioneers, excitement spread through the ranks. It had been months since their last chance to be with mixed civilian company.

The dragoons quickly set up camp and ate their evening meal. They waited for Sergeant Watson to finish. He seemed to be enjoying taking his time. He kept up a conversation with Corporal Rolling that lasted too long for the impatient dragoons.

The conversation finally came to an end. "Well, Rolling, I guess we should be gettin' over to meet with the wagon master. What was his name again?"

"His name is Sherwood."

"Then gather up the dragoons. Tell the men I won't stand for no trouble, and remind 'em, we are the U.S. Dragoons."

"Yes, Sergeant, I'll tell 'em again."

"Who'd you post for sentry duty?"

"Starke volunteered."

"Have somebody relieve him at nine o'clock."

They entered the wagon train circle through the area where the oxen and horses had been gathered. Several men were stationed to watch the animals, and they nodded to the dragoons as they walked past.

"This Sherwood is a good wagon master, keepin' his animals inside the circle. I guess he's learned something about Indians stealin' animals," Watson said to Rolling.

A few fiddles and banjos were tuning up near a large campfire as members of the wagon train began to gather, two and three at a time.

Rolling pointed out the wagon master to Watson as they approached the campfire. Watson extended his hand as he reached him and said, "Wagon Master Sherwood, Sergeant Hank Watson, United States Dragoons. Thanks for the invite. My men and me appreciate the hospitality."

"Good evening, Sergeant. Wilson Sherwood, out of Saint Joe. It's our honor to have you with us. It also makes me feel a little better knowing the government is out here protecting us from the savages."

Watson smiled and looked at Rolling. "We're here to serve, Mr. Sherwood. The local tribes in this part of the trail are friendly. You won't find any savages attackin' your wagons."

"Well, you never know. I don't trust any of them. Glad you and your men are here. How long will you be traveling with us?"

"Not long. Early in the morning we will leave ahead of you. Heading for the Cimarron Route."

"We are traveling the Mountain Route. Very few of these people or their animals could ever make it over the Cimarron. Never chance it. Too dry and too many savages."

Watson ignored Sherwood's second savage reference. He knew he couldn't change the man's opinion.

The fiddlers and banjo players struck up the tune "Camptown Races," and some of them began singing. The dragoons watched and enjoyed listening to the music. A few clapped their hands to the beat of the tune. More people gathered and a few dared to be the first to dance. Quickly the mood relaxed as more danced or sang. A few of the young women approached the men in blue.

One pretty one picked Dwight, who was singing the lyrics to the song he had first heard in Norwich before he left.

Dwight hesitated at first and glanced over to Sergeant Watson. The sergeant nodded and called out while he motioned for the tall, handsome man to dance, "Oblige the lass. I hope you dance good."

That was all Dwight needed, and he held the petite woman as he began dancing to the melody. They looked good together, despite the differences in height. Dwight towered over her by more than a foot. It didn't seem to matter as the young woman kept in step and enjoyed the attention, the song, and the man she was dancing with. More joined in as Dwight and his dance partner circled the campfire again. When the song ended, everyone clapped.

The music changed to a waltz. More men were asked to dance by the young ladies who had been given permission by their parents.

Dwight realized that he had not introduced himself. "I must apologize. I have not introduced myself properly. My name is Aaron Dwight Stevens."

The girl didn't answer him immediately. She concentrated on making sure the women who were not dancing had a good view of her as she danced past them. Dwight waited and suspected that she was enjoying having people watch her.

"I didn't catch your name, miss?"

"Well, Mr. Stevens, I haven't given it. You shouldn't have to apologize for not introducing yourself. Remember, I picked you to dance with." As she finished, she looked straight at him for the first time. Her bright green eyes reflected the bright light of the campfire.

"And your name is Miss…"

"It's Faith, Mr. Stevens. Faith Johnston."

"Well, Miss Johnston, I am very pleased to meet you."

"The pleasure has been mine, sir. You are a very good dancer."

"Taught by my older sister, Lydia. Fine singer and dancer she is."

He made a mental note to write her at the first opportunity.

The waltz ended and another song was struck up. It was a polka, and Dwight signaled that he would wait it out. Miss Johnston smiled and took him by the hand through the outer circle of spectators to a table of refreshments. Cool water, cider, some home-baked sweetbreads and pie were available. An elderly lady waited on them.

"Would you like a drink, Miss Johnston?" he asked.

"I'd like a cider, Mr. Stevens."

"Two ciders, please…and thank you."

The two walked away from the table sipping cider out of tin cups.

"May I ask where you have come from, Miss Johnston?"

"My family is originally from Philadelphia. We lived in St. Joseph while we were waiting for Mr. Sherwood to return from California. My father is a banker, and he financed this journey."

Dwight smiled at her answer.

"And you, Mr. Stevens?"

"Please, call me Dwight."

"I like Aaron better. I will call you Aaron."

Dwight snickered. He deduced that she was a pretty young lady who apparently had been accustomed to having her own way most of her life. "I lived in Norwich, Connecticut, most of my life."

"Never heard of it. Is it anywhere close to New York City?"

He smiled and nodded, but refused to carry the conversation any further.

"How long have you been a soldier, Aaron?"

"My first hitch was for eighteen months. I've been in the dragoons for five months now."

She looked confused as he finished. "How old are you?"

"I'm nineteen."

"I thought you were older than that when I picked you out from among the other soldiers."

"Miss Johnston, we are dragoons."

"Whatever you are, you are just a boy. I'm older than you. How could you be in the army for over two years? You aren't old enough."

"Well, Miss…" He paused to keep gentlemanly. "I enlisted in the First Massachusetts when I was sixteen. I lied about my age. I spent most of my eighteen months in Mexico. I spent some time in Norwich and then I just joined up for the dragoons in New York City in April."

"Mr. Aaron, or Dwight, or whatever you said, your story seems conflicting to me."

Dwight finished his cider and put the tin cup back on the refreshment table. He looked the petite but very high-strung young lady in the face and tipped his cap, then said, "Thank you for the dance and conversation, Miss Johnston. Have a safe trip to California." He bowed and smiled, then departed and disappeared into the crowd before the woman could say another word.

While Dwight made his way back to the camp, he passed Adolph, who had just been relieved from guard duty.

"You leave now?"

"Yes. I danced a few but I'm turning in." Dwight thought about Miss Johnston. He laughed to himself when he thought about the poor man that would ask her hand in marriage someday. He was almost convinced in his mind, even after his short time with the woman, that the poor soul would regret it until he took his last breath.

Dwight settled in for the night. He strained to read the print of *The Age of Reason* from the dim campfire light, but then put the pamphlet down as he caught himself dozing. He laid back and put his hands under the back of his neck. He stared out, looking at the stars and listening to the faint music coming from the wagon train. His mind cleared of all thoughts as he fell off to sleep.

Chapter Eleven

The Cimarron Cutoff

The dragoons mounted before the sun had cleared the horizon.

A few men kidded Dwight as to why he had left the cute little woman. Some asked why she returned without him and danced with several more of them. He only remarked that she was a charming young woman, but he was too tired to try to handle a woman as spirited as she was.

A few men laughed. One dragoon stated that she was a sassy one at that. He understood why Dwight had left early. He commented that he felt sorry for the man that wed and bedded her. More laughter erupted as the men waited to move out.

Sergeant Murphy motioned, and Corporal Rolling gave the call to move out.

Dwight saw some activity in the wagon encirclement as teams were being hooked up to the wagons and people moved about. As the dragoons passed them, several waved to the men in blue. A few dogs barked and ran alongside the two dragoon supply wagons for a few hundred yards, until they lost interest and returned to the wagon train. He also looked to see if Miss Johnston was watching the column departing. He laughed to himself that she would most likely be the last to rise, and that she would probably hold up the wagon train if she had her way. The dragoons would have over an hour's head start on the slow-moving wagon train.

Sergeant Watson and Corporal Rolling were overheard in conversation, hoping that Wagon Master Sherwood did not encounter any scouting or hunting parties of the Kiowa. The Kiowa tribes in the area were peaceful, and both men hoped that Sherwood wouldn't start any trouble.

On the twentieth day, in the late afternoon, Sergeant Watson yelled back that the column was approaching Pawnee Rock.[1] "Pass the word back! We camp at the rock tonight! We will be about one third of the way to Galisteo! Three hundred miles in twenty days ain't bad time with oxen!"

---

[1] **Pawnee Rock** are the beautiful sandstone rocks, and a famous landmark, along the old Santa Fe Trail in Kansas. They marked the approximate halfway point of the trail and were used by local Indians as a vantage point to locate buffalo or wagon trains.

The Kansas prairie hid the rock until the men saw it rise ever so slowly on the horizon. The rock grew higher and longer as the column approached from the east.

Watson yelled back again, "And stay out of the settlement on the other side. We ain't got no need to be buyin' any of the cheap goods they sell. Sherwood and his wagon train can spend their money on 'em. You keep your eyes and ears open while we camp here. The Pawnee don't like us much."

It wasn't until after the supper meal that the dragoons learned that Pawnee Rock was one of the most famous landmarks on the trail. The rock was famous for sheltering Indians who attacked travelers who stopped for supplies, as well as for bloody battles when different tribes encountered each other while hunting.

Rolling also spread the word about the rumors that early Spanish travelers had buried their gold and silver near the rock so the Pawnee raiders would not take it from them.

Sergeant Watson addressed the dragoons. "Stay away from the rock. We don't want a scouting party to pick one of you off if you go out looking and diggin' for buried treasure that ain't there. The corporal and me seen some scouting parties watchin' us for the better part of the day."

That statement startled everyone who heard it. The word passed quickly to those further back. Dwight was especially concerned when the corporal informed him that he had the midnight to 2:00 a.m. sentry duty. His stomach turned when he heard that Sam Sample would be with him. This was the first time in twenty days that the sergeant had instructed that a double sentry be posted.

Pawnee Rock
Public Domain photo

When Dwight and Sam relieved the midnight sentries, a half-moon illuminated the prairie, which eased the two men. Occasionally, a cloud would obstruct the moonlight for several minutes at a time, which only heightened their state of alertness. Sometimes their mind and eyes would play tricks on them. They were surprised when Corporal Rolling appeared with their relief.

"See anythin', Stevens?"

"No, Corporal, but my eyes seemed to play tricks on me sometimes."

"I know they can fool you. Your best bet is to keep your eyes moving from side to side. You ketch movement from the sides of your eyes where there ain't no straining. You can see the difference that way. Pawnee use it to their advantage. I've been watching for a spell myself. They ain't too interested in us." Rolling looked out over the prairie and then back toward the rock. "You know, us talking like this reminds me of how Pawnee Rock got its name. Back in the '20s, a snot-nosed kid named Kit Carson[1] was keepin' watch just like you two. His eyes played tricks with him too. He shot his damned mule, thinkin' it was a Pawnee. Been

---

[1] **Kit Carson** enjoyed a long, famous, and adventurous life in the American Southwest. He was a trapper, guide, military scout, Indian agent, soldier, rancher, and lawman, and is still a well-known legend of the West.

named Pawnee Rock ever since." He laughed a little. "Years later, Carson was a trapper and scout for John Freemont[1]. Carson became kinda famous back East in the penny papers. Don't know where he is now or what became of him."

"I remember Kit Carson. I read about him in those penny papers when I was home in Norwich," Dwight said. He returned to the encampment very relieved that the corporal was on sentry duty, but still he did not sleep soundly for the remainder of the night.

Kit Carson
Public Domain photo

At first light, the dragoons were underway. As Pawnee Rock slowly disappeared into the eastern horizon, Dwight wondered where a Pawnee

---

[1] **John Frémont** (1813–1890) was an American military officer, explorer, and the first candidate of the anti-slavery Republican Party for the office of president of the United States. In the Civil War, he had command of the armies in the Western Theater, but made questionable decisions (such as trying to abolish slavery without consulting Washington) and was relieved of his command.

scouting party would show up again. He found out about an hour along the trail. The scouting party was watching the dragoons just out of their sight.

During the ride, Corporal Rolling was overheard talking to Sergeant Watson. "Keep spottin' the same scout southwest of us. He's been shadowing us for a while."

"I've been watching. There could be two. One reportin' and one watchin'. They won't be bothering us. We got too much firepower for a day attack. Pass the word that we keep on the trail for another mile, then we head south to the Arkansas River to take on water before noon."

Dwight wondered whether the river would afford some defensive cover for the dragoons and their animals and wagons.

Several days later, the column was within a day's ride of the Cimarron Cutoff when word was passed up from the rear of the column that a stagecoach was quickly approaching.

Sergeant Watson ordered the column off the trail to let the stagecoach pass. The six-horse team galloped effortlessly by, and the dragoons noticed that, oddly, no protection had been assigned to the coach except a lone rifleman sitting outside next to the teamster. Six men inside the coach waved and hollered as they passed.

"Damn fools. Probably going out to dig for gold," Corporal Rolling remarked.

"I wish I had the time or money to try it. Thought about it in 'forty-nine when my hitch was coming up said Watson.

"Sergeant, you ain't going to be nothin' more than a military man until the day you die. I can't see you as a gold digger," Rolling said and laughed.

"Yeah, I guess you're right. I'm military through 'n through and that's the truth, ain't it? But right now I worry that our Pawnee scouts are still out there shadowing us." He turned and looked back at the column before he spoke. "Rolling, take Stevens and"—he looked over the dragoons—"Sample with you, and ride with the coach. I got a feeling those scouts might be interested in it once it is out of the range of our presence. Stay at the stagecoach stop at Cimarron for the night. I figure we'll catch up to you by mid-morning tomorrow."

"Stevens, Sample, follow me." Rolling waited as the two dragoons broke from the column. "At a gallop, ho!"

Dwight and Sam followed the corporal for approximately a mile before they saw the stagecoach's dust trail. Several minutes later they pulled up on each side of the coach as the teamster slowed it and then stopped.

"What brings the U.S. Dragoons, Corporal?" the teamster asked.

"Orders, sir. We are watching some Pawnee scouts trackin' us. My sergeant figures they might want to cause you some harm before you reach the stagecoach stop at Cimarron Cutoff."

"Thank you, Corporal, but they haven't been bothering us for a spell now."

"Orders, sir. We'll be with y'all until you reach the stop and exchange teams."

"Suit yourself, Corporal. Glad to have you around."

A few voices were heard from the passengers, who complained that they wanted to get going again. The teamster rolled his eyes as he snapped the reins to get the stagecoach moving. Before long the coach and dragoons were at a gallop again, heading toward the Cimarron Cutoff. Sam and Dwight flanked the coach as the corporal led the way.

Hours later the coach pulled into the Cimarron Cutoff stagecoach stop as dusk was quickly approaching. The teamster climbed off the stagecoach and thanked the dragoons for the escort. "We got some open space in the hayloft in the stable out back. See Wilson, the colored man. Tell him you're guests of the coach company. We got a hot meal for you once you stable your horses. It ain't that good, but it's hot."

"Mighty obliged, sir. My men and I can sure use a hot meal. It's been a spell."

Dwight and Sam looked forward to a little relaxation while they waited for the column to catch up with them in the morning.

Corporal Rolling motioned for the two dragoons to follow him to the stable. Within minutes they found Wilson, who was tending to the tired horses that had just pulled the stagecoach. "Wilson, I'm Corporal Rolling. My men and me will be sleeping in the hayloft. We'll be stablin' our mounts here. Any particular stable you want us to put them in?"

The elderly Negro only pointed to a large stall at the end of the stable.

Dwight smiled at the man as he passed with his mount.

Wilson never made eye contact with any of the dragoons.

"He ain't much of a talker," Sample remarked.

"No, I guess he doesn't have much to say," Dwight said.

The men unsaddled their mounts and began to brush them down when Wilson spoke up.

"Y'all be doin' no brushin'. Wilson be doin' that for ya."

"Thanks, Wilson," Rolling said as he flipped him a half-dime coin. "That's for the three mounts."

"There ain't no need for you payin' me. I am a free man and get paid by the company."

"Consider it a tip for your troubles, Wilson, from the dragoons."

The man bowed as he began to brush Rolling's mount.

The three dragoons entered the stagecoach house. A thick beef stew with hard bread was the meal for the six male passengers, teamster, coach guard, three dragoons, and several stage house workers. The conversations the men had at supper ranged from the local Indians, who had been mostly peaceful, to the dragoon's concern for the stage house being raided by renegade Pawnee, to gold in California, to the unrest that was developing in Missouri and Kansas. There were no arguments, only the sharing of information among the men.

Dwight never spoke and let Corporal Rolling represent the dragoons. He only talked about matters pertaining to military policy. Dwight realized that Rolling had experience with staying neutral on all of the issues when some of the men wanted to delve deeper.

The three dragoons returned to the stable for the evening.

Wilson had finished his chores and was eating alone at a small table. The Negro stopped eating and stood when the dragoons entered.

Corporal Rolling addressed him. "Wilson, we will bed in the loft and be no bother to you."

Wilson remained stoic with his head bowed.

Rolling decided to leave the man to his privacy.

To his surprise, Wilson commented, "There's no bother, sir. At ya service if ya be inclined to be needin' somethin'."

"Thank you, but we have all we need. Be out and on the trail by sun up," Rolling said.

Dwight watched the man sit back at his table and finish the meal. He noticed that Wilson was eating the same meal they had eaten at the stage house table. "You always eat alone, Wilson?" he inquired.

Wilson stood again as he was addressed. "Yes, sir. I eat alone. I stay out here. Not be proper. Don't want to upset none of the white folks."

"You should have come in and ate with us." Dwight was about to explain to Wilson that he would have liked to talk to the freeman and share a meal at the table, when Rolling interrupted him.

"Private Stevens, I think Wilson needs to finish his meal in peace. We need to turn in now. We leave early in the morning."

Dwight looked at Rolling and nodded. "Yes, Corporal." He turned to Wilson. "Good night, Wilson."

"Sir," was the only response the man gave.

The next morning the dragoons departed and headed out slowly, waiting for the main column to catch up.

During the slow walk, Dwight brought up Wilson. "Corporal Rolling, is Wilson really a free man?"

"Hell, Stevens, I don't know. He says he is, and probably he is. He just knows his place."

"Knows his place?"

"Stevens, this is Kansas. Full of settlers passing through and some stayin'. They come from all over. From slave states and free states. Wilson wants to survive without drawin' attention."

"Attention from whom, Corporal?"

"Christ, Stevens, you're from the North somewhere, ain't you?"

"Connecticut, Corporal."

"I'm from Maryland. We got free Negros and slaves as well. I learned to leave the free ones alone. You leave the slave owners alone and you'll be better off. Some of them will kill you if you mess with their property."

"Humans held as property is hard for me to go along with, Corporal."

"Stevens, I'm telling you only once. You're in the dragoons. Dragoons protect free- and slave-thinkers alike. Dragoons have pro-slavery men in the ranks as well as anti-slavery. Many of our officers are from the South as well, so you figure it out. Remember that." Corporal Rolling realized the conversation was becoming heated. He felt it as he looked at Stevens, who glared at him while he talked. He took a deep breath and calmed his tone.

"Stevens, something else you need to remember. Slavery in this country is legal and protected by the Constitution, whether you like it or not."

Dwight began to say something, but Rolling put up his hand. "I ain't finished. Listen! As dragoons, we are sworn to protect and uphold the Constitution. You remember that from when you took your oath?"

Dwight nodded as he maintained control and answered slowly, "Corporal Rolling, I do remember, but I didn't know at the time that I was swearing to uphold slavery."

Rolling didn't say anything for a few moments. Finally he looked at Dwight with a more serious look. "Well, between you and me, you're probably right, and we ain't heard the last about the slavery question. But where we are going, slavery ain't the issue. Indians are."

Sam Sample had been listening to the conversation, and he spoke up in an effort to change it. "Corporal, you think the scouting party will be bothering the stage house?"

"No, they are looking for easy prey. The few hands they got at the coach stop have enough weapons to keep 'em away."

Rolling looked over Dwight's shoulder and noticed dust rising in the east. "The sergeant made good time, dragoons. At a gallop, ho!"

That evening Sam and Dwight talked about Wilson again.

Sam knew he would never be able to convince Dwight that the Negros, free or slave, were none of their business. "Dwight, you can't carry on about folks like Wilson. The corporal was right, telling you that the army is out here to protect everyone from hostile Indians no matter where they come from."

"Are they protecting the Negros?" Dwight said.

"I guess we are. Wilson was protected livin' at the stage house."

"He's living in the stable, Sam."

"Yeah, the stable, but nobody is harming him."

"Why in God's name would anyone harm Wilson?" Dwight paused for a while, then with concern in his voice, he quietly spoke, "He doesn't even eat with the whites, Sam."

"No, he don't. Probably his choice. Ain't any white Southerner who pays good money to ride the stage to Santa Fe goin' to eat with him. Wilson's smart. He stays out of the way and nobody bothers him as long as he does his work and knows his place."

"It's not right for anyone to live that way."

"Maybe in your part of the country, Dwight, but out here it's the way of life. Let it go before you piss off some folks that don't think like you. They get pretty hostile when you start talking about their property rights. Remember, many Negros out here are escaped slaves that say they are free. They don't want any attention brought to 'em."

"Kansas is going to have to deal with people who think like me."

"Yeah, and they also going to have to deal with the types of people I just talked to you about. I figure we are going to be busy keepin' them from harmin' each other over it. You need to keep your thoughts to yourself."

Dwight did not like the message his close friend had given him.

Adolph had listened in on the conversation and had remained quiet until Sam Sample had finished. "Sam makes good sense. Not our business."

Dwight looked at Adolph, annoyed.

"Dwight, I no take sides. Not my business. You learn quick. Not your business, like Sam say."

Dwight did not answer as he walked away in an effort to control the rage he had started to feel inside. He cooled down and stood a while to watch the moonrise and the sky reveal its celestial show of endless stars. It calmed him, and he realized that he needed to appreciate what his friends were trying to say even if he couldn't have disagreed with them more. Insisting that "it was not their business" seemed to Dwight like nothing but passing the evil buck of slavery.

"Well, whose business is it?" he muttered to himself. He

remembered his church preacher saying, *It was easy for evil to rise up when good people did nothing to stop it.*

Two days later they reached the Cimarron Cutoff and camped for the night. The Cimarron Cutoff crossed the Arkansas River and became the direct path across the plains, used almost exclusively by the army to shorten the distance to Santa Fe by fifty miles. The trail would take them southwest across Kansas, through the corner of southeastern Colorado, and into the northeast corner of the Oklahoma panhandle. Once across the Cimarron River, the trail angled in a southwesterly direction, across desolate and unforgiving territory.

In the encampment that night, Sergeant Watson gathered the men and said he had a lot to tell them and they had a lot to listen to. He began by explaining that the trail would pass through the territories of the Kiowa, Ute, Navajo, Comanche, and Jicarilla Apache tribes. He expected every dragoon to be alert and prepared if any circumstance arose from unfriendly Indians. He also cautioned the dragoons that some tribes might show up as the column passed, out of mere curiosity. In some cases, rogue scouts could try to intimidate them. He also explained that the dragoons would not draw any of their weapons unless ordered to do so by him or Corporal Rolling. There would be no exceptions.

"There could be some trouble with the Comanche. We'll be crossin' the Comancheria first. That's what they call their territory. Sometimes they bother you, sometimes they don't. In the weapons wagon we got some trading goods if they are interested." The sergeant walked among the dragoons while chewing his cigar stub. He tried to light it, but, realizing it was too short, discarded it and continued talking. "The government has a contract with a company to run mail between Santa Fe and Missouri. We ain't seen any of 'em galloping through, but don't be shooting any of them, thinkin' they're Indians tryin' to attack us." He turned to Rolling and asked, "What's the name of the company hired to run the mail?"

"Waldo, Hall, and Company, Sergeant."

"You're going to experience some heat in the next few weeks. Keep your wits about you. Watch your animals. They drink before you, remember that. The gnats and black flies will eat you alive at night. Whiskey heals some of the bites, but I know no one's got any." He smiled. "For the next fifty or so miles, the weather is day to day. Clear and hot mostly, but if you see the clouds coming from the west, be prepared. It could be raining, hailin', or both sometimes. When you see and then feel it, watch the sky and listen. Sometimes it might be a twister. The Spanish call 'em tornados, but down here we called them twisters. The noise sounds like nothing you've heard before. I've seen four or so. There is no place to hide, so you got to hope you can figure out which way it is going. If it gets you…" He paused and looked around, then continued, "You won't live to tell about it."

He pulled out a fresh cigar, bit the end off, spit it out, and lit it. The glow grew brighter as he puffed on it. "The dust is constant. More than what you've seen so far. There's been sickness reported, the kind you don't see or hear about in the east. Malaria, dysentery, and the worst, cholera, is here. I had all three. You feel sick, tell somebody. There ain't too much we can do for you except keep you away from the rest." He continued to puff on the cigar when he paused, then continued, "The Indians that do want to trade, or just talk 'cause they are curious, sometimes have women with 'em. Don't even look at 'em. Most ain't much to look at, but there could be a good-looker once in a while. I've seen some that I could think about beddin'. Don't let your eyes tell your lust. The braves don't like the idea of any white man even looking at a squaw. You can take out your needs on some of the Mexican women that will be around at Galisteo when we get there." He looked at Corporal Rolling. "I miss anythin'?"

"Yes, Sergeant. Bugs."

"Oh yeah, bugs. We got ants that bite like hell. Watch where you bed down. Dig down a little with your sabers to make sure you ain't sleeping with any. Grasshoppers can make you itch. The bigger ones, the locusts, can blacken the sun when they move. Lots of beetles and rattlesnakes too. Rattlesnakes can kill you. You leave them alone, and they will do the same to you. Scorpions are the ones to watch for. The right sting can cause real sickness. You wear boots. Stomp on them. Don't handle them. The damn little black flies are always with you. Get used to 'em."

He looked over the dragoons, who remained still while listening about the insects. He puffed more on his cigar and commented, "Flies don't like cigar smoke." He walked around to the back of the assembly. Their heads followed him. "Black Widow spiders. The female be the one to watch. They are the bigger of the two. Their bite can sicken a man real bad. Sometimes it can kill. Stomp on 'em. Again, watch where you lay or sit."

He had reached one of the wagons and rested his free hand on it as he continued to smoke. He looked at the wagon, and then back at the dragoons, and started to talk a little faster. "We're gonna change things a bit, now that we are taking the Cimarron Trail. We stop midmornings to rest and water the animals while we eat the noon meal and rest some more. Teamsters, check the wagons. If they need fixing, you fix 'em then. We travel late until we can't see very well. We stop, build fires, and then sleep. Use the buffalo chips. They burn good. Not much firewood out here especially as we head further down the trail. Ain't much more to be talking about. A lot of nothing between here and Galisteo. Get some sleep."

Another week passed. Uneventful as it was, the men did notice that the nights were becoming colder as September of 1851 ended. After the first week of October had passed, the men had still not reached Galisteo. October 8th was the first day the column saw civilization.

Sergeant Watson pointed to Corporal Rolling as dust could be seen approaching them from the southwest. "Riders coming, pass the word."

Rolling broke rank and informed those down the line until he reached the wagons, then he turned his mount and galloped back to the head. "What are your orders, Sergeant?"

"We wait to see who they are."

The men watched as the figures became identifiable to Watson, who was watching intensely. "They are dragoons. Stand down and relax, men."

They all observed the six dragoons approaching. A lieutenant headed the patrol. He pulled up to Sergeant Watson, who saluted and waited for the officer to complete the military courtesy.

The officer spoke. "Sergeant. Preparing to engage?"

"Yes, sir, until I identified you as dragoons."

"Heading for Fort Union?"

"Fort Union, sir? Never heard of it."

"Well, you will soon. You'll come to it about five miles down the trail. It's still under construction. We've been out here for four months building it."

Both men exchanged quick salutes and the six dragoons galloped away.

They reached Fort Union in the late afternoon. The settlement had several stone barracks in various stages of construction and a completed stable and storehouse. Oxen-drawn wagons filled with rock and stone were being unloaded at various places around the site as dragoons who were stripped to their waists worked continuously.

Watson halted the column near the fort's tented headquarters. He found Lieutenant Colonel Sumner's aide, and reported in.

Later that evening, Watson was summoned to Sumner's tent to exchange military pleasantries. They talked of the battles of Cerro Gordo and Molino Del Ray, where Watson had served under Sumner during the war. Watson was also informed that his former commander had been appointed to military governor of the New Mexico Territory and that the fort was being built because of the continued problems with Indians in the Southwest.

Lieutenant Colonel Sumner[1] explained that the sporadic raiding of New Mexican settlements and their herds characterized the stormy coexistence between the Mexicans and Indians. When New Mexico became an American territory, it had swelled to alarming proportions. Attacks had increased on the wagon trains along the Santa Fe Trail because the Southern Plains tribes had grown increasingly resentful. Sumner reminded Watson of the White Massacre[2] of 1849, and the Wagon Mound Massacre of 1850[3] that the army had been criticized for not preventing. He underscored the need for some sort of military presence from his new base of operations and informed Watson that his men at Fort Union had spent much of the year so far engaged in active and aggressive campaigning against the Comanche, Jicarilla Apache, Navajo, and Ute tribes.

The column of dragoons left at first light, disappointed that there were no places to purchase a drink, get a hot meal, or sleep in a barracks bed. The conditions at Fort Union were no different from what they had endured for the past seven weeks out on the trail. One sigh of relief came when Sergeant Watson yelled back as they left Fort Union, "Pass the word, Santa Fe is only a hundred-fifty miles due west. When we reach there, we cut south to Cantonment[4] Galisteo."

The word was passed down to all the dragoons. Dwight did the math and realized they'd be at Galisteo in less than ten days. The mundane journey was coming to an end, and more than a little excitement stirred in the ranks. Conversations at the noon stop, and then again at the night encampment, concentrated on several of their basic needs, namely,

---

[1] **Lieutenant Colonel Edwin V. Sumner** established the first Fort Union on the Santa Fe Trail. He was known as "Bull" because of his loud and resonant voice. He was the senior officer chosen to accompany newly elected President Lincoln from Springfield, Illinois, to Washington, D.C., in March 1861.

[2] **White Massacre of 1849** – James White, a merchant traveling often between Independence and Santa Fe, decided to leave a wagon train and go on ahead with his wife, baby daughter, a Negro servant, and several others, after "the dangerous part of the trip was over." They were attacked by Jicarilla and Ute Indians. All were killed but Mrs. White, the baby, and the servant, who all went missing. Mrs. White was later found dead, but the baby and the servant were never found.

[3] **Wagon Mound Massacre** – In early May 1850, near the town of Wagon Mound, New Mexico, a band of Jicarilla and Ute Indians attacked a mail party of 10 men and killed them all. The massacre was not discovered until another mail party heading to the east came upon the site. The second mail party quickly returned to Barclays Fort and refused to complete the 150-mile trip without a dragoon escort.

[4] **Cantonment** was generally designated as a camp or fort under construction, or as a temporary fort.

good food, good drink, friendly women, and a hot bath.

Dwight amused himself with listening to the order in which some of the dragoons ranked their priorities.

Several days passed with little or no change in the routine, until one evening a shot rang out near the supply wagons. Several horses reared and the two sentries on duty ran to the source of the pistol shot. They found Private Scruggs cursing as he kneeled and held a pistol in his hand. Within seconds, Watson, Rolling, and eight or nine dragoons had scampered over to the site where Scruggs was.

"What in Christ's name is one of my dragoons shooting at? Somebody tell me quickly!" screamed the senior NCO as he held his pistol in his left hand and saber in the other.

One of the sentries spoke. "Scruggs shot a snake under the wagon."

"Damn it. What kind of snake, Scruggs?" Watson pushed Scruggs with the pistol in his left hand. Scruggs didn't answer, but sat back on his butt and then rolled to his side, grabbing his left calf.

Watson yelled to the sentry, "Check under the wagon carefully to see if Scruggs got the snake!"

Rolling checked Scruggs's calf. "The bite looks like it came from a good-sized rattler, Sergeant."

"Shit, let me look." Watson examined the dazed Scruggs, who grimaced in pain as he looked at the snakebite.

The sentry found the snake in two pieces. Scruggs's shot had cut it in half.

Watson yelled to Rolling to get one of the sharp hunting knives that was part of the trading items they were carrying. Within a few moments, Watson had several to pick from. "Hold 'im down." He looked at Scruggs, who had become a little disoriented. "This is going to hurt a bit." He looked at the four dragoons who had a grip on Scruggs's legs and arms, then cut into the bite site, then bent over and used his mouth to suck and spit out the blood and venom. He sucked and spit continuously until he felt he had removed most of the venom. He yelled over to Rolling, "Get my haversack! Pull out the pint I have in there and bring it here!"

Rolling hurried away and returned quickly and handed it to him.

Watson pulled the cork and took a large swig. He spat out, cleared his throat, and spat again. "Waste of damn good whiskey." He took a large swig again, but this time swallowed it. "Clear a space in the wagon. Make him comfortable. I hope the venom that stayed in his body ain't enough to kill 'im. Never lost a dragoon in transit, and I ain't going to start now. Y'all watch out. The snakes are looking for warmth, now that it is gettin' colder at night." He looked at Dwight. "Stevens, you saddle Scruggs's mount in the morning. Tie it to the wagon he's in."

"Yes, Sergeant."

Watson looked at Rolling. "I got the first watch. Relieve me at midnight." He looked at all the dragoons that had assembled to watch his medical treatment. "Starke, you relieve the corporal, and you take the teamster's job again. I need you to keep an eye on Scruggs while you're drivin' tomorrow. You understand?"

"Yah, Sergeant. I drive and watch."

Private Ryan Scruggs lay motionless in the supply wagon as Sergeant Watson occasionally cooled his brow with some of the barrel water. By midnight, Scruggs had developed a high fever. He moaned and occasionally talked incoherently.

Rolling relieved Watson. "He gonna make it?" Rolling inquired.

"Don't know. He's skinny, so it wouldn't take much poison to kill 'im. Watch and come get me if he has trouble breathin'."

Rolling took the watch until 4:00 a.m. When Starke relieved him, both men watched Scruggs's breathing, which had become shallower during the early morning. "Corporal, I think we should get the sergeant."

Rolling nodded and left the wagon.

A few minutes later Watson arrived to assess the situation. "There ain't much we can do except watch and give 'im comfort. Rolling, stay in the wagon while Starke drives. Keep 'im comfortable."

The entire column was up and ready to mount before sunup. No one had slept well, and everyone was awake as soon as Sergeant Watson was summoned to the wagon. Watson sensed the concern among the dragoons and ordered that the men move out immediately.

They were underway less than an hour when word was passed up for Sergeant Watson to stop. He immediately galloped back to the last wagon and dismounted. The look on Starke's face and the way Rolling stood outside the wagon indicated the worst.

Rolling softly said, "He's gone, Sergeant. He took his last breath a few minutes ago."

Watson stood motionless for a few moments. "Damn. Scruggs was a good man."

A spot was picked several hundred yards from the trail, and several men assisted in burying the dragoon with military honors, as best as could be performed.

No marker was made to identify where the soldier had been buried. Watson knew that graves were often disturbed by both Indians and white men alike, looking for valuables that may have been buried with the deceased. He measured the distance from the pile of rocks to the unmarked grave and recorded it. A team of dragoons would return to exhume the body sometime in the future.

The dragoons were very somber for the next several days as they slowly moved closer to their destination. The only physical reminder of Private Ryan Scruggs's existence was his black-and-brown Morgan tied to the back of the last wagon. Scruggs's saber belt, saber, and carbine had been slung over the saddle horn, and it was a stark reminder for Sergeant Watson that he had lost his first dragoon recruit.

Chapter Twelve

Galisteo, New Mexico Territory

The final week on the trail was solemn. The excitement of the eventual arrival at Galisteo was overshadowed by the loss of Private Scruggs. The relationship between the eighteen dragoons and their two NCO instructor-guides had grown strong over the seven-hundred-mile trip to the New Mexico Territory. Losing Scruggs affected the remaining seventeen in various ways; one dragoon had known him prior to their enlistment and they had signed together. He was the most saddened by his death.

All of them had appreciated his harmonica playing. Dwight had especially enjoyed singing with him at Jefferson Barracks and occasionally on the trip when Sergeant Watson had permitted it. The sergeant speculated that Scruggs had had all the makings to be a good dragoon. Some pondered if they would end up as he had, dead at twenty, buried in an unmarked grave.

They arrived in Santa Fe on October 17, 1851. The column moved slowly through the town in the late afternoon. Few people paid attention to the mounted men and two ox-drawn wagons traveling through their town. Sergeant Watson camped the group just outside the southern limits of the settlement. The men were allowed to visit the mercantile establishments on the main street and, while the cantina was not off-limits, Watson cautioned them that drunkenness would not be tolerated.

Most of the dragoons, including Dwight, Sam, and Adolph, visited it only for one or two drinks of whiskey. Some of them found more than just whiskey. It was the first time they were exposed to tequila. Dwight knew of its potency, having experienced it while in Mexico. Corporal Rolling, however, waited only a short time to enter the cantina and clear it of the dragoons before the tequila took hold of the inexperienced drinkers.

That evening at the encampment, numerous questions were asked about Cantonment Galisteo. Watson took the time to inform them of the place they would call home until the army decided to post them somewhere else. "The army picked the cantonment location because of its water supply. The Galisteo River supplies what we need. If you follow it, it leads to the Rio Grande. Galisteo is between the Sangre de Cristo and Sandia Mountains. This protected location between the mountains was used by the Indians and Spanish for hundreds of years as a trade center." Watson looked around at the men who had gathered to listen. "Many of the townspeople are dirt poor. An outbreak of smallpox happened a few years back, but it's been quiet for a spell. The townspeople won't bother you. But the Comanche will." He lit his evening cigar. "Corporal Rolling will post three sentries tonight. We don't want any of the townspeople stealin' the supplies we got in the wagons."

Rolling called out the sentry duty for the night. Luckily, Starke and Stevens missed the first shift. Sample grumbled that he got the midnight watch. The next morning, following a half-day's ride, the column reached Cantonment Galisteo after fifty-six days of travel. It was October 18, 1851.

The small encampment nestled near the Galisteo River afforded a good defensive position with access to an unlimited water supply. The eight-foot mud-brick walls with no windows were in their final stages of construction and offered good protection from hostile Indians.

Sergeant Watson reported to the cantonment commander, Second Lieutenant John Wynn Davidson[1], that he had delivered seventeen new recruits who were fully trained and ready for duty at the commander's discretion. He sadly reported that he had lost one dragoon to a rattlesnake bite and that he had the exact burial location in the event that a detail was sent to exhume the body and re-inter it at the cantonment.

The commander looked at the sergeant and said, "Sergeant Watson, I suggest that you relay that information to Lieutenant Colonel Sumner at Fort Union during your return east. He has the resources to retrieve the dragoon's body at his disposal." He paused for a few moments, then continued, "Further, Sergeant, it might take some time for the lieutenant colonel to send a detail, seeing that he is in the process of building Fort Union."

Watson's only response was, "Yes, sir. I will relay the location to him during my return to Fort Leavenworth." He vowed to himself that he and Rolling would take care of Scruggs themselves, if they had to.

The sergeant gave the roster of dragoons to the lieutenant. He looked it over, called in his sergeant major, and handed the list to him. "Disperse the men according to the needs of each company, Sergeant Major." He turned to Watson. "Thank you, Sergeant Watson. You and

---

[1] **Lieutenant John Wynn Davidson** was born in Virginia, graduated from West Point, and fought with the dragoons in the war with Mexico. After the Battle of Cieneguilla, he was promoted to captain in command of Ft. Tejon , California. When the Civil War broke out, he refused a commission with the Confederate army. Instead he joined the Union Army of the Potomac. He reached the rank of brigadier general. After the war, he returned to the west as a colonel in the 10th Cavalry known as the "Buffalo Soldiers," where he was nicknamed "Black Jack."

your corporal can find quarters from the sergeant major here. He'll see to your needs. That will be all."

Sergeant Watson came to attention and saluted. Lieutenant Davidson returned it, and Watson left his office with the sergeant major closely behind.

Outside, the sergeant major remarked, "Not much of a personality."

"Sergeant Major, glad to see you again," Watson replied and smiled as he extended his hand.

"As far as your dragoon goes, I'll make sure Colonel Fauntleroy knows of the situation back at First Dragoon headquarters. If he knows, then either Sumner at Fort Union, or us or the new cantonment we got near Taos, will get the boy. I promise you that. We also got a new captain coming out here soon. Name is Blake. I'll make sure he knows."

"Thank you, Sergeant Major. It will lessen my guilt."

"There ain't no reason for that, Sergeant. Out here, as you know, anythin' can happen. What's the boy's name again?"

"It's Scruggs. Private Ryan Scruggs. The boy's from New Jersey."

The sergeant major shook his head and then spoke. "Get your gear and your corporal. The NCO quarters are small, but we got room for two more. How long you stayin'?"

"I figure to leave with the two wagons and ox teams in a day or so."

"Leave the teams and wagons. We can use 'em here this time."

"I got a stable sergeant back at Leavenworth, and he will kick my ass if I don't return with his property."

"Yeah, Sergeant Jeremiah Delaney. Is that old fart still at Leavenworth? You know, I served with him before the war. I thought he would have retired by now. Tell 'im Sergeant Major Leonard Simms owns 'em now. I'll give you a conscription note to take back. He can get more animals. I can't out here."

"At your order, Sergeant Major."

"Delaney's still got only three stripes, huh?"

"Yeah, he still does. Should have more, but he kinda loses 'em sometimes."

"Yeah, I know. I've seen 'im in action. He's tough man. I can't remember anyone puttin' him down, for that matter. Now show me the new recruits."

The two NCOs went outside to the waiting dragoons. Watson stood behind Simms, who addressed them. "Welcome to Galisteo. You're under the command of Second Lieutenant John Davidson. I'm Sergeant Major Simms. When I call off your name, answer me so I can see you and assign you to a company." He paused and looked around at all the men. "Sorry for the loss of Scruggs. Your sergeant here told me he was a good man. I can assure you that the army will take care of him. Now listen up." He unfolded the list Watson had given him and began calling out names. He finished and the seventeen dragoons had been split up among three companies of the 1st Dragoons stationed between Cantonments Galisteo and Taos. Stevens, Sample, and Starke found themselves together in Company F, stationed at Cantonment Galisteo.

The three men headed to stable their horses and saddles. They found fresh grass in a wagon just outside the stable, where they noticed two dragoons sharpening scythes.

The dragoons watched the three new recruits approach. "Just in, are ya?"

Sam answered, "Yep, just about an hour ago. Sam Sample, from Lancaster, Pennsylvania."

"Marvin Church. Shreveport, Louisiana. This here's Jim Anders."

Anders raised the stone he was sharpening with as if making a mock salute and said, "From Savannah, Georgia."[1]

Sample motioned to Stevens and Starke.

Starke spoke first. "Adolph Starke. From Deutschland." He corrected himself. "From Germany."

Church and Anders only nodded. They looked at Dwight.

"Dwight Stevens from Norwich, Connecticut."

"Oh, a real Yankee," Anders commented.

Dwight looked at the man. "Yes, a real New England Yankee."

Both Southerners smiled, and Church put out his hand. "Welcome to Galisteo, asshole of the New Mexico Territory."

All the dragoons laughed as they exchanged handshakes.

"You look like you just come in from the fields. You cuttin' grass for the mounts?" Starke asked.

"Yep. Y'all will get your chance," Anders responded.

"We do it daily. Fill one to two wagons, depending on how many mounts we have stabled," Church added.

"How come you don't just string 'em and secure the picket pins or post a guard? They eat by themselves. That sounds a lot easier to me," Starke said.

Anders laughed.

Church continued, "Y'all don't know much about the local Indians,

---

[1] **The names and ranks of all the officers,** and the last names of all the soldiers in the U.S. Dragoons are real. However, the relationships and conversations are fictional.

do you? They are some of the finest horsemen you ever did see. They steal 'em right from under you. We bring the grass to the stables. We do it two men at a time. One scything and one watching. Y'all will get your turn, like I said."

The three new recruits realized that they needed to learn a lot more about the ways of the native Indians. They stabled their horses and gear, and were shown to the Company F barracks.

The one-story building was L-shaped and formed the northeast corner of the outer fort wall. There were no windows on the outer side, only ones facing the front courtyard. The ventilation was subsequently poor, and the dry heat made the barracks feel like the Lancaster iron foundry Sam Staple had enlisted in the dragoons to get away from.

Dwight picked an empty bunk and stored the gear from his haversack in the foot locker next to his bed. The new recruits spent the remainder of the day settling in. One of the chores that had been assigned to them was to procure a second uniform set. Each man was issued another jacket and set of trousers.

To the amazement of Sam, Adolph, and Dwight, their uniforms didn't quite match. Although designed alike, they found that the blue jackets varied in shades. Dwight commented that he had the war-issue dragoon jacket he had seen while he was in Mexico. He said that the other two looked darker than his. They all agreed that the orange striping on Dwight's jacket looked redder than theirs.

They were further amazed when some of the regulars began entering the barracks. Some had been stationed in Galisteo for several months and exposed to the intense heat and sunlight of the New Mexico Territory, and their jackets were several shades lighter than the ones that had just been issued to the new men.

Sam said, "U.S. Dragoons ain't really the army's elite. Looks like we get the hand-me-downs."

Dwight smiled. "It sure looks like it."

"Don't worry, mate. The sun will bleach yours into light blue if you survive here for a year or two," one of the men said. "Ronald Skelton, from Sheffield, England, by way of Toronto, Chicago, and now New Mexico Territory. Spent a few years in the Fourth Royal Dragoons." He extended his hand.

"Dwight Stevens. I'm glad to make your acquaintance."

The two shook hands, and Dwight introduced Skelton to Sam and Adolph while several more new recruits gathered around to meet Skelton. A few minutes later, more dragoons entered the barracks. It didn't take long for the new arrivals and the permanent party men to get comfortable with each other.

Sergeant Watson and Corporal Rolling departed Galisteo on October 20th. The two senior dragoons passed the men working on the south wall and main gate areas. Among the workers were ten of the seventeen dragoons they had led to New Mexico Territory.

A few of the dragoons called out to them as they passed, leading a pack mule loaded with supplies for their journey back to Fort Leavenworth. Some bantering was exchanged in good humor as the dragoons wished the two men a safe trip back to Kansas. Someone called out that they hoped the two didn't get lost on their way back.

Watson quickly responded, "Well, boys, Rolling and me will be in Leavenworth in thirty days. No need to be leadin' oxen while following wagon ruts and wet-nursin' recruits on the way out there."

Laughter erupted.

"We will be trainin' more of you by mid-November. Maybe see you in the spring. Do your duty." Watson yelled. The two men tipped their caps as they trotted out the unfinished gate of the cantonment.

The first snows had blanketed the landscape the morning Dwight Stevens was assigned his first patrol with a detail from Company F. Spirit was a little jumpy as he saddled the black Morgan. He hadn't been ridden regularly since Dwight's arrival, but Dwight's patience and love for his mount settled the spirited horse when he galloped him around the coral.

The other dragoons glanced up while they saddled their own mounts. "You in a hurry to get out of here, Stevens?" a voice from within the stable yelled out at him.

Dwight pulled up on the reins and slowed Spirit to a walk, although the animal sidestepped and tried to prance a few times. Dwight realized Lieutenant Davidson was addressing him. "No sir, just getting Spirit here calmed a little. I haven't ridden him in a while. Just bound-up energy."

"I expect all my dragoons to keep their mounts in good riding condition."

Dwight didn't make a remark. He looked at Sergeant Morrow, who would be the senior NCO on the patrol, with a bewildered look. The sergeant just slowly moved his head side to side.

"Private, did you hear my statement?" Davidson asked.

"Yes sir, I did. I can assure you that we are ready to respond to any situation that develops."

"Good, Private. I expect that from all my dragoons. New Mexico Territory is unforgiving. You must have a mount that is reliable and in good condition." As he finished his little lecture, he looked around to make sure all the other dragoons, as well as Sergeant Morrow and the scout, had heard it.

The detail left Galisteo and headed due north. The word was

passed among the men that it was a routine patrol of less than a week, and that their destination was at the discretion of the lieutenant. In a short time, the patrol found tracks of an Indian party. Davidson gave orders that they would follow. Sergeant Morrow advised the lieutenant that he should send the scout out ahead and, to Morrow's surprise, he actually took his advice. Several hours passed and still the mounted patrol never saw the party they were tracking.

They reached Cantonment Taos at dusk. The facilities at Taos were not as comfortable as those at Galisteo. The barracks was not large enough to accommodate all the men of the detail.

Dwight found sleeping quarters in the stable. The blacksmith stove afforded him the heat he desired after ten hours in the saddle on patrol. He relaxed in the warmth of the stable and its smells, which, as he drifted off to sleep, reminded him of his journey to join up in the First Massachusetts Volunteers years earlier.

The next morning when the detail assembled, they were informed by Sergeant Morrow that the scout had returned during the night and told Lieutenant Davidson that the party they tried to track was not a hunting party, but a group of twenty Apache braves whose purpose for quick and elusive travel had not yet been discovered. Morrow stated that the party had finally camped for the night around the time the detail had cut off their pursuit and headed for Taos.

The group waited for approximately a half hour for Davidson before he finally appeared from his quarters and informed Sergeant Morrow that the detail would ride to head off the Apache war party, as he had now labeled them.

Sergeant Morrow reminded Davidson, "Sir, the Apaches have been peaceful for over a year now and there have been no reports of any type of roaming war parties."

Davidson mounted his horse and turned to Sergeant Morrow. "Are there any questions to my orders?"

"No, sir. I just want to remind you that there have been no reports of any hostilities in over a year and our route will take us into the mountains where it will be difficult to track them."

"Duly noted, Sergeant Morrow. Prepare the detail to ride."

The temperature had risen by the time the detail had covered several hours of their patrol route. At that time, Davidson turned them west, in hopes of running into the Apaches. He also thought that the Indians could have slowed their movement, thinking no one was following them.

They finally intercepted the trail of the Apache party, but Sergeant Morrow figured that they had missed them. Davidson persisted in his pursuit, despite Morrow's advice to let the scout observe and report on the Indian's activities so they could get out of the foothills before dark.

An hour later they came to a flattened area that turned into a small pasture. The tree line was thinning, and Morrow realized that the detail would begin to encounter rough terrain. He relayed his concerns to Davidson, who was about to dismiss the sergeant's advice when he suddenly stopped his horse. Sergeant Morrow expected some chastisement, until he followed the lieutenant's gaze.

Tied to a small cedar tree out in the center of the pasture was the scout that Davidson had ordered to follow and track the Apache. Scout George, as the dragoons had always called him, was a half-breed Apache himself.

Sergeant Morrow called out, "Dragoons, draw your weapons and be alert." He ordered Private Skelton to approach the scout while the dragoons stayed out of the pasture clearing as they waited.

"He's dead, Sergeant. Two arrows in him. One through his neck. One in his chest."

"Untie him from the tree. We'll bury him here," Morrow ordered.

Skelton looked at Dwight to help him. He quickly dismounted.

Davidson watched and then said, "I think we better just move on, Sergeant. The animals will take care of the carcass."

"Sir, it will only take a short while to cover the body with rocks," Morrow replied.

"He was a scout, not a dragoon, Sergeant."

"He was a dragoon, sir. I knew Scout George for three years. He deserves a proper burial," Morrow said, raising his voice.

"Suit yourself, Sergeant, but make it as quick as possible," Davidson snapped back.

"Yes, sir."

No words were spoken over the burial site. No one knew if Scout George was a Christian.

Dwight prayed that his spirit was free and content. He also gave thanks that the Apache party had apparently moved on.

The wind began to pick up, and Morrow advised Davidson to withdraw from the mountain foothills before they were ambushed. Davidson didn't need any convincing this time. The patrol returned to Cantonment Taos late that evening feeling tired, cold, and mad about losing Scout George.

Dwight Stevens had completed his first patrol as a dragoon. Life in the New Mexico Territory was nothing like he had imagined.

In late December, Captain George A. H. Blake[1] arrived at Cantonment Galisteo. Immediately after taking command, Captain Blake changed the patrol tactics that the 1st Dragoons had maintained since Dwight's arrival. He had figured out, after being there for only a short period, that the native tribes knew approximately when and where the patrols of the dragoons would be at all times. He also increased the size of the patrols to include portions of several companies.

Col. George A. H. Blake with officers during the Civil War
Public Domain photo

Standing: 1. Lt. Ira W. Trask, 8th Ill. Cav. **2.** Lt. George W. Yates, 4th Mich. Inf. **3.** Lt. James F. Wade, 6th U.S. Cav. **4.** Lt. Henry Baker, 5th U.S. Cav. **5.** Lt. Leicester Walker, 5th U.S. Cav. **6.** Capt. Charles C. Suydam, A.A.G. **7.** Lt. Daniel W. Littlefield, 7th Mich. Cav. **8.** Unknown. **9.** Lt. Curwen B. McLellan, 6th U.S. Cav. **10.** Unknown. **11.** Lt. G. Irvine Whitehead, 6th Pa. Cav.

Seated: 1. Lt. Col. Albert S. Austin, Chief Commissary. **2. Col. George A. H. Blake**, (second from left), 1st U.S. Cav. **3**. Maj. Gen. Pleasonton. **4.** Lt. Col. Charles R. Smith, 6th Pa. Cav., Chief of Staff. **5.** Capt. Henry B. Hays, 6th U.S. Cav., Ordnance Officer.

On ground: 1. Lt. Woodbury M. Taylor, 8th Ill. Cav. **2.** Capt. Enos B. Parsons, 8th N.Y. Cav. **3.** Capt. Frederick C. Newhall, 6th Pa. Cav. **4.** Lt. Clifford Thomson, 1st N.Y. Cav. **5.** Surgeon S. L. Pancoast, U.S.V. **6.** Lt. B. T. Hutchins, 6th U.S. Cav.

On February 13th, a patrol left Cantonment Galisteo. Captain Blake brought along four dragoon scouts, as well as a dozen pack mules

[1] **Colonel George A. H. Blake** – Following his being disciplined for the drunken riot in Taos, New Mexico, Blake became Commanding officer of Ft. Churchill in the Nevada Territory. Later he became a brigadier general in the Civil War under General Philip St. George Cooke.

to carry food supplies and barrels of water. The scouts were ordered to keep in touch with the patrol as it headed due west and across the Rio Grande. Their journey was to alternate between northwestern and northeastern directions until they returned to Cantonment Taos, which had recently been renamed Cantonment Burgwin. The name change had occurred in honor of Mexican War hero and 1st Dragoon Captain John Henry K. Burgwin, who was killed during the siege of Pueblo de Taos in 1847. Eventually the patrol would return to Cantonment Galisteo. Captain Blake hoped to keep the Indians off-guard with his new patrol plan.

One week into the southerly patrol, Dwight was assigned to a hunting party. Captain Blake ordered the main patrol to proceed at a walk in order for the hunting parties to stay within a few hours' ride of them. Corporal Skelton and Privates Stevens and Morse were assigned as the Company F hunting party, while three dragoons from Company C were assigned to another. Their assignments were to hunt whitetail deer, mule deer, bison, and elk.

Both parties left before dawn in different directions as the main patrol moved slowly on. Unbeknown to the Company F hunting party, Company C shot, killed, and gutted a mule deer in the mid-morning hours, and had triumphantly returned before mid-afternoon with a one-hundred-fifty-pound dressed buck. The main patrol waited to see if Company F could produce the same.

Company F did not see any game until mid-afternoon, when Skelton found a cow bison with her calf. He could not bring himself to shoot the animal because of the calf. Dwight respected the corporal for his compassion. No further luck ensued until Private Morse signaled that he had game in his sights.

Dwight approached on foot to find him looking over a small knoll at a bull bison. The grass extended close to Dwight's secure position, and he decided to crawl over the mound and through the tall grass to shorten the range and increase the accuracy of his weapon.

Private Morse and Corporal Skelton crouched in the tall grass and watched as the novice hunter approached his prey. As he moved closer, the bison moved away and lengthened the range again. Frustrated, Dwight waited to see what his prey would do. As luck would have it, the bison moved to a new, closer grazing area. It shortened the range and afforded Dwight a clear shot. He aimed low and to the right of the front left leg of the beast, adjusted for distance, steadied his aim, and shot. The recoil stung his shoulder.

The bison dropped immediately. A short time later, as they prepared the carcass, Skelton confirmed that the shot had penetrated the animal's heart and killed him instantly. Company F would be well represented at the following day's supper meal with the two hindquarters of a respectably sized bull bison.

Captain Blake congratulated both hunting parties, but commented that he personally would have preferred some bear meat. "Gentlemen, you'll become real hunters when you stare down a charging bear and shoot him dead several feet from where you're standing."

Nobody who heard the boast said anything.

Sergeant Morrow rolled his eyes to Corporal Skelton, who did everything in his power not to laugh. Lieutenant Davidson expressed that he would enjoy hunting with his commanding officer when the opportunity presented itself.

After supper, Dwight approached Morrow and inquired as to whether or not he had ever shot a bear and eaten it.

"No, Stevens, I haven't shot one. I have tasted the meat. It's a little too greasy for my taste."

"It sounds like the captain is quite the hunter."

"Yeah, if you believe all he said. Maybe we'll get a chance to see what the man can do sometime on this patrol." Sergeant Morrow then walked slowly away.

"You got a feeling that he doesn't care much for the captain?" Sam remarked.

"I don't know," Dwight said.

On March 10th, the patrol reached the Mexican border. In twenty-five days they had not encountered any Apache hunting parties. The scouts reported that the tribes had settled on the west side of the Rio Grande basin for the winter. Captain Blake, upon hearing the reports, boasted to his lieutenants that his plan was developing. Several days later, on a northwesterly direction, the patrol encountered a small Apache hunting party that invited them to their winter encampment of approximately two hundred Apache Indians.

The chief invited the patrol to feast on deer and elk. Captain Blake and his two officers were asked to smoke in his tent. Blake brought along Scout McCoy, an Apache half-breed who had been with the dragoons for several years as an interpreter.

One interesting bit of information that Scout McCoy relayed to Sergeant Morrow that night was that the Apache chief had moved his winter encampment from the Pecos River basin to its present location two weeks before due to sickness. The scout's interpretation of the chief's description was that smallpox had broken out.

Morrow asked McCoy, "Any of the hunting parties you came in contact with show signs of sickness?"

McCoy just shook his head no.

"Did our other two scouts have contact?"

The dragoon scout thought a few moments and responded, "Both not return."

"They should have met up with us by now," Morrow said. He left the conversation and headed for Captain Blake's tent. "Excuse me, sir, when do you figure the remaining scouts will be reporting in?"

"They should have been here by now. I'm sure they will report during the evening, Sergeant. Why do you ask?"

"Scout McCoy informed me that the chief said that sickness had been reported."

"Yes, he did. The chief said he moved on when he heard about the sickness, to avoid any contact."

"Yes, sir, I understood that as well. Did anyone confirm what it was?"

"Not really. The chief implied that it could have been smallpox. No proof of that, though."

"Sir, don't you think it was strange that we did not see any winter encampments along the Pecos River basin during our southerly route?"

"Sergeant, what are you getting at?"

"I don't know, sir. I will feel much better once we talk to the two remaining scouts."

The following morning before the patrol had mounted up, Sergeant Morrow searched to see if the two scouts had returned. He became more concerned when he found out they hadn't.

Captain Blake maintained his daily schedule, and the dragoon patrol was mounted and underway by sunrise. The patrol continued to move in a northwesterly direction until Captain Blake turned the patrol northeasterly around noon. Within an hour, the rear guard reported that riders could be seen approaching. When the word reached Blake, he stopped the patrol. They saw that Scout Morning Cloud was riding alone, but with another horse in tow.

Sergeant Morrow's feeling that something was wrong became a reality.

Scout Morning Cloud stayed away from the main patrol and rode parallel to it. When he reached the head of the patrol and was within shouting distance from Captain Blake, he stopped his horse. Blake recognized that Morning Cloud had a body slung over and tied to the horse.

"Morning Cloud, is that Brown Bear?"

"I stay away. Brown Bear die today."

"Of what?"

The scout didn't respond.

"I asked a question, scout!" Blake yelled a little louder.

"Pox. I bury now."

Captain Blake waved the patrol ahead, and the dragoon scout watched the patrol pass.

Dwight asked Skelton why the captain had left the scout in the middle of the wilderness to fend for himself.

"He probably has it already, and knows it. I fear we might get it ourselves now that we have come that close to Morning Cloud and Brown Bear."

"You ever had the pox, Corporal?" Sam asked.

"No. If you get it and survive, though, it is good odds you won't catch it again, I hear."

Grumblings down through the ranks were heard as the dragoons moved north.

They camped that evening next to the riverbank of the Rio Grande. Captain Blake summoned his lieutenants and NCOs to his tent. He waited several moments before he spoke. "Gentlemen, besides today, when was the last time we had contact with Morning Cloud and Brown Bear?"

No one answered, and he looked around for a reply.

Sergeant Morrow spoke first. "Sir, I think our last contact with the two was five days ago, when they reported that they had only seen one small group of Apaches heading south along the Pecos River basin."

Lieutenant Davidson replied, "That's what I remember as well. Based on that, I figure Brown Bear was already infected with the pox and failed to mention that he was feeling ill to Morning Cloud."

"What will happen to Morning Cloud, sir?"

"I don't think he's had smallpox before. He'll have to survive on his own. If he returns to the Apache encampment, he'll infect them all. He knows better than to come here to us again. He came once to warn us. He was a good friend."

"He ain't dead yet, Captain," Sergeant Morrow remarked.

"Keep a watch on the men. Keep a good ear open. They'll talk among themselves on how tired or sick they feel. If you hear that, inquire. If one gets too sick to ride, tell me. We'll stay quarantined out here next to a water supply."

The next morning, the dragoons awoke to find that two men had rashes on their face, hands, and arms. One of those was Adolph Starke.

Dwight saw the German struggling to pack his haversack with his sleeping blankets. "Let me help you, Adolph," he offered.

"I feel not so good. Got headache and feel weak."

Sergeant Morrow overheard the complaint and investigated. He reported to Lieutenant Davidson, who passed the information upward, and Captain Blake quarantined the patrol. By the second day, six more dragoons had become ill, including Captain Blake and Corporal Skelton. Those dragoons that had not been infected were sent out in half-day hunting patrols to shoot any game that they came across. By the beginning of the second week, pustules and scabs had developed in different stages for those infected with the virus.

Of the nineteen that had been infected, seventeen seemed to be recovering well. Adolph Starke was one of the two who seemed too sick to recover.

Dwight had been unable to get any serious amount of food into his stomach and his fever made him delirious at times. He had been sick for over a week now, and most of the men of the patrol worried that he would not survive.

One death occurred at the river's edge. Private William Marks, twenty-three years old from Youngstown, Ohio, died one month short of his twenty-fourth birthday. A small cross was erected with his name, year of birth, and date of death carved into it.

Captain Blake ordered that *smallpox* be carved on the back of the cross. Several more days passed, and Adolph began to gain strength.

On Blake's orders, Sergeant Morrow built an Apache travois from driftwood gathered at the riverbank and blankets stitched together. He attached it to Starke's horse. They loaded the weak dragoon and Dwight led the mount with Starke on it.

The patrol started on their northerly route again after twelve days at their smallpox encampment. Several days passed and Adolph was strong enough to mount his horse and ride with the patrol. They returned on April 7th with forty-nine dragoons and two scouts after fifty-four days on patrol. Waiting for them at Cantonment Galisteo was Scout Morning Cloud. He face was scarred, but he was fit and smiling.

Sergeant Morrow was pleased to see him. "You made it back. I'm glad that you did," he said.

"Mourning Cloud glad too."

"Where did you stay?"

"Spent time near Apache camp. They sick too."

"How bad?"

"Maybe twenty die. Some children."

Morrow shook his head as he looked down. A few seconds passed and he said, "We lost one dragoon. His wife doesn't know yet. The captain's going to tell her." Morrow left Morning Cloud and walked to headquarters.

"There, Lieutenant, your savior has arrived," Blake said as he entered.

Morrow looked confused. "Excuse me, sir?"

"Lieutenant Davidson was just sharing his concerns with me. I ordered him to inform Mrs. Marks of her husband's death, and he thinks that you should notify the woman, seeing you're his sergeant."

Sergeant Morrow became angry but held his temper. "Sir, I don't have any problem with telling the woman, but I think it would be more appropriate that you, as the commander, inform her."

Blake realized that Morrow was glaring at him and waiting for a reply. "Well, Sergeant, I completely disagree. You are ordered to inform the woman. Also, Sergeant Major, please make the arrangements for her departure from the cantonment."

"Army regulations permit widowed women to stay as long as they choose, sir," the sergeant major informed him.

"I know the regulations, Sergeant Major, but I have my own. Get her to a place of her choosing, but get her out of my cantonment. It's bad for morale of the men and their families. Do you have anything else on your mind, Sergeant?"

"No sir." He left immediately.

Corporal Skelton saw Morrow leaving the headquarters. He saw the irritation in Morrow's face and called out just as Morrow was about to mount his horse. "Sergeant Morrow, can I be of assistance?"

"No, Skelton, I'm off to see Mrs. Marks."

"Aye, you have the assignment. I figured as much. I will accompany you. I know Maggie Marks better than you."

Morrow waited for Corporal Skelton to reach his horse.

The sergeant major called out to both of them. "Dismount, both of you! Walk with me! We'll all go to see Maggie! It's the least we can do!"

Dwight and Sam heard the conversation between the three NCOs of what the officers had said to them concerning the widow. Dwight looked at Sam and shook his head in disbelief that no officer from the cantonment had offered their condolences to the wife of a deceased dragoon. They watched the three NCOs walk to the permanent-party family quarters to inform Mrs. Maggie Marks that she was now a twenty-one-year-old widow.

"Dwight murmured, "That should have been Blake's responsibility." Sam shook his head in disbief.

That evening, Sergeant Morrow and Corporal Skelton sat in the NCO quarters. Each man had just emptied a whiskey shot glass. "How long did Blake give the sergeant major to make arrangements for the poor woman to leave?" Skelton asked.

"He didn't. He just told him to get her out as soon as possible,"

Morrow replied.

"The bastard. What the hell difference does it make how long she stays?"

"It makes no difference to me or any other dragoon in the cantonment. Just to Blake."

"He should give the poor woman time to mourn. Maybe in a month or so, the sergeant major could take her and the child to Santa Fe. She could catch the stagecoach back to Kansas and a riverboat to Ohio. She must have family back there."

"Carrying a baby with her? I don't think so. I need to talk with Simms and arrange something nearby. The child needs to grow more before traveling that distance."

Skelton poured more whiskey into each man's shot glass.

There was silence for a few minutes as they each thought about what they had witnessed that afternoon.

Skelton spoke first. "It doesn't seem right, soldiering for a man who could care less about a soldier and his family."

"You mean Blake? He proved he has less respect and feeling than Davidson does."

"It's going to be hard to serve under men like that."

"Yeah, it will be," Morrow remarked.

"Maybe we can change that?" Skelton said and looked at Morrow.

"Well, we ain't going to kill either one of the bastards. I sure would like to, but I can only hope that the Apaches do."

"We can hope on that. But maybe there could be another choice," Skelton said as he poured another glass.

"Desertion would never cross my mind. I can outlast the likes of Davidson and Blake," Morrow said as he waved off Skelton's attempt to pour him another glass.

Corporal Skelton never responded to Morrow. He thought, *There will be a time when it will be easier to convince this man to come along with me.*

A service was held for Private Marks several days later. Captain Blake attended, but did not eulogize the fallen dragoon. That task, usually performed by the commander or an officer picked by the family, was bestowed upon the sergeant major.

Upon completion of the service, all those that participated passed Mrs. Marks and gave her their condolences. Captain Blake was one of the first to go by and pay his respects, although he chose not to partake in the social gathering after the service.

The word had spread that the sergeant major had made arrangements for Mrs. Marks to stay in Santa Fe until her child was deemed old enough to safely travel back to Ohio. Her accommodations were mostly paid for by donations from Companies C and F. Captain Blake was not informed, nor did he inquire, about the arrangements Simms had made. His actions greatly lessened the respect the dragoons had for him.

That evening Dwight and several dragoons discussed the services that had been held for Private Marks. Some men were concerned, and now hesitant, about bringing their families out to the cantonment while Blake was in command.

"No man should keep you from bringing your families out here."

"That's easy for you to say, Stevens. You ain't got a wife or lady friend back home you are thinkin' about bringin out here," Marvin Church said.

"That's right, I don't. But the sergeant major took care of Maggie Marks and her baby. There are at least some good leaders here who care for us."

"I sure hope I don't get drunk one night and find Blake alone. I don't know if I could resist kicking the shit out of him. I've never seen such a heartless bastard like him in my three years in the dragoons," Jim Anders said and looked at Marvin Church.

Church put a hand on Anders's shoulder. "Careful, you can't be making statements like that, Jim. You could be brought up on charges if Simms, Morrow, or even Skelton heard you mouthin' off."

"I say we all calm down and let this pass. Blake must have had a reason, and as long as the sergeant major took care of things, we can't be bitchin' too much," Sam Sample remarked.

"I say Sam right. We have to let it pass," Adolph said and walked away.

"It don't settle good with me how Blake was so cold in handling this." Anders said, turning away from the gathering.

The group of dragoons disbanded, and Dwight was left to his own thoughts. *I do not have any respect for this man. Confidence in him will come hard for me and most of the others. This man could be real trouble for us all.*

Chapter Thirteen

Duty, Desertion, and Death

Captain Blake ordered more patrols within a week of when the fifty-six-day patrol had ended. Companies C and F were assigned to support ten-man patrols, and these were scheduled for a week's duration on alternating weeks.

Dwight Stevens found himself on patrol the week of April 21, 1852. Led by Second Lieutenant Davidson, and with Sergeant Morrow and Corporal Skelton, Dwight felt confident in the abilities of the two NCOs to guide Davidson with safety and purpose.

The assignment was to follow the Pecos River basin and investigate what effect the smallpox epidemic had on the Apaches. None of the dragoons were pleased with Blake's orders to send patrols back into the smallpox-infected area, since most could not have cared less if the Apaches had been wiped out.

Dwight did not feel that way, but he knew that his feelings about Indians as well as blacks did not set too well with some of the dragoons. Most thought that the Apaches were not only a nuisance to the army, but also a constant threat to the settlers. Many dragoons had argued with Dwight that their non-existence would benefit the military and civilians. Even Adolph and Sam found it difficult, at times, to defend Dwight's thought process.

One night at an encampment near the Rio Grande, a conversation between Jim Anders and Dwight Stevens turned ugly. Anders approached and asked what Dwight was reading. Stevens did not acknowledge the man, as he was fully engrossed in the book.

Anders was known for being impatient, and he grabbed the book from Dwight's hands when he did not respond. "What the hell is so important in this book, Stevens?"

Startled, Dwight angrily rose from where he was sitting near the campfire, stood face to face with Anders, and grabbed the book back.

Anders didn't anticipate the quick reaction. "What the hell are you all fired up about, reading that goddamned book that you never put down?"

"It's none of your business. Don't ever do that again, Jim."

"And what would you do if I did?"

"You wouldn't want to know."

Anders foolishly made a mock attempt to grab the book back from Dwight. Dwight's quick temper had already heightened his reaction time and clouded his judgment. He spun Anders and caught him with a short, hard punch to his ribs.

The dragoon couldn't catch his balance from the blow, and he fell into the campfire. Luckily, he was able to roll and only caught the side of his jacket and part of his trousers on fire. The dragoons that saw it quickly doused the flames. Anders recovered and stood up, yelling and swearing. Several more dragoons stepped between the two men just as Sergeant Morrow arrived.

"What the hell is going on here? Everyone, at ease!"

Marvin Church spoke up. "Anders tripped on Stevens's feet. Clumsy bastard that he is. No harm done."

Anders just nodded his head that he agreed.

Dwight spoke up, realizing that Anders' close friend had just saved both of them from disciplinary action. "That's right, Sergeant. My feet tripped him and it was an accident. My apologies, Jim."

Anders unbuttoned his jacket and viewed his side. His undershirt was burnt, but he had no blisters on his skin.

Morrow looked at Dwight, not saying a word, then turned and walked away, not believing the story. Sergeant Morrow knew it wasn't an accident, but could tell the lieutenant that it was if he asked.

The men watched him walk away and out of hearing range.

"What's so important in that book, Stevens?" Church whispered.

"It's an opinion on God, religious organizations, and subjects of that nature."

"Is that where you get your ideas about freeing the slaves? I hear the men talking, Dwight."

"Not in this particular book. But slaves are men too, Marvin. Just like us. They were born like us, they laugh and cry just like us, and they live and die like us." He paused to control his emotions and lowered his voice before he continued. "They love like we do, and long to be free the same as we do. And Marvin, they hate slavery just as much as you would if things were turned around."

Marvin Church raised his voice. "You don't know shit about slaves, Yankee! If you lived in the South, you'd see we treat 'em well. They're not smart people who can take care of themselves, so we do them a favor by taking care of them. In return, they work in the fields."

"It's slavery." Just as Dwight's voice was getting louder, the two men heard a voice behind them.

"Both of you shut the hell up. There ain't going to be no more arguing about slavery, religion, politics, or any other shit that causes you to fistfight and wake up every goddamned Apache for miles around," Sergeant Morrow said through clenched teeth as he worked his way between the two men. "This is the second time I've had to come over and separate you from other dragoons, Stevens. Put the book away. Read it in your bunk at Galisteo. You hear me?"

Dwight looked at the glaring sergeant. "Yes, Sergeant."

"Good. Don't have me tell you again, because I'll put you in chains and you can walk behind the patrol until we get back. You'll spend a month in the guardhouse after that."

Dwight knew he had pushed the sergeant to his limit. He didn't dare say a word.

Church smirked, and Morrow caught the facial expression. "You'll be right next to 'im, Church, so back away. I don't want to hear your opinions on anythin' either. You understand?"

"Yes, Sergeant. I understand."

"Good. Now the two of you report to Skelton and inform him to change the midnight to two o'clock sentry duty. Tell him you two got it." He turned and walked back to his blanket near the campfire.

"Sergeant Morrow, what was that all about?" Lieutenant Davidson inquired.

"Nothing, sir. Just two dragoons having a disagreement on something. They were getting too loud, and I shut 'em up."

"It sounded like more than that to me, Sergeant. Is Stevens a troublemaker?"

"No, sir. Like I said, it was just a disagreement that was gettin' too loud."

"I hope you have control of your men, Sergeant."

"Complete control, Lieutenant. I wouldn't worry about it."

"Then carry on," Davidson said and returned to his blanket to turn in for the evening.

Corporal Skelton waited until Sergeant Morrow had relaxed. He whispered, "The boys are a little restless tonight, Sergeant?"

"No, it's just Stevens stirring the shit with his Yankee beliefs and a few of the Southern boys reacting to it."

"That seems to be a growing problem in this country, I have observed."

"What do you mean, Skelton?"

"Well, being an Englishman, I have observed you have three distinct Americas. One North, one South, and one West. Slavery seems to be the difference. The North seems to be against it mostly, the South embraces it, and the West will be split because of it."

"You don't know shit. Go to sleep, Skelton."

The Englishman never responded to his sergeant's last statement, but thought to himself, *This issue could be powerful enough to split the whole country in two someday.* He obeyed the sergeant's last order, and just as he began to make himself comfortable for the night, he was interrupted when Stevens and Church reported to him that Sergeant Morrow had changed the sentry duty roster.

The next day the patrol reached the Apache encampment that had been reportedly infected. Lieutenant Davidson halted his men on a knoll overlooking it. "They look like they made it through the epidemic. We'll move on and circle back toward the cantonment."

"Aren't we going to see if they need assistance, sir?" the sergeant asked.

"Assistance for what, Sergeant?"

"Food, for one thing. We don't know if their men were affected and haven't been able to hunt. We could hunt for them."

"Sergeant, I have no orders to feed them or hunt for them. I was instructed to see if they survived the epidemic. I can see that they are still here, so they survived it. I have fulfilled my orders. We move on. Do you understand?"

"Yes, sir."

"Good, now no more Apache sympathy. Move the men at a gallop and follow me."

Word spread down the ranks at what happened between Davidson and Morrow. Dwight kept his opinion to himself, but he agreed with the sergeant. The majority of the men agreed with Davidson. They were pleased they were moving away from the encampment.

Several days later, the patrol returned to Cantonment Galisteo to find Captain Blake making final preparations to move all the companies to Cantonment Burgwin. Davidson, along with Sergeant Morrow, reported that he had that confirmed the Apache encampment near the Rio Grande had survived the smallpox epidemic.

"Were there many that survived, Lieutenant?" Blake asked.

"From what we could see, a good amount seemed to be walking around the encampment, sir." Davidson said.

Morrow put in, "Excuse me, sir. We never went into the camp and talked to the chief. We don't know how many people he lost or whether he needed food or not."

"Sergeant, you are out of order. I'm reporting to the captain, not you. You are dismissed."

"But, sir …"

"You heard the lieutenant, Sergeant Morrow. You are dismissed. Leave my office at once," Blake barked.

"Yes, sir."

Morrow left, grumbling incoherent sentences.

The captain turned to Davidson. "Please continue with your report, Lieutenant."

Morrow passed the sergeant major as he was coming into the office. Simms could see the anger and frustration in Morrow's face and inquired about what had happened. Morrow motioned him back and out of the office so he could explain, but Simms offered no comments. He just shook his head, which indicated his disapproval of the position the captain and lieutenant had taken.

Morrow returned to the NCO quarters a few hours later, after he had cooled down.

Skelton was waiting for him. "You look angry, ole boy."

"Skelton, it's 'Sergeant.' Not 'ole boy.'"

"My apologies. Sergeant, you look a little upset."

"I am. Those two horse's asses treat me like I'm some kind of…of…" He searched for right the word.

"'Underling' I believe is the word you are attempting to use, Sergeant."

Morrow glared at him, but realized the man had correctly explained who he felt he was.

"Yes, underling. That's the word. Those two bastards don't have an ounce of brains between 'em. They could not have cared less about the people in that camp. Wouldn't the humane thing have been to at least inquire as to whether or not we could have done somethin' for them?"

"You would think that, Sergeant."

"I don't know why I put up with shit like this."

"You don't have to."

"Skelton, I don't want to hear any more." The corporal walked away.

Skelton left the NCO quarters and walked to the supply house to inventory the cantonment supplies that were to be shipped under guard to Cantonment Burgwin. He also checked with the paymaster to ensure all the company funds would be collected, recorded, and contained in a small safe, under guard, to be transported.

The next day, the 1st Dragoons, with the complete complement of Companies C, E, and F and their dependents, left for Cantonment Burgwin. Galisteo would be abandoned, but would remain intact for reoccupation if required.

Within a week, Captain Blake reorganized Burgwin's six companies, A through F. Sergeant Murdock Quinn of Cantonment Burgwin's Company F had been junior to Sergeant Morrow while Company F had been split between the two cantonments. Quinn was made the Company F sergeant by recommendation of Lieutenant

Davidson to Captain Blake. The change was immediately approved.

Sergeant Morrow was reassigned to commissary and supply, over the objection of Sergeant Major Simms. The sergeant major was informed that there would be no objections to the new reorganization.

Most of the dragoons assigned to Company F soon realized that Quinn was no equal to Morrow. His actions in the field were only reactionary to Davidson's orders. He was not as experienced as Morrow in Indian matters and was not a free thinker when situations on patrol warranted it. Most men thought of him as only a "yes" man to Davidson. Dwight, Adolph, and Sam went on numerous patrols with Quinn and found him to be a marginal NCO at best.

Morrow remained at Cantonment Burgwin and was constantly at odds with Captain Blake when certain supplies failed to arrive. Despite having Skelton to assist him in maintaining the commissary and supply warehouse, the constant belittlement and harassment plunged the man into a deep resentment for both Blake and the army. By the winter of 1852, Sergeant Morrow had made up his mind. He had had enough.

One morning Captain Blake requested that Sergeant Major Simms order Sergeant Morrow to report to his office on the double. An hour later, the sergeant major returned to Blake's office to inform him that he had been unable to find Morrow.

Blake immediately sent two armed dragoons to escort Morrow to his office. The men searched for several hours, but to no avail. Corporal Skelton was summoned when Morrow could not be found, but no one could find Skelton. By mid-day, the entire command had been put on notice to find both dragoons.

That evening, Sergeant Major Simms reported to Captain Blake that Sergeant Morrow, his horse, and belongings could not be found. Blake inquired about Skelton and was informed that he also had not been found. Blake ordered Simms to record that both dragoons were suspected of desertion and were now subject to military law and disciplinary action.

A report was generated to Fort Union and Fort Leavenworth that the two dragoons had deserted. Several days passed before Sergeant Simms had to report again to Blake on the missing dragoons' presumed desertion.

"What is it, Sergeant Major?" Blake asked with irritation.

"Sir, I have an incident to report that needs your attention."

"What is it, Simms? Somebody else desert?"

"No, sir. It concerns Sergeant Morrow and Corporal Skelton."

"You mean the two deserters, Sergeant Major. They are no longer ranked dragoons."

"Yes, sir."

"Well, speak, man. What about them?"

"Sir, a review of the cantonment safe found it was empty. Two-hundred forty-seven dollars is missing."

"You telling me that someone stole our money?"

"Yes, sir. Morrow, Skelton, and myself were the only three with access to the safe."

"Put that into a report and send it to Forts Union and Leavenworth. I also want them both shot on sight if any of our patrols come in contact with them. Do you understand?"

"Yes, sir. I will inform all patrols prior to their departure of your orders."

Several days later, Morrow and Skelton stopped at a stage house en route to San Francisco, California. They paid for meals and stabling of their horses for the night. No names were given, or asked, when the two men ate there. They left the next morning before sunrise. Morrow and Skelton were never heard from again. Word spread among the troops quickly. A few commented on the theft of the money, and most speculated that they had set out for the California gold fields.

The desertion of the two NCOs affected the dragoons of Company F for several weeks, as Sergeant Murdock Quinn tried to settle into his position as Company F sergeant. Unknown to the dragoons, Captain Blake had requested and received two replacements for deserters Morrow and Skelton. Both were corporals.

One was placed to oversee the supply house and commissary, while the second was assigned to the position of corporal for Company F. Corporal Richard May was the Company F replacement and a native of Baltimore, Maryland. He had been in the dragoons for five years. His most recent post had been Fort Union.

Almost immediately, the morale of Company F started to improve with the apparent experience May brought to the company. The men watched how May handled working and reacting to orders from Davidson and Quinn while on patrol and at the cantonment. May was very knowledgeable of the Indian tribes in the territory and very skillful in handling his superiors. He was a master of suggestion, and that usually kept him from being at odds with Quinn or Davidson. The men, especially Dwight, appreciated May's abilities, which included assisting in the leadership decisions while the company was on patrol.

Another noticeable ability was May's voice. Like Dwight, he was a strong baritone, which became apparent one evening when the dragoons were playing and singing in the barracks. May visited the barracks when he heard Dwight and several other dragoons singing and playing instruments for themselves. When he could, he joined in with them. One day he suggested that the company put on a musical play. He let it be known that he had experience in musical plays and variety shows in Baltimore, before he joined the dragoons. May also volunteered to direct the plays and suggested that some of the dependents of the dragoons join them to put on a show.

Corporal May suggested a play in which he had participated in 1844, while still a civilian. The play was called *The Drunkard*[1] and had been a very funny play that was part of a temperance movement popular in Baltimore at the time. Several dragoons had no idea what the temperance movement was all about.

"It is a social movement urging reduced use of alcoholic beverages," May explained.

The dragoons, including Dwight, laughed.

"Seriously, the temperance movement criticizes excessive alcohol use. Some people in the movement promote complete abstinence. There is even pressure put on the government to enact anti-alcohol legislation. It hasn't happened yet, of course, but the play was popular with the public and fun to do. That's why I suggested we get some of the dependents to be in the play. It will be fun for us to do. I remember some of the songs. It wouldn't be Baltimore, but who would know or care if it was a little different? We're out in the middle of nowhere." He looked at the faces of the dragoons listening. He quickly spoke as he saw increased interest. "I'll ask permission of Sergeant Quinn and Sergeant Major Simms. We all know the army's regulations on drinking and buying liquor. How could they turn down a funny play where singing is involved?" Corporal May looked at the men standing around him again, and waited for some reaction.

Marvin Church spoke first. "It's June second. Do you think we could have a play ready in three or four weeks? I was thinking that July Fourth would be a good time."

"That's a great idea. I'm sure we could be ready," Corporal May stated.

The men began to speak all at the same time, until the corporal brought them under control and began making plans for the play to be held at Cantonment Burgwin. Within several days, May had obtained the permission he needed and began developing his version of *The Drunkard*

---

[1] ***The Drunkard* or *The Fallen Saved*** (from Wikipedia) is an American temperance play first performed in 1844. A drama in five acts, it was perhaps the most popular play produced in the United States before the dramatization of *Uncle Tom's Cabin* in the 1850s. In New York City, P. T. Barnum presented it at his American Museum in a run of over 100 performances.

as best as he could remember.

The anticipation of the play lifted the spirits of the dragoons even higher as more members of the other companies heard about it and asked to be part of it. Corporal May held try-outs and picked out the six main character actors that were needed for the play. Anyone who had tried out and was turned down for a part was not turned away, but simply absorbed into the chorus that was headed, and being organized, by Dwight. Marvin Church led the organizing and music arrangement in the instrument section.

The mundane life at the cantonment changed when the men became involved in the play. It was something to do that didn't involve Indians, orders, military routines, or differences in politics. It occupied everyone who participated.

Dwight was so involved that he didn't have time to read. Directing the chorus reminded him of the days he spent in his father's choir, and of his loved ones at home. He realized that it was time to reconnect with them. One evening after a chorus rehearsal, he sat with pen, ink, and paper in hand on the edge of his bunk. It was quiet because most of the men had stayed outside to smoke and talk. Dwight concentrated on what he should say to his sister. He had not corresponded with her since he left to join the dragoons.

In fifteen months, he had trained hard to become a dragoon, traveled halfway across the country, experienced contact with severe weather, dangerous snakes, annoying insects, diseases, and both peaceful and warring Indians. He wondered how he could explain all that to his sister. He began to write,

Cantonment Burgwin
New Mexico Territory
June 21, 1852

My Dearest Sister,

I truly apologize for my tardiness in my correspondence to you and our family. Please tell them first, that I am well and prospering in the year and three months since I last bid everyone farewell. I arrived in the New Mexico Territory in October of last year. I have met new friends from different parts of the country. They are a very interesting lot, I must say. Despite our regional differences, we have become a close group of men with the same purpose. That purpose is to protect the settlers from the Indians and sometimes the Indians from the settlers.

I have eaten all types of game that are found in abundance here. One acquires a taste for the game, but that I am still developing. I have been fortunate to be assigned a beautiful black Morgan horse who I have named Spirit. I swear he is the most

intelligent animal in the cantonment stable. I take great pleasure in riding him. His speed affords me the security I need when a situation to act quickly presents itself, and his gentleness the comfort I yearn for while I ride on long patrols through the Territory.

It abounds with majestic mountains, open plains and plentiful game. Everywhere, one can turn his sight to find beauty bestowed by God. But one does not have to look far to see the danger from insects, reptiles, and large animals that exist in this untamed territory.

The Indian tribes only become warring when provoked by each other, or by the whites who do not understand their ways and customs. I have seen that firsthand of officers and dragoons alike. The men here are very talented. They could sing in Father's choir anytime. Some play musical instruments. We are fortunate to have a corporal who has had experience in musical plays. He has organized us to perform the play The Drunkard for the cantonment. It first played in Baltimore a few years ago. Maybe you have heard of it. We all are enjoying our preparation for our show on July 4th. I wish you were here to see it. Please pass my love to our parents and siblings. I miss you all. I will write again soon.

Your devoted brother,
A. D. Stevens

Dwight finished the letter and addressed the envelope. He felt content that he had made the time to finally correspond with his sister. He hoped that his letter was informative, but not too alarming to the dangers he briefly touched upon. He did not want them to be constantly worried that he was in harm's way. He could never lie to them, but he also realized that he did not have to tell them everything. He put the letter in his footlocker to be posted at the commissary's mailroom as soon as he was free from his daily duties. He rested well that night.

On July 4th there were no patrols scheduled. Captain Blake ordered a celebration for the country's seventy-sixth birthday. A schedule of events had been posted for the dragoons and civilians at Cantonment Burgwin. One major event was the review of all the companies passing Captain Blake and numerous invited civilian guests and their families.

Companies A through F spent the previous day polishing boots, washing uniforms, and grooming their mounts. After the review, a feast was held at noon, organized by the commissary and the wives of the married dragoons. The afternoon was filled with demonstrations of marksmanship and riding skills. The evening highlight was the musical play *The Drunkard.* Those that participated in the play received a standing ovation. A social gathering after it afforded the townspeople, military dependents, and dragoons a chance to mix in conversation and to dance to the music Marvin Church had organized.

Dwight Stevens, dressed in his cleanest uniform, mingled among the townspeople. The tall handsome man had his first opportunity to socially meet some of the single and unescorted women from Taos. Many dragoons invited some of them to dance. Dwight watched as his friends enjoyed themselves with the single ladies. One specific young woman continually smiled at him while he watched the festivities. He became aware of her observation as he stood at the edge of the dance area and sipped apple cider.

As he watched, several dragoons approached the mysterious woman and were politely rejected. She continued to watch him. He got up the nerve to try his luck in asking her to dance. He waited until Marvin's band played a waltz to make his move toward the dark-haired, brown-eyed beauty. As he walked toward her, a dragoon cut in front of him and asked her to dance. She turned the dragoon away and walked directly to Dwight.

They faced each other on the dance floor and she spoke. "I assumed that you were coming to ask me to dance, *señor*?"

Dwight did not answer, even as she softly touched his left hand with her right and placed her other hand on his shoulder.

"You are going to dance with me, are you not, *señor*?"

"Yes, miss. Excuse my clumsiness." He began to lead in the slow waltz. "I thought you were going to dance with that other dragoon."

"In Mexico…" She paused, and then corrected herself, "In New Mexico Territory, our custom is to address an unmarried woman as *señorita*."

"My apologies, *señorita*, for not acknowledging you are Spanish."

"There are many Spanish people in Taos, *señor*."

"Yes, I'm sure there are. But none as beautiful as you are."

"Your flattery is better than your dancing," she said, then smiled and laughed at his facial expression.

"I'm afraid you are right. We don't get to do this very often," he said with obvious embarrassment. He couldn't take his eyes off of her. "May I ask your name?"

"It's Señorita Maria Gonzales y Maritta."

"May I call you Maria?"

"*Sí*, as long as you tell me your name."

"Dwight Stevens."

"Well, Dwight, I am very pleased to make your acquaintance."

"The pleasure is mine, Maria."

They danced until the waltz ended. Church's band struck up a faster dance, but Maria led Dwight over to the refreshment table. He poured her cider, and they spent the next several hours getting to know each other. As time went by, they became closer and laughter came easily and often. One specific bit of information Dwight found out was that

Maria's brother had been killed during the war fighting for Mexico. He offered his condolences and confessed that he had also been in the war. She questioned his age, and he explained. He described where he had been in Mexico as her beauty mesmerized him.

The conversation ended when Maria noticed her father observing her. The man turned his head in an obvious beckon for Maria to come to where he was standing. Dwight saw her facial expression change as she looked away from him. He turned to see the stocky gentleman standing next to Captain Blake, who was talking with a woman and the town's sheriff.

"Does that gentleman know you, Maria?"

"*Sí*, he is my father. I must go now."

"Your father is a guest of the captain?"

"*Sí*, he is. Captain Blake invited me and my mother as well. I truly have to go."

"Where do you live, Maria? I would like to call on you when I have some time to leave the cantonment and come to town."

"Ask for the doctor's house. You will find me there, but I warn you that my father does not favor American dragoons."

"Did he come tonight by invitation of the captain?" Dwight asked.

"*Sí*, but he was only being courteous now that you occupy our land."

Dwight was struck by the soft animosity she exhibited in her eyes as she spoke. She bid him good night as she quickly walked to the side of her father. She turned back to look at him as she stood next to the doctor. Dwight watched as she, along with her mother, father, and the sheriff, were escorted by the captain away from the dance. Maria glanced back again at him and smiled.

Señorita Maria Gonzales y Maritta had made a large impression on Dwight. He wondered how much he had impressed her. His main concern now would be to try to impress *Señor* Maritta if he got another chance to do so.

Thoughts of meeting Maria again were put on hold when Dwight was informed that he had been ordered by Sergeant Major Simms to report to the cantonment quartermaster's office. While at Quartermaster Sergeant Lockhart's,'s he informed Dwight that he had been picked to work for him, based on his military record that indicated he'd been a machinist by trade before joining the dragoons.

Dwight explained that he had spent a little over a year as an apprentice but did not feel confident to work on his own.

Lockhart would not hear any excuses. "Stevens, I need someone with machinist experience, however little he has, to make some things that take too long to order and get here from the east."

"Sergeant, I haven't touched a machine in over eighteen months."

"Get yourself familiar with them in here."

"Sergeant, I'm scheduled for patrol tomorrow at sunrise."

"You ain't now. Your orders came down from Captain Blake. He wants you here, working for me. I want you here tomorrow at seven a.m. You work until four p.m. and earn an extra buck a month for your machinist skills. So, as you can see, the army is making it worthwhile. That's all, Stevens."

Dwight returned to the barracks a little disappointed that he was not going out on patrol with the company. He relayed his disappointment to Adolph and Sam.

Sam was the first to respond. "You're disappointed? What the hell is wrong with you? Nine hours a day in a machine shop. No insects, snakes, Apaches, or Davidson. You got to be shitting me. I'd trade you in a heartbeat if I had your skills. Too bad they don't need a foundry man."

"Sam right. Good job in shop. Maybe you get some time to see Spanish lady after work, yes?" He smiled as Dwight looked embarrassed.

Dwight thought to himself, *Maybe Adolph is right. I could spend some time going into Taos, and try to see Maria.* He didn't want to admit he was somewhat taken with the Spanish beauty. He looked at his friends and tried to deny his interest. "No, I wouldn't do that. She made it clear that her father doesn't like American dragoons."

"So why would that stop you, Stevens?" Sam questioned him with a huge smile.

"You lucky to get machine job. Make good use of it," Adolph said and slapped Dwight on the back as he walked away.

Dwight knew his denial was phony. He was concerned that he had feelings for a woman who couldn't have come from a more different lifestyle and background. That night he kept thinking about Maria. He knew he had to see her again. He needed to be tactful in his attempt to find out if she was as interested in him as he already was in her. He also needed to be diplomatic and not offend *Señor* Maritta, who could bring additional trouble for him with both his commanding officer and the town's sheriff.

Sleep did not come easy as he continued to plan how he could be discreet and not draw attention to his attraction to *Señorita* Maritta. He couldn't remember ever feeling so excited about a woman. Finally, he realized the one thing he had to do was fall asleep. He needed to be alert for the new assignment.

The next morning, Dwight reported to the quartermaster sergeant.

"Well, good morning, Private Stevens. You ready to work?"

Sergeant Lockhart said as he finished a cup of coffee.

"Good morning, Sergeant."

"You want a cup of coffee? I keep a little pot on the stove in the back room. Get it while it's fresh. By noon, if it ain't drunk, it's thick and strong."

Dwight watched the man hobble over to a stool and sit. "No, thank you, I've had my cup for the day."

"Let me show you what I have for machines. It took three years to get some of these beauties out here. Some were broke and I had to fix 'em." The sergeant walked him around the small shop, pointing out the machines he had been able to get. "That's my 1818 Whitney milling machine. She's an old one, but she works well. She'll cut down on the time you need when filing. Over there is my Fox, Murray, and Roberts planer I got from Leavenworth. She's almost as old. I got a decent drill press over there."[1]

Dwight noticed a young Mexican boy standing in the doorway to the back room. "And who might this gentleman be, Sergeant?"

"Oh, that's Miguel. He's the foot and hand-power for the machines. He oils them, cleans up the shavings and other things around the machines. I pay him a quarter a week out of my pocket. His family has a small farm outside of Taos. He uses the money to help them."

"He doesn't go to school?"

The sergeant shook his head. Then added, "He don't speak much American, either."

"What type of work do you mostly do in the shop, Sergeant?" Dwight asked.

"Repair work on wagons, like making new axles and things like that. Sometimes I make parts for muskets. Just recently, I made some parts for the captain's grandfather clock he has in his office. It is a German clock his family has had for years. We couldn't get parts for it. That's why you're here."

"What do you mean by that?"

"Well, my hands don't work as well as they used to, and I get bouts of the gout and can't stand for long periods. So when I fixed Blake's clock, he asked me if I needed anything. I told him I needed a helper. He promised he would do something about that. So, here you are."

The two men talked for a while longer, until Lockhart started showing Dwight how to run the machines and communicate with Miguel.

---

[1] **The machines mentioned were known at that time** and could have been available at the Fort.

Before he knew it, the end of the workday had arrived. Dwight asked Lockhart what type of schedule he expected him to work.

"Well, we work Monday through Saturday. On Saturday, I like to close up shop by noon. I like to spend time with my wife. Sunday is the Lord's Day. Unless we got an emergency, the shop's closed."

"So you would have no objection to me going to town on Saturday after work, or Sunday for the day?"

"No, Private, unless your company sergeant has other duties for you to do."

"No, Sergeant. Sergeant Major Simms ordered me to report to you, and Sergeant Quinn has made no fuss about it."

"Well, enjoy your time, Stevens. I expect you back at seven a.m. tomorrow, fit and ready to work."

"Thank you, Sergeant, I will. I will see you first thing in the morning."

Sergeant Lockhart only smiled and nodded.

The rest of the week passed quickly as Sergeant Lockhart gave Dwight different tasks to perform. That following Saturday afternoon, Dwight left the cantonment mounted on Spirit in his cleanest uniform for the ten-mile ride to Taos. The black Morgan got him there quickly.

The inquisitive dragoon found his way about the town, and was able to find the house of Doctor Maritta. The white stucco house with an orange tile roof sat near the center of Taos. Off to the side and connected to the house was a clinic where several people lined up to enter. Dwight had waited for several minutes when the side door opened and Maria stepped out. She never noticed him.

He decided to wait in line behind several of the prospective patients.

Several minutes later, Maria reappeared, only to be startled when she saw him standing in line. He immediately took off his hat when she spoke to him.

"*Señor…*" She paused. "Dwight, what are you doing here? Are you sick?"

"No. I came to see you, Maria."

She spoke Spanish to the next person in line and directed him where to go inside. She turned to Dwight. "I was serious when I told you that my father did not like American dragoons. You know why he feels that way."

"I do, and I understand, but do you feel that way, Maria?"

"It does not matter what I feel. My father would never approve of us even talking like we are now, never mind you visiting my home."

Both turned when they realized her mother had opened the clinic entrance door and was standing there looking at them. She spoke in Spanish to Maria. Just the look on her face was enough for Dwight to realize the uncomfortable position she was in.

Dwight bowed slightly when Maria's mother had finished speaking. She did not acknowledge his politeness, but only glared at Maria for a few seconds and then left.

"My mother is upset that you have come. She is very upset with me. You must leave now. Please do not come here again."

Dwight's face reddened in his embarrassment. "My apologies, Maria. I just thought that maybe I could see you again, and even talk with your father and ask permission to visit you properly."

"Dwight, please listen to me. I know it is not your fault that my brother was killed." She paused to gather her thoughts and to look around to see if her mother had returned. "Actually, I believe the two of you would have been friends. You are the same in so many ways." She pulled him aside, close to the outside wall of the clinic so they would be at least partially out of sight. "Listen to me. You must believe me." She stared into his eyes. "I think of you all the time. You are with me always since we met. My heart is in such pain." Her eyes filled with tears. She blinked, and one tear flowed down her cheek. Dwight gently wiped it away. "Until I can change my father, we cannot see each other. I will not deceive him for any reason. Although he is wrong about this, I love him. Please leave now. Maybe in another time before the war, or before my brother's death, my father would have been a more reasonable man. That time may be gone forever. You must understand."

She turned and entered the clinic door.

He left, and eventually found himself at the local cantina. He sat at a table with a drink and thought about what Maria had said. Several dragoons entered the cantina and were becoming loud as they ordered rounds of tequila. Dwight finished his drink and left as the sun began to set.

He heard someone calling him as he walked to Spirit. It was a female voice. He turned, hoping that Maria had found him and wanted to talk. His eyes followed the sound of a voice as it called again and saw a local brothel he had heard about. The attractive young woman motioned him over. He stepped inside the doorway and thought about leaving, but her gentle and soft hands pulled him closer. He followed her to a room, where she opened the door for him. After he passed through, she closed the door behind him.

Dwight occasionally visited Taos in his free time, but he went with friends to keep from thinking about catching a glimpse of Maria at the clinic. Although embarrassed and hurt by her reaction to seeing him again, he understood the animosity her father had for the dragoons.

On one Sunday a couple of months later, Dwight, Sam, Adolph, and several other dragoons saddled their horses and left the cantonment with the intent of spending some time in Taos. Several miles from town, they came upon the sheriff and deputy on the main road. A few hundred feet from meeting the approaching riders, the sheriff raised his left hand up in a sign for the dragoons to stop. They all had apparently ignored his signal and continued riding. They immediately stopped when he fired his pistol into the air.

He yelled to the men, "I'm Sheriff Kit Carson! We have sickness in the town and I am ordering you to stay away. Tell Captain Blake that the town will be off-limits."

Sam Sample inquired, "Sheriff, what kind of sickness?"

"The town's doctor says it's cholera. It started about four days ago. We got a lot of sick people, and we don't need to be spreading it to the cantonment. Turn around and tell your captain and surgeon what I said."

Sam saluted the sheriff, turned to the dragoons, and said, "You heard the man. We gotta get back and tell what's happened."

Dwight froze in his saddle as he thought about Señorita Maria being right in the middle of the epidemic. He didn't respond when Sam called to him to turn around.

Dwight yelled to the Sheriff, "Did Dr. Maritta report that, Sheriff?"

"He's the only doctor in town. Tell your surgeon he needs help."

Dwight prayed to himself, *Dear God, please protect Maria.*

Word spread quickly in Cantonment Burgwin. Captain Blake ordered double guards to ensure that no locals came from town and entered the cantonment. Patrols around the cantonment were increased to a two-mile radius to assure isolation from the epidemic. The only person allowed to leave was the cantonment surgeon and his wife, to aid Dr. Maritta. Captain Blake sent wagons of clean water and food supplies to within one mile of the town. The teamsters would leave the wagons and ride back on mounts that they had tied to the wagons. The sheriff got men in town to drive the wagons to the clinic and other places that served as temporary areas to treat the epidemic. The military population waited for news from town. A week went by, and reports began to reach headquarters that a third of the town had come down with cholera. Of those, half had succumbed to it. Dwight prayed that Maria and her family had survived.

When permission was granted to enter Taos, Dwight left the following Saturday directly from the machine shop. He rode to the clinic to find many townspeople still on cots under large canvases to protect them from the sun. He passed the cots and entered the clinic. He found the dragoon surgeon and his wife still attending to patients.

The surgeon looked at Dwight and asked, "Private, why are you here?"

"Sir, I've come to find Señorita Maritta."

The surgeon looked away and put down the cloth and basin he had been holding. Dwight waited for the man to speak. The surgeon paused and looked at his wife.

Dwight looked as both stood in silence.

The wife spoke first. "They are all in the back, past the garden. We are alone in here."

The surgeon turned and began to treat another patient. Dwight looked at his wife.

She began to turn her back on him as she assisted her husband, but she stopped. She extended her arm, pointed, and said, "Look behind the house. She is with her family in the garden. They are all out there."

Alarmed by her solemn explanation, he followed where the surgeon's wife had pointed. In a short time he found the garden and searched until he found what the surgeon's wife had been pointing to. At the edge, he found the small family cemetery. A stone marked the grave of Juan Miguel Gonzales y Maritta. He knew it was the grave of Maria's brother.

He froze when he realized there were two fresh graves on either side. He fell to his knees and thought to himself, *That is what the woman was trying to tell me. They are all here.* He felt numb, nauseated, and weak, as he found himself sitting in the dirt staring at the fresh graves. He prayed for all their souls.

He heard someone behind him. He didn't turn, thinking it was the surgeon's wife. Then he heard her voice.

"You have come. I had hoped you would, though I could not blame you if you never wanted to see me again."

He turned to see Maria standing there. She looked exhausted and pale. But her slight smile was the most beautiful sight he could have ever imagined. He stood up and ran to her. They embraced, and he held her tightly as she began to sob. They stood in the garden until she stopped and lifted her head to speak.

"We could not save either of them. My mother and father are gone. We saved many people, but could not save the two that had saved the most."

He did not say a word as he let her explain what had occurred in the past three weeks. When she finished he asked, "What can I do to help you?"

"You already have, my love. You have come to comfort me."

He realized what she had called him and held her again and did not let go until she gently pushed him away. "You may help us today with the last of the patients we have at the clinic. The surgeon and his wife are exhausted too. Your help would be greatly appreciated."

He stayed the rest of the afternoon and late into the evening, until it was time to go back to the cantonment. Before he left, he asked, "May I come again to see you, Maria?"

She smiled, touched his hand, and then gently kissed him on his cheek. "Yes. Please call on me when you are free from your duties."

He was happily encouraged by her kiss and pleased at what he heard. "I will come tomorrow. I am free on Sundays."

"No, tomorrow I will attend Mass with my uncle. I have not attended for several weeks."

"I will come next week on Saturday, after I am free from my duties."

"Yes, that would be fine. But I must warn you, my uncle Roberto Gonzales will not be pleased to see you."

"I assume that he is your mother's brother?"

"Yes, he is that, and my godfather as well. He is also a very good friend of our sheriff and tells that to everyone. But I will tell him tomorrow that you will be calling. He won't be a bother, for I am of age, but he does feel responsible for me, as you must understand."

"I do and I will be the utmost gentleman in his presence."

"Only in his presence, *señor*?" She smiled and looked into his eyes. He blushed. He was about to explain when she gently touched his lips with her index finger. "Do not explain. I was only trying to be amusing."

He smiled and slightly bowed while grabbing her hand. He gently kissed it.

"Dwight, I will look forward to seeing you. Thank you for your help and friendship."

"It was my duty to offer help, but I do want to offer more than friendship, Maria."

She smiled. He left her standing at the entrance to the clinic. He mounted Spirit, waved to her as she stood watching him, and galloped away. He didn't remember the ride back to the cantonment, but before he knew it he was passing through the front gate. All he could think of during his ride was Maria Gonzales y Maritta.

Chapter Fourteen

The Battle of Cieneguilla

Dwight awoke on Sunday morning to find the barracks stirring with activity as the dragoons prepared to go on patrol. Sam and Adolph said that they were surprised to see him.

"Why would you say that?"

Both men smiled as they looked at each other. Sam spoke first. "Well, when you rode out yesterday, hell-bent on seeing that Spanish lady, we figured on not seeing you for a couple of weeks. We're going on patrol to the border to check on some reported Mexican crossings into American territory. The captain is leading us himself. Three companies, I hear."

"Our entire company is going?"

"Yep, all but you and a few that are in the dispensary. We got a new second lieutenant named David Bell[1] from Fort Union. He seems to be pretty sharp. He's got some Indian experience. Got a level head too, I hear. Bell will be in charge of the cantonment while Blake takes Davidson and two of the other company officers[2] with him on the patrol. Sergeant Major Simms will be here to make sure things run smoothly."

"I wish I could go with you."

"And miss Spanish Lady?" Adolph said and then smiled.

Dwight laughed at his German friend. He was right. Dwight really didn't want to go with them. "See you when you get back."

"Guard the cantonment for us," Sam said, and Adolph laughed.

Dwight watched the three companies mount and depart. While he did have a feeling of envy, his thoughts continued to focus on Maria, and before he realized it the companies were out of sight. He stayed in the cantonment for the day. He tempted himself with a trip to Taos, but went to the commissary instead. He found several new books that had just arrived with supplies from Fort Leavenworth.

Moby Dick and *Uncle Tom's Cabin* seemed strange names for novels, but Dwight read a little from each and decided on the latter. He read Stowe's book until he finished it. He couldn't get enough, and was sad to

---

[1] **Lieutenant David Bell** formally accused Lieutenant Davidson at the Battle of Cieneguilla of needlessly risking the lives of his troops.

[2] **Dragoon officers' names are real,** and each served at the time in the U.S. Dragoons in New Mexico.

finish it. He considered it enlightenment for anyone who would read it, and thought the book was the most informative and important novel he had ever read. When his company returned, he figured he would recommend it to all his friends.

Monday morning brought several tasks that Quartermaster Sergeant Lockhart needed completed quickly. That meant he would need pedal power from the young Mexican boy. As the work proceeded during the day, Dwight realized that the youth could be of assistance to him outside the shop as well.

"Miguel, do you understand English better than I understand Spanish?"

The youth did not respond as he pedaled on the 1818 Whitney milling machine.

The Quartermaster Sergeant overheard his question to Miguel, and said, "He understands a little American a lot better than you do any Mexican, Stevens. Don't you, Miguel?"

Miguel only smiled.

Dwight understood that he would have to gain the friendship of the boy if he was going to communicate with him as Lockhart apparently could. Dwight continued to talk politely to him when he needed assistance and maintained this despite the boy's silence.

Several hours into the afternoon, Miguel finally answered Dwight. "*Señor* Stevens, you talk all day. I understand."

Dwight smiled. "Miguel, I need a favor from you. I want you to teach me some Spanish. I want to say polite things to a lady friend of mine. Do you understand?"

"*Si, Señor. Yo comprendo.*"

Dwight looked surprised and then realized Miguel had done exactly as he had requested.

"You probably are wondering why I have an interest in learning a little Spanish."

"No, *Señor. Comprendo usted tiene una novia,*" he said and smiled.

"What did you just say, Miguel?"

"He said he understood, and that you have a girlfriend, Stevens. Christ, listen to the kid," Lockhart said, then laughed and walked back into the backroom.

A closer relationship began that day between Dwight and Miguel as the boy began to teach him the basics of the Spanish language. By the end of the week, Dwight Stevens had a better understanding of the language. However, it would be months more before he felt comfortable enough to have even a limited conversation using Spanish.

Saturday afternoon came, and Dwight saddled Spirit quickly. The

Morgan galloped into Taos and directly to the home of *Señorita* Maria. He arrived, dismounted, walked casually to the front door, and knocked softly. He waited for what seemed to be an eternity until the door slowly opened and Maria stood there in a pretty blue dress and a beautiful smile. She motioned for him to enter.

He obliged and found a gentleman standing in the foyer, hat in hand and with what seemed to be a frown on his face.

"*Señor* Dwight Stevens, may I introduce my godfather and uncle, *Señor* Roberto Gonzales. Uncle, this is my friend Dwight, who has come to visit me." She moved from between them so the two men could meet.

Dwight extended his hand and said, "I am very pleased to meet you, *señor.*"

Gonzales did not extend his hand, but asked, "What are your intentions with my niece, *señor*?"

"My intentions, sir, are honorable. I seek your permission to visit, maybe have dinner with Maria, or even walk with her in town. Anything that is appropriate."

Her uncle was taken aback by Dwight's tone and noticed the politeness in his delivery. He looked at Maria and then back to Dwight and spoke. "That is an honorable request, *señor.* I will give you my permission to visit, dine, and walk on the street with her. I will not agree to much more than that. Do you understand?"

"*Si, señor. Yo comprendo.*"

"Good. I see that you are attempting to learn our language. I also must inform you that I am very friendly with our sheriff. *Señor* Carson will be informed of your intentions."

"I know of him and his reputation. He was a dragoon like I am and a scout during his career in the army."

"I am aware, *señor*, of *Señor* Carson's character. He has proven his honor and integrity to me. You must do the same."

Dwight answered with a nod that he understood.

Señor Gonzales turned to his niece, kissed her on the cheek, and walked past Dwight out the door.

"He will get to like you in time," Maria said.

"What makes you think he will?"

"Because he has always given me what I have requested. He will like you because I like you. He is a good man, as you will learn." She smiled again as she put her hand in his, and they stepped off the stairs leading to the street. They spent the day together, including having dinner at the hotel café. He walked her home in the dim dusk light.

Dwight said that he would like to see her the next day. Maria agreed that he could, after she attended Mass. She asked that he come in the afternoon.

Thus began a relationship that was pursued weekly for several months. In that time, Dwight learned more Spanish from Miguel, and Miguel learned better English from Dwight. When Dwight was not with Maria, he was either working in the shop or reading on the weeknights in the barracks. He read Herman Melville's *Moby Dick* and Nathaniel Hawthorne's *House of Seven Gables*, which he enjoyed more than he expected. Some dragoons, including Corporal May, took Dwight's suggestion and read both novels. Dwight suggested that everyone read Stowe's novel, but a few of the Southerners would not read *Uncle Tom's Cabin* when they learned of its content.

The romance was temporarily halted when Quartermaster Sergeant Lockhart completed the backlog of machine work and Sergeant Major Simms reassigned Dwight back to full-time duty with Company F. Almost immediately, the company was called to patrol the Mexican border again when outbreaks of hostilities were reported between the Apaches and settlers from Las Cruces to Yuma.

The patrols usually lasted a week to ten days, but Dwight returned and visited Maria as often as time and his newly scheduled patrols permitted. Their happy relationship continued through the winter of 1852-53.

Colonel Fauntleroy at Fort Union ordered Captain Blake to patrol the border between Mexico and the United States, specifically the land that was still under dispute between the two countries.[1] It formalized the southern border for the first time since the end of the hostilities in 1848, and also served as the right of way for the new railroad that was being planned for the territory.

The dragoons welcomed the news that boundaries would finally be set between the two countries, opening up settlement space for pioneers moving into the area and pushing the Indian tribes out of the way of the new railroad. Rumors were heard in the barracks that the new patrol would take approximately a month. Dwight didn't want to go on one that lengthy, knowing how much he would miss Maria.

On a Saturday, the day before the company was scheduled to depart, Dwight told Maria that he would be gone on a long patrol. She took the news in stride as they walked together that day.

The couple had become a common sight. The sheriff, as well as

---

[1] **The Gadsden Purchase -** is a 29,670-square-mile region of present-day southern Arizona and southwestern New Mexico that was purchased by the United States in a treaty signed by James Gadsden, the American ambassador to Mexico at the time, on December 30, 1853.

Señor Gonzales, had grown accustomed to them walking arm and arm in the streets and having dinner together in full view of the town's citizens. But on this particular evening when Dwight prepared to leave Maria for the night and go on patrol, Maria held him even tighter and kissed him longer than was usual. Dwight could see she did not want him to leave. After several moments of deep thought, while gazing into Dwight's dark eyes, she made a decision. Maria smiled up at him, blushing slightly, and told him to lead his horse around to the clinic entrance.

He obliged but was curious as to her request.

"Tie your horse over there and wait here for a minute, then enter the clinic. I have a gift for you."

He followed her instructions and returned to the clinic door and entered. Several candles were lit, indicating the path he should follow. They ended at a door that was slightly opened. He entered and realized it was her father's medical library. In the corner of the room was a single bed that had been used by the physician when he had patients in the clinic overnight.

When Dwight's eyes adjusted to the light of a dim candle, he saw Maria lying in bed with a linen sheet covering her. He watched as she slowly uncovered and exposed her beauty to him. He had never beheld such beauty in his life. He began to approach when she motioned for him to stop and said, "Please, undress before you lie with me."

He slowly obeyed as he looked upon her. That sight would be burnt into his memory forever. They made love until the pre-dawn hours and parted, vowing that they would keep their union a secret.

Dwight returned to the cantonment just as the dragoons began to prepare for their patrol. As Dwight fumbled with his gear, the scent and sight of Maria was still with him. He was smiling as he prepared to depart. His comrades noticed it. Neither Sam nor Adolph ever asked why he had returned late, but one look at him and they had no need.

The patrol took almost four weeks to complete. The winter temperatures at night dropped below freezing. Fresh game was hard to find as the patrol moved along the new boundary, and the men began to grumble about the hard tack, jerky, and the occasional elk they had to eat.

On one occasion they were able to shoot a bear. The male specimen weighed over four hundred pounds and had apparently been flushed from his hibernation, became disoriented, and ended up in someone's sights. The carcass was dressed and the meat roasted on an open fire.

Dwight found the meat very greasy and hard to enjoy, despite his hunger. It was apparent that even Captain Blake did not enjoy the meat as the men had expected him to, given all his boasting of his experience with killing bears. Word spread quickly that he actually didn't take kindly to eating fat, as he had said he had gladly done to survive years earlier. His reputation became very questionable in the eyes of some of the men.

Captain Blake and the dragoons returned to Cantonment Burgwin almost one month later. Dwight did not have any time to visit Maria because he was immediately assigned temporary duty to Fort Massachusetts,[1] some eighty-five miles north of Taos.

The stay at Fort Massachusetts during the late winter and early spring of 1853 took its toll on the dragoons. Only fifty dragoons could be billeted at one time due to the constant influx of passing settlers. Spring afforded some relief to the occupancy as the settlers, however, left to build settlements. The location was strategic but hazardous during the summer months. A large swamp was located nearby, which spawned mosquito larva and malaria.

In the spring of 1853, Dwight and part of Company F were replaced by another contingent. Sam Sample and Adolph Starke were in it. Sample and Starke began patrols in the San Luis Valley, where malaria began to affect the settlers, soldiers, and Indians alike.

Sam and Adolph were ill during those months, but were ordered to go on patrol despite their sickness. The surgeon of Fort Massachusetts prescribed high doses of sulfate quinine to treat them, but that treatment later killed two dragoons in Company F.

Sam continued to be affected more than most and almost died when he was administered too much of the medication. Adolph helped nurse him back to health. The two deserted from Fort Massachusetts one night and were never heard from again. Dwight learned of his two best friends' desertion only after the Company F contingent returned.

All told, two dragoons had died, two had deserted, and seven were still feeling the effects of malaria. It would be five more years before Fort Massachusetts was abandoned due to the many cases of malaria.

Dwight and Maria continued their relationship under the watchful eyes of *Señor* Gonzales, who made privacy for them rare. The townspeople and the sheriff enjoyed seeing the happy couple walking through the town and frequenting the general store and hotel café.

Maria attended Mass on Sunday mornings while Dwight stayed at the cantonment until noon. Discussion of their individual religious beliefs were avoided, though Maria slowly began to perceive that Dwight's

---

[1] **Fort Massachusetts** was established in 1852 on the banks of Ute Creek in what is now Colorado, to protect the travelers and settlers from the local Indians. It was a poorly chosen location for a fort due to a nearby swampy area, and the fort was no longer in use after 1858.

opinions were different from hers. She never questioned or attempted to read *The Age of Reason*, however, and he never felt the need to attend Mass with her. They occasionally enjoyed privacy when *Señor* Gonzales was on business out of Taos.

When not on patrol, Dwight spent his free time with Maria or working with Corporal May to organize more musicals in 1853. Marvin Church and his small band organized and played for the dances that were held a few Saturdays a month, which Maria often attended.

Second Lieutenant Bell became a proficient patrol commander, and most of the men in Company F had complete confidence in him. This came about as the result of Corporal May's continued assistance during patrols when he was assigned to accompany Bell. Longer patrols that required larger numbers of dragoons were assigned to recently promoted First Lieutenant Davidson, along with Sergeant Quinn.

Dwight avoided the larger patrols as often as he could by volunteering for the shorter and more frequent ones when they were scheduled. The shorter patrols tended to remain relatively uneventful, as the purpose was to simply maintain a visible presence with the Indians. Recently promoted Major Blake scheduled the longer patrols to seek out areas where cattle and horse stealing had been reported, usually blamed on renegade bands of Indians.

Dwight was fortunate to maintain this type of patrol duty throughout the winter months of 1853–54. However, on March 26, 1854, approximately sixty dragoons under the command of First Lieutenant Davidson left Cantonment Burgwin under strict orders from Major Blake to patrol the Rio Grande basin and report on the Jicarilla Apaches. They were supposedly camped with an unknown number of Ute Indians and had moved south from the Colorado Territory during the winter.

Major Blake ordered Davidson not to engage unless attacked. His orders were to sight and report on any movement the combined tribes made. Dwight Stevens, Jim Anders, and Marvin Church were assigned to this patrol. The patrol followed the Rio Grande, and on the morning of the 29th, First Lieutenant Davidson ordered Scout Jesus Silva and Dragoon Jeremiah Maloney to scout ahead and observe any Apache or Ute movements. Their main objective was to arrive at the Embudo crossing of the Rio Grande and report any movement made by the defiant band of Indians. Dwight watched as the two men galloped away in a southwesterly direction, as they continued at a trot following the river.

Second Lieutenant Bell and Corporal May rode out ahead of the patrol that was several hours behind the scouts, looking for a suitable campsite that afforded a good defensive position next to the river. An encampment was picked by Bell near a swampy area of the Rio Grande that the Indians call Cieneguilla, or little swamp. The March weather was cool and calm that night.

A heavy guard was posted and changed every two hours. During the pre-dawn hours, Scout Silva and Dragoon Maloney reached the crossing and found no evidence that any tribe had been there. They did see distant campfires twinkling atop a ridge to their northeast, however, and returned to the dragoon encampment at Cieneguilla to report. When First Lieutenant Davidson was informed of the Indian's position, he immediately broke camp and ordered the patrol to prepare for a surprise assault on the Indian position.

While the men saddled their mounts, checked their weapons, and awaited their final orders, First Lieutenant Davidson and Second Lieutenant Bell met to discuss the plan to engage.

Before the conversation commenced, Bell led Davidson away from their NCOs, who stood nearby awaiting Davidson's orders. "Sir, I would suggest a more appropriate approach by ordering our scouts to watch the Indian encampments on the ridge. We could remain here in a defensive position, waiting to see what direction they take from the ridge. If they seem peaceful and ignore our presence, all we do is parallel their movements."

"They are not peaceful, Bell. I do not want to wait for the scouts. I believe surprise is to our advantage. You and I both know that they will be sleeping and will maintain a minimal posting of guards. We will break up the Jicarilla Apache and Ute union before it can become an effective threat."

"Sir, we have no information as to the size and position of the Indians. This was not in the orders we received from Major Blake."

"I am aware of Major Blake's orders, Lieutenant. He instructed us to find the defiant band of Apaches who were reportedly joining forces with the Ute Indians."

"Yes, sir. We found them, but I believe we should gather more information as to their size and intentions. This could be the mere remnants of Lobo Blanco's cattle thieves that I dealt with last month, but now they have an unknown number of Ute warriors with them."

"I am well aware of your encounter with Lobo Blanco[1]. He's dead, but I am sure someone else has taken command and has now joined up with a group of defiant Ute Indians. Like I said before, Lieutenant Bell, these Jicarilla Apache warriors are puny cowards. They will be

---

[1] The **Jicarilla War** began in 1849 and was fought between the Jicarilla Apaches leader, Lobo Blanco, who was killed, and the United States military in New Mexico.

overwhelmed by fear at our surprise assault."

"Sir, they will hear and see us coming well before we reach the ridge."

"I doubt that. And even if they do, they are only armed with bows and arrows, and maybe a few flintlocks. Lieutenant, you are forgetting that we are United States Dragoons. We are better trained, have significant firepower over our enemy, and they are a primitive people with primitive fighting skills."

"Sir, again, I must warn you that these Indians have not provoked us and are possibly in a good defensive position to cause us trouble if we try to dislodge them if they stand and fight. They could ambush us before we reach the ridge, and they do possess formidable fighting ability."

"So noted, Lieutenant Bell, but we have the element of surprise and superior firepower. Each dragoon will do his duty. This engagement should be over in minutes. Now, if there are no more objections, get your men ready to engage."

"Yes, sir." Bell walked back to Corporal May and gave orders. "Corporal, see that the men are ready to mount up immediately."

"Yes, sir." May turned and walked to his dragoons. "You heard the lieutenant. Prepare for the command to mount up." May walked back to where Bell was saddling his mount. "Sir, what's the plan the lieutenant has in mind?"

"He wants a frontal assault on their position before they are awake."

May looked at his pocket watch. "It's five-thirty, Lieutenant. It will take us some time to get sixty men close enough to engage them. By that time, they will either be gone or be waiting in ambush for us."

"I know, May. Just follow your orders." Obvious frustration laced Bell's voice as he mounted his horse and looked at May to do the same.

Dwight heard the last few words of the exchange between Bell and May. He looked to another dragoon named Jim Bennett. "Did you hear what Bell said?"

"Yeah, part of it."

Marvin Church heard the conversation and looked to Jim Anders. "I don't like what I'm hearin', Jim."

"Let's hope the assault scares the shit out of 'em and they just scatter. Most of them will be on foot then and we can easily cut 'em down. We'll get most of them that way. Maybe we get their horses too, and that will be it."

"I heard them say that they don't know the number of 'em."

"Shit, Marvin, we should be able to kill two or three apiece. That should wipe them out if there is that many."

The men heard the order to mount and form in columns of two. Within minutes, First Lieutenant Davidson led the patrol of sixty men toward the ridge.

It took an hour for the patrol to slowly ascend the ridge. The slope was steep and forced them to move parallel until a more favorable and less sloped area could be found. The weather had warmed and the sky, which had previously threatened rain, cleared.

Davidson noticed that the two scouts had stopped ahead. He slowed the patrol.

Lieutenant Bell rode up and asked, "Sir, are there signs of Apaches?"

"I don't know yet. The scouts are returning. We'll stop and wait for their report."

Private Maloney and Scout Silva told Davidson, when they arrived, that they suspected an ambush could be up ahead.

"Is there, or isn't there, an ambush, Scouts?"

"Sir, Scout Silva and I believe that we could be going into one."

"Did you see Apache or Ute warriors?"

"I can't say we did, but we saw signs that an ambush might be their intention."

"Private, if you or Scout Silva have not seen any warriors, we will continue on ahead."

"Yes, sir." Maloney saluted, turned his horse, and galloped back with Scout Silva.

Second Lieutenant Bell drew a breath. "Sir, maybe we should …"

"Return to your men, Lieutenant Bell," Davidson said. "Be prepared to engage. We move ahead. Sergeant Quinn, give the order."

Bell returned to his secondary position and ordered May to prepare the men for a possible engagement. The look on May's face indicated that the worst could possibly be about to unfold for the dragoons. May looked at the landscape and realized the dragoons would be mostly in the open if the enemy chose to fight there. He shouted orders to check weapons.

Dwight's stomach turned in anticipation of the coming battle. He understood Bell's concern that the Indians now knew how many dragoons were approaching them. He looked over at Bugler Cook and checked his smoothbore carbine to ensure it was loaded, then checked his pistol. He double-checked his rounds. He hoped he carried enough for what he feared would happen.

Davidson ordered the column to proceed with caution as they rode at a walk. Several minutes slowly passed, and then suddenly Sergeant Quinn took an arrow to his right thigh. Several more arrows found their mark in his horse. The mount reared, lost his footing, and fell while the sergeant tried to maintain his position atop the horse. Several shots from flintlocks were heard, and the dragoons began to break away from their column position and spread out in a defensive location on the slope of the ridge.

Bell saw the initial engagement and looked at May and pointed. Bell ordered the dragoons forward at a gallop to support and stop what looked to be complete confusion in Davidson's leading column.

Bell's arrival allowed the confused dragoons to dismount, seek cover, and begin to answer the enemy fire. Davidson was still on his horse when his mount suddenly dropped from under him as three arrows stuck out from the horse's neck and side.

Bell's dragoons were now under fire from shot and arrow. He yelled, "Dismount, dismount!"

Within a minute, the heavy fire being produced by the Apache and Ute warriors had pinned down the entire dragoon patrol. Their whooping and hollering sent chills down the spines of the dragoons as they began to concentrate fire on those they could see.

Lieutenant Bell realized that the dragoon mounts were being butchered by the flintlock fire and numerous arrows that were finding their mark on the screaming animals. He ordered, "Horse handlers, to the rear!"

Several dragoons got the reins of their horses and quickly began pulling them to the rear and out of harm's way. The order was fruitless for one dragoon as he gathered the reins of a few horses, then fell dead from an arrow to the neck. Some other dragoons managed to collect six or seven horses that still continued to receive arrow wounds as they led them to the rear.

Lieutenant Bell screamed at his men to seek cover from the continual onslaught of the Indian attack. He worked his way to Davidson, who had found protection and was firing his pistol. "Sir, we need to sound a retreat and find a better position to defend ourselves."

Davidson didn't respond at first as he continued to fire his pistol.

Bell screamed into his ear, and the man finally turned and nodded his head to sound the retreat.

Bell yelled to Sergeant Quinn, "Find Bugler Cook! Tell him to sound the retreat!"

Quinn looked at Davidson, who began to back away from his cover and fall to the rear. He stood up while grabbing his wounded leg to move and find Cook, then fell from an arrow wound to the chest.

Bell ran and checked the sergeant. He was dead with his eyes open and a puzzled look on his face. The arrow had apparently pierced his heart. Bell found Cook, who had taken cover behind the falling trunk of a dead and rotted fir tree. "Sound the retreat. Fall back several hundred feet down the trail and keep blowing that damn bugle until I tell you to stop."

Cook picked up the bugle and sounded the retreat.

Bell watched as the dragoons slowly and carefully withdrew from their positions. He was proud of the way they carried their wounded and were still able to return concentrated fire at the Indians. Several warriors ran at the retreating dragoons, trying to kill those who were carrying the wounded. The dragoons cut them down as they approached. The firepower held the Indians at bay until the dragoons could find a better place to defend themselves.

Scout Silva finally found Davidson. He informed his commander that he estimated there were several hundred Apache and Ute warriors engaged in the ambush. Davidson did not acknowledge him. He just kept firing as quickly as he could reload his pistol.

Corporal May overheard the scout yelling his assessment and relayed the information back to Bell, who was trying to set up a defensive position and take the wounded out of the line of fire. He encouraged the wounded that could still shoot a weapon to keep it up.

May glanced at his pocket watch and realized that the ambush had lasted only about fifteen minutes. He estimated that Bell's dragoons had seven or eight dead, with ten or so wounded. He couldn't estimate Davidson's casualties because both his sergeant and corporal were dead. Corporal May moved about, trying to assess the strength of Davidson's men as the firing slowed and the dragoons regrouped.

Lieutenant Bell reached Bugler Cook and signaled for him to stop blowing the retreat. He moved among the men to assess ammunition needs, wounds, and positions, and screamed at them to conserve ammunition.

First Lieutenant Davidson regained his composure when he found Second Lieutenant Bell returning from his quick appraisal of the situation. Davidson gave him orders. "This is a good position. We'll hold here and see if they expose themselves. We'll cut them down during their advance."

"I think we should not wait any longer, sir. We should disengage and move slowly but defensively back, before they outflank us. They could be doing that right now. We don't want to be cut off from our horses. I don't know how many we have left, or all the casualties yet either."

"Lieutenant, I'm not running away from these bastards. Let them come, now that we know where they are. We'll cut them down as they charge us."

"Sir, we don't know how many there are. Silva estimates over a hundred, maybe more. We don't know how many we have killed, so we must withdraw down the ridge and back toward our encampment position. If they choose to follow us and attack, we will be in a better position. Right here we are still blind."

"No. We stay and defend from their attack that I know is coming. Alert the men to take careful aim and make every shot count."

"Sir, we should withdraw from this!" Bell screamed at him.

Davidson stiffened. "Alert your men to make every shot count. That is all, Bell."

Lieutenant Bell sent Corporal May to count horses and see to it that there was ample protection to assure that the warriors could not kill or steal them. May posted several more dragoons to protect the animals. Bell counted only twenty horses. He prayed that more had trotted down the trail when the firing began.

Several minutes passed, and Bell's prediction of an Indian flank attack came true. Bell yelled to Cook to blow his bugle and alert the men to withdraw in an orderly manner. He then took eight or nine dragoons with him to counter the flanking movement the warriors were attempting.

Dwight followed Bell, Church, and six other dragoons to engage in the attack. The blanket of fire laid by Bell's dragoons was effective enough to stall the attack. Dwight knew he had killed or wounded several warriors and quickly estimated that a dozen or more had been cut down by his fellow men. He felt pain in his right thigh and realized a ball had grazed it. He saw Church pull an arrow from his right upper boot. The boot stopped most of the arrow's impact, but his boot was now full of blood.

Anders had been shot from his horse. His wound under his left arm was not serious and he was able to hold his weapon, but it was painful. Their efforts slowed the advance of the warriors still trying to cut off the dragoons from their horses. Bugler Cook sounded the call to retreat. The wounded were quickly thrown on or over the horses and led away by mounted dragoons. Fire was concentrated on any of the warriors that attempted to stop the orderly retreat.

The dragoons moved off the ridge, anticipating the warriors would not follow. Lieutenant Davidson still had hopes for a victory and found a better position to salvage the day. During the lull in the action, Bell observed him assigning the men in groups of three and four to defensive positions. Bell, in the meantime, had assessed that by now there were approximately thirty or more horses rounded up. Corporal May was still determining the number of wounded. He had reported fifteen confirmed dead.

Then another combined Apache and Ute attack started. Bell returned to his men as Davidson's dragoons opened fire on the advancing warriors, who screamed and ran straight at them. The surge was quickly halted with considerable warrior losses. Another advance came within minutes of the first. Again the dragoons were successful in stopping them.

Lieutenant Bell saw that the warriors were attempting another flanking movement. He also realized that the movements were developing in unison with the frontal attacks. Bell ordered his dragoons to counterattack, hoping that Davidson could sustain his defense. His tactic worked, and both warrior attacks wavered and then quickly retreated with heavy casualties.

Davidson would have remained, but he knew he had sustained heavy losses. He saw five dead and six or seven more wounded immediately around him. He yelled at Cook to sound another retreat.

Bell ordered May, Stevens, Church, Anders, and six other dragoons, to protect the organized retreat back to their Cieneguilla encampment. They had engaged a combined band of approximately two hundred warriors for almost three hours.

Corporal May reported that he could not account for twenty-two dragoons. Of the names he listed, most were confirmed dead by the other dragoons. Thirty-eight dragoons remained after the engagement, and thirty-six had various wounds. No supply horses were found, and they were assumed dead or taken by the warriors.

The patrol limped back to Cantonment Burgwin late in the afternoon. Major Blake was aghast at the amount of casualties his dragoons had suffered during the battle. He immediately assigned Sergeant Major Simms to find out what had happened, while he went to receive the report from Lieutenant Davidson.

It was late into the evening before Dwight received medical attention for the wound to his thigh. Anders remained in the dispensary from the wound that he had received to his armpit. Marvin Church bitched that the arrow had ruined a good pair of boots. He was also thankful that the thickness of the leather had slowed the arrow in penetrating his calf.

A report on the battle was held in Major Blake's office with only the three officers present. No one would know of the conversation that took place that evening until a few weeks later when Brigadier General John Garland announced that a formal inquiry had been requested in Taos. Second Lieutenant Bell had filed an official accusation that stated First Lieutenant Davidson had risked the lives of his dragoons when he did not have to fight the warriors, and could and should have avoided the ambush. Garland disregarded the accusation and praised Davidson and his dragoons for gallantry in the face of hostile Indians.

Major Blake sent a large patrol of one hundred men back to the battlefield to collect as many dead dragoons as could be found. The men were buried at Cantonment Burgwin.[1] Most of the dragoons, including Dwight, felt that Davidson's report to Major Blake was not accurate. But it was the only report recognized up the chain of command. As a result, Second Lieutenant Bell was transferred back to Fort Union. He filed another accusation there. His second request turned into a formal Court of Inquiry, held exactly two years later. The results were similar to the version General Garland had given. Lieutenant Davidson was vindicated of all accusations.

Dwight returned to the arms of Maria and was lovingly pampered as his thigh wound healed over the next few weeks. Corporal May had given all the wounded combatants extra time off from duty so they could heal properly. Dwight and Maria used the time to rekindle their love.

Eventually, Maria asked questions about the loved ones he had back in Connecticut. He described all the members of his family to her. Dwight had to laugh as he fondly remembered his father. He explained to Maria that his father ran a "tight ship" with his choir. He tried to describe what his father and his choir were like.

"He must have given you that beautiful singing voice you have," Maria said.

"Yes, I inherited that from him. But he did try to perfect it. You had to sing the hymns and songs he taught to absolute perfection or suffer the consequences. He was very strict during rehearsals."

"He must have been very strict, since you turned out to be a good singer."

"Oh, so you like the way I sing, do you?"

"You know I do." Maria smiled and asked him more about his childhood. "Were you a quiet child, always staying obedient to your father? You describe him as a very stern man."

Dwight laughed. "Oh yes, he was, and still is, a stern man. But I was too stubborn at times, and it caused me some unneeded whippings. If I had been a little less obstinate and a lot smarter, I wouldn't have undergone the stick so much."

She laughed. "Yes, that I can understand. You are a persistent young man."

He smiled and held her. The smell of her being close to him

---

[1] **Modern Version of The Battle of Cieneguilla** — Recently a grant was given to help perform an archaeological excavation of the battlefield. After a year of working to locate the exact site, the survey was accomplished. The findings are in Douglas Scott's *Fields of Conflict, Vol. 2*, and they support most of Lieutenant David Bell's accusations concerning Lieutenant Davidson's actions. They also concluded that the dragoons had been thoroughly routed.

awakened every sense within him.

She continued. "So, what else can you tell me about *Señor* Aaron Dwight Stevens? No, let me tell you. You were always in trouble at school, yes?" She poked him in an attempt to tickle him.

He laughed as he evaded the attempt. "I always got in trouble with the schoolmaster, and my bad temper usually made things worse."

She seemed more interested than just kidding him now. Her face turned a little serious. "Please, tell me how bad you were. I think I need to hear about it." She looked deep into his eyes and squeezed him to pull him closer.

"Well…" He paused and looked at her. She looked like a little girl as she waited intently for him to begin his story. "Well, when I was getting toward the end of my education, a young friend named Edmund Clarence Stedman[1] got into trouble with our summer schoolmaster, Mr. Aikman, who threatened to take a feruling to him for a comment he had made. I forget exactly what Stedman had said, but it made Mr. Aikman very mad. I didn't like Aikman because of the way he treated us, so when he yelled that he was going to give Stedman something he'd remember, anger came over me and I yelled out that if he gave a licking to Stedman, he'd have to lick me first."

Maria giggled and asked, "You didn't do that, did you? You really said that?"

"Unfortunately, I did. The old man was taken aback and asked me what I had said. I repeated it."

"What happened next?"

"He said he was giving me and another boy who had also opened his mouth ten demerits, and to hold out our hands. So I put out my hand for Aikman to hit."

"And did he?"

"No. I guess the look on my face kept him from following through with it. But he went after Edmund. He missed, and the ferule fell to the floor. Edmund picked it up and handed it back to Mr. Aikman in

---

[1] **Edmund Clarence Stedman** (1833-1908) and his family moved from Hartford to Norwichtown, Connecticut, when he was a young boy. It was Dwight Stevens who stuck up for Edmund when an overzealous teacher gave him trouble. Stedman became one of the foremost early American poets, and was one of the first seven people to be placed in the American Academy of Arts and Letters. He memorialized Dwight in his poem "How Old Brown took Harper's Ferry," with these lines: "It was the sixteenth of October, on the evening of a Sunday: "This good work," declared the captain, "shall be on a holy night!" It was on a Sunday evening, and before the noon of Monday, With two sons, and Captain Stephens, 15 privates black and white, Captain Brown, Osawatomie Brown, Marched across the bridged Potomac, and knocked the sentry down…"

defiance. This infuriated the schoolmaster, so he took Edmund over his knee and thrashed him with the ferule as he sat on a stool. Edmund was a smart kid, and he used his leg to push against the stove and upset Mr. Aikman and him on the stool. We all laughed as they both fell over. Mr. Aikman could not hold onto Edmund because he was trying to hold onto his wig."

"A wig! He had a wig?!" Maria exclaimed delightedly, as she was very amused by this story.

"Yes, he had a wig, and didn't want to lose it in front of the class. This gave Edmund time to skedaddle out of the schoolhouse. I couldn't help but laugh out loud."

"So then what happened?"

"Mr. Aikman regained his footing and got the laughing students under control. He knew he would deal with Edmund later. He kicked me and the other student named Joe Case out of the school for the remainder of the day. I guess our sassing frustrated him. I didn't care, though, and was glad to get out of his class for the day. What we didn't know was that after we left, he told the class that he was going to ferule both of us at the beginning of school the next day. Somehow, a wager was made that Joe Case would be able to pull off Mr. Aikman's wig while he tried to ferule us. The next day when we reported to school, I got feruled first. It stung my hand, but it was over quickly and I hoped we could get on with the school day. He called Joe next. As Joe came up to get his punishment, he grabbed at the wig. Mr. Aikman was too quick, and deflected the attempt. The next thing I knew, they both were rolling on the floor.

Mr. Aikman ended up grabbing the rawhide he used to ferule us with and got it around Joe's neck. Joe reached for a poker to hit him. Both of them could have killed each other, as I recall it now. It became one of the biggest fights talked about in Norwichtown. Joe finally succumbed to Mr. Aikman. Aikman suspended him, and me too, even though I had already been disciplined. I never returned to school. I hated that man. I ended up working at the Wilcox Saw Mill for a while until I grew bored. That winter I ended up joining the First Massachusetts Volunteers and went off to war."

She hugged him, and he laughed. She asked him if there was anything that he was afraid of. He pondered for a few moments and looked into her eyes. "I'm afraid of beautiful women."

She punched him lightly in the arm. "No, seriously. Are there things that frighten you?"

"Well, I don't like big dogs. They make me uneasy. I didn't like them when I was a child. When I was out hunting, I hated to see wolves. If they came close, I would not hesitate to fire to scare them off. If they did not heed my warning, I would kill them."

She made the sound of a wolf and growled at him.

He laughed and held her close to him. He kissed her on the forehead.

Maria asked about his family life when he was a child. She marveled that he was fortunate to have so many siblings and friends back home. She explained how she missed her brother and told Dwight that he should always keep his family and friends close to his heart. She inquired as to when he had last communicated with them.

He confessed he had only written one letter since he had come out West.

She encouraged him to write as soon as he returned to the barracks, while he was away from her and back on duty.

Dwight completely recovered from his wound and returned to active duty in April. It was at this time that he was informed that he had been promoted to bugler for Company F. The promotion came after Bugler James Cook deserted, and it was otherwise mainly due to the musical abilities he had demonstrated with several instruments. He went on more patrols during the summer and fall months in his new position and saw three Apache and one Ute tribe sign peace treaties with the army.

Only a few cattle and horse-stealing incidents were reported in the area around Taos during the months after the tribes had signed. The army did not investigate them and left the peaceful tribes alone. Months passed, and Maria would occasionally ask Dwight if he had heard from his family.

He never lied and always told her that no one had sent him a letter, though he did fail to tell her that he hadn't written one. He finally obliged, eight months later when his conscience bothered him enough that he wrote another letter to his sister.

Cantonment Burgwin
New Mexico
November 9, 1854

My Dear Sister,

I have a few leisure hours at present. I take pleasure in writing you a few lines hoping they will find you in good circumstances. The reason I didn't write before was because I have been tramping nearly all the time cince last April, and now I have just returned from a chase after the Paches and was gone for a month, but we didn't find them. We enjoyed ourselves though very much. We had got antelope and one bear. The bear was so fat that we could hardly eat it. The fat was six inches all over it.

Our company has had two fights with the Patches, this year,

and had 9 men killed and 11 wounded. And another company 19 killed and 13 wounded. And another 4 killed and 5 wounded and another 2 killed and 3 wounded making all 34 killed and 36 wounded, and as luck would have it I have got off safe so far. But they might get me yet. We have made four tribes come to a treaty cince I have come to this country.

I wonder how pore Jim is now. I expect he is in the Pacific soaking and tumbling about. I would like to see him very much. I suppose he has got to be quite a man. I hope he will do well, and live till we shall meet once more. What would you think to hear that I had got married to a Spanish lady. Well I haven't yet.

Your loving brother,
A. D. Stevens[1]

[1] **Actual letter from A. D. Stevens** to his sister Lydia.

Chapter Fifteen

Riot at Taos

Fort Massachusetts in the winter months was tolerable for the three-year veteran, despite his separation from Maria. The 1854–55 winter was uneventful, except for some of the hunting trips Dwight went on to help supply the fort with meat. Elk and deer were plentiful, and occasionally a bison was taken. The dragoons and the Ute and Apache hunting parties kept their distance from each other.

No outbreaks of malaria occurred that winter. Sub-zero blizzards kept everything frozen and the fort unreachable for days due to the deep snow. Patrols were limited until mid-February, when the snow had melted enough to allow for some short-range patrols to check on the settlers and Indians in the area. Dwight was eventually ordered to return to Cantonment Burgwin at the end of that month, which pleased him because he knew he would be able to see Maria as soon as time permitted.

Just as he arrived at Burgwin, another blizzard occurred, snowing him in for a second time that month. His thoughts of spending some free time in Maria's warm, loving arms were quickly dashed when news arrived of an uprising. The dragoons at Burgwin were ordered to take action against the Ute Indians as soon as weather permitted. A brief stay in the town allowed the dragoons to gather information on the numbers and location of the Ute tribes, as well as gather supplies. Dwight did not have any time to see Maria during his unit's short stay.

On March 8, 1855, as the dragoons of Burgwin were planning to depart Taos, an incident occurred that would change the life of Dwight Stevens forever. The soldiers of Company F were ordered to collect supplies. Privates John Cooper, Joseph Fox, and John Steel had been given specific duties by Lieutenant Robert Johnson[1], who then accompanied Majors Blake and Thompson on other duties. Bugler Dwight Stevens had been ordered to hold the reins of Major Thompson's horse and his own. Other dragoons of Company F had also been directed to await the return of the officers and NCOs.

Privates Cooper, Fox, and Steel watched Majors Blake and Thompson enter the local cantina accompanied by Lieutenant Johnson,

---

[1] **Lieutenant Robert Johnson** was charged with not assisting in the suppression of the Taos riot, but was later acquitted. He was ultimately given command of a Confederate division under General Longstreet during the Civil War.

while Sergeant Thomas Fitzsimmons waited on his mount outside. The privates apparently took advantage of this situation and visited another local watering hole several streets over for a few swigs of whiskey. The men had figured they would have enough time for whiskey and still be able to complete their task before the officers returned to the company.

Both the officers and the enlisted men finished their drinking, and all left their establishments under the influence of too much alcohol. When the two groups met on the street in front of a store, words were exchanged. This exchange developed into an altercation that included a drunken Major Blake being pushed to the ground by three inebriated privates. Sergeant Fitzsimmons broke up the fight with assistance from Lieutenant Johnson and Major Thompson, who were also obviously drunk.

Dwight Stevens was not involved in the first altercation between the major and the three privates, other than to tell other soldiers watching to not join in. Dwight maintained his position of holding the reins of the two horses. While he despised Major Blake for his many shortcomings, Dwight had never seen him this bad before, even when he would get drunk and either challenge or berate the soldiers. Dwight had not been a target of his venom until today.

Blake regained his composure and decided to address the entire company concerning the incident that most of them had just witnessed. He was still under the effects of alcohol when he spoke to the men and loudly stated ***"I can whip any son of a bitch from the right to the left of this company."***

Dwight was disgusted by both the appearance and slurred statement the major had just made, and he took the statement as a personal challenge. ***"By God Major Blake, you shant say that to me or anyone here."*** Dwight drew his revolver and cocked it.

Corporal Vandivice saw what was happening and stopped Dwight by grabbing and pushing down the cocked weapon. He yelled at him to hand over the gun and back down.

Dwight obliged, unlocked his hold on the revolver, and handed it over to him. He backed away as Blake watched. The corporal told Dwight to fetch the horses that had gotten away from him when he dropped the reins to draw his revolver. Dwight walked slowly to the horses, took the reins of both, turned around, and stared at Major Blake.

While Dwight fetched the horses, Judge Perry Brocchus[1] and

---

[1] **Judge Perry Brocchus was** appointed the Utah Territory Judge in 1851 by Millard

Sheriff Carson arrived, seeing the end of the first altercation and Corporal Vandivice's disarming of Dwight. The judge offered to quell the incident, realizing that both parties of the first fight were apparently drunk and that the second had been sparked by Blake's brashness.

Sheriff Kit Carson reminded the Judge of Stevens's association with the Gonzales y Maritta family as Dwight returned with the horses.

Judge Brocchus said in an effort to sooth the matter, ***"Major, let me speak to this man. He has a good countenance and seems to be laboring under excitement."***

Blake nodded and let the judge approach Dwight. The judge took him aside, and within a short period, Dwight agreed to apologize. The judge escorted Dwight back to the waiting major and motioned for the two men to approach each other to settle the incident. Judge Brocchus said, ***"This man appears to be sorry for what he has done."***

Major Blake, hearing the statement, stepped closer and said in a condescending way, ***"If this man is willing to take back all he has said..."***

As the major finished his statement, Dwight's temper got the best of him again, and he screamed back as he drew his Sharps rifle, cocked it, and aimed it at him, ***"No! By God Major Blake, I am as good a man as you."***

Major Thompson and Sheriff Carson were surprised by Dwight's reaction. They immediately subdued him and took the rifle away. Dwight did not resist and surrendered the weapon with no incident.

Sheriff Carson addressed him. "Son, what have you done? You can't draw your weapon on an officer. I'm afraid that I will have to put you in jail to cool your temper. You'll have to answer for your actions later. Come with me now."

Carson led Bugler Stevens to the Taos jail. Privates Cooper, Fox, and Steel were also escorted to jail by Lieutenant Johnson, Sergeant Fitzsimmons, and Corporal Vandivice, following directly behind Carson and Stevens.

The four dragoons were incarcerated in the Taos jail for a week while Blake, his officers, and the several companies from Cantonment Burgwin campaigned in the Ute territory. Days after the Taos event, *Señor* Gonzales was informed by Sheriff Carson that Dwight Stevens was in jail for mutiny and was awaiting trial by court-martial.

Fillmore. He conflicted with the "Latter Day Saint" settlers and later left the post in September of 1851 to head east. He was described as "at times disarmingly charming, at other times bitterly sardonic."

When Maria was informed, she immediately went to the jail. The sheriff anticipated her arrival and moved Dwight into a separate cell to give more privacy to his friend's niece.

She entered the jail visibly upset. "*Señor* Carson, may I see Dwight, please?" she asked, barely holding her emotions.

"Yes, *señorita*, but please do not stay long."

"*Sí*, I understand. Thank you."

Sheriff Carson escorted her to Dwight's jail cell and announced her arrival.

"I'm sorry that you have to see me in this place, but I am happy you came. I have thought of nothing but you since I have been here," Dwight said, only occasionally glancing at her due to his embarrassment.

"What have you done? Is it true that you drew your weapon on an officer?"

"Yes, and I am not proud of it. My temper got the best of me again like it always does when I fail to control it".

"Do you realize what could be done to you if you are found guilty?"

"Yes, I think I do."

"I fear that I will not see you again. My heart has ached since my uncle informed me of this. He is upset as well. He was just beginning to like you, but now he has forbidden me to see you. I will have to ask the sheriff when I leave to lie and say that I was not here. You have made my uncle, and even the sheriff, wonder why you have done this. I will pray for you today, and every day, that your trial and punishment will be quick and minimal for your actions. Oh, Dwight, I do love you and miss you so much." She broke down and wept. In agony, she slowly slid down to a kneeling position as she held onto the cell bars.

Dwight followed her down as he attempted to ease her emotions by telling her that everything would be all right.

"No, things will not be all right. You are in very serious trouble. Trouble that I dare not think about, trouble that could be…" She strained to control her emotions.

Dwight did not challenge her. He waited until she stood upright again and had wiped the tears from her face. "Maria, I have a good service record. I might be demoted and may have to serve some time, but I am sure that the army will treat me fairly and that this incident will be behind both of us soon."

As he finished his statement, Sheriff Carson informed Maria it was time to leave.

She acknowledged him and then kissed her index finger. She pushed it through the bars and touched Dwight's lips. She turned and walked away quickly, failing to hold back her tears.

Dwight heard her sobbing and could only watch with frustration as she departed. He wanted so desperately to hold and comfort her. He was mad at himself for hurting her. He sat on the hard cot and agonized over the pain he had inflicted on the most important person in his life.

The following week, after several more secret visits from Maria, Dwight and the three privates were transferred back to the guardhouse at Cantonment Burgwin. Dwight Stevens, John Cooper, Joseph Fox, and John Steel would remain in the guardhouse until May 21, 1855, when a general court-martial was convened in Taos. They were to appear that day at 10:00 a.m., when the charges would be presented to each individual mutineer, starting with Bugler Aaron Dwight Stevens.

Military Judge Captain Isaac Bowen[1] presided and read the charge against Dwight. "Will the prisoner please rise."

Dwight immediately stood at attention and the charges were read.

"Charge 1st – Mutiny. Specification – In this that Bugler Aaron D. Stevens of F Company, 1st Dragoons, U.S.A., did begin, excite, cause or join in a mutiny or sedition against Major George A. M. Blake, 1st Dragoons, U.S.A. This at Don Fernandez de Taos, New Mexico on the 8th of March, 1855." Bowen paused, and then further addressed the accused. ***"Charge 2nd – Violation of the 9th Article of War. Specification 1st – Aaron Stevens did draw a pistol and attempt to shoot his superior officer Major George A. M. Blake – he being in the execution of his office and was down and defending himself against other men of Company F, First Dragoons, and did attempt to strike his superior officer, on the 8th of March, 1855. Specification 2nd – That Aaron Stevens did raise his rifle, cock it and swore he would shoot his superior officer Major George A. M. Blake. He being in the execution of his duties…Aaron was in the act of bringing his rifle to aim when it was forcibly taken from him. These were signed by Major George A. M. Blake."*** Judge Captain Bowen took off his glasses and addressed Dwight. "What say you to the accusations read by me at this court-martial?"

Dwight responded to each charge. "Sir, not guilty to specification, first charge. Not guilty to first charge. Not guilty to first specification, second charge. Not guilty to second specification, second charge. Not guilty to second charge." He remained at attention until the judge ordered

---

[1] **Captain Isaac Bowen** was a native of New York. He attended West Point and then served in the Mexican War where he received two brevets for outstanding performance. In 1850 he was made captain and was stationed in New Mexico.

him to be at ease and to be seated.

Dwight glanced around the room to see if Maria had come to the proceedings, but there were no women present anywhere. He did make eye contact with *Señor* Gonzales, who sat next to Sheriff Kit Carson. He noticed that *Señor* Gonzales only shook his head in disbelief at what he was witnessing.

Major Blake took the stand and repeated his earlier statement that three dragoons had attacked him, and that he could not recollect provoking them in any way. He did state that Dwight was not of the original group that had attacked him and also that his argument with Stevens occurred on two separate occasions. The first was after the initial incident with the three dragoons who had knocked him down. Blake stated that Stevens attempted to aim a revolver at him and that Corporal Vandivice took it away. Judge Brocchus had witnessed the incident and had had words with Stevens just prior to the second incident. Judge Brocchus walked away from Stevens. The judge thought that Stevens would apologize for his statement, but instead he drew his Sharps rifle and cocked it. As Stevens attempted to aim in his direction, Sheriff Carson and Major Thompson took the rifle away from him. Then Sheriff Carson arrested Stevens and, along with the others, led them to the Taos jail.

Dwight shook his head as he heard the major, under oath, give his statement to the court.

When the major was finished, Dwight was given permission to ask the major a question.

He asked, ***"Sir, did you not declare on several occasions that you could whip the whole company?"***

Major Blake paused while he looked at Stevens. He looked away and then back at the general audience and stated, ***"I said that they could beat me but could not whip me or words to that effect and the remark was not in a tone of challenge."***

Judge Bowen spoke up and asked Major Blake, ***"Did the prisoner make any apology?"***

Major Blake looked directly at the judge. ***"No."***

Dwight could feel his face begin to warm, and he knew his contempt for the man was showing. He looked away from Blake as he was excused from the stand.

Sergeant Thomas Fitzsimmons was called to the stand next. He gave a very different account of the incidents that had occurred that day. Dwight felt a little vindicated as the sergeant described the events. Fitzsimmons explained that he had been mounted and saw Major Blake addressing the dragoons while Stevens held the reins of some horses with one hand and his Sharps rifle in the other. He further stated that after the riot, Major Blake addressed the troops and boasted that he could whip or thrash any man in the company with a gun, pistol, or saber. Fitzsimmons also stated that Major Blake dared any man who thought himself fit to challenge him. He stated that Stevens immediately challenged, but that the major did not answer and walked away. He said that Stevens followed him, but stated that he did not hear any further words exchanged between the major and Stevens.

Judge Bowen asked the sergeant, ***"At the time Major Blake was in conflict with the other men, did you hear the prisoner use any words encouraging the men against him?"***

Sergeant Fitzsimmons paused and looked at both the major and Stevens. ***"No."***

Judge Bowen then called Lieutenant Robert Johnson to testify. The lieutenant stated he observed a riot caused by the men of the company. He saw Major Blake rise up from the ground after scuffling with several men. The major walked away toward the store in the plaza where the prisoner was standing, holding the reins to some horses. The lieutenant stated that he heard the major state that he could whip any son of a bitch from the right to the left of the company. He saw the prisoner drop the reins to the horses and yell at the major. He stated that Stevens said, "By God, Major Blake, you shan't say that," or words to that effect. The lieutenant confirmed that the prisoner then cocked the revolver he had in his hand. Corporal Vandivice then ordered the prisoner to surrender and took the revolver from his hand. Johnson also stated that he told the prisoner to fetch the horses that had gotten away from him.

Lieutenant Johnson went on to state that he witnessed Judge Brocchus' attempt to quiet the incident by asking the major if he could speak to the prisoner. He had agreed, and the judge spoke to him. They returned a short time later and the judge told the major that the prisoner was willing to apologize. Then the major responded that he would be satisfied, as long as the man would take back all that he had said. At that time, the prisoner became angry and said, "No, by God, Major Blake!" The lieutenant then said that Stevens cocked a Sharps rifle and aimed it.

The lieutenant paused and then remembered what the prisoner said while aiming it: "By God, Major Blake, I am as good a man as you." He stated that he thought Major Thompson grabbed at the gun and that Sheriff Carson had then come to assist in taking the rifle away from the prisoner. The prisoner was then led away to jail.

More witnesses were called by the prosecution, which included Sheriff Kit Carson, Judge Brocchus, and Major Thompson. Thompson stated that Bugler Stevens was his orderly for the day and had been assigned to hold his horse's reins. There was no mention of the cantinas or the condition of either Major Blake or the three dragoons prior to the fight. There was also no mention of Major Blake's personal history of boasting or his periodic belittlement of the dragoons. No acknowledgement of this was recorded in the trial, which could have exposed the resentment some men had for Blake.

There were no witnesses on behalf of Aaron Dwight Stevens. If there had been, two important facts could have been brought to light: the inebriated condition of the three dragoons accused of fighting with the major, and that the major and the officers that were with him also had consumed a large amount of alcoholic beverages. Judge Bowen did allow prisoner Stevens to make one remark to the court.

Dwight rose, cleared his voice, and spoke slowly and directly at Major Blake and Judge Bowen, ***"I did not join in the attack on Major Blake, but was some distance from him. I used my influence with and succeeded in keeping two or three from joining those who were on the Major. When he spoke to me after Judge Brocchus advised me I was willing to apologize if I had done anything wrong and told the Major so, but he turned away with a sneer which made me very angry and I made some exclamations and did things for which I am sorry."*** Dwight sat down, continuing to look at the judge and then back at the major.

There were no expressions from either man.

The judge closed the proceedings for a short period of time while the accusations and testimony were reviewed. When the court resumed, Judge Bowen announced, "The prisoner will stand at attention."

Dwight stood as ordered, and awaited the judgment.

The court was quiet as the judge spoke. ***"The court was closed and after careful and mature consideration on the testimony…finds the prisoner:***

Not guilty of the specification of the 1st charge
Not guilty of the 1st charge
Not guilty of the 1st specification of the 2nd charge
Guilty of the 2nd specification of the 2nd charge
Guilty of the 2nd charge."

Judge Bowen looked up at Dwight as he finished reading the verdict. He spoke to several dragoons, who had custody of the prisoner. "The prisoner shall be returned to his confinement until a sentencing shall be administered by this court tomorrow at ten o'clock in the morning. Remove the prisoner."

Dwight thought about the guilty verdict and assumed that he would be demoted and sentenced to time in military prison. He also considered that he would then be dishonorably discharged from the army.

It sickened him to think of the shame he would have to endure as a prisoner and then as a dishonored dragoon for the rest of his life. But he thought of Maria. *I hope she will wait for me for as long as it takes to serve what time is given to me. Two, maybe three years could be the sentencing. Deserters who are caught never spend more than six months in the guardhouse. I have seen that with my own eyes. Maria would wait for me, I am sure. We could live a good life together away from the army.*

He hoped that he could somehow get word to Maria while he spent the night in the Taos jail. He was mistaken. He was put in irons with a heavy ball that he had to carry to a wagon, which took him back to Cantonment Burgwin's guardhouse alone. The three other dragoons were still in court. He did not eat or sleep while he waited for morning and his return to the court in Taos.

The next day at 10:00 a.m., Judge Bowen ordered that the prisoner stand before him at attention as he administered the sentence. He spoke slowly and directly at Stevens. "The court has given its sentencing to the prisoner, Bugler Aaron D. Stevens. With two-thirds of the members concurring, the prisoner is…" He paused and looked at Dwight. ***"To be shot to death at such time and place as the President of the United States shall direct. The prisoner is to be kept in double irons until the execution of his sentence."***

Shot to death!? Within seconds of listening to the words, Dwight was not hearing, seeing, or feeling anything. Nothing existed but his thoughts, and they were jumbled and not making sense. The sentence could not possibly be what he just heard. Dwight was paralyzed, not from fear but from shock. *This is all wrong,* he thought. He had never even considered this outcome. Standing like a thousand-year-old crumbling statue, he completely shut down.

He was led from the courtroom, oblivious that it was even happening. He never remembered leaving the court or his ten-mile wagon ride back to the cantonment in double irons. He finally came to as he was being locked in his single cell. His plan to spend his whole life with Maria would not happen. He felt the loneliest he had ever felt in his life—lost, alone, and betrayed, mostly by himself. He hoped that his death would be administered quickly, because the thought of never again seeing, smelling, touching, or loving Maria was too much for him to endure.

His grief turned to rage as he felt that God, nature, the army, and everything that was right and just in the world had failed him. He remained depressed for many days until his hunger overcame his grief and thoughts of escape entered his mind. He knew he had to regain his strength to execute whatever plan he made. Several weeks passed, and one day he was given a letter as he was served the noon meal. He immediately recognized the handwriting and quickly opened the short letter.

April 20, 1855
Fernandez de Taos, New Mexico

My Dearest,

I write to you with a heavy heart, thinking of your future. It has taken me this long to be able to get Señor Carson to agree to deliver this letter to you. He has done so without the permission of his good friend, my uncle Roberto. He only did it because he feels that you have paid too high a price for your actions toward the officer you threatened, and also because he has as little respect for him. He regrets he had to testify on what he saw that day in Taos. This is why I was fortunate to be able to get this letter to you. I, and you as well, should thank him for his assistance.

I pray to the Virgin Mother, the Baby Jesus, and God himself every day that a miracle will be granted that spares your life. My thoughts of you overwhelm me to extreme bouts of depression, which causes me to be ill. My uncle has taken me to our doctor to see what illness had overtaken me. The doctor told him that there is no cure for what I suffer. I need you. I will wait and pray that my miracle happens and that you will be spared. Keep in your heart knowing I will love you always, no matter what God decides that your fate will be.

Your loving Maria

He cried as he read the letter several times. He could smell the scent of Maria on the paper. He carefully placed it back in the envelope and put it on the blanket of his cot. He hoped the scent would remain longer that way. He read the letter over and over until he could recite it by memory. He would smell and kiss it each day, until he could not smell her scent anymore.

In late August, Maria's prayers were answered and her miracle occurred. A letter arrived that indicated the President of the United States had made a decision. Dwight was notified of the letter's arrival and summoned to the cantonment headquarters along with the three other sentenced men.

All four stood at attention in irons in front of a group of officers who had assembled at the headquarters building. Not present was Major Blake. Captain Bowen, the presiding military judge at the Taos court proceedings, read the letter.

War Department
Washington, August 8, 1855

A general Court Martial held at Taos, New Mexico, on the 21st May, has passed sentence of death on Privates Aaron D. Stevens, John Cooper, Joseph Fox, and John Steel, of Company F, 1st Dragoons, who were engaged in a drunken riot in that town, when the company entered it on their march to join a military

expedition against Indians, and who mutinied against a Major of the regiment, when, being present in the town, he interposed his authority to bring them to order. The case is a clear one under the 7th and 9th Articles of War, upon the law and the facts; and the President would feel it his duty to order the execution of the sentence of death, if he were not compelled to find something to mitigate the crime of these men in the general condition of their company, and in the misconduct of their officers. It is proved that the commander of the company, and many of the company, then under arms, on a march, were drunk when the riot and mutiny broke out. It appears that no proper discipline had been previously maintained in the company, and that the Major of the regiment, under whose command they had been serving, was greatly responsible for the utter want of discipline which would have cost him his life in this mutiny, if he had not been rescued by the civil authority; and that part of the violence he suffered, in the riot, was invited by his challenging the company to fight him, man by man. Under these circumstances, however imperative the President will not visit the whole consequence of this mutiny upon the four soldiers who have been convicted, nor execute in this case the sentence of death. The sentence pronounced against Privates Aaron D. Stevens, John Cooper, Joseph Fox, and John Steel, are hereby mitigated to hard labor for three years, under guard, without pay. They will be sent out of New Mexico, in irons, by the first convenient opportunity, and will be put to labor with ball and chain at Fort Leavenworth.

Captain Bowen looked up at the four prisoners standing before him after he had finished reading. He did not smile, but those observing and listening as he read to the prisoners observed his facial expressions change. With a slight relief in his tone of voice and a gentler look to the prisoners, he said, "You have heard the decision of our president. Guards, you will escort the prisoners to the guardhouse, where they will remain until transferred as ordered to Fort Leavenworth. Prisoners, you are dismissed." He waited until the four men were escorted out of the headquarters, then looked around at the officers that had been ordered to be present for the reading. "Gentlemen, I will now ask you all to remain to hear the entire letter that has been sent from the Secretary of War ." He turned to Sergeant Major Simms. "Sergeant Major, please ask Major Blake to enter the room."

"Yes, sir, at your command."

The sergeant major walked to the door of an adjoining room and opened it. Within a few moments, Major Blake appeared.

Captain Bowen waited until the major reached some seats that had been left vacant. "Major, please sit down while I read the remainder of the Secretary's letter." He read, ***"I, Jefferson Davis, Secretary of War hereby disband Company F of the 1st Dragoons. The men will be placed in other companies in the regiment."*** Bowen stopped reading and looked up and directly at Major Blake, who sat relaxed. The captain cleared his throat and continued reading. ***"As Secretary of War, I also have called for Court Martial proceedings against Major Blake and other officers of the company 'implicated' in this affair. Jefferson Davis, Secretary of War."***

Captain Bowen looked around the room and then looked at Major Blake, who had stood as soon as he heard that court-martial proceedings were being made against him. Before Bowen could speak again, Major Blake burst out, "That is outrageous, Captain."

"Sir, as the military judge in this proceeding, I advise you under the Military Code of Justice to refrain from any further comment," Bowen said. "I will advise you and those other officers involved in the previous incident in Taos." He paused and looked at the other officers in the room. "Major Thompson and Lieutenant Johnson, you will be advised as well when the proceedings are given a time and place as directed by the secretary of war. I advise you to seek counsel as soon as possible and inform my office as to the name of the counsel you have retained." He looked at everyone and stated, "This proceeding is closed. Gentlemen, thank you for attending."

Dwight was shocked that President Franklin Pierce had spared him. He thought of Maria and the letter she had sent. Her miracle had come true. He felt that the entire weight of the world had been lifted from his chest. He could breathe. He could begin to envision a future with Maria, after he had served his sentence. He began counting the days before he would be released into her arms.

He realized it was a long time away and that there was the chance that she would forget him or find another. He convinced himself, however, even before he reached his cell, that her letter was proof that she would wait for him. He hoped that Sheriff Carson would hear the news and relay it to her immediately. He also hoped Roberto would find out and at least tell her of the changed sentence. He was sure she would somehow find out the news.

Dwight ate everything given to him while in the guardhouse that night. He found himself either pacing back and forth, despite the ball and chains, or sitting idly and waiting for the army to transfer him back to Fort Leavenworth. He wondered when the time for his three-year punishment would begin. Would it start here or at Leavenworth?

The following morning one of the guards told him that Major Blake and the other officers involved in the fight were undergoing court-martial proceedings to investigate their conduct in the affair.

"By God, Maria has received two miracles from her gracious prayers," he said aloud. His depression lessened as he felt vindicated that Blake could possibly receive punishment for not only the Taos incident, but for all the things he had said and done to officers and men under his command. He thought, *Maybe with the grace of God, the man will no longer be able to command in the army again.*

But mostly Dwight cared about getting to Fort Leavenworth, serving his sentence, and leaving as a free man to return to Taos and be with Maria for the rest of his life. He hoped that she would give him some message that she knew of his new sentence and that she would wait for him.

Another week passed as he waited to hear from Maria. Sheriff Carson, as well as *Señor* Roberto Gonzales, had heard the news of the letter from the secretary of war. Roberto decided not to tell Maria and hoped that time would distance her from the dragoon. He suspected that the positive change in her attitude and mood was directly associated with her receiving news of the stay of execution that Stevens had been granted.

But he did not want his niece wasting her youth on a man who would not be released for three years. He would instead encourage Maria to look elsewhere for love and forget the undependable prisoner. He also felt he could convince her that after three years of prison, Stevens would be a changed man, and not for the better. Many other men from good Mexican families were still interested in her. Her attraction to, and public association with, the American soldier still had not hurt her reputation.

Roberto suspected that someone would help her communicate with the dragoon. He found out that the sheriff had earlier pitied his niece and helped her send a letter. He asked the sheriff to help him make sure that Maria could not contact the dragoon ever again. He explained that he felt it would be in her best interest if she no longer associated with a man who would be spending three years of his life in prison, and who would have no immediate means to support her when he was released. Sheriff Carson agreed to respect his good friend's wishes.

When Maria approached Carson days later to have another letter sent to the cantonment guardhouse, he agreed, but took the letter and handed it to her uncle. Roberto destroyed the letter in front of the sheriff.

Dwight waited and never received even a note from the woman he worshiped. He suspected that her uncle may have been responsible for her silence. His suspicions would be confirmed months later.

Chapter Sixteen

Shackled in Disgrace

In September of 1855, Privates Aaron D. Stevens, John Cooper, Joseph Fox, and John Steel began their seven-hundred-and-forty-two-mile journey back to Fort Leavenworth, Kansas, under guard and under the command of Captain Richard S. Ewell.[1]

Dwight felt worse than he could ever remember. He was thoroughly sick inside. His life was now a complete failure and his future seemed nonexistent. The only thing he still had to hold onto was his memory of Maria. He could remember everything about her even though he had not seen her for months. He could still hear her voice. He could see her brown eyes and her face smiling up at him, her lips before he kissed them, and her beautiful body that she had shared with him. He could see her across the table at the hotel restaurant, laughing at some private joke between them.

He was miserable, and what made it unbearable was that it was his fault. Getting mad and losing control of himself had quite possibly ruined his whole life. This problem wasn't going to go away. This was going to change his life, and he couldn't even guess at the full extent of them yet. Actually, at this time, he found he didn't much care, except he wanted his life to include Maria. That was what he held onto as he trudged mile after mile in shame and humiliation.

The first day became the second, and then became the third as the miles slowly passed. The heat was intense, but he had pretty much gotten used to it over the last several years. He was not used to his heavy leg irons, however, and constantly being in the heat and sun for the duration of each long day.

After the first couple of days, he knew which dragoons on the travel detail were going to treat him well and which were going to be trouble. Captain Ewell and his companions did not lower themselves to address him, or even consider him alive, during the trip. He was nonexistent to them. However, the rest of the dragoon party had to feed the prisoners and tend to their needs along the way. Most were civil, but a

---

[1] **Richard S. Ewell** was a career U.S. Army officer and Confederate general during the Civil War. He achieved fame as a senior commander under Stonewall Jackson and Robert E. Lee, and fought effectively through much of the war. His legacy has been clouded by controversies over his actions at the Battle of Gettysburg and at the Battle of Spotsylvania Court House.

few weren't. For those that were not civil, Dwight had less hate for them than he did for himself. He simply considered them as part of his own private punishment. Most of the time, the prisoners weren't really guarded so much as watched. Everyone knew that there was nowhere to go, especially in the heavy chains.

Day by day they covered the over seven hundred miles to Fort Leavenworth. After a long period of depression and self-loathing, Dwight came to the realization that he was revisiting places and scenery that were somehow familiar to him. He finally understood that he was retracing the steps he had taken in 1851 along the Santa Fe Trail when he was traveling to New Mexico as a new and inexperienced dragoon.

He considered the irony of the situation. On the way from Fort Leavenworth years ago, he remembered himself as being excited and full of life, with adventures ahead of him. Now he was an embarrassed, lost, and beaten man, trying to hang on. What was so sad about it all was that he had loved being a dragoon. He actually enjoyed the life, and even the hardships, along with the camaraderie of the other men. Now his horrible mistake threatened to ruin everything.

Confederate General Richard S. Ewell during the Civil War
Public Domain photo

One day, a week or more into the trip, Dwight thought of someone he had not thought of for years—Private Ryan Scruggs. Out of nowhere, while the slow-moving party passed an area that looked like the place where the dragoon had died from a snake bite, he remembered Scruggs.

Dwight thought of Sergeant Watson and Corporal Rolling, who had tried to save Scruggs, but how he absorbed too much venom and didn't survive. It was Sergeant Watson's first casualty while taking recruits out to the New Mexico Territory. Dwight wondered if he would run into Watson and Rolling when he was jailed in Leavenworth. He hoped not. What would he say to them?

As the summer heat lessened each day, Dwight began to feel stronger and was not in as much pain, physically and mentally. It was still horribly embarrassing to have to be attached with chains to another man for days at a time, especially when performing things usually done in private. However, the chains didn't feel quite so heavy and walking mile after mile was not as difficult as it had been earlier.

A small but important change had occurred along the way, as the prisoners were allowed to quietly talk with each other as they marched along. There was no formal announcement of the change. It had just happened. One pleasant night, as the prisoners were all together and talking of dragoon stories and old times, Dwight told them the story of what he had first been told New Mexico was really like. Sergeant Watson had given the speech at about this same place along the Santa Fe Trail four years ago.

All the prisoners had a good chuckle at the story he told that night. The three others told their own versions of going through much of the same introductions on their journeys to New Mexico Territory. It was actually the most enjoyable evening they had all shared on the trip so far. Dwight thought about Dragoon Scruggs again before he closed his eyes that night and wondered if he had been re-buried as promised.

The weather was changing gradually as October began. It was not as hot as it had been, and the daylight seemed shorter now. But, generally, each day was just like the one before. Everyone was up at daybreak and on the trail with a small breakfast behind them. From that point until an hour before dark it was nothing but walking for the prisoners. Captain Ewell was always mounted, and his family and friends were usually in the wagons while all the dragoons were on horses at a slow walk. There were too many well-armed dragoons for any Indian trouble, and other than putting out guards every night, there was not much concern for danger from local tribes. There were occasional wagon trains going in the opposite direction and several stagecoaches.

Dwight dreaded seeing them. People would either try not to look at him at all, as if he had a terrible deformity, or the opposite, staring at him and wanting to know all about who he was and what terrible things he had done. They stopped one night at a stage stop that he remembered very well. He looked around the area for Wilson, the black man who had worked at the station caring for the horses and doing odd jobs. Wilson was no longer there, and Dwight felt satisfaction that the man had moved on. That night, as he lay in the barn on foul-smelling straw along with the other prisoners, he thought of Wilson, a man he hardly knew at all and yet who had been a constant symbol of black oppression to Dwight since meeting him that night four years ago. He could picture it all as if it had happened only last week and wondered whatever became of the gentle black man. He realized that Wilson, if he was still alive, probably had a better existence than himself. He sincerely hoped Wilson was happy, wherever he was, but still it depressed him and he forced himself to think of other things.

Several days later, after reaching the mountain fork of the Santa Fe Trail, Pawnee Rock grew on the horizon out of the flat grassy plains. Dwight remembered doing his first guard duty as a dragoon at that place and how scared he had been.

The party kept on traveling as the weather became colder, and sometimes forbidding, as the days in November passed. Another week went by, and still more flat prairie was all that could be seen. Dwight began to recognize places as they got closer to Fort Leavenworth. He didn't know if he should look forward to the fort and the end of the trip or if he should dread it. He had no idea what lay in front of him for the next three years while he served his sentence at hard labor. He was feeling stronger, and his outlook on life had improved along the trail. He did not concern himself so much with what others thought of him, but only with serving his time and returning to Taos and Maria.

The times the four prisoners spent reminiscing were probably the single biggest help to Dwight's mental recovery. He enjoyed listening to the others tell of their adventures, and he also found that he was finally able to laugh again. The prisoners had also been joined by a few of the more friendly dragoons at times, and they also contributed their experiences.

Dwight found that he had a talent for storytelling and liked doing it. On one cool night as they gathered after the meal, Dwight told them all how he met the lovely and precious Miss Johnston on his way to New Mexico. When he completed the story, all the prisoners and guards were laughing loudly. Dwight thought it ironic, and laughed out loud when one of the guards remarked that the poor soul that married her would regret it until his last breath.

It was during those nights that Dwight thought about how excited and proud he had been when he had joined the dragoons. It seemed such a short time ago that he had struck up new acquaintances, honed his military skills, and learned the ways of the dragoons. *How everything has changed,* he thought, sitting now with the other prisoners. He looked out at the western horizon. The sun had sent illuminating bright reds, oranges, and yellows streaking across the sky. He glanced east. It was dark already. He felt it was a sign of the darkness he would have to endure until he was released.

It had been another exhausting day. He looked over and saw the glow of the large campfire warming the dragoons and civilians. It captured his curiosity. He strained to make sense of the muffled noises. He was too far away to hear any conversations, but he could hear some laughter from a few children that were still awake. He still wasn't sleepy yet, so he stared toward the fire and eventually fell off to sleep thinking of other men he had met in the dragoons.

The next morning he felt a hard kick to his right boot. It was from a guard. As he cleared the sleep from his head, he heard the other prisoners being awakened to the same treatment. Within a short time they were taken to a secluded area to relieve themselves. Dwight had many experiences in the army, but performing the morning constitutional while chained to another man was one of the most difficult and degrading experience he had ever had to endure. The one positive thought he had was that it was one time less in the three years he had to endure this type of degradation. After yet another small breakfast consisting of bacon fat spread on a biscuit, he was tied to the wagon and the trip continued. This day seemed uneventful until the party passed a column of dragoons heading west.

Dwight saw the officer in charge of the column salute Captain Ewell as he passed. He tipped his hat to some of the women he saw riding on the wagons. Dwight watched him as his dragoons approached where the prisoners were tied to the trailing wagons, then looked up to see if he knew him. It was a mistake.

The man glared at him and shook his head. There was a look of complete distain on his face. Dwight wanted to break his chains and drag him off his horse. Reality set in as he suddenly thought, *That very behavior is why I am in this predicament. But he still deserves it.*

Many days later, he knew they had to be getting closer to Fort Leavenworth, though he didn't know how many weeks he had spent on the trail or how many days were still left to go. He forced himself to keep a calm attitude and remain quiet. It was getting easier for him to control the one emotion he knew was his downfall. He saw mustangs appear on the horizon and realized how much he wanted to be free. He fantasized that the horses were calling to him. *Maybe*, he thought, *in my next life I will return as a wild horse, free to roam at will in the wilderness.*

The mustangs disappeared, and he thought back to the early days in the dragoons when he'd prepared to go west. He thought about Spirit and welcomed the memories as he slowly moved east, shackled to a wagon, stinking of sweat. His mind drifted back to the first day he had seen Spirit.

Several more days passed, and the next morning began as just another day. It was colder now and the sky threatened snow. Approximately two hours along the trail, Dwight recognized that a river ran parallel to the party. He perked up and whispered over to Steel, "There's the Missouri River. You see it?"

Steel nodded and then smiled and said, "We're close now. It can't be more than two more days of this shit."

"Keep it down over there!" a guard coming up from behind them called out.

Dwight remembered filling barrels of water from the river on the second day he was on the trail going west.

That night the prisoners confirmed with the guards what Dwight had recognized. They would be at Fort Leavenworth before sunset the next day. There was relief and happiness at the prospect of ending the eight-week trip, but also apprehension and sadness for the prisoners as they thought of their imprisonment and long hard-labor workdays.

That night no one talked during the supper meal or prior to turning in. Each man was thinking of what it would be like in prison. One positive thing Dwight could think about was that he would be in prison among prisoners. No one except the guards would think of him as anything other than just as a man who had broken an army regulation. He would not have to endure scorn, derogatory comments, evil looks, or an occasional kick to get moving.

The next morning, they rose to another cold and damp day. The weather couldn't make up its mind whether to rain or snow, so instead it did both all morning until it finally changed to snow in the afternoon. Captain Ewell hastened the pace for the party, hoping to reach the protection of the fort before the weather worsened. The prisoners benefited from his orders. They were allowed to sit in one of the three-quarter-empty supply wagons for the remainder of the journey.

Because of poor visibility, and being the last wagon to enter the fort, Dwight could not see the fort until they had almost reached it. The guards wasted no time in turning them over to the Fort Leavenworth prison guards, and Dwight Stevens soon found himself in a damp stone and cement cell.

"Get up, Stevens. I can see you're awake!" He heard someone yell to him. The sound cleared as he became more conscious. "Get up, goddamn it! We ain't got all day!"

He tried to move quickly, but he was stiff from the cold and dampness in the prison cell. He managed to stand upright and stretch. He looked at the guard who had yelled to him. Under different circumstances, the man would have been bloodied and unconscious by now, waking him that way. Dwight noticed that he towered over the idiot by a foot and outweighed him by fifty pounds. He thought, *The little bastard needs a good whipping.* He stared at him all the time he was stretching. The guard kept his distance behind the locked cell door just in case the look on Dwight's face was any indication of what he wanted to do to him.

"Here's your breakfast, Stevens."

"Thank you," Dwight managed to say.

"The warden wanted to make sure y'all had food in you for today's work detail."

Dwight kept eyeing the little weasel. "I guess we don't waste any time around here, do we? Who is the warden, by the way?"

"You'll find out soon enough. Now eat and shut up," the man said as he handed Dwight a tin of coffee and a plate of food through the opening in the barred door. "You eat out in the field for midday rations. We feed you again at six o'clock. Make sure you eat everything, or you'll have the rats botherin' you."

Dwight looked at the food. It was bacon, biscuits, and several eggs. He had a utensil this time and ate slowly. It was the best meal he'd had since being in the cantonment prison cell.

Dwight was assigned his daily labor details. There was no leisure time. The workday was twelve hours, seven days a week. His duties consisted of latrine cleaning, grounds keeping, stable cleaning, and field clearing, all the while chained in ankle irons that were attached to a forty-pound iron ball. He had approximately an eight-foot circumference to work with before he was required to pick up the iron ball and move it to a new location to continue his work.

On occasion, when out in the field moving heavy rocks and timber with the assistance of a team of oxen or workhorses, the ball was detached for maneuverability. Several soldiers, armed with pistols and muskets with bayonets attached, guarded him and the other prisoners during these times.

Just after Christmas of 1855, Dwight received the only letter he would ever receive at the Fort Leavenworth Military Prison. At first he thought it could be a note from Maria, but the handwriting was unfamiliar. He quickly opened it to find a short but informative letter from *Señor* Roberto Gonzales.

December 1, 1855
Fernandez de Taos, New Mexico

Prisoner Stevens,

I am informing you that my niece, Señorita Maria Gonzales y Maritta, is aware that your sentence to die for your crimes was mitigated by a presidential directive. Your stay of incarceration of three years is also now known to her. I have encouraged her to move on with her life by convincing her that your life together would never be one with the social and material standards that she is accustomed to. I also warn you to never return to Fernandez de Taos. I have notified the local authorities that your return here would be considered a threat to me and my family. I have the political, social, and monetary abilities to enforce my accusations against a known convict.

Maria has been welcomed back into the affluent society that she was born, bred, and destined to live within, as planned by my dear late sister and her respected husband. If you have any respect and dignity left in your being for my niece, I ask that you never contact her, and consider this communication final.

Roberto Tomas Gonzales

Dwight ripped up the letter and threw it into his waste pail. He hoped for bad things to happen to Gonzales, but finally realized that he couldn't expect Maria to wait for him with all the attention she had around her in Taos. He couldn't compete with the affluent Mexican men while in prison. They courted her with both permission and encouragement from her uncle and guardian. He had mixed emotions for several days after reading Gonzales's letter, but in the end, he held no hatred against anyone.

The work details in that month lessened as the holiday season drew closer. Some furloughs reduced the number of soldiers available for guard duty and increased the demand for prisoner labor. Dwight was fortunate enough to be guarded by soldiers who treated him humanely, knowing both his depression and his reason for imprisonment. They treated him fairly when he was in the field or working within the prison, cleaning or repairing items. The guards usually paired prisoners together who seemed to get along and work without incident.

Dwight was one such prisoner, despite his depression. John Steel was another one that worked and never caused any trouble. They were paired together. Steel did not converse very much, instead working hard and only speaking when spoken to. His response to the soldiers that guarded him was even less. A simple "yes, sir" or "no, sir" was all that could be expected.

Corporal Vandivice visited Dwight shortly before the new year of

1856. The corporal had returned from Taos, New Mexico, to report for duty. During his short visit, he informed Dwight that Major Blake and Major Thompson had been summoned to court-martial proceedings for their participation in the incident at Taos. Major Blake had been removed from command and banished to California with no other details of what his position and duty would be. Major Thompson had been cashiered out of the dragoons and was somewhere in Nicaragua, last he had heard.

"Corporal, are you telling me Blake got off and Major Thompson was cashiered out of the dragoons?" Dwight asked.

"Yeah, Stevens, that's what I just told you."

"How did that son of a bitch stay in the army while Thompson had to leave?"

"I guess he had some contacts back here in Fort Leavenworth, or in Washington. I don't really know, but everyone at Burgwin is glad he's gone."

"California is where he is. You don't know exactly where, do you?"

"No, Stevens, I don't, and if I did I wouldn't tell you. You'd be pigheaded enough to go there and shoot 'im, if I know what you're thinkin'."

Dwight laughed for the first time in months. The corporal had to laugh himself, as he saw the joy in Dwight's face.

The guard outside his cell yelled for them to keep their voices down.

"They keep a good eye on everything you do, don't they?"

"Yes, you can't piss or shit without them watching your every move. It's no way to exist."

"I can't speak for you, but it is better than the first sentence they gave you."

"I know. You're right. I'm thankful for that."

"Where you going after you get out?"

"I'll probably stay out here in Kansas or Missouri. It won't be back to Connecticut. I know that."

"Kansas is becoming a real pain in the ass for us, if you haven't heard. That's why I was sent back here, to keep the settlers from killing each other. If I was you, I'd head further west again, but stay away from Blake."

They both laughed until they heard the guard warn them for the second time.

"What do you mean about the trouble here in Kansas?"

"The anti- and pro-slavery people are shooting each other. There's a move on both sides to bring Kansas into the union as either a slave or free state."

"God, I hope the free state people win."

"Don't be thinkin' of joinin' them. We've been arresting both sides when they break the law, Stevens. You don't need another stay in jail now, do you?"

Dwight smiled as he contemplated what could be going on in Kansas as he rotted in jail. Vandivice's visit had been very informative. The news spread to the other three dragoons, which gave them a little vindication that at least something had been done to the officers involved in the fight. Those few days after Vandivice's news were the best days of Dwight's imprisonment. It was also fitting that he was a little upbeat for the New Year.

On January 2nd, Dwight and John Steel were assigned field-clearing duty. It was during these work assignments that the prisoners were not chained in irons. They were free to work and move about without any interference from the leg chains or the forty-pound ball. The leg iron clasps were the only part of their irons that were left on.

A wagon, a teamster, and two workhorses had been assigned for use by the prisoners to load rocks for transport to a central area. Each teamster was well armed, and a mounted dragoon was stationed in the vicinity to watch every move the prisoners made. The twelve-hour work day began at 6:00 a.m. The men worked almost continually, except for the ten-minute breaks they were allowed every couple of hours. Dwight and John Steel filled several wagons during the course of the morning and afternoon sessions.

Steel mentioned to Dwight that the mounted dragoon was the only one assigned to watch the five wagons and the ten or so prisoners clearing the field.

Dwight looked at Steel with a mock-surprised look. "I didn't know you knew that many words, but now that I think about what you said, you are right."

"Watch and observe, Stevens. The mounted dragoon is several hundred yards away right now, and at times isn't watching us. Our teamster, who should also be watching us, is half the time smokin' and bullshittin' with another one."

"So you think you can just run away, and the teamster or the dragoon is just going to watch you disappear in the open prairie?" Dwight smiled as he bent down to pick up some rocks and throw them into the wagon.

"No, smart ass, I don't. But I do think we could slowly unharness the workhorses without the teamster paying attention, and each get on one and skedaddle out of here."

"Don't you think the dragoon would chase us down?"

"No. If we do it fast enough, he might get confused whether to stay and watch the rest of the prisoners or go chasing after us. He ain't going to do both."

Dwight continued working as he contemplated what Steel had said. "We're taking a chance that he might draw a bead on us and fire."

"Dwight, this dragoon is fairly new. I've been watching, and they always use the newest men for guard duty. He might be one of the ones waiting to go out West."

Dwight threw more rocks in the wagon as Steel bent down to pick up more. They both continued to watch what the teamsters were doing as they worked.

"The mounted guard could still chase us down even if he didn't fire his weapon," Dwight pointed out. "You know that his Morgan can outrun a workhorse."

"Yep, I know that, but will he chase us, and for how long? If we can hold him off for a mile or so and he can't see the fort, he'll turn back. I'm sure of that. Plus, these workhorses can run for a long time. Our weight ain't nothin' for 'em."

Dwight did not reply as he thought through the facts and assumptions Steel had made.

"It's almost quitting time. If the same kid is guarding us tomorrow and we can get the team unharnessed, I think your plan will work."

"Then tomorrow we go?"

Dwight smiled and nodded as he bent down to pick up a heavy rock and place it on the wagon. He raised his hand and waited for the teamster to address his signal.

"What do you want, Stevens?"

"Sir, the wagon needs to be emptied."

"Get on and I'll drive to the pile for unloadin'. I'm glad to end this day. Unload it quickly so I can get back to the stable and go home."

Dwight never responded as he got onto the wagon with Steel to unload it so they could return to their prison cells. He did not get much sleep that night as he planned how he and Steel would escape to freedom and tried to figure out what he would do if they were successful.

Chapter Seventeen

Escape to a New Life

January 3, 1856, was cloudy and overcast. The temperature had dropped, and the threat of snow was in the air as the prisoners assembled near the wagons. By midmorning the teamsters and the same mounted dragoon took turns standing near a fire for short periods. They had started the fire with the wood-gathering assistance from the prisoners before work commenced.

During the guards' noon break, more wood was gathered and fed to the field fire by Dwight and the other prisoners, who had quickly eaten their meal. The teamsters and guards took turns going to eat. It was during that time that John Steel, who had agreed to let Dwight pick the right time to make their escape, managed to loosen the harnesses of the two workhorses.

The wind picked up in the afternoon, driving the teamsters to gather at the fire while the mounted dragoon patrolled the five wagons being filled with rocks. When Dwight saw that the dragoon was heading away from his wagon and that the teamster that was assigned to them was still soaking up the warmth of the fire, he made his move.

Dwight pointed at Steel and motioned for him to go to the horses. Dwight continued to work as he watched. He loaded several more rocks onto the wagon while Steel dropped the harnesses from the horses. Steel quickly unhitched the horses as Dwight moved slowly toward them. Steel waited until Dwight reached his workhorse to mount. Both men got on in unison and kicked the horses with their boots and galloped away from the wagon.

There was no reaction from the teamster at first, as the winds began to blow and cover the noise of the horses as they galloped away. They had gone about thirty yards when one of the teamsters noticed the flight of the two prisoners on horseback. One teamster took aim with his musket and fired.

Dwight heard the shot and whiz of the ball passing near his head. He glanced back to see if the dragoon had started to chase after them. There was no movement from the mounted dragoon as another shot was heard. He calculated they were now two hundred yards away from the men with weapons. The workhorses carried them quickly and effortlessly as they put more distance between themselves and their captors. Dwight laughed to himself, thinking that he would have been in real trouble if his workhorse had acted like Crazy Bay when he'd first arrived at Carlisle

Barracks. Then thoughts of Spirit entered his mind. He missed that horse. He wondered what had become of him since his arrest in Taos. That was another thing that depressed him. He had lost his horse, too, because of his temper.

He cleared his mind. He had to concentrate on his escape, and on survival on the prairie. They headed south until dark, then slowed the horses to a trot until they found water at a small stream. The two men stayed there for enough time to water and rest the horses.

Steel laughed as he bundled up his overcoat to ward off the wind. "That was a good escape, Stevens. Somebody will get an ass chewin' for that."

"Yes, probably."

"Where you plan on going?"

"I don't know. I didn't think about it much. Maybe I'll go west to California or I'll stay in Kansas. I don't really know."

"Not me. I'm heading back east. No Indians, no dragoons, and no one who knows me," Steel said.

"We need to get to somewhere where we can find some different clothes. These Army uniforms with the large white *P* painted on our backs are a sure sign we don't belong anywhere around here."

"Right, we need to add clothes stealin' to the horse stealin' we already done," Steel said and laughed.

"We don't have a choice. We need to change fast and get rid of these workhorses," Dwight insisted.

"Where we gonna get clothes, Stevens?"

"There is an Indian camp down here somewhere."

"You mean the Delaware[1]. They ain't got the kinda clothes we need."

"At least they're not Army blue with large white *P*'s painted on them. I'm heading south and hope to find them before the army finds me."

"Sorry, Stevens, I ain't going with you to the Delaware. Good luck."

John Steel mounted his workhorse, gave Dwight a half-assed salute, smiled, and disappeared into the darkness of the prairie night. Dwight drank some more of the cool running water and mounted his

---

[1] **The Delaware Indians,** at the time of Dwight Stevens, lived on lands in what is now Kansas, west of the Missouri River and north of the Kansas River. The main reserve consisted of about 1,000,000 acres. About 1,000 Delaware lived on the Delaware Reservation in Kansas, many in log cabins, but some later built substantial farm houses with outbuildings.

horse. He headed him into the stream and followed it for a while to keep the army from following his tracks.

He didn't think they were following, but it was better to be careful. He figured they would head east and track Steel while he gained distance from whomever might be tracking them during the day.

After a mile or so, he just rode parallel to the stream and south toward where he thought the Delaware might be encamped for the winter. The night winds cut into him as the temperature dropped. He noticed that some ice had formed on the edge of the stream. It reflected the light of the full moon that had appeared. The overcast clouds seemed to be breaking up. It indicated that tomorrow would be a clear day, which meant the army might send out a patrol to try to find him and Steel.

He continued to trot his workhorse through the night, occasionally stopping to water the animal. At daybreak, he found what he had been looking for. A Delaware hunting party was heading north. They were a good distance away and didn't notice him. He followed their tracks south and found their winter encampment nestled in a low valley of the prairie. The valley protected their teepees from the cold west winds. Several streams drained into the valley and formed a small pond that afforded them water.

Several men ran toward the lone rider as he approached, and Dwight raised his hands to indicate he was unarmed. He kept them up as several men with drawn bows were at the ready in case he acted aggressively. One Delaware brave grabbed the bridle of Dwight's horse and led him toward the center of the camp. He relaxed a little when he realized they were taking him to an area where several large fires were lit for the morning breakfast.

Another brave motioned for him to dismount. He obeyed quickly and stood still with his hands held up. An older man exited a large teepee and looked over at Dwight as the brave that had fetched him explained what had occurred.

The older man approached as several braves surrounded him to assure protection. He pushed several of the braves aside and spoke to Dwight, but Dwight did not respond. He then looked back to some of the braves near him and spoke. One brave quickly departed and soon returned with a young dark-haired woman. The older man spoke to her for a few moments.

She turned to Dwight and said, "Our chief asks why you come?"

Dwight was surprised to find someone who spoke English. "I need clothes to change into and something to remove my ankle irons, and then I will go. I have escaped from the army prison."

She turned to the chief and translated what had been said.

The older man broke into a smile and then laughed and spoke quickly to the woman. She turned to Dwight after he had finished. "My chief asks why you in prison?"

"Tell him I threatened an officer. He was not a good man, and I have already spent several months in prison."

She relayed the answer.

The chief talked to several men before he responded. He spoke again for a longer time, and Dwight began to feel more and more uncomfortable.

The chief finished, and the woman turned to Dwight. "Chief say you can have clothes if we find big enough to fit you. You big man and you eat much. You can stay if you hunt what you eat. Army not come here."

Dwight smiled. "Tell your chief he is a good man, and that I thank him. I will make what you give me fit, and when I hunt for food I will share anything I kill. I will be no bother."

As she spoke to the chief, he smiled. He motioned for Dwight to follow him. He led him to a teepee shared by three young men. He was given food, water, a buckskin shirt, and a bison hide coat.

The woman stood around as he took the items the chief had provided. She explained that the men who shared the teepee were preparing to become warriors of the tribe and that he would not see much of them until they had completed that rite.

With assistance from a warrior, Dwight managed to remove the leg clasps. A flintlock musket in poor shape was provided to him for hunting and protection. After he had changed and eaten, he cleaned the musket as best as he could so he could depend on it. He then traded the army workhorse for an Appaloosa. The patch-marked horse was predominantly white with black and brown patches, and looked to be several years old.

Unknown to Dwight, the workhorse was immediately butchered and the meat divided among the women. He found out later that the tribe had no use for it and their supply of meat was low. He felt bad that the animal that had carried him to freedom became a Delaware Indian staple and would never have given the horse to them if he had known its fate.

He stayed in the encampment for several days, assuring himself that the army would not venture close in an attempt to hunt him down. Soon he was allowed to accompany a hunting party heading south to hunt for game. It would be several days before the party would find a small herd of elk. They split up into two groups, those with firearms and those with bows and arrows. The latter would chase, and hopefully direct, the herd of elk toward those armed with muskets who were concealed just behind a hill. The plan worked, and Dwight was able to shoot a buck elk.

Several others were taken that day, which allowed him to keep his promise to share his kill with anyone that needed meat.

And so went the weeks as Dwight hunted with the Delaware parties. When he was not hunting, he busied himself making a set of clothes that fit better him. After a time, he felt a little better about never seeing Maria again, although Dwight continued to have dreams about her. It angered him that his subconscious would not let him get her out of his mind.

By March, as the weather began to change, he wanted to return to the white man's civilization. But before he ventured back into that world, he would need an identity change. He couldn't be Aaron Dwight Stevens anymore, due to the risk of being caught by the army.

It came to him one night as he lay in the teepee. He would call himself Charles Whipple. His cousin and best friend would never know he had used it, and he realized there could be other people in the country named Charles Whipple. He recalled that he had known several men during his years in the army who were named Whipple, and it would be an easy identity to maintain as his own.

He knew all the particulars about Charles Whipple, including that no one, especially his family, ever called him Charlie. It was Charles Whipple from Norwich, Connecticut, and his new identity was established. The Delaware Indian tribe that he was staying with couldn't have cared less. Soon he would test it out in his world and make people believe he was Charles Whipple.

Dwight left the Delaware encampment, leaving a freshly killed elk near the chief's tent as thanks for the hospitality he had received. He headed southwest and farther away from Fort Leavenworth. Twenty miles from the Delaware encampment, he reached the outskirts of Lawrence, Kansas. He camped for the night and prepared to enter the town in the morning. He cooked, ate, and turned in early. The March night was cool, but indicated that Kansas spring was in the air.

Sleep did not come easy as he rehearsed the details of his new identity as Charles Whipple, just discharged from the army and originally a native of Norwich, Connecticut. He rose before dawn, broke camp, and was in the town as the sun peeked over the horizon. There were few people about as he slowly passed the general store, bank, and other establishments on the main street.

He noticed a bulletin board near a small telegraph office. He stopped when some large lettering on one of the posted papers caught his eye. He began to read and suddenly realized how out of touch he was with what had occurred in Kansas and the surrounding territories during his many months of imprisonment. The bulletin read:

Kansas Militia
In need of Volunteers.
Military Experience Preferred for Selected Positions
Inquire to Colonel James Lane
Free State Hotel

Dwight read more postings and understood that Lawrence was an anti-slavery town that supported a free state entry into the Union. It did not take long for him to find the Free State Hotel. He entered and found a night clerk busily fussing through papers strewn about his small desk behind the counter.

He inquired, "Excuse me, sir, where can I find Colonel James Lane?"[1]

Col. James Henry Lane
Public Domain photo

The clerk looked up and was slightly perplexed when he saw the tall young man dressed in animal skins but speaking with a polite New England accent.

He stared a little longer than Dwight cared. "Sir, if you would be so

---

[1] **Colonel James Lane** was born in Lawrenceburg, Indiana. He fought in the war against Mexico with the Indiana Volunteers. After his return, he went into politics, becoming the Indiana lieutenant governor in 1849. He moved to Kansas in 1854, and became well known as the leader of the free-state and anti-slavery militias and soldiers during the era of "Bloody Kansas." In the Civil War, he rose to the rank of brigadier general of volunteers and served until the end of the war. In 1865, he was elected to the U.S. Senate; however, he lost much of his support and finally shot himself in the head on July 1, 1866, and died 10 days later.

kind to direct me to Colonel Lane."

"Please excuse me. I was taken aback by your accent. New Englander, isn't it?"

"Yes, Charles Whipple. Norwich, Connecticut. Fresh out of the army. I spent some time hunting with the Delaware. I guess I look like one of them, the way I'm dressed." Dwight smiled to relax the man.

"May I inquire about your business with the colonel?"

"Yes. I am considering volunteering for the militia."

"Ah, the colonel should be down for breakfast at six o'clock. I will point him out when he shows. You can wait at one of our tables. Will you be having breakfast?"

Dwight remembered that he had no money. The clerk looked and waited for a response.

"We serve a very good breakfast, Mr.…Whipple, wasn't it?" He paused and waited for Dwight to respond.

"Yes, it's Charles Whipple. And no, thank you. I will just wait for the colonel."

"The coffee is free, sir. My gift to you for joining the militia. Would you care for some?"

"Why yes, I would. Thank you."

"No thanks needed. My name is Edward Callahan. It's my pleasure. You are doing a great service to this territory. It needs good men in the militia. The causes of anti-slavery and pro-slavery are pulling our territory apart. We in Lawrence support a free state. We don't want slavery here. But we need the militia and men like you to keep things civil, let votes count, and leave intimidation out."

Dwight realized how personal the issues were in Lawrence. He looked at the hotel clerk and said, "I, too, strongly support the anti-slavery cause, but keeping the peace must be a priority as well."

The clerk departed and Dwight relaxed, feeling more welcome despite his appearance.

The black coffee was brought to him a few minutes later. It was the first good cup of coffee he had had in a long time. He thought back to sitting in the Taos jail awaiting transport back to Cantonment Burgwin in chains. He remembered Kit Carson had given him a decent cup just before his departure. His next thought was of Maria, and he instantly fought to get her image out of his head.

He heard someone calling him and realized that the hotel clerk was trying to get his attention.

Dwight snapped out of it as he heard the clerk address Colonel Lane. "Good morning, sir. Will you be taking breakfast as usual?"

"Yes, Edward. Thank you. A cup of your good coffee to start the morning will be fine, and some bacon and eggs, as well, when you are ready."

"Yes, sir. Right away."

The colonel moved to the rear of the small dining area and sat down. He looked over in Dwight's direction and nodded. He opened up his breast pocket and checked his pocket watch with the Register clock that hung over the main desk. The time was 6:05 a.m.

Dwight slowly rose and walked over to where the colonel was receiving his cup of coffee. The colonel looked up as he saw him approach. Mr. Callahan also looked at Dwight and smiled as he left the table.

"Excuse me, Colonel. I apologize for disturbing you, but would you allow me to introduce myself?"

"By all means, young man." The Colonel stood up.

"My name is Charles Whipple. I was in the U.S. Dragoons in the New Mexico Territory for several years. I heard about your need for experienced military men."

The colonel smiled and replied, "Yes. I am looking for good men. Colonel James Lane, Second Volunteer Regiment, Kansas Militia." Lane extended his hand. Dwight shook it. "Where are you from, Charles Whipple?"

"Originally from Norwich, Connecticut."

"Glad to make your acquaintance."

"It is my honor, sir, to meet you."

"Please continue, Mr. Whipple."

"Well, sir, I am here to offer my services if you are interested. I would like to join your free state militia. I have experience fighting Indians with the dragoons, and I am proficient with all issued army weapons, including sabers."

The colonel smiled as he heard the details. "First, Mr. Whipple, I must explain that the Second Volunteer Regiment is our official name and we are a mounted one. We are called the free state militia because we are all anti-slavery, and most of us come from Lawrence and the surrounding area. But you must understand, we are part of the Kansas Militia and subject to the commands of our territorial government."

Dwight nodded. "I enlisted in the First Massachusetts Volunteers under Brigadier General Caleb Cushing. I'm sure you have heard of him."

"I have, Mr. Whipple. So you are a veteran of the Mexican War?"

"Yes, sir. Forty-seven through forty-eight."

"I was too. I resigned my commission to enter politics in Indiana in forty-nine. I was lieutenant governor for four years and served in Congress for two more. I came to Kansas in fifty-four because of the slavery issues that plague this country."

"My credentials are not of your stature, Colonel, but I can help you in training and operating the militia."

"I must inform you, Mr. Whipple, that I am in the process, with other Kansas legislators, of forming a constitution in Topeka so that Kansas may enter the union as a free state. But I have been asked to stay neutral so that a Kansas militia can keep the peace between the Missouri ruffians and the New England settlers carrying their Beecher's Bibles[1]. There is no room for slavery in this territory, or this country, in my opinion. Are you prepared to train men to keep the peace in Kansas?"

"Yes, sir. I would agree to do that. I am anti-slavery like you."

"Good. I need experienced military men. I am prepared to offer you a commission in the Second Regiment of Volunteers, if you will accept one under my command."

"Colonel, I was only a bugler in the dragoons. I was not an officer."

"Mr. Whipple, I need men with experience to run this regiment. Most are Kansas farmers or transplanted easterners that ride horses for transportation, not mounted military maneuvers and encounters. I can use you. I am offering you the rank of lieutenant. If you prove yourself competent, more promotions will be in order. Will you accept my offer, sir?"

Dwight stood back and sipped the last of his coffee. He looked at the colonel and smiled. "Sir, I would be honored to serve under your command as your lieutenant." Dwight extended his hand, and the two men shook again.

"Good, I am delighted. Can I offer you some breakfast?"

Dwight hesitated, embarrassed to have to explain that he was broke. He didn't want to lie. The only lies he was guilty of so far were his name and the fact that he had not mentioned his recent escape from prison.

"Lieutenant Whipple, would you like breakfast? I am offering it courtesy of the Second Regiment of Volunteers of the Kansas Militia."

"Well, yes, thank you, sir. I would be honored."

"Good."

The colonel smiled and looked up just as Mr. Callahan approached with his breakfast. "Edward, breakfast for Lieutenant Whipple, please.

---

[1] **Beecher's Bibles** was the name given to the breech-loading Sharps rifles that were supplied to the anti-slavery immigrants in Kansas. The name came from the Connecticut minister Henry Ward Beecher, and the rifles were provided to settlers moving to the Kansas Territory to fight slavery.

Lieutenant, order anything you would like."

"The same as the colonel, please."

Both men exchanged information and stories of their days in Mexico.

After that, Lane changed the subject. "Lieutenant Whipple, your task to train my men will be challenging, but I'm sure you, my staff, and I can accomplish that in a reasonable time and prepare them for any possible opposition. The unorganized pro-slavery ruffians that have been harassing, stealing, and sometimes beating anti-slavery settlers are a true nuisance. That is a major concern to me, but our worst concern is in the territorial government."

"Sir, I don't quite understand."

"Our territorial governor is the problem. I understand from my sources that the president is considering removing Governor Wilson Shannon. He is pro-slavery. This is good if it happens, but we do not know who the president will appoint as his replacement." He looked at Dwight and lowered his voice. "It is speculated that the pro-slavers will be trying every means possible to get another of their men appointed to the governorship."

"Can you tell me who you suspect?"

"I have heard names, but if Governor Shannon is removed, his lieutenant governor, Daniel Woodson, will be sworn in immediately. He's no different from Shannon and will be easily manipulated by the pro-slavery factions."

"I understand now, sir."

"Yes, as you can see, we are part of the Kansas Militia and despite our open support for a free state, we have to obey the governor's orders to keep the peace. That will mean making sure that settlers entering the territory are protected, whether or not they are pro- or anti-slavery. If we cross that line, we will be disbanded."

The conversation lasted for over an hour, until the colonel invited his new lieutenant to the small stock house that had been converted into a makeshift armory. Dwight was able to find some articles of clothing to replace his Delaware skins, and he met several men who were introduced as part of the colonel's staff. Only a handful had any military experience.

Aaron Dwights Stevens
As he may have appeared as Charles Whipple in Kansas
Kansas State Historical Society

Several weeks passed, and Lieutenant Charles Whipple organized the men into two companies. Their numbers fell short of the full complement required to make a regiment, but Colonel Lane insisted that more men would soon be added to total the one thousand required. He hoped they would join as the reputation and experience of their outfit became better known in the territory.

Dwight didn't bother himself with the numbers, but rather focused on the quality of instruction they received from him. He scheduled rigorous training in horse handling, riding, and weapons handling, including firing at targets. The militia recruits observed that Lieutenant Whipple was a crack shot with a musket, Sharps, or pistol.

He also taught all the men some simple techniques of saber handling. He demonstrated how to advance and defend with a saber while mounted. His abilities truly impressed the recruits during instructional periods. News quickly spread that the large, handsome man known as Charles Whipple was not a man you wanted as an enemy.

Dwight explained the effect of close-order marching and drilling despite the fact that the regiment was a mounted one. He drilled them over and over in practiced military maneuvering in different formations, including controlled firing. The new lieutenant expressed the need for his men to be organized and knowledgeable of military tactics on foot or mounted. He could not emphasize enough the need for them to realize that cover increased their odds of survivability in engagements. He likened that success to the ways of the different Indian tribes he had fought against in the West. Dwight's success in shaping the regiment was certainly noticed, and greatly appreciated, by Colonel Lane, who quickly promoted him to captain. Dwight was now the second in command.

News of the experienced captain teaching and drilling the regiment spread quickly in the vicinity of Lawrence, to free state and pro-slavery factions alike. It wasn't long before the reports of an organized and formidable regiment reached the governor's office. Governor Daniel Woodson had temporarily succeeded Governor Shannon, and desperately needed to activate the 2nd Volunteers to maintain the peace. He immediately promoted Colonel Lane to Major General of the Kansas Militia, despite Lane's free-state affiliation. Lane then promoted Charles Whipple to colonel by the end of April of 1856.

With Whipple's promotion, advancement within the militia was extended to some other members as well. One was John Henri Kagi[1], a young attorney originally from Virginia who had moved to Nebraska. Kagi had practiced law in Nebraska until his interest in the anti-slavery cause overwhelmed him and he joined the Kansas Militia. His strong anti-slavery beliefs and his organizational and administrative abilities did not go unnoticed by Colonel Whipple. He promoted Kagi to lieutenant immediately following his own promotion. The two became inseparable during the next few years. One who knew John Kagi well later described him as, ***"Thoroughly educated, with a long and angular build, scanty hair and cold, leaden eyes. He was a logician of more than ordinary ability, and in an address or discussion would stand slightly bent with hands behind his back. The solid thinker would not tire of listening to him."***

Incidents continued to occur in Kansas between the free-state and pro-slavery factions during the spring and summer of 1856. Transportation of goods was controlled by the pro-slavery factions, causing considerable hardship for the free-state settlers. The deficits also affected the regiment. Dwight considered taking the supplies by force, but waited until other factors contributed to his decision. In May of 1856, an incident brought territorial attention to Colonel Charles Whipple.

An individual reached Topeka, where the regiment was stationed under Whipple's command, and stated that he had been confronted by a large group of pro-slavery ruffians. He stated that they had threatened his life and then stole personal property from him. In reaction, Colonel

---

[1] **John Henri Kagi** – See 10 raiders who died at Harper's Ferry.

Whipple and a company from the 2nd Volunteer Regiment returned to Indianola, Kansas, where the suspected ruffians had originated, and sacked the only dry goods store in the city. The men that guarded the entry to Indianola saw Whipple and the company approaching on horseback.

Lieutenant Kagi had devised a plan to enter the town, assault the dry goods store, and take supplies while Whipple attacked the ruffians and drove them off. Colonel Whipple ordered sabers drawn when he saw an organized number of men mounted near the dry goods store. He ordered the bugler to sound the charge while Kagi's men waited.

Immediately, at the sight of the charge, the mounted ruffians retreated out of town. The news spread quickly of the arrival and presence of the mounted militia, headed by the notorious Colonel Whipple. The ruffian guard force did not return to Indianola for several days, and Whipple and his company departed with their supplies unopposed. Dwight did not realize until later, when informed by Kagi, that the name and reputation of Colonel Charles Whipple had become so famous with both factions in Kansas.

More trouble occurred when a pro-slavery faction of approximately eight hundred men, led by Sheriff Jones[1], sacked Lawrence, Kansas, and burned down the Free State Hotel. Also, in Washington, Senator Charles Sumner of Massachusetts[2] was caned and almost killed by South Carolina Congressman Preston Brooks, after Sumner finished a speech entitled "Crime against Kansas." The speech was extremely critical of several senators, including Brooks's cousin, Senator Andrew P. Butler, and condemned the sacking of Lawrence. The free-state thinkers hailed Sumner for his condemnation of the incident, and the pro-slavery thinkers idolized Brooks for his aggressive behavior in caning him.

---

[1] **Sheriff Jones and the sacking of Lawrence Kansas** – The non-fatal shooting of Douglas County Sheriff Samuel Jones on April 23, 1856, while he was attempting to arrest free-state settlers in Lawrence, is believed to have been the immediate cause of the violence. Lawrence residents drove Jones out of town after he was shot. Building on a proclamation and a finding by a grand jury that Lawrence's Free State Hotel was actually built as a fort, Sheriff Jones collected a posse of 750 southerners to enter Lawrence, disarm the citizens, wreck the town's antislavery presses, and destroy the Free State Hotel.

[2] **Senator Charles Sumner (R-Mass.) and Representative Preston Brooks (D-S.C.)** – In 1856, South Carolina Representative Preston Brooks nearly killed Sumner, beating him with a cane in his office following a speech in which Sumner ridiculed slave owners as pimps in his vitriolic denunciation of the "Crime against Kansas." Brooks was upset that Sumner had verbally slandered his cousin, **Senator Andrew Butler (D-S.C.),** pro-slavery co-author of the Kansas-Nebraska Act of 1854. After three years of medical treatment, Sumner returned to the senate as the Civil War began.

The division between the two factions was driven further apart when abolitionist John Brown and his four sons attacked and killed five pro-slavery men in retaliation for the Lawrence, Kansas sacking. The incident became known as the Pottawatomie Massacre[1]. Brown became even more popular, and feared, when he successfully led his anti-slavery forces in capturing twenty-two pro-slavery men. He and his men used them as hostages in an effort to retrieve his two sons, who had been captured following the Potawatomie Massacre. That incident became known as the Battle of Black Jack. The five-hour-long battle resulted in the exchange of Brown's two sons and another member of Brown's men for his pro-slavery hostages.

By July of 1856, the Kansas Legislature had been dispersed by acting Governor Woodson, causing the President of the United States to appoint a new governor. During July, August, and September, Colonel Charles Whipple led three more expeditions to Tecumseh, Osawkie, and Lecompton, all in the vicinity of Topeka, to procure food and supplies for his troops. The act of sacking for the supplies, however, did not go unnoticed.

By September, newly appointed Governor John Geary[2], upon hearing the news of the raids for food, ammunition, and other supplies by members of the militia, disbanded the entire Kansas Militia. He appointed a U.S. marshal named I. B. Donalson [3] to investigate the raids and the killing of one member of the militia during those raids. The governor relied heavily on support from the U.S. Army troops at Fort Leavenworth.

---

[1] **The Pottawatomie Massacre** occurred during the night of May 24 and the morning of May 25, 1856. In reaction to the sacking of Lawrence, Kansas, by pro-slavery forces, John Brown and a band of abolitionist settlers killed five settlers along Pottawatomie Creek in Franklin County, Kansas. This was one of the many bloody episodes in Kansas, which came to be known collectively as Bleeding Kansas.

[2] **Governor John W. Geary** was born in Mt. Pleasant, Pennsylvania, in what is now Pittsburgh. He enlisted in the volunteers for the Mexican War, where he was wounded five times. At 6 feet 6 inches tall, he was a good target. In 1856, Geary accepted an appointment to be governor of Kansas Territory. Pro-slavery forces were not happy with the appointment and, fearing for his life, he left Kansas in early 1857. During the Civil War, his Pennsylvania regiment fought in several of the largest battles on the Eastern Front, including Gettysburg and Chancellorsville. They were then sent to the Western Front, where he fought at Chattanooga, Tennessee. After the war, he served two terms as the governor of Pennsylvania.

[3] **I. B. Donalson**, a United States Marshal of Kansas Territory, was advanced in years and decidedly in favor of the slave party and one of its members, but was not of the rabid sort. His surroundings, however, were in every way unfavorable to a proper and just discharge of his duties. His deputies were all violent pro-slavery men, younger and more active than himself, and he became responsible for many of their illegal acts.

Colonel Charles Whipple now found himself wanted as a criminal for the raids he'd led. Many supporters of the anti-slavery cause looked to him as a modern-day Robin Hood who stole from the ruffians and gave to the anti-slavers while protecting them. Those in the pro-slavery Kansas government pushed Governor Geary to capture and arrest the dangerous criminal. It was ironic to Dwight that Marshal Donalson and his deputies were searching for Charles Whipple, while he was still being sought by the U.S. Army as Aaron Dwight Stevens. Incidents continued to occur rapidly in Kansas. In September of 1856, Governor Geary disbanded all armed units in Kansas except for the U. S. Army.

With the Kansas Militia dissolved, James Lane was compelled to move to Nebraska City with the majority of his anti-slavery followers. The distance of a hundred miles north of Fort Leavenworth, and on the west side of the Missouri River, afforded some protection from the U.S. troops as they tried to quell the trouble in Kansas. During his stay in Nebraska City, Lane held strategy sessions with the notorious John Brown. It was at one these strategy sessions that John Brown, Charles Whipple also known as Dwight Stevens, and John Kagi met.

The encounter revealed some interesting information that all three men would share until their deaths.

Lane introduced them. "Mr. Brown, welcome to Nebraska City. May I introduce two key men of my staff to you?"

"Yes, I would welcome the opportunity to meet them, General."

Lane began his introductions. As he approached John Kagi, he remarked, "Mr. Brown, may I present my strategist and administrative arm, the recently promoted Captain John Kagi."

Kagi quickly spoke. "My pleasure, Mr. Brown. It is an honor to finally be able to make your acquaintance."

"The pleasure is mine, Captain. I look forward to hearing your strategies on the different subjects we are here to discuss."

A few more exchanges were made between the two men, and Lane remained courteous and patient. Lane then introduced his famous colonel. "Mr. Brown, it's my pleasure to introduce Colonel Charles Whipple."

Brown spoke immediately. "I am honored to meet you at last."

"Likewise, Mr. Brown," Dwight said.

"After our session with the general, I would like to talk with you further, Colonel. That is, if it is permissible with you, General?"

Dwight was surprised by Brown's interest in talking with him privately, and Lane was also curious.

Major General John Geary
During the Civil War
Governor of Kansas Territory in 1856
Public Domain photo

As Dwight looked at John Brown, he saw a man as tall as himself, if not a bit taller. He also saw a man who was weather-beaten with a face that looked like it had been carved from wood. Brown was thin and wiry. Dwight wondered if he had ever smiled in his whole life, for he was certainly a serious-minded man. He had an obvious and overwhelming magnetism, with an undeniable personal strength emanating from him. Dwight immediately respected Brown and felt he could trust this man. He found himself wondering if the man in front of him could have butchered five pro-slavery men only months ago.

He stopped his thoughts and concentrated on the conversation as he heard Lane state, "By all means, Mr. Brown. The Colonel does not need my permission to talk with any man in private."

"Good." Brown turned to Colonel Whipple. "Then, after the session, I would like to talk with you as I return to my camp."

"I would be honored to accompany you there, sir," the young colonel said. "And, Captain, I would appreciate it if you were to accompany the colonel as well."

"Yes, sir. I will accompany Colonel Whipple," Kagi responded.

"Mr. Brown," Lane said and laughed. "I hope you will return my trusted staff to me upon finishing your conversations."

Brown smiled and motioned to Lane to begin his strategy session. Kagi looked at his colonel and frowned slightly as a sign of uneasiness concerning the upcoming conversation. The meeting ended several hours later.

As Lane's staff broke up, Brown motioned to Whipple and Kagi to follow him. No words were spoken until all three were alone in the street. "Gentlemen, my men and mounts are yonder." Brown pointed. "I will wait for you to fetch your horses to accompany me back to my camp. Please accept my hospitality to dine with me and my family."

Both Kagi and Whipple nodded as they went to retrieve their horses. The ride to Brown's camp was short, but during that time the three of them shared personal facts.

"Colonel, I understand you are from New England—Connecticut, to be precise."

"Yes sir," Dwight said. "Born in Lisbon and raised in Norwich."

"You are of a Christian faith?"

"I was a Congregationalist, Mr. Brown, until I joined the army."

"So you have changed your affiliation?"

"No, sir. I believe that I now consider myself a spiritualist. I have read the Bible and many other great works, but my spiritualist beliefs have been fortified by my reading of Thomas Paine. I carry his *The Age of Reason* in my jacket and refer to it at my leisure."

"Ah! *The Age of Reason.* I have not read it, nor do I intend to. I am a Calvinist."

Colonel Whipple responded, ***"I have had to look elsewhere for religion and found it in the great Bible of Nature."***

Brown looked over at Whipple riding next to him. "Tell me more about yourself, Colonel Whipple."

"Well, I seldom curse, I do not lie, and you already know my position and actions against slavery."

"I like those qualities in a man, Colonel Whipple."

"Sir, my Christian name is Aaron Dwight Stevens. My alias is Charles Whipple."

Both Kagi and Brown stopped their horses as soon as Dwight had made the statement.

Kagi spoke first. "I have heard, and read on a poster somewhere, of a dragoon named Stevens that was wanted by the U.S. Dragoons of Fort Leavenworth."

"I am the same, John."

"I have not heard of the name Stevens," Brown remarked.

"Does General Lane know this?" Kagi inquired.

Before he could answer, Brown replied, "You stated that you did not lie."

"Mr. Brown, in that case, when I joined the free state militia, I stated a name that the general accepted. It allowed me to perform my duties and train his men. That was my relationship with the general and the militia then. I am telling you my real name now so you understand that it does not matter which I use. The U.S. Army still pursues me because I attempted to shoot a drunken major who challenged me. I spent time in a military prison until I escaped. The major was relieved of his command and banished to an outpost in California. Now I am hunted by a U.S. Marshal of the territory by order of the governor." Dwight continued, "I have led several raids to procure supplies to feed and sustain my men and maintain a balance against the pro-slavery ruffians of this territory. I am no different from you, Mr. Brown, in the eyes of the established government here. We are both considered dangerous men. Don't you agree? I tell you this because I do not wish to lie to you."

"I respect your honesty." Brown hesitated for a second or two, then smiled and said, "I do believe we are both considered dangerous men, Mr. Stevens."

"I prefer 'Dwight,' sir. That is what my family called me."

"Dwight it shall be."

The conversation continued as all three men approached the Brown camp. John Brown moved on to specifics about John Kagi as they prepared for supper. Just prior to eating, Brown introduced the two men to his sons and followers. After the introductions, Brown asked both men to join his following. Both accepted under the condition that they first serve out their commitments to General Lane.

Brown agreed to maintain Dwight's alias for several reasons. One was his reputation as a fierce and noble leader in the anti-slavery cause in Kansas, which further aided Brown's reputation. Everyone in Kansas knew Whipple. Secondly, Brown did not want it known that Aaron Dwight Stevens was part of his following, as that could possibly cause the U.S. Dragoons to pursue Brown in hopes of arresting Stevens. No one knew Stevens except for the army.

John Brown
Around 1846
Public Domain photo

Marshal Donalson was an older pro-slavery gentleman with young deputies under his command at Lecompton, Kansas. Both the marshal and the deputies were hesitant to venture far from Lecompton to pursue Colonel Whipple. After Indianola and the other raids he orchestrated, Colonel Whipple's reputation grew to the point that both sides exaggerated his abilities for good or evil.

By October, Governor Geary became frustrated that the renegade colonel had not been arrested and brought to justice. Marshal Donalson and Governor Geary exchanged several letters on the subject of the arrest of Colonel Whipple.

September 17th, 1856
To his Excellency, John W. Geary
"Governor of Kansas Territory"

Sir: Finding the ordinary course of judicial proceedings, and the powers vested in me as United States Marshall of the territory, inadequate to execute a warrant placed in my hands, from the Hon. Samuel D. Lecompte, Chief Justice Supreme Court of Kansas Territory, for the arrest of one Charles Whipple and others, I respectfully request, that a posse of United States troops be furnished me to assist in making said arrests, and for the due execution of a number of other warrants, now in my hands.

Very respectfully, your obed't sev't
I. B. Donalson
U.S. Marshal, Kansas Territory[1]

Marshal Donalson made more requests for troops. Finally, when Governor Geary was completely confused as to the status of his requests to capture and arrest Colonel Whipple, he sent this follow-up letter.

I. B. Donalson, Esq.,
United States Marshal K.T.

Sir: You have at sundry times made application to me for requisitions upon Col. Cook, for men to assist you in the execution of warrants upon persons charged with offences against the peace of this territory, viz:

On the 17th inst., for two hundred dragoons to serve a writ upon one Col. Whipple and others;

On the same day, for five dragoons to arrest certain parties not named in your application;

On the 20th inst., for ten dragoons to execute a warrant upon Thomas Kemp and others;

On the 22nd for six dragoons to aid in securing sundry persons charged upon the complaint of James B. Lofton; and

On the 23rd, for ten dragoons to arrest Col. Whipple and many others.

As I have received no official information respecting the results of the above named requisitions, you will oblige me by reporting at once, in writing, whether they were complied with, and if so, whether the objects for which they were made have been accomplished, and all other information relative to the subject that you have the means to communicate. Yours, &c,

JNO, W. Geary
Governor of Kansas Territory[2]

The marshal's response was unsatisfactory, and Governor Geary stopped using him for pursuing, finding, and arresting Colonel Charles Whipple. Whipple and Kagi returned to Nebraska City and resigned from the free state militia a short time later.

Lane accepted their resignations with regret, but understood both men's extreme belief in the abolishment of slavery and new association with John Brown. Lane, on the other hand, wanted to concentrate on

[1] **Actual** letter.
[2] **Actual** letter.

forming the government and legislation to bring Kansas into the United States as a free state. He needed to distance himself from any further hostilities as he sought, and would eventually attain, promotion to senator from the State of Kansas in 1861.

Chapter Eighteen

A Noble Cause

In early October of 1856, both John Kagi and Charles Whipple had resigned their commissions and disappeared from sight, laying low at different locations until Brown returned to Kansas. Dwight kept busy reading more about John Brown and other famous abolitionists. He planned to keep a very low profile until Brown returned with the needed funds, weapons, and supplies to develop the army Dwight had been asked to train. No one knew where Stevens was as he moved from one location to another, performing odd jobs.

However, by November of 1856, Dwight's friend and previous companion, John Kagi, had been arrested by Governor Geary's marshals with the assistance of the U.S. Army. There was no bail set because his crimes were considered capital by the heavily stacked pro-slavery courts. He was jailed in Lecompton, Kansas, and eventually moved to a prison in Tecumseh, Kansas, during the winter months of 1856–57.

Dwight contemplated visiting him in jail, but knew it was too risky. He also knew that once he was caught, the army could learn his real identity as deserter Aaron Dwight Stevens. He knew it would mean a death sentence, especially if both crimes were combined. He decided to not even send a letter to Kagi.

John Kagi was released from prison in January of 1857, just in time for a pro-slavery convention at Lecompton. Kagi attended several other pro-slavery legislature sessions in an effort to observe and record their strategies and procedures. It was during one of these sessions that Kagi was arrested again, though this time he was fortunate enough to secure bail through anti-slavery friends who heard of his arrest.

The pro-slavery legislators and courts failed in their attempt to keep Kagi from interfering in their business, and they tried to find other ways to keep him at bay and away from their pro-slavery legislative sessions. Word soon spread about Kagi's anti-slavery leanings and his intentions to follow everything concerning the pro-slavery movement. A few of his friends advised him to leave Kansas as soon as possible due to death threats he had received. Many of them feared that Kagi could be lynched by a mob or shot by any pro-slaver he met who happened to be irritated, drunk, or just plain hateful. It didn't take long before Kagi was manhandled by a mob intent on lynching him. Again his anti-slavery friends came to his rescue, protected him, and insisted that he leave Lecompton.

Dwight was shocked one day when he read that John Kagi had been shot. The article stated that his old friend had slandered a pro-slavery judge named Elmore by accusing him as the prime influence for the mob that had attacked Kagi. Dwight also read in the newspaper how Judge Rush Elmore[1] was offended, and when Kagi appeared at a public meeting, the judge attacked him with a cane. Kagi received a severe blow to the head. Eyewitnesses stated that John Kagi drew a pistol and shot Judge Elmore.

The ball from his pistol critically wounded Elmore, but despite his serious pain, Elmore fired back and wounded Kagi in the side. The newspaper reported that Kagi's injury was minor compared to the judge's. Dwight did not attempt to contact his friend, but learned that his wound was serious enough to lay him up for a while.

Dwight moved to a different location and another job, continuing to look for other incidents in the newspaper that involved his friend. Dwight learned that Kagi had recovered and that he had been appointed by the Topeka Legislature to take the census for the northwest part of the territory. It was during this time while Kagi took the census that Dwight chanced seeking out his old companion. By February of 1857, the two men had made contact with each other.

The following month, Dwight read the supreme court's ruling on the Dred Scott case[2]. He had been following the case for a while, and became distraught when he read that the Court decided that ***"people of African descent brought into the United States and held as slaves were not protected by the Constitution of the United States and could never be U.S. citizens."*** He read on, to where the Court also held that, ***"Congress had no authority to prohibit slavery in federal territories and that, because slaves were not citizens, they could not sue in court."*** When he read that the court, ***"ruled that slaves, as chattels or private property, could not be taken away from their owners without due process,"*** he crumpled the newspaper.

---

[1] **Judge Rush Elmore** moved from Alabama with his family and 14 slaves when he was appointed associate judge of the supreme court of the Kansas Territory by President Franklin Pierce. Despite his strong pro-slavery views, he was a solid unionist in favor of keeping the country together.

[2] **Dred Scott Case** – An African American slave in the United States sued for his freedom and that of his wife and their two daughters in the *Dred Scott v. Sandford* case of 1857. His case was based on the fact that although he and his wife, Harriet Scott, were slaves, he had lived with his master, Dr. John Emerson, in states and territories where slavery was illegal according to both state laws and the Northwest Ordinance of 1787. The United States Supreme Court ruled seven to two against Scott.

He became furious, thinking that the pro-slavery factions had succeeded again in making their cause the law in the country. He spoke to himself out loud, saying, "The only way to counteract this type of law is to vigorously break it."

He was anxious to meet with John Brown and his followers as soon as possible, to discuss their reaction to the hideous decision rendered by the highest court in the land and to begin a plan to change it. It would not be until August of 1857 that Dwight would have the opportunity to be with John Kagi and John Brown. More importantly on Dwight's mind was the need to start training Brown's men. He knew military action would be needed to overturn the present law on slaves.

Dwight received disappointing news from Brown when he met him upon his return, namely, that he would become second in command to a new principal military trainer Brown had asked to join his cause.

Dred Scott
Public Domain photo

"Hugh, this is Dwight Stevens, the man that I told you all about during our journey here."

Both men shook hands as Dwight smiled but did not say anything.

"Mr. Stevens, I have heard a lot of good things from Mr. Brown."

"I haven't had the same courtesy of being informed yet of your military service, sir, but I am sure your credentials are impeccable if the Captain has asked you to join our cause."

John Brown informed Dwight that he would report to Hugh Forbes commencing immediately, and that he needed the two of them to put together a training plan for his men as soon as possible. Brown emphasized that there was haste needed in the training.

Dwight's stomach turned as he heard of his demotion, but he did not let Brown, Kagi, or Forbes know of his disappointment.

Brown also announced that John Kagi would become his counselor and strategizing partner again.

Forbes pulled Dwight aside as Brown talked with Kagi. "Dwight, Mr. Brown convinced me to join his anti-slavery group, but most importantly because of my military background and this book that I want you to read. I understand that you are an avid reader. This will help you understand my military tactics and what I want to instill in the army we will be putting together for our cause." He handed the book to Dwight.

Dwight read the title to himself: *Manual for the Patriotic Volunteer; On Active Service in Regular and Irregular War; Being the Art and Science of Obtaining and Maintaining Liberty and Independence.* He said to Forbes, "Sir, this is the longest title I have ever seen." He smiled. "But I will read it anyway."

"Good, Dwight. I will give you time while I settle in and talk more with Mr. Brown about my plans for you and our military training together."

Dwight only nodded. He was still disappointed in Brown for bringing Forbes in to lead the training, but he also realized that Captain Brown must have admired the man. As Brown continued to talk, Dwight flipped open the book and read a quote that Forbes had written: *To form any army, it is not sufficient to collect men and put arms in their hands.*

Dwight thought that he would hold back his opinions until he had read the book entirely and worked with it for a reasonable time. That evening, Dwight read intensively. The only personal information he knew about Forbes was that he was a former British Army soldier, brought here by Brown to teach the men of his army. His background and experience was in foreign campaigns against opponents that had different fighting skills and tactics.

Dwight resolved to learn as much as he could from the book, while also hoping to expose Forbes to some of the tactics he had learned while fighting the Indians. Within a few days, Dwight had finished the book and had started working with Forbes on their plans to develop a training schedule for the men.

As they began to institute the training plan, Kagi's contacts alerted him to the fact that warrants for both John Brown and Dwight, under the name of Charles Whipple, had been re-issued. Acting upon the information he received, Kagi began to keep up with the U.S. Army movements in the area and was constantly on the lookout for both men.

By the end of September of 1857, Kagi's sources alerted him that the army was closing in. He heard several reports that Lieutenant Colonel Philip St. George Cooke had been reported in the immediate area and was intent on arresting them.

During an evening meeting at Brown's camp on October 5, 1857, a discussion was held to decide where the band of abolitionists would go to avoid the approaching Cooke and his men.

Kagi suggested to Brown that they should leave as soon as possible. He was further concerned because Brown had been ailing from some type of fever over the past week. He addressed Brown. "Sir, the latest reports I have received indicate that we must leave here and head north and out of Kansas. I suggest Iowa."

Brown did not answer as he sat on a stool near the campfire.

Kagi continued when he did not get a response. "As I understand the reports, sir, Lieutenant Colonel Cooke is in pursuit with two warrants that I know of. There is one for you and one for Dwight as Charles Whipple. Both of you are outlaws in the territory of Kansas, per order of the governor."

"I agree, John. Tabor, Iowa, would be good place to go. We shall visit a known supporter and good friend to our noble cause when we arrive there," John Brown finally responded.

"And who would that be, sir?" Kagi asked.

"Jonas Jones[1]. Many people call him Quaker Jonas Jones. Maybe you have heard of him?"

"No, sir, I have not, but to stay with a supporter of our cause would be a great benefit."

"I should be able to correspond from there, and procure the supplies and weapons we will need. We shall leave in the morning." Brown turned and glanced at Forbes, but then looked at Dwight. "Notify the men that we are preparing to leave in the morning."

Dwight realized the order had been directed at him and quickly responded. "Yes, sir. I will also send two men out in the early morning

---

[1] **Quaker Jonas Jones** was an abolitionist and friend of John Brown in Tabor, Iowa. It was at his home that Brown received his mail concerning his plans and where Dwight did his military training.

hours to scout ahead and assure we do not meet up with Cooke. I saw the man in action in New Mexico against the Jicarilla Apache. He is a formidable officer, and we should stay clear of any contact with him."

John Brown nodded in agreement.

Owen Brown[1] spoke up. "Father, maybe you should stay a few more days to regain your strength. You have been ill for a while, and I believe travel will only weaken you."

Brown smiled and looked at his son. "Owen, my health would be better in Tabor, Iowa, than it would be in Colonel Cooke's guardhouse in Kansas. Stevens and Kagi are right. We must stay away from the colonel, and that will be accomplished if we head for Tabor."

Brown looked around at those in attendance and said, "If you all will excuse me, I will retire for the night. My efforts to defeat the border ruffians, and their pro-slavery institution, and free this country from the stain of slavery must not be interfered with by an irritating fever, or Cooke and the U.S. Army."

John Brown struggled to get off the stool, but then managed to walk to his tent and get onto his cot. Owen Brown waited for an hour and then checked on his father and saw that he had fallen asleep. He felt his brow and informed both John Kagi and Hugh Forbes that his father was feverish but resting.

John Kagi went to Dwight, bypassing Forbes, to discuss their plans. He found Dwight instructing two scouts on their early morning task to watch the movements of Colonel Cooke. Kagi waited until the scouts had departed. "Dwight, you need to know a little more about what has been developing between the captain and Hugh Forbes. Lately, there have been some disagreements concerning the salary the captain had agreed to pay Forbes, and you are well aware that money is a problem. Forbes has made it known that he is disappointed in the captain for not paying him on time. He has stated numerous times that his family, at home, is suffering because of the captain's inability to pay the salary he had expected. I have witnessed some uncomfortable arguments between the two of them, and I have kept them quiet until tonight when I saw the captain turn to you. I think he has some serious doubts about Hugh Forbes."

"John, I don't know about that, but we must leave in the morning. Cooke is a good cavalryman, and he will be closing quickly. He has experience tracking Indians, so I am very confident he will be tracking us easily. I hope that the scouts I ordered out in the morning will give us

---

[1] **Owen Brown** – See 5 raiders who survived the raid.

time to take action if Cooke does come our way. I would not want to fight a superior force with inferior men and an ailing leader. The results could be disastrous for everyone in this camp."

"I know you are right," Kagi said. He paused for a few moments before he spoke again. "I'll have Owen wake his father at four o'clock so we can be underway before dawn."

The party left as planned the following morning. By mid-afternoon, one scout returned to inform the group that he estimated Lieutenant Colonel Cooke had just arrived at the campsite they'd left ten hours earlier.

Brown turned to Dwight. "Well, Dwight, you were correct. Our colonel showed up, just as you predicted."

Dwight smiled but did not answer.

Hugh Forbes did not comment as he stared straight ahead.

John Brown turned to Kagi. "John, how far till we arrive at Tabor?"

"About thirty more miles, sir. We should arrive in the evening hours tomorrow."

"I hope Cooke is not hell-bent on my capture." He turned back and asked Dwight. "Will he pursue us?"

"I doubt it, sir." Dwight paused and pointed toward the Missouri River directly in front of them. "If he does, crossing the river and the rain that is approaching will cover our tracks. I believe he will stay in Kansas. I'm guessing he has too many commitments to the governor to be pursuing anyone, including us, west of the Missouri River."

"You are probably right, Dwight. I wish you had some insight on the weather, but I guess only the Good Lord knows that."

Brown smiled, and Forbes again did not say a word. Brown buttoned up his rain slicker as the storm approached.

Forbes was irritated. He mentioned it to Kagi, out of the range of Brown's hearing, as they rode toward Tabor, "I must inform you that I am not interested in staying at Tabor, or anywhere else, because of Captain Brown's inability to pay me the one hundred dollars a month we had agreed upon."

John Kagi did not respond for a few moments as the rain began to increase and the party of abolitionists continued riding. "Sir, I am sure that after we have settled and reorganized in Tabor, the captain and you will come to an agreement as to your salary, position, and any other matters that need to be addressed."

The next day, the group reached the home of Quaker Jonas Jones and was invited to stay as long as they needed. Both Kagi and Stevens hoped that Brown's first night of having a warm, comfortable bed and a good night's rest would be the medicine he needed to combat the ill health he had experienced.

Brown's fever broke sometime during the night, and he felt much better the following morning at breakfast in the company of Jonas and his wife.

After breakfast, John Brown sat with Jones, his wife, Kagi, and Stevens to discuss plans to leave Tabor and travel back East. Hugh Forbes did not attend the meeting, even though he had been summoned. During the meeting, Brown's friend Reverend John Todd[1] visited to inform Brown that he would assist him in any way possible while he stayed at Tabor.

Brown's only request was to have Reverend Todd agree that any packages or crates sent in Todd's name would be opened, cataloged, and stored by any of his men present as they saw fit. He explained to all of them that the packages would contain supplies or weapons for the cause. John Brown stayed with the Jones family until he felt fully recovered from his illness.

Several days before he left the Jones home, John Brown summoned Dwight. "We will be leaving in a few days."

"Do you want me to inform and prepare the men?"

"No, they will stay here for now. Hugh Forbes will continue to train and run the military part of our operation, if he decides to stay on with us."

"Is he planning to depart, sir?"

"I don't know yet, but that is not a topic I wanted to discuss with you. You will be my personal bodyguard. There are more pro-slavers out there that want me dead than there are slaves and anti-slavers that want me to succeed. I need protection, and you are the man I trust with my life. My family and followers trust you as well. Are you prepared for that responsibility?"

"Yes, sir. I have been prepared ever since you allowed me to be part of this movement."

"Good. Then it is settled. I will give you all the details when Mr. Kagi and I finalize my trip."

---

[1] **Reverend John Todd** was a Congregationalist minister and co-founder of Tabor College in Tabor, Iowa. He was a leading abolitionist and a conductor on the Underground Railroad. He was also one of the founders of Tabor, and the Congregational Church, of which he served as pastor for more than 30 years. Reverend Todd's home in Tabor served not only as a station on the Underground Railroad, complete with a concealed room in which escaped slaves hid until their next ride arrived, but also as a storehouse of weapons, ammunition, and other supplies for John Brown.

In late October of 1857, John Brown left with Dwight Stevens, as his personal bodyguard, and traveled until they reached Springdale, Iowa. At Springdale, a predominately Quaker town, Brown visited more acquaintances that lodged him and Dwight for several weeks. Brown wrote correspondence to potential suppliers and weapons backers, while Dwight searched the area for places to house Brown's followers for training during the upcoming winter months.

By December of 1857, the entire Brown party had reached Springdale, Iowa, from Tabor and settled in for the winter. Brown departed east shortly afterward, to visit the six individuals he hoped would introduce him to the right contacts to supply his needs. They would gain notoriety later as the Secret Six[1]. It would be while Brown was still back East that he learned Hugh Forbes had left Tabor, disgruntled over not being paid.

Within a few months, Forbes turned against Brown while Brown was still trying to raise money and supplies. The news of his anger, his slander of Brown, and his loose lips among politicians and other groups soon got back to John Brown.

After much consideration and speculation on the damage Forbes had done, Brown knew he could no longer move forward with his plan. He decided to postpone any strategy he had made until he knew exactly what Forbes had revealed.

Dwight continued to train the Brown party as it grew in Springdale. Intense military training continued as new men joined the ranks during the winter. The ten or so men spent the evenings in Springdale during the winter months of 1857–58, reading John Brown's letters of his plans and having spirited conversations ranging from religion, slavery, Spiritualism, Quaker customs, the Kansas–Nebraska Act, Missouri Compromise, horse breeding, and the latest books that had been published. Any subject was open to debate.

Dwight made a ledger of the men and their progress. He rated each one accordingly as their training moved forward. Dwight used a handbook that Hugh Forbes had given him, called *Forbes Duty of a Soldier*. It was one book that his former commander had written that he felt was worthwhile. He kept an account of the training he performed, three hours every day except on Sundays. His intent was to have this ledger available for Brown and him to evaluate the men, should Brown decide to promote

---

[1] **Secret Six** were the financial support behind John Brown. They were: Dr. Samuel Gridley Howe (his wife Julia Ward Howe wrote "The Battle Hymn of the Republic"), Thomas Wentworth Higginson, Theodore Parker, Franklin Sanborn, Gerrit Smith, and George Luther Stearns.

them as circumstances presented themselves.

John Kagi, Dwight's closest friend, didn't need much training. Kagi could shoot and ride with the best of them. Next on Dwight's ledger was John Cook[1]. He was a Haddam, Connecticut, native from a well-to-do family. As an attorney, he generally assisted Kagi in legal matters, but lacked ability learning military tactics.

Dwight, remembering his own problems, repeatedly warned Cook that his impulsiveness and recklessness would get him killed. Another member, Charles Plummer Tidd[2], joined the ranks of Brown's party at that time. He very quickly learned about weapons handling and military tactics. The Maine native's marksmanship improved over the winter, and Dwight rated him as one of the best shots and best prepared. Tidd would later be promoted, based on Dwight's records and his own personal recommendation, as Brown's party grew.

There were two brothers who constantly visited the farmhouse while Dwight instructed. Edwin and Barclay Coppoc[3] trained with the group. They lived nearby and did not stay at the farm. The twenty- and sixteen-year-old boys marveled at Dwight's military abilities with a saber and pistol. Since both were locals, their main tasks while training with the group were to procure supplies in town and help around the farm. The Coppoc boys were invited for supper many times, and were content listening to the discussions and arguments that occurred following the evening meals.

William Leeman[4] was one of the youngest of Brown's men at Springdale. He was another Maine native who had joined Brown, having fought with him at Osawatomie when he was just seventeen. William proved invaluable and was retained for further training despite his youth. Dwight liked him and often commented that Leeman had good intellect with great ingenuity.

Dwight made a separate list for John Brown's sons. He felt a need to keep them separate so that Captain Brown, as all of them had begun to call him, could evaluate his sons' abilities to carry on his cause in case he was injured, fell ill, or worse.

Both the family and group relied heavily on Owen Brown, the third son. Owen had a mindset that mimicked his father's, and he could be

---

[1] **John Cook** – See 6 raiders who were executed at Charlestown.

[2] **Charles Plummer Tidd** – See 5 raiders who survived the raid.

[3] **Edwin and Barclay Coppoc** – See 6 raiders who were executed at Charlestown and 5 raiders who survived the raid,, respectively.

[4] **William Leeman** – See 10 raiders who died at Harper's Ferry.

even more determined, at times, in his desire to succeed in freeing the country of slavery. Dwight figured he would be the heir apparent if Captain Brown ceased to be in charge for any reason.

Watson Brown[1], the youngest son, spent most of the winter in marital bliss with his new bride. He trained when he could, but did not live on the farm with the rest of the group. He was heavily relied upon to handle family matters, while his brothers trained full-time and his father was involved in communications and traveling to raise funds.

Dwight continued the training at the farm until the last week in April of 1858, when Brown returned from his eastern trips and called a meeting for all of his followers. He announced, "I have received help from a distinguished Canadian and one of the most prominent black physicians known in the area. Dr. Martin Delany[2] supports our plan to recruit blacks as members of the anti-slavery convention we have decided to hold in Chatham, Ontario, Canada."

Brown detailed the location of Chatham as being on the other side of Lake St. Clair from Detroit, a little ways into Canada. "I will be leaving soon to go north to plan and hold this convention."

Dwight listened and then asked a single question. "Sir, do you plan to have any of us accompany you to Chatham?"

Brown looked around the room. "I will expect most of you to come with me. We will be part of the white contingent that develops and votes to accept the anti-slavery constitution I plan to develop during the convention. You, Dwight, will come with me. I will need your protection and abilities to assure that I am safe." Brown looked around the room again. He continued, "Some of you will stay here, but John Kagi will figure out the details to that. You all will be informed of your tasks." He looked over to Kagi, who just nodded. "This will be a great day, gentlemen for our country to be able to read a constitution that truly represents everyone no matter what their color, creed, or gender is."

The men in the room clapped when he ended his speech.

Brown smiled, indicating that the meeting was over, and left the room. Kagi and Dwight discussed some of the details of the trip. Brown and his group would travel from Springdale, Iowa, to Chicago, Illinois,

---

[1] **Watson Brown** – See 10 raiders who died at Harper's Ferry.

[2] **Dr. Martin Robinson Delany** was an African American abolitionist, journalist, physician, and writer, arguably the first proponent of American Black Nationalism. He was one of the first three blacks admitted to Harvard Medical School. He became the first African American field officer in the United States Army during the American Civil War. Trained as an assistant and a physician, he treated patients during the cholera epidemics of 1833 and 1854 in Pittsburgh, when many doctors and residents fled the city.

and Detroit, Michigan, by rail, carriage, and then by boat to Chatham, Ontario. Kagi could not emphasize enough how vulnerable Brown would be to any pro-slaver, marshal, or hired assassin who wanted to harm him during the trip.

On April 27, 1858, Brown and eight others left for Chicago. During the train ride, Brown made it known that after the convention at Chatham, he planned to begin another tour east to raise more money, and, more importantly, to present the written constitution to his potential backers.

The train ride lasted through the night, and the group arrived in Chicago at 5:00 a.m. They exited the train, and Brown immediately sought out a place to have breakfast for his tired and hungry entourage. He picked Chicago's Massasoit House[1]. The men entered the establishment, sat, and began to order breakfast.

The lead waiter approached Richard Richardson, one of Brown's black followers, and told him that he would have to eat by himself in another part of the restaurant reserved for colored only. Brown sensed that something was wrong. He got up and approached, catching the last words of the lead waiter: "You will have to leave or follow me to the colored area to order and eat your breakfast."

"Excuse me, sir, is there a problem here?" Brown asked..

"No problem, sir. I was explaining to this colored gentleman that he was not allowed to eat in the white dining area. I'm sure you understand."

"No, I do not. This man is with me and my companions, and he will order and eat with us."

"I'm sorry, sir, but that is not possible. We have other white guests here that expect this gentleman to leave voluntarily or he will be removed by force."

Brown looked at Dwight, who immediately stood up and opened his dress coat enough to reveal the handle of a .45 Navy Colt revolver.

The lead waiter saw the exposed handle. "Sir, I can't change the rules of the house."

Two rather large gentlemen slowly began to move toward the group. The entire entourage stood up as the two Massasoit House employees neared the tables.

---

[1] **Chicago's Massasoit House and Adams House –** Both establishments were built during the mid-1800s in Chicago's huge development period prior to the 1871 fire, which destroyed them both. These were two of several luxurious Chicago hotels, and they had such modern luxuries as steam heat, gas lights, elevators, and French chefs.

Kagi anticipated an altercation and loudly spoke for everyone in the room to hear. "Gentlemen, please sit down. Captain, I would suggest that we find another establishment in which to order our breakfast."

Brown looked at his men and made a motion with his hand toward the door. He then said, "Gentlemen, please leave. We are not welcome. And now that I know their policy, I would not want to eat here. Mr. Stevens, please lead the men out."

A few chairs were kicked over in disgust by several of Brown's men as the group departed. The entire dining room was quiet as Brown and his party left the Massasoit House.

Kagi spoke to Brown after they all were on the sidewalk. "I would like to have seen Dwight shoot that arrogant son of a bitch in his chest for the comments he made to Richardson, but I guess it is better not to draw any attention to us."

"You are correct, as always, John. But I would have enjoyed it also."

The group found the Adams House, where Richardson was accepted. They ate breakfast and departed Chicago for Detroit on an afternoon train. During the twelve-hour ride to Detroit, the men talked a little about Richardson's reception at the Massasoit House.

Richardson asked Dwight, "Mr. Stevens, would you have used your pistol?"

"If the two men that backed the waiter had gone for their weapons, I would have."

"How'd you know they had weapons?"

"I knew that there would be people hired for security. Once I saw the two men approaching, the bulges in their coat jackets told me they were armed. I would have shot them dead if they had tried to draw their weapons, but the captain and Kagi defused the situation. I liked eating at the Adams House better anyway, just because of their policy to accept all customers."

Richardson never said another word. He knew he was with the right group, going to the right city, to be part of a right cause.

On the April 29, 1858, the group reached Chatham, Ontario. Captain Brown had several of his men write to prominent abolitionists back East to invite them to the convention. Of the several letters that Dwight had the privilege to write, one was to Frederick Douglass.[1]

---

[1] **Frederick Douglass** was born a slave with the name of Frederick Augustus Washington Bailey, in Talbot County, Maryland. He had no accurate knowledge of his age, as he never knew when he was born. He escaped north on the Underground Railroad through New York

They wrote the letters to no avail. None of addressees showed. At the convention, Dr. Martin Delany would remind Brown of the words he spoke to Delany at their first meeting: ***"Men are afraid of identification with me, though they favor my measures."***

Dwight overheard Delany's comment to the captain. He realized that the distinguished doctor was right. The abolitionists favored Brown's willingness to cause trouble, but none of them would publicly back him for fear of retribution, both politically and personally.

Dwight attended the convention with eleven other whites. Thirty-four blacks, mostly from Canada, also attended. The black-to-white ratio did not discourage Brown as he addressed the opening session of the convention. It was at this time that he announced his plan during the first day's session. Dwight sat with the men that had followed Brown, and listened as the captain declared, ***"It is time to take action against the evils of slavery."***

They glanced at each other as they listened to their leader explain the plan he had envisioned, for the last two to three decades, to dismantle the institution of slavery in the United States. All the members in attendance rose and clapped in unison when Brown detailed the news of his invasion. They wondered where it would be. He only mentioned that it would be an active slave section in Virginia.

City, where he met and was helped to freedom by black abolitionist David Ruggles. Douglass was an important part of Washington in the 1860s, and he became one of America's most outstanding writers, speakers, and social reformers.

A young Frederick Douglass
Public Domain photo

Brown stated that the slaves in the area where he planned to invade would see his actions as the start of liberation, and that they would spread the word. He went on to state, ***"The blacks will rally to the cause and escape with us to the mountains to form colonies that would terrify the slave holders into submission. Free blacks in both the North and the South will rush to join the revolution while the anti-slavery whites will rise and apply political pressure to abolish slavery."***

Sketch of Nat Turner
Public Domain

John Brown paused and looked at the members of the convention before he continued to speak. "You must all remember this. The deepest and most constant and terrifying fear for all of the slaveholding South is a slave revolt. There have been violent, deadly revolts in the past, such as the Denmark Vessey[1] Revolt and the Gabriel Prosser[2] Revolt, as well as the Nat Turner Revolt[3]. There was even a violent bloody revolt in the early 1800s in South Carolina. These slave uprisings have never left the Southern memory, and the constant fear that slaves could rise up and kill their masters is the soft underbelly of a slave-dependent society. That

---

[1] **Denmark Vessey** spent 20 years as a slave prior to buying his freedom in 1800, when he became a carpenter. In 1818 he was allegedly preaching rebellion to the plantation slaves in the Charleston, South Carolina area. He defended himself at his trial very well, but was still sentenced to be hung with about 35 others on July 14, 1822.

[2] **Gabriel Prosser** was an enslaved blacksmith who could read and write. He planned a slave rebellion in early 1800, and on August 30th of that year, the action had to be postponed due to a terrible storm. Before he could lead the effort the next day, two other slaves told their owners about the uprising and it was stopped before it began. Gabriel and 23 others were captured and hanged in August 1800.

[3] **Nat Turner** – On August 21, 1831, Nat and 6 others met in South Hampton County, Virginia, at the home of the Travis family and killed them in their sleep. He continued to kill until the militia was called out. In all, he and his group killed 55 whites.

never-ending fear should tell a moral man that slavery must be wrong. But the message is being ignored. We can strike directly at this paralyzing fear and perhaps put this country on a path to do away with this evil practice before it is allowed to spread and entrap more black men, women, and children."

Dwight listened and agreed that the plan could work. The black colonies could function like guerilla units. He thought about the small Indian parties that were able to hold off larger dragoon forces during his Indian-fighting days. He dreamed a little and pictured himself as one of Brown's leaders, teaching the runaway slaves and the free blacks that joined them in military guerilla tactics.

As he thought about this, Brown mentioned Haiti. Dwight regained his attentiveness and listened while Brown explained that the rebels in Haiti had been heavily outnumbered, but they still they were able to defeat the imperial powers of Spain, Great Britain, and France, driving them from their island.

At that point, the entire session broke into applause. Brown seemed ecstatic that everyone there appeared to agree with his plan. He then went on to detail the type of government and constitution that this revolutionary army would need to govern fairly and effectively as it spread.

Dwight realized that Brown saw this new constitution no differently than the one that had guided the country since its inception in 1776. The only difference was that the institution of slavery would not be allowed to corrupt it. A constitution was adopted toward the end of the convention, but the invasion plans Brown was going to detail were delayed due to the committee of backers urging him not to proceed.

Rumors and unconfirmed accounts spread through the convention that Hugh Forbes had let it be known that Brown planned to cause disruptions somewhere in the South. The committee urged him to return to Kansas as soon as possible. They hoped that his return to Kansas would keep his enemies confused. They would think he had returned to continue his cause to free Kansas from slavery. Brown should keep any thoughts of a Southern disruption secret until it was time to be initiated.

Brown and his group stayed in Chatham for another month and then departed on May 11, 1858. All their personal funds had decreased and they needed to replenish them. Dwight saw how depressed Brown's followers were when they disbanded a week after the last session of the convention.

They would have to wait an undetermined amount of time before

Brown could signal to begin the Virginia invasion. Dwight and George Gill[1] went to find work in Cleveland, Ohio. They earned enough money to return to Springdale and wait for Brown to complete an Eastern trip.

While Brown had some pleasurable times while with his family in New York for a few weeks, he yearned to return to the cause as soon as his business was complete. As Brown traveled back to Springdale, four crates of rifles arrived at the Springdale farm for Dwight to store. Brown had delivered one of his successes. Two hundred new top-quality Sharps rifles were now stored in a basement in Springdale, Iowa.

Brown was pleased to be reunited with Kagi and Stevens when he returned in June of 1858. He did not join in on the drills that Dwight had started, but he watched the exercise routine Dwight had developed and looked over the tactics he had chosen to concentrate on. Brown, who had started to grow a beard while at Springdale, left abruptly with plans known only to Kagi.

Meanwhile, the group continued drilling, exercising, and strategizing, but also used personal time to hold debates, mock legislatures, and other programs of amusement and instruction. In addition, time was spent making personal calls on the women in the area. The age of all the men ranged from eighteen to thirty, and no one objected to them calling on the Quaker maidens.

Most members of the town, including many of Brown's men, thought it would just be a matter of time before they returned to the Kansas conflict. Even though things seemed to have quieted down, Kagi and Dwight knew otherwise.

The Brown party left Springdale, Iowa, with heartfelt sadness, saying good-bye to the Quakers who had accepted them into their community. They left quietly, as ordered, for their return to Kansas. They camped outside Lawrence, Kansas, and awaited their captain.

Brown met up with the group in late June, traveling under the name of Shubel Morgan. His white beard had grown considerably and he looked completely different. It was at this time that Brown disbanded the group until he thought they would be needed for his new plan. He dispersed money to the men to use until they would reunite.

John Cook was sent to live in Harpers Ferry, to report back on the

---

[1] **George B. Gill** was active with John Brown and his raiders, but was not at Harper's Ferry. It was Gill who said "Stevens—how gloriously he sang! His was the noblest soul I ever knew. Though owing to his rash, hasty way, I often found occasion to quarrel with him more so than with any of the others, yet I can truly say that Stevens was the most noble man that I ever knew."

community as well as any military movements in the area. Some men were sent to New York to spy on Forbes. Brown would spend the fall of 1858 in southern Kansas, biding time for his big movement to Virginia. Brown, his sons, Kagi, and Stevens began to make secret plans for the invasion of Virginia.

Things had changed in Kansas, and the era of "Bloody Kansas" had passed. However, some atrocities still occurred before Brown's return to Kansas, but he did not take action to avenge them. Even though Brown needed to practice tactics for his brash move to attack Virginia, he did not use the violence he had been informed about as an excuse to implement any military action.

Instead, in September of 1858, Brown concentrated on constructing a fort that he would call Fort Bain[1]. It was just before building of the fort that Dwight wrote home to inform his brother of his situation and to reestablish contact with his family.

Spring Dale Cedar Co. Iowa
August 2, 1858
My Dear Brother,

I think I told you before that I was in the cause of human freedom, but did not give you the particklures. We left Kansas to strike slavory at the heart, and we had things all arranged to do it, and would of done so, but for a trator One of the party had a falling out with the head one and for gold turned trator to himself his country and his god; you may think it not best to do it by the sword, but I tell you it never will be done away except by the sword, and every year it is getting worse, and then think of the thousands who are murdered yearly, you are aware of how they do things down south.

I suppose that they work there slaves on those big plantations hard enouf to kill them in seven years, they can make the most of them in that way, so you see there is thousands of them yearly, and would you not think it best to do away with Slavory in a year or two losing a few thousands in war than to have thousands of them murdered yearly for god knows how many years, and to think how many of them have been murdered before this.

I am against war, except in self defense, and then I am like

[1] **Fort Bain** was a non-official military fort. It was little more than a log cabin, built by abolitionists John Brown and Captain Bain, to protect the area from pro-slavery forces during the Kansas–Missouri Border War. It became a rendezvous point for not only John Brown, but also anti-slavery leader Captain James Montgomery, and also a site on the Underground Railroad.

Patrick Henry, when he sayd "give me liberity or give me death." I do not think we shall be able to go on with this year, but I think the time is acoming when it will be done. It leaves us in rather bad circumstances for we had sacrificed all we had to the cause, but we are willing to give up life itself for the good of humanity.

Give my love to your wife, and tell her I should like to see her very much. You must excuse me for writing this short letter.

I will send my likeness. It is not a very good one, but then you can see how I look somewhat. I wish you would send me yours and you will greatly oblige.

Your loving Brother
A. D. Stevens
(Please write as soon as you get this.)[1]

The fort was useful to the group, as they were able to defend against any pro-slavery forces that might have attempted to dislodge them from the area. The fort at Little Sugar Creek afforded them several options to continue operations in Kansas, or to invade Missouri when and if they needed to.

In December of 1858, an incident modified Brown, Kagi, and Dwight Stevens' plans. A Negro slave named Jim Daniels informed George Gill that he needed the help of John Brown. Gill brought Daniels to the fort. Brown listened to Gill and became infuriated while Daniels stood by.

"Captain, this man says his wife is goin' to be sold the day after tomorrow." Gill paused to regain his thoughts as he saw Brown's face begin to show signs of rage. "Sir, he fears for himself, his wife, and their two children that they will never be a family again. He told me another man is goin' to be sold the day after tomorrow with her. Captain, can you help this man, his family, and their friend escape? They are owned by Mr. Hicklan."

Brown looked at Gill and then to Jim Daniels, and said loudly, "I will help you, sir. I will bring your family here tonight, and we will be discreet about it."

Daniels also told Brown that a slave named Jane, on the Cruise Farm just south of the Hicklan Farm, wanted to be set free as well.

Brown turned to Kagi and said, "Saddle up ten men, and you and I will lead them north to the Hicklan Farm to make sure the man returns with his family and friend, and find others that want to be free."

---

1 **Actual letter** from Aaron Dwight Stevens to his brother.

Dwight watched as Daniels quickly departed.

Brown turned to Dwight. "We now have information on others who want to be liberated. Let us move before they are sold like this poor man's family. Take eight men and go to the Cruise Farm. Free this woman named Jane and anyone else that wants to be freed."

Stevens and Kagi both stood and looked at each other.

Brown realized their apparent reluctance to follow his orders. "Is there a problem, gentleman?"

Dwight spoke up in defense of both. "No, sir. It was just a surprise that we would be freeing slaves this early."

Brown smiled. "I have stayed very quiet and have not avenged any atrocities that have been put upon us these several months since my return. I have prayed to the Almighty and have listened to the advice of many prominent men who have stressed that my quickness to violence has hindered our cause. This is not violence, gentlemen. It is an act of mercy for these poor souls. We will take these slaves to freedom with hope that no violence will occur. If we encounter violence, we will meet it head on. If we do not, we will be simply doing God's work to free these people. Please carry out your orders."

Both men smiled and jumped to their duties. In a short time, they were ready to leave for Missouri and carry out the captain's orders.

Chapter Nineteen

The Battle of the Spurs

Jim Daniels had told his story to George Gill in the middle of December. When John Brown heard it from Gill, it was almost as if a gift had been sent from heaven. It was an opportunity for Brown to accomplish several goals. First, it would allow Brown and his men to get back into action. Second, it would be payback for the recent atrocity which occurred at Marais Des Cygnes, Kansas, on May 19, 1858.[1]

On that day, approximately thirty Missouri pro-slavers rode into Kansas and captured eleven unarmed free-state men. The ruffians lined them up and shot them. Five people died and six survived. Revenge for this action was certainly on Brown's mind. Additionally, and perhaps most importantly, if Brown could take the slaves that Gill had informed him of from their masters and deliver them to freedom, his backers in the East would certainly be impressed in a very positive way. Brown saw his actions as both a semi-peaceful way to demonstrate to his backers that he could act without extreme violence and as a prelude to his ultimate plan for Virginia.

On the night of December 20, 1858, John Brown, Dwight Stevens, John Kagi, and seventeen other men rode into Missouri. Brown, Kagi, and their group of ten went to the farm owned by slaveholder Harvey Hicklan, while Stevens and seven other men headed to the farm of slaveholder David Cruise.

Brown and Kagi succeeded in surrounding the Hicklan Farm, freeing Jim Daniels, his wife and two children, and another slave, while taking horses, oxen, wagons, and supplies. They then went to the farm of John Larue and took more slaves and supplies after threatening to smoke Larue out after he refused to surrender to them.

At the same time, Dwight found himself in different circumstances. He approached the Cruise Farm and halted his men just out of sight. He announced his intentions to his men. "I will try to convince this man to give up his slave without any violence. I fear for the safety of the slave as

---

[1] **Marais Des Cygnes, Kansas** – Considered the last significant act of violence in "Bleeding Kansas." A roving band of pro-slavery men captured 11 free-state men, none of whom were armed, and led them into a ravine where the leader, Charles Hamilton, ordered the men shot (he fired the first bullet himself). Five men were killed. The incident horrified the nation and inspired John Greenleaf Whittier to write a poem on the murders, "Le Marais du Cygnes," which appeared in the September 1858 *Atlantic Monthly.*

well. I'm going to enter his front door and try to reason with him."

The men did not discourage him, but did caution that he was giving the slave owner the advantage if he failed to cooperate.

"I understand your concern, but the captain does not want any bloodshed while we free this woman."

Dwight dismounted and slowly approached the farmhouse. He reached the front porch and drew his pistol, then slowly opened the door. He saw a slave woman there and whispered, "Are you Jane?"

She just nodded.

Dwight could see the fear in her face. "I am not here to hurt you or anyone. Where is your master?"

"In with the missus, sleepin'."

Dwight moved in the direction she had pointed. He opened the bedroom door. Cruise and his wife lay in bed, asleep. Dwight stepped away from the open door and into the shadows. He made noise to awaken the two.

He heard Cruise speak. "I don't know who you are out there, but you're a dead man if you come to do harm here."

"I come in peace, Mr. Cruise. I want to talk to you about your slave you have on the farm."

"She ain't for sale if that's what you're looking for. You got men out there with you?"

"I have men outside, sir, and I have instructed them to stay under cover while we talk."

"Talk about what?"

"Talk about you giving up your slave without any trouble."

"Who are you, asking me to give up my property to take anywhere?"

"My name is Charles Whipple."

"I know the name. You're one of those free-staters, stirrin' up trouble." Cruise slipped his hand under his pillow and gripped a pistol. "Come on in, Whipple, but do it slowly so I can see you."

Dwight held his hand tight on his .45 caliber revolver as he slowly stepped closer to the bed.

Cruise began to move the pistol from under the pillow. "Move over to the fireplace where I can see you good."

He did as Cruise instructed, but kept his eyes on the man. Cruise fumbled with the pistol as he pulled it from under the pillow.

Dwight moved quicker. He sidestepped to his right as he raised his Colt. In seconds he had the pistol pointed at Cruise, who didn't realize what had happened. Before Dwight could tell him to drop his pistol, Cruise panicked and began to cock it.

Dwight succeeded in cocking his pistol sooner, and in the flash of a second, shot the man dead. Cruise fell back onto the bed with a mortal wound to the chest just above his heart.

Dwight didn't say a word, but moved back to the bedroom doorway. Mrs. Cruise got out of bed and found her corncob pipe. Without saying a word, she packed the pipe with tobacco and lit it. Blue smoke rose from the pipe. She drew in the smoke and passed it out through her nose.

Dwight found Jane. "Come with us as quickly as possible. Gather what you can carry. You are free now."

Jane walked passed Dwight and looked in on Mrs. Cruise, who now sat on the bed next to her husband.

Both women exchanged glances, and then Mrs. Cruise spoke. ***"I told him many a time to quit going to Kansas and murderen and stealin and cuttin' as he did 'cause sometime it would come back on him. Now it has."***

No other words were said as Mrs. Cruise moved her head side to side and began to cry.

Dwight yelled out to several men, "Take any livestock and provisions we can use."

During the ride back to the camp, Dwight felt remorse for having to kill Cruise. He thought to himself, *There was no need for that man to have died. He could have given up his slave and lived to be an old man. This country is doomed to horrible bloodshed if a man will risk his own life to keep another in the chains of slavery.*

Brown was not happy. "The men told me you shot Cruise dead in his home," he said as soon as he saw Dwight unsaddling his horse.

Dwight explained to Brown and Kagi what had happened. "Yes, sir. It was an unfortunate incident. I had no choice in the matter."

"I believe you, son, but do you realize that when the story is told, there will be even more soldiers and marshals looking for us? I am sure the story will not be told in a way that is kindly toward us. No one in Missouri will ever believe you didn't murder him."

Dwight did not answer but only nodded in agreement.

Kagi approached the two men and spoke as he heard the end of the conversation. "Captain, we should post a heavy guard for the night and leave here first thing in the morning. The fort will not be defendable with the amount of men that could be sent from Missouri as word begins to spread of our raids."

"I agree. We will leave at first light. I will pray on what our next move shall be. I welcome your advice as well." He looked at Dwight. "Both of you think on it, and we will discuss our plans in the morning. I will go and pray, and then rest."

The results of the raids had two immediate consequences. First, when Brown and his two parties liberated the eleven slaves, they forced the authorities to put a price on their heads. The President of the United States put a $2,500 bounty on John Brown, while the Governor of Missouri offered $2,000 for his arrest. Secondly, the farm invasions were not popular with many Free-state residents, who now feared that the Missouri pro-slavery groups would be attacking their homes and farms in retaliation for Brown's raid.

Within the week, Brown had moved north toward Topeka in an attempt to put some distance between him and possible retaliation from either the authorities or the pro-slavers. He did not want any more violence, which he knew would hinder his cause, so he decided to take the eleven freed slaves to Canada. He counted heavily on the assistance of his many friends and supporters along the way. Their first stop was Topeka, where they procured warmer clothes, food, and supplies.

Brown split up his men shortly after they arrived. Most returned to the fort when they found out that no authorities or ruffians had actually done anything. Brown, Kagi, and Dwight began a long trip escorting the slaves to their new freedom.

The warrants for their arrests grew as the authorities were unable to locate them after the raid. Each bounty had increased by $500 as the group headed north. By the time they reached Holton, Kansas, there was a new fugitive; on the 29th of January, Mrs. Daniels gave birth to a baby boy she named John Brown Daniels.

The three men escorted the now twelve slaves to a home owned by Albert Fuller, who they knew as a prominent abolitionist and participant in the Underground Railroad. Fuller's home afforded them rest and comfort from the heavy rains that made the local roads difficult for travel. Fuller and his wife had immigrated to Kansas from Lebanon, Connecticut, and Fuller's father-in-law was a deacon from Griswold, Connecticut.

Dwight's connections with the couple provided him several hours of relaxation, conversing with the Fullers on his Connecticut ties. Later, Dwight decided to water his horse and take a look at the nearby river they would soon have to cross. "Captain, I'm off to check on the river. Keep an eye out for me. I should be returning alone shortly."

John Brown acknowledged him, while Kagi went to the front window to watch Dwight go toward the river's edge, which was several hundred feet away.

The January rain had slowed to a drizzle, with flakes of snow occasionally falling with it, as Dwight reached the river's edge and began watering his horse. As his horse drank, he touched the water. He figured it was close to freezing. The river was still swollen, but there were areas where he thought the party could cross without major difficulty, even the horses pulling the wagons.

He heard a noise to the right of him and turned to see two men on horseback emerge from the riverbank underbrush. One of the men yelled out to Dwight, "Have you seen some wagons with slaves around here?"

Dwight paused until he could see both men clearly before he answered. He realized that they were deputy marshals by the tin star badges that they wore. The same deputy asked again, "Have you seen wagons with Negro slaves around here?"

"Yes, there are some over there at that cabin. I saw them before I watered my horse. Why do you ask?"

"They're escaped slaves helped by John Brown, and we've come with Marshal Wood to track 'em down."

"I'll go with you and help you get them," Dwight offered.

One of the deputy marshals instructed the other to stay with their horses as Dwight accompanied him back to the cabin, leading his own horse. He walked slowly and continued to ask questions on where the deputy marshal had come from in a tone that was a little louder than he normally spoke. The deputy marshal was oblivious to Dwight's plan to alert Brown, Kagi, and the others of his approach with a strange man.

Dwight slowly hitched his horse to a post outside the cabin, continuing to talk loudly. As the two entered the front door, Dwight yelled out, ***"There they are, go and take them."***

The deputy marshal was startled to see the muzzles of several pistols and rifles pointed directly at him. He next heard Brown call out, ***"Come in here and be quick about it."***

The deputy marshal was quickly made their prisoner. They questioned him, and found out that he was part of a nearby posse that had been formed by Marshal Wood to track and apprehend them. It wasn't long before the deputy marshal back at the river realized something was wrong. He returned to Marshal Wood and informed him.

The marshal was afraid to attack the cabin, not knowing how many he was facing. He also was very aware that John Brown, and probably Charles Whipple, were in there together. Their reputations as fierce fighters were well known, but he refrained from sharing his thoughts with his men.

The marshal decided to stay outside on the opposite edge of the river and wait for them to depart. He sent men out to scout different areas of the Straight River to make sure that Brown and his party could not sneak away. The marshal hoped to either take the group in the open or while they were vulnerable crossing the river.

While the deputy marshal was being held captive, Dwight suggested that Brown send a messenger to get help to fight off the posse. Albert Fuller snuck out during the night and went to Topeka. He was able to get about twenty men to saddle up with weapons and ride back to the Fuller farm to help John Brown.

Marshal Wood did not rest easy as he watched the cabin, and he too sent for reinforcements. Within a day, he had a force of about forty-five men.

No shots were fired as both groups positioned themselves under cover for an eventual battle. On January 31st, Wood's posse observed Whipple and Kagi hitching horses up to wagons, which looked to be an attempt by the Brown party to cross the river. Wood sent the word for his men to prepare to engage.

Upon hitching the horses and returning to the cabin, Kagi and Whipple informed Brown that they were ready. The other men who had come to assist Brown began to ask him questions about what he was doing.

Brown answered, ***"I intend on crossing over the river and moving North."***

Some of the men began to argue as to the best way to avoid the posse and cross the river. Brown, Kagi, and Whipple listened until Brown spoke up and silenced the arguments. ***"There is no use of talk of turning aside. Those that are afraid may go back, but I will cross at the Fuller crossing."***

John Brown turned to Kagi. "Get them into the wagons as quickly as possible." He looked over to Dwight. "Those that choose to fight, have them positioned near the wagons as we move across the river. Those that want to leave, have them stay until we have crossed." With that statement, he turned and mounted his horse.

Marshal Wood watched from his vantage point on the other side of the river as Brown and his men began to cross. He sent the orders to begin their engagement, which was never carried out. Word had spread quickly that John Brown had Charles Whipple with him. Both men had achieved notoriety that far exceeded reality.

Brown's reputation was because of his Potawatomie butchering, and Whipple's because of his size, strength, and well-known ability with weapons. Both were feared by these farmers and shopkeepers, who knew they were no match for Brown and Whipple. Quickly, the volunteer deputies began leaving their positions to mount their horses, and before Marshal Wood realized it, almost all of his men had left the area.

Dwight saw the men leaving their positions. He expected a last-minute attack while they were in the middle of the river and completely exposed. He was prepared for the worst. When he realized that they were riding off in the opposite direction, he spoke to Brown, who seemed oblivious to what was happening on the other side of the river's edge. "Captain, they seem to be riding away from us. I expected a confrontation, but it looks like they have chosen to run. You must have intimidated them, sir."

Brown kept his head straight and spoke. "I think they are afraid of the infamous Charles Whipple."

Dwight smiled briefly and continued to brave the cold waters of the Straight River. Occasionally he would glance to the rear to make sure the wagons were following.

The marshal sat on his horse, helpless to stop them. He and four deputies were all that remained of the forty-five-man posse. The marshal watched two men who had panicked and grabbed the tails of their horses; they were dragged a few yards until they were able to get them stopped and mount them. He commented to the four that were near him, "Look at the damned fools. They're scared to death of Brown and Whipple."

Finally, the marshal turned the reins of his horse and left in the same direction that the rest had gone. The last four men watched the marshal leave. They stood on the river's edge as Brown and Whipple approached.

Dwight had drawn his .45 caliber Colt. He was surprised that the men did not move. He spoke to them when he saw they had put their weapons on the ground and stood there with their arms folded. He called out, ***"Do you surrender?"***

"Yes you may take us," one yelled to him.

Another yelled out, ***"We simply wanted to show you that there were some men in the Wood party who were not afraid of you."***

Brown heard the entire exchange and ordered Dwight, "Take them prisoner. We'll use them as hostages if needed."

The men were eventually released once Dwight assured Brown, by scouting behind the party, that no other posses were pursuing them. When the four men were released and returned home, they reported what had happened to an Eastern correspondent named Richard Hinton[1]. After

---

[1] **Richard J. Hinton** was born in London and came to New York City in 1851, where he became a reporter for several newspapers. He was a strong anti-slavery advocate. He went to Lawrence, Kansas, to report on what was going on there. In the Civil War, he helped recruit and then served with the 1st Kansas Colored Regiment as 1st Lieutenant, and later as Captain for the 2nd Kansas Colored Regiment. After the war, he served on several high appointed positions in the Federal Government. He wrote the book *John Brown and His*

hearing their story, he reported in jest on the "Battle of the Spurs."

Hinton named the incident that because the only weapons effectively used were spurs on the horses as they rode away. He also made note that not a single shot had been fired by either side.

A few days after the river crossing, and about a day's travel from reaching Tabor, Iowa, the group relaxed, knowing no one was in pursuit of them. The slaves, as well as their escorts, were tired and cold from the winter wind that constantly blew.

Dwight found a suitable campsite situated in a valley thick with evergreens and relatively obscure. He, Kagi, and a few of the male blacks quickly cut branches from the trees and made several makeshift huts. They lined the floors with fur branches and laid blankets over them. Dwight's days with the Delaware Indians paid off as he remembered their quick but efficient way to build the huts.

By dusk, the party was warming at fires next to the huts and preparing to get their first decent night's sleep since crossing the Straight River. Luckily for the group, a doe wandered too close to the party and was shot and quartered by Dwight. A hind section was prepared for supper as snow began to fall. The fresh white powder covered any tracks they had made to their small isolated encampment and gently fell as the wind subsided.

As the supper meal was roasting, Jim Daniels started a conversation. "Massa Whipple, you be a good shot to shoot that doe. She be almost out of range when you got her."

"The wind had died down, so I took the shot." Dwight paused for a few seconds, looking into the fire. "Jim, call me Dwight. My real name is Dwight Stevens. You don't need to know why I use a different name, but I do."

Jim looked confused for a few moments, but he accepted Dwight's explanation. "You, the captain, and Mr. Kagi be good people to take a chance on gettin' killed for us."

"It is a pleasure, and I think a duty, to help you escape. No man, woman, or child should ever have to live in slavery," Dwight replied.

"You're different, sir. I can see that you feel Negros are equal. Not many white folk do that."

Dwight paused before he answered as he cut a piece of venison from the hindquarter. He blew on the meat and then looked at Daniels. "Jim, you say white folk like us are different from you. I'll grant you that only a blind man and a fool can't see that you are black and I am white.

Men: With Some Account of the Roads They Traveled to Reach Harper's Ferry.

But a man should also see that God and nature has made red men and yellow men too. Some have been made tall, and some are fat, and some have black hair while others have none at all. They are not all men, as you know. There are women. This is all good, and it is the way of nature. It is when man decides one color or some other difference is better than another that everything goes to hell. Nature and God have put an infinite amount of color and variety of species in the world so that it would be beautiful and alive for all to share. The world operates best that way. God never made one color to be the king of colors. He never made one flower the best flower, nor did He make one color of man better than another color. It is all supposed to work together in nature. Too many people seem to have trouble with this. I wonder how we have managed to keep ourselves from extinction. To come this far without killing each other off is a wonder, although that may still happen."

Jim poked the fire as Dwight continued to talk.

Dwight realized that he was preaching and stopped. He smiled at Jim and looked over to his wife as she fed her son. "Look at that beautiful baby boy suckling his mother's breast. He's one with nature right now. He doesn't know anything else but what is natural. If I have my way, he'll grow up knowing only that he is a free man, and that he can do anything he puts his mind to. My life is worth it if he never feels the evil, pain, and degradation you have had to endure since you were weaned from your mother's breast."

John Brown listened while Dwight talked to Daniels. He never entered the conversation, but smiled when Dwight stated that his life was worth freeing another man.

Kagi approached the fire and cut a piece of venison off. He raised the piece to Dwight before he ate it and then looked at Jim. "Jim, I couldn't have said it more eloquently than Mr. Stevens has. I salute you, my good friend." Kagi raised his knife in a mock salute as he ate the meat.

Dwight smiled.

After the meal, the group turned in early and got a good night's sleep. The snow stopped and there was no wind as the temperature dropped to the mid-twenties. The huts had performed as hoped and kept the party warm during the night. The storm had passed by daybreak, and the group proceeded on to Tabor.

Many discussions, songs, and prayers were shared during the trip that enriched them all. Dwight learned more about slavery and the twelve ex-slaves as time went by. It was almost as if they were all truly family members. They shared laughter and some tears with Dwight, but each one left a mark on his heart that only death could erase.

One night as they all sat around the fire warming from the cold,

Jane asked Dwight a question. "Why you not afraid of anythin'? I see you at Massa's house and you not scared a bit. I see you at the river when y'all rode at 'em and they all done run away. I think you not scared o' nothin'." She watched as he sat down and got comfortable. He smiled at her as she continued, "I be scared o' everthin'. Been scared all my life. Scared o' bein' sold, scared o' bein' punished, scared o' bein' made with child, scared o' bein' a slave, scared o' tryin' to escape. I be scared o' a lot more too every day o' my life. But not you. Lord, I wish I was you."

Dwight's smile disappeared. He looked into the fire and thought for a long time while everyone around waited to see how he would answer. He took in a deep breath and looked at Jane. "I think after we get you and the others to Canada and freedom, most of your fears are going to leave you. The horrible fears you have now will die away and be replaced by different ones. You will probably think more about how you will make a decent living, maybe find a good man who will help to put food on the table for the family that I know you will have some day. I don't know if all these things are in front of you or not. You will still have to deal with some unknown things, just as we all must do in life, but I will say that you will never again have those same dreadful fears with which you all have lived with for such a long time." He looked at all of them as he finished his answer to part of Jane's question.

Jane kept staring into the fire and said, "I hope you are right, but you did not answer me why you was not afraid o' anythin'."

He laughed a bit and then he became more serious. "There is a fear I have. It is real and constant, and it drives me, and even more since I have met all of you. It is the fear that I will have lived my life in the dark shadow of the greatest evil known to mankind, slavery, and I did not do enough to rid this country of it." His tone began to turn and his eyes grew wider as he talked. "I've never been afraid of other men and what they could do to me. You have witnessed that while we have been together. I don't expect that to ever change." He stood up from the fire and looked around.

No one spoke for a while until Jim Daniels asked a question. "How many white men feel the same as you?"

Everyone remained silent until John Brown stood up and looked directly at Dwight, then looked down at Jim Daniels, and over to Jane. "Well, Jim, more and more all the time. It will come to a battle very soon, in your lifetime maybe, and much blood will be spilled. But I believe the Lord will decide who is in the right, and slavery will be wiped away."

As the group continued traveling, it became evident that Jim Daniels, who had told Charles Tidd the story about his family being sold into Texas, was a funny and lovable storyteller. He never ran out of games to play with his kids and stories to tell them. However, he could stretch the truth further than anyone Dwight had ever known.

There were many times Brown's men did not know if he was telling the truth or if he was kidding them. In any case, they didn't mind because his stories were funny, harmless, and always easy to listen to.

Dwight often wondered if the story Jim told about his family going to Texas was even true or if he had stretched that truth too. As far as Dwight was concerned, if they could all get to Canada safely, it wouldn't matter.

Jim Daniels loved his wife, Narcissa, a lovely and quiet girl who was rather opposite of him. She was a doting mother and a very religious person who told her own Bible stories to her children. Jim and Narcissa's children, as well as the other two children, were mysterious to Dwight and John Kagi, who had never spent very much time around young children. They had absolutely no idea what to do with children when they talked to them or even how to act around them.

As time went by, however, they became a little more comfortable dealing with the youngsters. Captain Brown, on the other hand, enjoyed all children, especially the small ones. He was a father and grandfather to many children, and he enjoyed watching Kagi and Stevens try to figure out how to deal with them.

Samuel, who had been brought along from the Hicklan farm with the Daniels family, was about eighteen years old and a strong young man. Unfortunately, this made him prime property and a valuable slave. He, unlike Stevens and Kagi, was very familiar with the Daniels children and was like one of the family. During the trip to Canada, Samuel would grow closer to the thirty-five-year-old woman taken from the Larue farm. Her age didn't seem to matter to Samuel, who also grew close to her children. He would eventually marry the woman when they settled in Canada.

Kagi and Stevens found they could better relate to the older children, who could talk and actually carry on a conversation with the two bachelors. Their mannerisms were generally quiet, and they would not speak until spoken to. It was probably due to their many years of keeping quiet while trying not to draw attention to themselves.

Jane helped the other mothers as best she could all the long way to Canada. She took turns watching the youths while the mothers got some sleep when the opportunity presented itself. The health of the children during the extreme cold nights was a priority for all. But the women took turns making sure the needs of the children came first.

When there was a free arm to cuddle a child, the women made sure it wasn't free very long. Dwight and Jane's friendship grew closer as the trip continued. She confided in him that she had a husband who had been sold to another slave owner. She never saw him again. She often talked to Dwight about him. He reciprocated with stories of a woman he would never see again from New Mexico.

They continued on for the entire month of February to reach Grove City, then on to Des Moines, Grinnell, Springdale, and eventually Iowa City, Iowa, by the end of the month. At every stop they were welcomed, housed, fed, given money, and seen as heroes when they explained what they had done to free the slaves they had with them. The most difficult times were while on the road, slowly moving no more than fifteen miles a day in freezing rain, snow, strong winds, and temperatures ranging from below zero to no higher than thirty or forty degrees.

In Grinnell, John Brown and John Kagi spent several days giving speeches, while Dwight guarded the former slaves in a barn close by as they gathered their strength. The two men gave orations on how they had succeeded in freeing the slaves they had with them.

That packed the local meetinghouses, where they received loud applause and considerable contributions for their expenses as they traveled north. At Iowa City, John Kagi sought out W. P. Clark before the party arrived. Kagi secretly entered the city dressed in disguise. Clark was influential in obtaining a railroad freight car in nearby West Liberty, some seven miles south, which would be used to transport the party to Chicago, Illinois.

Dwight arranged for the twelve former slaves to be transported to the railroad freight car during the night of March 8th. The two wagons and their escorts arrived just before midnight at the West Liberty rail yard. Hay and blankets were spread on the floor of the freight car to help insulate against the cold.

When the last escapee was loaded, Dwight turned to John Brown. "I would advise you to ride in the freight car. We cannot risk anyone seeing you as a passenger heading to Chicago." Dwight looked at Kagi for support in his request as he continued to talk to Brown. "John and I will sit in the passenger car closest to the freight car. We'll be able to observe it at all the stops."

John Brown nodded and then was helped into the freight car. Food supplies were loaded as soon as he was set, and the door was locked from the inside.

The eastbound Chicago train approached several hours later. It stopped long enough to hitch up the freight and passenger cars containing Brown and the escapees. Kagi and Stevens sat in the partially full passenger car, concealing their weapons as the train departed. No one said a word as the two men found seats facing the rear. They expected no trouble as the train passed through Illinois to Chicago. John and Dwight remained alert the entire trip. At each stop, they would casually move about the passenger car and occasionally step off in an effort to stretch their legs. The main intent was to watch the freight car containing Brown and the escapees.

Just before arriving in the Chicago rail yard, John Kagi turned to Dwight. "We've come a long way since leaving the fort. I lost count on how many days it's taken us to get this far."

"It's been eighty days," Dwight answered.

"You kept count?"

"Yes, eighty days and almost a thousand miles, John."

"We didn't get shot, caught, or even stopped, my good friend."

Dwight looked at him and smiled before he spoke. "We were lucky on all three. The captain would never let me scout ahead, and I feared that there would be an ambush before every town we approached. It seemed no one had the stomach for an engagement. I never heard a shot fired except for hunting, come to think about it."

John Kagi laughed. "You were probably the reason nobody engaged or took the shot. You scared the fight right out of them."

Dwight chuckled, but then his face grew serious. "Maybe I contributed, but the look the captain has on his face when he is angered concerns me occasionally."

"He can be intimidating. I'll agree to that."

Both men settled back, knowing they had about another hour before they reached Chicago.

Dwight spoke out from under the tipped hat he had pulled down over his eyes to get some rest. "Do you think this Allan Pinkerton[1] person is trustworthy, and a good contact?"

"I know he is trustworthy. I am told by reliable sources that he is a detective and a man of his word. The Pinkerton house is a well-known safe house for runaway slaves. He was recommended by some of the captain's closest financiers."

"I hope so, John. I would hate to be almost at our destination and have to confront some law enforcement agent trying to become famous by capturing John Brown."

---

[1] **Alan Pinkerton** was originally from Scotland and created the first detective agency in America. His home in Chicago was a major stop on the Underground Railroad. He served as head of the Union Intelligence Service 1861–1862 for General George McClellan during the Civil War. This was the forerunner of the U.S. Secret Service.

Allen Pinkerton during the Civil War
Public Domain photo

"Dwight, I do know that he is a master detective who always surrounds himself with concealed protection. I would advise that you relax and trust him. I would not want to see you shot dead by one of his detectives."

"I'll stay back and observe. You meet him and show him to the rail car. I'm sure some of his men will expose themselves as they escort the captain and the escapees from it."

John Kagi did not dispute Dwight's plan. He knew from experience that the man was cautious and had been very much responsible for successfully getting the party this far in their escape to Canada.

The train arrived at the Chicago rail yard. As the passengers departed, Kagi observed an enclosed wagon pull up to the rail car that John Brown and the escapees were still inside. Dwight watched from a distance, assuming it was a Pinkerton wagon, but was concerned how Pinkerton's wagon driver knew where to place it. Kagi approached a man that Dwight would later be introduced to as Alan Pinkerton. They both walked to the freight car and opened it.

Brown jumped out and shook hands with him. The escapees were quickly escorted into the wagon. When all of them were in, Brown turned to Kagi. "Where is Dwight?"

Before Kagi could respond, Dwight appeared.

Pinkerton smiled and spoke to John Kagi. "I think the notorious Mr. Whipple has arrived. I think he was untrusting. I admire your caution, sir."

Dwight turned to him and said, "It's Dwight Stevens, Mr. Pinkerton."

"Ah, but I knew that, Mr. Stevens. I make it my business to know a lot about people."

"I admire you, sir, your reputation precedes you. How did you know what freight car to drive up to?"

Pinkerton smiled and pointed to a young woman approaching. "Miss Wilson informed us when she departed the train. She watched you load the poor souls in West Liberty."

Dwight smiled and said as he tipped his hat. "I admire your caution too, sir."

They stayed in Chicago several days while Pinkerton made arrangements for another train to take them to Detroit, Michigan. Pinkerton and his brother housed, fed, and supplied both clothing and goods for them. When it was time to leave, Pinkerton and his men moved the ex-slaves and their escorts quickly and proficiently.

When they reached the rail yards, the Pinkerton wagon moved to another freight car which was noticeably guarded by several plain-clothed detectives. Brown and the escapees were loaded into it. As the last escapee was assisted onto the rail car, Pinkerton turned to Brown and declared, ***"I detest slavery…it is the curse of America."***

John Brown smiled and extended his hand. The two men shook.

Pinkerton spoke again, "Sir, it has been my pleasure to assist you in your noble accomplishment. I do know that your destination will be reached with no further problems."

"I'm sure there will be none, Detective. Thank you, and may God bless you."

Pinkerton nodded and tipped his hat. He turned to Dwight next. "You may relax, Mr. Stevens. I can assure you that your journey will be uneventful, so please enjoy some rest. I will have detectives onboard and I can guarantee you will arrive safely."

Dwight shook hands and left to board the passenger car. For the first time in quite a while, Dwight slept well.

The train arrived in Detroit the next morning. The escapees were escorted to a ferry on which to cross over into Canada. It began to sleet and rain on that March day, but it did not dampen the happiness everyone felt as they were about to board. After hugs, kisses, handshakes, and many misty eyes, the freed slaves boarded the ship to their freedom.

In all, it had taken them eighty-five days and over 1100 miles to accomplish this feat, despite the attempts of slave catchers, bounty hunters, U.S. Marshals, and the army to stop them. John Brown, John Kagi, and Dwight Stevens would never know how the escapees' lives, and those of their offspring, would turn out, but one thing that all of them shared, was the freedom to make choices in their future. It was a satisfying moment for the three men, but only the beginning in their next step to free every slave in the country. The rest of the year would be spent preparing for the upcoming raid.

In a hotel room in Detroit, Brown, Kagi, and Stevens sat and discussed a ledger Kagi had in front of them. It listed the men that Brown would organize and lead on his raid.

"How many are committed to Harper's Ferry, John?" Brown asked.

"Sir, we have less than twenty for you to lead there."

"Besides my sons, Watson, Oliver, and Owen, and you and Dwight, who else is on the list?"

John Kagi read from the list. When he was finished, he looked at Brown, who seemed to be in deep thought. "Sir, are you worried about the men?"

"No, but I had hoped there would be more. Will they be ready?"

Dwight spoke up, "Captain, I can assure you that all will be ready for the invasion. There will be no doubt about their readiness."

Brown continued to pull on his beard as he thought for a few more moments. "No Dwight, that is not my concern. I have no doubt that these men will be ready when the time comes. We have been the force that has awakened the abolitionists in this country. It has been through our actions that we have succeeded in being a force to reckon with. We must plan this correctly, because we will want it to terrify the pro-slavery faction." He stood up and walked to the window and looked out.

Kagi and Stevens looked at each other and waited for their leader to speak.

He turned and said, "We will eat a fine supper tonight to celebrate our accomplishment. We will then begin to plan the awakening of the slaves in this country to revolt. We should contact John Cook now and inform him that we will be coming soon."

John Kagi would assist Brown in the plans for the raid at Harper's Ferry. Dwight Stevens went to West Andover, Ohio, to stay with friends of Brown and to await his call to participate in the raid. It would be in West Andover at the home of Mr. and Mrs. Lindsley that Aaron Dwight Stevens would begin to fall in love for the second time in his life.

John Cook had moved to Harper's Ferry in the previous summer of 1858. Brown had sent him there, even before he had successfully taken the twelve slaves into Canada. Cook was the advance person Brown needed to scout out the town, and was hired as a worker at Lock 33 of the Chesapeake and Ohio Canal. After being in that position for almost an entire year, he was free to move about the town and gather intelligence as to movements of commerce, troops, and weapons to and from the Armory, as well as anything else that might be useful for the captain to know about prior to his invasion.

During his time in Harper's Ferry, Cook managed to impregnate, and then marry, a woman named Mary Kennedy. They had a son. It would be later in 1859 that John Brown would make his final plans to attack the Armory at Harper's Ferry.

Chapter Twenty

Jenny Dunbar

Ashtabula County, Ohio, became a sweet refuge for Dwight Stevens in the late spring of 1859. The towns of Cherry Valley, West Andover, Wayne, and Williamsfield made up the balance of Ashtabula County, a stronghold for the Underground Railroad.

Dwight was sent there to live at the home of Mr. and Mrs. Horace Lindsley[1] of Cherry Valley, who were close personal friends of Brown. He had periodically used the Lindsley residence as a place to receive and send correspondence, and to board his sons. He also used the house to store supplies and weapons that were received from his anti-slavery financial backers.

Dwight's duties, while he waited for Brown and Kagi, were to open any correspondence, packages, or crates received and addressed to "I. Smith and Son," a cover name for John Brown. He also prepared to begin another training session after Brown recalled all his men. It was during that time that Dwight Stevens met Miss Jenny Dunbar.

Jenny regularly came to the Lindsley home to give music lessons twice a week to the children. Dwight became fond of the pretty young teacher as he watched her. She was always invited to stay for the noon meal while she worked. Occasionally, she would also stay for the evening meal, which frequently climaxed with her playing the piano and singing for the family and guests.

It was during those times that Dwight requested particular songs for her to sing. He would occasionally join in and sing with her, to the delight of the Lindsleys and their other guests.

One evening in late May, Dwight watched Jenny as she prepared to mount her horse to return home. "May I be of any assistance, Miss Dunbar?"

"No, sir. I believe I can handle my horse. He's a gentle one and has never been uneasy all the time I have had him. But I do thank you."

"Maybe an assist to the saddle mount?"

She looked at his kind, handsome face and couldn't find any reason to not accept his offer. "Well, yes, I could use your help. Thank you for

---

[1] **Horace Lindsley** was born in 1811, taught school as a young man, and was a lifelong successful farmer and the father of eight children. The family was a great support to the Underground Railroad and supplied food, clothing, and shelter to many on their way to freedom in Canada.

the offer."

He guided her left shoe into the stirrup and then gently put his hands around her waist. As he lifted her, he figured she could not weigh more than a hundred pounds. The slight scent of her stirred his senses. He had forgotten how wonderful it was to have those senses awakened.

"That was very thoughtful, Mr. Whipple. Thank you."

"May I accompany you for part of the way to your home?"

"I can assure you that I will be fine. It won't be necessary."

Dwight paused for a few moments, smiled, and decided he needed to be more forthright with her. "I know it isn't necessary, but I thought maybe I could accompany you for a while and we could just talk. Would that be all right?"

She looked down at him from her horse and hesitated before she spoke. "I guess that would be all right, Mr. Whipple, if you wish. But you don't have your horse with you."

"I do wish, and I can walk very fast if need be. Please, call me Dwight."

"Thank you for the permission but, if it is all right, I will continue to call you Mr. Whipple until I know you better. I am a little confused, though. Is Dwight a nickname?"

"No, it is my middle name."

"Oh, I understand now."

He felt a little dejected that she would continue to call him Mr. Whipple, but he realized that she was a very proper young woman from a good family in a small community; that was obvious by the way she acted, spoke, looked, and by her recent hiring by the Lindsleys. She began to ride her mount at a walk as Dwight walked beside.

The May evening was warm, but a gentle breeze kept the mosquitoes away and made it pleasant. Even though the sun was setting, there were several more hours of sunlight remaining. As they walked along, there was silence between the two except for an occasional glance by each.

Dwight broke the silence when he asked, "How many instruments do you play, Miss Dunbar?"

"I play mostly key instruments. I do love the piano the most, though."

"I can assure you that you are one of the most accomplished pianists I have ever heard."

"You are too kind, Mr. Whipple."

"No, I really mean that. My brother owns a music store in Norwich, Connecticut, and I have had the opportunity to be around many musicians. You are one of the best I have heard play the piano."

"Thank you."

"I would have loved to hear you play the organ in my father's choir."

"Oh, so your father is a music teacher?"

"No, but he has been the choir director in our congregation in Norwich for close to fifteen years."

"Do you play an instrument, Mr. Whipple?"

"Yes, I play several. I enjoy the banjo and the guitar, and I was a bugler for a short period while I was with the dragoons. I also like to sing while I play. Some people have told me that I have a decent baritone voice when I do. Occasionally I play the piano, but I certainly do not have the ability you exhibit."

"Why, Mr. Whipple, your flattery is almost embarrassing."

Dwight's face flushed. He stumbled a little in his response. "I did not mean in any way to embarrass you."

She recognized how sincere he really was and came to his rescue. She smiled as she looked directly at him. "Then, Mr. Whipple, I will take your comment as a sincere one."

"Please do, please do. I meant no disrespect."

She noticed that he avoided eye contact, so she tried to reduce his uncomfortable state. "Mr. Whipple, maybe in a few days when I return, we both could sit at the piano and work on a duet together. I'm sure the Lindsleys would like that." She saw the instant relief in the young man's expression.

"Yes, I would very much enjoy singing a duet with you," Dwight said.

"Good. Then I can expect you to join me at the piano when I return the day after tomorrow?"

His face brightened as he looked directly at her. "Yes, I will surely enjoy that opportunity. I look forward to it."

They walked along for a few minutes until Jenny began to feel uncomfortable with the silence again. "Mr. Whipple, tell me a little about yourself. You said something about the dragoons. How exciting."

"Well, I'm just twenty-eight this past March. I spent time in the Massachusetts Volunteers during the war with Mexico. Then the dragoons in the New Mexico Territory until I joined up with the free state militia against the pro-slavery forces in Kansas."

"I'm impressed. You are a military man by profession, I presume."

"Yes, you could say that. I do prefer peace at any cost, but I will fight for a just cause and do my duty as I see fit when it presents itself."

"And what just cause has presented itself in Ohio?"

Once again he laughed and then smiled as he looked up at her.

"There is no cause here. I am a guest at the Lindsley home until Captain Brown returns with instructions as to our next campaign."

"Your next campaign. What could that possibly be?"

"I do believe that you have heard of John Brown."

"Yes, I have indeed heard of him and his anti-slavery position. He is a popular abolitionist here and in many other places in the country, I am told."

"You may have also heard of me as well."

"I believe so. I have read about a Charles Whipple associated with John Brown, but nothing recently about him. Are you the same Mr. Whipple?"

"Yes, I am the same. But my real name is Aaron Dwight Stevens."

She looked confused. "I have not heard of a Mr. Stevens."

"I do hope that you are not uncomfortable because I use an alias?"

"No. On the contrary, I admire Mr. Brown and the men like you that he leads. If you need an alias, then I understand. I admire the cause you have all undertaken, but I do not condone violence to accomplish it. I do support what I hear the Lindsley family has done to assist many Negros as they pass through here to freedom."

There was silence as the two continued to walk. Dwight contemplated defending the use of violence to free slaves, but he did not want to become argumentative. Dwight finally spoke and said, "Believe me, Miss Dunbar, when I say that I do not condone violence as well. I have seen too much of it in my lifetime during war with Mexico, fighting the Southwest Indians, and confronting the pro-slavery ruffians in Kansas."

They continued their walk for several more minutes until Dwight realized that he would rather leave her thinking about something else than their discussion about violence. He reached for the reins and tugged on the bit to halt the bay. "Miss Dunbar, I believe we are very close to the split in the road that leads to West Andover. You will be able to continue your ride at a faster pace if I leave you here and return to the Lindsley homestead. I have enjoyed our conversation and truly look forward to your return and our duet. I will think of some songs we may be able to sing together. Would that be agreeable to you?"

"Yes, it would. I look forward to seeing you again. Thank you for escorting me. I enjoyed our conversation. Good evening, Mr. Whipple." She playfully paused and smiled. "Or should I say Mr. Stevens?"

He tipped his hat, smiled, and then remarked, "The pleasure has been mine. Good evening, Miss Dunbar, and you may call me either and I will answer."

"Then Mr. Stevens it shall be." She slapped the bay on the rump and the horse trotted away.

Dwight smiled as the beautiful lady disappeared around the bend on the Hayes Road that led to West Andover. For a brief moment, his mind found its way back to Maria lying in her father's office. He had not thought about her in a long time. He remembered her uncle's letter and realized it didn't hurt or anger him anymore. He wondered if meeting Jenny Dunbar had done that for him, or if it was simply time that had healed him. He ran back to the Lindsley homestead. When he arrived, he wasn't even winded. All he thought about during his run was Jenny Dunbar.

"I saw you accompanying Miss Dunbar as she was leaving. She is a fair one at that, wouldn't you say?"

Dwight turned to see a smiling young Edward Peck, the Lindsley's youngest farmhand, seated on the porch swing.

"I would say that you need to be careful when speaking to me about Miss Dunbar, Edward."

"No offense intended, Dwight. I just meant that she is an outstandingly beautiful woman. I envy you being able to acquaint yourself with her. I know if I was a bit older, I'd make an effort to accompany her anywhere."

Dwight thought the youth was simply paying a compliment. "She is a pretty one, I'd say that for sure. She is also very smart, of good character, and a fine person to talk to."

"So that's your only interest, talking to her?" the smiling young man teased and rolled his eyes.

Dwight could feel his temper coming on. He took a deep breath to control it. He wanted to box the ears of the little pain in the ass, but controlled his urge. "Edward, you must have chores to complete."

"Nope, I'm done for the day. I checked with Mrs. Lindsley and she has no more for me to do."

"Fine, but don't be making comments about Miss Dunbar. Now be off with you."

The young man laughed and immediately removed himself. He had previously learned when and when not to joke with Dwight. He sensed that there was more than just conversation between Miss Dunbar and Dwight Stevens, at least as far as Dwight was concerned.

Dwight entered his room. Sitting on his writing desk was an unopened letter addressed to "I. Smith and Son." Only Mr. Lindsley and Dwight knew the coded address was correspondence from John Brown. He knew Mr. Lindsley must have placed it there, and quickly sat down and began to read.

"How was your walk with Miss Dunbar?"

Dwight looked up and saw Peter Miller, the Lindsley farm foreman, standing in the bedroom doorway.

"Doesn't anyone mind their own business in this homestead?"

"I wasn't meddling. I saw your door open and I was just asking a civilized question."

"My walk with her was just fine. We talked about books, authors, and things of that nature, that's all."

"Then I will guess that you do not mind if I ask you when will she be back to teach the Lindsley children?"

"She returns the day after tomorrow. We are planning to sing a duet together."

"Wonderful, I will look forward to it."

Dwight glanced back at the letter and folded it so Peter could not see any of it.

Peter inquired, "Is that from a relative or someone?"

"Yes, a relative. Mr. Lindsley left it here for me to read. It's just a note to let me know what is going on back in Connecticut."

"I hope all is well?"

"It is, and thanks, Peter."

Peter Miller seemed satisfied with Dwight's answer and continued down to his room to clean up prior to dinner.

Dwight finished reading the letter and decided to find Mr. Lindsley to see if he also had received correspondence from the captain. He found the elder gentleman sitting in his study with pen in hand, writing a letter. "Excuse me, sir. I have received correspondence from the captain."

"Yes, I know. It was addressed to I. Smith and Son. I knew to leave it on your writing desk in your room. You weren't around when we received our mail this afternoon."

"Oh, that's all right. I was wondering if you received correspondence from him as well."

"No, your letter was the only one. May I ask what it contained?"

"Yes, sir. The letter stated that John Kagi and the captain have completed their plans for the next campaign." Dwight knew that he was not at liberty to divulge the information that the raid on Harper's Ferry was imminent.

"And when would that be, son?"

"Mr. Lindsley, with no disrespect, I feel that the captain should tell you that."

"I understand. No disrespect taken. During these times discretion is needed. Maybe I will be informed later by John Brown as to his plans."

"Sir," Dwight ventured to say. "One thing that I can divulge is that I am to send the weapons we have stored here to an address he disclosed in the letter."

"Well, I will help you with that. I will have the farmhands assist you when you are ready."

"Thank you, Mr. Lindsley. I appreciate it."

"It is the least I can do for my old friend, John Brown."

Dwight left Lindsley's study and thought about the letter he had just received. Brown did not specifically state in his letter when the Harper Ferry's raid would commence. Yet he had specified that the supplies he had stored in Ashtabula County labeled "fence castings" needed to be prepared to be shipped to Kagi in Chambersburg, Pennsylvania. He also explained that Kagi would ship them to a farm owned by the heirs of Dr. Booth Kennedy in Maryland, when ordered by him. The letter also stated that he had sent communications to the other men and ordered them to prepare to arrive at the Kennedy Farm before the end of August, alone or in groups of no more than three.

Dwight's first concern should have been how to ensure the weapons were sent to Kagi as requested. It wasn't. Instead, he only thought of the next few days when he would see Jenny Dunbar again. He knew he had a limited time to get to know the woman before he would have to leave for the Maryland farm in August.

Jenny Dunbar returned, as scheduled, two days later. Dwight stayed clear of the Lindsley household during the day as he diligently prepared to move the weapons. He could faintly hear her teaching piano lessons from his work area. Lunch came and went, but Dwight remained at his work until the dinner bell rang from the farmhouse kitchen for everyone to come and eat.

The main dining room was strictly for the Lindsley family and their invited guests. Dwight and farm foreman Peter Miller were the only two that had been invited. Tonight would be a special night with Jenny Dunbar in attendance.

With the meal completed, the Lindsleys invited their guests to the parlor, where several instruments were located. A new Gilbert and Company piano[1], which Mr. Lindsley had purchased only a few weeks earlier, sat in the corner of the room.

Jenny Dunbar was the first true pianist to play the new piano. A six-string classical guitar was also positioned in a holder next to the piano,

---

[1] **Gilbert & Company Pianos** was run by Timothy Gilbert, an American piano manufacturer, abolitionist, and religious organizer in Boston, Massachusetts. In 1856, the company advertised they had made upward of 6000 pianos, and they were awarded a bronze medal for the third best grand action piano at the American Institute Fair, after Chickering & Sons and Steinway & Sons.

but very few members of the household or guests staying there could properly play it. Mr. and Mrs. Lindsley asked Jenny to play something on the piano as they took their place together on the parlor couch. Dwight and Peter Miller found chairs to sit on while the children found places to stand in the room or sit on the floor.

Mrs. Lindsley spoke again as Jenny situated herself at the piano. "Have you decided what you will entertain us with this evening, Miss Jenny?" That was the name that the Lindsleys insisted that their children call her. They felt it gave the young beauty more a sense of being family than of being just an employee.

Jenny thought a few moments and was about to announce her selection when Dwight spoke. "Miss Dunbar, I would love to hear 'Wait for the Wagon.' I haven't heard that song in many years. I first heard it while I was at Jefferson Barracks training to be a dragoon. Do you know it?"

"Why yes, Mr...." She paused, then added, "Mr. Stevens. I do know an arrangement for it. Maybe you could accompany me?" She looked over at the guitar and added, "Maybe play a few strings as well?"

Dwight smiled, knowing he had been tricked into being the one who would get the most attention, since she knew no one had played the six-string guitar while she had been teaching there. Dwight walked over to the guitar and picked it up. He strummed a few strings and said, "I haven't played as fine an instrument as this since I worked in my brother's music store." He looked at her and strummed again, making several small adjustments to tune it. She played some notes for him to tune in on, and in a relatively short time he seemed to have the guitar ready.

"Do you think you are ready to play, Mr. Stevens?"

He nodded and waited for her to begin. She played an introduction to the song and Dwight picked up the melody quickly. By the time she began to sing, he had gotten in sync with her. After the first chorus, he joined in and sang. Their voices sounded superb to those that sat in amazement at how two people could sing that well together without any practice. They sang the lyrics and played in unison to the enjoyment of everyone. The couple received rousing applause when they finished.

Chants of "more, more" came from the children, while the adults smiled and nodded in approval. Dwight grinned and looked straight at Jenny. She blushed with all the attention. Several more songs were suggested for the duo to play and sing. They obliged all requests.

At one point, Jenny declined to play a song she was not familiar with and had no sheet music for. Instead, she looked over at Dwight. "Mr. Stevens, maybe you could play a tune on the guitar? I do enjoy string music, and you have shown you have talent."

He smiled and knew he had been drawn into a situation where, again, more attention would be on him. "I think I will sing and play 'Camptown Races.' I'm sure you know the lyrics. Join in, all of you." He strummed a few strings and began. In less than a minute, the parlor was filled with singing and laughing.

Jenny Dunbar enjoyed watching Dwight play and sing. She couldn't keep her eyes off him as she watched his every move. Several more songs were sung and the evening ended with Jenny playing a classical selection Mr. Lindsley had requested.

With the singing and playing over, Dwight found himself asking, again, if he could accompany Jenny back home. She accepted, to the delight of those overhearing the request, especially Mrs. Lindsley, who stopped Peter Miller, who had offered to fetch her horse. "That won't be necessary, Mr. Miller. Dwight can see to that chore. I need to see you on some farm matters. Would you accompany me to Mr. Lindsley's office?"

Peter Miller reluctantly acknowledged her request as the Lindsley children prepared for bed. Mr. Lindsley sat on the couch until his wife touched his boot with her shoe as a signal to accompany her and Peter Miller. The elder man struggled out of the couch and began to follow them to his study.

As he slowly walked by, he turned to Jenny and Dwight. "Thank you for a wonderful evening. I shall request an encore when you return, Miss Jenny. Good evening." He looked at Dwight and winked. "Good evening, Mr. Stevens."

The two found themselves alone in the parlor.

"Mr. Stevens," she said, and in a lower voice, "I should say Dwight. I had a great evening. You are a gentleman and a very good musician at that."

"Thank you for the compliment, but especially for calling me Dwight."

"You may call me Jenny. Miss Jenny when we are around the children, if you don't mind?"

"I thank you, Jenny, and it will be Miss Jenny when I see you with the children."

They left the parlor together. Dwight fetched her horse and brought it to her. This time he borrowed Mrs. Lindsley's mare to accompany her back to West Andover. Within several minutes, they were trotting their mounts and carrying on a conversation.

It was a joyful ride for Dwight that summer night. They talked about music, musical instruments, and the popular songs they had heard. In a very short time they reached the boarding house where Jenny was staying. He assisted her to dismount. They stood talking to each other in front of the boarding house stable.

"Thank you, Dwight, for accompanying me. You are a real gentleman, and I have truly enjoyed your company this evening."

"Thank you. I have enjoyed yours as well."

"I look forward to seeing you on my next visit. I will make a list of some of the songs I do not need sheet music for. Hopefully you will be able to accompany me again."

"I would enjoy that, Jenny." He anguished inside as he thought that in a few short months he would be away, but didn't want to bring up the subject. He decided that he would wait until later to inform her that he was leaving.

She sensed he was thinking about something else when he did not immediately continue their conversation. "Dwight, you seem to have something on your mind. Is there anything wrong?"

"Oh no, Jenny, I was thinking about music and selections. I'm excited about your invitation to be able to accompany you again."

She was apparently happy with his explanation. "You must go now. I'm sure the boarders or the landlord know we are outside talking."

"Yes, I'm sure they do. I look forward to being with you for another performance. I would also like to see you on other occasions, if you become comfortable with me this summer, Jenny."

"The summer is short and I will not be here in the fall, Dwight. I will be back at my father's house. Finding me there could be difficult."

"I would like to see you no matter where you reside, if that is permissible to you?"

"I think it will be, Dwight, but we will see how this develops during the summer." She touched his hand and pulled him closer. She kissed his cheek gently then said, "Good night, Dwight." She turned and walked her bay to the stable.

Dwight stood for a few moments as he registered what she had just done. He quickly mounted Mrs. Lindsley's mare and kicked her. The mare responded as he looked back at Jenny with a huge smile on his face and raced off with the mare.

Jenny Dunbar laughed as she heard the commotion. She realized she hadn't ever kissed a man on the cheek, except for her father. She smiled again as she unsaddled her bay. She hoped that the time would pass by quickly until she saw Dwight Stevens again.

May ended, then passed to June and much too quickly to July as far as Dwight was concerned. Every day that he saw Jenny, he fell more in love with her. The days that she was not at the Lindsley homestead, he longed for them to end. When she did teach at the farm they spent the evening together, either in song or sitting on the Lindsleys' porch swing in pleasant conversation, occasionally holding hands. They would sometimes walk the homestead grounds, which included the flower and vegetable gardens.

One evening, Dwight lent Jenny his copy of the *The Age of Reason.* She commented when she returned it a few weeks later that it was interesting reading. He never challenged her on any specifics written in the book that he had almost memorized. He wondered if she had even read some parts of it, but did not risk debating, arguing, or even suggesting that she had not read the whole book.

Some of the younger Lindsley children playfully hinted to Jenny that she had a beau. When Mrs. Lindsley overheard one of her daughters making that statement, she chastised the child, to the embarrassment of Jenny. Mrs. Lindsley's only comments after the chastisement were, "Miss Jenny, children can be irritating at times in matters such as this. But they do sense things. My disciplining was for her forwardness, not for her intuition." She smiled at Jenny and walked away.

From that point on, and for the rest of the time Jenny Dunbar and Dwight Stevens spent together, no Lindsley child would ever say anything about their relationship again. No farmhand or foreman said a word as well. Mrs. Lindsley was a matchmaker and she made her opinion well known that the couple should be left alone with no joking or fun at their expense. She would remain a matchmaker for the couple until the events leading to Harper's Ferry forever changed her efforts.

On August 1st, Dwight and Jenny sat on Mrs. Lindsley's porch swing. The mood was light and the conversation was about the day's events. More questions about their younger days were then asked, and other experiences before their acquaintance were discussed. Jenny sensed that the conversation was becoming one-way. She also thought that Dwight was not as attentive as he usually was during conversations. She stopped mid-sentence to see his reaction, but there was none. She further tested his attentiveness. "Mr. Stevens. Mr. Whipple. Aaron." They were three names that he would have immediately responded to if he had been attentive. He failed. She waited.

He finally responded, but a little confused. "Excuse me. I'm sorry, but what did you call me, Jenny?"

"I called you three names that you should have at once commented upon. I called you Mr. Stevens, Mr. Whipple, and then Aaron, because you were not listening to anything I was saying. Where are your thoughts?"

"I'm sorry, but they were obviously not with the conversation you were carrying on. I am truly sorry."

"You don't have to be sorry. What seems to be bothering you? Is there something wrong?"

"I must confess that I have not been forthright with you."

Jenny Dunbar became uncomfortable. She wondered what he could have held from her since their first introduction. She then thought the worst and asked, "Are you married, Dwight?"

He was startled that she would even suggest that. "No. No, Jenny. I'm not married, nor have I ever been married, or even engaged to be married."

She relaxed for a moment when that registered. "Then what has you in this state of mind tonight?"

"Jenny, I'm sorry for my inattention. I will be leaving in a few days. I have been summoned by Captain Brown to report as soon as possible. I will need travel time to arrive as scheduled, so I must leave very soon. I was trying to find a way to tell you."

"Just be honest with me and explain yourself. Do you know how long you will be away?"

"Several months will be the minimum."

"Where shall I be able to write you?"

"You will not be able to write to me. All I can say is that I will be in Maryland."

"Maryland?"

"Yes, Maryland. I will write to you as soon as I am able."

"Apparently this is a secret assignment for Mr. Brown?"

"Yes, that is all I may say."

"When will you leave?"

"The day after tomorrow."

She stood up from the porch swing, fixed her dress, and turned to him as he stood. "Well, I guess this evening will be our last."

"No, Jenny, I said the day after tomorrow. That's when you will return to teach the children. I will be able to be with you then."

"No, Dwight, your planning is wrong. I will not be coming for more than a week, because Mr. and Mrs. Lindsley will be taking the children on holiday to Conneaut Lakeshore during that time. They leave the day after tomorrow. Apparently you did not know?"

"No, I did not."

"Well, Mr. Miller knew. He even asked me if I was accompanying the Lindsleys on the trip to the Pennsylvania lake."

Dwight was speechless, and then angry, that Miller had never mentioned the trip to him. He was also irritated that Mr. and Mrs. Lindsley never divulged a word of their plans to him either. He realized that she had started to walk toward the stable. "Jenny, where are you going?"

"I'm going home. I'm tired and wish to retire for the evening."

"I really would like to spend more time with you. Please stay."

"I'm sorry, but I am tired and have to go."

"As you wish. I'll saddle your bay."

"No, Dwight, I can accomplish that myself." Jenny turned to him as she reached the stable. "I wish you well on your trip to Maryland. I will be at my father's home when and if you have time to write and explain what you have been doing. Mrs. Lindsley has the address. She will forward your letters to me. I do hope that you will have a return address by then."

Dwight was motionless as she placed the horse blanket on the bay. He then backed away and watched her finish the saddling. Jenny pulled at the reins of the bay and walked the horse out of the stable. She mounted on her own and adjusted herself on the saddle and looked down with tears in her eyes, then said, "Be careful, Dwight. I wish you well." Jenny slapped the bay with her riding crop and trotted away.

Dwight was dumbfounded. His stomach turned as he watched her disappear down the road. "Well, that was unfortunate, Stevens." Then he turned to see Peter Miller, who obviously had seen and heard everything, standing just outside the stable doors, grinning. "Why didn't you tell me the Lindsleys were going on holiday to Pennsylvania?"

"I guess I didn't think it was important for you to know. You're leaving in a few days anyway, so why would you care?"

"That's why. Didn't you see her leave?"

"Yep. She'll be back when the Lindsleys return. Oh, that's right, you won't be here."

Dwight's rage got the best of him as all he could see was Miller's grin. In a flash he threw a right-handed punch and hit him square in the face. Miller was floored from the blow. He moaned as he rolled over onto his side, spitting blood and then a tooth onto the ground. He was too dazed to challenge Dwight and just lay there.

Edward Peck saw the entire incident and ran to the house.

A few minutes later, Mr. Lindsley found Miller staggering to his feet and still trying to regain his senses. He inquired and heard the same explanation from Miller as he had from Peck. He then found Dwight in his room. "Mr. Stevens, you know our position on violence in this homestead."

Dwight stood as he heard the elder gentleman speak. "Yes, sir. I apologize but the circumstances..."

"You will pack your belongings and depart my home immediately," he said. "Your work for the captain is finished, so there is no reason for you to stay. You are no longer a guest, based upon your latest action striking my foreman."

Dwight attempted to explain again, but Mr. Lindsley cut him off. "My word is final. Leave immediately. You can purchase a horse at the stable in Cherry Creek." Mr. Lindsley left the room and passed Mrs. Lindsley, who had been updated on the disturbance from Edward.

She went to Dwight's room as he finished packing his belongings. "Dwight, I'm so sorry."

"It's my fault, Mrs. Lindsley. There is no one to blame but me and my short temper. Thank you for your hospitality. This place was like home to me." He nodded to the lady as he passed her to leave.

"Dwight."

He turned as he approached the stairs to go down to the first floor.

"Take my horse. I don't ride anymore. You take one of the farmhand saddles and reins and be off with you. Serve the captain well and stay safe, and control that temper. I'll talk to Miss Jenny and explain what transpired. Now go with God."

He exited the house and saw Miller sitting on the stone wall next to the stable. He watched the foreman as he passed, making sure he didn't try to challenge him now that he had regained his composure. Miller never moved as he held a cloth to his mouth. Dwight saddled the mare and mounted.

Miller called out to him, "I hope ya have permission to take the missus's mare? Or are ya a thief too?"

"Check with her, Miller."

"I will, and ya better be telling the truth or…"

Dwight stopped the mare in front of him. "Or what, Miller?"

Miller never said a word as he continued to nurse his mouth.

"I will return to seek Miss Jenny's affection either here or at her father's home. I do not want to hear that you have been in any way involved with her. Do you understand?"

Miller did not say anything until Dwight began to dismount from the mare. "I heard ya, Stevens. I understand."

"Good, because I don't want to be responsible for…"

Mrs. Lindsley cut him off mid-sentence. "Dwight, be off with you. You've said and done enough for one evening. Leave the farm now."

He tipped his hat and kicked the mare with his old dragoon stirrups he had donned. The mare instantly responded, and he disappeared into the darkness of the night.

"He's a damned crazy one, that Stevens is, ma'am," Miller said.

There was no response from Mrs. Lindsley as she turned to enter the house.

"He'll end up in trouble somewhere, you know that."

Mrs. Lindsley stopped and turned to him. "Peter, you are a good foreman, but you never know when to keep your mouth shut. That gap in your teeth might be a reminder for you."

"Mrs. Lindsley, that man is a wild one and—"

She stopped him. "Go clean yourself up. I heard what Dwight said to you. Stay away from Miss Jenny for your own safety. Dwight Stevens is an honorable man, with a temper, I know, but an honorable man who is also in love. He might really shoot you dead if he ever hears that you have wronged this house and anyone associated with it, especially Miss Jenny. Now come with me to the house." Mrs. Lindsley looked up at the quarter moon that was just rising. She hoped that the misunderstanding that took place this evening between Jenny and Dwight was reconcilable, and wondered if she would see Dwight Stevens again. She hoped so. She knew that she would probably hear more about him and his association with John Brown as the weeks and months passed.

Mrs. Lindsley stopped before she entered the house and turned to Miller. "Peter, we have received word that more are coming."

"How many this time, ma'am?"

"Mr. Lindsley says that there are six. Two are children. Two are adults. There will be two escorts with the family. They will arrive while we are at Conneaut Lakeside. Keep them in the stable during their stay."

"How long, ma'am?"

"One, maybe two days. That's all. They will arrive at night. Depending on the rest needed for the children, the escorts will decide when they are ready to depart. Miss Strong will prepare meals from the kitchen, which Edward will bring to them while they are here. Let the escorts sleep in the bunkhouse. If anyone comes by and asks, they are extra hands needed for a few days. They will depart with the family during the night."

"Yes, ma'am. I'll see to it."

"Good. Mr. Lindsley and I expect that. Good night, Peter."

"Good night, ma'am."

Aaron Dwight Stevens walked his horse along during the night, thinking of Jenny Dunbar. He vowed that as soon as he was able, he would write and explain how he felt about her. He did not want her to slip out of his life like Maria had. He couldn't bear that again. Jenny Dunbar was the woman he wanted to be with for the rest of his life. He didn't know what the rest of his life would be like, but he knew she needed to be in it. He felt saddened that he had to leave the Lindsleys on such a bad note, but he felt he could patch that up in time.

He even felt a little sad about Peter Miller. He knew that he was a good man. He had to be, to be willing to hide runaway slaves and be associated with the Underground Railroad like the Lindsleys. He cursed himself for throwing that punch. At the same time, he hoped Peter was scared enough to stay clear of Jenny. But he knew he was powerless to keep him away. He couldn't blame him for his interest in her. What normal man wouldn't want to spend time with her?

He cleared his thoughts and hoped that as soon as the Harper's Ferry plan was executed, he could concentrate on his personal life, of which he wanted Jenny Dunbar to be a large part.

Chapter Twenty-One

The Farm

The farm as it looks today
Photo by Tommy Coletti.

It had been two days since Dwight Stevens left Jenny Dunbar in Ohio. Over all the miles behind him he had mostly thought of nothing other than her. However, there was one other unwanted thought that kept forcing its way into his mind. It was like an ugly, unwanted, and despised relative coming around to pester him once again. He couldn't help but think that his lack of self-control over his anger might have done it again.

"Why do I do that?! What's wrong with me?!" he shouted out to no one.

His horse perked up a bit but gave him no answer.

Dwight just shook his head. He had a hard time believing that he could keep making the same stupid mistake over and over again. He had lost his temper completely with that drunken fool Major Blake and then lost Maria because of it. Actually, he damn near lost his life because of it.

Now he'd done it again and gotten mad at that idiot what's-his-name. Now Jenny, the most beautiful, wonderful woman in the world, might not think as well of him as she had before. He couldn't live with himself if he was so hopeless as to have done it again. He thought that Jenny would give him another chance. He had to believe that she would. Thinking back on it, though, she didn't seem all that happy with him when she left. He just shook his head again, looked up at the sky in silence, and felt like hell.

After several more miles of being upset at himself, he thought he might try to examine his anger problem and see if he could figure out where it came from and why it haunted him as it did. If he could find out why he got so mad and what caused the powerful anger, maybe he could do something about avoiding it. He felt a little better devising this little exercise, rather than doing nothing and admitting defeat. Besides, he had plenty of time and miles to do it.

Remembering back to his childhood, he could see himself in several fights with other kids. Those events mostly seemed to be childish disagreements and silly confrontations to determine who was tougher. He also saw himself being a pain in the ass to his parents, especially his father, but that he also considered to be somewhat of a normal thing. Yet there was a possible issue with the fact that his father was such a strict disciplinarian. Dwight recalled that he was certainly very mad at times, especially when he thought his father had been unfair. Not that Dwight was an authority on children, of course. He remembered how the young children on the way to Canada had made him and Kagi uncomfortable, much to the delight of John Brown and the other adults.

The first time he remembered being so terribly upset and losing control was in school, when the teacher was harassing a younger student. He had laughingly told Maria about the incident, but looking back on it now, he knew he was staring directly at the problem. Even now he could feel the heat rise inside of him at the unfairness of the situation.

The young student was helpless and had no defenses. He was depending on the teacher to do the right thing because the kid couldn't force the teacher to be reasonable. The teacher was stronger, older, and more experienced. The teacher was also the authority in the classroom, but unjustly forced his will upon the helpless student.

"I can't stand that," Dwight mumbled to himself. He noticed that his fists were tightly balled around the reins of the horse. He thought of other times when he had lost control and looked for similarities. He thought of the bully at the machine shop in Norwich. Once again, there had been a man in a position of authority over the younger apprentices who depended upon him to help and teach them. The apprentices would not fight back, fearing that they would lose everything they had worked for if they confronted him.

Dwight had completely lost it that day. He could have killed that man and thought nothing of it. That was how low he considered the guy to be. The same scenario was present in Taos when Dwight, blind mad and unthinking, threatened the often-drunk Major Blake after he challenged and demeaned the whole company. That action and the resulting trial had been the turning point; it was what had put him on the path to where and what he was at this moment.

Dwight considered that these factors might be a large reason behind why he hated slavery so much. There were so many reasons to despise it. However, the anger flowed because of the unfairness and evil being waged against people who could not defend themselves. These same people, held in slavery against their own wishes, were completely dependent upon their masters. The master could visit upon the slave a show of compassion or nothing but misery. The master's hand held it all, as well as life itself. Even now, as a lone traveler on a quiet road in Ohio, Dwight trembled with rage and yelled out, "God help me, what kind of man can do this to another?!"

He felt better as he considered that he might be getting somewhere with this series of memories, until he thought of the last time he had lost his temper. Dwight had been mad so quickly that once again, without thought, he had struck Peter Miller with one powerful blow and sent him to the ground. Dwight was puzzled about this event because it didn't seem to fit in with the trend of his other actions. He knew damn well the reason he was so mad, and it wasn't because Miller was a slaveholder or a bully. No, it was because Dwight was seriously jealous. *Well, this time is surely different,* he thought.

The only thing that made any sense, after racking his brain for several long miles, was that when those things and ideas that he held most dear were threatened, he would react in a rash and violent way. What he could never figure out was why it was so unthinking and aggressive.

As he thought about it, he wasn't really feeling that bad about the teacher, Major Blake, or the bully. They all had it coming as far as he was concerned, and in each case they had paid some kind of justice. Dwight didn't understand himself any better now than he did hours ago. *I guess that's just how I'm made,* he thought.

It was a bad answer, and he wasn't happy with it, but he had no other thoughts on the problem at this time. He only hoped that the next time he would be able to control himself enough to think about the consequences.

Dwight's trip to Maryland took less than a week. In that time he constantly reflected on his relationship with Jenny Dunbar. He convinced himself that the relationship was only on a temporary hold until the slave revolt was well underway. He planned to be able to get away from it for a short time and return to Jenny to rekindle what he hoped was a developing relationship. He fantasized that it could quickly progress into something more serious.

Dwight did not contemplate marriage for the near future, but wished to think that it could be possible for the future. He considered Miss Dunbar to be the perfect woman: smart, beautiful, talented, and a joy to be with. There were none like her in his mind. He imagined returning to Norwich some day with the most beautiful woman a man could ever hope to be with. Additionally, he would be treated with respect as one of the men who helped John Brown free the country of slavery.

These thoughts helped him bide his time as he slowly guided his horse over the hot and dusty roads through Pennsylvania and into Maryland. He pondered how he would correspond with her once he was settled with the rest of the captain's small group.

He began to mentally go through the list of men he knew the captain should have summoned along with him. As the military instructor, he began to rank their skills and mentally note what he would concentrate on when he began training them again at the farm. He hoped he would have a reasonable amount of time to hone their military skills. In order to accomplish this, he visualized an open space where he could hold drills for weapons and saber handling and, most importantly, re-instilling military discipline in the band.

While he camped at night, he wrote notes to himself about each of them and their progression in military training. The thought that he would probably have new men to train crossed his mind. He contemplated splitting the men into two groups, those previously trained and the new recruits the captain had solicited. Dwight wondered how many new faces he would see.

Other matters were also on his mind as he camped alone. Uneasiness came across him as he wondered about the status of the weapons he had shipped from the Lindsley homestead to John Kagi in Chambersburg, Pennsylvania. Dwight contemplated going to Chambersburg to visit him, but decided against it. He disciplined himself to keep to John Brown's orders to come to the Maryland Heights address where the Kennedy Farm was located. He crossed into Maryland on the 5th of August. The trip had been uneventful. He drew no attention in the towns he passed through, even when he stopped to purchase food. He looked no different from any other traveling person, and using an alias never entered his mind. No one cared to even ask who he was.

Dwight reached Maryland Heights on the evening of August 6, and stopped in front of a dry goods store. A person exited onto the wooden sidewalk with a broom.

He asked for directions. "Excuse me, sir. Could you direct me to the Kennedy farm?"

The middle-aged man was just starting to sweep the wooden sidewalk when he stopped to answer. "Did you say the Kennedy farm?"

"Yes, sir. I'm reporting for work there."

"Oh, I didn't know Isaac Smith was hiring. Is he going to work it now? I didn't know cattle buyers liked to farm."

Dwight was cautious. "I think he wants me to help out around the place."

The man looked Dwight up and down. "You look big and fit enough to help the old man. Lord knows he could use the help out there. The place is a bit rundown."

Dwight received the directions and went on his way. He realized that the man didn't mention any others who had arrived ahead of him. It wasn't long before he came upon the farm at dusk. It looked to be in disrepair, especially when compared to the Lindsley homestead he had left a week ago. The fields had not been attended to and the vegetable garden near the road was heavy with weeds. Several fences needed repair, and he saw no horses or cattle on the property. He dismounted, and was slowly approaching the front porch when he stopped, seeing a person sitting on it.

He started to speak when he heard, "Identify yourself."

Dwight slowly reached around and found the handle to his Colt pistol. "Dwight Stevens is the name. I'm looking for Mr. Isaac Smith."

"He's in the kitchen, Dwight."

"Edwin Coppoc, is that you I hear talking?"

"Yep, one and the same. You can relax a bit. No need for that Colt you're itchin' to pull out."

Dwight laughed as he walked onto the porch. He saw the Sharps rifle Edwin had laying across his lap. "I see you picked up a decent rifle."

"The captain has a lot more of them in Chambersburg."

"I know. I shipped them for him. When will Kagi be able to ship them here?"

"I don't know. It's good ya brought another horse. We can use 'er now to fetch them when they come to town. The captain says to look for crates marked farm equipment and addressed to him when we are sent to fetch them. Barclay and me will go to pick 'em up. We don't have to worry about the one horse we got to pull the wagon. We got two now."

"How many men have shown up so far? Are you telling me nobody else came by horse? By the way, the place looks very rundown. Tell me, Edwin, what's going on here?"

"Slow down, Dwight. I'm trying to tell you."

Dwight's patience was limited, but he controlled himself so that the youth could begin to answer his questions. "To answer your first question, Barclay and me got here about two weeks ago. We were the first two to come. The next week William and Dauphin Thompson[1] came. I can't remember if Watson came the day before or after them, but we will use his horse with yours now to pull the wagon."

"Where are they, Edwin?"

"They're out back. We wait for the evening to come out. Orders from the captain."

Dwight turned to leave and head in the direction Edwin had pointed to.

"Dwight. Don't leave yet. You stay here and watch for anyone coming up or down the road. I'll go through the house and tell 'em you arrived. I don't want you getting shot going around to the back of the house. They're a little spooked now, so wait here." Before Dwight could ask more questions, Edwin disappeared.

It wasn't long before he reappeared with Albert Hazlett[2].

"Good to see you, Dwight." Albert extended his hand.

Dwight smiled and shook it. "Glad to see you, Al. This is quite the place we have here."

"Come with me. I'll show you where to tie up the horse." Hazlett walked off the porch and headed behind the house.

Dwight began to follow, but stopped and turned to Edwin. "You here all night?"

"No, Barclay relieves me at nine o'clock, and then Stewart Taylor[3] at midnight. I can't remember after that. We have three-hour watches set up by Tidd."

Dwight relaxed, hearing Tidd's name. Charles Plummer Tidd and he were good friends since the early Kansas days. They were of the same temperament, and Dwight respected Tidd for having more control of his temper than he did. The two usually got along, but there were times they argued; on a few occasions, they'd almost come to blows. But Dwight had respect for him and knew his watch schedule was probably thoroughly planned out.

Hazlett spoke up. "Dwight, we need to get the horse out back. We don't need Mrs. Huffmaster asking questions about seeing a horse and rider coming to the farm. She's been a pain in our asses ever since we

---

[1] **William and Dauphin Thompson** – See 10 raiders who died at Harper's Ferry.

[2] **Albert Hazlett** – See 6 raiders who were executed at Charlestown.

[3] **Stewart Taylor** – See 10 raiders who died at Harper's Ferry.

came here. She's the neighbor lady who is too nosy for her own good. I'll tell you more about her later."

They rounded the house. Dwight could see several men outside sitting near a fence as his eyes tried to adjust. There were no lanterns or torches lit, and the dusk was turning into night quickly. Fireflies were the only source of light flickering among the men standing as Hazlett and Dwight approached.

Albert called out, "Say hello to Dwight, gentlemen!"

Charles Tidd was the first to call out, "I thought you'd forgotten about us, Stevens! What kept you?"

"I didn't get the word from the captain until a week ago. I came as soon as I could."

Tidd stood up from a barrel he had been sitting on and approached Dwight. He smiled when they could see each other's face. He hugged him and slapped him on the back. "Good to see you, Dwight."

"Glad to be here."

Several other men stood around the two. Dwight recognized William Leeman, Stewart Taylor, and Jeremiah Anderson[1] and exchanged greetings. There was also a black man he did not know. Dwight was introduced to him. "Mr. Dangerfield Newby[2], I'm pleased to see you here," Dwight said as they shook hands.

"The pleasure be mine, sir. I had to be here with ya." Newby said.

Dwight held his hand a little longer so that he could look the black man face to face and smile before unleashing his grip.

He turned to the others and said, "Doesn't anyone know how to light a lantern? Why are you all sitting in the dark?"

"Captain's orders. We keep a very low profile here," Leeman said.

"The neighbors think that Isaac Smith and his sons are the only ones here," Tidd cut in and explained.

"Damn, I told the storekeeper in town that I was a hired hand for Isaac Smith," Dwight explained.

"We should tell the captain so he knows how to handle any questions if he's asked about you. He's in the kitchen with Owen and Watson."

"Is Kagi with them?"

"No. He stays in Chambersburg and corresponds with him. You better report in and let him see you. I'm sure Edwin has alerted him to your arrival already."

---

[1] **Jeremiah Anderson** – See 10 raiders who died at Harper's Ferry.

[2] **Dangerfield Newby** – See 10 raiders who died at Harper's Ferry.

Hazlett took Mrs. Lindsley's mare to the stable. Dwight and Tidd walked into the house.

John Brown rose as soon as he saw Dwight enter. "I'm pleased to see you, son. I assume you had an uneventful ride from the Lindsleys."

Dwight immediately thought about the punch he gave Peter Miller and the expulsion from the Lindsley homestead by both Mr. and Mrs. Lindsley. He chose to not mention the incident. He knew the Lindsleys had no way of reaching him unless the captain initiated correspondence. "I do have to report that I had a conversation with a man outside the general store."

"About what, Dwight?"

"I asked for directions to the farm and explained I was a farmhand."

"That was understandable. It was probably George Strong, the owner. If he asks when I'm in town, I'll confirm it."

Dwight looked over to Brown's sons, who were waiting to welcome him. Brown gestured for Dwight to finish the greetings. Pleasantries were exchanged, but Dwight could see that Brown had documents and other papers in front of them. It looked to be family business, and he excused himself to go back outside and be with the men. Before he left, he said, "The Sharps are with Kagi in Chambersburg, I just heard."

"Yes, now that you are here, I will send for them immediately."

"Where is Oliver[1]?"

"He's back in Elba. He'll return soon." Brown could see the apprehension on Dwight's face. He attempted to calm his trusted lieutenant. "Dwight, I know it will be difficult for you to train and prepare the men in the next few months at this place. But we have too many interruptions, and are very limited in accommodations, to perform open training, in my opinion. Most instruction will have to be accomplished during the evening and night hours. I have instructed the men to stay out of sight during the day."

Dwight heard all that the captain said, but decided to reserve any opinion or advice until he assessed the accommodations and talked to Tidd and the others. "Yes, sir. We'll follow your orders. I will report back once I have been with the men and have understood the situation."

Brown only nodded.

Dwight gave Tidd a glance that said they needed to talk as he passed him. Tidd followed behind quickly. Dwight did not say a word

[1] **Oliver Brown** – See 10 raiders who died at Harper's Ferry.

until the two were well away from the house and the men sitting outside near the fence. "How am I…" he began, "I mean we going to train fifteen to twenty men in a confined area and after sunset?"

"We ain't, Dwight. We have to hope the training you have given all of us has been retained."

Dwight's frustration was evident. "Damn! We don't even have weapons to work with."

"You heard the captain. He'll send for them now that you're here."

Dwight wasn't happy. "What about the new men the captain plans to bring in?"

"Trust in the Almighty that they have some military experience or can at least handle a weapon."

Dwight shook his head. "This is a poor location to set up a training camp. We should have all stayed at the Lindsleys' and then gone directly to Harper's Ferry from there. We could have moved at night and in small groups, and descended on it unnoticed. I'll go and talk with the captain in a day or so, and suggest we leave here."

Tidd never responded. Whether he agreed or not, he didn't show it. He did give some advice in an attempt to cool Dwight and the apparent frustration he felt. "Let's go and be with the men. See what they have retained. Get a good assessment of the situation before you approach the captain. Give your evaluation then."

Dwight realized that Tidd's patience and suggestion was the right thing to do. "Yes. Let's do that. I'll take the time to assess the situation, and hopefully I can get to see John Kagi soon and air my thoughts."

"Dwight, John has not been to the farm once. He has stayed in Chambersburg. You will have to ask permission from the captain to see him. Do your assessment first. Give your evaluation to Kagi then, if you get the authorization. If not, at least you can give the captain your appraisal based on fact and not frustration."

The two approached the group of men, and soft laughter and banter ensued. Dwight was happy being back with them. For a short, enjoyable time he did not think of the situation he had found at the Kennedy farm, or even of Jenny Dunbar.

In the early dawn hours, the men ate breakfast outside, served from the kitchen. Eggs, bacon, and hard bread were served by the Brown sons, but not before the captain read from the Bible. Satisfied that they had given proper thanks for their meal, Brown returned to the house to eat alone in the kitchen.

Dwight noticed that Owen was having difficulty trying to carry multiple plates of food with his crippled arm. He remembered hearing the story of how Owen was injured in Kansas. He stood to assist him in carrying out some of the tin plates.

Owen realized what Dwight was doing. "Thanks. It gets difficult carrying things sometimes."

"It would sure be better if we had some womenfolk here to help do these chores while we get on with the business that is needed," Dwight said.

"My sister Anne and Oliver's wife, Martha, will be here shortly. Father wants the semblance of normality here. He feels that having women around will keep the nosy Mrs. Huffmaster and sorts like her from coming around too often and asking questions."

Dwight realized Oliver Brown must have been away to fetch the women. "Mrs. Huffmaster. I've heard the name before. Who is she?"

"A true pain in our ass. Damned busybody. Her and her snot-nosed kids show up at any time for no reason. I've never seen Mr. Huffmaster myself, but he needs to keep his wife and kids corralled up at home."

"I'm pleased to hear that the women will be here soon. I'm going to ask your father if we can perform duties around the place to clean it up and make it look like a functioning farm."

"We've stated the same, Dwight, but so far it's falling on deaf ears."

Dwight dropped the subject. He'd wait for the right opportunity to approach the captain, who had too many other things to worry about. He finished his breakfast as the sun began to rise. Dwight could feel the heat and humidity starting to increase as the men slowly assembled and entered the house.

Several men entered the one bedroom on the main floor. It was a temporary arrangement until the two Brown women would arrive to occupy that room. Dwight followed the rest to the attic, where he observed that blankets and bedrolls had been placed close together. The attic was already too warm. He couldn't imagine what the heat would be like by mid-afternoon, when the August Maryland temperature would reach ninety degrees or more.

All he saw for relief from the heat were two small open windows, one at each end of the attic. There was very little movement of air as the hornets and flies flew about freely in and out of the two openings. He found a small area and laid out his bedroll. He realized how tired he was as he finally reached some minimal comfort on the warm wood floor. He drifted off to sleep for several hours, until he woke drenched in sweat.

Tidd spoke softly to him once he saw that he had awakened. "Hot, ain't it?"

Dwight only nodded.

"We're lucky today. It's a bit overcast. Maybe get some rain in a few hours," he said as he moved to look out the attic window.

"My Lord, Charles. How hot has it been up here?"

"Over the one hundred mark, I'm sure. We send Edwin out to draw fresh water from the well regularly. He just came back. Drink some." He pointed to a large pail with a ladle in it.

Dwight took some and drank slowly. He didn't remember being this hot even when he was in Mexico City or the New Mexico Territory in the summer. He looked at Tidd. "Charles, are we going to go through August and September like this?"

"Hopefully not."

Tidd realized he had spoken too loud. A couple of men stirred after his comment. He squinted his eyes and then whispered, "We better keep quiet until dusk."

Dwight turned back over and tried to sleep. The heat was almost unbearable. He stayed as still as he could in the hope it would reduce the profuse sweating he was experiencing. It didn't, but he did manage to fall back to sleep for several more hours until later in the afternoon.

He lay on his damp bedroll until the light began to fade outside the attic window. He had survived the first full day at the Kennedy farm. He did not want to have to endure many more days like this one. He began formulating a plan to change some of the accommodations. He would present his plan as soon as he had thought it all out.

It rained that afternoon and cooled the house, and especially the wood shingles covering the attic. The smell of wood helped to cover up some of the human odor left by the men sleeping there. When it was dusk, the men began to stir and slowly exit the attic. Dwight noticed that the Brown women had arrived and were settling into the house. He was pleased that they had come, but it quickly dawned on him that the attic would be even more crowded as the men who were staying in the bedroom would join them now that the women were here. He knew he would need to devise a plan and present it to the captain as quickly as possible.

During the evening meal, Dwight was able to approach John Brown about reorganizing sleeping times and living arrangements at the farm. He suggested that the men retire at mid-night and rise before noon. That way they would not have to endure the stifling heat of the afternoon, especially in the attic. He also mentioned that he was working on a plan to drill the men in the afternoon for a few hours to try to keep them sharp. He assured Brown that he would set up a rotating watch to ensure Mrs. Huffmaster, or someone else, would not be able to sneak up on them during those exercises.

Brown smiled as he listened.

Dwight continued as he realized he was actually getting through to him. He explained that the small shed that was located across the road opposite the farmhouse could house several men and keep them out of sight during the day. The two horses could be tied up over there as well. He advised that more men be placed in the woods behind the house. It would be difficult if poor weather came, but he explained that they could deal with it on a day-to-day basis.

He stressed the need to greatly reduce the amount of men in the attic now that the Brown women had arrived, and also emphasized that the women should have privacy in the one room and Oliver would have to stay with his brothers. He told Brown that he was planning for several men to sleep in the stone basement once the weapons crates were delivered, but he'd wait to see how much room was available. He also stated that his plan would greatly reduce the tension and irritability of the men at the farm. Dwight suggested that Brown and all his sons sleep in the small parlor off the kitchen. He explained that the root cellar offered a cool place for a man to sleep during the day as well.

Brown was impressed and agreed to the changes. He initiated the plan immediately.

The men were pleased with the arrangements Dwight had worked out with John Brown.

He paused and looked at them after giving out the assignments.

Tidd saw the look on his face and remarked, "There is apparently something else you want to talk about. What is it, Stevens?"

Dwight smiled and spoke. "There is one thing always unpleasant for a soldier. That is latrine duty. I looked over the outhouse, and it will not support the constant use of the men, never mind the addition of the two women that have joined us. The outhouse will be off-limits to all the men. It will be for the use of the women only. No exceptions." He turned to the Coppoc brothers. "Edwin and Barclay, you will cover the waste with soil this evening to reduce the smell and make the facility more acceptable to our young ladies. The rest of you will work with me tonight to dig a latrine trench out back of the stable hidden in the woods. We are going to make one similar to the military's." He looked at them and explained further, "You will all cover your waste with soil each time to reduce the smell and the flies. When the trench is filled we will dig another one together. We begin tonight."

There were some groans of discontent, but the men obeyed and worked for the duration of the evening to complete the digging.

Dwight was relieved that John Brown had let him change the accommodations for the men. He was also pleased that he could keep busy working around the farm, clearing and repairing items that were in need. It was during the hoeing of the vegetable garden that Dwight met one of the Huffmaster children.

He could hear something moving in the high grass that surrounded the garden. The movement reminded him of how the Delaware Indian boys learned to sneak up on their prey. He didn't know who could be quietly approaching, but he assumed the worse. Dwight realized he did not have his pistol. He continued working with the hoe, but was prepared to deal with the intruder if he had to.

It was evident from the noise the intruder made that it was someone inexperienced. In his peripheral vision, Dwight watched for some movement. He finished rowing the potatoes and turned away. He hoped the prowler would show himself now that his back was toward him. He did, and Dwight turned and looked at a boy no older than ten.

The youth froze when Dwight addressed him. "Who are you, young man?" Dwight moved quickly toward him before the shock of seeing each other eye to eye wore off and the youth began to run. The boy regained his composure and attempted to flee, but Dwight grabbed him. "Not so fast, mister. I asked who you are. What is your name?"

"Let me go. I live down the road."

"Oh, so you are one of the Huffmaster children Mr. Smith told me about."

"Who are you?" the boy asked.

"My name is Dwight and I work for Mr. Smith. You, my little vagrant, are trespassing. I should bring you into town and let the sheriff put you in jail for trespassing."

"I didn't do anything wrong. I was just watching."

Dwight released him. "Go home and don't let me find you sneaking around here anymore."

The barefoot youth quickly ran off. Dwight knew he probably had not seen the last of him. He expected one of his parents would visit the farm as a result of the meeting. He notified Brown and the women in the house that he expected one of the Huffmaster parents to show up.

Several hours later Brown summoned the Coppoc brothers to hitch up the wagon to prepare for the trip to fetch the rifles. Brown had received a note delivered by one of George Strong's stock boys that some equipment marked farm machinery had arrived for Isaac Smith.

Brown stayed in town while the brothers completed the task to fetch the weapons and return to the farm. They unhitched the horses and left the wagon near the farmhouse to be unloaded into the cellar during the evening hours. Edwin returned to town with both horses saddled to fetch Brown when he was done with his business there.

It was that afternoon that Mrs. Huffmaster paid a visit to the Kennedy farm. Anne Brown[1] observed the portly woman entering the front yard and notified the family. The woman continually looked about and ignored the young girl standing on the front porch.

Anne Brown was a mature fifteen-year-old and courteously greeted Mrs. Huffmaster. "Good afternoon. It's a beautiful day, isn't it?"

"And you are who, miss?"

Anne Brown quickly played along. "I'm Anne Smith, Isaac Smith's daughter. Welcome to the Smith farm."

"This is the Kennedy farm, missy. Your father ain't bought it yet. If I reckon, he's renting."

Anne knew who the woman was, but answered, "Can I help you with something, missus?" She waited for a response.

"I'm Mrs. Huffmaster. I live down the road. One of my boys was half scared to death by one of your men. My son says he was a giant."

"Well, Mrs. Huffmaster, my brothers are not giants. They don't pass much taller than five feet seven inches, as I recall. How big is your son?"

"Never mind how big my son is, young lady. He was scared out of his wits by a large man that works or lives here. He saw him in the garden." She moved forward, trying to get a better look at the rear of the house, when Anne stepped off the porch and confronted her.

"Well, he must have seen our new hand. He is a tall man and I know my father assigned him some garden chores. Would you like me to get him?"

"No, that ain't necessary. I must warn you that I will report this to the sheriff in town if this occurs again."

"I will relay your message to my father, but I would encourage your son to stay out of our garden. That way he will not run into our new farmhand. His name is Mr. Stevens, by the way."

"You just relay my message to Mr. Smith."

"Yes, Mrs. Huffmaster, I'll relay the message to him when he returns from town on business."

"Who did you say you were? I have never seen you here before."

"I'm Anne Smith, Mr. Smith's daughter. I came here a few days ago with my brother's wife, Martha."

"Oh, well, you relay my message."

---

[1] **Anne Brown** was one of John Brown's daughters. She was about 15 years old at the time she stayed at the Kennedy farm. She played a significant role assisting her father and his raiders.

"I will, Mrs. Huffmaster. It was very nice to make your acquaintance."

"I'm sure it was, young lady. Good day."

Anne smiled.

The overweight and unkempt woman began to depart and stopped to observe the unloaded wagon. "I see you have some equipment to unload. Is Mr. Smith planning on doing some renovations to the old place?"

Anne Brown
Daughter of John Brown
West Virginia State Archives

"I really don't know, Mrs. Huffmaster. You would have to ask my father."

Dwight appeared from behind the house. He knew Mrs. Huffmaster had been talking and looking around, so he said, "Good day." He tipped his hat.

Mrs. Huffmaster looked at the tall, handsome, and bare-chested man looking at her.

Dwight looked to Anne. "Miss Anne, I'll unload the equipment with Mr. Oliver after I'm finished out back."

Mrs. Huffmaster remarked, "You must be the giant that scared my son."

"Yes, I guess I am, if your son was the boy hiding in the tall grass and making more noise than a flat fish out of water. He ran away too quickly. I could have used a hand rowing the potatoes." Dwight looked at Anne. "Is there a problem, Miss Anne?"

"No, Mr. Stevens. Mrs. Huffmaster was just leaving."

The woman wasn't about to leave yet. She remarked, "I see that you have quite a bit of laundry hanging out to dry, Miss Smith. How many men live here?"

Dwight realized that this woman was a real busybody, but before he could remark, Anne quickly replied. "My father and brothers did not wash clothes often enough. My sister-in-law and I had quite a bit of washing to catch up on when we arrived. Three men and now Mr. Stevens can quickly build up laundry for two women. You surly must understand that yourself."

Mrs. Huffmaster only smiled and nodded.

Anne smiled back.

Dwight could hardly retain his laughter. He could see by the looks of her son and herself that Mrs. Huffmaster hadn't done laundry in a while. The woman departed slowly, but continually kept looking for something.

She was well out of hearing range when Dwight turned to Anne and said, "You handled her very well, young lady. The captain will be proud of the way you stood up to that silly busybody." He paused, then added, "And you did it so nicely, too." He smiled.

Anne Brown smiled back, almost embarrassed.

Oliver Brown appeared with Martha[1] as Anne acknowledged the compliment. "We heard the whole conversation. Dwight is right. You did a fine job with her. It looks like you have a new friend."

They all laughed.

Later that evening, Dwight and several men stored the weapons in the partial cellar of the farmhouse. In several of the fifteen boxes of rifles were the Maynard pistols Dwight was looking for.

When John Brown returned that night, he was informed of Mrs. Huffmaster's visit. The captain was also very pleased with his daughter. He thought that Anne should continue to be the contact with the nosy lady and that all the others should do everything in their power to avoid her.

---

[1] **Martha Brown** was daughter-in-law of John Brown by her marriage to Oliver Brown.

The living and sleeping arrangements continued as planned for the rest of August. Mrs. Huffmaster visited the farm often. At times she would be accompanied by several of her children, who loved to roam about while Mrs. Huffmaster talked with Anne. On these occasions, Dwight and one of the Brown sons would join up together to watch the boys and make sure they did not stray too far from their mother.

Dwight drilled the men one to two days a week for several hours during daylight. Several men stood watch during the trainings to ensure that the Huffmasters, or any other stranger, did not come by. He also assigned readings for the men from the military manual of arms that Hugh Forbes had written. The manual was the only good thing that Dwight thought Hugh Forbes had contributed to the cause. Practice with rifles and pistols using live ammunition was held to a bare minimum due to the unexpected visits from Mrs. Huffmaster.

On August 18th, John Brown announced his final plans for the trip to Chambersburg, Pennsylvania, to meet with Frederick Douglass. In addition to his sons Owen and Watson, the captain requested that Dwight also accompany them. The four men utilized the wagon and two horses to make the trip. Upon their arrival, they visited with John Kagi, who updated Brown on his attempt to get more volunteers to join the small group. He gave Brown a list of several blacks who he expected to join him at the Kennedy farm and detailed the plan to solicit more black men from Canada once the revolution had started. Correspondence and other business matters were attended to while Dwight stood guard. With their business completed, they drove out to the old Chambersburg quarry to meet with Frederick Douglass.

The quarry was isolated and seldom visited by the locals. The men met and talked of Brown's plans to attack the Armory at Harper's Ferry, and Dwight witnessed how Douglass vehemently opposed Brown's plan. The meeting lasted for over an hour as Dwight cased the area to ensure no one was listening or could come close enough to harm either man. With Frederick Douglass was an escaped slave named Shields Green[1]. Dwight had the opportunity to meet and talk with Shields as their two leaders conversed and sometimes argued.

After Dwight was satisfied that the quarry was safe for the two men to talk privately, he struck up a conversation with Green. "Dwight Stevens." He extended his hand.

"Shields Green." The other man reached out to shake his hand.

"Did you escape, Mr. Green?"

---

[1] **Shields Green** – See 6 raiders executed at Charlestown.

"That be true, Massa Stevens."

"Call me Dwight, please."

"Just habit, massa." He corrected himself. "Dwight. Respect keeps folk like me safe."

"I understand, Shields. If I may, can I call you by your name? I remember hearing the same thing from a man named Wilson a couple of years ago."

"Calling me by my name is welcome."

"Good."

The two conversed about general subjects as they got to know each other. They stopped talking at times when they heard their respective leaders arguing about certain parts of Brown's plans. Toward the completion of the meeting, both men overheard Brown raise his voice and pump his fist into the air. ***"When I strike, Frederick, the bees will swarm, and I shall want you to help hive them."***

Both Shields and Dwight heard Douglass respond to Brown when he yelled back, ***"Virginia will blow you and your hostages sky-high rather than you hold Harper's Ferry for an hour."***

The argument continued as the men walked too far away for Shields and Dwight to hear more of the conversation. The Brown sons and John Kagi also distanced themselves from the two men, as they felt uncomfortable.

Eventually the two men returned and stood near the others. They heard Douglass repeat his position that he would decline Brown's invitation to join him in the raid. Douglass turned and looked at Shields in an effort to signal that he was ready to leave the quarry. Shields did not immediately respond. Douglass saw his hesitation and asked, ***"Do you wish to return to Rochester or join Mr. Brown?"***

"I b'l'eve I'll go wid de old man."

All who heard it smiled, except Douglass. Dwight spoke quickly to reduce any tension between Douglass and Green. "I will fetch your carriage, Mr. Douglass. Shields will drive you back to Kagi's. He can come with us from there, if that is acceptable, sir."

Douglass smiled and responded, "It will be, Mr. Stevens."

Dwight looked at Brown and then Green for any objection. There was none, and he left. When Dwight returned, Shields assisted Douglass into the carriage. Neither Brown, his sons, Kagi, nor Dwight knew what the two talked about during their return to Chambersburg.

Douglass looked at Shields and said, "Go and be safe. I envy your quick response, courage, and determination. I hope I do not regret my return to Rochester alone." Douglass shook Brown's hand and then hugged Green. Mist was evident in Douglass's eyes as he turned to shake hands with the rest of the men.

Shields Green accompanied John Brown, his sons, and Dwight back to the Kennedy farm, arriving on August 23rd. Kagi remained in Chambersburg while Douglass returned to Rochester later that week.

September came, and Dwight managed to continue sporadic training with the men, who had endured the August heat and cramped quarters. Their disposition was good despite a few altercations that occurred between them but were quickly broken up. Dwight's plan to train during specific hours of the day and then continue during the early evening hours progressed well and seemed to work despite the constant snooping from Mrs. Huffmaster. Anne's thorough watching aided in keeping training operations ongoing. John Brown did not partake in the training, but steadily wrote supporters back East, encouraging them to continue sending money and supplies for his plan.

It was during this month that John Brown was able to completely pay Charles Blair[1] to produce the remaining pikes of the one thousand he wanted. Brown planned to distribute them to the slaves when they revolted. Nine hundred and fifty were delivered to the Chambersburg, Pennsylvania, storehouse. Eventually Kagi shipped them to the Kennedy farm. They were stored in the cellar with the Sharps rifles and Maynard pistols.

John Brown felt more comfortable each week as new members arrived at the farm. During this time, John Copeland[2], Lewis Leary[3], and Osborne Perry Anderson[4] arrived. All three were blacks and had been in contact with John Kagi, who gave them instructions on where to find Brown and his followers. The arrival of these men caused still more logistical problems.

Dwight and Brown both knew that extra white men seen at the farm could be explained away, but new black men would not be. All three were carefully hidden in the back fields on the other side of the road from the farm where there would be little chance of the locals seeing them. The

---

1 **Charles Blair** – During a trip east in 1857, Brown contracted with blacksmith Charles Blair of Collinsville, Connecticut, for several hundred pikes (weapons with long wooden shafts ending in pointed steel heads, used by foot soldiers). Blair was a forge master working for Collins and Company who made quality edged tools. He agreed to make 1000 pikes for Brown at $1 apiece. After making 500, Blair halted production because Brown had failed to pay him. Blair held the pikes for two years. In 1859, Brown showed up at Blair's door with the money to purchase 954.

2 **John Copeland** – See 6 raiders who were executed at Charlestown.

3 **Lewis Leary** – See 10 raiders who died at Harper's Ferry.

4 **Osborne Perry Anderson** – See 5 raiders who survived the raid.

three men understood, and Shields Green volunteered to stay with them to help explain the situation they were coping with. The last thing that anyone in the group wanted was the impression that blacks were treated any differently than the whites. Francis Jackson Merriam[1] was the last man to arrive at the farm. Meriam brought John Brown $600 in gold that he had received from his abolitionist grandfather, Francis Jackson.

The twenty men were the only ones Brown could expect to arrive at the farm after he received correspondence from John Kagi that all solicitations to join the raid had been exhausted. With Kagi, and counting himself, John Brown's emancipation army consisted of twenty-two men. A far cry short of the numbers he expected.

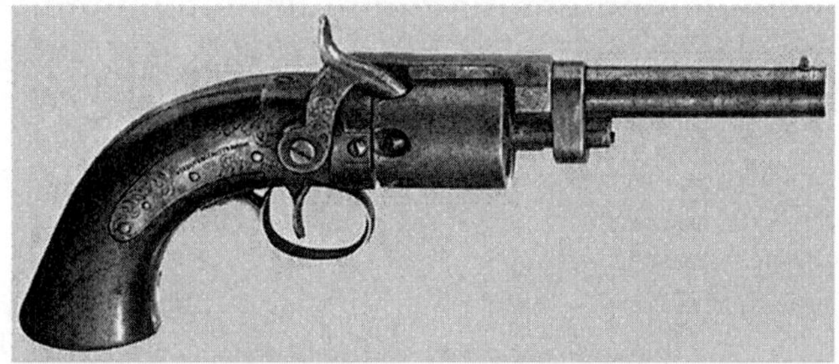

Maynard .31 caliber pistol
Public Domain photo

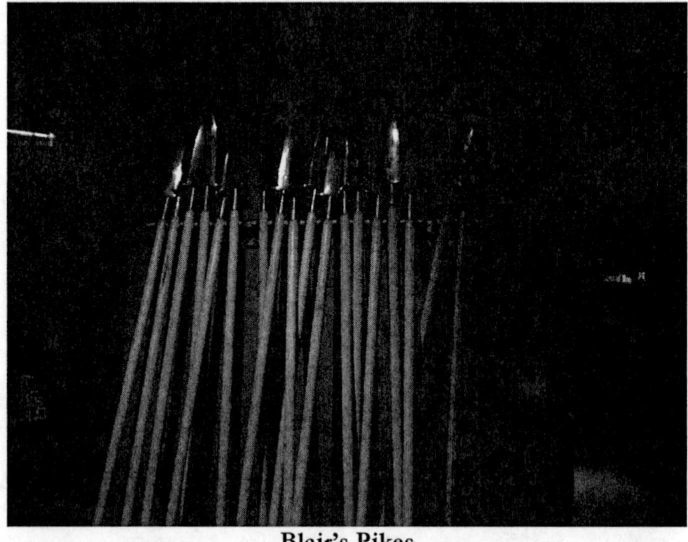

Blair's Pikes

[1] **Francis Jackson Merriam** – See 5 raiders who survived the raid.

Photographed at Harper's Ferry Museum by Tommy Coletti

On September 30th, Brown sent John Cook on a reconnaissance mission. He instructed Cook to gather information concerning the slaves in the area. He waited several days until Cook returned to the farm. Upon seeing Cook's return, Brown asked, "What have you to report?"

Cook, who was sipping water in the kitchen, smiled and said, "Captain, I have seen and spoken to many of them. Those that were not afraid of my questions said they were ready to follow you to their freedom."

Brown questioned him further until Cook convinced him that all was ready to descend on Harper's Ferry.

"Captain, they are discontented and ***are ready to swarm like bees."***

With that statement, John Brown informed the women that it was time for them to return to Elba, New York. He instructed Oliver to escort them to Chambersburg and then return. The women would eventually reach Elba by train. He then told Dwight that it was nearing the time to go to Harper's Ferry.

Dwight asked Brown to have Kagi informed of his decision, and he agreed. Oliver would tell Kagi to return with him to the farm. Both Brown and Dwight knew that John Kagi's presence was needed there to listen to the last-minute plans before the descent on Harper's Ferry.

On the night of October 7th, Dwight used the kitchen table to write a letter he had thought about for many months. The night offered him a chance to collect his thoughts about the woman he loved. The evening walks, duets on the Lindsleys' piano, the touch of her hand sitting next to him on the front porch swing, and the slight scent of the perfume she wore were pleasant memories. His time at the Kennedy farm had passed quickly, and he knew it wouldn't be long before his captain would give the word for their assault on Harper's Ferry. The lantern flickered as someone entered the small kitchen. Dwight looked up and saw John Brown looking at him.

"You could not sleep?"

"No, sir. Just writing a letter to a beautiful woman I met while at the Lindsley home. I hope Mrs. Lindsley will forward the letter to her."

"I'm sure she will, son. She liked you."

The captain left Dwight to compose his letter.

Near Harper's Ferry, Oct. 7th/59

Jenny,

I sit down to write you a few more lines not knowing but that it may be the last time that I Shall have the pleasure of writing to

you. But I trust I shall live to see thy lovly face wonce more. I hope you are well both in body and mind. I have not got a lettor from you yet, but am looking for one with all my eyes. You cannot tell how much good it would doo me to get a lettor from you. If it was nothing but a friendly one, and if it was one of love I Shall not attempt to tell you how I should feel.

Jenny, I hope you will not feel sick nor think I am a flatterer, if you do, you do me injustice. For you seeam to fill my soul with what a woman ought to be. If you can love as poor a mortal as I am, it will be more than I expect, but if you doo I Shall strive to never have you sorry for so doing, for no love intrusted in my boson shall ever complain. I hope your heart will be with me in this cause, Oh! There is so much happiness in trying to make others happy. I feel at times that I am in heaven. There is hard and trying times, now and then, but it is thrice washed away by the happy feelings that spring from the thoughts that we have not lived for naught, that is we have accomplished some good in the world, and instead of keeping our fellow beings back, that we have healped them forward. Jenny I doo long to see you so that I am almost dead, and hear you play and sing some of those songs. I am very sorry that I did not get better acquainted with you for then I should feel bettor, but I hope that I shall have the pleasure of seeing you before a very long time. And now good by until I have another opportunity of writing to you which may be some time, for we commence work in a few days, give my love to all inquiring friends, and if you see our girl give her a half a dozen kisses for me

With very good wishes I remain for ever your love.
C. Whipple
Good By[1]

He posted the letter several days later when he went into town for some supplies for the farm. He hoped Mrs. Lindsley would oblige his request. He also wondered if she had ever mentioned the incident at the Lindsley home to John Brown in any correspondence. He felt that she hadn't, or else John Brown probably would have said something to him about his temper affecting his judgment. He returned to the Kennedy farm hoping Jenny would respond.

Early in the afternoon of October 14, 1859, John Brown, Dwight Stevens, and John Kagi were the only ones sitting at the kitchen table.

---

[1] **Actual letter** written by A. D. Stevens. Research didn't reveal why he signed it C. Whipple and not A. D. Stevens.

Everyone else had been politely asked to leave. Brown wanted to go through their overall plan one more time before the raid began.

Brown pushed his chair back and stood. He addressed his two lieutenants. "The general plan I have sold to our backers is very simple and has not changed significantly over the last two years. We will establish a strong presence in the surrounding Blue Ridge Mountains to assist escaped and runaway slaves. From our bases and with a growing slave army, we will be able to launch attacks on slaveholders throughout a large area and free more slaves in the process. We should be able to fully arm them with the weapons we will soon seize from the Armory and rifleworks in Harper's Ferry, as well as the pikes and weapons we already possess. Are we in agreement so far?"

John and Dwight only nodded.

Brown continued. "The coming raid will be to accomplish several things. It will provide us with the weapons we need and raise awareness of our existence. It will also draw the freedom-loving slaves to us as bees to honey. Fear will be struck in the hearts of the slaveholding South, and this raid will begin the long, hard, and possibly bloody path to the end of slavery." Brown was walking in circles around the small room as he spoke. He would stop occasionally when he wanted to make a point. "Dwight, we have discussed this before. You will have complete responsibility for training the slave army, and conducting the Indian-like raids against the slavers. You also will help me develop the defenses which will protect our bases, and those who side with us."

He sat again and addressed Kagi. "John, you will continue as my second in command, my organization specialist, and our point of contact for all correspondence. You and I will try to raise money to support our cause as best we can." He paused, looked up, and closed his eyes for a few moments before he looked back at his lieutenants. "Dwight, tonight you will need to go over the details of the raid with the men again so that all will run smoothly. Make sure each man knows his assignments. We will make adjustments as needed."

Dwight acknowledged the order and stood, preparing to leave.

Brown addressed both men one more time. "We have gone over this many times and we have developed a good, bold plan that should work but also could cost us our lives. Every man here understands it is a possibility. The time for action is near. Do you have any last-minute questions or suggestions?"

Kagi stood next to Dwight, but both were quiet. Kagi then answered for the two men. "Sir, we are ready."

During the night of October 15th, all the men were sitting outside the stable laughing and bantering, knowing the raid was imminent. The cool night was welcome after the hot and humid summer evenings the men had endured.

Brown sat, listened, and enjoyed the spirit he saw that night. He thought about how well the training, sleeping arrangements, meal planning, and general welfare of the men had been handled by the efforts of Dwight Stevens. He was also pleased that Kagi, his planner-administrator, was at his side again. Despite not getting the number of volunteers he had expected, he was happy. John Kagi had performed admirably in Chambersburg with the correspondence to solicit funds and supplies. Now that the women were safe at home in Elba with his wife and children, Brown became content and relaxed, enjoying the moment at the farm. He left the gathering noticed only by Dwight and Kagi, who watched him return to the house.

"Why didn't he stay and enjoy the night?" Kagi asked.

"If I know his ways, he has returned to read Scripture and pray to the Almighty that the raid goes well."

"I hope the Almighty is listening tonight when he prays, Dwight."

"John Brown is convinced that he is, and that is all that counts. In a little while we'll need to break up this joyous time and retire so we are rested for when he gives us the command to go."

"Amen to that, Dwight."

Dwight only smiled and returned to the where the men were gathered.

The night sky was beginning to cloud over, obscuring the stars. Dwight felt that the universe was signaling to him that John Brown had spoken with the Almighty and everything would be changing forever. That night as Dwight tried to sleep, rain began to fall. He thought to himself, *It is going to be a raw, wet day tomorrow.* That didn't bother him. He had gone into battle many times in worse conditions to fight Mexicans, Indians, and pro-slavers. He knew that a damp and raw day would not hinder the battle he was about to undertake.

Chapter Twenty-Two

The Failed Cause

Aaron Dwight Stevens still lay motionless in his unconscious state after being shot. As he recoverd consciousness for the first time, he was overtaken by excruciating pain. All his vivid memories quickly evaporated as he came back to reality. He continually fell in and out of consciousness, not being able to hold on to it for any length of time. He could hear voices, some yelling at times, but couldn't focus long enough to see anything clearly. The taste of blood filled his mouth, sometimes choking him and forcing him to swallow in an effort to breathe. He was nauseated and his face burned.

The extreme pain he felt in his neck and chest only subsided when his awareness left and darkness overcame him again. His unconscious state was periodically halted as bouts of consciousness interfered. In unconsciousness, happiness existed. His sister Lydia came to him, smiling and caressing his head as she had done many times immediately after his mother had passed. In those days she had practically raised him until his aunt entered his home and became his stepmother.

He could also see his grandfather laughing at him as he picked himself up from the ground after being knocked down from the force of the old musket. Dwight could feel his chin, face, and shoulder hurting, but he had learned a valuable lesson on loading the correct amount of powder and preparing himself for the kick of the weapon.

As consciousness came again, the pain in his face and neck were real. Blurry figures passed in front of his eyes, but darkness overcame him again. Glimpses of Maria came to him, but the face of her uncle kept making her disappear. Pretty Jenny came in short, quick glimpses. He could only see her face. No sound came from her moving lips, but he knew how she looked when she sang. As awareness came, her face disappeared and only the sounds of people talking and yelling filled his ears. His face, neck, and chest throbbed, and relief came again as the darkness returned.

Joseph Brewer found John Brown holding on to his son Watson. The abolitionist never acknowledged Brewer's return, only rocking his semi-conscious son in his arms. Several of the prominent prisoners asked Brewer why he had returned, but Brewer never explained his actions. He did relay that there was more violence in store for the raiders now that the Jefferson Guard and local militia had arrived and taken up strategic positions.

Colonel Washington suggested that they all move to the corner farthest away from the thick oak door and wait. Washington hinted that maybe the captain would lay down his arms and surrender now that one of his sons looked to be dying.

Brewer took the initiative to ask Brown, "Sir, your son is gravely wounded. I could get help for him. There are good women already taking care of the man you call Dwight. Shall I go and ask to quarter this man as well?"

"You are most kind, sir, but I feel that my son can bear the pain of his wounds. His Heavenly Father has not summoned him. Until then, I shall comfort him." Just then Watson went into unconsciousness in Brown's arms, and he ordered a few men to gently move him to a corner of the room to lie in peace. It would be another day before Watson would painfully succumb to his wounds.

Young William Leeman had watched in horror as Dwight Stevens was cut down by blasts from a shotgun. His idol and mentor was grievously injured, perhaps even dead. The Maine native had seen enough. He decided he would not end up like Dwight. He thought to himself, *This crazy old man will have all of us killed. Why would he send Dwight out with a flag of truce only to be cut down? His plan must have failed. I must escape now that Stevens is probably dead and Kagi is nowhere to be found.*

He moved from his position as most of the others were watching Dwight being taken away. He found an escape route out of the Armory, climbed the back portion of the fence near the railroad tracks, and crossed them, heading for the river. He looked up and down and realized that wading and then swimming was his only choice for escape. He jumped in and waded across the river until it became too deep.

A few militiamen spotted him and rushed to the spot where he had jumped in. They began firing at him, but missed. He swam hard, scared that one shooter would finally get lucky and hit him. He found a large rock in the middle of the river and, exhausted, he pulled himself onto it to rest and wait for someone to surrender to. He waited on the rock as several men approached.

One of them, G. A. Schoppert, drew his pistol and aimed it at the youth. William Leeman attempted to surrender to him, but the man cocked his pistol and shot him point-blank in the head. Leeman fell backward, half in the water. His boots anchored his body to the rock as the water quickly turned red. He had died instantly. Leeman's body was not moved from the spot where he had been killed for several days. Occasionally, late-arriving militia and numerous drunks took aim at the corpse for target practice. Forty years after the killing, conflicting accounts of his death and the target practicing incidents still existed.

Liquor and beer were abundant at the Wager Hotel and the Galt House as more and more armed men arrived. The excessive drinking of some of the men correlated with the amount of bullet holes that ripped into the dead body of Dangerfield Newby, still lying where he had fallen earlier that day. Some approached the body and kicked it with their boots. Others thrust the butts of their muskets at the head of the dead man. His face became unrecognizable to any of those who knew him. His boots were even removed and carried off by one of the barefoot attackers. The day was overcast with periodic drizzle, keeping the exposed body cool and protected from bloating in the sun.

Later in the afternoon, Harper's Ferry endured a downpour. The rain slowed the activities on both sides, but as fast as the downpour started it also ended, allowing movements of men to increase again.

It was during this time that the Mayor of Harper's Ferry, Fontaine Beckham, made a bad decision to get closer to the conflict. Edwin Coppoc watched the mayor as he ever so slowly worked his way closer to the Armory. He waited until the man was in range of his Sharps rifle. He shot off a round and the mayor died instantly. It would be some time before the citizens of Harper's Ferry knew that their mayor had been killed.

A few minutes later, around 3:00 p.m., Oliver Brown, who had witnessed Edwin Coppoc's shot, took the same position as he spotted another target close to the same area. As Oliver raised his rifle and aimed, he fell mortally wounded from a bullet his prey had fired at him just a second earlier. John Brown saw him fall and immediately went to him. He now had two sons dying within his sight.

As Brown held Oliver, he began a hasty conversation with Colonel Washington. It ended with Brown proposing that Washington convince the guard and militia to give him and his men ample time to escape with selected prisoners. At a point approximately a half-mile outside town, Brown would free his captives and disappear into the mountains. His last words on the proposal were, ***"Every man for himself and the devil take the hindmost."***

While Brown negotiated with the colonel, word that Mayor Beckham had been killed spread quickly throughout the town. The townspeople and militia, whether drunk or not, were tired of kicking and shooting Newby's body lying in the street. They were also getting bored of taking shots at the body of Leeman, still half-submerged in the river. Now that the mayor had been killed, they were angry and their priority became avenging his death.

The word spread that a raider was still held captive in one of the rooms of the Wager Hotel. An unruly mob headed by George Chambers, the man credited with shooting Dwight Stevens, entered the hotel in search of the raider. Assisted by the nephew of the killed mayor, Harry Hunter, they found the room William Thompson had been held in. He had been surrounded and captured while carrying the first flag of truce earlier in the day.

Their attempt to grab and drag him out of the room was temporarily interrupted when Christina Fouke, sister to the hotel owner, had put herself between the mob and Thompson. Her attempt to change the minds of the mob leaders failed, and she was pushed aside. Thompson was carried from the hotel to the nearby bridge. He was forced to walk part of the way over it until Chambers and Hunter both drew pistols and shot him in the head. He tumbled over the bridge railing and somersaulted toward the water.

During the fall, his body was riddled with more bullets from men firing at will at the moving target. They were not satisfied with that kill. They returned to the Wager Hotel to replenish their liquor needs and plan for another target. Word quickly spread that one of the wounded leaders of the raiders was also in one of the hotel rooms, being treated. The mob set out to find out where this man was.

Volunteers shooting insurgents, *Leslie's*, October 29, 1859.
West Virginia State Archives

Amid all the yelling, chanting, and drunken stumbling, the mob managed to find the room where Dwight Stevens lay semi-conscious, suffering heavily from his wounds. He awoke to hear the commotion the mob made as they were coming in his direction. His eyes had cleared enough that he could see the anxious looks on the faces of the men who were guarding him and the attending women. Dwight thought to push himself up to be in a better position to brace himself for what was about to come through the door, but he was too weak to even attempt it. He knew his time had come.

He wished he had his pistol so he could have taken several of them to the afterlife with him, but he found himself simply hoping the end would come quickly. When Harry Hunter came through the door, the sight of Dwight covered in blood sickened him. He froze in his tracks and was bumped several times by the men that immediately followed him. Hunter put out his arms to stop those that attempted to go around him. Dwight heard him speak.

"Let 'im be. By the looks of 'im, he'll be dead soon enough." A few more men tried to slip past his outstretched arms. He yelled this time. "Ya heard me, let 'im be! He ain't got long!"

Several more men behind those who had entered the room stretched to see the wounded man and managed to get by Hunter's outstretched arms. They approached his bed as Dwight found enough strength then to prop himself up and look directly at his would-be attackers. Whether it was sheer adrenaline, anger, or a combination of both, Dwight stared at them a few feet from his bed for several moments. He expected them to drag him from his bed and end what he felt was inevitable—his demise at the hands of the unruly mob.

Someone yelled, ***"Look, he prepares to fight us."***

Another remarked more softly, ***"By the look and size of him, we should be content that he is wounded. It would take many of us to remove him if he were not."***

One man put the muzzle of a loaded gun to Dwight's head with the expressed determination to kill him instantly. Dwight was unable to move a limb, but he fixed his eyes on the would-be murderer and by the sheer force of the mysterious influence they possessed, he compelled the man to lower the weapon and refrain from carrying out his purpose.

Throughout his life, that man continued to state that he did not know why he stopped, but that he had felt such an irresistible fascination that bound him as strongly as any spell.

Hunter yelled for a third time to clear the room. They all turned and left, grumbling among themselves as the guards ordered to watch Dwight relaxed slightly seeing the mob go. The attending women remained with him. Dwight collapsed back onto his bed while one of the women shook her head as he began to bleed through his bandages.

The mob continued to mill in and out of the Wager Hotel. There had been no attempt to rush the raiders, especially knowing the accuracy and ability of the weapons possessed by them. Whether Brown thought he still had an advantage because of his weapons, no one really knew.

Kagi was still boxed up in the rifleworks while Brown sat dormant in the Armory engine house with two mortally wounded sons and his prominent prisoners.

The situation changed when the misdeeds of the drunken mob convinced a company of railroad tonnage men to launch an attack of their own. Two of the tonnage company leaders were E. G. Alburtis and Evans Dorsey. Both men were known to be very energetic and fearless, but most importantly they knew the layout of the buildings that Brown and his men held.

They were initially successful, despite the heavy fire from the Sharps rifles, and managed to reach the watch house. They freed some of the prisoners that Brown had left there and turned to head for the engine house. The firing from the raiders continued and eventually took its toll on the tonnage company men. Evans Dorsey was killed along with several others. Captain Alburtis ordered a retreat as soon as he witnessed Dorsey fall, shot through the heart.

Dwight could hear the sounds of the battle raging. He distinguished the muskets from the Sharps rifles being discharged, and he knew that the Sharps were firing faster. He wondered if Kagi had managed to stem off another attack. He fell back into a semi-conscious state as he felt a woman changing his chest bandage again.

Dwight would eventually learn that his friend, John Kagi, met his death later that night in the river along with John Copeland and Lewis Leary. The three men, one white and two black, had managed to hold the rifleworks until the evening, when they were overrun by the Charlestown irregulars. They tried to escape, but failed in their attempt to cross the Shenandoah River and flee to safety. They had no idea that the irregulars had not only successfully stormed the building to flush them out; they had also surrounded the buildings that bordered the river. As Kagi, Copeland, and Leary began to wade into the river, they were subjected to continuous musket fire. As the river deepened, they began to swim.

Kagi managed to reach a rock that stuck out midway. As he attempted to pull himself up, he was hit by several bullets and died instantly. Leary saw what had occurred to his lieutenant and was able to move away from the concentrated fire. He managed to go another fifty feet before he was struck and wounded. He floated downriver and managed to hit a shallow area, where he lay. Copeland had managed to reach the same rock Kagi had been shot on, but he stayed clinging to it when he saw the irregulars forming on the opposite side of the river. They had crossed the bridge and waited for the raiders to reach the other side.

James Holt, one of the irregulars, swam to where Copeland was hanging onto the rock. His rifle was wet, which saved Copeland's life.

Holt managed to bring Copeland back to the river's edge, where others jumped in and dragged the black man out. Immediately they screamed to lynch him. Some looked for a rope while others prepared to shoot the man dead.

Dr. Starry, who had returned from Charlestown, observed the entire incident and put his horse between Copeland and the irregulars who were beginning to become unruly. He ordered that Copeland be arrested and that no man was going to take the law into his own hands. The men slowly moved away and returned to an area in town to muster. Dr. Starry also ordered several clear-headed irregulars to fetch Leary, who still lay mortally wounded in a shallow portion of the river. They placed him on the river's edge. No one attended to him, but no one mistreated him. He was left to die, and did so later that evening.

Dwight awoke sometime in the early evening. He could occasionally hear weapons being discharged, but they were not Sharps. He guessed that the captain was still holding out and that the discharges he was hearing were probably from the militia taking aim at the Armory. He looked around the room at the several men who stood leaning against the walls as a few women bent over him. He felt the sheets move as a stocky woman pulled the blood-soaked linen out from under him. He saw her smile at him as she gently turned him on his side.

The pain in his chest was excruciating, but she said that she was only trying to put fresh linen under him.

He whispered, "Thank you, my good lady."

She smiled and ordered the younger woman who had started to assist her to hasten the job they were performing.

He realized that he had only his pants on. His boots, socks, and shirt were nowhere to be seen. He could see that he had several bandages on his chest. His face and neck still burned, and he raised his hand to touch them.

The woman cautioned him, "You have bandages on your neck and face. Do not disturb them. We have managed to stop the bleeding."

He obeyed, but softly asked both women, "Tell me please, what are my wounds?"

The older one paused and then spoke slowly. "You have been shot with buckshot, young man. You have a wound to your face, one to your neck, and several to your chest. Your left arm has been injured as well. We are waiting for a doctor to come. Be still. You have lost too much blood."

He looked over to one of the guards and asked, "What time of day is it, please?"

The man looked at another guard, who said, "Give the man the time."

He reached into his coat pocket and pulled out a watch. "It's half past seven o'clock on October seventeenth."

Dwight softly thanked him and then looked toward the one window in the room. The window was partially open, and he heard the rain splattering on the windowsill. One of the woman attendants noticed he was looking at the window and closed it. He was about to fall back to sleep when the door opened and several men entered.

"Who are you?" one of the guards asked.

"We are reporters. We've come to interview your prisoner and find out who he is and what he is up to."

The guard shrugged his shoulders, backed away, and let the men pass.

Dwight didn't say a word as one of the reporters grabbed a chair, spun it around, and sat on it backward, resting his arms on the back. "Now tell me, mister, who are you and what is the purpose of your attack on this town?"

Dwight spoke slowly and softly but was very clear. "Sir, John Brown and his men are here to free the slaves of this area."

"Is that your sole purpose, mister? Do you have a name?" He looked at Dwight, expecting him not to reveal his identity.

"My name is Aaron Dwight Stevens. My captain is John Brown. Our sole purpose is to free slaves in this town."

"How big of an army do you have, Mr. Stevens?"

"We are but twenty-two men. Seventeen white and five Negros. Our captain calls us the army of the Lord."

The reporter smiled as he jotted down the statement while gently speaking it.

Dwight became exhausted and passed out.

The two reporters stopped taking notes and looked at each other. One called out in a loud voice to awaken the unconscious man, "You said the army of the Lord. Is that right, Stevens?"

The reporter tried several times to awaken him until the senior lady attendant spoke up. "Leave him be. He goes in and out of consciousness. He's gravely wounded, and it's time for you two to be gone."

The reporters left the room but were told that another raider who was at the rifleworks had been shot and was still alive down by the river. They were led to Lewis Leary by a few of those who had witnessed his shooting. They found Leary shivering from the wounds he had received and the cold of the drizzle that still fell on him. In his last dying breath, Lewis Leary confirmed that Captain Brown called his men the army of the Lord.

The reporters left to file their stories at the Charlestown telegraph station.

As night descended on the town, occasional shots could still be heard as militiamen took aim at shadows in the semi-darkness in the street, thinking the raiders were moving to attack or escape. As eyes adjusted, they realized that it was some hogs that had escaped and were running the streets freely. Several hogs smelled the body of Dangerfield Newby, who still lay where he had been shot.

A few townsmen threw stones at the hogs to keep them from biting at the body or worse. The rock throwing failed, so they resorted to a few closely placed shots to chase off the hogs. It was at this time that they realized shots were being fired at them. Flashes could be seen coming from a hill across the river. They organized and concentrated their fire in the direction where the flashes had been last seen.

Several minutes of concentrated fire awakened everyone in the town, who feared a new battle was taking place. As quickly as the firing had started, it ceased and no more flashes could be seen coming from the hill. No militiamen attempted, or were ordered, to investigate, and the night quieted.

The firing had come from John Cook. He had managed to stay on the opposite side of the river, but away from Tidd and the rest of the men at the schoolhouse where the weapons were being temporarily stored. He became busy visiting residents he knew to obtain information on what had occurred in town. As the evening approached, he witnessed the militia shooting toward the engine house. Enraged and frustrated, he climbed a tree and fired several times at the militia. He quickly realized they were returning fire as bullets caught branches in trees next to him. As he exited, a bullet hit one of the branches he was using to support himself. It broke, causing him to fall fifteen or so feet to the ground. He was uninjured and retreated to safety as more bullets could be heard peppering the tree.

After finding temporary refuge at another resident's house, he later returned to the schoolhouse to find it still full of the weapons. Realizing he was all alone, he left down the Boonsborough Road back toward the Kennedy farm.

More town militias and companies arrived at Harper's Ferry. Organization of the groups under one commander would not be obtained until the arrival of the U.S. Marines. Before that, several commanders vied for control of the forces.

The first one to take temporary charge was Colonel Baylor, who had been sent by Governor Wise[1] to relieve Colonel John T. Gibson, who had been unsuccessful in controlling his troops and had failed to drive John Brown from his position. Baylor took command and immediately sent a messenger named Samuel Strider to John Brown. Baylor's message was short and simple. He demanded Brown surrender immediately before any more blood was shed.

Brown replied, ***"In consideration of all my men, whether living or dead, or wounded, being safely in and delivered up to me at this point with all their arms and ammunition, we will then take our prisoners and cross the Potomac Bridge, a little beyond which will set them at liberty; after which we can negotiate about Government property as may be best. Also we require the delivery of our horses and harness at the hotel.***

John Brown"

Strider returned with the message. Colonel Baylor fumed when he read it. He dictated an response to one of his subordinates to hand back to Strider.

"Sir:

The terms you proposed I cannot accept. Under no circumstances will I consent to a removal of our citizens across the river. The only negotiations upon which I will consent to treat are those which have been previously proposed to you.

Robert W. Baylor, Co. Commandant
3rd Regiment Cavalry."

Sporadic firing continued from both sides into the evening. John Brown held Oliver until he became unconscious. Brown had him moved to the opposite side of the room from where Watson laid, also unconscious and breathing shallowly.

Brown and the men with him, including the prisoners, failed to see Stewart Taylor die a short time later. He was the victim of a shot by one of the highly skilled marksman that had accompanied the militia into town. Despite being red-eyed from consuming varying amounts of alcohol, many were still very skillful with their muskets and unhappy that they had not been able to get a clear shot at a raider. Stewart Taylor, however, had afforded them a shot when he sat too close to a partially

---

[1] **Governor Henry A. Wise** was an American statesman and governor of Virginia. One of his last official acts as governor was to sign the death warrant of John Brown. Wise served as a brigadier general in the Confederate army. He commanded the Confederates during the Battle of Roanoke Island. His decision to surrender the island, when faced with much greater Union forces, was unpopular with the Confederate leadership.

opened door. A tipsy marksman noticed, aimed, and pulled the trigger. Taylor was killed instantly from a shot through the heart. No one noticed he had died as he lay propped up, still in his cross-legged position near the door, until he did not respond to an order from Brown to move away from it.

During this time, Albert Hazlett and Osborn Anderson seized the opportunity to make their escape. Both witnessed a messenger from Colonel Baylor arrive, depart, and arrive again. From the arsenal they had been assigned to guard, they made their plans to escape. With darkness upon them and the main attraction of the negotiations centered on Brown's location, they executed their escape.

The two slipped between the ranks of the rowdy and undisciplined men. Despite the color of Anderson's skin, they went unnoticed and managed to leave the troop-infested town. They eventually worked their way back to the Kennedy farmhouse and spent several days camping in the woods nearby. One of the two would eventually maintain his freedom.

Dwight awoke again. He asked for the time from a new man that was now guarding him. The man ignored his request until one of the women attending him turned and spoke. "The man asked you for the time."

The new guard seemed embarrassed by the tone of the woman. He pulled out a pocket watch and said, "Ten minutes to nine o'clock, the evening of the seventeenth."

Dwight acknowledged with a weak wave of his right hand in appreciation. He wondered what was occurring. The noises coming from the street and through the floor beneath him indicated that a large number of men had gathered very close to his room. He recollected that they had come once but had then left, and he thought he remembered talking to someone before he fell into unconsciousness. Dwight tried to move and sit up, but resolved to keep still when the pain in his chest and neck became overbearing.

The lone woman who was attending to him yelled, "Be still, man! Be still! You've started to bleed again!"

He could feel the pressure of her hands pushing on the bandages covering his chest. The pain nauseated him, and he asked for some water.

The woman obliged him, but when he took a drink, he began to choke from the dried blood in his mouth and throat. The sight unnerved he guards as they watched him choke and vomit up the fluid he most desperately needed to retain. They moved outside in order to regain their composure.

After Dwight cleared his throat, the sheer exhaustion to accomplish it and the excruciating pain he had to endure caused him to black out again. He could not hear the scolding he was being given by the woman who had to redress his wounds that had opened again.

The evening progressed with loud noises coming from the Wager Hotel and the Galt House. Another attempt was made to bring the crisis to an end. With most of his men watching from cover, Captain Sinn, a subordinate of Colonel Edward Shriver of the Frederick Cavalry, made an attempt to reach John Brown just as Oliver was begging his father to shoot him and put him out of his misery.

Captain Sinn approached the entrance to Brown's compound and requested permission to enter under a sign of truce. Brown obliged. The two men talked for almost an hour on their views of slavery and what had occurred during that day. Sinn departed with a different view of the gentleman-soldier he had just met, but the significance of his visit was his agreement to return with a surgeon to assist in the treatment of Brown's two sons.

The surgeon treated and dressed Watson's wounds as he lay semi-conscious on one side of the room. He then turned to treat Oliver. He quietly told Brown, "There is nothing I can do for this man except make him comfortable." He supplied some more folded blankets for Oliver to rest on. Oliver screamed at his father again to end his life, but before he fell off into a semi-conscious state, Brown responded to his young son, ***"You must die."*** He paused as he looked at him. ***"Die like a man."***

Captain Sinn accompanied his surgeon after treating Brown's sons. They stopped at the Wager Hotel so Sinn could confer with his company officers. While in the hotel, whether it was providence or sheer luck on Stevens' part, Captain Sinn heard a ruckus on the next floor that attracted his attention. He inquired of his junior officers what was occurring. They informed him that some of the civilians were harassing one of the raider leaders being held under guard.

Infuriated with his officers, he asked why they hadn't intervened to protect the prisoner. Their response was that the prisoner was under the jurisdiction of the militia and was not a concern of the cavalry. Furious with their response, Captain Sinn drew his pistol, commanded his junior officers to follow him, and climbed the stairs to the second floor. There he found a small crowd of highly intoxicated men pointing pistols at the wounded man.

Dwight had heard the mob ascending the stairs for the second time. He knew there would be more trouble than the first time as the noise from the floor below him had grown louder and more rowdy during the course of the evening. As the mob crashed in the door, the men assigned to guard him pulled back and did not warn or raise their weapons in any threatening manner. He forced himself to sit up with his chest bare and his right fist clenched. He sat still with blood-soaked bandages and stared at this new threat.

The attackers drew their pistols and pointed them at him, yelling and waving them as if they were going to shoot. Dwight kept his composure and glared at his tormentors. The women in the room screamed, but the guards never moved from their frozen position against the far wall of the room.

Captain Sinn couldn't believe what he was witnessing. He yelled at the men who were closest to Dwight, ***"If this man could stand on his feet with a pistol in his hand, you would all jump out the window. Now get out of here."*** He drove the "crowd of cowards," as he called them, from the second floor. His officers followed.

Dwight collapsed, completely exhausted but thankful to the cavalry officer for saving his life.

The women again attended to his wounds. One woman called to both guards to leave at once. They obliged her, but stood outside the door instead. Several minutes later at midnight, two cavalrymen replaced the useless guards with orders from Captain Sinn to shoot anyone who attempted to storm the room and threaten the prisoner.

The town then became quiet. The drizzle continued to fall, and drunken and sober men alike found dry places to sleep off the liquor or tiredness they felt.

It was the early morning hours of October 18th. The fact that the majority of the men were resting helped suppress the news of the arrival of Lieutenant Colonel Robert E. Lee, his assistant, Lieutenant J.E.B. Stuart, and ninety-three U.S. marines. Captain Sinn had been informed of their arrival from his superior, and he relayed the information to Brown. Sinn had hoped Brown would now see the fruitlessness of his cause.

John Brown looked at his watch as he debated the issue of slavery with Colonel Washington. Realizing he had not heard any moaning from Oliver, he called over to him. There was no response. Brown walked over and looked down at his son, but saw no breathing. He checked his pulse and found none. He softly removed his cartridge belt and straightened his limbs. He spoke in the direction of his prisoners, ***"This is the third son I have lost to this cause."***

Most knew that Frederick Brown had been murdered at Osawatomie. Those present had seen Oliver die from the wounds he received under a flag of truce, and they must have realized that Brown knew that his other son, Watson, would soon die from a lucky shot taken by a militiaman.

As the hours passed, Brown waited for the inevitable appearance of the U.S. Marines. He surmised that they could attack and destroy his small army of the Lord quickly, but he pondered whether the officers in charge would chance the lives of the hostages he held.

Not far away, Lee and Stuart discussed the same concern. Lee informed his officers and men that he would communicate with the raiders first. Then, if his communications failed to convince the leader to surrender, he would wait until daylight to help distinguish the hostages from the raiders. He would then assault the building with bayonets to keep from having any stray bullets injure a hostage. With the plan set, he waited until just before dawn to communicate with John Brown.

Dwight Stevens awoke about 3:00 a.m. on the morning of the 18th. His wounds had stopped bleeding, and an exhausted woman who had stayed with him during the night awoke when she heard him move in the bed. The iron springs creaked as Dwight attempted to turn the oil lamp up to lighten the room.

She spoke to him. "You better keep still, young man."

He was startled at hearing a voice coming from the dark corner of the room, then saw the older woman wrapping a shawl around her shoulders to ward off the cold and damp. There was complete silence as she bent over and turned up the wick on the oil lamp.

"You've slept soundly for several hours. You should try to do more of the same. Your wounds have stopped bleeding, but you still need a doctor to attend to them."

Dwight motioned for some water to sip. The kind lady assisted him to drink from a small glass. He wet his mouth and swallowed very cautiously, remembering the incident when he had choked and vomited water and blood all over himself. He successfully managed to swallow the cool liquid before he spoke. "Thank you. Where have the guards gone?"

"Not far. They stand guard out in the hallway."

He grimaced as he attempted to laugh. "They didn't do very much to protect us the last time. I saw them scared to death over in the corner of the room."

"They are not the same two men. A captain has posted two cavalrymen outside your door with orders to shoot anyone who attempts to force his way in here."

"I remember a captain yelling at some men who came to pistol-whip me, or whatever they had planned."

"One and the same."

Dwight looked amused after hearing about the captain who had saved his life. The woman saw his expression and asked what he was smiling about. Dwight just shook his head. The woman seemed to be waiting for an explanation and Dwight sensed it. "It's just ironic that a cavalryman saved me, for I was one myself years ago."

The woman instructed him to remain still and try to go back to sleep. No sooner had she instructed her patient, a musket was fired off down the street.

Dwight asked her, "Are they still held up in the engine house?"

The woman looked confused.

Dwight asked his question differently. "Are my men still holding hostages?"

She nodded before she turned the lamp down. "Yes, nothing has changed since you came in here except that more men have been wounded or killed on both sides."

Dwight thought to himself as he tried to relax and get more sleep, *Kagi must have received the weapons he needed. He now holds the army off, but for how long?*

Dwight heard the woman return to her chair and attempt to get comfortable. He waited for her to settle in. As he lay there, he began to think of a plan to escape. Dwight knew he had two cavalrymen stationed outside his door, and he began to plan a way to overtake them. His thoughts came to a quick halt when the pain in his arm and chest became excruciating at his attempt to move to a more comfortable position.

He heard the woman call to him, "I can hear you moving! Be still, man, for your own sake! You will die if you lose more blood!"

Dwight succumbed to the realization that he could not even get out of bed, never mind overtake two cavalrymen by surprise in order to escape out of a hotel full of men aching to kill him. He had beaten many odds during his days fighting in Mexico and in New Mexico. He had managed to stay alive as a free-state militiaman and so far in John Brown's army, but he realized the odds were overwhelming for this fight. He fell back to sleep from sheer exhaustion.

During the night, Dwight felt something pull on his face. Then there was pain. He reached up with his right hand and felt it being forced back down to his side. He opened his eyes to see a strange man attending to him as the woman he had talked to earlier watched from behind. "Who are you, sir?"

He didn't receive an answer immediately. He tried to move his right arm but realized it was pinned. Dwight tried to move his head in that direction and was stopped.

"Be still, man. Be still."

Dwight could see the man clearly now. He heard, "You there, woman, put some pressure there to stop some of the bleeding."

He felt pressure on his face as the woman moved over to apply it. The man spoke to someone who had been holding his right arm. "Let the arm be. Hand me that instrument."

He realized that the one holding his arm was the other woman he had seen sometime during the night.

"This one, doctor?"

"Yes."

She handed it to the doctor.

"Now you put some pressure right here." The doctor called to the older woman, "Fetch the basin. Keep it close."

Dwight realized a military doctor was attending to his wounds. The man wore a cavalry officer uniform. He then felt pain in his face.

"Don't move. I almost have it out."

Pain shot through his face and he then heard the sound of metal clanking in the tin basin that the woman was holding. The doctor spoke to her. "Press on that wound. I'm going for the other piece of buckshot. You, step away but keep the bandage ready."

Dwight continued to feel pain, but it was less intense. He heard another clank in the basin.

"That's both of them in the face. I'll wait until you dress both. Then I want you to turn him to his right side. Watch his left arm. I'll check that later."

He fell off into unconsciousness. Shortly later, he became conscious again. He felt the bandages on his face and neck. When his eyes cleared, the doctor was working on his left arm. He heard him say, "Lucky bastard. It missed the bone. He'll live to use it again. I'm ready for some bandages now." Dwight saw the doctor reach for the clean torn linens the older woman handed him.

Within minutes, Dwight's arm was cleaned and bandaged. A conversation went on between the two women and the doctor. Dwight could only make out a few words as the noise out on the street and from below the floor of his room fluctuated. He recognized that men were talking and moving about. His concentration on the noises was broken as the women removed the bandages on his chest. Some of them stuck painfully to the wounds. He noticed that they were beginning to bleed as the doctor prodded the wounds and wiped away the blood.

"Hand me that instrument. Yes, that one. They don't look too deep."

Once again, Dwight felt intense pain as the doctor prodded the first chest wound. He heard him remark "Stuck in between the ribs. Lucky. This one glanced off one." More intense pain followed until he heard another clink in the basin the older woman still held. More commotion could be heard outside and below the room. The doctor remarked, "What's all the noise about?"

Both women only responded by shrugging their shoulders.

Dwight felt more pain as the doctor probed the second wound in his chest. Several minutes later he had finished. Dwight felt nauseated and weak from the pain and probing the doctor had performed. The surgeon moved away, and Dwight could now see him clearly.

The doctor washed his hands in another basin as the younger woman poured water over his hands and wrists. "Keep pressure on the wounds, ladies. I've gotten all the lead out of him that I can see and feel. He could have one of two more pieces in him, but I couldn't feel them. We'll know in time. They'll either fester or lay dormant. It's too early to tell. He's lucky. If whoever shot him had been closer, he'd be out there in the street, dead."

The doctor opened the door to the room and asked the two guards, "What the hell is all the noise about?"

"Not sure, sir. All we could make out was that some marines had arrived."

He took out his pocket watch. The time was 5:15 a.m.

Chapter Twenty-Three

The Marine Assault

At 6:00 a.m., Lieutenant Colonel Robert E. Lee rose from the chair he had been resting in while awaiting daylight on the morning of October 18, 1859. He was still in the same civilian attire he had been wearing when he was summoned by the secretary of war less than twenty-four hours earlier. He checked his watch and looked to the eastern horizon.

A glimmer of light was peeking over the mountains. He had been hoping for more light at this time in the morning, but the overcast sky and continuous drizzle prohibited it. Lee walked to a vantage point where he could observe the entire area within the iron fence in front of the engine house.

He had ordered the local militia and government soldiers to take positions around it. The vicinity controlled by John Brown was surrounded by the troops Lee had organized as part of his plan. The sounds of the men forming that morning was relatively quiet. Only rattles from sabers, thumps of boots marching in unison, and an occasional command could be heard. It seemed quietly eerie once all of the militia was in position.

All who had assembled then heard the distinct march of the U.S. Marines as they turned the street corner and headed directly to the gate in front of the engine house. All who witnessed watched in amazement as the marines, in their striking uniforms, came to a smart halt in front of Lieutenant Colonel Lee. The blue frock coats and matching trousers with white belts stood out among the drab uniforms of the guards and militia.

Marine Lieutenant Israel Greene[1] came to attention and saluted Lee. "At your command, sir. My men are ready."

Lee returned the salute despite his civilian attire. "Thank you, Lieutenant. Stand ready."

Greene took his position next to Lieutenant Stuart, standing a few feet away from their commander.

---

[1] **Lieutenant Israel Greene** was born in New York, raised in Wisconsin, married in Virginia, and a marine for most of his life. He declined several appointments from both sides in the Civil War until he accepted a captaincy in the Confederate States Marine Corps based in Richmond. He was captured and paroled in 1865, and then left for the Dakota Territory (now South Dakota) where he lived until 1909.

Lee and his staff couldn't help but notice the continuous influx of citizens arriving from their homes to witness what was about to take place in their town. He sent orders to the guard and militia commanders to post the necessary sentries to keep the civilians a safe distance from the hostilities he hoped would not start. Lieutenant Colonel Lee requested that Colonel Shriver of the Maryland volunteers join him with his staff.

When the colonel arrived, Lee addressed him. "Sir, you being the commanding officer of the Maryland volunteers and me believing that this situation is a state matter, I am offering you the opportunity and honor of opening up the attack."

U.S. Marine Lieutenant Israel Green
In his Confederate Marine Uniform during the Civil War.
The rank insignia is of a major in the Confederate Army and Marine Corps.
(Marine Corps Art Collection at the U.S. Naval Institute)

Colonel Shriver looked at Lieutenant Colonel Lee and pondered his offer for several moments before he answered. "Lieutenant Colonel Lee, I am personally honored that you have given my volunteers the privilege of the attack, but I respectfully decline for their sake." Shriver cleared his throat, and Lee waited for the colonel to continue. ***"These men of mine have wives and children at home. I will not expose them to such risks. You are paid for doing this kind of work."*** Shriver bowed out but told Lee, "Sir, I will summon Colonel Baylor, the ranking officer of the Virginia militia, for you." He saluted Lee and left.

Lieutenant Stuart approached Lee and whispered, "Sir, no one has the stomach to engage."

Lee put his hand up next to his ear to indicate he did not want to hear anymore. Colonel Baylor of the Virginia militia approached and saluted. Lee returned the salute and said, "Colonel Baylor, I have stated to Colonel Shriver that this incident is a state matter. I offered him the privilege to lead the attack, but he declined. I am offering the same privilege to the Virginia militia."

"Lieutenant Colonel Lee, I will decline as Colonel Shriver has done. ***I defer the attack to the marines. They are the mercenaries."***

Lee looked at Lieutenant Stuart. Stuart looked back, expressionless. Both men seemed to know what the other was thinking. Lee turned to Marine Lieutenant Greene and said, "Lieutenant Greene, form a storming party of twelve marines. Supply three sledgehammers to the storming party to beat down the door. I want another dozen in reserve."

"Yes, sir."

The young lieutenant turned and barked the names of the specific marines he wanted in the initial storming party. He paused and named the reserve group next. He yelled over to one of the corporals who had not been called to either party to commandeer three sledgehammers. Within minutes, Greene's men were formed in front of Lee and Stuart.

Lee walked to the assembled men and slowly and patiently told the men what he expected of them during the assault. The gentleness and confidence this man radiated in battle would be experienced by countless men many times over in the years to come. "I want you to assault using only your bayonets in order to avoid wounding or killing any of the hostages. Is that understood?" Lee looked around to assure that everyone did. The two groups of twelve nodded almost in unison. "You should be able to recognize the insurrectionists. The hostages should be grouped together with minimal guards around them. Do not bother with the Negros unless they become hostile." He looked around again to assure himself everyone understood his orders.

He then turned to Lieutenant Stuart. "Lieutenant Stuart, you shall approach under a flag of truce. Instruct their leader that I offer a peaceful solution to this matter. Do not negotiate, but be prepared to wait for a written response to carry back to me. If he is uncooperative and will not negotiate, signal to me by raising your hat and waving it."

Stuart smiled. "Yes, sir."

Lee looked at his pocket watch. It was 7:15 a.m.

Stuart smartly saluted, turned, and began his walk to the engine house, carrying a white flag of truce. His spurs jingled and the plume in his hat sagged from the continuous drizzle. Despite the conditions, Stuart looked sharp as all the U.S. Marines did.

It must have been noted by the remaining raiders in the Engine House that although this was the third time a flag of truce was shown, it was the first time that it was honored. Stuart yelled as he approached the heavy oak door, "I request a *parley* with the leader of the raiders!"

The door slowly opened, and Stuart saw a tall old man appearing before him. He knew of him from his days on duty in Kansas and confirmed that it was John Brown. He now knew who was in charge. Brown stood in such a manner that Stuart could not see inside past him. He told him Lee's surrender demands. Brown listened carefully, and when Stuart finished, he shook his head and began to argue.

Stuart remained still as John Brown explained, demanded, vented his temper, and finally refused to surrender to the government troops. Lieutenant Stuart had heard enough from Brown after several minutes. He turned toward where he knew Lee would be observing and nonchalantly removed his cavalry hat and raised it above his head. Lieutenant Stuart did not say any more to John Brown, but turned and walked toward the marines forming for the attack.

Brown watched for several moments as Stuart left, and he saw the marines begin to approach. He closed and boarded the thick door, then gave orders to his men to prepare for an assault. The raiders awaited their fate and the hostages huddled together.

Dwight was awake now after sleeping for several hours since the surgeon had removed the lead shot from his body. His wounds ached but were considerably less painful since receiving the physician's care. The older woman had apparently departed, but the younger one still sat looking out the window of the room. He called out to her, "What is happening?"

She startled when she heard his question.

"I'm sorry, miss, I have startled you."

"It's all right. I was watching to see when the marines were going to storm the Armory."

"Marines? We have marines here?"

"Yes, they came last night."

Dwight did not respond as he wondered what Kagi and Brown would do. He figured nothing had occurred since there had been no gunfire. He made an attempt to sit up, but his strength failed him.

The young woman spoke as he lay back down. "Your wounds will open up again. You must be still."

"Can you assist me to get up? I need to see."

"I'm sorry. You would not have the strength to get up, much less walk to the window. Your wounds will open up, and I will be blamed for the bleeding."

"I will not hold you accountable, young lady."

"Guards. Guards, please come in."

Storming of the Engine House *Harper's Weekly,* November 5, 1859.
West Virginia State Archives

Within moments two cavalrymen entered. She addressed the first. "Explain to this prisoner that he may not attempt to rise from his bed and look out the window."

The two cavalrymen just looked at Dwight, who lay motionless with an irritated look on his face. The senior man, a corporal, spoke to her. "I will stay inside the room to make sure he ain't movin' from the bed. My private here will stay just outside of the room's door." He motioned to the private to leave.

Dwight lay there wondering when he would hear shots being fired, knowing that for every shot, one of his men could be on the receiving end. It was not long before he heard the noise of the crowd coming from the street. He looked at the corporal, who was looking out the window with the young woman. "Can you tell me what's happening?"

The corporal looked back at him. "They are preparing to charge the Armory. It will be over soon."

But there were no shots. The crowd grew louder. The several minutes that followed seemed like an eternity for Dwight as he lay in the bed. Then he heard a shot, then several more. He recognized the sounds of the Sharps rifles being fired. He knew Kagi must have been putting up a fight. He watched for a reaction on the corporal's face to give him some idea of what was occurring, but his expression didn't reveal anything. The young woman only held her hand across her mouth as she watched.

More firing was heard but not as concentrated as Dwight thought it should be. As quickly as it had started, it was over. There were no more shots. The two watchers didn't react at first after the firing stopped. Dwight waited anxiously for an account of what had taken place.

The corporal finally turned from the window. "That didn't take long. Three or four minutes, I reckon." He moved back to his position in the corner of the room.

"They're bringing them out," the young woman said.

The corporal moved back to the window to look again. "Yep, by the looks of it, they killed quite a few. Looks like a dead marine as well. These men will hang for sure, now that a federal soldier has been killed."

Dwight felt helpless as he listened carefully to the corporal. The noise from the crowd had lessened, but he could hear cheering at times.

"They're bringin' out the hostages now. They look to be all right," the young woman remarked.

The marines had successfully charged the engine house, smashing in part of the large door to let their men through to enter the building. One marine lost his life in the initial entry, but they soon overcame the small army within.

Unknown to Dwight, John Brown had been knocked unconscious and was bleeding profusely as he was dragged and laid out in the yard in front of the building's entrance. Dauphin Thompson and Jeremiah Anderson lay dead from bayonet wounds. They were also dragged into the street and laid out for all to see.

Watson Brown lay unconscious and was moved from the Engine House and laid next to his father. Watson would die later that day. The marines continued to remove bodies. Oliver Brown came next, followed by Stewart Taylor. They were also exhibited. Edwin Coppoc and Shields Green were the only two men, one white and one black, who survived the U.S. Marines attack, aside from John Brown. They were led out under guard. Private Luke Quinn[1], the lone marine killed in the attack, was carried away by several of his fellow marines.

Dwight could hear the crowd cheer again. He wondered why, but didn't ask the corporal or the young woman. He didn't have to after he heard the young woman say, "There's Colonel Washington. They saved him. He doesn't look harmed."

Dwight's heart sank. He knew for sure that the raid had failed. He pictured all the men he had known and trained in the past years. He lay in pain as all his emotions pulled him in different directions. The woman closed the window and returned to his bedside, then bent over him and checked his bandages. "Good, you haven't bled any more. I'm going to get some broth. Do you think you can eat anything?"

Memorial to Quinn
Photographed at Harper's Ferry by Tommy Coletti

Dwight never responded, and closed his eyes as if going off to sleep.

"Let him starve, lady. He's going to hang soon enough, if he don't die

---

[1] **Private Luke Quinn** was the only U.S. Marine killed in the Harper's Ferry Raid. Private Quinn was fatally shot in the abdomen as he stormed the Engine House at the command of Lieutenant Colonel Robert E. Lee. Quinn was an Irish immigrant who had joined the marines in 1855. In October 2011, a monument was erected in his honor near the site of his death in Harper's Ferry.

first. Let 'im be," the corporal remarked as he took his position next to the door.

The young woman waved her hand for him to be silent. "I'll go downstairs and will return soon."

Dwight opened his eyes and only nodded to acknowledge her persistence. It was something his sister would have said and done. He appreciated that in the woman and resolved to be respectful to her kindness. He was nearly overcome as the pain in his chest and face persisted. He knew he could do nothing but either wait to die, or begin to heal and face whatever charges would be brought against him. Dwight fell off to sleep from sheer exhaustion and distress.

Bringing prisoners out, *Leslie's,* November 5, 1859.
West Virginia State Archives

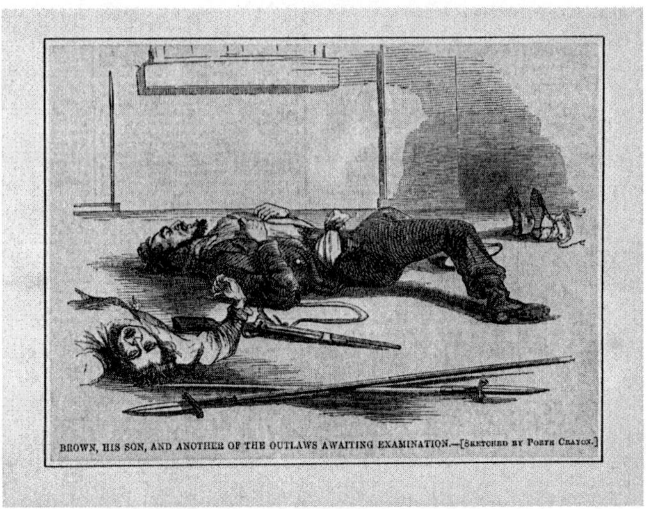

Brown and son awaiting examination
Harper's Weekly, November 5, 1859
West Virginia State Archives

Dwight was awakened by the young woman, who returned with a small bowl of chicken broth. "Sip this slowly. It is not too hot. You need some nourishment, so eat as much as you can."

He smiled at his caretaker and obliged. He sipped it and swallowed. The slightly salted liquid soothed his parched mouth and throat. He managed to take a second sip slightly larger than the first.

"That's good. Sip some more. You need nourishment."

As he sipped and swallowed, Dwight heard approaching footsteps coming down the hall to his room. It was quiet for a few seconds until the outside guard opened the door and two marines entered. The sight of their uniforms impressed him. He remembered seeing his first marine onboard ship on his way to the Mexican War. Both men stood at attention as a marine officer entered and spoke. "Aaron Dwight Stevens?"

Dwight nodded in acknowledgement.

"I am Lieutenant Israel Greene, United States Marines. By order of Lieutenant Colonel Robert E. Lee, commanding, you are under arrest for treason. You are to be removed from this establishment and confined at a temporary prison until formal charges can be placed against you. Do you understand me, sir?"

"Yes, I do."

Greene ordered the two marines to pick Dwight up, but the young woman stopped them.

"Lieutenant Greene, this man is unable to walk."

"He will be assisted by my men."

"He needs a litter, sir. His wounds could open again. He has lost a lot of blood already. Check with the surgeon who treated him. He can verify his condition."

Greene barked orders. "Get a litter made quickly! I do not have time to consult the surgeon!"

Both marines disappeared as Greene walked out of the room. He stayed outside with the cavalryman.

"Finish the broth. Do it quickly if you can." She steadied the bowl as he sipped it. The marines returned several minutes later. They carried the litter into the room and laid it parallel to his bed. One marine took his shoulders, the other the waist, and one of the cavalrymen took his feet.

Lieutenant Greene ordered, "On my command, lift him. One, two, three, lift."

Dwight moaned as the pressure to his chest increased and his body sagged from being lifted. His neck hurt as his head fell backward, unsupported. Quickly he found himself on the litter. The young woman threw a blanket over him.

The marine Lieutenant ordered, "Take him to the paymaster's office in the watch house as ordered."

Dwight watched the ceiling of the room and then that of the hallway pass as the marines carried him on the litter. His descent on the stairs afforded him a good look at the many people watching him as he was being carried out of the Wager Hotel.

About halfway down the stairs someone cried out, "You'll hang soon enough, traitor."

Cheers arose from the remark. Dwight ignored all of it.

Within moments the marines had taken him out of the hotel. Lieutenant Greene followed with his ceremonial sword drawn as the two marines carried Dwight. To ensure protection, the two cavalrymen originally assigned to guard Dwight followed the marine Lieutenant. Dwight felt the coolness of the light rain on his face. The sky was overcast, with light and dark gray clouds mixed together. He never heard any more yelling as the men made their way to the paymaster's office in the watch house. Dwight remained conscious until he reached the entranceway. The pain from his wounds was overwhelming. He slid off into unconsciousness as they set the litter down on the wood floor. It would be several more hours until he awoke.

The smell of damp wool and linen was prevalent. Dwight slowly turned his head to see people walking past the office door, gazing in at him. Few people said anything, and if they did it was inaudible whispers. He quickly realized he was on display. Disgusted, he turned his head in the opposite direction and saw that John Brown was lying next to him. He too was covered with soiled and damp wool blankets, but did not have the luxury of a litter to lie on. Brown lay on the cold wood floor with no bedding. Dwight could see that he had not received any medical treatment for the bruises and cuts on his face, neck, and head. The blood had dried. But Brown was still alive going by the slow expansion of his chest under the blankets.

Spectators filed past the open door. They had come to stare, point, and comment on the two men. He heard John Brown's voice. "You have survived, my son. I am pleased that the Lord has spared you."

Dwight could not respond at first. He composed himself before answering. "Captain, your wounds…? Are you…?"

Brown interrupted, "I have been spared by the Almighty. I have no bullet wounds, only cuts and bruises from the officer who tried to kill me with his sword. I lost consciousness during the conflict. I do not know the status of the men." Brown winced as he tried to move onto his side toward Dwight. Some less courageous people scurried past quicker because of Brown's movement.

Before either could talk further, Lieutenant Colonel Lee, Colonel Lewis Washington, and Lieutenant Stuart led in a group of men to the office.

Dwight could see by their dress coats and hats that these men were of some importance. Conversations and pointing motions were observed until a man knelt down next to John Brown and spoke. ***"Mister Brown, as you might remember I am Lieutenant Colonel Lee. I am personally responsible for your detention, but also for your welfare. I can order anyone from this room if they cause you any suffering or annoyance."***

Dwight observed some color return to Brown's face after hearing Lee's kind words. ***"I am very glad to make myself and my motives clearly understood."***

As Dwight lay beside Brown, he could hear the talking his captain was engaged in. As men talked with John Brown, Dwight heard the names of Governor Wise, Senator Mason, Representative Charles Faulkner[1], all

---

[1] **Charles J. Faulkner** was elected to the United States House of Representatives, for Virginia, serving from 1851 to 1859. He was appointed by President James Buchanan as minister to France in 1860, serving until he was arrested in August 1861, on charges of negotiating sales of arms for the Confederacy while in Paris, France. Faulkner was released in December, after negotiating his own exchange. Afterward, he enlisted in the Confederate army and was assistant adjutant general on the staff of General Thomas J. "Stonewall" Jackson.

from Virginia, and Representative C. L. Vallandigham of Ohio[1], while he also observed several reporters scribbling notes.

Reporters and Congressional delegation waiting to question John Brown
West Virginia State Archives

Dwight fell into and out of consciousness as Brown, his face and beard still covered in dried blood, spoke in heated conversation on why he had initiated his raid on Harper's Ferry. It seemed to go on for hours, as the men were relentless with their questions and arguments. Lieutenant Colonel Lee stayed for some of the questioning, but periodically would leave to check on the other prisoners he had under guard. After several

---

1 **Clement Vallandigham** was an Ohio Copperhead anti-war Democrat during the Civil War, and served two terms in the U. S. House of Representatives. He "publicly" denounced the "wicked and cruel" war by which "King Lincoln" was "crushing out liberty." He was arrested and tried by a military court and convicted of "uttering disloyal sentiments" and attempting to hinder the prosecution of the war. He was sentenced to two years' confinement in a military prison. Lincoln, not wanting to make him a martyr to the Copperheads, ordered him sent to the Confederacy and he was taken under guard to Tennessee. He then went by blockade runner to Bermuda and then to Canada, where he declared himself a candidate for Governor of Ohio, subsequently winning the Democratic nomination. He lost the 1863 election for Ohio governor in a landslide to pro-Union war democrat John Brough. He died in 1871 at the age of 50, after accidentally shooting himself with a pistol. He was representing a client in a murder case for killing a man in a bar room brawl when he attempted to prove the victim had in fact killed himself while trying to draw his pistol from a pocket when rising from a kneeling position. Grabbing a pistol he believed to be unloaded, he put it in his pocket and enacted the events as they might have happened, shooting himself in the process. Vallandigham proved his point, and the defendant, Thomas McGehan, was acquitted.

hours, Lee stopped the questioning so that water and food could be given to the two prisoners.

Brown thanked Lee as if he had been a gracious host at an evening social. The congressional delegation seemed irritated that Brown and his subordinate were being treated so well by Lee. Lee allowed the questioning again about an hour later. Eventually, he brought in a military surgeon from the Virginia militia to check both prisoners' wounds. The surgeon requested that he be given some help to clean both men. Lee found some of the women who had volunteered with the first casualties of the raid to assist the surgeon in their clean-up. The congressional delegates left as the process began. They would return later in the evening with the reporters to continue their questioning.

A woman volunteer removed Dwight's bandages so the surgeon could evaluate what the first physician had done. Dwight appreciated the gentle touch the woman exhibited as she removed his face and neck bandages.

The surgeon remarked, "Wash the dried blood away from the wounds. The bleeding has definitely stopped, and there is good color. I don't think there is any more lead in his face. We'll need to keep watching for any swelling, and signs of infection."

"Is Dwight doing well, Doctor?" Brown asked with great concern in his tone and facial expressions.

"Yes sir, considering the wounds that were inflicted and the amount of time that it took him to get proper medical care."

"Then you feel he will survive this ordeal?"

"I'm not sure. He is very weak and has lost a lot of blood. He needs to be cleaned up, and needs many weeks of complete rest."

Brown graciously nodded and said, "Thank you, Doctor, I understand." Brown lay back on the cold floor and stared at the ceiling.

The surgeon looked at Dwight's chest wounds and then his arm. He instructed the woman to clean and dress those wounds like she had his face and neck. The surgeon called to one of the guards stationed outside the paymaster's office door. "Tell one of your officers to find two beds with mattresses and linens, and deliver them here."

The guard quickly responded and left.

John Brown spoke softly to the surgeon. "May God bless you, sir, for your compassion."

"There is no need to thank me, sir. It is my duty to treat all my patients as well as I am able. Now, sir, I would like to examine your wounds."

Brown nodded and with great effort pushed himself up into a sitting position. He removed his outer garments so the surgeon could treat him. Dwight heard the comments the surgeon made to Brown as he examined him. "You have blunt wounds to your neck, left shoulder, and rib cage." Brown winced as the surgeon touched and prodded the areas.

"I believe you have some cracked ribs. We will wrap them to give you some relief from the pain." He called to the woman who was finishing with Dwight. "Find some more bed linens, and cut them into strips. We need to clean and wrap this man's chest."

As he finished his instructions, several marines arrived carrying parts of iron beds with two mattresses. The surgeon instructed where he wanted both beds to be placed. Several minutes elapsed as Dwight heard the noises of the marines assembling them.

"Where did you get them from so quickly?" the surgeon asked.

"Lieutenant Stuart commandeered them for Lieutenant Greene from the Wager Hotel," one marine responded.

Dwight heard the surgeon command the men to gently remove him from the stretcher. He opened his eyes to see four men lift him off the stretcher and place him on the single iron bed. The pain he endured in his chest came and went quickly as the four marines completed their task. The woman who had dressed his wounds offered water. He obliged her, but soon fell asleep.

The two prisoners were left alone for several hours until the congressional delegation and reporters returned to resume their intense questioning. Dwight was awakened by the talking near Brown's bed. At times, he could distinguish Brown's voice arguing. As Dwight's head cleared from the deep sleep, he heard a question from Senator Mason. ***"Who supplied you with the money to undertake this raid?"***

Brown was taken aback for a moment, hearing the pointed question. ***"I raised much of the money myself."***

There was silence for a few moments. A newspaperman took advantage of it and asked, "Mr. Brown, why did you stay so long?"

Senator Mason seemed irritated that the newspaperman had cut into his interrogation and asked the question again. "I want to know who supplied you with some of the money then."

Brown spoke but responded to the newspaperman, ignoring the senator. ***"I should have gone away but I had thirty-odd prisoners, whose wives and daughters were in tears for their safety, and I felt for them. Besides, I wanted to allay the fears of those who believed we came here to burn and kill. For this reason I allowed the train to cross the bridge and gave them full liberty to pass on."***

Dwight thought completely different to himself as he heard Brown's explanation. *If he had listened to me or John, we could have been in the mountains a long time ago, planning our next raid to free slaves.* He realized that he had not heard anything about John Kagi, or any of the others for that matter. He resolved to ask Brown, or even his captors, to find out what had happened to each man as Senator Mason responded to Brown's previous statement. ***"But you killed some people passing along the streets quietly."***

Brown paused and then stated, ***"Well sir, if there was anything of that kind done, it was without my knowledge. Your own citizens, who were my prisoners, will tell you that all possible means were taken to prevent it. I did not allow my men to fire, nor even to return fire, when there was danger of killing those we regarded as innocent persons, if I could help it. They will tell you that we allowed ourselves to be fired at repeatedly and did not return it."***

Dwight fumed inside. He wanted to tell Brown that he should have returned fire quickly and often to frighten them and show how deadly accurate the Sharps rifles were. He refrained, realizing that even if they had cut down numerous amounts of militia, it wouldn't have changed the fact the slaves never came.

The senator asked Brown, ***"What was your object in coming?"***

"We came to free the slaves, and only that."

"How do you justify your acts?"

Brown looked over at Dwight, who looked to be asleep, before he answered, looking straight at the senator and then glancing around to all that were listening, ***"I think, my friend, you are guilty of a great wrong against God and humanity – I say without wishing to be offensive – and it would be perfectly right in anyone to interfere with you so far as to free those willfully and wickedly held in bondage. I do not say this insultingly."***

Senator Mason responded, "I take no personal insult in what you have said."

Brown continued, ***"I think I did right and that others will do right to interfere with you at any time and all times. I hold that the Golden Rule, 'Do unto others as you would that others should do unto you,' applies to all who would help others to gain their liberty."***

One of the newspapermen asked, "Is your movement a religious one?"

"It is, in my opinion the greatest service a man can render to God."

"Do you consider yourself an instrument in the hands of providence?"

"I do."

Dwight could not lay there any more with his eyes closed.

Brown thought he had just come to. "You have awakened, my son.

I hope your pain has lessened."

Dwight attempted a smile, but his face still hurt.

Several of those in the room only glanced at Brown's subordinate before they turned back to Brown. "Upon what principle do you justify your acts?"

"Upon the Golden Rule. I pity the poor in bondage that have none to help them; that is why I am here, not to gratify any personal animosity, revenge or vindictive spirit. It is my sympathy with the oppressed and the wronged that are as good as you and as precious in the sight of God."

Dwight looked at the faces of the men who were listening. There was no indication that they had the slightest form of agreement.

One of the congressmen Dwight could not see spoke from behind the senator. "So you have no belief that the South could end slavery?"

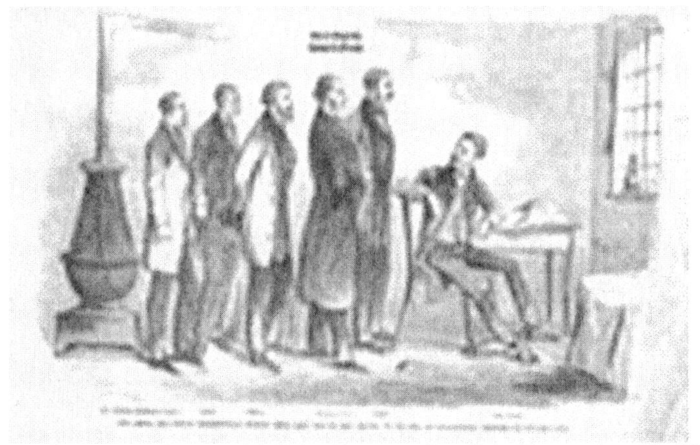

News Correspondents with John Brown, *Leslie's*, December 10, 1859.
West Virginia State Archives

Brown paused and looked at Dwight, who stared at him, waiting for a response. ***"I don't think the people of the slave states will ever consider the subject of slavery in its true light until some other argument is resorted to than normal suasion."***

Dwight looked at the men who had just heard Brown's statement. There was a look of concern on a few of their faces.

Congressman Vallandigham from Ohio asked, "Did you expect to hold Harper's Ferry for any considerable time?"

Brown looked toward Dwight as his lieutenant shook his head ever so slowly. ***"I do not know whether I ought to reveal my plans. I am here a prisoner and wounded, because I foolishly allowed myself to do so. You overrate your strength in supposing I could have been***

taken if I had not allowed it. I was too tardy after commencing the open attack – in delaying my movements through Sunday night, and up to that time I was attacked by the government troops. It was all occasioned by my desire to spare the feelings of my prisoners and their families and the community at large."

Dwight wanted to yell at his captain for confessing, at last, why he had not taken the advice of Kagi and him during the entire raid. Dwight managed to raise his head enough to let Brown notice that he had reacted to that statement.

The other newspaperman, who identified himself as being from the *New York Herald*, asked Brown, ***"I do not wish to annoy you but if you have anything further you would like to say, I will print it."***

To that statement Brown replied, ***"I have nothing to say, only that I will claim to be here in carrying out a measure I believe to be perfectly justifiable and not to act the part of an incendiary or ruffian, but to aid those suffering great wrong….You had better – all you people of the South – prepare yourselves for a settlement sooner than you are prepared for it. The sooner you are prepared the better. You may dispose of me very easily; I am nearly disposed now, but this question is still to be settled – this Negro question I mean. The end of that is not yet."***

The Governor of Virginia smirked, then remarked, ***"Mister Brown, you should now begin to think about eternity."***

Brown looked into his eyes and said, ***"Sir, we both here before you are prepared for it. We thought about that preparation before we came here."*** Brown looked at Dwight and smiled.

Dwight did not respond. He closed his eyes and wondered if Kagi and the others had made the journey already.

When Dwight awoke again, the government officials and reporters were gone. The room was dim, and he realized evening was quickly approaching. A lamp near Brown's bed was lit. Dwight focused his eyes to see his captain sitting up and reading in bed. He saw that Brown had managed to hold onto his old Bible.

The captain looked over at him when he saw movement coming from the bed. "You are awake. I hope you have been able to regain some of your strength."

Dwight attempted to answer him, but he choked when trying to speak. The movement was painful in his chest. He forced himself to stop coughing and eventually replied, "Could you get me some water? I am parched."

Brown slowly but steadily got out of bed and walked to Dwight's bedside. He poured some water into a tin cup and handed it to him. He watched as Dwight sipped the water.

"I will call the guard and ask him to send food for you."

"Just liquids. I cannot chew very well right now."

Brown nodded, smiled, and called for the guard. He explained what he needed. Dwight heard that it would be several minutes before anything would be supplied. When Dwight motioned that he had sipped enough water, Brown set the cup down and went back toward his bed.

He had begun to read scripture again when Dwight asked, "Have you heard any news of the men, Captain?"

Brown looked over, was silent for several moments, and then responded sadly, "Yes, my son, I have. We will talk about them later. Once you have regained your strength."

Dwight painfully shook his head and coughed a few more times. "Captain, what has happened to them?"

"You are weak. We will talk of this later."

"Captain, please."

Brown looked at his young lieutenant. "I have been informed from Lieutenant Colonel Lee that Watson has succumbed to his wounds. Oliver died shortly after you were shot. I do not know where Owen has gone. I have not said anything to Lee that he was with us. The Thompson brothers have been killed as well."

Dwight's stomach turned after hearing the fate of Brown's sons, and of the others. He found enough strength to turn partially on his side and asked, "And the others? Kagi, Cook, Hazlett? What has happened to them?"

Brown turned away from his young companion. Whether he was too upset to look at Dwight or felt guilty for their fate, Dwight didn't know. Brown continued, and said in a voice that wavered, "John Kagi has died. Lieutenant Colonel Lee stated that he has sent troops to look for John Cook. I do not know if that applies to Albert Hazlett, because I did not mention his name."

Dwight felt tears roll down his exposed cheek at the news of his best friend. "The others?"

Brown spoke slowly, with his eyes turned away from Dwight. "The whereabouts of one of the Coppoc brothers is unknown to me."

"Which one?"

"Barclay. I have been informed that Edwin is in custody of the government troops. Shields Green is with him. Lewis Leary, Dangerfield Newby, Stewart Taylor, and William Leeman are all dead. No one knows of Francis Merriam and Charles Tidd, and I do not know their fate. Jeremiah Andersen was killed. I do not know of Osborne Anderson's fate, nor have I asked, in case he has also escaped."

Dwight thought to express his condolences to Brown for the death of his sons, but no words came to mind. He did not speak any further with John Brown until the next day.

Early the next morning, Lieutenant Colonel Lee entered their room with Lieutenant Greene and four U. S. marines.

Brown looked up from his bed as the men entered. "You have come to take us, but where?"

Lieutenant Colonel Lee overlooked Brown's question and spoke directly to Lieutenant Greene. "I want two men to carry Stevens carefully on his mattress. Do the same for Mr. Brown."

"Yes, sir," was Greene's response.

Lee turned to Brown in a delayed response to his question. "Mr. Brown, I feel that your safety could be compromised here in Harper's Ferry. It would be in your best interest for you and your men to be transported to Charlestown. You will be taken by rail coach along with other members of your group immediately."

Bringing Brown and Stevens to the Railroad Station
West Virginia State Archives

Within a few minutes, both prisoners were loaded into a wagon waiting outside. The marines encircled the wagon and then marched with it as it was driven to the railroad coach that had been commandeered to carry Brown and his men to Charlestown. Spectators lined the street to see the event unfold. Dwight observed some of the dignitaries that had questioned Brown following their wagon, protected by the marines. He also saw Copeland, Coppoc, and Shields Green for the first time since before he had been shot. "Captain, there are only three that are still with us."

Brown never replied as several men watching the wagons approach the rail line yelled out, "Lynch them! Lynch them!"

The marines were ordered to keep the spectators at a distance from the prisoners. As the marines moved toward the crowds, they quickly retreated and dispersed. There were no more incidents as the train began to move toward Charlestown.

Chapter Twenty-Four

Jail

The train ride to Charlestown was uneventful. No words were exchanged among any of the prisoners. Dwight chose to close his eyes and listen to the train moving slowly along on its route. The sound of the wheels was almost hypnotic as they clanked on the steel rails.

For a few minutes, he thought of his youthful days when he had hid onboard a train seeking adventure in 1847. He remembered how scared yet excited he'd felt when he left Greenville, Connecticut, to join the Massachusetts Volunteers on that cold night. There was no comparing that to this train ride. He was almost twice that age now, wounded, doubting he would even make a full recovery from his wounds, and unsure of his fate with the courts, if he did recover. He dozed in and out of sleep.

When the train finally stopped, the marines escorted the prisoners out of the coach and into the Charlestown jail. Dwight was carried on his mattress by orders from Lieutenant Colonel Lee. He was surprised at how small the jail building was, but more surprised that a contingent of militia stood guard on each side of the entranceway.

A man that looked to be the jailer held the door open as Dwight was carried in. He heard the man say, "Put him and the mattress on the bed in the corner of the cell. Put the older man with him. He can use the cot that is already there."

Dwight was gently placed there, as ordered, and then Brown was escorted in. Within minutes Brown and Dwight were by themselves , with the exception of the jailer, who briefly watched them through the iron bars before he spoke. "Gentlemen, you have been placed in the Charlestown jail. I am John Avis, jailer and deputy sheriff for this city. I am also a captain in the militia. Governor Wise has ordered that you remain here until further notice. He has also decreed that half of the county's militia guard this jail, the city courthouse, and their entrances, to ensure that you remain here under arrest."

John Avis
The Good Jailer
West Virginia State Archives

Dwight did not respond to the information Avis had just given, but did react with a small request. "Sir, could you be so kind as to fetch some water?"

"By all means, son. I'll bring it to you right away." Avis looked at Brown, who just nodded to indicate that he was thirsty as well. Within a minute's time, Avis handed Brown a pitcher of water.

The old man helped Dwight to drink. Exhausted from the trip from Harper's Ferry to the Charlestown jail, Dwight then closed his eyes.

"The boy looks like he is at death's door," the jailer said.

"Yes, he has some serious wounds. Wounds like that would have killed most men. Dwight is strong, and with the help of the Almighty, he'll recovery quickly," Brown replied.

Avis shook his head in a doubting manner. "I don't know. I've seen men in better shape than him die from their wounds."

Brown ignored Avis's remark and pulled out his Bible and began to read. Avis turned away but stopped when he heard, "I'm not dead yet, Mr. Avis."

"No offense intended, young man."

"No offense taken, sir."

"Well, in that case, Mr. Stevens, if you are up to it, I'll ask the missus to bring over some of her beef stew with dumplings. It's mighty tasty, if I say so myself. It will help you regain some strength."

Dwight made a weak attempt to smile, despite that fact that his facial bandages were still on.

The jailer looked at the young man with real concern. "I'll also ask Dr. Kent to stop by and change your bandages." Avis looked at Brown and said, "You too, Mr. Brown. I'll get a washbasin with water and some soap and washcloths."

As the man left the jail cell, Brown acknowledged his personal kindness. It wasn't long before John Brown had cleaned his face and attempted to get some of the dried blood from his white beard. Dwight had to wait several more hours before Dr. Kent, who was not happy that he had been summoned to care for these particular prisoners, arrived.

When the Charlestown physician entered the cell, the attitude he displayed talking with Avis in his office changed when he saw Dwight's condition. "Son, I'm going to look at your wounds and change these soiled bandages."

Dwight never responded, but just lay there thinking about how he must have looked to the doctor.

Dr. Kent removed the facial bandages and said, "This will burn and hurt a little, son, but I feel these wounds might heal more quickly if just a little cleansing can be done." He went about his task, watching Dwight's reactions as he cleaned the wounds. When he had finished, he said, "Son, I'm leaving the facial bandage off. You'll be better off without it. You will be scarred, but maybe a beard will cover them, if you decide to grow one." He then began to work on the neck bandages. He discovered the condition to be the same and again left the bandages off. The chest and arm wounds were cleansed and bandaged. When he finished, he called out to Mr. Avis, "After he has rested a while, bring in the food you have. See to it that he eats as much as he can. Whatever you do, get food into him."

The deputy sheriff only nodded.

John Brown had eaten his meal and continued to watch Dr. Kent finish treating his young subordinate. "Thank you, Doctor. It's good to see the handsome face of this young man again. The Lord has been merciful to him. His good looks will remain."

Dr. Kent looked at Brown. "Well, he is certainly not out of danger, and he needs nourishment to regain his strength. Encourage him to eat when he has the ability to do so."

Brown nodded and prepared for the physician to examine him. Within the hour, Kent had left. Brown then assisted Dwight in eating the stew Mrs. Avis had prepared for them. Dwight ate most of the broth with Brown's encouragement, despite his inability to chew the meat. He then fell off to sleep feeling a little better but completely exhausted.

Both men managed to sleep through the night, despite the constant noise of militia marching up and down the street in front of the jailhouse. Militia guards were changed every four hours and positioned inside the jail per order of the Virginia governor. They had been assigned to Deputy Sheriff Avis, whether he wanted them or not.

For the next several days, more reporters and officials questioned John Brown. Their questions were often repeated, and Brown's disposition became strained. Mr. Avis recognized that Stevens needed more quiet to sleep and recover, so he limited the questioning to several hours a day to allow more privacy for the prisoners.

The limited hours wrought havoc on the deputy sheriff, who was immediately identified as a raider sympathizer by the Southern press and Virginia government officials. To most people in Charlestown, however, Mr. Avis was known as a good man and a law-abiding citizen who used good judgment when doing his job.

Several days passed before Dwight awoke early one morning and, with great difficulty, sat up on his own. He pushed himself around and up on his mattress. For the first time, he put his bare feet on the cold stone floor.

Brown, who had been reading his Bible, looked over and watched him get into that position. "Good morning, my son. You look a bit better. It looks to me that you are attempting to stand on your own? Should you be doing that?"

"Captain, I need to relieve myself. Is there a chamber pot in here?"

The need was taken care of, which was a positive sign that Dwight was slowly recovering.

After the event, Dwight remained alert and asked Brown questions. "Is there news of any of the men we have not accounted for?"

Brown slowly shook his head.

"Is there any communication with our backers?"

Again Brown shook his head, but he then spoke. "Jailer Avis has informed me that the nation's newspapers are rampant with our story. Mostly negative in the major Southern papers, and he states that the townspeople are irritated by what the Northern papers are saying about our raid. They have quoted me verbatim in some papers, according to him. He has promised to provide us with those articles when he can."

"Do they list the names of the good men we lost during the raid?"

"They have listed my sons."

"Are there any others?"

"John Kagi has been mentioned."

"There were twenty-two of us, Captain."

"I know, Dwight. Let us allow Mr. Avis a little time to gather and give us what has been written."

Dwight looked at Brown and thought, *You read them, old man. I do not have the stomach to read about the men I trained, marched, fought with, and then lost on account of indecision and poor leadership.* He didn't respond with what he was thinking. He still had respect for the captain, and he realized that he, too, was at fault with the leadership. He should have demanded withdrawal as soon as he and Kagi had realized the slave revolt was not happening and that the militia was arriving in town. He did respond after several moments. "Captain, I am tired now. I need to rest for a spell. We can talk about the men later."

Brown suspected that Dwight had more to say. "Yes, we shall discuss what went wrong. I have thought about nothing else."

It wasn't long before the exhausted lieutenant was back in a deep sleep.

Jailer Avis remained true to his promise to obtain more newspaper articles on the Harper's Ferry raid. Brown read every word that was supplied to him, while Dwight slept most of the day.

That evening, Dwight was awake long enough to eat a small amount of his meal and ask for a few details of what Brown was busy reading.

Brown gave him the news. "It says here that the governor's son is asking for the Virginia militia commander to be investigated for cowardice. Another article indicates that the Virginia governor has authorized several companies to remain in Charlestown to guard you, me, and some of the men."

"That many men are needed to make sure we cannot escape from their prison?"

Brown laughed when he heard Dwight's response. "It's more than that, Dwight. I think the Virginia governor needs to guarantee several things. One is to keep people who hate us from lynching us as quickly as possible, and second is to assure that no group of Northern sympathizers comes down here to free us and the other men."

Dwight lay there listening as Brown read a few more articles. Then he stopped the man.

"Captain, it seems that what we have done may be causing an even bigger split in this country. This could be a far greater divide than what we experienced in Kansas."

"I agree, son, but I will need to read more of the Northern papers to confirm that. Mr. Avis has stated that he would try to see if he could get some of those papers."

While Dwight rested, he remembered what Dr. Kent had said about his face. For the first time, he reached up and felt where the lead had entered. He wondered how much disfigurement there was. He needed to ask the jailer if he could supply a shaving mirror. He wondered if the man would consider giving him one, because mirrors could be broken and used as a weapon. He didn't get the chance to ask, as he heard the noise of the cell door being unlocked.

"Tomorrow morning you both will be required to be at the courthouse. You must be ready by quarter till eight o'clock," Avis said.

John Brown responded with, "We shall be ready."

Avis acknowledged the response, but then Dwight said, "I would like a small mirror to see my face. Would that be possible?"

Avis paused for a few moments and looked at him and said, "I have a small shaving mirror in my desk. I will get it for you." He locked the door and left, but soon returned with the mirror Dwight had requested. He unlocked the door as Dwight attempted to get up slowly. Avis said, "Stay in bed, son. You're too weak." The jailer moved next to his bed and handed the mirror to him.

"Thank you, sir."

Dwight studied his face in the mirror for a while as Avis stood and watched. Brown had also stopped reading to watch his cellmate.

Still looking in the mirror, Dwight said, "It doesn't look as bad as it feels. A beard will cover most, or maybe even all, of the scars."

"Son, you need to think about recovering and regaining your strength. Now hand back the mirror."

Dwight obliged and half smiled at his jailer. He lay back and looked at the ceiling. Brown waited until Dwight looked comfortable and then commented, "You have said very little. I do not know if it is your pain that keeps you from conversing for any length of time, or if you have more to say that you are keeping to yourself."

Dwight slowly sat back up on his bed. "I do have more to ask, Captain."

"Then, by all means, ask."

"Why did you not heed the requests that both Kagi and I made to you to leave and make our escape? Right now, we could have been planning our next move to spark the slave revolution we had planned for Virginia."

Brown slowly put down a newspaper and said, "I have thought of my indecisions ever since the marines stormed our fortifications. I had hoped that the slaves just needed a little more time to come to our support. I felt confident that, with the firepower the Sharps rifles exhibited, the untrained militia would not dare to attack us. I did not calculate that the federal government would react as quickly as they did and send marines to Harper's Ferry. I was also unaware that so many of the locals would rally for the defense of their city and hold us at bay until the federals arrived."

"Captain, we cautioned you that we thought we were going to be surrounded, whether by inexperienced militia or the federals."

"I rejected your concerns. I should have known better. I read too much about Napoleonic tactics, but should have read more about Napoleon's errors. I failed to do that. I am responsible and sorrowful for what has happened to the cause, our men, and my family. Every day I hope that the sorrow I feel and the guilt that I retain will be lifted from me as I read the Bible. If nothing else, it will prepare me to face our Creator, who already has gathered beside Him the men that we have lost. I will not have to explain my errors to them. There will be no need." He looked at Dwight, who was misty-eyed after hearing the confession his captain had just made. Brown looked directly at him and said, "Dwight, I pray every waking hour to the Almighty that you should live to tell our story and be spared the gallows."

Dwight did not say anything as John Brown looked away and then lay down on his cot. He remained quiet for several minutes until Dwight spoke.

"Thank you for your prayers. I understand now what you are going through, and apologize to you for not performing my duties better during the conflict. I…"

Brown raised his hand to stop him from talking. "You have no fault, son. It is I who made the final decisions. I was a general who failed his army. Please, let you and I not talk of this anymore."

Dwight closed his eyes and thought of what Brown had said. He admired the man for admitting his mistakes. He didn't like the result of his mistakes, but he accepted it. His mind drifted back to his days in the dragoons. He thought about the Battle of Cieneguilla and of Second Lieutenant Bell. He wished that he had acted as quickly as Bell had done during the battle to counteract the misjudgments First Lieutenant Davidson kept making. Bell's quick action had saved Dwight's life and those of the dragoons he was fighting with. He wondered what had happened to Bell. He thought to himself, *Maybe if I had been as forceful with the captain as Bell had been with Davidson, things could have been different.*

He resolved to admit that he was just as responsible for the defeat as was John Brown. He fell off to sleep, feeling better now that Brown had confessed his thoughts to him.

The next morning Dwight was awakened by the sounds of Avis unlocking the cell door.

"Good morning, men. It is half past seven o'clock. We leave in fifteen minutes for the courthouse." Avis turned to the guards outside the door and said, "Return in fifteen minutes."

Brown spoke up. "Sir, will you explain what we might expect?"

"Yes, I will. You have been summoned to the county courthouse by the grand jury to hear the evidence that has been brought against you."

John Brown rose from his bed and looked at Dwight.

Avis turned to Dwight and said, "Mr. Stevens, can you walk there?"

Dwight attempted to rise from his bed.

Avis observed how much effort it took for Dwight to move. "When it is time, I will have two militiamen assist you to a standing position." Avis left and returned in ten minutes with the militiamen to help him.

Dwight attempted to put his arms on the shoulders of the shorter men, but they refused to allow it. They, in turn, held him under each armpit and began to almost drag him out of the cell.

Avis called out, "Boys, the man is wounded and weak. Have some compassion. This is the first time he has been standing." Both militiamen looked at Avis, who reiterated his command with a nod of his head, and then said, "Help him walk, men."

Dwight acknowledged his compassion and tried hard to walk with their aid. Brown was led out first, followed slowly by Dwight and the deputies assisting him. Dwight realized they had stopped. He lifted his head and observed Edward Coppoc being manacled to Brown. He expected to be manacled the same way to Shields Green or Copeland, but he was spared. His captors realized he could not possibly run away. He watched as Shields and Copeland were then manacled together.

As they walked onto the main street, calls for a lynching, shooting, and hanging could be periodically heard from the crowd that lined the street. But as they got closer to the courthouse, the cries for their demise began to lessen. Dwight saw that people were looking at Brown and the other captives and turning away with disgust. He realized that all of them must have appeared wretched and haggard. He wondered how he looked, and quickly came to the realization that the pain in his left arm was becoming intense. The deputy who was assisting him had latched on to the wounded arm, causing more pain.

Dwight called out, to the surprise of all that were in hearing, "For God's sake, man, I can't use my arm! No need in trying to detach it from me."

The deputy understood what he was doing and loosened his grip.

Dwight became further weakened and found it difficult to climb the stairs to the courthouse, even though he was being supported. Most people observing at the courthouse looked on him more with pity than with hate as the five men were led into the main entrance.

Dwight quickly glanced around as he was assisted into the courtroom. The room was packed with people pointing, laughing, scowling, and occasionally threatening each prisoner as he was led in. He found it difficult to breathe in the heavy smoke and human odor that took his breath away. He found relief when he was laid on the floor of the courthouse. Dwight blacked out for a short period of time.

When he awoke, he could see Mr. Allstadt testifying on his account of the raid and his arrest. He had missed Colonel Washington's account and only managed to see Mr. Allstadt point at him before he blacked out again. Dwight continued to fade in and out of consciousness until someone shook his shoulder when he was addressed by one of the magistrates.

"Mr. Stevens, are you in need of an attorney?"

Dwight struggled to put words together to respond, when Brown intervened for him.

"He is a wounded man who should have been allowed to recover sufficiently from his wounds before you asked him to even be here to answer such a question."

The main magistrate turned to Brown and said, "Sir, the same question applies to you. Are you in need of attorneys?"

Brown paused, pulled himself up, and glared at the eight magistrates for what seemed to many observing to be a long time before he spoke. Dwight managed to stay alert for Brown's response: ***"Virginians, I did not ask for any quarter at the time I was taken. I did not ask to have my life spared. The governor of the State of Virginia tendered me his assurance that I should have a fair trial; but under no circumstances whatever will I be able to have a fair trial. If you seek my blood, you can have it at any moment, without this mockery of a trial. I have had no counsel; I have not been able to advise with anyone. I know nothing of the feelings of my fellow prisoner, and am utterly unable to attend in any way to my own defense."***

John Brown braced himself on a banister in the courtroom. He looked around the quiet room and continued, ***"My memory don't serve***

me; my health is insufficient, although improving, there are mitigating circumstances that I would urge in our favor, if a fair trial is to be allowed us: but if we are to be forced with a mere form—a trial of execution—you might spare yourselves that trouble."

Dwight watched as Brown moved along the courtroom railing, looking defiantly at each magistrate. Those that watched wondered when he would fall, seeing how unsteady his arms and legs were.

Brown realized he was losing his strength, and sat back down slowly. ***"I am ready for my fate. I do not ask a trial. I beg for no mockery of a trial—no insult—nothing but that which conscience gives, or cowardice would drive you to practice. I ask again to be excused from the mockery of a trial. I do not even know what the special design of this examination is. I do not know what is to be the benefit of it to the commonwealth."*** John Brown looked at his lieutenant as he lay on his mattress. Dwight had heard all he had said without passing into unconsciousness. But Brown was not finished. He spoke a few more words. ***"I have now little further to ask, other than that I may not be foolishly insulted as only cowardly barbarians insult those who fall into their power."***

When Brown had finished, he braced himself on the chair that he sat upon. There was silence in the courtroom until one of the magistrates ordered that the five prisoners be escorted back to the Charlestown jail. Their return to the jailhouse was uneventful. There were no calls for them to be lynched, shot, or otherwise eliminated. Brown's speech had quieted the crowd long enough for the prisoners to reach the jailhouse and be safely locked up again.

Upon Dwight and Brown's return, Avis had a meal fixed for them. The looks of cold meat, several slices of bread, and a cup of coffee did not appeal to Dwight's appetite. He still was having difficulty chewing and swallowing, and he fell off to sleep for a short time. Brown, on the other hand, was regaining his strength and appetite. He ate most of what was offered by the "good jailer," as they were beginning to call him.

When Dwight awoke, he managed to take several bites of bread from the meal. The coffee helped to soften the bread and wash it down.

The next morning, after being served coffee and bread, the two prisoners were notified that they would be taken to the courthouse again to face the formal charges from the magistrates. Brown became upset upon hearing the news and said, "They have not listened to a word I have said to them. I know my fate. I do not need, nor will I endure, another travesty in their court today."

Dwight did not respond to Brown's declaration at first. He knew from experience that the militia or sheriff's deputies would carry them to wherever the magistrates ordered. Brown was still mumbling his dissatisfaction on hearing they were summoned to court again when Dwight called over to him, "Captain, we will have no choice in the matter. They will do as they want with us. Think of it as an opportunity to express more of our cause when you are before them."

His comment stopped Brown from rambling. He turned to Dwight and remarked, "We will make it difficult for them. They will have to carry us like the pharaohs of Egypt." He smiled.

Dwight closed his eyes and awaited the sound of Jailer Avis unlocking their cell door. Before long, the jailer arrived with several deputies and announced, "Gentlemen, you have been summoned by the magistrates to appear within the hour."

Brown called out, "Mr. Avis, I am not capable of attending an invitation of the magistrates this morning. I am too weak. You shall inform them that I will consider appearing at another time."

Avis looked at the deputies and ordered, "Go get the other four outside and instruct them that we will need to carry both prisoners this morning."

Dwight heard the instructions and lay back on his mattress. He waited to see how the jailer would handle Brown and his objection to attending the summons. Several moments later, four deputies appeared next to Avis.

"Carry Mr. Brown, cot and all."

As ordered, the four deputies approached Brown's cot. The old man looked defiant as he lay on the cot stiff-legged and with his arms crossed. He never said a word as the men lifted him on the cot and carried him outside.

Dwight watched with some amusement as Brown was carried out. He attempted to smile but his face hurt. Several moments later, he too was carried out on his mattress. The trip to the courthouse was uneventful this day. Most of the bystanders had already crowded into the building, which held approximately six hundred people. No calls for them to be lynched or harmed were heard all during their route to the second hearing. The four deputies placed John Brown on his cot in front of Judge Richard Parker.

Before the judge could begin the proceedings, Brown spoke to him. "Sir, if you would allow me a few moments before you commence this proceeding." Judge Parker was about to question why, when Brown continued, "Sir, I ask for a very short delay. I have agony in my kidney wound, and a temporary loss of hearing due to the beating I endured from the marines."

Judge Parker looked down at some papers he had before him. One was a signed document from the physician that had treated Brown, swearing he was fit to stand trial. The judge spoke to Brown in a raised voice, but slowly, so everyone in hearing distance could understand him. "Mr. Brown, I have here a signed examination document from the physician that treated your wounds. He states that you are healthy enough to stand trial. I respectfully deny your request."

Brown lay back on his cot and did not say anything for a while as the proceedings continued. Dwight remained awake through most of the proceedings that day. Occasionally he would fall into a deep sleep and those closest to him could hear his soft moans of pain.

On one occasion, Dwight yelled loud enough when he woke up that the judge stopped the proceedings and called for a physician to examine him. The physician reported the prisoner was in some pain from his wounds and that his exhaustion had put him into a deep sleep and probably in some state of dreaming.

Judge Parker asked if Stevens could remain in court to hear the evidence presented against him. The physician agreed that he could, but no one ever mentioned that the prisoner was asleep half the time and was thus not aware of what evidence was being brought against him.

Thomas C. Green and Charles J. Faulkner were appointed as counsel for the prisoners. Dwight did not know, nor did he care, if he received counsel. He had no faith in any court based on his past experiences and resolved to himself that he would be found guilty of treason no matter who defended him.

To his surprise, he did manage to stay awake when a young, beardless attorney volunteered to assist the two appointed counselors for the prisoners. George H. Hoyt, from Athol, Massachusetts, had come to Charlestown originally as an abolitionist spy but had taken interest in the trial of the raiders. The court questioned his credentials, but sufficient proof was presented that he was an attorney in good standing.

Judge Parker allowed Hoyt to assist in counsel, despite the objection that Hoyt was considered a spy. The proceedings ended with a reading of charges for treason and first-degree murder against the prisoners. It was also determined that each man would be tried separately because of the injuries to Dwight. Brown would be tried first.

During their return to jail, Dwight observed the numerous guards that had been placed both inside the jail and around its perimeter. The men also created a constant noise of militia marching up and down the street leading to the courthouse. On one occasion Dwight remarked to Jailer Avis on the number of deputies and militiamen he observed in Charlestown while on his way to and from court.

Avis replied, "Governor Wise wants to make sure you and the others don't get freed."

Dwight countered with, "Mr. Avis, it would take a brigade of cavalry to free us."

"There is a plan, we hear, for some abolitionists up North to come to Charlestown and free you, Mr. Brown, and the others. Governor Wise will not let that happen."

The next morning, October 27, 1859, Dwight awoke to observe John Brown reading his worn Bible. Brown looked over to Dwight and set his Bible down as he slowly stood up from his cot and spoke. "Today, my son, the mockery begins. I do pray that it ends quickly."

Dwight stretched carefully before answering his cellmate, "Captain, the new attorney from Massachusetts may be of help. You should listen to his counsel. He might know of a way to reduce the charges against us."

"Mr. Hoyt is who you speak of. He tells me that he is considered a spy. He also told me that he is being watched even by the two court-appointed counselors he has been allowed to assist."

Mr. Avis and a four-man contingent entered the cell to escort him to his first day of trial.

"Mr. Brown, it is time for your trial."

Brown sat on his cot with his arms crossed.

Avis wasted no time in ordering the deputies to lift the cot with Brown on it. He asked one more time, "Mr. Brown, do you feel able with our assistance to walk to the courthouse?"

Brown only lay down on the cot.

Avis shook his head but did not comment. He motioned for the deputies to lift the cot while Brown defiantly stared at him. Dwight watched as the captain was carried away.

Approximately seven hours later, John Brown returned to his cell. He was brought in with almost the same expression he'd had when he departed. After his cot had been positioned in the cell and the deputies and the jailer had left, Dwight inquired, "Captain, do you care to inform me of today's proceedings?"

Brown's stoic expression changed to a frown and then almost to rage as he looked at Dwight. "Do you know what my court-appointed counsel had the audacity to insinuate?" He paused before he continued. "That my family in Akron is insane. He read a cockamamie letter that stated I had relatives there that had been put in an insane asylum. He declared that insanity was the curse of my family, and that I should be sent to an asylum."

Dwight remained quiet to keep Brown from getting any madder.

Brown cooled a little after a short while and said, "I told them that

I looked upon it with contempt more than otherwise. Insane persons, so far as my experience goes, have but little ability to judge of their own insanity."

Dwight only nodded. He did think that the counsel was only trying to save Brown's neck from the gallows, but he did not attempt to defend his counsel or try to reason with him. Brown began to cool down and then looked at Dwight again, this time with concern. The rage was gone. "John Cook was captured yesterday in Chambersburg. It was announced during the proceedings today."

Dwight shook his head and lay back on his bed.

Brown whispered to him, "I have been informed that Hazlett was with Cook. I will state that I do not know Hazlett. I will get word to the others to say the same. It could be enough for the authorities to release him."

"You may do that, Captain, but I feel it will make no difference to the authorities."

"We must try, Dwight. We must try." Brown was not finished. "Dwight, during my escort between the courthouse in both directions, I noted a cannon positioned pointing directly at the courthouse. I thought of this maneuver as strange."

Dwight asked him to repeat what he had just said. He listened intently to every word and responded, "Our captors are concerned that a force will come here and rescue us. I think they feel the use of a cannon will deter any attempt. I am a little confused as to why they would aim the cannons at the courthouse, though, which could kill many of the good citizens they are trying to protect."

Brown paused and smiled. "Yes, I see your point. Good observation. Let us hope no one comes to save us. I'll pray on that."

Neither man knew that Governor Wise had ordered the cannons to be pointed at the courthouse from four different positions. The artillerymen manning them were under strict orders to begin firing on anyone attempting to free the prisoners while in court. No one seemed to consider that more Southerners in the courthouse would probably be killed than Northerners who were trying to free the raiders.

Several more days of trial ensued for John Brown. Dwight could only listen to the captain as he raved and ranted about the poor excuse of a counsel he had been given. This culminated with the expulsion of his court-appointed counsel and the acceptance of the twenty-one-year-old Hoyt as his attorney. The trial continued until November 1st.

Dwight listened to Brown describe the testimony of Captain Sinn, the cavalry captain who had helped Dwight. The testimony of Captain Sinn, and one specific sentence he spoke, convinced the jury that John

Brown should be sentenced to meet the Almighty. Brown paused as he recollected the exact words Sinn had stated. He looked at Dwight and said, "In another time this man could have been a friend where we could have defended our different views of slavery in front of as many as would have cared to see the debate. But he came to state the truth as a gentleman and a soldier. He did that."

Brown stared at the ceiling and, almost verbatim, repeated the words Sinn had spoken, ***"I have no sympathy for the acts of the prisoner or of his movement but I regard Captain Brown as a brave man. As a Southern man I came here to state the facts about the case, so that Northern men would have no opportunity of saying that Southern men were unwilling to appear as witnesses in behalf of one whose principles they abhorred."***

Brown remained quiet for several moments until he looked over at his lieutenant. "That was my conviction. I have the Sabbath to pray and reflect, because on Monday, I will be sentenced on that statement alone."

Brown closed his eyes until Jailer Avis entered with the evening meal. Brown ate well, read more from his Bible, and seemed content with life. Sunday was more of the same for him. While Brown read, Dwight slept to regain his strength. Every day that passed was slightly better, physically, for him. The constant pain was slowly diminishing.

On Monday, November 2, 1859, John Brown was found guilty of treason in advising and conspiring with slaves and others to rebel against the State of Virginia, and of murder in the first degree. Judge Parker announced that John Brown would be hanged on December 2, 1859.

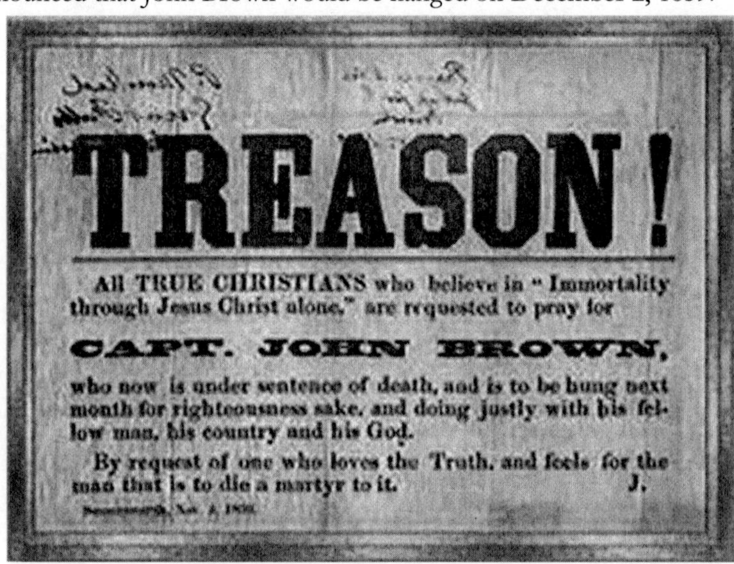

"Treason" Broadside, 1859 November 4,
Public Domain

The judge asked Brown if he had anything to say.

Brown slowly rose and addressed the court. ***"I have, may it please the court, a few words to say. In the first place, I deny everything but what I have all along admitted—the design on my part to free slaves. I intended certainly to have made a clean thing of the matter, as I did last winter, when I went to Missouri and took slaves without the snapping of a gun on either side, moved them through the country, and finally left them in Canada. I designed to do the same thing again, on a larger scale. That was all I intended. I never did intend murder, or treason, or the destruction of property, or to excite or incite slaves to rebellion, or to make insurrection."***

He paused, cleared his throat, and looked around at those quietly listening. ***"The court acknowledges, as I suppose, the validity of the law of God. I see a book kissed here which I suppose to be the Bible, or at least the New Testament. That teaches me that all things whatsoever I would that men should do to me, I should do even so to them. It teaches me further to 'remember them that are in bonds, as bound with them.' I endeavored to act up to that instruction. I say, I am too young to understand that God is any respecter of persons. I believe that to have interfered as I have done—as I have always freely admitted I have done—in behalf of His despised poor, was not wrong, but right. Now if it is deemed necessary that I should forfeit my life for the furtherance of the ends of justice, and mingle my blood further with the blood of my children and with the blood of millions in this slave country whose rights are disregarded by wicked, cruel, and unjust enactments.—I submit; so let it be done!"***

There was quiet as the abolitionist slowly sat. Only a few dared to talk quietly as John Brown was taken back to his cell.

In that month's time, Dwight's wounds improved due to the excellent care Jailer Avis and his wife provided. Brown wrote and read for most of the time between his sentencing and hanging. The conversations between the captain and his lieutenant covered all subjects, including family, religions, memories, friends, and the afterlife. When they were not engaged in conversations, Dwight rested and Brown wrote letters to family and friends.

Almost daily, Jailer Avis brought in letters to John Brown from many who sympathized with his cause, and he informed him that they had written for his pardon from the governor of Virginia. Although appreciative, Brown knew nothing could save him.

Dwight watched as Brown was given three or more letters that he knew the captain would answer as soon as possible. Avis retained one letter and called to Dwight, "Mr. Stevens, this one is addressed to you."

Shocked, he remarked, "Captain Avis, are you sure?"

"Yes, sir. It says A. Dwight Stevens." He brought the letter over to him.

Brown spoke up and said, "It could be a letter from your family in Connecticut."

Dwight knew it could be, but he truly hoped it was from Jenny Dunbar. He studied the handwriting on the letter and realized it was a woman's.

"What are ya waitin' for, son? Open the letter," Avis said, smiling as he turned and started to leave the cell. He stopped, paused, and said, "I almost forgot. I have some toiletries for both of you."

Brown looked up and asked, "From who, my good jailer?"

"A woman who has requested permission to see you specifically, sir. My supervisor is contemplating giving her permission as we speak."

Brown seemed perplexed but then went back to reading the first letter he had been handed.

Dwight slowly opened and read his letter.

November 2, 1859

Aaron Dwight Stevens

Care of Jailer

Charlestown, Virginia

Dear Dwight,

I'm sure you never thought you would hear from your old army friend Avery. I never thought I would be writing you either. When we parted in '49 I thought you would become famous. But not this famous! I hope your wounds are not as bad as described in the newspapers. I pray you heal quickly.

If you are wondering why this letter is so perfect it is because my wife Catherine is writing what I say, but in the right way. She is also my secretary and really she is who runs the business. I met her through my Aunt Katie and her husband Robert Morrison. We have a daughter and a son now, as well. She is eight and he is four. We named her Emma and I named him Dwight for a good friend I knew back during the war.

My uncle set me up in business. I have a company that loads and unloads goods on ships sailing in and out of Boston. I couldn't get away from the docks. I could have used a smart man as you seemed to be to help run this business. I inquired to your family in Norwich, and they replied that you were off in the dragoons. Whatever made you do that? Now I read in the Boston papers that you had an alias and called yourself Charles Whipple. I read up on Whipple. He had quite the reputation in Kansas.

Whichever you are, I wish you well and hopefully you will get a reduced sentence for your crime against the institution of slavery. I can tell you that the sentiment in Massachusetts is one of awe and support for you. I wish you well.

Your affectionate friend,

Al

Alfred Avery

President

Continental Shipping

Wharf D

Boston, Massachusetts

"Ten years," he said out loud.

Brown looked over to him briefly as he continued to read the letters he had received.

Dwight thought to himself, *Al Avery, after all these years, with a wife, family, and a business.* He felt happy for the first time since before he left the Kennedy farm. Dwight re-read the letter. He wondered how much different his life would have been had he stayed home and responded to Avery's request to come back to Boston. He soon dismissed the thought, realizing he had loved the dragoons, Kansas, and what he had seen and done with John Brown. It far exceeded running a shipping company.

He remembered that he had needed to get away from the established "hum-drum" society that went to work every day except the Sabbath so they could have the material goods they so desperately thought they needed. It was just not the life for him.

What Avery did was exactly what he had decided not to do. Going into the dragoons had solved that. He felt good today, and writing a letter to his best friend during his army days was now a priority. He knew that he would need to ask someone to help him. He thought about the problem. *Maybe Mrs. Avis could help me?*

Another week passed, and he had not yet asked Mrs. Avis to help him. He felt improved enough to attempt to write a letter on his own when he heard Avis call to Brown that a visitor had come to the jail and requested an audience with him. A discussion ensued that Dwight figured would result in the unknown visitor being escorted out of the building. Several moments passed as he concentrated on his slow, painful writing. Finally, he heard the cell door being unlocked.

He looked up and saw a petite woman and a boy enter the cell.

Brown seemed surprised, as well, at the sight of them. There were a few uncomfortable moments until the woman broke the silence as she held a handkerchief to her nose. The boy stood stoically next to her.

"Mr. Brown, I am Rebecca Buffum Spring[1] of Eaglewood, New Jersey. This is my son Edward."

Brown looked up at the woman and said, "And do I have the privilege to know you, madam?"

"You do not, sir, but I am here in support of what you have done against the evils of slavery. I am a friend of your wife, who awaits a visit with you as soon as it can be arranged."

"Why have you come here, Miss Spring?"

"It's Mrs. Spring, Mr. Brown. ***When men fight and hurt each other, women should go and take care of them."***

Brown smiled at the woman and remarked, "I am taken care of, Mrs. Spring, but I do welcome news of the outside. You can tell me of what you have seen, heard, and read. Can you tell me of my dear wife? Have you any news as to when I should be able to see her?"

"I do not have all the answers, but I can assure you I will do my best to respond to your questions."

Brown's eyes lit up. "You, madam, are the caring soul that sent us the toiletries, are you not?"

"Yes, Mr. Brown, I am responsible. I had hoped to present you with them at my first meeting, but had to endure a wait for Sheriff Campbell to grant me permission to visit you. He did allow the items to be delivered."

"I am pleased that he has allowed both now, Mrs. Spring."

Dwight tired and could not stay awake during Mrs. Spring's entire visit with John Brown. But his strength grew as days passed, and she became a regular visitor through the month of November until Brown's execution. During that time, she became acquainted with Dwight and on several occasions when he was feeling stronger had lengthy conversations with him. She also helped him write a letter to update Al Avery on everything he had done and gone through since their departure in Boston. After he had completed that letter with her help, there were three other people that he vowed to write: his almost adopted sister, Anne, the daughter of John Brown; his sister Lydia; and, most importantly, Jenny Dunbar.

---

[1] **Rebecca Buffum Spring** was a Quaker woman who worked in education reform for girls. Her father, Arnold Buffum, was the first president of the New England Anti-Slavery Society. She was married to Marcus in the spring of 1840. Rebecca and Marcus were avid abolitionists and became intensely involved in social politics, advocates for girls education, and involved in the transcendentalist movement. They also corresponded with William Lloyd Garrison and Ralph Waldo Emerson. In the late 1850s they founded Eaglewood Military Academy, where Stevens and Hazlett were both buried for a while.

Years later Mrs. Spring would write about Dwight, ***"Stevens was an old crusader in spirit, and yet he was loving and gentle as a child. He was only dangerous to wrong the oppression."*** In her memoirs, she also wrote that, ***"He was a gentle man by pointing out his love of God, of nature and of good people and his manly courage in the face of death."***

Dwight looked forward to her visits, and through her he was able to obtain information on one very important woman in his life. A few weeks after having Avery's letter mailed by his new friend Rebecca, Dwight slowly put pen and ink to paper and addressed Jenny Dunbar for the second time since he had seen her at the Lindsley homestead.

Rebecca had managed to supply him with an address where she was sure the letter would reach Jenny. Dwight thought for several days what he would say to the woman who still held a special place in his heart. He decided to get to the point so that she would know he was truthful and could compare his heart-felt expression to what may have been written about him in the newspapers.

Charlestown, VA
November 1859
My Dear Friend,

Having got nearly well of my wounds, I will try and write you a few lines, hoping, that I am not forgotten although in prison, for Murder, Treason and other charges. I do not feel guilty in the least, for I know, if I know anything, that there was no evil intention in my heart. I thought I should be able to do, more good for the world, in this way, than I could do in any other. I may have erred, as to the best way, but I think everything will turn out for the best in the end.

I do not expect to be tried, until next Spring, when I expect I shall be hung, as I think, all the rest will, Slavory: demands that we should hang for its protection, and we will meet it willingly, knowing that God is Just, and is over all.

There seems to be no mercy, for those who are willing, to help those who have none to help them.

My heart, feels like bleeding, to think, how many thousand's are worse off in this land as I am now. Oh that I could see this country free, I would give a thousand lives if I had them to give. When I say free I mean both North and South.

O, how I wish I could hear you play and sing, some of those sweet songs, once more, but I suppose I shall have to wait until we meet in the spirit land.

What joy there is in feeling, that we shall meet at our friend's, sooner or later in a world better than this is: where the chances of

doing good, are better than here.

I will not write any more at present, for fear that I am intruding upon your time and patience.

Remember me to Mr. and Mrs. Lindsley and family, and give the little one a few kisses for me. She is such a sweet little girl, how I would like to see her!

If you will write to me a few lines, in answer to this, you will confer, a grate favor on one of your warmest friends, and well-wishers.

Also remember me to Wellthy, Alvi and all enquiring friends.

Yours for all the good of mankind,

A. D. Stevens

P.S. If you write, direct to Capt. Avis, Jailor

Charlestown VA [1]

When he had finished writing the letter, he wondered if she would respond. He waited until Rebecca visited to express his concerns.

She explained to him that he was a hero and a knight in shining armor to most women of the North. She smiled and told him that he should pay more attention to all the young women parading by the jail. "They aren't walking by here just to see John Brown. They are very interested in the handsome Mr. Stevens." She thoroughly convinced him that he would hear from Jenny soon.

That anticipation overshadowed his knowledge that the captain would be hanged in less than a week.

Lately, during the evening meals, Dwight had begun to actually sit up unassisted and eat his meals on his own. The jailer brought softer food when Mrs. Avis heard of the difficulty Dwight still had when chewing. She took the time to boil potatoes for Dwight. Other types of soft foods were also added to his diet. Fruit preserves and apple sauce aided in supplying nutrition and some relief to Dwight's sensitive jaw and numb facial muscles. The change in diet greatly contributed to the young man regaining his strength.

Another week passed and Brown, Avis, and the men that guarded the jailhouse remarked on how quickly he was recovering. By the end of November, just before John Brown's execution, all the bandages had been removed. Dwight's beard had grown considerably and covered most of his facial wounds.

Jailer Avis had procured clothing for both prisoners and had a large tin tub brought into the cell for the two men to share for Saturday

---

[1] **An actual letter** written by A. D. Stevens to Jenny Dunbar.

evening baths. Mrs. Spring had suggested both, and Mrs. Avis demanded it when she visited and saw the clothing the men were wearing and smelled their body odor. Dwight was able to bathe by himself, but depended on Brown to assist him with getting in and out of the tub.

BROWN AND STEVENS IN THEIR CELL, THREE DAYS BEFORE THE EXECUTION.

Brown and Stevens in jail cell, *New York News*, December 10, 1859.
West Virginia State Archives

Chapter Twenty-Five

A Journey to the Gallows

After Brown's conviction, Attorney George Hoyt visited both men almost daily. But he spent more time with Dwight, asking for the details of what had happened from the time the raiders left the Kennedy farm until Dwight was rendered unconscious from his wounds. Hoyt would sit and speak softly, trying not to interfere with Brown's reading and letter writing.

During several meetings Hoyt had with Dwight, Rebecca listened and occasionally commented. She also encouraged Dwight to write home to his relatives to ease their concerns as best he could. Rebecca, in a small way, acted like his sister.

John Brown never interfered with the meetings Hoyt scheduled. If a meeting was underway and Rebecca had come to visit, Brown would spend time with her so the two men could converse quietly. Both Hoyt and Brown wanted Dwight to be spared the gallows that Brown was preparing himself for. The days in November quickly passed and everyone, whether it was those in the city or those in the jail, exhibited anxiety and unrest as to what would transpire on December 2nd.

During this time, rumors spread continually. Governor Wise was sure, based on the reports he had been given, that an insurrectionist army was close by and would descend upon the quiet city to pillage and burn it and free the prisoners. Four hundred more militiamen were ordered to Charlestown to defend the city.

There was an immediate shortage of room to accommodate the added troops. The new men were lodged in the churches and schools in the city as best as they could. Some meals were cooked in the courthouse, schools, and churches, but most meals were prepared and cooked outside. Any visitor of Charlestown during the trial of John Brown, and through to his execution, would have thought the city was under siege.

When Brown learned that he was to be visited by his wife in the next few days, his temperament and personality changed. He began to speak softly and smiled more than anyone who visited him had seen him do before. One night he sat staring at his desk with quill in hand.

Dwight noticed and remarked, "Captain, are you ill?"

"No, my son, I am physically much better than the day before. Each day I feel grateful that I have almost completely recovered. I ponder what I shall say in this letter to my wife, my sons, and my daughters. I must think of the words to express my love for them that they may read again and again after I am gone."

Dwight never replied. He knew this was a private time for John Brown. He watched as the captain wrote for what seemed like an hour.

Upon completion, Brown put down his quill and looked at Dwight. "I would like you to read this and only comment if I have not said the right things in what will probably be my last letter to them." He stood up and walked to Dwight's bed and handed it to him. He slowly walked away, sat at the desk again, opened up his Bible, and began to read quietly.

Dwight read,

As I now begin what is probably the last letter I shall ever write to any of you; I conclude to write you all at the same time. I am waiting the hour of my public murder with composure of mind & cheerfulness; feeling the strongest assurance that in no other possible way could I be used to so much advance the cause of God; and of humanity: & that nothing that either I or my family have sacrificed or suffered: will be lost. I have now no doubt that our seeming disaster will ultimately result in the most Glorious success. So my dear shattered and broken family be of good cheer & believe & trust in God; with all your heart & all your soul. Do not feel ashamed in my account; nor for one moment despair of the cause; or grow weary of well doing. I bless God; I never felt stronger confidence in the certain and near approach of a bright morning & a glorious day.

Your Affectionate Husband & Father
John Brown

Dwight reflected on the words. He slowly got up and walked to the desk where Brown sat reading. He placed the letter on it, made no comment, and retired to his bed. Dwight vowed to write more letters to those close to him.

On the morning of December 1st, carpenters' hammers could be heard banging in the early morning hours. Despite being a good walking distance from the jailhouse, the still morning allowed the noise to be heard throughout the town. As the noise of horse and wagon traffic increased by the jailhouse during the day, the prisoners were sometimes spared the eerie sound of the construction of Brown's death platform.

The uncomfortable atmosphere ended when Mr. Avis came in and began to unlock the cell door. "Mr. Brown, you have a visitor."

John Brown did not react, thinking that another newspaperman or politician was there to see him. Many had come and gone in their effort to question him, argue with him, or bestow accolades on him. Some came just to be able to say they had met and talked with the notorious John Brown.

"Mr. Brown, you have a visitor!" he announced again, this time in a louder voice.

Brown paid attention to Avis's statement this time, and asked, "Who is here to visit me, sir?"

He watched Avis unlock the cell door and remove himself to the outer office as a woman passed him. It was Brown's wife, accompanied by two deputies. Dwight watched as she entered the cell and embraced Brown. Both stood still for a lengthy time, with neither expressing any words. It was a delightful sight for Dwight, who also felt uncomfortable witnessing the love between the two people. In only a few hours, each would have to wait until both were in the hereafter to meet again.

Avis yelled to the two deputies, "There will be no need for you two to be standing here watching them! Get outside and leave 'em be."

The two men scurried off, hearing the orders.

Dwight turned away from the couple as they embraced again. He stayed in that position for a few minutes until Brown called to him.

"Dwight, I would like to introduce my wife, Mary, to you."

Dwight turned and began to get up to greet the woman, when he heard her say, "Please be still. I know of your wounds and condition. Do not get up on my account."

Dwight either ignored her or was too focused on concentrating his strength to get up to greet the woman. Before she could reiterate her concerns, he stood with his hand extended. "I am honored to make your acquaintance, Mrs. Brown. I am Dwight Stevens."

"I know who you are, young man, and I am pleased to have met you at last. My sons talked of you many times in their letters home. My husband cannot talk more highly of you. You are a son to him." She walked toward Dwight, passed by his extended hand, and embraced him as a mother would have done her son. He melted into her arms and held back the tears as best he could as he felt the swelling in his eyes.

Whether it was an expression of the loss of her sons, or the imminent demise of her husband and the father of her remaining children, or his want of affection from a mother-like figure, he did not know. He found tears wetting his beard. He held her gingerly and enjoyed the embrace. When they had finished, she kissed him on his cheek and turned back to her husband.

The three talked for only a short period until Jailer Avis returned and addressed the Browns. "My wife and I would like to offer you our hospitality. Would you please join us for dinner at six o'clock this evening at our home? I do have to inform you that you will be taken to our home by carriage and under an armed guard. I apologize for that, but it is necessary. I hope you understand."

Mrs. Brown looked at her husband and asked, "Do we accept?"

Brown smiled and said, "Of course, my dear. I would like you to meet the woman who helped nourish me and Dwight back to health. Mr. Avis, we accept your hospitality, and thank you."

Avis smiled and nodded. He bowed and returned to the outer office.

Dwight lay back on his bed, satisfied that there was at least some honor still left in the world, even though it came from the jailer who would also be responsible for John Brown's death the next morning. Dwight would wonder, until his own death, what was said at the Avis homestead that evening as the two couples from completely different backgrounds shared a meal.

Brown returned to the cell after 10:00 p.m. After his remarks of appreciation for his host, he sat at his desk as Dwight lay still in the dark.

Dwight could hear Brown getting up to scratch a match and saw the light from the small oil lamp he had lit. He then heard him yell, ***"Mary, God bless you and our children. Do you hear me my love? God bless you and our family."***

The arrival of Mrs. Brown in Charlestown,
***New York News*, December 17, 1859.**
West Virginia State Archives

THE LAST SUPPER. JOHN BROWN AND HIS WIFE IN THE PARLOR OF MR. AVIS. FROM A SKETCH BY OUR OWN ARTIST.

John Brown and wife, *New York News*, December 17, 1859.

West Virginia State Archives

JOHN BROWN'S LAST INTERVIEW WITH HIS WIFE IN THE JAIL AT CHARLESTOWN, VA.

John Brown and his wife's last interview

West Virginia State Archives

Dwight realized his cellmate was yelling to his wife. He could hear the sound of the many horse hoofs pounding on the cobblestone as the carriage drove away.

Brown sat back down and only briefly looked at Dwight. No words were exchanged. Brown went back to shuffling through the pages of his Bible, looking for the best passages or verses to read as the hours of his life quickly passed.

Dwight decided to leave him alone and, in doing so, fell asleep until around 4:00 a.m., when he awoke to hear Brown quietly praying. He remained still until Jailer Avis entered the cell an hour later and announced that he would take Mr. Brown's request for breakfast.

Brown paused and then stated, "Mr. Avis, I would like eggs, bacon, and some of that homemade bread your wife served with dinner last night. Could she heavily butter it if possible? And also, my good man, a cup of very hot coffee."

Avis acknowledged his request and turned to Dwight.

Before he could ask, Dwight smiled and said, "Hot coffee and some of that bread the captain has requested, thank you."

"Your requests will be here within the half hour. Good morning, gentlemen."

Dwight thought how polite and proper the day had begun as the three men seemed to avoid what they knew would be happening within a few hours.

Brown ate his meal with Dwight in silence. When he had finished, he called to Jailer Avis. When Avis arrived, Brown asked if he could visit with the other prisoners. Avis stated he would give him ample time to say good-bye to his men before he was led out.

An hour later, the time was near for Brown's execution and Avis led him to the others. Brown handed each man a quarter-dollar coin. It was the last bit of money he still had in his possession. Dwight, Edwin Coppoc, John Copeland, and Shields Green wept as the captain bade them farewell. He nodded to Cook and ignored Hazlett as they all had done.

Dwight knew Brown was irritated with Cook, who had twisted the truth to attempt to save his own neck, and Brown ignored Hazlett in his attempt to maintain the illusion that no one knew him, hoping he would be released.

Brown performed two last acts before his execution. He handed Dwight a small note he had composed right after breakfast and said, "Read it when I have gone." Dwight also noticed that Brown had handed Jailer Avis a note as the two men walked outside toward the wagon that was waiting to take him to the gallows. That would be the last time

Dwight saw Captain John Brown. He opened the note and read it.

Charlestown Jail, Dec. 2nd, 1859

John Brown to Aaron D. Stevens

He that is slow to anger is better than the mighty, and he that ruleth his spirit is greater than he that taketh a city.

Dwight gently folded the letter, sat, and reflected. Within several hours Jailer Avis returned. His duty had been accomplished, but he did not speak of it. He entered the cell room and handed Dwight the note John Brown had given him. Avis never said a word as he turned and left. Dwight slowly opened the note and read it.

I John Brown am now quite certain that the crimes of this guilty land: will never be purged away; but with Blood. I had as I now think: vainly flattered myself that without very much bloodshed it might be done.

Dwight decided to hand the note to Rebecca Spring when she returned to visit him so that his captain's last words would be known to more than just two men. He thought on his leader's last thoughts and wondered how accurate his prophecy would be. He wrote a letter to Mrs. Spring, just in case she did not return soon to visit him.

Farewell between Brown and Stevens,
***New York News*, December 10, 1859.**
West Virginia State Archives

Dear Mrs. Spring:

The Captain was as cheerful on the morning of his execution as I ever saw him; I think he is better off than any of us now, and I almost long to be with him in the Spirit Land.

Dwight sat alone on his cot most of the rest of the day until he heard Jailer Avis come in and unlock his cell. "You have a new cell companion, young man."

Before Dwight could ask who the companion was, he saw Albert Hazlett being led into his cell. Dwight first wanted to greet him, but refrained until the jailer had left. He too had hoped he could keep the charade going that no one knew Albert Hazlett. Confident that Avis could not hear them, he whispered, "Al, I am pleased you are with me."

"I am as well."

He said nothing about his time with John Cook, and Dwight did not inquire. Brown's reaction had been enough for both men to realize Cook was not at the same level as they were in his eyes.

As Dwight continued to recover from his wounds, he diligently wrote to as many people in his family as he could. One particular letter he wrote was to his Uncle James, just before the sentencing of the remaining four raiders.

Charlestown, VA: Dec. 11th/ 59

Uncle James,

It is under rather adverse circumstances that I sit down to write you. I hope you do not think that I have forgotten you, nor Aunt Meather. I suppose you have seen by the papers about the Harper's Ferry affair, & that I and several more, are about to as they say to dance on nothing. It is rather a queer way to leave this world. But as a person must die because he loves man & justice why I think it because one of the best of deaths.

Death is something we all must meet and I rather die for trying to do good than evil.

I received six wounds at the Ferry and the Docs thought at one time that I would not live. I underwent a great deal of hard pain, but am quite well now and very cheerful.

It is true I should like to live a few years yet here in this world, but if my time comes now, I shall meet it cheerfully and it will not be many years until I shall have the pleasure of seeing you all in the other world. The old man passed off in good faith and the rest of the men are, I think quite cheerful and happy. There time is close at hand. And man gets to the end of his chain when he takes life, that is it's all he can do. It is a long road that never turns they say.

I think now, from what I have seen, that the way we were

trying to do away with Slavery, is not the best way, but I had to get this experience before I knew it. I think the ruling power of the universe is working in all these things and we shall all get our just reward. There is a feeling in my bosom for the oppressed, and I can not help it, & I am very thoughtful for it.

If you have time, it would give me pleasure to have an answer to this. Give my love to your wife & boys & all kind friends.

Yours for the right.
A. D. Stevens

Several more weeks passed before Dwight saw John Cook, Edwin Coppoc, Shields Green, and John Copeland pass by his cell en route to the courthouse and their trials. The trials did not last long, and all four were sentenced to be hanged on December 16th.

The night before the four raiders were scheduled to be executed , Cook and Coppoc made an attempt to escape. Dwight did not know of their plan until the next morning, when Jailer Avis came into the cell and put heavier and shorter-chained leg shackles on both him and Hazlett.

Dwight questioned the act. "Mr. Avis, why the different irons?"

"By order of Sheriff Campbell."

"Have we not been model prisoners?"

"Two men tried to escape last night."

"Who has tried?" Hazlett inquired.

"Cook and Coppoc. They failed, but now I am under scrutiny. It will not happen again."

Shortly after the four men were fed their last breakfast, they asked that they be allowed to say their good-byes to Stevens. Dwight stood and greeted them as they entered his cell and bid him farewell. They talked for a brief time as Avis stood by and watched. After a short period, the jailer told them that it was time.

Upon hearing that, Hazlett extended his hand to them as they began to pass by. Only a quick handshake was exchanged between Hazlett and the four men as they passed. Dwight wanted to encourage each man to be brave, but he remained silent. His throat tightened and he was temporarily unable to speak as they passed and shook his hand for the last time. It was especially hard for him to watch young Edwin Coppoc go to his death with the three others.

Once the last hand had been shaken, he regained his voice and said, ***"Good-bye friends! Cheer up! Give my love to my friends in the other world!"***

Stevens and Hazlett kept quiet for the remainder of the day. Dwight spent his time reflecting on the friendships he had developed with the men he had trained and now had seen walking to their death. As with

Brown's execution, Jailer Avis returned after the hangings had been completed and did not say anything.

During the late afternoon, slaves were brought into the jailhouse under guard. As was the normal procedure for the county, slaves were held in jail when they were captured, to await their owners. Dwight and Hazlett saw firsthand the perils of slavery as two young men and a woman were herded into jail cells to await the wrath of their masters who would come to claim them. One male slave was very rebellious, causing Mr. Avis to remove him from the jail and take him away.

Later, he was returned barely alive from the whipping the deputies had inflicted. It sickened Dwight to see this. Moans could be heard coming from the adjacent cells as the evening progressed.

Later that night, both men heard horses and wagons making considerable noise passing outside the jailhouse. After several hours of this, Avis came into the cell area to make his last check on his prisoners and the now-silent slaves.

Dwight called out to him. "Sir, there has been considerable noise throughout the evening! What is happening? It sounds as if an army has come here."

"On the contrary, the noise you hear is the various militia and federal troops leaving our city. With John Brown and the four men that were executed today now in the presence of their Maker, the governor believes there is no need for the number of men he had requested to protect Charlestown and Harper's Ferry."

Dwight acknowledged the information and did not respond. He and Al Hazlett turned in for the night. They were both resting comfortably when they were awakened by loud sounds. A drunk was being vulgar and obnoxious with Avis. They could hear the man yelling in the outer office.

"I am Silas Soule[1]. I coulda kicked any ass in that place if they hadn't jumped on me. They're a little unfair. One on one I could've whipped 'em. I'm a bit drunk, but that don't mean ya'll have a reason to lock me up."

As Jailer Avis manhandled the drunk, he said, "This drunk will be with you two for the night. I can't put a drunken white man in with the

---

[1] **Silas Soule** came from an abolitionist family that moved from New England to Kansas to fight against slavery. The Soule house in Kansas was a stop on the Underground Railroad, and John Brown visited often as he and Silas's brother were close friends. In 1861, Silas enlisted in the 1st Colorado Volunteers and fought in the infamous Battle of Sand Creek. Silas refused an order given by Colonel John Chivington to attack defenseless women and children, and later testified against Chivington for his atrocities.

slaves. There ain't any room anyway."

As he started to unlock the cell door, he explained to Dwight that there had been charges brought up against this man for starting a fight while intoxicated and resisting arrest.

Dwight just hoped that the loudmouthed drunk would quiet down quickly as he attempted to fall asleep.

Soule didn't. He kept being obnoxious until Avis threatened to crack his skull open with a nightstick or put him with the runaway slaves if he didn't quiet down. He really didn't want the man in with Dwight and Hazlett, who were still upset over the four executions earlier that day. He also didn't want people hating him for putting a drunken white man in with the runaway slaves. Additionally, he was concerned for Stevens, who was still recovering from his wounds and needed more rest.

Silas Soule remained loud and annoying, but kept it just below the limit, preventing Avis from striking him. The jailer was a large man, and Soule knew enough not to push him past his tolerance.

Dwight looked to Hazlett, who spoke as Soule was grabbed by Avis and pushed into the cell. "I guess we have a visitor."

Soule looked at Dwight, then remarked, "And who might you be, mister?" Soule slurred and staggered a bit as he said it.

"Never mind who he is, shut your mouth and behave or I will have your hide," Jailer Avis yelled as he pushed him further into the cell. Soule fell onto the floor facedown and didn't move. "I guess he'll be quiet now for a spell. Call for me if he awakens and is a bother."

Dwight only nodded and went back to lying on his bed. He watched the man move and moan once or twice as he lay on the floor. With no more interest, he turned away from the drunk and tried to go to sleep.

"Has the jailer left?"

Dwight didn't respond at first.

"Stevens, is the jailer gone?"

He realized the man was talking to him. "Yes, he has, but I was hoping you would lay there and sleep off what you have drunk tonight."

Silas Soule turned over and smiled. "That's one of the greatest impressions of a drunk I ever did. It got me in here, and that's what I wanted."

Dwight was confused initially, but he quickly went into a defensive posture as he got out of his bed. The action hurt muscles that he hadn't used in a while, but the adrenaline he produced overcame the pain.

"No fisticuffs required, Mr. Stevens. I'm here to help, not to harm either of you."

Hazlett remained confused, while Soule tried to convince both of them that he was a friend and not a foe. Soule whispered when he realized that his voice was beginning to carry in the cell. "My name is Silas Soule. I do a little acting and mimicking. I also have experience in guerilla fighting which you, Mr. Stevens, know all about." He looked in several directions and continued to whisper. "I came here with Captain Montgomery[1] to rescue you two. I'm sorry that we were too late for Captain Brown and the others. May God rest and bless their souls."

"Who put you up to this? What was your name again?" Hazlett asked, while Dwight stood still but ready to strike.

"Silas Soule. My name is Silas Soule. I came here with Captain Montgomery, and we have a plan to break you two out of this jail." He grimaced and lowered his voice again and said, "The guards for this jail, the courthouse, the entire town have been reduced considerably since the execution of…" He paused and never said Brown's or the others names. The sight of Stevens still ready to harm him made Soule whisper faster.

When Dwight realized that the man was harmless, he backed down and asked, "Who has paid you to come here and free us?"

Soule relaxed and pointed to the chair that was by the desk. "May I sit?"

Dwight nodded, but remained standing as Hazlett sat on the edge of his bed staring at Soule.

Soule spoke clearly and slowly. "We were paid to come here by a group that continues to support Mr. Brown and this cause. Even with Mr. Brown's demise, and now that of the other four today, there is still support to free Brown's trusted lieutenants. You gentlemen are heroes to many people in the Northern States."

---

1 **James Montgomery** was a Jayhawker during the Bleeding Kansas period, and a sometimes controversial Union colonel during the American Civil War. Montgomery was a staunch abolitionist and used extreme measures against pro-slavery populations. In 1857, he organized and commanded a "Self-Protective Company," using it to order pro-slavery settlers out of the region. The most famous of his operations during the Civil War, was a Raid at Combahee Ferry in which 800 slaves were freed with the help of Harriett Tubman.

Silas S. Soule
During the Civil War
Public Domain photo

"Your group was too late to free our leader and friends," Dwight said softly.

"I know, but this town looked like an army camp with all the militia and federal troops stationed at every street in and out of it. We hoped that the number of troops would diminish, but that didn't happen until after the four were…" He looked at both raiders and just nodded. Both knew what he meant. "Mr. Stevens, you have seen me before. I visited here with the many others that wanted to see John Brown and his men. You, sir, are very popular with the ladies, and many have come by just to see you alone."

"Silas, I believe you are getting away from your original point."

"You're right. Captain Montgomery is waiting to initiate our plan once I have reported back to him. It should take me no more than a day or two to be released with a small fine. If it takes longer than that, the captain will come in and bail me out. He plans to tell them that I'm a lost soul and my family wants me back home."

Hazlett asked him, "How are just two men going to free us?"

"When either I am released or Captain Montgomery has come to bail me out, we will overtake the jailer and tie and gag him. If there are a few guards outside, I can lure them in and both of us will have no problems overtaking them as well. None of the remaining guards we observed look to be seasoned deputies."

Dwight shook his head. "The jailer, Mr. Avis, is a kind and generous friend, but I am sure he would put up a spirited fight to keep the two of you from freeing us. He's also a very large man if you haven't noticed, and it would take a considerable effort to overtake him."

Silas Soule nodded in agreement. "In that case, I would kill him, Mr. Stevens, and as soon as I did, Captain Montgomery would kill the other guards outside. It is not what we planned, but it will be done to free you both if it is necessary."

Hazlett watched as Dwight finally sat on the edge of his bed and began to relax.

Dwight shook his head several times before he spoke. "Mr. Soule, I particularly do not want more deaths on my conscience, especially that of Mr. Avis, who has been so kind and fair to all of us here in this jail." Dwight looked to Hazlett for his comments.

His new cellmate paused for a few seconds but nodded his head in agreement before he spoke. "I agree with Dwight. There has been enough killing."

Soule frowned at first, but changed his facial expression as he began to talk. "Gentlemen, if you do not allow Captain Montgomery and me to free you, then you both will surely die on the gallows, just as your leader and your friends have done."

Dwight looked at Hazlett. Both were locked in an agreement that Soule could see in their eyes. The part-time actor, mimicker, and guerilla tried in vain most of the night to convince the two men to agree to his plan to free them. It was to no avail.

The next morning, Silas Soule was led before a justice of the peace for his arraignment, where he was given a lecture on the evils of drink. He left for Harrisburg the same day. Upon his return, he met with Captain Montgomery and both men decided to adhere to the wishes of the prisoners.

Later that month, they informed their employers that an attempt to free the prisoners would have been very difficult with the amount of federal and state troops in the immediate area from Harrisburg to Charlestown. There was a general consensus that the chances of successfully freeing the two men would have been very low, and the cost in lives very high.

The day after the executions of the four raiders and the departure of Silas Soule, Dwight put quill and ink to paper and wrote Rebecca.

Charlestown, Dec. 17th,

The four young men who passed yesterday met their fate like men. They seemed to feel a little badly about parting with friends, about the same as I have seen them several times before, for they

had very warm hearts.

Cook and Coppoc undertook to escape the night of the 16th but were caught before getting out of the jail yard. This has hurt Capt. Avis and Sheriff Campbell, and has brought more irons on me and the other man who is in here with me. But no one can blame them, for life is sweet to all.

Your friend,
A. D. Stevens

As he asked for his letter to be posted by Jailer Avis, several slave owners showed up at the jail to reclaim their property. Dwight watched as a relatively small man entered the cell area, accompanied by several deputies. He saw him point and say, "That tall buck is mine. Shackle him good. This is the second time he has run away." The man looked at Dwight and shook his head. "So you're one of them that were going to free the slaves." He laughed and turned away to watch them shackle his property.

The tall slave was still rebellious despite his whipping the night before, and he made his shackling difficult for the deputies. Finally the deputy pulled out a nightstick and hit the slave several times about the head and neck.

The owner yelled out, "Damn, man, go easy. I need him quieted down, not dead. If he dies, the county will owe me fifteen hundred dollars. He's got good stud qualities, which is one of the only things that keeps me from killing him myself."

Dwight thought, *In a different world, this slave would have broken this small man in half. In a different world, this man would have never even thought to challenge the tall slave.*

He watched as the little man and his chattel left.

As the days passed, a few more slaves were incarcerated in the jailhouse. And almost each day, an owner would arrive to claim his property. On one particular day, two men came into the jail and pointed out their slaves. Dwight heard a conversation ensue where the men began to bargain. The conversation included one owner asking the other to let him buy a particular female.

"Why you so interested in the woman?" one asked.

"She looks like a good breeder. She don't look more than twenty."

"She's eighteen."

"Light-skinned, too. She got white in her?"

The owner did not comment.

"I'm offerin' you four hundred fifty for her. My slave women are gettin' old. I could use some new blood around the place."

The owner thought about the offer and replied, "No, I think I am going to have to pass on ya offer."

Not to be rejected, the other man said, "How about four hundred seventy-five for her? Just think about it."

He looked at him and remarked, "Ya make it five hundred and ya got a deal."

"Done."

They shook hands as the slave woman was given to the new owner. He looked her over, felt her breasts, and then turned her around. He cupped her buttocks and said, "I think I got a good deal."

"I know ya have," the other one said and then laughed, winking his eye.

As the previous owner counted the greenbacks the new one had handed him, Dwight was utterly disgusted as the men, slave, and deputies passed by his cell. The wide-eyed, petrified look on the young woman stayed with him.

Just seeing that exchange alone convinced him that his participation in John Brown's raid had been worth it. Dwight was unable to sleep that night as he thought of nothing but the woman slave's terrified eyes.

Dwight soon became concerned about his affairs after his death. With his relatives many miles from Charlestown, he took it upon himself to make his final arrangements as easy as possible for them.

He received a letter from Rebecca Spring, written a few weeks after the death of the four raiders. Her letter included an offer to bury him at her Eaglewood Academy property in New Jersey. He replied to her immediately.

Charlestown Jail, Dec. 31st, 1859

My dear friend:

Your long letter of Dec. 25th I have received through the kindness of Capt. Avis. He says you must not think it any trouble for him to read your letters, it is a pleasure. And if it is a pleasure for him, I shall be willing to give you a sketch of my life under different circumstances. This much I can say. I passed a happy life up to nine years, under the care of a kind mother. She was taken from me at the age of nine. Since then I have passed through many scenes, have had many happy hours and days, and also hardships and sufferings. I do not see any part of it to throw away; it has been a great lesson. And now, as I have just learned to live I am about to go back to childhood in another state of existence. I have a dear father, a very kind and benevolent man. He came on as far as Baltimore when I was first brought to the jail, but the excitement was so great he came no further. I have two sisters and two

brothers, all very near and dear to me. My oldest brother is a music teacher; in fact, we all understand music more or less. My father has led a Church choir ever since he was fifteen, he is now about sixty.

I have written to ask my father if he will want to claim my body if I am sent to the Spirit Land through the kindness of Virginia. It makes very little difference to me what becomes of the body after the spirit leaves it. My father is a poor man, and may not be able to come for my body, I hope he will comply, if not, please accept my thanks for your kind offer.

I hope you will not hesitate a moment about speaking to me of death, for it gives me no more pain than it would to talk about living. It would give me much more pain, to have you tell of some poor human being trodden down by some tyrant. Death has no terrors for me, at the same time; I should like to live as long as I can do any good.

Your friend to the end of time,
A. D. Stevens

Dwight wrote more letters to Rebecca Spring before and during his trial on the subjects of religion, his interest in music, difficulties with the heavy shackles he had to wear, and his improving health. In one specific letter he wrote before his trial began, he mentioned his concern with Jenny Dunbar. Dwight had desperately hoped to hear from her. However, as time passed and his trial would soon begin, he was afraid that he would never hear from her again. It was his one deep regret.

Charlestown Jail, VA., Jan. 31, 1860.

My Dear Mrs. Spring:

I have received your letter with the Poems "Abou Ben Adhem", and "St Pavon". Please accept my thanks, they are beautiful, both of them.

My trial comes on tomorrow, and I shall soon know my destiny. I have not much hope of anything short of the Better Land.

That question you ask me I will answer: There is, her name is Jeanie Dunbar, very kind, benevolent lady. She is like me deprived of a mother, except such as we find through kind motherly sympathy, she is a music teacher, and very industrious, having to earn her own living.

My health is very good. I get along very well under the care of good Capt. Avis and his wife.

The time seems very short since I have been here. True happiness I think comes from helping the poor and needy.

Your loving friend through endless time,
A. D. Stevens

As Dwight Stevens waited for his trial to begin, he noticed more visitors passing by his cell. Dwight went about writing, singing, and sleeping as sometimes dozens of Virginians passed to see him in his cell every day.

On one occasion Dwight asked Avis as he was securing the outer doors to the jailhouse, "Mr. Avis, why do you allow people to come through here?"

Avis paused for several seconds as he secured and double-checked the door. "Mr. Stevens, most of the people that have come through here are free minded. They don't believe everything they read in the newspapers, whether they were printed in the South or the North. They believe their own eyes. They have come to see what you look like. Some dread coming in, and tell me as they leave that you are dangerous and should be chained to the floor. Some come with admiration and bring gifts which I have passed to you when appropriate. Those people leave with kind words about you."

Dwight did not respond.

Avis paused before he left and said, "My own guards even enjoy their guard duty because they get to listen to you sing. You have a real effect on the townspeople. They seem to either love you or hate you, and some are just plain scared to death of you."

On February 1, 1860, Aaron Dwight Stevens was brought before the Honorable John Kenny of Rockingham, presiding, and Judge Parker of Hampshire County. Judge Kenny delivered the charge in reference to the Harper's Ferry Invasion to Trial Foreman R. V. Shirley, just after he was sworn in.

Dwight listened as Judge Kenny spoke to Shirley, saying, ***"It is known to you, and is now a part of the history of the country, that on the night of the 16th of October last past a band of traitors, murderers and incendiaries stealthy made a decent on the soil of Virginia, in the County of Jefferson, and wantonly murdered several of our citizens and people, with the design to incite our slaves to revolt and to subvert our Government. Some of these desperadoes, and others the dupes of designing cowards, were captured, tried, and punished according to their deserts. But there are some engaged, or supposed to have been engaged, in this foray who have not as yet been apprehended, and others who are believed to have been actively engaged in this tragedy, but who are not yet known to the public. It will be your duty, and I believe your pleasure also, to inquire who were guilty of polluting our soil and attempting to dishonor the sovereignty of Virginia. I deem it unnecessary for me to recommend to you to conduct your inquires with that coolness,***

justice and good sense which has distinguished your predecessors in their inquisitions, and which have met with the approbation of the good and patriotic citizens of our common country. So conduct your inquires that the bright escutcheon of our beloved State not be dimmed by passion, prejudice or groundless suspicion, and also let them be connected without fear, favor or affection, that you may elicit the truth, the whole truth, and nothing but the truth."

The court was silent as the jury was then instructed to leave the room and the witnesses in the case of the Commonwealth vs. Aaron D. Stevens were called in. Dwight was informed that a Mr. Sennott had been appointed by the court as his and Hazlett's attorney. A Mr. Andrew Hunter represented the Commonwealth.

Dwight sat and listened while Sennott and Hunter bantered back and forth on procedures and the rights of the accused. And so went the day until Dwight was escorted back to his cell.

The walk between the courthouse and the jail was approximately a hundred yards and within the same block in town. As Dwight and Hazlett were escorted, the large manacles that had been placed on them hindered their walking pace. The shortened chains made them stumble at times, while hundreds of bystanders watched the two walk by them. Dwight occasionally smiled back at some of the women who smiled at him as he passed.

The next day Hazlett was left in the jailhouse as Dwight was brought to court in a new suit that had been provided for him. The dark gray suit, starched white collar, and black tie, made the handsome prisoner more distinguished than ever before. As word spread of the clothing and good looks of Aaron Dwight Stevens, the street leading to the courthouse became even more crowded with bystanders.

Complimentary calls to Dwight could be heard among them. Even from afar off, spectators could witness the handsome prisoner being escorted to and from the courthouse. In some cases he was a head taller than many of them and easily seen as the crowds grew to three and four people deep trying to catch a glimpse of the notorious lieutenant.

Dwight enjoyed the chance to see people who, in most cases, seemed polite and interested in what he looked like. Sporadic questions were asked of him from different newspaper reporters who were covering the famous case. Dwight answered them in short words, never saying more than a sentence.

As expected, Aaron Dwight Stevens's trial did not last very long. On February 4, 1860, at 4:00 p.m., the jury returned to court after only fifteen minutes of deliberation, with a verdict of guilty on all counts. Upon hearing the verdict, Dwight smiled at the jury members who, in most instances, did not look at him as he eyed every one of them. Those that did meet him eye to eye reflected that he did not show hate or discontent toward them for their verdict.

The judge rendered the punishment that Dwight would be hanged on the gallows until he was pronounced dead, on March, 16, 1860. The judge then asked Dwight if he had anything to say. He nodded. Everyone waited.

"May it please the Court; I have a few words to say. Some testimony given against me was untrue. One witness stated that I said 'Let's kill the ___ of ___ and burn the town!' To those who know me it is useless to make denial of this charge, but deny here, before God and man, ever having made such a proposition. I wish to say I am entirely satisfied with the conduct of my counsel, Mister Sennott. I think he did all in his power in my behalf. I desire also to return my thanks to the officers who have had charge of me, for their universal kind treatment, and to my physician for the services rendered me whist suffering from my wounds. When I think of my brothers slaughter and sisters outraged, my conscience does not reprove me for my actions. I shall meet my fate manfully."

No one there, except Dwight, realized that he would make it to his twenty-ninth birthday the day before his life would be snuffed out by the hangman's noose. He counted the days walking back to the jailhouse as some women cried, some men called out, and many others just watched in silence.

He had forty days and forty nights until the sentence was carried out. Maybe it was a biblical sign, he thought. Whatever it was, he was happy the trial was concluded. He wished only to see the friends he had written and hoped they would grant his requests to come and visit before the hangman completed his assignment.

No sooner had the verdict been given with the sentence and the date of death set, Dwight's sister, Lydia, came to see him. Unknown to Dwight, Jailer Avis had been informed that Mrs. Lydia M. Pierce had been given permission to visit with her brother as soon as security measures had been undertaken by order of the governor through Sheriff Campbell.

Jailer Avis and his wife agreed that Mrs. Pierce should be allowed to see her brother without the confines of his shackles. Avis told Dwight that he was to have a special visitor in the morning. Hazlett, who was taken out of the cell and transferred to one of the other cells not occupied at the time, remarked that it must be a very special visitor if he had to be removed before the guest arrived.

Avis came in and said, "Your special guest will be here shortly. I have been informed that she will be coming from the hotel."

It was the first time Dwight understood that the special visitor was a woman. "Good jailer, may I inquire as to who this woman is?"

"You will find out soon enough." Avis opened the cell door and approached Dwight. "Sit and be still. I am removing your shackles for this visit. I have trust that you will not contemplate escape during her visit."

Dwight was taken aback as Avis unlocked the shackles and removed them out of sight. He rubbed the areas where the shackles had been and waited for the woman to arrive. His thoughts wandered. *It can't be Mrs. Spring. Her letters indicated it would be some time before she returned to Charlestown.*

His anticipation ended quickly when Lydia entered his jail cell. Both of them studied each other for several moments. Dwight was amazed that she had not changed in thirteen years. Although thirty-six now, she looked to be in her twenties.

Her impression of him was that he had grown into a very handsome man of twenty-eight. He was taller and darker than she had remembered, but his dark eyes still sparkled as soon as he recognized her. His clothes were impeccable for a man who had been in jail for almost six months.

They stood and looked at each other for a short period before Dwight finally took her hands in his. He couldn't speak. He tried several times. He squeezed her hands and pulled her toward him. They embraced without a word until she said, "You look very well. I shall inform Father and our family immediately of this."

He still couldn't talk until she pulled away and looked directly into his eyes. "I am here, my dear brother. I have come to comfort you in any way that I can."

He nodded. "I am happier than you know that you have come to see me." Tears rolled down his cheeks and into his full beard, where they disappeared.

She blotted his cheeks with a scented handkerchief and remarked, "My dearest brother, what have you gone and done?"

"I have done what I thought was right, and now I will pay the consequences for my actions. This is a simple case of right, which is not understood, and of wrong, which is a way of life in the South."

She didn't respond to his statement, but only hugged him again until he slowly pushed away and inquired, "Our brothers and sister, are they well?"

"Yes, Dwight, all are well. They send their love."

"I have not seen any of them since I left for the dragoons. That seems a long time ago, and many things we would have shared have passed."

Lydia did not say anything to him as he spoke in a soft and sometimes strained voice. Finally, he stopped his reflections and allowed her to speak. "Henry is doing well. His business has become very successful. Lemuel has grown into a handsome young man. He's twenty-four now and as tall as you, I think. Susan is a beautiful young woman who has taken the good looks of both her parents. She will be twenty-one very soon, Dwight."

He sat down and shook his head. "So much has happened, and I have missed it all." He paused and asked, "And Father and Stepmother?"

"They are fine as well, but they worry about you. You know Father came as far as Baltimore before he turned back for home, don't you?"

"Yes, I was informed that he inquired about me as soon as he found out what had happened and where I had been taken to recover. And Charles, how is he?"

"He sends his best. I have addresses for all so that you may correspond at your leisure."

He laughed.

"Have I said something amusing, my brother?"

He smiled. "You talk of leisure. I guess I have been given much as most will believe, but to me, it has been torture to see my captain, my friends, and many slaves pass through these cells to the other world or to more years of slavery."

"Let us not talk of your imprisonment. Let us talk of what we have seen and experienced since our last meeting. We have so much to discuss, and we don't want to waste time reflecting on tortuous incidents."

He hugged her again. They began to catch up on the many years that they had missed in each other's lives. Jailer Avis occasionally looked in and offered refreshments to them. They gratefully accepted. He served them tea and small cakes that Mrs. Avis had made when she heard that Lydia had come to visit her brother.

Lydia returned several more times that week, and on one occasion, Mrs. Avis fixed a proper meal of chicken, garden vegetables, and freshly made bread that her husband delivered for the evening meal. Lydia did not talk about Dwight's conviction until the last week of her visit. After they had been interviewed by several newspapermen and had pictures taken together in their Sunday best, she waited until all of them had left before she informed Dwight of her plans. "I will be traveling to Richmond to see the governor. He seemed to be a fair individual when he granted his permission in a letter for me to visit you here. I will approach him again, in person this time, to ask that you be given a pardon. I am sure…"

Dwight held up his hand and stopped her mid-sentence before she could continue. "Lydia, I do not want you subjected to any rejection by the governor. There are too many problems, legally and politically, for the governor of Virginia to allow you to convince him that I should be pardoned. The public in Virginia would hang him right alongside me if he even considered it."

Lydia burst into tears. He melted at the sight of her crying and held her. He tried in vain to comfort her as she whimpered, until she finally was able to control her emotions. "Dear brother, I must try, for you, me, our family, and our country. At home you are seen as a hero who has undertaken a large step in making the country realize the evils of slavery."

"What you say could be true, but Lydia, it is in the North that you hear this. The South will never freely accept the abolishment of slavery."

"It shall someday, because of men like you and John Brown."

"No, Lydia, it won't. The only thing that the captain, Kagi, and I have accomplished is to further divide this country over the institution of slavery. It will take many lives someday, both North and South, to end it. Maybe ours are just the first."

"You talk of war with that statement."

He nodded. "The captain said it before he died."

"Well, John Brown could be wrong."

"Lydia, please do not waste your time and subject yourself to being rejected by the governor of Virginia. Your time with me is too precious to waste on fruitless attempts to sway him."

Lydia promised him that she would not see the governor, but she did not mention that while she was in Charlestown she would continue to write letters almost every day to have Dwight pardoned. She also did not tell him that many others were also writing the governor directly or signing petitions that were being sent to him on behalf of Dwight.

During this time while Dwight was jailed in Charlestown, one hundred and fifty miles further south in Richmond, the new governor, John Letcher,[1] had a problem. He had just taken over as governor from Henry A. Wise on the first of the year in 1860.

As the trial of Aaron Dwight Stevens concluded, his office was overwhelmed with mail from towns all over the North asking for him to have compassion and not hang young Dwight. Many of the letters were just a page or two from individuals asking him to be lenient. Problems came from the growing numbers of requests consisting of page after page of hundreds of signatures from entire towns to free the prisoner.

---

[1] **John Letcher** was elected the 34th governor of Virginia and served from 1860 to 1864, through most of the Civil War. His home was burned down by Union troops in 1864.

The governor had absolutely no thoughts of mercy for Stevens and was not about to give up Virginia's right to hang this man who had admittedly tried to start a slave uprising. Letcher knew that many Virginians considered Stevens to be even more dangerous than John Brown. But more than that, the band of outlaws had embarrassed Virginia in front of the whole country, having held off the Virginia militia with only twenty-two men.

It was a cold, bright morning in February when the new governor cornered his administrative aide and scolded him, "What the hell are you going to do with all these petitions that keep coming into my office? They are not going to change my mind, and I do not wish to have them stacked on my desk every day."

The old clerk, who would not be cowed by the new governor, responded as he looked up and over his glasses, "Sir, ya can't just ignore 'em and throw 'em out. They're official documents, not personal. We got to keep 'em until you're long gone, even if ya ain't about to look at 'em."

The governor did not like the response and shouted out, "But look at the mess! I've got letters from places I have never even heard of. Look at this one from Norwich, Connecticut, where the motherless son of a bitch was born. Obviously, everyone there signed the damned petition."

The clerk paid no attention as he recorded the documents. The governor rambled on as he entered his office. The clerk thought, *How could this man be motherless and a son of a bitch at the same time?*

Very few of the petitions sent to the governor of Virginia were ever read.

The reporters continued to come in the jail to see Dwight day after day. They kept asking him the same questions in different ways, hoping that he would denounce John Brown as a poor leader who had caused the raid to fail.

At first, Dwight simply refused to answer the questions. However, he came to realize that it was important to give a good answer to this particular question. He finally resolved to speak to them in the small, cramped room. "You need to fully understand that I loved and respected John Brown. I am strongly devoted to the same cause that we fought for in Kansas as we did here in Virginia. We have been through much together, and we have both lost friends, loved ones, and dreams that none of you will ever know about. I only wish that the raid had been successful and that we had freed many slaves. I will not say a bad thing against John Brown." He paused for a few moments and then continued as the reporters wrote down every word, "Certainly, I wish I was not here discussing our failures with you. Here is what is real. We have been tried for treason, found guilty, and sentenced to die. I must ask you who are gathered here today, how can a nation enslave so many and think God is not looking?"

After Lydia's visits, Dwight spent his time crossing off names of relatives he knew he must write to before his death. One such letter was written to one of his brothers.

My ever dear Brother,

I sit down for the last time, without doubt, to communicate a few thoughts to thee… I should like to see you my Dear Brother very much, but shall have to wait until we meet in the Spirit-world. What joy it will give me to meet you and all other kind friends there.

I hope Dear Brother you will investigate the spiritual theory for it is such pleasure to know that we shall all meet sooner or later in the Spirit-land, than mere belief.

I hope you will be one of those lovers of truth and right, and help redeem the world from sin and oppression of all kinds, and as you love yourself as you love man, as you love woman, as you love God, work with your head, heart, and hands, for the happiness of yourself and all the world. Be careful and not think too much of self, this is one great thing we should all conquer….

Farewell my Dear Brother we meet agin beyond the tomb, God bless you and yours.

A. D. Stevens

After a morning visit by Lydia, Jailer Avis informed Dwight that another woman was there to see him. At first, he thought Mrs. Spring had come now that the weather was beginning to change, which made it easier for her to travel. He accepted the notification with no other reservations and waited for her to enter.

He could not believe his eyes as Jenny Dunbar, dressed in a dark green dress with cream trim and a shawl, entered the jail and awaited Avis to unlock the cell door.

Dwight rose and walked forward, but almost tripped from the shackles that had been placed back on his ankles after Lydia had left. Avis realized by the look on Dwight's face that she was someone very special to him. He immediately removed the shackles as Jenny stood back and continued to smile at Dwight. Avis exited quickly, as he felt awkward standing between the two as they gazed at each other.

"You have come at last. I am so grateful. You look well, and your dress is beautiful."

"I made it just for this occasion." She paused for a few seconds. "Your wounds. They are healed?"

"Yes. Well, almost completely. I do have trouble eating and smiling sometimes, and my face doesn't respond as it used to."

"I think you look well. I like your beard. You didn't have it when we last parted."

"I know. I never had any use for a beard, even in the cold of a Michigan winter. But I grew one because it hides the scars."

Both of them stopped talking for a few moments while Jenny looked down at the floor. After a deep breath, she lifted her beautiful face to Dwight. He could see the tears in her eyes as she began to talk. "I came after Mrs. Spring informed me of your request. I must admit that I hesitated in coming to see you. But as I read in the newspapers of what you had attempted to do and how everyone felt about it, I changed my mind. You are a hero in the North, Dwight. I have seen, firsthand, the amount of letters and petitions that have been sent on your behalf. I stopped on my way here and had an audience with the governor of Virginia. It took me over a week to get that audience, or I would have been here earlier. He turned down my request to have you pardoned. I knelt before him asking for leniency for you. He would not pardon you."

"I am sorry that you had to endure that rejection on my behalf."

She smiled and kissed his cheek, then held both his hands. "I have missed you since we parted at the Lindsleys'."

"I am sorry that I could not confide in you and been forthright."

"I know, and I understand now."

"Let us speak of it no more. We need to spend our time catching up on what we have missed in each other's lives."

They spent their meeting in relative quiet until the press and locals found out that another woman, not a relative, was visiting with the popular prisoner. The rumors quickly spread through the town and into the newspapers that Jenny Dunbar was betrothed to Dwight and they were to have been married.

When Lydia and Jenny visited together on occasion, small crowds were attracted to the well-dressed women as they walked from their accommodations to the jailhouse on the busy Charlestown streets. As they strolled the several blocks, many of the town's citizens followed. When small crowds developed, the press was always around, reporting of the visits in the newspapers. The stories carried to other cities far away in both the North and South.

When the women were visiting alone or together with Dwight, spectators and curious folks from out of town streamed pass the jail to get a quick glance at the handsome prisoner and his attractive female guests. These activities brought more newspapermen to interview Dwight and Hazlett as the time of their scheduled demise grew closer.

Few hateful or derogatory pieces were now being printed in the local newspapers. The articles posted in Charlestown seemed more social as they described who had visited with John Brown's lieutenant. The large Northern and Southern city newspaper reports dealt primarily with public opinion and sentiment. The North expressed understanding of the actions of John Brown's raiders, while the South further separated itself from the North by condemning John Brown as a traitor, murderer, and insane man. With the final conviction of Stevens and Hazlett, and a hanging date soon approaching, sentiment for their respective opposing positions on slavery was solidly in place.

The first week in March arrived, and Lydia and Jenny were both still in Charlestown. Dwight thought that they should leave before his appointment with the gallows. They refused, even after several attempts on his part to persuade them to leave. He was pleased that he could experience the love and warmth of both women, who visited him separately based on an agreement they had made between themselves. Both women realized the different type of love he had for each of them, and both were willing to allow him to express that love to each in his last days on Earth.

On March 15, 1860, Aaron Dwight Stevens turned twenty-nine years old. A quiet gathering with the two women in the Charlestown jail was probably one of the happiest days of his short life.

The local press heard the news that his birthday was one day before he would die. Several pictures of Dwight sitting with two women, one on each side of him, were printed in the county newspapers. As questions about his raid with John Brown, his position on slavery, and the past incidents in Kansas were asked again, he acknowledged one thing that they had failed to ask him.

He stood up during the picture-taking and questioning and said, "Gentlemen, you ask me questions that I have answered many times before. I have not changed my position on them, but you have failed to ask me one important question."

One newspaperman challenged him, "What question have we failed to ask you, Mr. Stevens?"

"You did not ask me how I am feeling while I have two beautiful women visiting me."

The room grew quiet for a few seconds, as all the eyes and attention turned on Lydia and Jenny. Dwight smiled and spoke to break the silence. ***"I did not believe anything so good could come to me. I did not expect to spend my last hours with dear friends. I think more of these women than I ever did before."*** He turned to Jenny first and said, "I thank this dear friend that she has ventured to my side from Ohio. I remember when I first met her, and she informed me that she taught music. She also sang to her students, and I wish she would sing for me today. I long to hear her sweet voice."

At first, Jenny's voice was a little raspy as she began to sing a song dear to Dwight in front of the newspapermen. Within moments, she gained her voice and sang to the enjoyment of all who heard her. All three's spirits were lifted from the sorrow that had been building, knowing the end was near.

They sang for a considerable time, until Jailer Avis informed the newspapermen it was time to leave. Once they had left the jail, he told the prisoners and guests that dinner would be served. Hazlett, Dwight, Jenny, and Lydia ate while engaging in conversation and singing a few more songs until it was time for the women to go.

Lydia was first to leave that evening. She knew that her brother should be with Jenny. Lydia approached him, controlling her emotions with great difficulty. He held her close and bid her farewell for the evening.

Jenny looked at Hazlett and started to say something. He shook his head and smiled briefly. He understood that she needed to spend as much precious time with Dwight as she could. Hazlett did say that he was pleased to have met her. He removed himself to the far end of the cell to allow some privacy for the two.

"You have made me a happy man, Jenny Dunbar. I only wish that I had more time on this Earth to spend with you, but that cannot be done."

He hugged her for the first time, which caught her by surprise. She never moved away, instead hugging him back. They drew back to look at each other, and Dwight hesitated as if he were contemplating kissing her. The gentlemen's code he had grown up with held him back. She let no codes hold her back. She gently kissed him on the lips as tears flowed from her eyes and down her cheeks.

Dwight could smell the sweet scent of her and taste her tears. His eyes watered and she temporarily blurred in his vision. He blinked and cleared them. The most beautiful woman in his world turned to leave, one of her hands grasping his until she walked away. She did not turn back to look at him. He watched as she disappeared from his view. He did not know that Lydia and Jenny would accompany each other back to their residences and talk about him. He was happy thinking that he would see both of them one more time.

Early the next morning, around 4:00 a.m., Dwight was doing a lot of thinking. He knew that many people in Virginia considered him to be more dangerous than John Brown and had contemplated that thought many times during the night. Dwight reached the same conclusion. They were right. He loved Captain Brown and respected him for what he stood for and did, but Dwight also knew that he was the one that was younger, stronger, and better trained. Those qualities made him more dangerous in the eyes of the Virginians.

At that moment, sitting in his cell, Dwight did not feel threatened. It was early morning of his last day on earth. He had remained awake the entire night, thinking. He realized he wasn't afraid, but more curious and reflective. His imminent death was an overwhelming thing to understand, and he pondered what it would feel and look like in the place he would be later in the day.

Between his thoughts and reflections, he continually kept repeating a poem he had memorized years earlier and quoted portions of it to friends in letters he had written from jail. The poem was titled "The Messenger Bird,"[1] and it helped him feel more confident on what lay ahead:

Thou art come from the spirits' land, thou bird!
Thou art come from the spirits' land!
Through the dark pine-grove let thy voice be heard,
And tell of the shadowy band!
We know that the bowers are green and fair
In the light of that summer shore,
And we know that the friends we have lost are there,
They are there—and they weep no more!
And we know that they have quench'd their fever's thirst
From the fountain of youth ere now,
For there must the stream in its freshness burst,
Which none may find below!
And we know that they will not be lur'd to earth
From the land of deathless flowers,
By the feast, or the dance, or the song of mirth,
Through their hearts were once with ours;
Though they sat with us by the night-fire's blaze,
And bent with us the bow,
And heard the tales of our fathers' days,
Which are told to others now!
But tell us, thou bird of the solemn strain!
Can those who have lov'd forget?
We call—and they answer not again—

[1] **The Messenger Bird** was written by Felicia Forthea Hermans (September 25, 1793 – May 16, 1835), an English poet from Liverpool, England. Portions of the poem were written from memory to Rebecca Spring, a friend of Dwight's, while he was incarcerated in Charlestown, Virginia.

Do they love—do they love us yet?
Doth the warrior think of his brother there,
And the father of his child?
And the chief, of those that were wont to share
His wanderings through the wild?
We call them far through the silent night,
And they speak not from cave or hill;
We know, thou bird! That their land is bright,
But say, do they love there still?

On his last morning, Dwight arranged with Jailer Avis for the prisoners and their guests to eat breakfast together in the hall outside of the prison room. Hazlett's brother had also arrived during the night, and that made him as cheerful as Dwight.

Avis and his wife, as before, did the best they could to accommodate the five of them. As Lydia returned that morning to the jailhouse, she walked past the gallows that were in their final stages of construction. When she met Dwight she was upset. Dwight asked her to control herself for one more day. Jenny arrived a few minutes later, also upset after seeing the gallows being built.

Dwight put on his charm, and before breakfast had finished he had made the two most important women in his life laugh through their occasional bouts of tears. The breakfast concluded too quickly for everyone that attended. They all knew it was time to say their last goodbyes.

As before, Lydia was the first to depart. Before she could speak, Dwight said, "I love you, and give my love to the others. Tell our parents that I often think of them and wish them a good and prosperous life until we all meet someday in a different place."

Lydia attempted to say something again, and he gently placed his fingers to her lips to stop her. With his other hand, he wiped the tears from her cheeks. "Go now, and may God travel with you."

She turned and nodded to Hazlett and his brother. They both smiled and watched her as Avis escorted her out of the jail.

Jenny broke down, realizing she would never see Dwight again, and cried as she watched Lydia being slowly taken out. She began to speak and, as with Lydia, Dwight stopped her and said, "I know there should be much to say, but it will fulfill no purpose. In a different time, things could have been wonderful for us. It did not happen because of me."

She started to speak again, and he stopped her. Realizing this was the end, she held him close and kissed him on the lips for an extended time. He felt her warmth, tasted her tears, and thanked the Almighty that he had lived long enough to hold and lovingly kiss Jenny Dunbar.

She quickly turned and almost ran out of the cell.

Avis attempted to follow her, and Dwight urged him on with a request: ***"Get them away as soon as you can, I can't bear this much longer."***

Avis watched as the two women entered the carriage to take them back to their accommodations. Lydia and Jenny continued to comfort each other as they left Charlestown later that morning for Harper's Ferry, where they waited until after the execution to board a train. They both traveled north together and stayed at the home of Mrs. Spring.

"It is time," Jailer Avis announced. He entered the cell and applied the shackles he had left off both men as they bid good-byes to their loved ones. He was courteous enough to ask each man if they were ready to walk to the wagon that would take them to the gallows. Both Dwight and Hazlett informed him that they could walk and would not have to be helped by his deputies.

Hazlett was led out first. No words were said by any of the spectators that lined the street.

It was now Dwight's turn to exit the jailhouse where he had spent six months. He had entered it as a wounded, bleeding man, and exited it in a fine suit, almost as healthy as anyone his age could expect to be. It was ironic that the same society that almost killed him had nursed him back to complete health, only to then execute him.

As he appeared to the waiting crowd, whispers from the men and sobbing from a few women could be heard. He stood tall and looked over the crowd as the guards assisted him into the wagon with his shackles. Hazlett and Stevens met eye to eye as they sat facing each other, but did not speak. They both continued to look at the people on the street as the wagon began to move slowly past the courthouse.

The time to reach the courthouse was much quicker now, compared to when he had to shuffle under the pain of his wounds to appear in court with Captain Brown. That seemed like ages ago.

The wagon turned left and passed a bank he never knew existed. He realized he had never had the opportunity to see Charlestown except for the hundred yards or so it took to get him from the jail to the courthouse.

Within a short time, the wagon turned to the right. There were people still standing on the street as they passed. Dwight laughed to himself and thought, *Are they here to see Hazlett and me, or to watch the mounted cavalry escort ahead and behind the wagon as we journey to the gallows?* He paid it no mind. He heard and noticed several spirited mounts in the cavalry escort. One particular one reminded him of Spirit. He hoped that the army had taken care of that precious horse. His mind quickly went to the day he found Spirit waiting for him following the Battle of Cieneguilla. Spirit had been one of the few horses not killed, wounded, or stolen. Dwight laughed to himself that Spirit probably had kicked some unsuspecting Indian who had attempted to ride him. He hoped he would see him again soon in the spirit world.

The thought left him as he looked at the fine houses and white fences lining the cobblestone road. As they traveled further, the road turned to dirt. He noticed a hotel sign that stated *Vacancy.* He wondered if Lydia and Jenny had stayed there. Then the scenery changed as the cavalry moved off the road and the wagon turned left into an open field.

He saw the gallows for the first time. He was surprised that it did not frighten him.

He waited for the deputies to assist him and Hazlett out of the wagon. A few young boys ran too close and were yelled at by the deputies to get away. He laughed inside, thinking that he and Charles Whipple would have probably done the same thing if they had lived here and witnessed this event.

It was a short walk to the gallows stairs. Hazlett walked up first. Dwight did not hesitate and followed closely behind. Before their heads were covered, they smiled at each other and then embraced. Neither man showed any fear. Dwight looked out over the crowd. Everyone's eyes were fixed on the two of them.

The scene quickly went dark as a black cloth was put over his head. He felt the heavy and coarse rope being slipped over his head. He then felt the knot being placed directly at the back of his neck. He waited, then felt the floor from under him fall away. A brief second, and then he felt extreme pain. It was the worst pain that he had ever experienced. His face wanted to explode from the strangling he was experiencing, his neck ached terribly, his eyes burnt as if they had been on fire, and he couldn't breathe.

He viciously moved his body in hopes of getting some air. It was to no avail. The knot pushed deeply into his neck as the noose tightened. He couldn't yell and began to feel faint.

It was a welcome feeling now, compared to the pain. He spit a large amount of fluid from his mouth and recognized the taste. It was blood. He knew the end was near as he began to black out. The hurt in his neck subsided. He knew nothing more. He was gone.

The End

Afterword

The raid on Harper's Ferry was a complete and utter failure. It did not accomplish any of its objectives. However, the South, and especially Virginia, had been horribly embarrassed as Brown and just a few other men had achieved a stand-off against several hundred militia troops, if only for a short time. This fact had a large bearing on the trials being Virginia state functions rather than federal functions, even though the arsenal was federal property. Seventeen men had died in the raid at Harper's Ferry. Ironically, the first to die was the African American baggage master Hayward Shepherd.

Additionally, the raiders killed three white townspeople and one U.S. Marine named Luke Quinn. Ten of the raiders, including two of Brown's sons, were killed. Two slaves who had been liberated by the raiders also died. However, several of the raiders who had stayed at the Kennedy farm escaped. A few of them were captured in the following weeks and brought back to Virginia for justice.

For John Brown, Aaron Dwight Stevens, and the three others who were taken alive during the raid, it was in this precious short time, between the raid and their deaths, that they made their case to the public, both North and South. They became heroes and martyrs in the North, while they were assumed to be treasonous, dangerous, and even mentally unstable by the South. But both the North and South could only respect the dignified, courageous actions and the thoughtful, passionate trial testimony of John Brown, Aaron Dwight Stevens, and the other raiders, which were carried so diligently to the public by the newspapers throughout the country.

The raider's actions, testimonies, and fates were more earthshaking and more important to their cause than a successful raid could have ever been. John Wilkes Booth, the young actor and future assassin of President Abraham Lincoln, had to admit as he watched the hanging of John Brown that Brown was ***"a brave old man."***

It was this small but important chapter in the lives of John Brown and Aaron Dwight Stevens that finally divided the North and South, so much so that they were not united again until well over 600,000 men had died and the nation suffered through four years of civil war, disease, and destruction.

John Brown wrote this terrible, yet powerful prophecy on a note he gave to his jailer as he had walked to the gallows.

The following is an account of the hanging of Aaron Dwight Stevens and Albert Hazlett, as printed in the *Norwich Courier.* On Saturday March 24, 1860, the *Norwich Courier* published the following account of the executions from the *Charlestown Jeffersonian* newspaper.

Execution of Stephens and Hazlitt – ***The Charlestown Jeffersonian is the only Virginia paper which gives any intimate account of the execution. In its issue of the 17th instant it says:-***

The near approach of the day of execution seemed to have but little effect on the prisoners, and for the past few days they were unusually cheerful. Stephens declaring it was his wish to be free, and therefore desired the day for his execution to arrive. Mrs. Pearce, the sister of Stephens, was with him up to yesterday morning, and made a fine impression on all with whom she was thrown, by her lady-like deportment and conduct. On Thursday a Miss Dunbar, of Ohio, arrived in town. It is said she was engaged to be married to Stephens at the time of the Harper's Ferry invasion, and had corresponded with him since his imprisonment in this town. She is a lady of much intelligence and beauty.

A brother of Hazlitt, who resides in Armstrong county, Pa., also arrived a few days ago, and was present with his brother until yesterday morning. He advised Hazlitt to make a full confession of his connection with the Brown party, and counseled him to abandon all hope of a reprieve or commutation of punishment.

Yesterday morning the table was set in the passage for the criminals to eat, and seated around were the two men, who in a few hours were to be launched into eternity, a sister, and betrothed of one, and the brother of the other. A solemn feast and one which was seemingly enjoyed by but two – the condemned.

After breakfast had been partaken of, the friends of the criminals bade them a long farewell and took a carriage for Harper's Ferry, where they remained until the bodies of the executed reached that place.

At eleven o'clock the field on which the scaffold was erected was occupied by a large number of spectators, a still larger number, however, remaining in town to accompany the sad procession. Col. John T. Gibson was in command of the military, which mustered twelve companies.

At 10 minutes to 12 o'clock the prisoners made their appearance on the field, escorted by three military companies. The prisoners walked to the scaffold. Hazlitt was in advance, and ascended the steps with an easy, and unconcerned air, followed by Stephens. Both seemed to survey with perfect indifference the large mass of persons in attendance, and neither gave the least sign of fear. A short time was spent in adjusting the ropes properly around the necks of the prisoners, which was improved in taking an

affectionate farewell of the Sheriff, jailer and jail-guard, after which the caps were placed over their heads, and Aaron D. Stephens and Albert Hazlitt were launched into eternity, to be dealt with by a Judge "who doeth all things right."

There was no religious exercise with the prisoners, as they declined all offers from the clergy. Just before the caps were drawn over their heads, Stephens and Hazlitt embraced each other and kissed.

The fall broke the neck of Hazlitt, and he died without a struggle, while the knot slipped on Stephens's neck, and he writhed in contortions for several minutes. They were permitted to hang about half an hour, when they were examined and pronounced dead.

Obviously, Aaron Dwight Stevens did not die easily on the gallows. Unfortunately, the knot that Jailer Avis had tied, following the friendly competition between Stevens and Hazlett to have him be the one to tie it, slipped. Dwight died a difficult death as a result, and violently struggled for several minutes before life finally left him.

Following the hanging, and according to the agreed-upon arrangements, the bodies of both Albert Hazlett and Aaron Dwight Stevens were placed into wooden boxes and taken to the Harper's Ferry train station. They were then shipped to Perth Amboy, New Jersey, where they were both taken to the Eaglewood Academy grounds, owned by Mr. Marcus and Mrs. Rebecca Spring, who were both deeply involved in the abolitionist movement.

When the plain wooden caskets containing Stevens and Hazlett arrived at their destination, it was found that Stevens had bled profusely in death, while Hazlett had died rather quickly with a broken neck. Despite the large quantity of blood covering much of Stevens' head and face, a lady named Mrs. Thomas took some scissors and cut off a lock of his blood-soaked hair. She washed it clean and kept the lock of hair, later taking it home to Norwich, Connecticut, with her.

That lock of hair taken from Aaron Dwight Stevens is kept today at the Daughters of the American Revolution (DAR) Faith Trumbull Chapter in Norwich, Connecticut, along with several other mementos of Aaron Dwight Stevens.

At Eaglewood, many people gathered to say farewell to Dwight Stevens and Albert Hazlett. Several of them had come from Norwich, Connecticut, including the Reverend Hiram P. Arms from the First

Congregational Church[1]. Dwight's sister Lydia Pierce and Jenny Dunbar also were in attendance.

It was here that Aaron Dwight Stevens was laid to rest until 1899. The final action, on behalf of Dwight, occurred in that summer, when a project was undertaken to recover the bodies of as many raiders as possible and bury them all in North Elba, New York, with John Brown.

The remains of eight men had been recovered earlier in the year. They were: Oliver Brown, William Thompson, Dauphin Thompson, Stewart Taylor, John Henri Kagi, William Leeman, Dangerfield Newby, and Lewis Sheridan Leary.

At the last moment, Mr. E. P. Stevens of Brookline, Mass., son of Aaron's brother, Henry, found out about the plan and asked that the remains of his Uncle Aaron and Albert Hazlett also be re-buried in North Elba, New York, with their friends. It was accomplished, and all remains of the now ten men were placed in one handsome casket, which was donated by the town of North Elba, New York. It had silver handles and a silver plate inscribed with the name of each man, and the date of burial, which was August 30, 1899. Aaron Dwight Stevens proudly rests there to this day.

It was interesting to see that most all of the newspaper accounts had spelled Stevens's last name with a "ph" instead of a "v." It was as if one writer wrote it that way, and all the rest followed without ever really checking the correct spelling. Even accounts in Norwich had the last name spelled as "Stephens."

It is also interesting to note that all the Stevens family members buried in the Yantic Cemetery in Norwich, Connecticut, are all spelled "Stevens." All other records through his life had his last name spelled with the "v," except of course when he used the last name "Whipple." The "Stephens" spelling appears to have been used only by the Harper's Ferry press.

Additionally, it was mentioned several times that even though a religious-type service was constantly offered, the men, including the staunchly religious John Brown, refused it at the hanging. It was a point made specifically by John Brown and the others that they wanted no ceremony performed by any priest or reverend from the South. While their reasons were based on the fact that they knew a Southern preacher would preach, and believe, that slavery was something God supported or

---

[1] **Reverend Hiram P. Arms** was born in Windsor, Connecticut, in 1799. He was ordained in Hebron, Connecticut, and became pastor of the First Congregational Church in Norwich, Connecticut, serving from 1829 to 1882. He remembered Dwight as a boy.

wanted for his sons and daughters on Earth, none of the reporters seemed to think this was important and let it all go by, simply saying, "They didn't want religious help on the scaffolding, or during the execution process."

In our research for this book, and especially in the effort to write it, several conscious decisions had to be made which determined critical paths we would rigorously follow. We had to answer questions about Aaron Dwight Stevens and use what was available, even though data was sometimes conflicting, to bring forth a believable, factual personality from over one hundred and fifty years ago.

In the South, and especially in Missouri, Stevens, as with John Brown, has never been a hero to many and is still considered to be more villainous or terroristic. Using letters from people who knew him during different phases in his life, military records, a personal account by one of the slaves he helped to escape to Canada, newspaper articles, and many letters from Dwight, we can clearly see a heroic man who had flaws just as we all do.

He was certainly impetuous, with a lifelong temper problem. He was also a physical presence, and so many references called attention to his size, strength, and good looks. Because of his upbringing in a home and church that appeared to be decidedly against slavery, his attachment to Thomas Payne's *The Age of Reason*, his own letters, and the words of others who knew and lived with him, by the time of the attack on Harper's Ferry Aaron Dwight Stevens was certainly an avid anti-slavery individual. He considered slavery to be the worst evil in the world.

Some references do not follow this line of thinking, though. References found in Missouri, Virginia, and West Virginia (part of the state of Virginia at the time) were not complimentary to Stevens and instead describe a different man than we have portrayed. We, of course, do not know which source is correct, and so we made a decision based on the preponderance of data we found.

We were fortunate enough to discover that Aaron Dwight Stevens was a good letter writer, and that many of his letters are still preserved in various places. Some can even be easily found on the Internet. These letters provided a wonderful, clear, and steady picture of him as he went through different phases of his short but interesting life. Throughout his letter writing, he never wavered on his views on slavery, his love for his family, and his obvious care for Jenny Dunbar.

Before we progressed very far into the book, a real effort was made to define who Aaron Dwight Stevens was and what he was like. We decided that, from what we knew about him, he most closely fit into the ISTJ (introverted/sensing/thinking/judging) personality and was generally what would be called "The Duty Fulfiller."

His personality traits would include: somewhat quiet and reserved—not pushy, strong internal sense of duty, air of seriousness, loyal, faithful and dependable, dislikes doing things which make no sense to him, has strong opinions and maintains standards for his own behavior and others, not naturally in tune with his own feelings and the feelings of others. Maybe most importantly, this type of personality will stop at nothing to do his or her duty and willingly give support as needed once he or she commits to a cause or idea. This trait is what took him to Harper's Ferry.

The relationships between Aaron Dwight Stevens, John Henri Kagi, and John Brown were completely constructed by us for the book. Their real relationship is not known, other than that John Brown was obviously their leader and they did as he wished. It was certainly John Brown, as a dynamic speaker and somewhat successful fundraiser, who was the face of the effort. He was also well known, at least by reputation, from the Pottawatomie Massacre in Kansas, while Stevens, Kagi, and the others were only soldiers.

It is our contention that John Brown was a very intelligent man with a magnetic, strong personality who also knew some of his own limitations. He would encourage religious discussions and arguments among his band of raiders, even though few of them agreed with his Puritan religious views.

All of them were intelligent, knowledgeable men and could hold their own in any debate, although John Henri Kagi was probably the best at it. Kagi was almost completely anti-religious, while Stevens was against the organized religions of the day and more of a naturalist, following the views he had learned from Thomas Paine.

John Brown appeared to be unafraid of opposing views and did not appear to think less of those who did not agree with him. It is not a far stretch to believe that John Brown gave quite a bit of responsibility to his two able lieutenants and, furthermore, probably trusted them both in their own specialties—Stevens militarily and Kagi as a planner and organizer.

John Brown had seen his own shortcomings in military affairs, and it is reasonable to think he would include them both on the preparation and execution of all his plans, as well as the Harper's Ferry raid. It is interesting that the real plan included taking the slaves who were to join them in Harper's Ferry and going off into the Shenandoah Mountains to wage guerilla-type warfare on the slaveholding South. The one man in John Brown's raiders who could militarily pull that off was most definitely Stevens, not Brown.

We believe Aaron Dwight Stevens to be an original American hero who gave his life to a cause he believed in. It could have been Stevens that President Abraham Lincoln eloquently described as having "firmness in the right, as God gives us to see the right." Perhaps now more than ever before, every one of us needs real heroes to emulate and to look up to. Young, strong, daring, adventurous, and honorable, Aaron Dwight Stevens is a good one.

Vic Butsch and Tommy Coletti

Photo Album by Tommy Coletti

Front view of the courthouse in Charlestown, West Virginia

The site of John Brown and Aaron Dwight Stevens's hanging

The Engine House at it appears today

Co-author Vic Butsch in the Engine House

Aaron Dwight Stevens's Sharps Rifle
As displayed at the Harper Ferry Museum

The area of the Shenandoah River where John Kagi was killed while crossing

John Brown Statue
At the Brown Farm, North Elba, NY

John Brown Homestead
At the Brown Farm, North Elba, NY

Gravesite of Stevens and other raiders
At the Brown Farm, North Elba, NY

The Co-authors Vic Butch and Tommy Coletti at the John Brown Raiders Memorial
At the Brown Farm, North Elba, NY

Bibliography

"A History of Cherry Valley, Ohio." First published in *The Ashtabula County Historical Society Quarterly Bulletin*, Vol. 6, No. 4, December 15, 1959. Katherine H. Talcott, editor. http://home.comcast.net/~kms2135/cherry_valley_history.htm.

"Aaron Dwight Stevens." *The Norwich Aurora.* October 29, 1859.

America's Best History U.S. Timeline, The 1850's. The 1850's–Expansion and the Looming Divide. http://americasbest history.com/abhtimeline1850.html.

America's Historical Newspapers. "Massachusetts Regiment of Volunteers." *Barre Gazette.* Feb. 19, 1847. Volume XIII, Issue 34, Page 2. Barre Mass.

Africans in America, Resource Bank, Historical Document. "Dred Scott Case: The Supreme Court Decision." http://www.pbs.org/wgbh/aia/part4/4h2933.html.

America's Historical Newspapers. "The Massachusetts Regiment." *Farmer's Cabinet.* Feb. 18, 1847. Volume 45, Issue 27, Page 2. Amherst, New Hampshire.

Ancestry.com. "Meech Family Tree" http://trees.ancestry.com/tree/3702786/person/-1697851226/family/pedigree/print. 1/7/2011.

Anderson, Osborne P. Electronic transcription, "A Voice From Harper's Ferry: A Narrative of Events at Harper's Ferry: with Incidents Prior and Subsequent to its Capture by Captain Brown and His Men." http://www.libraries.wva.edu/theses/Attfield/HTML/voice.html.

Barry, Joseph. *The Strange Story of Harper's Ferry With Legends of the Surrounding Country.* Chapter IV: The Brown Raid, A firsthand account. Thompson Brothers, Martinsburg, WV, 1903.

"Battle of Cieneguilla." From Wikipedia, the free encyclopedia. Oct 8, 2009.

Bettmann, Otto L. *The Good Old Days–They Were Terrible.* New York Random House, 1974.

"Blackjack Battlefield & Nature Park," copyright 2009, The Black Jack Trust, Inc., http://www.blackjackbattlefield.org/

Bosse, Tom. *Aaron Dwight Stevens, Abolitionist. A Native of Lisbon, Connecticut.* Lisbon, CT. Historical Society. 2009.

Brigden, George Billings. *Reminiscences.* In Otis Library, Norwich, Connecticut. G 9 B763.

Brown, John. *The Life and Letters of Captain John Brown who was Executed at Charlestown, Virginia, Dec 2, 1859, for an Armed Attack Upon American Slavery; With Notices of Some of his Confederates.* Printed by Alfred Webb, great Brunswick Street, Dublin. Digitalized by Google.

Brown, John Brown "Provisional Constitution and Ordinances for the people of the United States." Introduced at the Trial of John Brown by his lawyer Samuel Chilton. http://law2.umkc.edu/faculty/projects/ftrials/johnbrown/brownconstitution.html

Cahill, Kevin I. *Biography of Silas Soule.* http://www.kclonewolf.com/history/SandCreek/Bio/silas-soule-biography.html

"Connecticut History Online–A Century of Transportation." www.cthistoryonline.org.

Cooke, John E. *Confession of John E. Cooke, Brother in Law of Gov, A.P. Willard of Indiana, and one of the Participants in the Harper's Ferry Invasion. Published for the Benefit of Samuel C. Young, a Non-Slaveholder, who is Permanently Disabled by a Wound Received in Defense of Southern Institutions.* D. Smith Eichelberger, Charlestown, Va. 1859.

Copeland, Lewis, Lamm, Lawrence W. and McKenna, Stephen J. *The World's Great Speeches, 4th Edition, 1999.* Dover Publications, Inc., Mineola, New York. 1999.

"Copies of numerous letters sent to Governor Wise & Virginia Governor's office to pardon Aaron D. Stevens." Provided by Library of Virginia, 800 East Broad St., Richmond, Va. 23219-8000. Archives Research Services.

Creitz, William F. *Letter to Col. James Redpath, Holton, Kansas, Dec 17, 1859.* Pages 1-8. Territorial Kansas Online – Transcripts http://www.territorialkansasonline.org/cgiwrap/imlskto/index.php?SCREEN=show_transer.... 9/18/2008.

Cushing, Caleb. "Order #69 From Col. Cushing, concerning those involved and accused in Garrison Court Martial." Massachusetts Historical Society. April 13, 1847. 1

Cushing, Caleb. "Headquarters, Matamoros, orders for a detail to proceed to Palo Alto and arrest teamster Henry Aldrich for assault." Massachusetts Historical Society. April 16, 1847. 1

Cutler, William G. *History of the State of Kansas, Jackson County.* Part 2, Southeast quarter of section 10, Township 6, Range 15. Home of Albert Fuller. 12/6/2008.

"Descriptive and Historical Register of Enlisted Soldiers of the Army," Pg. 222. National Archives & Records.

"Descriptive and Historical Register of Enlisted Soldiers of the Army," Pg. 222. National Archives & Records. "#139 Stevens, Aaron D. deserted 2 Jan, 1856."

[Additionally, numerous sources record the fact he escaped from Ft. Leavenworth.]

Digital History: Back to Hypertext History: *Our Online American History Textbook.* "Westward Expansion, War Fever and Anti War Protests. 1820-1860."

http://digitalhistory.uh.edu/database/article_display,cfm?HHID=318.

"Enlistment records of Aaron D. Stevens, in New York, New York, April 1, 1851, Form 86 military Service Records," National Archives & Records. [no other address is given other than Town of New York and State of New York]

"Events of the Harper's Ferry Raid of 1859. Timeline for the John Brown Raid on Harper's Ferry, Virginia 1858-1859." http:/transvideo.net/~rwillisa/Ferry_Raid.htm. 1/24/2011.

Expo Museum / "The 1851 Great Exhibition of the works of Industry of all Nations, London, United Kingdom." http://www.expomuseum.com/1851/

Feather, Carl E. "Insurrection at Harper's Ferry: The Ashtabula County Connection." *The Star Beacon*; Ashtabula, Ohio. October 18, 2009.

http://starbeacon.com/currents/x546364794/Insurrection-at-Harper's-Ferry-The-Ashtabula-Connection.

Fitchett, Margaret Pinkerton. "The Early Pinkertons." Pinkerton Resource Page
http://freepages.geneology.rootsweb.ancestry.com/~pinkerton.

George Stammerjohan and Will Gorenfeld. "Chronicles of the 1st U.S. Dragoons, 1833-1861, Dragoon Uniforms." http://musketoon.com/?

Gill, George B. Kansas State Historical Society, "Gill Manuscript #28973," KSHS MSS Coll. Hinton / notes for John Brown & His Men / Box 8.

Gorenfeld, Will. "The Battle Of Cieneguilla: Anatomy of an Army Disaster." April 5, 2008. http://musketoon.com.

Hamilton, James Cleland. "John Brown in Canada." Reprint from *Canadian Magazine*, Dec. 1984. KSHS #K/B/B81/Pam/v.1. [As told by Samuel Harper, one of the eleven slaves taken to Canada.]

Hinton, Richard J. *John Brown and His Men, Volume 2.* As

published in 1894. Page 494. Published by Digital Scanning Inc. Scituate, Ma. 02066.
http://www.digitalscanning.com and http://www.PDFLibrary.com.

Hodges, Graham Russell Gao. *David Ruggles: A Radical Black Abolitionist and the Underground Railroad in New York City.* The University of North Carolina Press, 2010.

Holcombe, R.I. *History of Vernon County, Missouri.* "Hicklin, Harvey G., Statement regarding the taking of his slaves by John Brown 12/20/1858." Kansas Historical Society, 977.81, V59, H71.

Holcombe, R.I. *History of Vernon County, Missouri.* "The Robbery and Murder of David Cruise." Kansas Historical Society, 977.81, V59, H71.

Hughes, Patrick J., Ph.D. *The Life of the Dragoon Enlisted Men.* Kansas Collection Articles, Produced by Susan Stafford. http://www.kancoll.org/articles/dragoons.htm,

Johanessen, Severn T. "Did You Know That…" *Bicentennial Sketches of History and Nostalgia.* 1959.

"John Brown's Right Hand Man: The Story of A. D. Stevens as written for the *Boston Sunday Journal* Newspaper by His Next of Kin." (Nephew of Mr. E.P. Stevens of Brookline Mass.) Copied by Faith Trumble Chapter D.A.R., Norwich Ct. (no date of article) D.A.R. stamp dated 1893.

Keller, Allan. *Thunder at Harper's Ferry.* ACE Books Inc. New York, NY. 1958.

Kiene, L.L. "The Battle of the Spurs and John Brown's Exit From Kansas." Kansas historical collections. http://www.kshs.org/publicat/khc/1903_04/kiene.htm. 12/6/2008

"Lines of Fire: A Last Letter From Prison." March 27, 2006. Letter From A.D. Stevens to His Brother written in March 1860, just prior to his hanging. http://www.military.com/forums/0,15240,92376,00.html

Lowe, Percival G. *Five Years a Dragoon ('49 to '54) And other Adventures on the Great Plains.* 1906 Reprint, Norman, University of Oklahoma Press, new edition 1965.

Lurie, Maxine N. *A New Jersey Anthology.* New Jersey Historical Commission, Newark New Jersey. Page 179.

Massachusetts National Guard, Military Museum & Archives: "The First Regiment Massachusetts Infantry in the Mexican War." Historical Sketch by Fred W. Cross, Feb. 1920. Military Archives division, The

Adjutant General's office.

Massachusetts National Guard, Military Museum & Archives: "The First Regiment Massachusetts Infantry in the Mexican War." Historical Sketch by Fred W. Cross, Feb. 1920. Military Archives division, The Adjutant General's office. List of Deaths in the First Regiment Massachusetts Infantry, taken from the records of the Adjutant: San Angel, Mexico, March 20, 1848.

Massachusetts National Guard, Military Museum & Archives: "The First Regiment Massachusetts Infantry in the Mexican War." Historical Sketch by Fred W. Cross, Feb. 1920. Military Archives division, The Adjutant General's office. From enclosed copy of *Boston Daily Times* and *Bay State Democrat.* "Return From Mexico of the Massachusetts Regiment of Volunteers and Their Encampment at Cambridge Crossings"

McClellan, George B. *On Volunteers in the Mexican War.* http://www.aztecclub.com/1846-Volunteer-McClellan.htm

Newsletter created by Charles and Jean Carder. "Aaron Dwight Stevens." *The Norwich Arms Gazette.* Published by The Guns of Norwich Historical Society, Inc. Sept – Oct 2007.

"Oldest Railroads in North America." Wikipedia.org/oldest_railroads_in_North_America.

Paine, Thomas. *The Age of Reason.* Citadel Press, Kensington Publishing Corp. New York, New York. 1948.

Reader, Samuel James. *Diary and Reminiscences of Samuel James Reader.* Edited by George A. Root. Kansas Historical Quarterly—The First Day's Battle at Hickory Point. Nov. 1931 (Vol. 1, No.1)

[Additionally, numerous sources record the fact he lived with the Delaware Indians along the Kaw River following his escape from Ft. Leavenworth.]

Renehan, Edward. *The Secret Six: The True Tale of the Men Who Conspired with John Brown.* University of South Carolina Press, 1997. Pg. 134.

Reynolds, David S. *John Brown Abolitionist The Man Who Killed Slavery, Sparked the Civil War, and Seeded Civil Rights.* Vintage Books, New York, 2005, Page 194.

"Sentences of Steven and Hazlitt." A letter from Charlestown, VA., Morning Bulletin, Norwich, CT, Monday, February 22, 1860.

Stammerjohan, George R. "Letter from State Historian II, State of California Dept of Parks and Recreation, to Mr. David L. Larson, Ranger Harper's Ferry National Historical Park. May 14,

1991." Page 2 of 6. [From wonderful Kansas Researcher Kim Barber.]

Spring, Rebecca. "The Rebecca Spring Papers." Stanford University Libraries Dept. of Special Collections and University Archives. Ca 1830-1900. Special collections M0541. Pages 142–146.

Stevens, Aaron Dwight. *Letter to Uncle James, December 11, 1859.* Library of Virginia, Archives Research Services. 800 East Broad Street, Richmond, VA.

Territorial Kansas Online 1854–1861. "Letter from Paul Shepherd to James Redpath, Jan 3, 1860." http://territorialkansasonline.org.

The American Colonization Society. http://personal.denison.edu/~waite/liberia/history/acs.htm

"Horace Lindsley." *The History of Ashtabula County, Ohio With illustrations and Biographical Sketches of its Pioneers and Most Prominent Men.* Published in Philadelphia by Williams Brothers in 1878.

http://freepages.history.rootsweb.ancestry.com/~arkbios/Ashtabula/lindsleyh.txt

"The Kennedy Farmhouse, John Brown's Provisional Army." http://johnbrown.org/provisionalarmy.htm

The New York Times, "News by Telegraph; Trial of Stephens and Hazlett at Charlestown. Charlestown, Va. Wednesday Feb. 1, 1860." Provided by The Culture Center, 1900 Kanawha Blvd. E, Charlestown, WV. 25305-0300.

"The Record of Service of Connecticut Men in the War of the Revolution II War of 1812 III Mexican War, Under the Direction of the Adjutant General 1885–1889, Hartford 1889."

To take a virtual tour of the Kennedy Farmhouse – http://johnbrown.org/take_a_QTVR.htm.

U.S. National Archives & Records Administration: Form 86. Military Service Record: Aaron Dwight Stevens, Mexican – American War (1846–1848). Joined for Duty Feb. 6, 1847, and Muster Rolls.

U.S. National Archives & Records Administration: Form 86. Military Service Record Aaron Dwight Stevens, Mexican – American War (1846–1848). Joined for Duty Feb. 6, 1847, and Muster Rolls – Muster Out.

U.S. National Archives & Records Administration. RG 153: Records of the Judge Advocate General (Army), Entry 15: Court-Martial Case Files: 1809-94 Box#222, HH-497 (Private

Aaron D. Stevens, 1st Dragoons, Company F, 5/1855-5/1855. Charges against Bugler Aaron Dwight Stevens.

U.S. National Archives & Records Administration. RG 153: Records of the Judge Advocate General (Army), Entry 15: Court-Martial Case Files: 1809-94 Box#222, HH-497 (Private Aaron D. Stevens, 1st Dragoons, Company F, 5/1855-5/1855. Testimony of witnesses.

U.S. National Archives & Records Administration. RG 153: Records of the Judge Advocate General (Army), Entry 15: Court-Martial Case Files: 1809-94 Box#222, HH-497 (Private Aaron D. Stevens, 1st Dragoons, Company F, 5/1855-5/1855. Verdict.

U.S. National Archives & Records Administration. RG 153: Records of the Judge Advocate General (Army), Entry 15: Court-Martial Case Files: 1809-94 Box#222, HH-497 (Private Aaron D. Stevens, 1st Dragoons, Company F, 5/1855-5/1855. Sentence.

U.S. National Archives & Records Administration. RG 153: Records of the Judge Advocate General (Army), Entry 15: Court-Martial Case Files: 1809-94 Box#222, HH-497 (Private Aaron D. Stevens, 1st Dragoons, Company F, 5/1855-5/1855. General Order No. 12, War Department, Adjutant General's Office, Washington, August 9, 1855. Letter from Jefferson Davis, Secretary of War.

West Virginia Division of Culture and History, West Virginia Archives & History at: http://www.wvculture.org, was extremely valuable with a tremendous amount of data including trial testimony of many key individuals.

"Witnesses and Testimony at the trial of John Brown." From *The Life, Trial and Execution of Captain John Brown. Known as "Old Brown of Osawatomie," with a full Account of the attempted Insurrection at Harper's ferry.* Robert M. DeWitt, Publisher. 1859. http://www.civilwar.org/education/history/john-brown-150/witnesses-and-testimony.html.